'Here now . . .' she screeched at him like a fish-wife. Angela couldn't believe this was the gentle Minthami. Her eyes were red and swollen with weeping and her hair unbound and dishevelled. She looked like a wild woman, not the beautiful princess of the Zat performance. 'She is here . . . Amagyi-Angel is here . . . you tell her. She is brought by your evil spirit to hear this thing to sadden her . . . go tell!'

'Minthami, what on earth's wrong?' Angela glanced from one to the other in bewilderment and embarrassment.

Minthami glowered at her husband; 'Tell her, *kala*!'

ALEXANDRA JONES

MANDALAY

Futura

A Futura Book

ISBN 0 7088 3680 1

Reproduced, printed and bound in Great Britain by
Hazell Watson & Viney Limited
Member of BPCC plc
Aylesbury Bucks

Futura Publications
A Division of
Macdonald & Co (Publishers) Ltd
Greater London House
Hampstead Road
London NW1 7QX
A member of Maxwell Pergamon Publishing Corporation plc

To my husband,
my mother and my
sons.

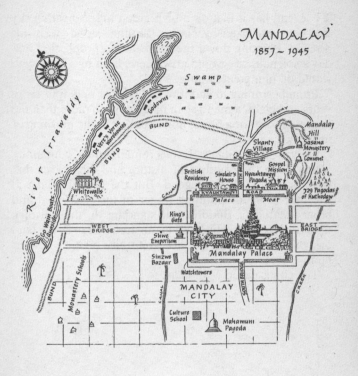

MANDALAY
1857 ~ 1945

River Irrawaddy

Swamp

Godowns

BUND

BUND

BUND

Dr Vert's Horse Warehouse

Go Water Boats Quayside

Whitewalls

PATHWAY

Mandalay Hill

Shanty Village

Sasana Monastery

Convent

British Residency

Sinclair's House

Gospel Mission

Kyauktawgyi Pagoda

NORTH ROAD

KYAUKTAWGYI

Palace

Moat

729 Pagodas of Kuthodaw

CANAL

King's Gate

WEST BRIDGE

EAST BRIDGE

Shwe Emporium

Mandalay Palace

Sinzwe Bazaar

SOUTH BRIDGE

Watchtowers

MANDALAY CITY

BUND

Monastery Schools

CANAL

CREEK

Culture School

Mahamuni Pagoda

Legend has it that on a high green hill, beneath a sky blue as water-hyacinth, Buddha stood with his disciple. Pointing down the hill Buddha prophesied one day a splendid city would arise there, built by a King who would do him great honour.

From beginning to end it would last for only four score years and eight, a man's span in history, no more than the haunting scent of a bhodi flower culled in the morning of its glory.

Only indestructible red walls remain today, containing within them the dry dust of history and those lives that were once part of the legend. But the legend itself will live forever in the pointing finger of the great gold and bronze statue of Buddha still standing on the hill of a thousand temples. His hand is outstretched over the land on which there once stood a great city built to honour him.

The city is called Mandalay.

Part One

Part Two

INTERREGNUM

September 1878

In his old man's dying dreams he saw his life's ambition fulfilled; sixty-two thousand pounds, British sterling, sitting on the Shwe Dagon Pagoda in the shape of an umbrella. A diamond orb, a jewelled vane, lotus petals and golden bell to earn him merit with Siddhartha Gautama Buddha. A serene smile curved King Mindon Min's pale, generous lips as he relived the banana-bud of all his earthly endeavours embodied in that wonderful hti, his own umbrella of devotion.

But set apart from that charitable gift to the Sangha, there had been another momentous act by him. One to earn him a far greater glory than any materialistic donation, for it was a spiritual one that would ensure him a place in the hearts of the devout, as well as immortality in Nirvana. He had gathered together 2,400 monks to read together the sacred Tripitaka Texts comprising the whole book of Buddha's teachings. In all the centuries of the Buddhist Faith, only four such gatherings had ever been convened. Now, the Fifth Buddhist Synod would be immortalized in tablets of stone that had taken all those monks, in non-stop relays, six months to finish reading.

The serene smile became almost plebian.

In the past, the Raj had refused him permission to preside over the inauguration of his wonderful panoply of devotion, since they were strategically able to exercise their whims when the mood took them. Yet now, they could not prevent those precious gems from scintillating beneath the hot Burmese sun to dazzle the eyes of the foreigner, the kala, stepping ashore at Rangoon. They could not disallow the Authorized Text engraved on 729 slabs of white marble at the foot of Mandalay Hill from being known for evermore as the Kuthodaw, THE WORK OF ROYAL MERIT. They could not, above all, refute that which had already been decreed for him, a place in Nirvana . . .

Yes, Nirvana! A safe harbour on an even brighter shore.

At last, he, the King of Burma, Lord of the White Elephants, could dispense with the patronage of the lordly Raj.

Where he was going, they could not follow!

'Tranquil and led by the good doctrines, I would hatred calm,' he murmured the words of sacred Pali inscribed in the Shwegugyi Temple by an ancestor.

Yes, a peaceful reign! So now it remained with him, as a matter of final settlement, to ensure that the next generation also lived in peace. He could not relinquish completely his mortal hold on The Golden Kingdom when one more urgent matter required his Kingly attention. Such a *quodlibet* of importance had been left in abeyance until now because it had been expedient, a matter concerning none other than that illustrious personage, his favourite son, Prince Nyaungyan Min ...

Nervously the King plucked the black silk cover on his bed. He felt the rough metalic touch of gold. His fingertips absorbed that glorious kiss of spun gold, and all the power and the glory that was his kingdom filled him once more with strength and devotion to leave his mind clear in the final moments before death. He recalled the name the British had given his chinthes, his emblem, the emblem of Burma. The British had renamed them Crested Lions. He recalled with sad indignation how his Dragon Throne had become the Lion Throne. He sighed with frustration over the Imperialistic desire to rename anything remotely resembling the British symbol, be it dragon or lizard, a lion!

The King of Burma raised his head from his silken pillow, crooked his index finger on chinthes embroidered in threads of gold, saw them as mythical beasts more akin to dragons or griffins than crested lions, and finalized his last defiant act against the invader. In the ever attentive ear of Queen Sinpyumashin, his Chief Queen, King Mindon Min murmured his last request.

PART ONE

The Golden Road
1878-1879

CHAPTER ONE

ONE

Mandalay trembled behind red-brick walls. Tiered roofs, spires and steeples bent in golden refraction. The Burmese sun intrigued upon white pagodas, melting them into isinglass. The Irrawaddy river slowed its arterial pulse to the heart of the fevered plains. No breath of air fanned the silken tail of the King's Peacock Banner, for this was the hour of noon, a time to rest.

Yet, the city boiled in a heat-haze of midday activity. Earthern ramparts and crenellated walls shuddered to the incessant passage of bare feet as holy monks in saffron robes crossed and recrossed the five wooden bridges leading to the moated palace. The atmosphere lay hot and heavy with the murmurings of many prayers, one-hundred-and-eight telling beads in the hands of the devout smoothing for the last time the path of King Mindon Min on his final journey to the 'oneness with the all', Nirvana.

Royal Troops in uniforms of red, white and magenta guarded the city within a city. Closely watchful from their wooden pyatthat pavilions above main gates and embattled parapets of palace walls, the hour for caution had come. Plots and counter-plots prevailed, rumour was rife everywhere, murmurings of assassinations, conspiracies, intrigues, rebellions and sorcery. ...

It was rumoured King Mindon Min had left it too late to name his successor; it was rumoured he had appointed as the new Einshemin, Prince Nyaungyan

17

Min, and that the Crown Prince was being kept a prisoner of the British in Rangoon. Then it was rumoured he had been assassinated at Sagaing while on his way to claim the Dragon Throne of his father, the rumour embellished further by accounts of the Shwe Nat of Mandalay having been paid in rubies to get rid of Prince Nyaungyan Min.

'Tell me again, Captain de Veres-Vorne, why you were smuggling rubies out of the country. This time I'd prefer an honest answer.' The Queen of Burma sat on the King's throne beneath the Western Portal of the King's Audience Chamber.

Matthew Sinclair of the Indian Civil Service sweated a little more in that glass-grotto held within a fretwork of entwining dragons' tails, chinthes, crocodiles, manuthiha — half lion, half man. Coming from a gentler culture, he found his brain becoming confused, his imagination uncomfortable in the potency of his surroundings. Feeling like a fly caught up in a web of spidery craftsmanship, he witnessed how absolute power corrupts.

'I've told you, Madam, all I know,' Nathan Vorne said angrily, 'Without being clairvoyant, I can tell you no more.'

The Burmese called him the Shwe Nat of Mandalay, the golden devil. To them he appeared a spirit-creature, a god, a giant, a being of fire as his remarkable blue eyes attacked the Queen of Burma when it was forbidden to raise one's eyes to look at her, let alone battle with her. Matthew, observing the proceedings with a heavy heart, hoped Nathan Vorne wouldn't earn them all the death sentence.

'I'm not accustomed to being ignored or answered back in that tone, Captain.' The voice and manner were sweetly bland, the Queen of Burma exercising her English, though the American spoke fluent Burmese, picked up in his ten years as a trader on the Irrawaddy. Everyone present in the Hall to witness the American's trial was aware it would be a grave mistake to crack the

18

crystal quality of that voice, for here despotism ruled supreme. Within Queen Sinpyumashin's tiny frame savagery lurked as surely as in the tattooed breasts of the two Spotted Faces who earnt their keep in useful employ to the Court of Ava. Known also as the Children of the Prisons, Spotted Faces were criminals whose death sentences had been commuted to life imprisonment, their distinguishing marks branded circles on cheeks and foreheads.

Through a pair of gilded opera-glasses, the Queen of Burma scrutinized the crouching man humbled at her feet. His hair was fair and thick, rich in the diffused rays of sunlight filtering through lattice and mosaic glass, his fresh complexion glowing even more healthily from reflections of vermilion lacquer and gold-leaf embellishing the teak pillar around which his chains had been fastened. She lowered the opera-glasses after her close consideration of him and, pursing her mouth into a tight Burmese rose, signalled to the Spotted Faces to chastise the prisoner a little more in the hope he might be a little less obstinate afterwards.

Wooden cudgels knocked him to the ground, blood trickled from the side of his face. Matthew Sinclair wanted to protest but when he opened his mouth no sound emerged.

The Shwe Nat, unable to right himself again, bound as he was hand and foot, was dragged back to a kneeling position by the Spotted Faces. He got his breath, chest heaving and eyes blazing, a volume of abuse contained in the look he gave Queen Sinpyumashin.

His voice husky with temper, he said: 'Madam, any rubies found aboard my boat were put there deliberately by someone wanting to make me look guilty.'

'A very plausible excuse, Captain. But you're not a man to be trusted and have told me nothing so far but a pack of lies. So, why were you taking your boat down to Thayetmyo, if not to smuggle rubies across the border?'

'Rice, Madam, not rubies.' His sigh, emphasized by the acoustics of the high-arched Hall, was heard throughout in all its devil-take-her attitude. He shifted his position and, in the silence, Matthew heard Nathan Vorne's knees crack. 'I have an export licence for the sale of rice, granted me by King Mindon Min ...'

'You lie, Captain! You stole rubies from my mines at Mogok without concessional rights to them, therefore you are a thief. You are a thief, a liar and the perpetrator of treasonable offences for which the punishment is death!' Her voice had risen to a crescendo of indignation. Queen Sinpyumashin wriggled forward on the great carved throne of Burma, her dainty bare feet scarcely able to reach the brocade footstool of the throne as she pointed an accusing finger at the American: 'You insult me, Captain, and I will have your head.'

'Bullshit.' The muttered abuse from Nathan Vorne made Matthew Sinclair wonder if the man was not altogether insane in dallying with a Queen who had the power of life and death in her hands.

Nathan, said aloud, 'Fabrication Madam. I had nothing to do with stolen rubies.'

Matthew kept his eyes downcast on the soles of Captain Vorne's dirty, cut feet. What a pity, Matthew thought, King Mindon had left it so late to name his successor. If he had done so earlier, the Einshemin would now be seated on the Dragon Throne, not the Queen. But Matthew knew why King Mindon Min had not appointed a successor any earlier. A dozen years before, Mindon Min's brother, the then Crown Prince, had been brutally murdered in a Palace rebellion. Since that time, King Mindon Min wisely had decided to keep everyone guessing as to which of his forty-eight sons would be the new King. It had been the King's own safety precaution to prevent any more bloodshed in the royal family. It appeared now, as the hour of noon was struck on heavy brass gongs outside the palace, that Vorne was going to be made the Royal Family's scapegoat.

He had the temerity once more to raise his ice-fire eyes to the Queen. She jerked her finger at him; 'No!

Don't look at me. You have no right. I don't like your English blind eyes that show me the emptiness inside your head. Neither do I like your lies, Captain.'

'I'm American, not English, Madam,' he corrected her.

'Your disrespectful manner won't save your head, Captain, English or American.' A tornado of viciousness, she nodded to the Spotted Faces.

Matthew found his courage. He raised his voice but not his eyes; 'Madam, I beg you, the British Resident will be very unhappy to know the prisoner is being ill-treated. We have an understanding about the treatment of our people which includes, Madam, Captain Vorne's nationality on account of there being no legal representation for him at this time in Mandalay.' It was all Matthew felt he could do, pretend to a little power.

The Queen swivelled opera-glasses upon him: 'Don't interfere, Mr Sinclair. You may report back to the British Resident that the Queen of Burma is equally unhappy because the foreigners in her Kingdom only make trouble for the Burmese. Why don't you people mind your own business! You are here to witness, Mr Sinclair, not make comments, since the affairs of an American are no concern of the British — as I've already been informed.'

Put in his place he fell silent. His head ached. Hot, so very hot still, with the southwest monsoons not yet supplanted by the cold season. What misery this weather, how amiable the cold — even if cold in Mandalay meant the equivalent of a warm sunny day in England. How wonderful that word sounded, England!

Matthew's thoughts strayed, the Queen's strange accents washing over him while reflections of the girl he was going to marry provided a more pleasing picture. Her letter had arrived by dâk-post that morning. What she had written had at first excited then alarmed him.

Angela wrote to say she had decided to join him in Burma. Since her father's death in Delhi, almost a year ago now, she had lost direction working with the Hindus.

21

They who dedicated their girl-children to the temple-gods were no nearer Christianity than the Misses Bloxhams at the Academy were near to marriage. She wished to start again among the Buddhists in Burma.

Such news filled Matthew with trepidation. He made up his mind to write a letter that very evening to warn her about the dangers she would meet in Burma. At least, under British rule in Delhi, she had little to fear. Out here in a land so very different, so untamed, she would be exposed to all sorts of dangers against which he would be powerless to protect her — even as her husband. On that score, Matthew felt he really ought to hurry up and set a date for their marriage, otherwise she might tire of waiting for him. He remembered their wonderful voyage together aboard the *SS Tahara*, phosphorescent trails of flying fish in the wake of an ocean-liner, beside him, a stunning girl with green eyes and sungold hair. It was all rather like a dream now, a beautiful dream far away from Mandalay ...

Nathan Vorne was being as stubborn as ever, refusing to give the Queen the information she sought. She might chastise his body, but she would never subdue the spirit which had earned him his name.

The Queen moistened her lips with the tip of a pink tongue, rather like a little snake. Matthew guessed she was tossing up in her mind what to do with this foreigner who spurned the laws of Upper Burma and insulted the Court of Ava. Everyone in the Audience Chamber was aware that outside in a private courtyard lay four garotted river-pirates removed along with the Captain from his boat the previous day. But to have the American's head as well, would not be a prudent thing to do in the circumstances; not prudent at all.

'Take him,' she instructed the Spotted Faces. 'Since he cannot be truthful, and seeks only to make the Court of Ava look foolish, his boat shall remain impounded and he can rot in the Sagaing prison.'

Escorted by her female guards in their long skirts called longyis, Queen Sinpyumashin and her ladies-in-waiting, to the crash of gongs and cymbals, left the King's Audience Chamber.

TWO

Outside the wooden palace with its fairytale architecture, Matthew found his shoes and socks and put them on. He was rudely pushed aside by the Spotted Faces leading out Nathan Vorne on the end of his chain. Unwilling to cooperate with his gaolers, and even while his arms were still bound behind his back, he lashed them with feet and tongue, ducking their cudgels with a kind of grim glee in a game in which he was the loser. Why, oh, why did he have to complicate matters? Matthew found himself wondering again while he wiped his steamy glasses and side-stepped the Spotted Faces.

'Minthami ...' Nathan said desperately to Matthew, before the Spotted Faces pummelled him against a closed wooden cart that would take him down to the riverside three miles away, and thence by boat to Sagaing.

'What?' said Matthew. Rendered helpless by the politics of a country too feudal to come to terms with in the space of a few months, Matthew could only owlishly repeat, 'Sorry, I don't understand what you mean.'

'Minthami, tell her to get out of Mandalay ...'

The Spotted Faces then managed to toss Nathan Vorne into the enclosed ox-cart. They went off with him across the wooden bridge leading to the South Gate while Burmese soldiers in their pyatthat pavilions shouted down to the gatemen to let the cart through.

Matthew reconciled himself to having seen the last of Captain Nathanial de Veres-Vorne of a dubious Navy.

Past noon, on the streets of Mandalay the monsoon weather was debilitating. The dense dust of the plains seemed to settle inside monsoon clouds to be tipped all over Mandalay in this month of September. Against the retaining walls of the Palace, pinnacles, tiers and pyatthats reflected in the wide hyacinth-strewn moat, women wailed as they were given back the corpses of the executed dacoits. Matthew hastened to get away from their fly-blown stink. He hoped the Lord of the Eastern House would appear before it was too late for Nathan Vorne. No one had ever escaped from the punishments inflicted inside the Sagaing Fort, so that it had come to be known as the prison of death. Neither did Matthew like getting 'involved' in Nathan Vorne's private affairs. This business of going personally to warn Minthami that the Spotted Faces were likely to be after her next, spelt danger for himself.

The British Resident had warned him very strictly to observe impartially and not to participate — the British had to maintain a neutral stance where Americans were concerned lest the Burmese lump them all together.

Deep in thought, Matthew did not see lying across his path the long wooden handles of a Burmese cart. He tripped over them knocking the cart over. Landing in the dust, his precious glasses disappeared somewhere underneath it. Wicker baskets ended in the roadway, demented chickens began to fountain feathers and confusion everywhere. From the other side of the street a fat Burmese girl with her longyi stretched taut across her buttocks, came running. Ma Ngwe, interrupted in her business of bartering chutneys and chickens for joss-sticks and sandals, looked at the clumsy Englishman sitting in the dust. A long thin cigarette between her fingers, she giggled and a flake of tobacco clinging to her lower lips fluttered with her laughter. Annoyed, Matthew peered up at her shortsightedly.

'What's so funny?' he demanded, his dignity bruised.

'You, Mr Englishman Sinclair,' she answered. She extended her hand to help him up. 'Look, see what you do to Ma Ngwe chickens? You make them go crazy. Not good for curry now. That will be five pyas each hen and five hens make one kyat for chickens.' Slanting dark eyes regarded him saucily.

Matthew Sinclair drew himself up, brushed himself down and stopped short of telling her what he thought of her inflated arithmetic. 'Can you see my glasses anywhere?' he asked, speaking in her language, which he had studied in his Indian Civil Service examinations before joining Mr Hawes in Mandalay.

Ma Ngwe smiled at his mispronunciation of her language, though she did stoop to retrieve his glasses. She kept them dangling just out of reach, taunting him with all the coquetry inbred in her.

'Come on, Ma Ngwe,' Matthew said irritably, 'you'll break them — if they haven't been smashed, already.'

'No, they still alright, Mr Sinclair. You buy please chickens for Residency and Ma Ngwe give you back glasses.'

She skipped off with them, exasperating him with her childish behaviour. Matthew would have gone after her had he been able to see his way decorously across the road without making a fool of himself again, but he was a blindman without his second eyes. He waited until she had done her shopping, fuming the while at the hard core of the Burmese inability to accept no for an answer. He'd give her a good piece of his mind presently ...

By the time she got back, crossing over to him with her arms laden and throwing her purchases on the pavement beside her chickens, he was in no mood for any more of her nonsense. In English, Ma Ngwe meant Miss Silver. He thought how right her mercenary name was for her: 'Look here Ma Ngwe,' he said irately, 'I suggest you stuff your chickens in the cart and go to the Sinzwe bazaar with them. You'll get a better price there than any I can give you. Besides, the British Resident's tired of chicken.'

'I go already. They got plenny chickens too and don't want Ma Ngwe's hens.'

'May I have my glasses back.' He put out his hand demandingly, the girl making a laughing stock of him in front of a small crowd of amused onlookers. Matthew, very conscious of his exalted position as a member of the Raj, did not care to be made a public spectacle on account of his own glasses. 'Come on Ma Ngwe, don't be irresponsible.'

'You buy my chickens, I give you back glasses,' she maintained stubbornly.

He felt inclined to slap her plump rump instead but, ruling against it in view of Mandalay's staring population, Matthew realized diplomacy was called for here. Suddenly an idea struck him, and he fished out his wallet. 'Ma Ngwe,' he said, extracting from it three pyas, 'go and deliver a nice fat chicken to Minthami the Burmese dancer who lives out at Go Wain. Tell her its her supper sent from Captain Vorne since he'll be eating his with the Spotted Faces at Sagaing. Tell her the chicken curry will taste much nicer if she can cook and eat it far away from Mandalay. Captain Vorne's orders. Whatever you do, don't mention I'm responsible for buying her food. Got that?'

For a moment Ma Ngwe's wide flat face stared impassively back at him. He hoped by frowning at her she would get the message, see that the joke had gone far enough, and that he had far more serious business on hand than her silly teasing.

'Ma Ngwe understand Mr Englishman Sinclair,' she nodded.

Matthew was relieved she had managed to grasp the situation without anymore charades. 'Good, now hand me my glasses if you please.' Ma Ngwe soberly handed them back, mercifully still intact though a little bent. With relief Matthew hooked the wire arms over his ears, his vision clearing. He handed Ma Ngwe three pyas. She grinned widely, her teeth and gums brown with betel-juice as she made haste to re-load her sampan-like cart. The crowd began to disperse, sensing the show was over.

'You very nice Englishman like I like, not like others like you,' Ma Ngwe told Matthew. 'So Ma Ngwe like to give Mr Sinclair very nice present.' From her belongings she fetched out a small earthenware jar. She tried to thrust it into his hands but he was having none of it.

Gifts from the Burmese usually took on the significance of bribes, and bribes Matthew knew full well were strictly taboo from where he stood. Should it be

26

seen that he was accepting 'gifts' from Burmese girls, his job would be forfeit, he would be sent packing in disgrace, and his father would read the Riot Act all over again from a little book handed to all Officers and Gentlemen when alighting on the shores of the East, explaining the code of conduct expected of the said Officer and Gentleman.

'No thanks,' he said testily, his hands firmly behind his back. He looked to a point somewhere above Ma Ngwe's blue-black topknot of coils and bundles secured with tortoise-shell and silver combs. A number of heavy gold bangles on her wrists jangled noisily together while she held out her two hands to him in the hospitable Burmese gesture when presenting a gift. She smiled sweetly, beguiling him into acceptance. His patience sorely tried, Matthew knew he would be still standing there arguing with her when sunset lowered the flag over the British Residency. Besides, by denying her an opportunity of giving something away, he was preventing her from earning a little merit from her Buddha, the Buddhists believing merit was accumulated and blessings earned by the number of generous deeds one performed towards another living creature — any creature, including a mosquito. Neither did he want her calling up her wretched Nats in the middle of the night, those spirits or devils on which Burmese lore thrived. Looking over his shoulder sheepishly, his soft-heart getting the better of him in deciding not to be totally selfish, he took her offering with as much grace as possible for his three pyas. It turned out to be a jar of ngapi, the smell of which reached him even through its sealed lid.

'Thanks, Ma Ngwe,' he said, trying hard not to show his feelings about ngapi. 'Now, you won't forget about Minthami, will you? Or what Captain Vorne wants her to do?' He spoke to her as he would a child, an annoying child he'd forgiven.

'I not forget,' said Ma Ngwe picking up the long handles of her cart. 'Shwe Nat very good fellow and bring back plenny presents from across seas for everyone in Mandalay. So I do his woman favour as he very crazy about her and not wish her any harm. Don't worry Englishman Sinclair, Ma Ngwe know much — including leetle English. She tell Minthami get-to-hell out of Mandalay because of Spotted Faces. One day soon, you come see Ma Ngwe and Auntie who live in shade of White Monastery. Pyan-dor-may, Englishman Sinclair, goodbye.' With a dexterity her long tight skirt defied, she set off in the direction of the Irrawaddy river three miles away where the Shwe Nat and Minthami had a little stilted house at the water's edge.

Satisfied with himself, Matthew directed his footsteps back to the British Residency.

The Resident, Mr Hawes, was standing in the compound listening to the Burmese gardener who seemed to be engaged in vociferous complaint. Matthew paused politely in the background.

Without turning round, but his ear still attentively tuned to the unhappy gardener, Mr Hawes said: 'Maung Soe Tun tells me he put in a chitty for a new watering-can six weeks ago and hasn't received one yet. Since the poor man can't be expected to keep the flowerbeds in order with only spit to water them, would you see to it Mr Sinclair?'

Sola topi on his grey head, iron-grey moustaches drooping sadly, official baton tucked under his left arm held rigidly to his labouring heart, Mr Hawes' khaki zouave jacket was darkly drenched in perspiration.

'Yes, sir,' Matthew said, following Mr Hawes across the compound. Hands behind him, baton tapping the back of his left knee as he ascended the verandah steps, Mr Hawes swivelled at the top and regarded Matthew Sinclair at the bottom of the steps: 'Well,' he said ponderously, 'since death has been by Queenly decree rather than democracy, what has become of our intrepid Captain? Are they going to garrot him like the dacoits?'

The smell of ngapi wafted under Matthew's nose to make him wonder if the Burmese fished their fish out of army latrines before burying them in the ground to ferment for three years. 'They've taken him to Sagaing, sir.'

Adrian Hawes betrayed nothing. 'Then that's curtains for the silly ass,' was all he said.

'Yes sir,' said Matthew, agreeing wholeheartedly.

THREE

The British Resident went inside the dâk bungalow that served to house his important office. It reeked of kerosene, mildew and earth oil. Here was another domestic insult to Empire as far as he was concerned, this so-called Consulate of his. He smarted under many insults lately, not the least of them being that he had had to send his assistant to the Palace in his stead, since he had been banned from verbal and social audience with the King and Queen of Burma. Adrian Hawes poured himself a tumbler of lukewarm drinking water from the brass jug on his desk.

'I think sir,' said Matthew from the doorway, 'the matter is a little more serious than rubies — though neither party is admitting anything.'

Mr Hawes made no reply, but instead turned to the window while he searched for a glass phial of amyl-of-nitrate to inhale. He felt very irritable these days, hardly able to cope with himself let alone British affairs at the Court of Ava. More and more he longed for the velvet nights, the shining moon and stars beyond the open window. He longed to hear, see and smell the great Irrawaddy flowing irridescent beneath God's silver-blue umbrella — not Mindon Min's ...

He broke the glass carelessly and stupidly drew blood from his finger. The Portugese doctor was right, he ought to retire from this business altogether. His thoughts while he wrapped the tiny cut in a damp handkerchief, paid little heed to the prevention of infection. Adrian Hawes shoved broken glass and his frustrations back into his pocket. He turned around and seated himself at his desk.

Drumming thoughtful fingers on his blotting-pad he said: 'Captain de Veres-Vorne's death can only lead to even further diplomatic complications. You know and I know that ruby-smuggling was only a pretext for his arrest, and that Queen Sinpyumashin's real reason for wanting Vorne eliminated is much more sinister. She cannot, however, go too far in case we come down on her like a ton of bricks — hence that mummery trial convened this morning. If I'm right in what I believe is happening here in Mandalay, then God help us all. Mr Sinclair, I want you to secure me a passage on the next boat going down to Ava. I want to talk to Captain Vorne personally.'

Bemused, Matthew regarded his Superior.

'Don't look at me like that, young man! I haven't taken leave of my senses — yet. We have a duty to perform. We have got to find out why Queen Sinpyumashin is so interested in our American friend. If the sparks are going to fly, we want to know in which direction the wind is blowing, don't we?'

Matthew Sinclair had not come to Mandalay as Assistant to the British Resident without knowing something of the calibre of the 'old man'. What Adrian Hawes was required to do in the line of duty, he did — God, Queen and Country considered in that order before any personal safety. Banned from the Mandalay Palace on account of a diplomatic incident involving the removal of shoes, Adrian Hawes had not set foot inside Mindon Min's Palace for nigh on three years.

It had been considered by the British to be beneath the dignity of the representatives of Her Majesty, Queen Victoria's Government, to crouch barefoot in front of a native King. Henceforward, Britain declared, all such mode of obeisance would not be adhered to by the British. It had been their declaration of independence even though all foreign envoys to the Court of Ava, past and present, conformed to the required custom. For that reason, Mr Hawes had been debarred from Mindon Min's Royal presence. Although ostracized and beyond official circles of recognition inside the Palace, Adrian Hawes was still a force to be reckoned with outside it.

Matthew knew all that, and so he said: 'Yes sir, let's just hope we can put out the flames in time.'

'While you're about it, send word to the Gospel Mission on Kyauktawgyi Road and ask for that other Yankee fellow ... what's his name? Yes, that one, Edom Gideon. Ask him to attend on me here in the space of the next few hours in view of our mutual friend Vorne being unable to oblige. I also want to send off a telegraph to Rangoon. People in high places might as well know what we've to put up with during this changeover.'

'Yes sir.' Matthew despatched himself about his duties and altogether forgot about the letter he had been intending to write to his fiancée. But, in any case, she would not have received it. Angela Featherstone had already left Delhi.

CHAPTER TWO

Escaping the Ganges valley, currents of warm air struck the Khazi-Garo hills and then the Himalayas. Torrential rains fell without let up. Cherrapungi must be the wettest place on God's earth, Angela thought as the storm lashed them. Felicity Quentin grumbled accordingly, a whining, monotonous sound that was getting on Angela's nerves. As the most sensible means of precluding a sharp retort, she stopped her ears by tightening her rain-hood around her head and burying herself beneath a blanket.

Bedraggled, they set off again, moving indolently and with seemingly little purpose. Pack-ponies, armed escort and white folk — feringhi to the native bearers paid to protect and guide them through these hills — had scarcely made any headway at all since leaving Cherrapungi early that morning.

Five up-hill miles in five hours, at that rate Angela felt they would never reach Imphal let alone cross the Chindwin river into Burma.

Behind the closed and sopping curtains of her palanquin stoically carried by four bearers Dora Quentin bemoaned her dysentery. Angela began to feel pity for the poor unsuspecting Emperor of China, Kuang Hsu, who had unwittingly invited the American Baptist missionaries in the shape of the Quentins to his Court in Peking. He was in for a shock, thought Angela grimly. She had heard the story of how Farley Quentin had been invited personally by the Great Emperor of China, and how Kuang Hsu thirsted after righteous knowledge from

32

the West, and how Farley Quentin had been chosen by Almighty God to convert the heathen, until she knew it all by heart. Poor Farley Quentin, he was so näive! He would never reach Peking, not unless he got himself better organised.

'Halt! Halt!' The Minister once more shouted above the storm. They had come into a rocky Pass where boulders stood as high as houses. Angela drew the mule to a halt on the Minister's command. 'Dear Ichabod,' she murmured patting its soaking hide, 'let us pray.'

Farley and Dora Quentin had not envisaged the spreading of the Word of a Christian God could be quite so difficult. Argumentative and querulous, they were all at each other's throats, including the bearers and guides. Mostly hill-men of northern India, hardy individuals who hired themselves out as escorts to anyone brave or foolish enough to contemplate crossing the mountain barrier of northern India into an equally mountainous and jungle-ridden northern Burma. Not only did they have the prevailing wind and rain to contend with while they tried to pitch camp, they also had to cope with Minister Quentin's unhelpful instructions in its positioning.

He wanted it right in the teeth of the gale and it could not be done. And the hill-men had no wish to stop in the San Mukh, the Mouth of the Cow, where they could easily be picked off by devil-spirits above the Jainta Pass, among them human shaitans with guns.

Minister Quentin was adamant. They would pitch camp where they stood: the weather was too vicarious to carry on. Looking like Moses in the wilderness with billowing beard and tattered waterproof cape, his arms gesticulating in all directions, he issued his orders. But the high winds channelling themselves through the narrow gorge were stronger than the Baptist Minister's good intentions and, in the end, the tents were abandoned while they all huddled miserably under sodden blankets. Overshadowed by a brooding and dangerous overhang, Angela prayed an avalanche of loose rocks driven before the wind, would not compound their miseries.

TWO

Bo (leader), General Garabanda, scowled at Prince Yoe. Raindrops on his waxed moustaches and black beard glistened like fat translucent lice. He blamed Yoe for having brought him so far from home.

Crouched behind his own rock, Prince Yoe, low on the scale of Burmese princes, pretended he had not seen the look Garabanda had given him. His thoughts concerning Garabanda were unflattering. 'That illegitimate whelp of an unspecified warrior-chief from regions unknown, and Indian nautch-girl of places well inhabited, has illusions of grandeur most unpleasing to me.'

Yoe shook the water from his telescope end and retracted it since it was utterly useless to try and see anything with the rain lashing his face. His Burmese turban felt like a solid lump of wet-washing on his head.

Prince Yoe, encompassed within a triangle of bitterness, only tolerated Garabanda. He needed the Bo-leader in order to settle his quarrel with the Raja of Manipur and Sir Edwin Tennent-Browne who represented the British- the British being at the apex of Prince Yoe's triangle and the main target of his aggression. For four days now, they had waited for Sir Edwin to travel this route through the Jainta Pass. He was to preside over the Court of Public Appeal in Shillong where plaintiffs could dispute territorial injustices with her Britannic Majesty's India Government and the Raja of Manipur whose Princely buffer state lay under the protection of the British. But Prince Yoe had already represented his case to the Court of Public Appeal, a year ago, and the Boundaries Commission with Sir Edwin Tennent-Browne presiding, had dismissed his appeal for restoration of his land on grounds of insufficient proof of

34

ownership — a paltry excuse indeed! But now there would be no more public appeals, only private deals at the end of a gun. Holding Sir Edwin Tennent-Browne to ransom would be a feather in his cap, thought Prince Yoe smugly. The Raja of Manipur and the British would not fail then to restore his territory — not if they wished to save Tennent-Browne's hide. Yoe permitted himself a sly smile behind his Burmese scarf. Yes, indeed! Garabanda's rag-tag-and-bobtail band of mercenaries, the whole of Asia commingled, Eurasian, Arab, Muslim, Mon, Chinese plus many other obscure nationalities of no fixed abode or religion, would catch Sir Edwin Tennent-Browne!

'My Prince!' Garabanda's rough voice with always an edge of scorn when addressing Prince Yoe, startled the Prince out of his day dreams. Garabanda wiped a filthy hand across his face, his waxed moustache seeming to mock Prince Yoe as, even in the rain, it curled dutifully up at the corners to remind Prince Yoe of Mustapha the camel-dealer. 'My Prince, how many moons does it take to wrestle with your conscience? We are all awaiting your order to attack and regrettably, my lord-prince, catching pneumonia in the meanwhile!'

Prince Yoe, while resenting Garabanda's disrespect, felt his heart leap a little on the word 'attack'. He put his telescope to his eye and peered down into the pass. The downpour had eased and he could make out through the murky atmosphere, a small group huddled with their pack-animals in the lee of the rocks. This was hardly the kind of entourage Sir Edwin of the Calcutta Boundaries Commission would be travelling with! Prince Yoe was disappointed as he examined the people in the pass. He felt Lord Buddha had played a dirty trick on him by sending him missionaries instead of Sir Edwin. One could smell missionaries a mile-off, ill-equipped, weary, sick, incompetent, their zeal far surpassing their common sense, they were always easy pickings where Garabanda and his thugs were concerned. Prince Yoe knew that Garabanda would attack that small party of helpless travellers, if not for their women, then for the medicine they always carried to cure the shaking fevers. The camp had no more quinine and they needed quinine.

Prince Yoe eased his conscience; Garbanda and his men would do the actual dirty work, leaving his hands free of blood. Prince Yoe decided to give any money and jewellery they found in the missionary camp, to the phongyi-kaung in his village. In that way, Lord Buddha would be appeased. Any blood spilled would be in the line of duty — the kala had a word for it, Crusade. Prince Yoe decided it was a most suitable word for what he was indulging in, even though he did not carry a cross.

Prince Yoe's thoughts were an agony to himself: He would refrain from any order to attack such a helpless group cowering in fear and misery down below. He would refrain from any lustings of the flesh, for he was a good Buddhist, or at least tried to be, and there would certainly be women in the missionary party, for it was the women more than the men who desired to convert the heathen — the heathen like Garabanda ...

'Who says we attack without our lord-prince's permission? Who says we leave him to his strange dreams while we count the loot?' Garabanda rallied his men boisterously, standing up on a rock and brandishing his rifle in the air as though he were on a Holy Crusade, while the assenting growls from behind the rocks were from the throats of animals: Prince Yoe also stood stiffly. He retracted his telescope. He pulled his wet scarf away from his face, but did not look at Garabanda when he spoke to him:

'Whatever my wishes might be, you, in the end, will do exactly as you please — as you always do,' he muttered to Garabanda before moving away from the edge of the precipice.

Garabanda's lusty laugh reverberated off the rocks, carrying to Yoe, 'Never mind, Yoe! You have a good General able to command the souls of devils who would eat their little Prince alive given half a chance. We'll bring back the red-haired woman for you. Through my glasses I have examined her well and she's a pleasing creature. You can teach her to perform the tricks of Buddha instead of her Jesus Christ.'

He was vile! Prince Yoe cringed inside his cave, shivering with the cold dark dampness all around. Even after his man-servant had removed his wet garments and wrapped him in warm dry rugs, he shivered with the knowledge of what was to come. His conscience grew heavier. He disliked the wanton desires of the flesh even more than the actual spilling of mens' blood. The destruction of innocence was a greater torment to his soul than the bullet in the gun; he knew, he had seen it all before where Garabanda and his animals were concerned.

Prince Yoe opened his texts. Sacred Theravada Scriptures might just make him forget he had in his employ an outcast animal called Garabanda, Bo-leader of rebel thugs!

THREE

The light was poor even though it was only mid-afternoon. Angela huddled deeper into her saturated blanket, pulling it over her hood under which strands of her bright hair had worked loose to be whipped across her face by the wind. She was hungry. They had had nothing hot to eat all day as the lethargic cook had been unable to get a fire started earlier, only cold dal for breakfast eaten from a communal dechi before setting off from Cherrapungi. And here they were, crouched in the lurid shadows of God's wrath like some super-imposed engraving taken right out of the Good Book. Any moment now she expected a stone tablet to come hurtling down from the mountain. Felicity, she saw, was crying, the girl's tears adding to the water in the world as well as the Reverend Quentin's ill-humour.

'Don't cry, Felicity,' Angela said, reaching out a hand to comfort her.

37

'I feel just like a child of Israel. My father and mother might place their faith in a God from whom all things flow, but as far as I'm concerned the only thing flowing is the monsoon.'

Angela could not restrain a little smile; poor Felicity, tormented in all directions.

'How lucky you are,' Felicity continued miserably, 'to be going to Mandalay to marry a nice handsome man.'

'Yes, Matthew's nice, but he isn't what one might call handsome. Though he does have a certain kind of attractiveness about him when he removes his spectacles. But that's not important, what is important is his wonderfully kind nature and warm personality.'

'Tell me again how you two met,' said Felicity eagerly, snuggling closer to Angela.

Angela laughed, 'Felicity dear, I've told you about Matthew and myself hundreds of times already. You must surely be bored with it all.'

'No. I'm only bored with myself. I shall probably marry a Chinaman. I'll never meet anyone on a romantic ship sailing to Bombay.'

'The ship was rather overcrowded and noisy. And Uncle Adrian Hawes made no bones about the fact he was my chaperon taking me out to my father and not into the arms of a "noodle of a young fellow" to use his words.' Angela smiled in memory of her Uncle Adrian who had been on leave in England, returning to Mandalay and looking ten years younger after his much-needed holiday in Bath. Dear man, thought Angela, at least he had been good enough to put in kind words on the 'noodle's' behalf when Matthew had applied for a job in Mandalay. And there they both were, in Mindon Min's fairytale city about which she had heard so much through Matthew's letters.

'You'll be in Mandalay long before I reach Peking. I wish I was going to Mandalay with you.'

'I shan't be heading for Mandalay straightaway,' said Angela. 'You must remember I told you about going to see my Aunt Lydell in Loloi first. I have to pay my respects to her as she's my mother's sister. After stopping off with her for a little while, I'll journey down to Mandalay via the Irrawaddy river. That will be exciting — but no less exciting than your travelling through China to be entertained at the Court of Emperor Kaung Hsu. Cheer up Felicity, we're all depressed because of this wretched weather, but once we get through these hills we'll make swifter progress. At least we're not at sea being lashed by the waves as well as the rain.'

'What about my father's tongue,' said Felicity bitterly.

'Cheer up do, you're making me miserable just looking at you. Felicity dear, life isn't that bad!'

Felicity thrust her small face closer, staring at Angela with eyes that burned fiercely; 'Angela, if I told you I hated my parents, would you be very shocked?'

Angela hesitated, 'No . . . no, I don't think so. I didn't know my parents, so I can't really be the judge.'

'They never really wanted me you know. I was an accident that came too late in their lives — I heard them talking about it once. Let me come to Mandalay with you, let me Angela.'

'Don't be silly.' Angela smiled and patted Felicity's hand reassuringly. 'Come on, one day soon you too will meet a handsome young man to sweep you off your feet . . .'

'A Chinaman,' Felicity scoffed with a little laugh. Again she leaned forward to peer into Angela's face, her own such a picture of misery and thwarted hopes, Angela felt sorry for the spirit that was being crushed. She knew that Minister Quentin would not allow Felicity even to look into a mirror for fear that her head might be turned through the sin of vanity.

Garabanda's bullet ricocheted from a shoulder of rock above the minister's head, almost killing him as it struck its own lightning from the granite. Felicity screamed, her hands over her ears in terror while the word *'Shaitans'* from panic-stricken camp bearers sent everyone diving for cover, some of the escort taking advantage of the confusion to steal away from the missionaries they were past caring about.

'Call them back, demand their return!' Dora Quentin's shrieks were whipped away by the wind to a pitiable lament, her up-raised bunched fists fighting the air: 'Farley, we are doomed if they desert us now. Do something will you,' she wept.

'Calm yourself dearest. I can do nothing if they're scared stiff and run off like frightened rabbits the moment a gun pops. Natives are most unreliable.'

'Then why in God's name did you pay them?' screamed the minister's wife who would have done something herself if she had not been afflicted with dysentery, terribly afraid to die in the Jainta Pass despite the promise of heaven. 'I knew we oughtn't to have paid them a pice till they'd proved themselves.'

'Let us pray,' said Minister Quentin, getting down on his knees and clasping his hands around his Bible. He, inadequate in his pious pratings, made Angela realize in that moment how Felicity must sometimes feel. His mild blue eyes blinking away a grey film of water, turned to her, his wet-whiskered face benign, his attitude one of infinite calm.

'Come, my child, kneel beside me and let us pray to God to help us. We must not let ourselves be panicked into a situation simply because our escort has run away. God will help us.'

Angela knelt, but instead of clasping her hands together in prayer, she clasped them round a 12-bore elephant gun she had brought from Delhi. She took careful aim through the sights, her slender arm all of a sudden amazingly strong and steady.

Garabanda, high on the rocks above, gave a low belly-laugh. His large discoloured teeth gaped the smile of a blood-thirsty shark. Someone down there had spirit. He was glad to see it was the woman with the sunset hair. 'Do not kill the women, only the men,' he ruthlessly ordered.

When the rattle of bullets from the San Mukh came, the missionaries' brave little stance was turned into a rout. Minister Quentin, still on his knees with his Bible in his hand, received a bullet through the head. The rest of the men lying dead around her, Angela, spattered with blood, knelt among them, her own gun empty.

Garabanda and his men filed down from the rocks like vultures to glean whatever they could find from the pathetic mess. Dora Quention and her daughter, their arms wrapped around each other, their faces hidden in the curtains of Dora's palanquin, were beyond knowing anything. Garabanda gave orders that none of the three women were to be molested in any way.

CHAPTER THREE

ONE

The *Coramandel*, a steamboat of the Irrawaddy Flotilla Company, chugged its noisy way south towards Amarapura, eleven miles from Mandalay. Aboard her was a noble retinue. Mr Hawes had been unable to secure a private interview with Captain Nathan Vorne in his prison, but Queen Sinpyumashin had informed him that two of her Atwinwun would be going to Sagaing prison to present to the Captain a document of indictment that required his signature. If Mr Hawes felt so inclined, he could accompany them to the prison and secure Captain de Veres-Vorne's signature in the presence of witnesses. Mr Hawes, with permission from the Queen, was also taking along his own witnesses, Edom Gideon, an American Gospel Preacher and his wife Nanette Hélène who was everybody's friend, including the Queen's. It had been a clever move on his part to bring Nanette along, for she gleaned and imparted information like none other in Mandalay — except perhaps the Shwe Nat himself.

Meanwhile, the golden devil was giving his tormentors a rough time. Nathan knew if he lost heart he would die, and so, to keep up morale, he sang:

'*Glory, Glory Hal-le-luuu-Yah*!' Happily, in foul confines where humanity rotted forgotten, the Shwe Nat survived.

'Silence, kala!' Tin-Sook-En shouted furiously.

42

Christened Uncle Grub by the Captain, he thrust his face into the prisoner's dirty face. The Shwe Nat sprouted a tempting beard and Tin-Sook-En was greatly tempted to chop it off there and then to keep him quiet. Instead, he raised his stump foot, amputated because he had brutally murdered a shopkeeper for no motive, and viciously kicked the Shwe Nat with the wooden prosthesis strapped to his ankle.

'Hey, Uncle Grub, have I ever told you what a whimper of a maggot you are?' Nathan spoke in English, deriving great satisfaction from abusing Tin-Sook-En without his understanding. He then said in Burmese; 'What a half-Chink bastard you are.'

'Silence kala!'

'*I have read a fiery gospel writ in burnished rows of steel* ... I know I oughtn't to sing such a song, not a good Confederate man like me, if one can call it singing. See here, Grub, cut lips, swollen blubber jaws of a dolphin. One day I'm going to pay you back, fly offal. Freedom I scream! Hey, Grub, let me out of the leperous colony of depravity and I'll buy you some ngapi.'

'*My country 'tis of thee, sweet land of Liberty*' he carolled with all his strength and hoped Grub was becoming more annoyed. '*Thy woods and templed hills, my heart with rap-ture thrills* ... hey, Grub, I want to pee in the bucket ...'

Tin-Sook-En had had enough of the kala who sang in a tongue he did not understand and insulted him in ways he did. He picked up the half-filled canvas bucket used for night soil and flung it at Nathan to the delight of the other Spotted Faces.

Only the other prisoners remained impassive, eyes closed against the harshness of reality and the noise the golden devil insisted on making. Their sentiments were that to fight only meant it took longer to die, and so they offered the Spotted Faces no resistance.

'Bloody barbarian, I want some water, I want some freedom and I want to be cleaned up,' Nathan bellowed.

'You're always wanting something, kala. I'll give you

43

something.' Tin-Sook-En began to flay the kala's back and feet with bamboo. Afterwards, he turned to the Spotted Faces: 'This golden-haired kala with the blind eyes is crazy! I hurt him, beat him, kick him, string him up and still he sings. Never has it taken so long to chastise anyone, and truly, he must be that Nat spirit of destruction. But I'm told I mustn't kill his body, only his mind and spirit, and that is not possible. I'll go to Father, and you, Lo Choon, can take my place. I'll see what else can be done to chastise this kala.'

But Tin-Sook-En was back sooner than expected. With him was the man they called 'Father', ruler of the Spotted Faces for this section of the prison. Father was angry.

He took his wrath out on Tin-Sook-En: 'Fool!' he shouted, beating him, 'He is to be taken to the noble Atwinwun. How can I present him in this state? Release him!' Uncle Grub began to strike off his fetters, none too gently, and the rusty rims dug into Nathan's bruised and torn flesh. He set his jaw, wondering what new diabolic-device they had in mind for him now. To his amazement he was taken into the yard where he was stripped and sluiced down with not altogether clean water but cleaner than he had been used to. Then he was given a ladleful to drink, and a clean shirt and trousers to put on.

He began to wonder if he were having hallucinations, especially when Father handed him a toothless comb for his tangled hair.

TWO

The Burmese officials from the Hlutdaw descended the worn gangplank to the dirty, smelly shore of Sagaing. The ferryboat had taken them from the Ava shore to that of Sagaing where the great fortress on the hill marked their destination. But prettier than the prison were the myriad white temples and pagodas gleaming through the green net of Burma's tropical splendour.

Flame-of-the forest trees scattered their pendulous scarlet blossoms in a flowered benediction on the heads and golden umbrellas of the little knot of important people ascending the hill-path.

'Good morning, Giddy, Nan ... Mr Hawes,' said Nathan, pleasantly surprised when he was finally brought before them. They were in a stone watchtower in the garrison section of the prison and from the slit of glassless window, Nathan could see his beloved Irrawaddy. He turned his back on it. They allowed him to sit because of his raw feet, but the delegation remained standing. Nathan, placed on a wooden bench before a long teak table in the otherwise bare room, felt conspicuous, especially as they all insisted in staring at him. 'Well, I guess this is the execution squad,' he said, pulling his ear, his forced smile rueful. 'Are you to give me the last rites and extreme unction, Giddy, while sweet Nan is to feed me my last meal and testimony?' He eyed the laden basket on the table. 'I hope you've included the rum ...'

Mr Hawes, momentarily nonplussed and greatly shocked by the American's appearance, found his voice; 'Captain Vorne, you're a bigger fool than I'd previously supposed.'

Nathan bowed his head. He had always entertained a feeling Adrian Hawes did not much care for him. But the old stickler to duty was a shrewd vulture and Nathan never for one moment underestimated the British Resident.

The Hlutdaw's interpreter translated the English conversation for the benefit of the Atwinwun who nodded at each other, in total agreement with Mr Hawes. Then a parabaik was produced, elaborately signed, sealed and beribboned. It was passed across to Nathan. He unrolled it, and, through swollen eyelids, perused its contents. It was written in English and Burmese.

'We ...' Mr Hawes indicated the four Europeans present, 'all speak Burmese, so let us speak Burmese and dispense with the interpreter. A lot easier.'

'Our Divine Majesty, the Queen Sinpyumashin, Chief Queen of our noble King and Lord, Mindon Min, commands that the American Captain place his signature to the document of confession.' The senior Atwin-wun indicated the parchment scroll.

Nathan ignored him and passed the document to Mr Hawes who already had his hand outstretched. The British Resident read the charges brought against the American. At length he looked up, lips thin beneath his mournful grey moustache. 'Mr Gideon, would you like me to read out the charges your countryman is accused of? I take responsibility in all this since he has no legal representation in Mandalay at the present time. I am sir, also a trained barrister,' he added. Edom Gideon shrugged his massive shoulders indifferently, a stocky, surly man, he didn't care what the American Captain might or might not have done, he was only there on sufferance.

'The charges brought against Captain Vorne are manifold,' Mr Hawes continued, and clearing his throat read them out; 'He is accused of stealing rubies from the Queen of Burma's Royal mines at Mogok. Trading illicitly and contravening the official Treaty of Yandabo. Consorting with foreign traders contrary to agreements with Upper Burma, thereby undermining monopolies of the King. The money received from ill-gotten gains used to further the cause of pretender princes to the Burmese throne. For inciting to murder and rebellion subjects of their Majesties the King and Queen of Burma. And in all such activities the said American Captain, Nathanial de Veres-Vorne, has incurred the very great displeasure of the Kaungbaung Dynasty and the Court of Ava. He is therefore an unworthy citizen of the realm. A sentence of death will be mooted to one of deportation if the American Captain, Nathanial de Veres-Vorne, were to sign the document of confession on the charges brought against him. That's it in a nutshell, gentlemen,' said Mr Hawes, ignoring Mrs Gideon's presence.

Nathan snorted in disgust and turning to the Atwinwun said; 'Keep your trumped up piece of paper Ministers. I sign nothing! That rubbish ...' he flicked his fingers in the direction of the parabaik, 'is so flimsy, a fly can wipe its ass on it. Your assurances mean nothing to me and you can go home and tell your divining Queen, I said so!'

Burmese faces darkened to a leathery glow at the rebuttal of all their good intentions. The American had insulted them. Mr Hawes, realizing Nathan Vorne's truculence was not going to be the salvation of his neck, attempted to remedy the matter;

'Would it not be possible for Captain Vorne to be given the status of a political prisoner in view of the fact he's been charged as one?' He asked the Atwinwun. 'He could then be taken out of the hands of the Spotted Faces to the garrison section of the prison where he might be better treated.'

'It is the wish of our Divine Queen that the American Captain remain in the care of the Spotted Faces,' the Senior Minister said with great dignity.

Nanette Gideon came to the rescue. 'In that case poor Nat will be starving! I've brought him food.' She went over to the tiffin-basket and took off the napkin. 'The Spotted Faces may search it thoroughly and see as sure as God made li'le apples I'm telling the truth. The Shwe Nat must be fed. If he dies, the Queen of Burma is sure going to be mad as hell. I'm her best friend on the whiteside of things, and I know what's in that lady's mind for sure! If I tell her Shwe Nat's been badly treated, she's going to be so incensed, she'll cut out every Spotted tongue around here,' Nanette Gideon warned, replacing the napkin over the tiffin-basket before beguiling the Atwinwun with soulful eyes. 'Maybe he'll sign that silly piece of paper when he's been fed.' She turned back to Nathan, cajoling him, 'Say yes honey, for my sake.' After a great deal of muttering between themselves, the Atwinwun agreed. The Senior Minister, frighteningly regal, addressed himself to Father and Uncle Grub; 'Feed the prisoner. Don't let him die, otherwise it will be the worst for you. You will be put to death slowly over the snakepit of your own devising if the Queen's prisoner dies before his time. The document of confession will be placed with the Commander of the Royal Guard to whom you are directly responsible.' He stared at Father. 'He will be taken out of the inner prison forthwith and confined in the stockade in the compound. When he is ready and willing, he is to sign the parabaik which must be brought to Mandalay immediately. Make certain we do not have to wait too long,' and upon that cryptic note he focused his unblinking eyes on Nathan. 'Captain de Veres-Vorne, you are a foolish man if you do not prefer banishment to death. After all, Rangoon I'm told is a very nice city, and has the advantage of being British.'

'Mandalay, sir, is where my home is,' Nathan retorted, 'citizenship granted me by no less a person than King Mindon Min!'

The Atwinwun inclined their Burmese topknots gracefully, and after the grand shikkos performed at their feet by the Spotted Faces, left the room. Nanette was the last in line to file out of the watchtower. At the entrance where two Burmese soldiers in their eye-catching magenta uniforms stood guard, she blew him a kiss.

Ruefully he fingered the front of his shirt. 'I guess Daw Khin Htay'll have a hard time of getting my dhobi-wash clean after they've made me sign away my life. But you make mighty sure, Nan, they bury me in a clean shirt, else I'll be back to haunt the hide off you. And thanks for tiffin, honey.' He gave her a wink with an eye already half closed.

48

CHAPTER FOUR

ONE

Prince Yoe was captivated. Not only did the woman with the green eyes and hair like burnished copper enchant him, but also her Fox-Talbot. He remained mystified by the seemingly empty box that had the power to put images on paper. He had never seen anything like it and was half afraid of the spirits it might contain.

'But where do the spirits that perform this strange magic transference of likeness live?' he wanted to know for the umpteenth time.

'It's really quite simple,' Angela patiently explained.

'In the hands of the ignorant the picture can be spoiled. Either light gets into the camera, it's shaken, or not properly focused; all sorts of mistakes can prevent a good picture developing.'

'Who gave you this magic box?'

'My father. He's dead now. But he left it to me. He was a very keen amateur photographer. In fact, here's one of his pictures I found amongst my things.' She handed Prince Yoe a Daguerretype taken years before by her father. It was of a tiger-shoot in Bengal. Prince Yoe took his time studying it, and was reluctant to hand it back.

'Tomorrow,' he said, 'will you take another picture of me?' He was like a child.

'I'd be delighted,' said Angela. 'That's if I've any plates left.'

'I'll buy you some more when we reach Mandalay,'

said Yoe, and Angela was touched by his consideration though it was the first she had heard of Yoe going to Mandalay. Prince Yoe sighed deeply. 'Alas, I fear, Miss Featherstone, General Garabanda also desires your magic camera. He keeps his picture pinned to the pole of his tent where he can see himself at all times.'

Angela hoped that would be all Garabanda ever wanted from her in the light of poor Felicity Quentin's fate. Garabanda had taken her for his own vile purpose and Felicity, after the first time of being subjected to him, had remained mute ever since, while her mother had turned grey overnight. Now, Felicity seemed not to care one way or another, and Angela wondered if the tragedy had wounded Felicity more deeply than she wished anyone to know. Angela was forever thankful she had Prince Yoe on her side. From that first day of their ignominious capture by these hill-ruffians, Yoe had taken her under his wing. That it was a good Buddhist one made Angela all the more grateful. She had nurtured the prince's platonic friendship, exchanging Fox-Talbot for Theravada Buddhism — about which she wanted to know a lot more. Prince Yoe took pleasure in being her tutor, teaching her all about the Tripitaka Texts, which he told her were the Three Baskets of the Sacred Pali Scripts of the Lesser Vehicle known as Theravada Buddhism.

Spending her time with him therefore, was far more pleasurable than being a prisoner in the women's tent listening to Dora Quentin's fevered ravings. Prince Yoe's cave in the San Mukh was more than just a bare hole. He had turned his temporary headquarters into an Aladdin's cavern of warmth and security. Thick Oriental carpets, silver candlesticks, dainty pieces of bamboo and lacquered furniture made it a welcome place to retreat to — as long as Garabanda was not there too.

Garabanda came often. He came now, thrusting his way unceremoniously into Prince Yoe's presence. He laughed in a coarse, lewd manner when he came across her speaking with Yoe. Angela hated his unwelcome intrusions and he always came besotted with toddy-palm liquor.

'Don't get too fond of the Fox-Talbot,' Garabanda warned Yoe. 'Remember our bargain, the camera for the woman's honour.'

Angela glanced at Prince Yoe who had turned aside, blushing deeply. In a way she was relieved, relieved and touched by Yoe's own code of honour, angry that Garabanda had forced them all into such a disgraceful situation. The murder of Minister Quentin and the few faithful retainers left in their party, she would never forget. It was a scene of bloodshed and waste that haunted her in her sleep — more so because of the cold-blooded and immoral way human lives could be dispensed with by those of a violent inclination like the unspeakable Garabanda.

'Now Yoe, I want this woman removed. Tell your guards to take her away and tie her up once more with the old baggage who has a whore for a daughter. We've something important to discuss concerning the Britisher who is himself the sweeper-boy of the Raja of Manipur. We don't want this English bitch listening to us with her ears flapping, do we?' He lifted a strand of her hair, his roving black glances lascivious.

Shuddering at his touch, Angela was glad to be led away by Prince Yoe's guards. They secured her with a double twist of coir rope round her waist to the central pole of the tent she shared with Felicity and her mother. In this manner, she had enough freedom to move as far as the entrance to the tent, but that was all.

Dora Quentin, dying with pneumonia and dysentery, lay on a damp blanket without even a straw pallet under her. She turned a stiff, fever-driven face to Angela, thinking it was Felicity returned after being with that loathsome creature who had put a bullet through her beloved Farley's head. Dora, in pain and anguish, wished the Lord had shown her the same mercy by having her finished off in the same way.

'Angela ...' she whispered, her eyes closing. 'I'm glad

it's you ... please ... a little water ...'

'Of course.' Angela propped up the sick woman's head and helped her to drink from the cup. Dora could only manage a few sips before dropping back in exhaustion and Angela heard the unmistakable sounds of the water immediately gushing out of her. No wonder she was so dehydrated. But Garabanda had refused them a doctor and medicines. The only mercy that could be shown her now was that she might die without any further pain. She sat by Dora Quentin and mopped the gaunt perspiring face. She had seen this women reduced from a buxom, fourteen stone creature when they set off from Delhi, to half that weight by the time they reached Cherrapungi. In the last few days, Dora Quentin had diminished to the proportions of a child so that it was hard to believe she was the same Baptist missionary's wife of such robust health and unflagging strength of character forever urging them all onward and forward. Dora squeezed her hand, light as a whisper; 'You're a good, stalwart girl, Angela Featherstone', she said, 'and God will bless you. I'm glad too, they spared you ... those men ...' her voice faded away and she fell into a fevered doze.

Angela, her spine pressed uncomfortably against the tent-pole, slept in an upright position.

TWO

While the Atwinwun and their entourage were borne away from the river shore to the city centre on gaily caparisoned elephants, Nanette, her husband and Mr Hawes walked from where the boats tied up at Go Wain, to Mandalay. The river journey and scenes at the prison had disturbed and tired him greatly, and Mr Hawes was glad to get back. The Gospel Preacher announced his fervent intention to return with all speed to the Mission Hall for his evening Bible Meeting. 'And I'm late!' he snapped.

He rushed on ahead of them, and since they were now alone Nanette remarked to the British Resident, 'They've beaten poor Nat till he doesn't remember anymore the things he should. Daw Khin Htay is an old and wealthy Burmese woman who lives on Mandalay Hill. She doesn't wash Nat's clothes, and never has done. Nor does Minthami, but Ko Lee's mother, Fee Tam does. You remember the Chinese boy he rescued from drowning some years back? Well, in gratitude, his mother does the Captain's washing and brings his shirts up like pastry. Nat's mighty particular about the way he looks and doesn't care for bugs in the clothes which give one the dhobi-itch. So all that nonsense about Daw Khin Htay doesn't make sense to me, since the only thing that old Burmese woman's done in her life is deliver babies. She's the royal midwife, you see, Mr Hawes.'

'Tell me more, Mrs. Gideon, about Daw Khin Htay.' Mr Hawes had a strange feeling Nathan Vorne had been name dropping for a purpose.

Nanette was delighted to talk: 'Like I said, Mr Hawes, she's the fat old midwife who lives behind the White Pagoda and its Phongyi-Kyaung up on Mandalay Hill. She showed me once a golden tray Mindon Min gave her. Its the Burmese custom to present royal babies to their father, the King, on a solid gold tray. Well now, after the successful birthing of one special prince, Mindon Min let her keep the tray. She showed it to me when I went to her for my own condition as Giddy's always bin mighty put out about my not producing no dukes of Gideon nor no duchesses either ...' She was going off at a tangent and Mr Hawes pulled her back in the direction he wished her to go. 'Mrs Gideon, which prince did Daw Khin Htay deliver to Mindon Min's Queen?'

'Now there you got me,' Nanette said shrugging lightly. 'I guess I've no idea at all since the name was never mentioned. There're so many of them in the Burmese Royal Family, what with all their lesser wives and concubines and whatnot going on behind their

Buddhist screens, its a job to tell one rabbit from another. Daw Khin Htay's a funny old thing but wise, especially in her midwifery practice. If I hadn't seen that golden tray with my very own eyes, I guess I'd have thought she dreamt it all — though a lump of solid gold ain't never a bad dream, eh Mr Hawes? But the Burmese are like that, from King to commoner. Generous to a fault in material things and real mean when it gets to things like the Spotted Faces.'

'Mrs Gideon, where can I find Daw Khin Htay? You mentioned some monastery . . .'

'Why sure I did, Mr Hawes, the White Pagoda, half-way up Mandalay Hill. Daw Khin Htay lives in a little wooden house up against its west wall, a grace and favour place given her by Mindon Min for services rendered. What with that and the gold, I don't reckon its a bad business being a royal midwife. But it's sure a mighty climb, Mr Hawes, and you oughtn't to do it, not with that bad heart of yours. Its two thousand steps . . .'

'Yes, yes, I'm perfectly capable of climbing steps, Mrs Gideon!' Mr Hawes said irritably.

'Well then . . .' she broke off to stare after her husband. 'Well now, I do declare, Mr Hawes, will you look at his bad manners! If Giddy does not wish to accompany me back home — as he so obviously does not by the way he's marching on with such ill-concealed zeal, then I feel under no obligation to attend his Bible Meeting. I'll take you to Daw Khin Htay myself.'

'I'm very grateful to you Mrs Gideon.'

Mr Hawes opened a white wicket gate leading into a garden bright and fragrant with jasmine, orange, red and yellow canna lilies and creamy frangipani whose essence compensated for the scentless asters. Being an Englishman who loved a garden, he was impressed by its well-tended beauty. Turtle doves browsed in unfathomable peace beside the mistress of this tiny paradise halfway up Mandalay Hill.

Daw Khin Htay snored beneath a Hopia tree,

wonderful in her immense size and serenity. She did not
stir when her visitors startled the young Phongyi medita-
ting on a prayer mat at her feet. His begging bowl, earlier
filled with rice and vegetables from his benefactress's
table, was held in the lotus cup of his lap.

Mr Hawes regarded monks who tramped the streets
of Mandalay begging a living with their black lacquered
bowls like the bald-headed vultures that crouched in the
trees — shaven heads, glittering eyes unblinking over
hooked beaks, brown scraggy arms clutching scraps in
black-bellied bowls — all orange birds of prey feeding off
others. However, this one at Daw Khin Htay's feet
appeared different. Plump and golden, his well-built
shoulders were sleek as silk, his saffron robe of better
quality than usual. Beneath the air of calm piety, sat a
well ordered and handsome young man who had been
bred to be very positive as to his station in life.

The cautious young phongyi bowed his head. The
hour for breaking his fast and his silence had not yet
arrived, and so he rose up on silent bare feet to slip away
to his monastery, leaving behind him an aura of curiosity.

Both Nanette and Mr Hawes were fully aware of the
Burmese belief that a sleeping person should not be
startled lest their spirit be lost forever to wander alone in
darkness, but Nanette knew Mr Hawes was in a hurry
and Daw Khin Htay was quite capable of sleeping on
until the moon set. She said to Mr Hawes when shaking
Daw Khin Htay's fat shoulder: 'Giddy's always waking
me from my sleep and he reckons he's saved my soul, so
I guess it won't do her much harm ... Daw Khin Htay,
wake up please, it's Ma Nan. I've brought an important
man to see you.'

Daw Khin Htay's white topknot secured with silver
and tortoiseshell combs tottered perilously with the
sudden rude awakening. 'Ma Nan ...' she mumbled
sleepily, her pendulous cheeks wobbling like pear-drops
while dozens of gold bracelets made music on her arms.
She yawned widely, blinked the sleep from her and woke

up to see two people leaning closely over her as if they would abduct her from her garden. She was alarmed at first, then her huge flat face became wreathed in smiles, pushing up her eyes into sloe-slits of Oriental welcome.

'Sit please.' She spoke a little English to them and indicated the coconut mat recently vacated by her special Phongyi who had come to give her his blessing. 'Ma Ngwe, who is niece of Daw Khin Htay, she will bring tea and cakes for illustrious guests. You sit down please. Daw Khin Htay very happy to see Breetish Resident and Ma Nan.'

Ma Ngwe soon appeared with tea and refreshments from the charming teak house built in the style of all houses in Mandalay, with tiered roofs and clever carvings, a verandah running all the way round, and shutters at the windows.

'Daw Khin Htay,' began Mr Hawes, wishing to get on with business straightaway, even though he knew it was impolite to hasten one's hostess before she had sipped her tea: 'I would wish to ask you a few important questions if I may, but I'm afraid my time is short so I can't stay too long.'

She understood. 'Ma Khin Htay,' she answered, referring to herself less formally 'pleased to answer any questions from Breetish Resident, if she know answers to them.'

'Daw Khin Htay, do you know an American gentleman by the name of Nathanial de Veres-Vorne?'

Daw Khin Htay frowned, and then Ma Ngwe bent over to whisper something in the old woman's ear, the teapot still in her hand. 'Ah yes!' Again her face was wreathed in wonderful smiles. 'You mean Shwe Nat of Mandalay, tall riverboat Captain? Yes, Ma Khin Htay know golden devil very well.' Then her expression clouded: 'Something happen to him?' She asked anxiously.

'Yes, I'm afraid so. He's in the Sagaing death prison.'

She exclaimed dismay on a long drawn out note. 'Ahhh, then proud riverboat Captain will die. No man

56

lives who is at mercy of Spotted Faces. He must do bad, very bad things, to be locked in there.'

'What things do you think he might have done, Daw Khin Htay?' Gently persuasive, he wanted to wheedle as much information from her as possible if only to confirm his own suspicions in a curious matter. Proof was what he required if he were to make them believe him in Rangoon, solid proof.

'I know not U Hawes. Everyone hear a lot of every-one else's business in Mandalay, Ma Khin Htay hear nothing of what Shwe Nat do now. When he come here, it only to bring fine silk from Siam, pearls from Ceylon and tea from India. Nothing more ... ah wait, there is one thing more,' she touched a pudgy finger to her fore-head. 'It always to talk to special Phongyi over there.' The finger indicated the white monastery wall bounding her garden, the monastery itself screened by thick Neam trees planted for good luck. 'Shwe Nat come to talk to Phongyi on many matters and always for long hours. Maybe riverboat Captain wish to become Buddhist monk!' Delighting herself with her own joke, she began to heave like a small volcanic implosion. Presently Daw Khin Htay calmed down and wiped her eyes on a dainty handkerchief given her by Queen Sinpyumashin who had embroidered her initials and crest herself.

Daw Khin Htay had obviously led a good life at the Court of Ava, thought Mr Hawes as he took stock of the happy old woman, and to be fat in Burma was a sign of blessed prosperity.

She added placidly, 'But Shwe Nat forgiven if he does not always come to see Ma Khin Htay for herself, for he have such preety eyes and handsome body.'

He was not interested in the Shwe Nat of Mandalay as much as the 'Special Phongyi'. 'Can you remember, Daw Khin Htay, the name of the Buddhist monk Captain Vorne comes to see?'

'Always Ma Khin Htay remember name, U Hawes, but she never tell.' Her benign face became enigmatic, full of secrets, and for her own protection, he knew her lips were sealed regarding the identity of the monk in whom Nathan Vorne appeared to have a vested interest.

His face must have betrayed his frustration, for the Burmese woman clapped her hands sharply and to take him off the subject, asked, 'You wish to see golden tray from Lord of White Elephants, U Hawes?'

'Delighted,' he murmured, his thoughts not on golden trays but on what business Nathan Vorne had with a Buddhist monk.

She instructed Ma Ngwe to bring the golden tray. 'Please to take more refreshment,' Daw Khin Htay told them indicating the little tea-table adorned with a spotless white cloth and napkins. 'Ma Nan, she see golden tray from Mindon Min, now you please to look at it U Hawes.'

When Ma Ngwe brought the famous tray, Mr Hawes bowed beneath its weight, and marvelled the girl could carry it across the lawn. It was indeed a thing of beauty, and as he turned it over, the setting sun caught and struck rubies, diamonds and emeralds from the solid gold, every ounce of it a King's ransom.

'When Ma Khin Htay die, she leave golden tray to White Pagoda monastery,' the old woman said. 'For moment, it brighten up dark places of Ma Khin Htay little house and this old heart which soon return to Buddha. It will not be long now, U Hawes, but Ma Khin Htay have very good life and much happiness. In next cycle of rebirth, she maybe have even better time, eh Ma Nan?' She nudged her niece lightly with her immense elbow.

Mr Hawes was not paying the old woman any attention. On the back of the tray was a Burmese inscription: 'Tranquil and led by the good doctrines, I would hatred calm:' and then the date and time of the royal birth. But there was no name.

Excited by what Daw Khin Htay was trying to tell him in a very subtle way, her lips that were indeed sealed, now spoke volumes through the golden tray. He had a date and a time and his own records would provide him with the name. He was shaking so much with nervous agitation he had to hand back the tray to Ma Ngwe.

'Thank you,' he said, wiping his sticky brow with a mildewed handkerchief, his grey whiskers quivering. 'You have been most kind and hospitable, Daw Khin Htay. And now forgive me, but I must get back to the Residency. Come Mrs Gideon.' He put out a hand and assisted her to her feet. 'A splendid tray, Daw Khin Htay, truly splendid, and I'm grateful to you for allowing me the privilege of seeing it. Goodbye.'

'Goodbye, U Hawes, Ma Nan ... Ma Khin Htay too fat and old to see you out, but Ma Ngwe do it for her,' and she added a Burmese benediction as they departed, 'May you go with happiness in your stride.'

In purple stealth, long evening shadows stretched across the scented garden like probing fingers searching out the white stone monastery whose walls bounded many secrets.

Royal gold for a Royal prince, were Mr Hawes' thoughts on the way back. Not a bad day's work at all! He murmured to himself.

'Mr Sinclair,' he barked, once sun-helmet and baton were on his desk and he had asked the bearer to fetch fresh drinking water, 'I want you to take this down. We must send off a wire at once — in code if you please — to the C.C. in Rangoon. Let's hope we receive a swift directive in answer ... and why are you in your dressing-gown?'

'I was about to go to bed, sir.'

'So early? Never mind, I don't wish to know. How much does my niece mean to you, young man?'

'Everything in the world, sir.' Matthew wondered where all this was leading.

'Then, young sir, this is not the time for Angela to set foot in Mandalay and you must write and tell her so — immediately! Thanks to our intrepid American Captain, I have begun to uncover a most sinister plot at the Court of Ava. And we're not talking about a few miserable rubies at stake, but a whole empire of wealth! Is there a

59

trustworthy European in Mandalay who can handle this for us? I really don't want to use the Burmese.'

'Yes sir. A chap named Buchanan recently arrived out here to set up a modern telegraph system for the Burmese.'

'Well, Mr Sinclair, I rely on your judgement. Now get this down. Let's see what the Chief Commissioner makes of it all.'

CHAPTER FIVE

ONE

A ngela raised the candle high and looked into the
sick woman's sleeping face. It was peaceful; too
peaceful. She held the candle nearer and saw the film-
dew of perspiration had become the waxy green-sheen of
death. No fluttering came from the thinly pinched
nostrils but only the stench of inner rotting from the
slack mouth. Half-closed eyes stared out eerily from
purple sockets and in that uncanny suspension of a living
soul, Angela did not know what to do. She knew nothing
about laying out a dead person and to have to do it to
the emaciated, foul body of Dora Quentin, repelled her.
Felicity would not do it, she knew for certain. In her
heart Angela could not be sorry Dora Quentin was dead.
She had led such a dreadful existence since that day in
the Jainta Pass.

She straightened Dora's limbs as best she could,
wondering at what hour during the night she had died.
Angela went to the tent flap where two sleepy guards
stirred irritably at her voice. She held out a bowl and
demanded water, the sponge she had used to bathe
Dora's fevered body in her other hand. The guards
objected, refusing to oblige. The language barrier was so
difficult Angela was at a loss how to tell them if the
corpse were not washed immediately and removed for
burial, they would all sicken and die. Turning to one of
them, a surly hill-man thickly muffled in bright woolen
garments, his face obscured in his manifold scarves, she

drew him with gestures inside the tent.

His shriek on seeing Dora's corpse must have been heard throughout the slumbering camp. During her travels Angela had learned about the superstitions of the hill-people, their belief in animism and evil spirits haunting places of death. Angela hoped it would serve to frighten off all the men from the women's tent now that Dora's sick body was no more an obvious deterrent. But she did in the end get water with which to wash Dora's body, and a cloth in which to wrap her corpse.

In the dawn light Felicity returned, escorted by one of Garabanda's guards. She did not look at the body under the sheet but sat cross-legged on the ground, her eyes vacant. Angela noticed the two high spots of colour burning the girl's cheeks.

'Felicity,' she whispered, 'we ... you and I have *got* to try and escape from this place. Now that your mother's dead, she can't protect us from those men through the very fact of her illness. You know they won't come anywhere near the bed of a sick woman. But now she's gone, things will be worse for us.'

'For you,' said Felicity torpidly. 'I haven't anything to lose. Garabanda saw to that ... but I don't mind. Not anymore. Not now I know what it's all about, and it isn't as bad as they say ... not if you don't put up any resistance and let your mind think of something else.'

'Oh, Felicity!' said Angela in exasperation, 'please don't talk like that. Your poor mother went through agonies on your behalf and was only thankful your father wasn't alive to see your humiliation at Garabanda's hands.'

Felicity's golden head jerked up, her blue eyes fierce and the colour in her cheeks deepening. 'It's easy for you to talk like that Angela Featherstone, they don't want *your* virginity. At least Garabanda is a man, not some ... some little boy like Yoe. ... Anyway, we can't run away. They'll soon catch us, and then it could get a lot worse. Garabanda has made me his woman and has promised that as soon as Prince Yoe ennobles him, he'll marry me and make me his princess. ...'

'Felicity!' Angela said impatiently, 'don't be a little fool! Only a King or Queen can ennoble anyone. Garabanda is a monster and his promises mean nothing. He's playing with you, and as soon as he tires of you he's going to throw you to the rest of the pack ...'

'Shut-up, Angela!'

In the silence, irrepressible tears trickled down Felicity's face. 'I wonder what you'd do, what you'd think and say in my ... my position after what I've ... I've been reduced to. Peking might have been better for me in the long run ...'

'Felicity dear,' Angela fell on her knees beside the girl, gathering her into her arms, 'My poor, poor child. We'll go to Mandalay together. We must, Felicity.' She held her at arm's length and looked into the stricken face. Felicity, whom she had taken to be a wanton little wretch, who indeed had seemed so willing to sell her soul to the devil, was at heart, terrified. 'Listen, we must make plans. We've been here six days now, and I've noticed the way the guards are slacking their vigilance — and how they've started to look at us. Garabanda won't be able to keep them at bay, not when he can't be bothered anymore. And no one pays much attention to Prince Yoe. Then, it's going to be much much worse for you, and me. So we've got to escape. Let's sit down together and work out how, please Felicity?'

She shook her head. 'No. It won't work. We can't escape, Angela, and it's no good thinking we can. If they catch us, then it *will* be awful, so I'd rather stay with Garabanda and know my future. I don't mind being a foreign princess or even a General's wife.'

Angela felt like shaking the silly minx. She stood up and looking down on Felicity's head said, 'I don't understand you at all, Felicity Quentin, but I do pity you. You're also a selfish little baggage because you know I won't think of escaping if it means leaving you here alone.'

'Then you'd better become Prince Yoe's concubine, hadn't you Angela?' she retorted, tossing her head so

63

that Angela could have slapped her hard. 'Now leave me alone. I want to get some sleep ... when are they coming to remove her ... her body?'

'Don't worry, Felicity, I'm sure your mother will have better things to do than return to haunt a daughter who's most certainly given her soul to the devil!'

Felicity suddenly burst into a flood of tears and this time it was she who threw herself at Angela. 'Oh don't ... don't! Please don't be beastly to me Angela. You're all I've got now ... and I'm so afraid of Garabanda, you don't know how afraid. That's why I obey him without question. But please don't be angry with me ... please don't. Anger is something I always had to bear from my father and mother, anger and preaching. Garabanda never preaches and if I'm good, he's never angry with me. Please try and understand Angela, please!'

Thrown together pitiably through a miserable twist of fate, gently Angela smoothed Felicity's tangled hair and said: 'I understand, of course I do ... but we must get away from here. You will think about it, won't you, Felicity?'

She nodded, 'yes, all right ... now will you ask them to come and take my mother's body away for burial?'

'I rather think, my dear, we're going to have to do it all ourselves as those superstitious rogues won't touch her.'

TWO

During the afternoon, while Felicity slept, Angela and Prince Yoe spent the time discussing photography and the Buddhist scriptures. She had no intimation at that time of what was to follow.

In the evening two guards came to their tent, she and Felicity having had a meagre supper of thin soup and rice. Hindi had become the mode of communication as a few men in Yoe's camp spoke the language, and so did she, if only a very little.

'Please come, His Highness Prince Yoe requires your presence.'

'He must mean you,' Felicity said with a sly smile as she wiped out her soupbowl with a piece of chupatty.

But inside the San Mukh cave Angela came before Garabanda and not Yoe. At once her nerves were set jangling. Garabanda sat on Yoe's camp-bed, but the cave had been stripped of its luxurious furnishings and in place of silver candlesticks, small butter-lamps gave little light and ominous shadows.

'What's become of Prince Yoe?' Angela asked, trying to put on a brave face despite a terrible fear seizing her.

Garabanda wiped the back of his hand over his thick red lips and stretched for some more of the toddypalm juice in a flagon at his feet. 'He's been recalled to Mandalay. His mother, only a minor princess at the court of Ava — despite Yoe's grand illusions and self-importance over a few yards of swampy territory he claims is his, wishes him to attend a royal wedding. Its a diplomatic union I'm told, the House of Ava wishing to consolidate its hold on the country. A fat lot that ineffectual dolt can do to consolidate anything. Here ...' he tossed a book at her. 'The Buddhist dolt who couldn't kill a fly wishes you to have this. May it do you a lot of good.'

Garabanda's laugh was a low rumble of bad intentions that reinforced her decision to escape from this loathsome camp — more than ever now in view of Prince Yoe's desertion. She took up the prince's gift. He had left her his beautiful book of Theravada texts and while she was touched by the gesture, tears of aggravation stung her; Why-oh-why hadn't he told her he was leaving and she would have begged to go with him! But in her heart Angela knew how much of a moral coward was Yoe who took the lines of least resistance where it concerned Garabanda. She looked round the cave and saw her Fox-Talbot placed on a camp-table in the corner — the camera for her honour. She wondered if Garabanda would indeed honour the bargain. In the next few seconds she received her answer.

'Come, tall lady,' Garabanda said, leaning forward to catch hold of her hand, 'I too would wish to make you a gift; myself.' His insinuation striking terror through her heart, she could not disguise her shockwaves of disgust. His wide shark's smile grew and grew in front of her eyes until she could only see the entire universe filled with those awful teeth. Stupidly she began to laugh, for all she could associate with the sight of those teeth in that treacherously ugly face, was the story of the big bad wolf wearing an old woman's nightdress ...

Hysterically, Angela became aware that she was adding fuel to fire by her ridiculous behaviour. Garabanda was no wolf, but a man ten times more dangerous than any wolf ...

Garabanda, nonplussed, then became furious. The last reaction he had expected from the white woman was that she should jeer at him. His face thunderous, he demanded; 'Why do you make fun of me, English bitch? Is it that you don't think I am capable of being that man you would not dare to laugh at? Come then let's laugh together ...'

'I'm sorry ...' she stepped away, her back to the entrance, as she cautiously faced Garabanda's wrath. 'Thank you for giving me Prince Yoe's book ... you may keep the Fox-Talbot, for I daresay I'll be able to get another in Mandalay ...'

Garabanda flung himself bodily at her, knocking her sideways and away from the pistol lying beside the Fox-Talbot. Angela's hand reached out towards the weapon, every muscle stretched taut in desperation while Garabanda pinned her to the ground. Terror gave her strength and, forcing one hand free, her nails ripped his face, wanting only to draw blood, to scar him as he did to others.

'You're an animal,' she spat in his face.

He forced her backward, his foul spirit-soaked breath on an uproarious burst of laughter cracking her last reserves of strength and nerve. Helplessly and hopelessly

Angela realized she had become Garabanda's latest victim. Slowly and deliberately he moved his weight off her. His words chilled her even more than his actions of tearing open her bodice and lifting her skirts. 'The yellow-haired bitch is not a woman but a child who desires to be a woman. She'll be granted her desires. But you, you are already the woman I seek, an entertaining creature when aroused. If I find pleasure in you, you will be rewarded amply and in all the ways a woman finds pleasing. I will give you clothes, jewels and satisfaction. If not, and you displease me, then you'll be given to my men like the other one who now tires me.'

God, God have mercy, Angela pleaded in silent final humiliation while, fumbling and groping, Garabanda forced himself into her, and all her prayers went unanswered. What had Felicity Quentin said, learned tragically in her own violation at Garabanda's hands; it isn't so bad if you don't think about it ...

Angela compelled her mind beyond the San Mukh cave to the S.S. *Tahara*, to a cream tulle ballgown and silken flowers laced through her hair. They would have been fresh flowers had she been at a party or ball in the royal city of Bath, but one simply couldn't buy fresh flowers aboard a ship bound for the East. She had danced in the careful arms of a young man who, if not exactly handsome, was pleasant, good and kind in temperament. 'What's India like?' she had asked him. 'An education,' he had replied. 'I'm so glad you're going to Delhi,' he had told her. 'I'm also posted to Delhi — at the moment, that is. One can't be too sure about any posting after one has been away on extended leave. I've been at home in Caversham, recuperating after a severe dose of malaria — wretched business malaria. Anyway, let's talk about you, not me. I know your father, a jolly nice man — not many District Magistrates are. Perhaps he'd allow me to call upon you sometime? Later on, when I've passed my language examinations I'd like to go for Burma. Your Uncle Adrian tells me Mandalay's like no other city on earth. It's supposed to be the golden heart of Burma. They say the streets are modern like Rangoon's, Mindon Min has had the city designed to very up-to-date specifications. The walls are six miles square would you believe, ten feet thick and twenty-seven feet high, they turn blood-red by sunset — amazing! The moat is so wide, royal barges can sail on it and everything is reflected in hyacinth-blue water so that Mandalay always has an adoring twin smiling up at it — forgive me for waxing lyrical but I've always had a yen to see the golden Buddha city of Burma. It would be even more marvellous were we able to see it together. Perhaps we can, one day?'

'Yes, I should like that very much.'

Oh God. Not now. Not ever. The beautiful adventure was over, to be replaced by brutality, hatred and ugliness. Never would she be able to feel anything except ugliness for the rest of her life.

THREE

The Mandalay moon rode like a golden paddlewheel the oceans of its sky. The river Irrawaddy in mackeral scales of silver put away its captured writhings of the fevered day and slept quietly under a moonlit canopy. In the compound of the Sagaing prison, mosquitoes took over from where the ants left off.

Nathan had survived ten days inside the death prison three inside and seven out in the bamboo stockade. He wondered how on earth he had managed it, while doubting his ability to survive another ten days, reduced as he was to the lowest of the low. Inside an indescribably foul communal cell, twelve feet by ten, the stench and agony of his fellow prisoners had been nauseating. Out in the compound the heat of the day and the insects crawling in his wounds was mind-bending. He wondered which was worse.

Tiffin baskets continued to arrive for him, sent down-river by Nanette Gideon whose heart was where he had known it always to be. On most days a boat stopped at Sagaing, bringing food for its inmates from relatives and friends. Otherwise the prisoners were in danger of starving to death. Spotted Faces always helped themselves first and then tossed what was left to the prisoners. Nathan never cared much for his food after filthy hands had been rifling through his tiffin. Nanette included tiger-balm ointment for his cuts and bruises, his wrists and ankles raw and swollen where he was shackled.

Confined within stocks only elephants had been able to move into position, arms and legs sticking through in a grotesque parody of a stage-puppet, Nathan Vorne wondered how much longer he would have to wait on the Queen's pleasure. Obviously Mr Hawes' and Nanette's petition had fallen on deaf ears. Nathan began to wonder why the Einshemin was taking so long to consolidate his position in Mandalay. The longer the Crown Prince waited, the stronger Queen Sinpyumashin became in the interregnum.

'Hey you ... Low-down-Choon, I want to use the bucket.' Nathan said to Lo Choon, who had had his nostrils slit for lying and thieving. 'Come here and unfasten these stocks.'

Half-a-dozen Spotted Faces, like a primitive tattooed tribe, hunkered on heels in a game of Chinese dice played by the light of an oil-lamp placed on the sandy ground. They were in very festive mood, laughing, drinking and eating Nathan's food sent by Nanette Gideon from Mandalay. This evening, the Spotted Faces wore blouses with their longyis, an issue that was, later on that night, to stand in Nathan's favour.

'Hey, Low-Down-Choon, I need the bucket badly,' Nathan called loudly, Lo Choon apparently deaf to the first request.

Angrily, Lo Choon left the game and came across to Nathan. 'What do you want now, kala?' he asked, kicking Nathan's injured feet, a bamboo stick poised to use on Nathan's head. 'You've asked for the bucket all day, kala. There you are ... take it ...' He kicked the half-filled bucket, spilling its foulness over the open wounds on Nathan's feet. In disgust Nathan swore long and loudly, the merest mention of the soil bucket always causing the Spotted Faces great fun. Lo Choon began to hop around in delight while the others joined in his mirth. Bounding over to Nathan he unfastened the top-half of the teak stocks to release his arms. 'There now kala, let's see you crawl on your elbows dragging the stocks behind you.' He leaned over and spat, then covered the holes of his nose. 'Let's see how straight your aim is, the bucket's here ...' he tapped it with his foot, then caught it with his ankle through the handle, lifting it high. As on the occasion with Tin-Sook-En, Nathan was revolted by the stench and the filth in which he once again found himself, only that on this occasion he could also smell whisky in the air. The Spotted Faces began to jeer, making fun of the golden prisoner who wished to relieve himself, yet could not because his white civilization prevented him from soiling his clothes, unlike the other barbarians not averse to doing it where they sat. Now he stank like the rest. In their sordid mirth, they rolled in the compound like drunken imbeciles — and that was what they had become. Nanette had given them whisky.

Four days before, a Scottish barque had sailed up the Irrawaddy river to Mandalay where a Scotsman of the East India Company had interrupted his journey on account of malaria. He had found shelter for the night with the Gideons of Kyauktawgyi Road, and over-whelmed by Nan's hospitality and Edom Gideon's gospel, had left them four bottles of his personal store of best Scotch whisky. When he had departed, his malaria cured, Edom Gideon, who regarded alcohol as the devil's own brew concocted for the downfall of men and women, told Nan to throw it out. She did, but not in the rubbish-bin. She included the four bottles of whisky in Nathan's tiffin-basket in the rightful assumption his need was greater by far. She was right — but the Spotted Faces had helped themselves first.

* * *

Eleven miles away, the streets of Mandalay were in the grip of Pwe. Gaily bedecked elephants paraded the nobility under golden umbrellas, Chinese fireworks turned the night sky into a flower-garden, music abounded and gilded barges sailed like a fleet of golden argos on a silver moat.

It was the eve of a Royal wedding. The following day, Prince Thibaw, a monastic man like his father before him, was to marry Princess Supalayat. She was Queen Sinpyumashin's second daughter. The young Prince and Princess were also half brother and sister. '

'Mr Sinclair,' said Mr Hawes, watching the sky illuminated with fireworks, the noise in the Mandalay streets deafening 'I don't like this, I don't like this at all. It all smacks of intrigue. Thibaw and Supalayat are mere puppets of Sinpyumashin whom she's marrying off with indecent haste. Doesn't that make you wonder?'

'It does indeed, sir. If it's not too presumptuous of me to ask, sir, what was the C.C.'s reply to our telegraph?'

'Oh yes ... by the way, how is the toothache?' he turned and regarded his invalid Assistant.

'Gone, sir,' Matthew beamed while nursing a swollen face. 'The barber yanked it out this morning ... er, the telegraph, sir? You'll remember I wasn't here ...'

'Ah, the telegraph from Charles ... we're to bide our time, Mr Sinclair. That was our directive. We mustn't interfere — as we have no right to interfere in the internal affairs of Upper Burma.'

'I say, that's a bit of a blow — especially to Captain Vorne.'

'I dare say, Mr Sinclair. But Vorne is not our priority. Thibaw is.' Mr Hawes grimaced, and took some amyl-of-nitrate from his pocket. His heart was beginning to spasm, and he knew the reason. Lately his cardiac condition had been troubling him more and more. In fact, ever since he had found out that the baby presented to Mindon Min on a golden tray had been none other than Thibaw, the monastic prince he had seen in Daw Khin Htay's garden.

CHAPTER SIX

ONE

G arabanda, exhausted, became careless. His physical desires satisfied, his body replete despite the wounds drawn from Angela's nails, he gave a grunt like a rutting pig and fell face down on his camp-bed. Through the haze in his mind, he realized she was not tied-up. He dismissed his negligence with the sleepy thought that the guards outside the cave would prevent her escaping.

He was hardly aware of the blow to the side of his head.

Angela, confounded by her action, was mesmerised by the sudden spurt of blood from Garabanda's head. She could only stare, paralysed, wondering how it had happened. Then she was aware of Garabanda's pistol in her quivering hand and with a cry of fright flung it from her. She began to rub her palms together. She had only meant to stun, never to kill.

Someone was mewing behind her, playing games with her. In terror she whirled. The hunchback moved, loomed larger, more menacing, wanted to pounce, hesitated, drew back, rocked towards her again, and blind fear once more clawed her insides. Then she became aware that the shadow thrown on cavern walls was hers alone, rocking back and forth in suppliant misery. Those mewing noises were coming from her own throat as an overwhelming blackness enveloped her. Stark, soiled emptiness in which only fear and revulsion prevailed,

72

and complete degradation cast her down into a hell of lost souls.

Angela reached for the jar of toddy-palm, so close, she only had to tip it to stiff lips if her numbness would support the effort. Crying to herself, she drank, gasped and choked on the burning liquor spilling down her chin. She wiped her arm across her mouth. In a little while she felt calmer, the warm glow of alcohol in a curious way putting her ugly world back into perspective. She felt she had done the right thing for shock — Dora despite her religious principles, had always believed in brandy for shock, but toddy-palm juice was obviously the next best thing . .

Angela looked at Garabanda though she did not want to. The fountain had stopped spurting from his temple, but his large head was hanging over the side of the camp-bed, his mongoloid eyes half-open as though watching her through their heavy slits. An inane smile on his pouting lips, she recoiled from that mocking stare, her fingers in her mouth while she tried to stifle the frightful panic welling up inside her all over again.

He wasn't dead, he was still leering at her through his thick black un-Burman beard, and she heard him mouth the word, 'Murderess . . .'

'Oh God . . . Oh God,' she began to whimper, unable to think rationally but only to edge backwards on her haunches, as far away from him as she could in case he reached for her again. Her eyes in fixation upon him, she realized that he did not move, that though he was not as yet dead his strange stop-and-start breathing whistling through his lips was the unconscious death-rattle she had heard in Dora Quentin's throat.

Feverishly her icy hands fumbled with her clothing. In her haste she was putting on articles of clothing belonging to Garabanda. She tore them off again — his shirt-blouse, jacket . . . her breath caught in her throat!

In sorting boots, blouse, stockings, all the clothes thrown haphazardly on the floor, an idea so startling came to her in her miserable panic, that she was made dizzy by it.

She began to talk to herself. 'Puttees ... yes, yes, puttees, pantaloons, military style breeches and jacket, yes, why not?' Desperately she fumbled. She was tall for a girl, five feet nine inches, only about two or three inches shorter than Garabanda, if that. 'Same size feet? Yes, yes, but narrower, never mind, quickly Angela quickly! Hurry before the guards come. Fifteen yards of turban ... oh God, how? Cover my hair, my hair! Now what else? Greatcoat ... beard ... what about the whiskers? God, God help me! The scarf, wind it round your mouth girl, quickly, quickly ...' Whispering madly to herself, she took possession of the moment and the wonderful opportunity to escape.

Angela wanted to laugh and cry, much like the moment when she realized Garabanda's intentions. What else? The gun, the gun ... her elephant gun stood in the corner, pistol, yes, loaded, yes ... what else, think girl think! Camera? Yoe's texts, in the greatcoat pocket ... oh my God, I'll never be able to carry all this. I'll never get away with it!

She crumpled to the floor, defeated. Her head in her hands, she knew she could not do it — and there was Felicity to consider.

A little voice inside her beseeched: You can, you can ... you can do anything you set your mind to, Angela Featherstone, you know that ... just don't show your face or open your mouth. How, how? She screamed inside her head. The cheroots, he smokes doesn't he? Put a cheroot in your mouth, walk outside for a breath of fresh air. Look at yourself in the mirror, in the darkness no one will know. What about Felicity Quentin? She's his paramour, isn't she? Then go and get her. You've got to *be* Garabanda, idiot, no two ways about it. ...

Angela reached for the toddy-palm, took a gulp and wiped the back of her hand across her mouth. The hands, the hands, look at your hands, woman!

Then keep them in your pockets, Angela, she told herself and braved the exit.

The two guards leaning against the rocky entrance to

the cave, saluted her sleepily. They did not challenge her. But why should they? she asked herself sternly. She was Garabanda, wasn't she?

Imitating Garabanda's heavy stride, she made for the tent she shared with Felicity. The girl was sound asleep. Her hand clamped tightly over Felicity's mouth, Angela brought her forcefully awake. Her blue eyes dilated in fear above Angela's hands.

'Felicity, it's me, Angela ... For God's sake don't scream or do anything foolish. Garabanda's dead, I've just killed him ... unintentionally. But when they find out, all the world will be after me. You've got to listen to me and do exactly as I say. Only then do we stand a chance of leaving this camp tonight. But we must be swift. We've only a few hours before it gets light and then they'll come after us. Will you be a good girl and do as you're told?'

Felicity nodded. Angela took her hand from Felicity's mouth.

'Good. We'll see Mandalay together, trust me. Now hurry and get dressed, we've got to get out of here at once.'

While Felicity was getting ready, Angela whispered instructions to her. Then, with Felicity hanging onto Angela's arm as though she were seducing Garabanda with her big blue eyes, they walked through the tents to where the horses were roped in for the night.

'Halt! Who passes?' The guards challenged them.

Angela had no idea what language was being spoken but assumed the man was telling her to stop. Beside her, she felt Felicity almost fainting against her and she whispered, 'Stand up, Felicity, stand up, for goodness sake: otherwise they'll wonder what on earth's going on. Pretend Garabanda is taking you for a moonlight stroll ...'

Felicity giggled. It was an involuntary reaction but the sound carried to the guards. Stiff fingers found Garabanda's cheroots, and Angela drew Felicity back into the shadow of a solitary pine. 'We mustn't say anything ... but if I choke on this cigar, you must laugh loudly to

75

cover my spluttering ... with luck those two will think Garabanda's taking liberties with you ...' her hands trembled so much, the match only flared at the third attempt. As she knew she would, she began to cough chokingly, her shoulders heaving on the heavy tobacco filling her lungs because she had mistakenly inhaled at full capacity.

'Oh my God, they're coming for us,' Felicity panicked, clutching Angela's arm convulsively.

Two men, with rifles poised, came forward in their soft sheepskin boots, long-waisted woven coats and cartridge-belts. Again they were challenged.

Felicity left Angela's side and walked straight towards the men. Angela, paralysed, could only stand and stare at Felicity's shadowy figure. She could not cry out to tell her to stop, nothing came from her agonized throat. Only her mind screamed, 'Traitor, oh you traitor Felicity Quentin!' The men stopped, Felicity gesticulated toward the pine tree. The sentries saw the figure of their Commanding Officer smoking beneath the pine tree. They knew at once what was expected of them — Garabanda wished to take his woman for a moonlight ride. They moved away, and when they thought they were out of earshot, the two girls heard their coarse voices and snickers behind the rocks. Men had to tell their crude jokes, whatever their race, and Angela thanked her lucky stars they did. Afterwards, she thanked Felicity for her presence of mind, ashamed of her own distrust. Stealthily they moved amongst the horses. Angela took Garabanda's and Felicity another that looked fleet of foot.

'I've never ridden bareback,' Felicity said.

'I've never smoked cheroots before or drunk spirits. Life teaches us the hard way, so mount. We haven't time to look for saddles. I'll help you up, and only hope I can get up alone.' Angela retorted briskly, quivering with torn nerves, and mind and body that ached for revenge. She prayed the guards were still looking in the opposite direction so as not to notice what an odd picture she and Felicity made.

But they were unwilling to show themselves again in case they incurred their Commanding Officer's displeasure as well as his rough justice, so they obediently minded their own business.

'We're not far from the Manipur border,' Angela said, hanging on to her horse's mane for dear life, the 12-bore elephant gun clamped precariously in front of her. 'I looked over Prince Yoe's shoulder yesterday when he and Garabanda were discussing tactics over a map. We have to ride due East. We must reach the border by daybreak. Garabanda's horse seems obliging enough. How's yours, Felicity?'

'It seems to know this rocky terrain. Garabanda and his men must haunt these hills. You do look funny in that outfit, Angela, but I don't think I like it. It reminds me too much of what we're trying to get away from. Dear God, I hope this isn't a dream ... which way's East?'

Angela, feeling drained, said: 'The way the sun comes up, I suppose. Just watch and see in which direction the sky begins to lighten. I wouldn't know one star from another, so it's no good relying on me to navigate by the constellations.'

She kept her worst fears to herself. Two unescorted females in a country of cut-throats, hills, rivers, mountains, jungles; their troubles were by no means over. The distant horizon was as jagged as her hopes of ever arriving anywhere, while the wolf and the jackal and the moonlight eye of the owl presaged their strange progress toward a very vague frontier known as Burma.

TWO

'Oh well, I suppose now it really is a matter of death us do part,' Nathan muttered in the moonlight.

'What did you say, kala?' Uncle Grub asked. His fingers greasy, he stopped eating to peer at Nathan like a

77

grinning Cheshire cat. Nathan grinned too: 'I said, worm-of-worms, where's the Chief of the Spotted Faces tonight?'

'He's with a woman of the prison, *kala*. A big fat one who grips with the thighs to make a man explode. Why do you want to know?'

'I want to sign the document of confession. Besides, I've something he ought to know.'

'What kala?'

'It's for Father's attention only.'

'But tonight I'm Father, so you must tell me.' His mouth full of rice, he dug a sleepy Lo Choon in the ribs. Lo Choon, his head on his chest snored, his blouse open and the tattooed elephant on his chest breathing with him. It was considered manly to have borne the pain of the tattoo needle in the flesh, and the greater the degree of tattooing, the greater the esteem. Elephants, pagodas, palm-trees and prayers against the Nats, adorned the bodies of the Spotted Faces.

'Wake up, Lo Choon,' said Uncle Grub. 'The *kala* doesn't know I'm Prison Ruler tonight. Go on, tell him, then perhaps he'll pay me more respect.'

Lo Choon grunted something unintelligible. Uncle Grub became angry. He started to bully him. 'Wake up! This *kala* wishes to sign the document of confession. Go immediately to the Garrison Commander and bring the parabaik requiring his signature. We must hand it to our gracious goddess, the Queen Sinpyumashin, according to instruction. I'll put it into her hands with my humble ones, and the *kala* may then sign it in her presence. Do you hear me, Lo Choon?'

Lo Choon was reluctant to move. He felt very peculiar, as though he were walking backwards through a monsoon with cicadas rubbing their hind-legs in his head.

While the others were sleeping off the effects of whisky, the reverse was happening to Uncle Grub. He became lively and talkative. Lo Choon, prodded into activity, slunk off to the Garrison Commander as Tin-

Sook-En had commanded, knowing it would be the worse for him if he disobeyed.

Of the four other prisoners in the stocks beside Nathan, three were beyond recall and the fourth kept Nathan company. A Burman who had stolen his neighbour's goat, he had had his hand amputated for theft. His stump sealed with hot tar, he writhed while he talked, the vermin in his clothes making him itch to distraction. The mind's reason had also departed in severe shock. He babbled incessantly, some of it making sense to Nathan, some of it not, he and Uncle Grub two of a kind that night.

Lo Choon returned with the parabaik requiring Nathan's signature. He threw it on the ground, threw himself on the ground and promptly fell asleep again.

'Hey ... hey ... you there Uncle Grub, stop drinking and listen ... Christ, are you deaf as well as stupid! I want to tell you something ...'

'What now, *kala*?' Uncle Grub squinted into the empty bottle before trying to focus on the Shwe Nat of Mandalay whose devil's head shone brightly in the dark. It kept receding and reappearing with strange monotony. 'What a pity you can't be silenced forever, *kala*,' he sighed. 'But the Queen of Burma wants you kept alive and Tin-Sook-En, as her humble servant, has no choice but to obey. Sign, *kala*, and please the Queen, also Tin-Sook-En who tires of your company.' Dragging the rolled parabaik by its ribbons and the empty whisky bottle by its neck, Tin-Sook-En crawled towards Nathan.

'You like rubies, huh Grub?' asked Nathan when the Spotted Face was within touching distance.

'What rubies?' His greed suddenly stronger than his thirst, he dropped the bottle and parabaik.

'Queen's rubies.'

'Where?'

'Hidden.'

'Where?'

'Find out.'

'You lie, *kala*!'

'Too bloody Irish!' said Nathan in English. Then, 'See here, if you don't believe me. Warts! Five big warts like bloody blisters where I've been bashed on my head so often. Come and see for yourself — if you don't mind the lice.' Obligingly, he dropped his head forward over the top half of the stocks.

Tin-Sook-En got to his knees. He picked up the whisky bottle. Holding it high he said: 'Tell me truly, are you the bejewelled Nat, King of all Nats they call *Thagya Min*, or are you the Shwe Nat of Mandalay?'

'I'm both,' Nathan said.

If the golden *kala* had said he was the *Thagya Min*, the chief of the Nats, Tin-Sook-En would have respected his wishes. If he had said he was the Shwe Nat, he would have struck him with the bottle. But to say he was both was confusing. He could not strike Thagya Min who would punish him with demons for ever more. Tin-Sook-En took his chances. He staggered and almost fell on Nathan, his hands tearing at Nathan's hair. He felt a hard lump, another, and another, five of them. Tin-Sook-En almost jerked Nathan's head off his body in his wild search for the Queen's rubies. When he had them all in the palm of his hand, he was delirious with joy. His new-found wealth would make Father envious, the other Spotted Faces his servants. He would be able to afford the luxury of fermented tea-leaves, ngapi. He could buy himself out of the community of criminals and have his brand-marks removed: he could afford to buy all sorts of things — including a woman of pleasure. Saliva trickled from the corners of his mouth, greed oozed from every pore. 'You are clever, *kala*, too clever for your own good. The sealing-wax to hold the rubies to the scalp was a good ploy, but not good enough. For deceiving the Spotted Faces, you'll be punished ...' He raised the whisky bottle, ready to strike.

'Wait!' said Nathan. 'All right, Grub, you can hit me and run off, but one more ruby will buy you the moon. ...'

'You have another?'

'Sure, help yourself.' Nathan bowed his head, hoping Uncle Grub would not use the bottle on it. But the power those rubies represented was too much for Tin-Sook-En, who succumbed to the final temptation. He leaned over Nathan, greedily.

Lo Choon had forgotten to put Nathan's arms back in the stocks earlier in the evening when Nathan had asked to use the bucket. The festivities had then gone to everyone's head, and the way thereafter was left clear.

The Chinese cord Tin-Sook-En had made to his own design, thin wire instead of silken cord, with two wooden handles to prevent the user from cutting his own hands, Nathan located in Uncle Grub's top pocket. It was a simple matter to bring it round Tin-Sook-En's neck, Nathan taking advantage of the only opportunity he was ever likely to get. 'Unlock my legs, son-of-a-leperous-whore,' he snarled in Tin-Sook-En's ear while keeping his strangle-hold on him.

Tin-Sook-En's eyes bulged. The rubies dropped from his hand. They lay in the sandy-dust, pigeons' eggs in size and pigeon's blood in colour, the moon endorsing their beauty.

The talkative Burman groaned in frustration. He wanted the rubies too, and recklessly began to heave to and fro in his stocks, shouting dementedly.

'My feet, damn you ... quick!' Nathan gave a jerk to the wire around Tin-Sook-En's neck and the Spotted face was so frightened, he soiled his loin-cloth. Scrambling his hands through the bunch of keys the Prison Ruler had left in his charge, he bent to unlock Nathan's ankles, the pressure around his throat unremitting.

'Now help me up, Grub,' Nathan said, 'and keep me up, goddammit!' He winced. The agony unbearable as all the fires of hell loosed themselves in his stiffened limbs.

But he had to do it, had to, or die ...

Nathan set his teeth while perspiration poured from his weakened body. He must do what the Buddhists were good at, put the mind beyond the torments of the flesh, outside the threshold of pain, he told himself. Holding onto the cheese-cutting device of Tin-Sook-En's, his life-line now, he drove himself to walk. He told himself he would walk out of the Sagaing death prison or die in the attempt. ...

'Englishman, Englishman ... take me with you, I beg you ...' the Burman shouted loud enough to wake the dead.

'For Christ's sake shut him up!' Nathan, his blood congealing, put the whisky bottle in Tin-Sook-En's hand, and with a jerk on the cord drew a thin line of blood around Tin-Sook-En's throat. Tin-Sook-En obeyed at once, clubbing the Burman into silence.

Nathan shrugged off the laws of the jungle, and in sibilant whispers enlightened Tin-Sook-En, 'Listen spawn of Satan, if I'm to die, you'll come with me. I've got nothing to lose. I want you to tell the Royal Troops manning the gates you're taking me to Mandalay with the document of confession the Queen wants from me, ... so pick it up! Right. Now I have here another document,' and he took from the pocket of his tattered trousers a forged note smuggled into him in one of Nanette Gideon's food baskets. 'Its an exit permit signed by the Hlutdaw, authorizing me to leave Sagaing in the care of a Spotted Face who will bring me to Mandalay. A boat manned by Royal Troops awaits us in the Sagaing inlet. I'm to be taken tonight because it's the eve of the Royal wedding and therefore an auspicious moment. Got that Grub?'

Tin-Sook-En carefully nodded his head. He felt the wire-cord bite his neck to make his flesh creep. Degree by degree, drop by drop, he knew without a doubt that the Shwe Nat of Mandalay would do to him what he, Tin-Sook-En had done to others. Certainly he would feel the warm blood trickle from his nose, his mouth, his eyes, his neck, and that his head could be severed with the merest tightening of the Shwe Nat's hand. In his fuddled mind, Tin-Sook-En knew all that, and trembled. A robust individual, he supported the Shwe Nat's weight.

Nathan, so much taller than Tin-Sook-En, draped his arm around Grub's neck, his hand dangling in a seemingly casual manner over the mandarin neckline of the ceremonial blouse Uncle Grub had kept fastened.

'Stop! What's the meaning of this?' A royal soldier came forward, prodding a long-nosed Pennsylvanian rifle at them.

Tin-Sook-En felt his neck squeezed until he thought his eyes would pop out. 'Now!' Nathan hissed in an agony of sweat and pain.

Nathan eased his strangle-hold. 'I have paper ...' Tin-Sook-En garbled. 'See here ...' The soldier took the rolled parabaik and permit of release without glancing at them. 'Who are you?' he demanded of Uncle Grub.

'I am Tin-Sook-En, second-in-command of the company of Spotted Faces. I have in my charge a prisoner of the Queen to be taken to Mandalay ...' Tin-Sook-En trembled so violently, Nathan felt the Chinese cord slipping through his perspiring hand.

'Wait here,' said the soldier. He went off with the documents, disappearing inside a sentry box at the main gates. Then two more soldiers stepped out from the darkness, carrying modern French repeater rifles.

'Tell them what you just told the other one,' said the desperate Captain to Tin-Sook-En.

'No ... no ... I will stay here ... you go ....' Uncle Grub was going to pieces and in a few more moments Nathan knew his chance would be over and so would his life.

Before the two new sentries could challenge them, the first one reappeared. He called for flares, and the two went running off to fetch them.

Panic-stricken, Nathan jerked Uncle Grub into action: 'Tell them ... tell them if you don't want to die, not to molest us. That we have a signed warrant by the Hlutdaw ... tell them ...'

'Fools! Open those gates at once! I am taking this prisoner down to the Sagaing inlet where our boat awaits. Fools, can't you read? By the orders of our Holy

83

Alaungpaya, ancestral husband of our divine Queen Sinpyumashin, the prisoner is to be released forthwith to the Hlutdaw. I am Tin-Sook-En of the Spotted Faces who has this Royal command.'

Nathan breathed again. Tin-Sook-En had excelled himself. Like a coward, he loved to inflict pain but never to receive it. Neither was the order strange. Many times the Spotted Faces took prisoners of the Court of Ava to Mandalay. They were more faithful than the soldiers. A Spotted Face contemplating running out on his life-sentence of service to the Royal household was soon brought back, given away by tattoo and amputation. Then his punishment would be far worse than anything that had gone before. Tin-Sook-En was the most loyal of all. Pardoned for his offences as long as he did what was wanted of him, he preferred to remain on the good side of the Hlutdaw. As a government employee, he was given a roof over his head, food to eat, and entertainment with those whom he guarded. Royal Troops manning the gates had heard all about Tin-Sook-En, his sadistic reputation having preceded him. Nor had they any fear that Tin-Sook-En would desert once he had deposited his prisoner in Mandalay, for he was one of the 'old faithfuls' of Sagaing death prison. So the order was given to open the gates. Documents were returned into Tin-Sook-En's possession, and the flares were used to light his way.

Moonlight slipped into dark spaces with the vanishing of the mooncloud. It lay like a pool of shimmering water into which Nathan and Uncle Grub stepped, outside prison gates. Only Tin-Sook-En's lunatic stutterings brought Nathan back to his senses, lost in the fleeting joy of finding himself free at last. Tin-Sook-En had dropped to his knees, and was performing deep shikkos at Nathan's feet, since he now firmly believed him to be Thagya Min, King of the Major Nats. It only required a whimpering, pleading, cowering Spotted Face, to draw the attention of the guards in their stone watchtowers above the gates. Nathan knew what he had to do. He did it without any compunction whatsoever.

In the deep shadows of great prison walls, with all his remaining strength, his hands jerked quickly in opposite directions. He never imagined it would be like slicing into soft cheese, the amputation of a head from a body, part of an idea born in Uncle Grub's own brutality, part of a Spotted Face's retribution by his own killing device.

Without a groan, Tin-Sook-En slipped down into the pool of watery moonlight at the Shwe Nat's feet.

CHAPTER SEVEN

ONE

Thanking God for the simplicity of the Burmese mind and their utter faith in Nat spirits, Nathan rolled into the water with a splash which mentally revived him. Only then, did he become aware of several sensations together, liquid liberty, the drowning of lice and putrescent odours, and solitude — no more Spotted Faces. He wanted only to stay and wallow in the magic moment.

But he knew he dare not. He had to put as much distance as possible between himself and the fort on the hill.

Any moment now the Prison Ruler would do his night rounds to find Lo Choon and the others in a drunken stupor, Tin-Sook-En missing with the keys and the Shwe Nat of Mandalay spirited away by Nat charms. Then, Nathan knew without a doubt, all hell would break loose. Father would gather to his side every Spotted Face available and together with Royal Troops not a stone would be left unturned. They would tear down every toywa beyond the Irrawaddy, every villager would be questioned. Steamers, barges, sampans, raft-villages and ferries would be rocked at their moorings, first in line being the *Belle Hélène*. Nathan did not know where Findebar, Ko Lee and the rest of his crew had got to; the last he had seen of them was their tail-ends disappearing the moment Royal Troops had boarded the *Belle* to search for smuggled rubies. Nathan was well aware that Father and his Spotted Faces' lives depended on him being found. Nathan prayed Minthami was not still in their little house-of-stilts in Mandalay.

But if only *he* could get to Mandalay, he knew one place where he could remain hidden, inviolable against Burmese threats. They still respected the British Resident and the tiny patch of ground he protected beneath a Union Jack fluttering from its flag-staff.

Every sound on the river seemed to be magnified a thousand times. The gentle water cleaving against river banks, boats sounding like an army of swimming Spotted Faces waiting to pounce the moment silver ripples presented his whereabouts. A monkey's high-pitched scream sent sharp tremors of fear through him. He began to swim away from the Sagaing shore, for swimming was something he could do without pain.

Helped by the current, Ava's flickering lights became synchronized with his breathing. A long sandy reef stretched across the bend of the mighty river, almost joining Ava and Sagaing, and he headed for it.

And then the moment he had been dreading happened. The hillside came alive. Darkness was illuminated, peace shattered. Match-like figures were thrown out of the main-gates, falling over one another, their shadows becoming giant-like in the glare of torches. Guns, pikes and cudgels were emblazoned on fort walls. The discovery of Uncle Grub's almost decapitated body would be only a matter of moments — and then he knew his fate would be sealed.

Nathan slipped under water, holding his breath while he swam toward the reef. If he could reach it before the Spotted Faces, he had a chance of escape. Otherwise both sides of the river would be cut off and he would be caught like a guppy in a net.

He swam with grim purpose toward the dark stretch of impacted sands rising from the water like some prehistoric sea-monster. Around that dead arm of sand, the Irrawaddy river swept through a narrowed channel, taking up more snake-like contortions in the S-bend that was the loop of river between Ava and Sagaing. All the waters of the north seemed to collect here and any man falling in the river had to take his chances. He had navigated this tricky stretch many many times, and had found that bad enough. He had never believed he would have to plough the Irrawaddy in this fashion. When Ko Lee, his Chinese houseboy, had almost drowned and he had jumped in to save him, it had been in a quiet stretch further north. But this was sheer suicide.

Then Nathan knew, as greater forces conspired against him, that fate was only dangling him on the end of its absurd string for its own entertainment that night. Cramp gripped him so viciously even the muscles of his jaw locked in spasm. Held in the steel vice of his own shortcomings, his depleted body driven too hard for too long, Nathan gave up the struggle. Grey clouds of rushing water swept over his head. He sank. The currents took him again, turned him over and over, a leaf, a straw, a foetus in a great womb of water.

He bobbed back to the surface. Sank again, heavy as a stone. He resurfaced, gasping for air until his ears, his mind, his lungs seemed to explode in burning fragments. Dragged under again by weeds anchoring his already fastened limbs, he knew he was drowning. A drowning man sees his life pass before him, Nathan heard only music in his ears. Below, above, all around, music engulfed him and he realized his eardrums must have perforated underwater. His heart battered against the bars of his ribs, his blood pounding to get out of his veins.

He did not know it, but he was only unconscious for a few moments — a lifetime under water. He was only aware of the world rushing past him and pinpoints of red-lights turning from light to dark to light again as the river, by its own power and capriciousness, untangled his limbs and cast him to the safety of a sandbank.

Nathan's cheek grazed a rough surface, his eyes opened and in painful sweetness he gulped fresh air into his lungs. He found himself lying on a gently sloping sand-bar in the middle of the Irrawaddy, the rest of his body still submerged. Cast upon the gently sloping sands of a Crusoe's island, he lay for awhile curled up like a baby against its mother's breast. Blinking the sand out of his stinging eyes, he saw again those red lights that had been haunting him underwater. They became larger, brighter, closer. Round and round, whirling like Chinese wheels of fire, yellow, scarlet, orange, crimson water-circles warning him how near the Spotted Faces were getting, spread out upon the sandbanks and coming after him through the water by those convenient low-water bridges. He closed his eyes again in despair. So, what the hell, he thought, he'd given them a good run for their money.

Unable to move another inch he braced himself for the clubbing, and hoped his end would be swift — though he had a disconcerting feeling that it wouldn't be.

Nothing happened except that the ringing in his ears grew louder and when he next opened his eyes found that he was looking into the face of dragons. Scintillating fiercely, they rushed down upon him at great speed through the river. What he had thought were the Spotted Faces' flares turned out to be the torches of Royal Sailors lining both sides of an elaborate barge heading towards Mandalay. From somewhere inside it music proclaimed its stately progress, everything done to clear a path for the royal vessel emerging through the night like a triple pagoda built into the hollowed back of a sea-dragon.

Nathan's cramp had eased considerably during those few moments of respite although the pain was still with him. Any further exertion would bring it back again, and so, when he flung himself back into the water, he let the currents take him where they would. Instead of fighting the mighty river, he gave himself up to it, regulating his breathing with the water rushing over his head. If he was as good a sailor as he hoped he was, he knew by his navigation charts he would be drawn toward the narrow Ava-Sagaing channel through which the river tried to squeeze itself on its way to the sea five hundred miles away. And the Stately Barge would have to come to a virtual standstill if it did not want to run aground.

In front of the Royal Barge, clearing the way for it in a rowing boat, forty-eight oarsmen in royal livery colours of red, white and magenta, cut the water, oars dipping and squaring with precision. Behind it, the ceremonial barge lay low in the river, groaning beneath the weight of gold with which it was embellished. A gigantic dragon prow reared from the water, flanked by chinthes with snarling jaws. Eyes set with a myriad of precious stones, the mythical monsters fired the night like flames from a setting sun, their beauty by torchlight defying the imagination.

Two important silhouettes, the focus of this waterborne festival of light and splendour, sat in the pagodaed centre beneath a tasselled awning of silver and gold thread. Nathan groaned in despair. After all this, only to be thrown back into the arms of Queen Sinpyumashin in the shape of her very own wedding-couple, Prince Thibaw and Princess Supalayat, was too cruel to contemplate.

The two boats slowed down, the man in the pilot boat taking readings of the water with a long gauge-pole. They were repeated in a loud voice by the leadsman in the State Barge.

Nathan flung himself towards it, his arms pumping against the current in one last desperate bid to save himself from drowning. If only he could haul himself onto the back of the State Barge and hang there undetected while the distance increased between himself and the Spotted Faces, then he might get away with his life. Tossed backward by the wash of the pilot boat, bumping waves battered his bruised body, adding insult to injury, and he knew he would not be able to last out much longer.

He prayed for a miracle, and he found it. Nathan's up-flung arms grabbed a lifebelt before the great arc of the paddle-wheel, drawing along midships chopped him into little pieces. With all the strength left to him, he dug in the backs of his raw heels to secure a leverage along the wooden gunwale and discovered to his astonishment that the Standard fluttering beside his nose was that of the Einshemin, Crown Prince Nyaungyan Min, Lord of the Eastern House.

As the Stately barge slid under the threatening shadow of the red Redoubt of Sagaing, Nathan Vorne fell onto the carpeted deck of the Einshemin's boat. The Burmese sailors at whose feet he landed, gaped in open-mouthed astonishment. Until Nathan began to laugh.

He lay on his back and laughed so deeply and so infectiously, clutching his sides and wriggling around like a landed fish, the Burmese sailors, despite their serious and business-like aspect for the protection of the Ein-shemin's person, underneath were only what their race made them, a happy carefree people to whom gravity was of secondary importance to laughter and happiness. They too began to smile. Their grins broadened, and then they were laughing heartily along with the strange man lying on the deck laughing up at them.

The voice of authority brought them up short and Nathan found a sword point at his throat. Foolishly he gaped at twenty bare brown toes. The man who had earned himself a reputation like none other among the people of the Irrawaddy river, encountered the stern looks of the Crown Prince and his younger brother, Prince Nyaung Ok. His spluttering died away.

'Seize him guard!' said Prince Nyaung Ok, the point of his sword at Nathan's throat.

'Prince Nyaungyan Min ... Einshemin.' Nathan, half-drowned, drew himself into a sitting position. 'I come in peace. Certainly not to harm you or your brother who holds me at sword-point — not at all a good Buddhist thing to do.' He shifted himself from the angle of Nyaung Ok's blade.

'Silence, *kala*!' said Nyaung Ok, more hot-blooded than the brother whom he was protecting. 'You address the future King of Burma with disrespect, also his brother, a Prince of the Court of Ava. I am Prince,

Nyaung Ok.' He drew himself up regally. 'What infamy brings you aboard a Royal barge?'

'I apologize. I mean no insult or infamy ...'

'You are a river-pirate, that is infamy enough ...'

'Wait,' said the Einshemin to his brother. 'Don't you see who this man is? It's the Shwe Nat of Mandalay. He's the only man who can come aboard a royal State barge in this fashion ... eh Nathan?' He looked down at the American Captain with a glimmer in his eye.

Nathan looked up into the dark eyes of his friend and felt free to grin. The Einshemin and Prince Nyaung Ok presented flat strong faces, reminding Nathan of two blank and unblinking barn owls. They were dressed almost identically. White satin blouses with tight sleeves and jewelled buttons, culotte-type pantaloons called putsos were made of silken checks which denoted men of grandeur. Brown legs remained uncovered, so did their feet. Long black hair was wound into elaborate topknots and fastened by jewelled pins, and a white muslin band across the forehead secured the arrangement. Both princes were adorned with many precious stones, diamonds, emeralds, rubies, sapphires, heavy gold and silver adornments, earrings, rings, bangles and insignia.

The hasty Prince Nyaung Ok pulled at his diamond earring sheepishly while the Einshemin extended his hand to welcome the Shwe Nat aboard his vessel.

'Come,' he said as Nathan attempted to get up and found the effort too great. The Einshemin bade his servants help the Shwe Nat to his feet without knowing what a torment those feet presented to Nathan. 'You are bidden to enter our presence with a little more dignity,' he encouraged Nathan with a smile. 'Prince Nyaung Ok and I wish you to regale us with more of your stories as they always make us laugh. But first you must tell us what kind of trouble you're in — by the look of you, I think you're in hot water, eh my friend? Help him, guards, and bring tiger-balm for his wounds. Also refreshment, he looks as if he requires some.'

'No, no refreshment, thank you Einshemin. Not at present anyway,' Nathan said, adding, 'I've just swallowed enough liquid refreshment from the Irrawaddy to last me a lifetime, so my thirst is well slaked. And go easy on the tiger-balm,' he told the Einshemin's servants.

Nathan was placed on silken cushions on a brocade carpet in the centre of the royal barge. His feet were bathed with rose-water and massaged with tiger-balm. He was offered halwa to eat, his favourite sweetmeat, and he almost burst out laughing all over again. Of all the luck in the world, he had stumbled aboard the greatest good fortune! For a moment, while he was drowning, he had imagined the two shadowy figures in the boat to be the wedding-couple, Thibaw and Supalayat, in which case he would have drowned. That it had turned out to be his friend, the Einshemin, Crown Prince of Burma, was wonderful. No one would dare stop the princely entourage on its way to Mandalay — least of all the Garrison Commander of Sagaing! Nathan, while wallowing in his good fortune, was also perturbed on the princes' behalves.

Mandalay, unfortunately, was not where the two princes ought to be heading. As though reading Nathan's thoughts, the Einshemin explained; 'We go, Prince Nyaung Ok and myself, to the wedding of our half-brother and sister, the Prince Thibaw to the Princess Supalayat in Mandalay.'

'You mustn't go to Mandalay on any account,' said Nathan.

The two princes regarded him in astonishment. 'Not go!' echoed Prince Nyaung Ok, 'Who are you to tell us what to do?'

'Forgive us, Shwe Nat,' said the Einshemin looking alarmed as well as perplexed, knowing the American Captain must have a very good reason to voice such a forceful opinion, 'but what are you trying to tell us?'

'Einshemin, you and Prince Nyaung Ok are in very grave danger. There's a plot afoot to rob you of the throne of Burma. You'll both be assassinated the

93

moment you set foot in Mandalay.'

'I do not understand at all,' said the Einshemin at length, his brother for once silenced by fear — a fear they had lived with for a long time. To hear the Shwe Nat of Mandalay, a staunch friend and servant, voice their worst fears, was disconcerting.

'Mindon Min's Chief Queen, Sinpyumashin, retains office until you're crowned King. In the meanwhile she's taken control of Mandalay and its environs. She's marrying Supalayat to Thibaw to gain more power for herself. Remember Prince Thibaw's mother was banished by Mindon Min on account of her adultery, and that Queen Sinpyumashin gave succour and protection to Thibaw's mother in the days of her disgrace from Court?'

'I know that the Queen has always taken a great interest in my half-brother Thibaw's upbringing amongst the Sangha,' the Einshemin added.

'My point exactly,' said Nathan. 'We all know he's a pious youth not cut out to bear the burden of high office. Neither has he any military, or civil authority, so he remains a pawn in Queen Sinpyumashin's hands. Gossip runs rife in Mandalay. Most of it can be discredited. It's the things one doesn't get to hear about that are alarming. I've found out — and you know my sources are always reliable.'

The Einshemin and his brother nodded.

'Queen Sinpyumashin has recently brought the Taingda on to her staff of Palace Advisors ...' Nathan continued.

'But he's Chief of the Palace Guard, that's all ...' Nyaung Ok interrupted angrily. Although rumours had reached him when in Rangoon, he still could not believe it.

'Not anymore. The Queen's reason for promoting the fellow is obvious. His hatred of foreigners is greater than hers. And she's putting a puppet and a doll on the throne of Burma because she'll have whom *she* can manipulate. You're too much your father's son to be manipulated, sir,' Nathan turned to the Crown Prince.

The Einshemin bowed his topknot at Nathan's well-timed flattery. 'Shwe Nat,' he murmured, fingering his buttons, his lower lip thrust out in contemplative attitude, 'you worry needlessly on my behalf. Naturally I'm grateful — and flattered, but I must still go to Mandalay. It's my duty to do so, whether my life's in danger or not. Mandalay is my father's holy city, built by him in the year of your peoples' suffering in the Indian Mutiny ...'

'I'm American,' Nathan said in gentle reminder.

'Forgive me, Shwe Nat,' the Einshemin said with a sheepish smile, 'I'm always confusing the Americans with the British. As nations apart, there's very little difference to my Eastern eyes between your people and theirs. Now, before you sidetrack me further, as I was saying, Mandalay is my father's city, and I, as his Crown Prince, must go there. If it's all as you say it is, then Queen Sinpyumashin, gracious lady, would not have requested me to attend the wedding of my half-brother and half-sister in Mandalay. She would have left me in Rangoon until my crowning, meanwhile strengthening her hold on Mandalay. I think therefore, your fears and suppositions are unfounded. Forgive me, dear friend, but that is how I see it.'

'It's not what I suppose!' said Nathan in exasperation. 'You have been away from Mandalay, and no doubt unaware of what's been happening here in the meanwhile. Believe me there's danger everywhere. There's to be a royal wedding, but that's not all. Forgive me, Einshemin, but I too must speak my mind. Now I'll tell you something I wasn't going to mention. You'll see that even Mindon Min was concerned about what would happen to Upper Burma after his death. A month before I was arrested by Royal Troops boarding my boat at Sagaing, I was in Mandalay on business. While there, I was asked to present myself in King Mindon Min's royal apartments. A frail old man, he realized he had very little time left in this world to sort out his affairs. He asked me, as a special favour to him, to remove six of his favourite younger children from the Court of Ava, to a place of safety.'

Nathan paused, allowing time for that statement to sink into the Einshemin and Prince Nyaung Ok. They certainly looked paler beneath their dark skins and Nathan felt pity for them. Danger, he knew, had been their constant bedfellows, since the day they had been presented squirming on their golden trays to their royal father. 'If you listen to me, you can escape from the Queen Mother's clutches. But to show yourselves in Mandalay is not prudent right now.'

'What happened to my brothers and sisters my father, King Mindon Min, asked you to take away from Mandalay?' Prince Nyaung Ok demanded, still trying to discredit Nathan Vorne's story.

'Mindon Min issued a declaration that he was banishing them to India to live in exile. You know he's done that often before, so no one at the Court of Ava suspected anything different. I had to do it without Queen Sinpyumashin's knowledge — which was mighty difficult. They had to be whisked out under her nose concealed in laundry-baskets and put aboard the *Belle Hélène*. The *Belle*'s never sailed the Irrawaddy so fast in her life, but we managed to get those royal children into the Northern Shan States without anyone knowing. When she found out, Sinpyumashin was after my blood — not rubies like she pretended. I was unloading at Sagaing, as innocent as the day's long, when her troops came aboard all ready to take me off. I've been in the death prison ever since.'

'Then how did you get out?' asked Prince Nyaung Ok. 'No one has ever escaped from the death prison — not that I know of anyway.'

'Then meet your first escapee, sir!' Nathan bowed his head, his manner lighthearted but respectful, as he would never have been discourteous to the Princes. He knew it was more than his life was worth to take liberties — even among friends from the Court of Ava. 'I managed to escape, and now they're after me.'

'It seems,' said the Einshemin, 'we're all in the same boat.'

'Yes sir,' said Nathan, smiling appreciatively since the

Crown Prince seemed to expect recognition of his wit, 'but don't let the Queen mother depose you. She and the Taingda are trying to oust you from your legitimate inheritance to give it all away to an ineffectual monk. Now is *not* the right time to go to Mandalay, believe me. It will be the worst act of stupidity to show yourself at the marriage of Thibaw and Supalayat.'

A long silence followed Nathan's heartfelt speech. He could sense the turmoil in the two mens' minds, neither of them wishing to break the thread of history by upsetting a marriage between members of their Royal House, themselves an integral part of that family union.

At last the Crown Prince took a deep breath and asked the man for whom he had great respect, 'What do you suggest we do, Shwe Nat?' He and the Shwe Nat had formed a bond through mutual interests — business and pleasure — and he had learned to trust the commoner far more than any of the sycophants around. The last thing on earth the Shwe Nat happened to be was a man who grovelled for favours — he simply took them.

'I haven't the resources at this present time to raise an army against the Queen Mother who commands the Royal Troops. I've just come with all speed from Rangoon to take up my office as my father's successor. Had I realized sooner the unrest and scheming going on behind my back, I would have remained in Rangoon until I'd made my position stronger with the British to back me up. They would have provided me with civil and military support.'

'All of us can be wise in retrospect, sir,' Nathan murmured like a wise counsellor. 'It's being wise in prospect that matters.'

A heavy dull silence ensued, filled with deep conflict in the minds of all three men. 'Then,' continued the woeful Einshemin 'my destiny seems to be only the play of sunlight on water, a brief glimpse of glory before the dark clouds come. Is it not thus, Shwe Nat?'

'It needn't be,' Nathan reassured, he too fighting against all manner of woes afflicting him, not the least that tiger-balm was playing havoc with his constitution by devouring his feet. He asked for the tight bindings to be removed, anything constricting reminded him too much of Sagaing. 'There's one man who might help us,' he said while servants did his bidding, 'one place where we'd be relatively safe.' A foxy smile hovered on the American's lips and while he waited for the servants to make themselves scarce, he popped halwa in his mouth to take his mind off his feet — and, possibly, his neck. Presently he murmured, 'A place right on the doorstep of your own throne-room, Einshemin where no one would dream of looking.'

Both princes exclaimed: 'Mandalay!'

Prince Nyaung Ok added in confusion, 'You have just opposed our intention of going to Mandalay. Now you've changed your mind, so I don't understand.'

'It's called the balance of power.' Nathan chuckled, helping himself to more of his favourite sweet. 'While I've been reclining here in all manner of comfort and woe, it appears that the safest place for a hunted man to hide is slap-bang in the middle of the enemy camp. That's Mandalay. Now we know very well Queen Sinpyumashin is a far from stupid woman, so she isn't going to deliberately antagonize the British who split Burma in two halves twice before. So here's my plan ...'

Nathan went on to explain it to the two princes who were wondering what the Shwe Nat was up to now. Nathan himself realized golden opportunities did not come along twice in one night, and was therefore about to make full use of them.

The Einshemin's royal barge slipped through bright water and came to rest in a secluded little inlet just above Amarapura.

TWO

'Good God!' Edwin Tennent-Browne exclaimed in the interval of removing his Havana and replacing it. 'It ain't possible, Miss Featherstone!'

'I assure you, Sir Edwin, every word is true. I and Felicity Quentin escaped in exactly that manner and once we reached Manipur found friendly people and fresh horses to get us here to you in Imphal. We would however be obliged if the *details* of our adventure went no further than this room.'

'But m'dear, I must make out a report ...'

'Then use the word *detained*, not rape if you please where Felicity is concerned. She has her reputation to think of, Sir Edwin.'

She looked him squarely in the eye. What happened in the San Mukh cave was purely between herself and her God. Felicity, no one, knew anything about it. And Garabanda was dead. Such was the power of her green gaze Edwin found himself acquiescing.

'Very well m'dear, I'll do my best ... but those ruffians will have to be found and brought to justice — can't have them perpetrating all these heinous crimes without the law being set on them.' Then he smiled at the preposterous native uniform and the young woman in it; then at Felicity Quentin, frightened, dirty, exhausted and obviously designed for something prettier than jungle-warfare. Edwin cleared his throat. 'Miss — er — Featherstone,' he addressed her specifically since she had made herself spokeswoman for the younger girl too, 'I know it's not customary for a gentleman to ask a lady, but for the purposes of my report, how — er ...?'

'I'm nineteen and Felicity's sixteen, if that's what you want to know. Felicity was travelling to Peking with her parents to the Court of Emperor Kuang Hsu. Now they're dead she feels she'd like to return to her own country. She has grandparents who'll look after her in Minnesota. We were intending to travel to Mandalay together, but she has no relatives there, unlike myself, so I persuaded her to return to the United States.'

'Very sensible of you, Miss Featherstone.' He turned to Felicity, 'm'dear, if that's your wish, no trouble at all. We'll whisk you down to Chittagong where you can board a boat that will take you to America in no time. What are your plans, Miss Featherstone?' Edwin knew she was bound to have worked out her own strategy.

'I'm trying to get to Loloi in the Independent Shan States. It's been difficult so far, I don't mind admitting,' she added with a rueful smile that softened her rather austere features, though there was something very arresting about that face, Edwin thought. 'Since leaving Delhi in company with Mr and Mrs Quentin and Felicity, I seem to have been travelling all my life. But I must pay my respect to my aunt Lydell in Loloi as promised, before proceeding down to Mandalay where my uncle Adrian Hawes is Resident. My er ... fiancé is also there, as uncle Adrian's Assistant.'

'But you're not thinking of travelling alone? Not after ... not after ...' Edwin did not like to glance towards Felicity Quentin seated rigidly with her hands clasped tightly in her lap, her expression vacant. 'No I'm not. My Aunt is a schoolteacher in Loloi. The Sawbwa of Loloi, a good friend of hers, has promised his own elephant escort to meet me in Lashio. Meanwhile, I'd like a thoroughly trustworthy company to get me from Imphal to Lashio. Preferably a contingent of British soldiers on their way to declare war on Bo Garabanda and Prince Yoe. Oh, and by the way, I wonder if we could be furnished with a change of clothing as these are about to fall away to rags. Mine preferably in the feminine gender?'

His voice appeared to stick again. 'Eh, I daresay my wife Blaize can kit you ladies out. She seems to do nothing else but spend my money on new clothes for herself.'

Angela put out her hand in gratitude. 'Thank you so much Sir Edwin. I can't tell you how I value your discretion — and your kindness and understanding.'

'Think nothing of it m'dear,' he mumbled, not knowing what to make of such an astonishingly resilient young woman who, despite her ordeal, had nothing lacking in her handshake.

THE BHODI FLOWER

1879

CHAPTER EIGHT

ONE

1879

The peculiar cry of the 'sick-bird' made Angela smile. 'I'm-ill-I'm-ill-I'm-ill' it carrolled lustily outside her window. She tossed aside Prince Yoe's beautiful book of Theravada Texts as well as the bed clothes, for nights were apt to be chilly in Loloi, and padded to the window. Angela hooked aside the kus-kus tatties at the glassless window and light streamed into the small bamboo-walled room.

The view from the window never ceased to amaze her. Flame-of-the-forest trees fringed the compound. Scarlet lily flowers in pendulous cascades from leafless branches scattered spent blossoms on the ground like droplets of blood. Clematis and tuber-roses, vines tying the grapebloom of the jungle, heavy purple bunches whose acid juices burned the unwary hand. She also saw bhodi flowers, their texture that of human flesh. A strange anther like the hooded cowl of a snake, rose up from the heart of the flower. It resembled the canopy under which Lord Buddha sat when he fell asleep beneath the tree of enlightenment. Long after the flower had died its perfume lingered, exotic and overpowering. Miss Lydell disliked its heady scent and discouraged the bhodi flower from being brought inside the house. Angela, in her first enthusiasm on finding herself in Loloi after two months of a living nightmare, had brought all sorts of flowers and greenery into the school-house including many poisonous varieties. She had since learned to distinguish what to pick and what not to — especially the exotic jungle orchids.

On the horizon, smoky blue hills rose tier upon tier to the borders of China. On a clear day as today, she felt able to reach out and touch the mountains. In the evenings, sunset tinted the landscape to a Chinese water-colour, a palette of gold, sugar-pink, delicate hues of mauves and blues, apricot and yellow. Angela had sighed with frustration that there was no camera invented to take coloured photographs.

Chattering voices in the compound below drew her attention to her aunt in her open-air classroom. Angela brought out the Fox-Talbot and placed it on the narrow windowsill to steady the cumbersome box. She had received a tripod, new plates and silver-nitrate for the developing process, thanks to Edwin Tennent-Browne. In her heart, Angela held much gratitude for Edwin and Blaize — especially Blaize once it was discovered that Felicity was carrying Garabanda's child. Angela tried not to think too much about those awful weeks in Manipur, but sometimes the memory of it ate into her mind like gnawing rats to wake her in the night in a bath of perspiration and hatred against Garabanda. Blaize had turned out to be what Angela called 'a brick', taking control when the world seemed a very black place indeed. 'Don't worry darlings,' she had declared in her piercing voice, 'I know of a positively evil old crone in one of Imphal's back streets. Of course I wouldn't allow myself to be touched by her filthy claws in her smelly house if Edwin gave me a million pounds *and* a new frock!' Angela could smile to herself now, remembering Blaize Tennent-Browne. But she hadn't been able to smile then, it was all too sordid and horrible for words. But the medicine had worked wonders, and in due course, Felicity was on her way to Chittagong without any tangible signs of what she had been through.

Terrified that what had befallen Felicity might happen

to her, Angela too had taken the evil mixture. She however, kept all that secret from Blaize who only knew about Felicity's tragedy, not hers. But Angela had made the discovery she must be made of stronger stuff than young Felicity, for juniper berries did nothing for her apart from giving her the mother and father of all stomach-aches. Yes, she was bitter — Garabanda had destroyed everything for her, her trust, confidence, love, as well as her marriage plans. She could never marry Matthew Sinclair now. Those 'forbidden fruits' which had only been whispered about at the genteel establishment to which she had been relegated from the age of six, had become for her a reality in its most violent form, and she knew in her heart she could never allow herself to be subjected like that by any man again — not even one as fine and decent and as moral as Matthew Sinclair. She had written to him accordingly, informing him without furnishing him with any reasons, her desire to break-off their engagement. She had not heard from him since.

Angela brought her mind back to the present. 'All finished, aunt Emmy,' she called into the compound where the children sat looking up at her, more interested in her camera than learning by rote their multiplication tables.

'Good morning, dear,' said Emmeline Lydell, glancing up at her niece in her vague way, the greying chignon on the nape of her neck contained in a snood, and her pince-nez in danger of slipping. She smiled. 'I didn't know you were taking a picture of us, you naughty girl!' She began to gather her things together, chalks, books and the small bamboo table placed in the compound alongside her blackboard and easel. It was time to go "under" the house as presently the sun would be too hot. She dismissed her class, 'Saba ... go find Moke, children.' The word 'food' sent them scampering off without further ado to have their breakfast.

'Aunt Emmy, I'm going to the Loloi pagoda again.' Angela informed her. 'You don't want me to take a class for you or anything like that, do you?'

'No dear. I can manage today. You go and do what you have to. Only watch out for the Loloi tiger. He's still on the prowl I'm told by the Sawbwa.'

'I thought only leopards haunted these hills.'

'Occasionally we get a man-eating tiger down as far as Loloi. Not often, thank goodness, but this one of "ours" seems a particularly nasty creature.'

'What with Loloi tigers and the wild-Wu living in the northern hills, *and* the giraffe women I nearly forgot to mention, I'm afraid to go beyond the compound.'

'Ah, but you're made of sterner stuff I think, and British armour-plate is a great advantage out here. One needs it, if only to keep off the mosquitoes.' Her kindly eyes behind her spectacles, twinkled. 'Just don't stray off the main road, Angela dear,' Emmy Lydell warned.

'What road, Aunt Emmy?' Angela asked with a little laugh. 'All I've encountered so far are dirt tracks — I have to wash my hair every other day it gets so dusty. Anyway, I'll be back this evening, so don't save me any lunch. I'll pick some fruit if I get hungry.'

'I suppose you're going to talk to your hermit-phongyi at the Loloi Pagoda?'

'He's a remarkable old man. I'm learning a lot from him. I'll be down soon, aunt Emmy ... goodness!' she said, sniffing the air appreciatively. 'Moke doesn't stint with the peanut oil when he's cooking bacon, kidneys and eggs, does he? I can't get used to peanut-flavoured English breakfast,' she said cheerfully before withdrawing her head from the window. Angela threw on a cotton wrap before joining her aunt and the children for breakfast.

Built on stilts in the usual fashion, the schoolhouse had bamboo walls and a thatched roof of rice straw which was cool in the hot dry season and remarkably waterproof during the monsoons. Around the whole building ran a verandah and underneath the house itself, Miss Lydell had utilized the space for a classroom. Here the children remained with her until about eleven o'clock in the morning. Then they had lunch. During the hottest part of the day, from eleven onwards, they stayed under or inside the shady house. At night the six 'boarders' rolled down sleeping mats and slept side by side in the living room. The house was always cramped, comprising one single L-shaped room. The smaller segment had been screened off to provide a bedroom for Miss Lydell and Angela, with only a reeded screen separating their two cots. Angela had discovered that a line slung across the room served the purpose of wardrobe. Clothes and towels were hung over it haphazardly. She never got used to the idea. Miss Lydell seemed to be immune to inconvenience and Angela, sometimes looking at her aunt, admired the way in which she had adapted to strange customs. Afterall, her aunt Emmy Lydell was a long way from home and the customs of Wimbledon were not those of Loloi! She drew the line however at hunkering on her heels to eat her food in the Burmese fashion, and, on that score Angela was thankful.

Moke, Miss Lydell's Thai housekeeper, was being trained to become a real English butler. Moke did his best and more. He swept, cooked and cleaned, guardian-angel of the 'boarders' and Miss Lydell. He was tall, loose-limbed, loose-jawed, black-toothed and with a doleful habit of sticking out his lower lip, cut a comical picture with his wire-brush tuft of white hair which sprang from an otherwise bald dome of head. He reminded Angela of a melancholy Capuchin monkey though his heart and nature were anything but melancholy. Gentle, loving, kindness itself. Angela was very fond of 'old Moke' as she referred to him. In return, Moke plied her with sweet sticky jaggery which he made himself from palm-sugar, like dark rich toffee.

After breakfast Angela got herself ready to go to the Loloi pagoda. Another thing she thought she would never get used to were the primitive bathroom arrangements. Situated in the compound, a flimsy rattan screen was all that afforded anyone any privacy. With her figure, taller than average, especially compared with Burmese women, Angela found she exposed bare shoulders and bare calves in rather large expanses. In this fashion, with only a tin jug and basin and three inches of water, she was expected to perform her daily ablutions. When she had washed, she donned a cream linen skirt and white lace, high-necked blouse with leg-of-mutton sleeves that had belonged to Blaize Tennent-Browne — all her wardrobe having been supplied by the extravagant Lady Bee! The only new items in her possession were her buttoned leather boots and thick lisle stockings purchased in Imphal. Over her rampant locks she placed her sun-helmet, again one of Blaize's cast-off sola topis. Apart from her Fox-Talbot she was ready to face the day.

Moke stopped her in the compound with the usual compliment of jaggery. Miss Lydell's voice from under the schoolhouse admonished him: 'Moke, Miss Angela can do without jaggery to ruin her nice white teeth.'

'Then she better off having none like Moke, Miss Emmy,' he grinned widely, exposing toothless gums in a bizarre smile.

'Thank you Moke,' Angela said, taking the jaggery despite the warning. 'Goodbye, Aunt Emmy, I'll see you this evening.'

'Take care dear,' Miss Lydell began to concentrate on teaching her class.

TWO

Loloi was a small but very pretty village of simple basha huts with the exception of one very grand teak house in the centre of the village. This was the Sawbwa's palace, and reminded Angela of a wonderfully carved and painted Swiss chalet in whose gardens Hannibal's elephants had wandered loose. An immensely rich man, he was a traditional Shan Chieftan whose ancestors were of the Siamese people. The wooden palace was roofed with the expensive dahni palm that had to be shipped up-river from the southern delta. Angela had met the

Sawbwa on several occasions; he took great interest in Miss Lydell and her pupils. As her patron, the Sawbwa of Loloi was proud of his very 'British' school of which he boasted greatly. Once seen, he was a man never to be forgotten, the size of a baby elephant, his teeth ghastly with the stain of betel-nut, his laugh outrageous in its spontaneity and in sheer delight at being alive to enjoy all Buddha's blessings.

The Loloi pagoda, built on a little grassy knoll as most pagodas in Burma, was surrounded by a thick grove of mangosteens, untidy plantains and bright acacia. Angela found her hermit-monk sitting in the roofed rest-area which every pagoda had for the benefit of its pilgrims, who ate, played, slept and prayed there. Angela had made the discovery that the Loloi pagoda was only a crumbling relic of the past, but still sacred ground. It did not possess a monks-school, as the pagoda in Ku, but it did possess its very own monk, an old man who had taken the vow of silence — and broken it — to talk to the English-girl called Miss Featherstone. Expediency, she was beginning to discover for herself, was the hall-mark of life in Burma.

He did not wear the saffron robes of a scholar monk, but the ochre robes of a hermit. He took no notice of the girl who had come to talk to him in the few sentences of Burmese she had picked up, but went on fishing into his bowl of drinking-water with a little net strainer. When Angela had first encountered him and saw him doing such a strange thing, she thought he was being unusually fussy in his habits. Until she discovered he was looking for any insect that might have dropped into his bowl. As Buddhists believed that to kill anything, even an insect as tiny as an ant, was a sin, he was looking to save the life of the flying-creatures. Only when he was satisfied nothing more lurked drowning in his bowl, he drank from it.

Since he was so preoccupied, Angela placed her camera and boots outside the pagoda entrance and on stockinged-feet entered its gloomy interior. She would talk to him afterward. In a little notebook she jotted down Pali inscriptions to translate when she returned to the schoolhouse. The floor was not particularly clean. It was stained deep red in places where past pilgrims had spat betel juice. Yellow dust, bird and animal droppings, and litter blown in from outside, marred the place. A huge spider scuttled over her toes, and after the initial shock at seeing it so close, Angela decided to ignore it. She was learning to control her feelings on such things, as, even an ugly spider was Buddha's own creature. But the Loloi pagoda always gave her an eerie feeling, sending shivers down her spine for some inexplicable reason. She could almost feel time stand still in its green gloom, hear battle cries, the clash of war-axes and dahs as the Thaton Mons and the Thais fought each other for Burma.

A tiny sound in the semi-darkness startled her.

Angela approached the stupa, confident that she had been the only one in the pagoda. But a girl whom she had never seen here, knelt before a time-worn Buddha effigy carved out of stone. Presently, she stood up to arrange some white asters and marigolds in the niche at Buddha's feet. The flowers glowed like small suns and moons in the dark temple when the girl put a flame to each joss-stick placed among the flowers. Then she knelt down again, keeping her forehead to the floor for so long, Angela thought she must have fallen asleep at her devotions.

Angela began to wander round again, peering closely at the letterings that had been completely obliterated in places by the passage of time.

'Stop! English lady, please stop.' The sweet voice, speaking English, rang like an echoing bell throughout the great pagoda, clear, precise, and obviously accustomed to issuing commands. Angela was taken aback. The girl said, 'Please do not approach any nearer or touch the place of Buddha's holy relics.'

In the light of the candles behind her she appeared like a temple goddess.

109

'Why not?' Angela asked in astonishment.

'It is not permitted for women to go where men only may tread.'

'What nonsense! I always come here to look round. I only wish to examine the stupa more closely.'

'Yes, but in the stupa lie Buddha's sacred relics, an eyelash and two fingernails.'

'Buddha must have been born with a thousand fingers and toes and a positive beard of eyelashes if one believes in all Buddha's relics dotted around Burma,' Angela said crossly. The girl could not have been more than fourteen or fifteen years old, and this further irritated Angela, for she seemed to be too precocious by far. Yet, she was one of the most lovely Burmese girls Angela had yet encountered. She had a chance to study her while they both stood confronting one another. Not only did she speak English well, though with a strange inflexion, she had the face and body of an exquisite doll. Thick blue-black hair was wound into heavy coils on top of her well-shaped head. Crimson and purple orchids decorated the elaborate hairstyle. A white eingyi, a transparent silk blouse with long tight-fitting sleeves, was worn over an underbodice. Her longyi was the colour of a midnight sky, blue-black like the girl's hair, and was studded with claws of bright gems embedded into the material. But her hands intrigued Angela most of all. While she had been paying tribute to Buddha, Angela had noticed how long and white they were. Tapered fingers appeared to have a separate entity from the body, each bending back and forth in the arrangement of her flowers as though they spoke to the flowers in a language of their own, the language of a dancer.

Angela wondered who the girl was, and said 'Why can't I examine the stupa?'

Thick lashes fluttered downward, the hands betokened an apology: 'There is line painted on floor. Women must not step beyond line painted by phongis.'

Angela had never noticed the demarcation line before. Grubby, almost obliterated in places, it was hard

110

to see it now even by the light of Buddha's flickering candles.

'Goodness me,' said Angela in exasperation, peering at the floor, 'why on earth can't women step beyond such a stupid line?' She looked up at the girl, her own manner equally imperious.

'Because women are considered impure creatures and therefore are not permitted to stand before Holy Prince Gautama who now is Lord Buddha.'

Angela snorted derision: 'Why, that's absurd! I've never heard such nonsense in my life. How can women be considered any more impure than men when they both come to worship him?'

'It is so. It is written.' The Burmese girl tried to explain in faltering English. 'It is for reasons of the cycles of the moon and the monthly outflowing of the woman's blood.'

'Oh!' said Angela, 'Oh, I see.'

She did not see at all. But she had no argument against a logic contrived by men. She only marvelled that the Burmese girl could accept her secondary status in life — but no, not even secondary, for in the eyes of Buddha, women held no status, having only the life-quality of a chicken or spider. In her religion, she would have to be born again as a man in her next recycle of birth, for, as a woman, there was no Nirvana for her. No heaven, no paradise, no everlasting life, no nothing, unless she returned as the male of the species to enjoy what her father and brothers and all the males of her family already enjoyed, privilege in this life and the next. Because she was upset and angry at the exclusion her sex was offered everywhere she turned, Angela was determined to know why.

The old hermit-phongyi had not mentioned such things, and as his was obviously the real life sitting out there in the sunshine thinking of Nirvana, she decided to question him further in the halting Burmese she had learned. She put on her boots and took the old man by surprise with the directness of her questions. Since the

111

self-assured, and obviously rich young lady giving orders inside the pagoda, had chosen to follow her outside, Angela put her to good use as interpreter, knowing how hopeless her own stilted Burmese would be in a discussion of importance.

The hermit-monk was obliging. He spoke clearly and slowly so that anything Angela did not understand, the Burmese girl could explain. 'There are five principle sins,' he said. 'They are, killing — for all life is sacred, including life of animals, birds and insects: One must not lie nor lust; steal nor drink alcohol.'

'But I don't do any of those things.'

'Then if you do not do any of those sinful things, in your next cycle of rebirth,' the old monk was saying, 'there's a chance you will come back as a man, able to partake of Nirvana.'

'But what about now, in this world?'

'You have had the misfortune to be born a woman,' he told her simply, 'and therefore, Nirvana is not yours in this life.'

'But I had little choice in the matter,' she pointed out, determined to have a fairer and more plausible answer. 'I was born a woman, just as you were born a man. To make Nirvana for yourself and not me, is grossly unjust. If one looks at it logically, unless your mother hadn't been born a woman, you wouldn't be here now, a Buddhist priest, with the certain knowledge of that Nirvana waiting for you. So, somewhere along the line, Buddha got his facts wrong. Either that, or he didn't care much for his mother.'

The little Burmese girl giggled in the translation of those fierce words. Angela stood up and squashed down her sunhelmet angrily on her head, the chin-strap catching under her nose to make her even more hot and bothered. The hermit-phongyi smiled gently, bowing his shaven head before the fiery Englishwoman who, in her turn, intrigued him. Her culture was so different to his, and when the two met, it was an education. All white folk he had discovered during his long life, did the

112

strangest things, thought the strangest things and said the strangest things. Many people had come to him to tell of their one true Christian God, and the reasons why he should give up his belief in Gautama Buddha for Jesus Christ. The disciple in him had smiled and accepted and was always receptive even if the disciple did not always understand. And, though he had taken the vows of silence long ago in his hermit existence, he also accepted that shared knowledge was a powerful exchange. So he welcomed the English lady's visits. Their discussions always proved to be most interesting.

At length, the little Burmese interpreter made signs that she could stay no longer. She pointed to the sun in the absence of any timepiece and declared; 'It get late. Maybe we talk again tomorrow. Goodbye. Pyan dor may.'

Angela squinted into the sun, observing her departure along a steep path that went through the mangosteen grove behind the pagoda. She had been so wrapped up in Buddhist doctrines, she felt a momentary pang of disappointment at not asking the girl the most important question of all; would she pose for the Fox-Talbot?

CHAPTER NINE

ONE

O n her way home in the late afternoon Angela, having spent her time sketching as well as taking photographs, was walking past a basha hut with a banyan tree in the front garden when, to her surprise, she saw the girl of the Loloi pagoda sitting on the verandah steps. Two small boys flanked her. The basha hut was sufficiently removed from the Loloi-Ku road not to be inconvenienced by it, pedestrians and bullock-carts providing light relief from total isolation, situated as the hut was, outside the village stockade.

To Angela's even greater surprise, the girl appeared to have been waiting for her. As soon as she saw her coming with her camera, she ran down the steps with the two boys in tow.

'I am very pleased to talk to English lady in Loloi pagoda today,' she said breathlessly. Then she gave a graceful curtsy with expressive hands held together as if in prayer: 'Tomorrow, you come please early, to take feast with family?'

'Goodness me ... a feast ... well, I would be delighted.' Overwhelmed by such an invitation, Angela was at a loss. The girl was an enigma. Against her basha-hut surroundings, she appeared out of place in her exotic clothes and very expensive jewellery.

'My name Minthami. I thank English lady for accepting humble invitation to eat in her house,' the Burmese girl said.

114

'My name's Angela. Angela Featherstone.'

'Miss Feath-the-stone,' she tried to get her tongue round the difficult word and Angela hastily interrupted; 'Please call me Angela, Minthami. Its much easier.'

'An-Gel,' she giggled nervously, 'An-Gel wish for sons to carry home luggage?' She indicated the camera.

'You ... your sons?' Again, Angela felt the wind taken from her sails. Goodness, the girl didn't look old enough! 'Oh, no, no ... its very kind of you Minthami, but really, I can manage perfectly well. I'm accustomed to carrying my camera around with me.'

'Camera?' Minthami asked, perplexed by another strange English word. 'What is such a thing, please?'

'It's a box which takes pictures of people, places and things, and transfers it all onto paper.' She tried to explain. 'If I take a photograph of you — that's what the picture's called, it will keep forever — I hope.' She smiled.

The Burmese girl's sweet face lit up in delight and she asked: 'Sons too?'

'Yes,' said Angela, 'sons too.'

'Forever?'

'Forever. Provided of course I don't make a hash of it in the first place. Its a very tricky procedure and ...' No, it would not do, she could not confuse the poor girl anymore.

'Then you take picture of Minthami and sons tomorrow when you come to feast, please An-Gel?' Minthami made the request boldly because she wanted a picture of her sons more than anything in the world, even when she knew desire was bad.

'Indeed I will,' said Angela beaming, happy to oblige, delighted too because she had not had to ask for her picture. 'Goodbye until tomorrow.'

'Come early An-Gel. Minthami look forward to company of English lady.'

'Thank you, Minthami.'

Once back at the schoolhouse Angela could not wait to tackle her aunt on the subject of Minthami. 'I met

115

someone today, Aunt Emmy. A Burmese girl called Minthami. She told me she has been living in Rangoon.'

'Oh, she's back is she?' Emmeline Lydell raised tired eyes, and, putting aside her pince-nez, rubbed the red mark it had made on the bridge of her nose as she regarded her niece. 'Minthami's the Sawbwa's daughter. He did mention to me once Minthami had been living in Rangoon with her husband. I believe it was some sort of political move at the time.'

'She's asked me to have lunch with her tomorrow. She called it a feast.'

'Knowing Minthami, it probably will be a feast. I'll tell Moke not to save you any dinner,' said Miss Lydell with a twinkle in her eye.

'Then, if she's the Sawbwa's daughter, that makes her a kind of Siamese princess, doesn't it?'

'A Shan princess.'

'Why does she live in that lonely basha-hut out on the Loloi-Ku road, and not in the village with her family?'

'Minthami was ostracized by the Sawbwa's wives for her unconventionality rather than for being a Court concubine, I believe, though there are other reasons ...'

'A what?' Angela stared at her aunt in disbelief. 'She isn't old enough!'

'The Court of Ava take them young — for various reasons. To give to their princes, to train as Zat dancers, or merely as hostages. Minthami was all three. Without my knowing all the details, Mindon Min took her as a child-hostage along with some of her brothers and sisters, to make the old Sawbwa, her father, behave himself. As far as I know, he was playing up at the time and inciting the Shan people to rebel against the Burmese.'

'Poor Minthami,' said Angela dismayed.

They were interrupted by Moke standing in the doorway. 'Chickens not lay anymore,' he said miserably. 'No eggs for breakfast. What I give kiddies for tum-tums in morning?'

He could not understand why the two English women burst out laughing.

116

The following morning, her hair washed and gleaming and Blaize Tennent-Browne's clothes given a good shake and a brush, Angela set off for Minthami's basha-hut, eager to renew their acquaintance.

'Minthami ...' she called, running up the steps and throwing down her sun-helmet and camera on the verandah, 'Minthami, are you there? It's Angela ... Hrrrh!' She fell back in fright, her hand instinctively going to her throat as a tall figure wearing a Burmese longyi and little else, stepped through the tatties at the doorway.

The bearded stranger took a pipe from his mouth and drawled, 'You must be Miss Lydell's niece, pleased to meet you. I'm Nathan Vorne, Minthami's husband. I scared you, I'm sorry.'

'Min ... Min ...' stupidly, she could not get her words out. What she had wanted to say was, Minthami's husband? But I thought she would have been married to one of her own race, a Shan, or Burman, never a European! 'How do you do Mr Vorne,' she said in the end, 'I'm Angela Featherstone, and yes, I am Miss Lydell's niece. Minthami-er-invited me to visit her.'

'Minthami's not here right this minute, she's gone to light her candles to Buddha. But she won't be long. She told me to make you welcome, so step this way Miss Featherstone ...' he moved aside and held back the rattans hanging in the doorway.

She went past him into a tiny room with two glassless squares of window giving a view of the compound. Inside, a small round table, only a foot above the floor, had been beautifully set for a meal. Brass finger-bowls, knives, forks and spoons, unusual to the Burmese way of eating, napkins and flowers made her realize that Minthami had been well brought up. Only two places had been set at the table.

'I hope I'm not intruding,' Angela began forlornly, feeling strangely exposed in the light of Nathan Vorne's direct blue gaze.

'Not at all, Miss Featherstone,' he drawled, 'don't mind me. I'll be getting out of your way, as I know you'll want to talk womens' business. I'm taking Sa-Lon and Roi off to Miss Emmy's school, and then the Sawbwa and me'll be doing a day's tiger-hunting. With luck we might catch him, though he appears to be a wily begger. You know about the Loloi tiger I assume?' An eyebrow quirked in her direction.

'Yes ... oh yes. I've heard about him from my aunt.'

She was not normally tongue-tied but he seemed to confuse her for reasons she could not explain. 'You're American,' she said, knowing it to be a stupid statement.

'Yes. I grew up in Baton Rouge, Louisiana, but I've made Mandalay my home ... ah, here comes Minthami with the boys. I'll be seeing you, Miss Featherstone, good day.' He replaced his pipe in his mouth and she observed him jog-trotting the two boys out of the compound. She noticed too, he had a slight limp, and white scars on his feet and ankles which his open-work Burmese sandals could not disguise. His wrists also bore the mark of fetters and she wondered what terrible crime he had committed to have been confined like that.

'An-Gel!' Minthami said in delight. 'It with pleasure I greet you in my humble home.' She made her graceful curtsy with one knee bent behind the other, her hands together as if in prayer. With orchids in her hair and wearing a pretty longyi, she made a charming picture.

Angela sat down on the silken cushion Minthami had placed for her on a coconut mat on the floor.

'First we drink tea and talk, and later we have food,' Minthami said, fetching from an alcove a Chinese teapot.

Angela asked with curiosity, 'where do you do your cooking, Minthami? I can't see a kitchen.'

Minthami gave one of her delightful giggles. 'Minthami cook outside where all kitchens are in Burma. They not inside house, but in little place in compound.'

When the food was put on the table, Minthami did

118

not share it with her, but hovered in attendance. Angela felt obliged to say: 'You've gone to a great deal of bother on my behalf, and I thank you sincerely, Minthami. Everything's so delicious, won't you please join me?' She felt very awkward eating alone while Minthami's hospitality precluded her from eating until her guest was satisfied.

'No bother,' said the Shan princess. 'Minthami not eat, but happy to cook for An-Gel anytime.' She finished the sentence on a high sing-song note.

'Angela, not Angel,' said Angela, oblivious of the Burmese custom of not disputing or correcting another person, something a polite Burmese man or woman would never do for fear of offending. Minthami, however, did not take offence but again gave her childish titters of amusement.

'Why do you laugh?' Angela asked as she selected food from the numerous side dishes placed in front of her.

'It is nothing, only something private which amuse Minthami. English guest might not understand and take offence.'

'Why should I take offence? But if you don't want to tell me because it's personal, I shan't pry.'

'Then Minthami tell because English guest wish to know. It is in English, a good spirit, the name An-Gel, yes?'

'Yes, an angel is a good spirit.'

'Now Minthami have good and bad spirit in her life. Shwe Nat, that is Captain Vorne, he called golden devil in Mandalay and that is bad spirit. Angel and devil, it is ... how you say in English, special pro-vid-ence?'

Angela changed the subject: 'Tell me about your sons, Minthami.'

'Sa-Lon, he big boy, he six years.' She held up her fingers. 'Roi, he four. They help in paddyfields yesterday, taking water-buffalo to gather rice-harvest. Today, Shwe Nat make them go school because he say he not want them under sore feet all day. Also they must learn.

119

In two years ...' again she used her fingers as an abacus, 'eldest son, he go to Phongyi-Kyaung to earn merit for family in dedication of Shinbyu. Till that time, he learn many things at Daw Lydell school, like once-three-three and two-twos-four.'

'Yes indeed,' Angela murmured, wondering whose sons Sa-Lon and Roi were. They seemed to be too dark, too Burmese to be Nathan Vorne's children. She dismissed them as being the offspring of the prince to whom Minthami had been given. She wondered too how old Minthami was, for she was certainly older than she looked. They were questions she was prevented from asking on the grounds of courtesy and delicacy. 'This is very nice, Minthami.' She indicated the dish from which she was helping herself. 'May I be very rude and ask what it is?'

'An-Gel never rude, only curious like all Ingalaik. Minthami like to please. It called 'mohinga' which is rice-noodles in Minthami own sauce. Very com-plic-ated ... of own making. So cannot explain in English, please.' She smiled apologetically, her English a strange blend of Burmese and American pronunciation.

'Then I must learn Burmese properly, if you'll teach me. I've made a start on my own, but its a struggle because Burmese words are so difficult to pronounce.'

'English too,' said Minthami, and their shared warmth of laughter presaged the blossoming of a happy friendship.

After the huge meal, Minthami brought more tea and a tray of condiments according to custom. Strips of ginger, roasted groundnuts, halwa of rosewater, ground rice and bananas, and many other delicious confections made from coconut, riceflour and crystallized fruits. Minthami also offered her the expensive delicacy which no respectable Burmese feast was complete without, pickled and fermented leaves of the wild teaplant. Angela much preferred the Burmese cake called Beik-moke, made by Minthami in her stone oven to the fermented tea-leaves, but was too polite to say so and offend her hostess.

120

'Minthami,' Angela said, 'you must let me do something for you in return for this splendid meal — and thank you for letting me see what goes on inside a real Burmese home.'

'Minthami not require anything in return. She happy to oblige.' And then the effort was too great and she blurted out eagerly. 'Perhaps picture of sons when we go to hot-springs?'

'Of course ... but what hot-springs?' Angela asked, curious. She had been in Loloi several weeks now and had not heard about the hot-springs. 'Minthami show An-Gel when sons come home from school. It in jungle. Not far. We go through compound and take pathway in bamboo-grove. Now we sleep on mats as it very hot, and then, when sun begins to go down we find water-pool.'

Happily Minthami brought out two sleeping mats and put them on the verandah where a pergola of trellised flowers and vines kept them cool, shaded and hypnotized by the heavy scents of an exotic garden.

THREE

When the sun was going down Minthami took Angela and her two sons to the rock-pool. The way led through her back garden, along a well-worn path and into the jungle. When Angela first saw the jungle-pool she wanted to rub her eyes to see if she were dreaming. Here was a natural theatre surrounding a place of gushing water. It flowed from tiered rocks, cascading down into a pool of steam. Luxuriant ferns and shrubs grew all around, screening the water-garden from the eyes of intruders. Only women and girls with their small children seemed to occupy this place of lotus-blooms, butterflies, orchids and laughter. Shan girls splashed themselves and each other in the water, all of them fully clothed in sarongs or longyis. Two Chinese women on stunted feet did their washing. So did Minthami.

'Minthami come every day,' she explained to Angela

while she pummelled her household laundry on the rocks and Sa-Lon and Roi played in the water with other children.

'Do the village men ever come here?' Angela asked.

Minthami shook her head. 'They not go places women go. They men,' she said.

'And I've been in Loloi practically two months and have had such trouble washing my hair in two inches of water. I'll give my Aunt Emmy a good piece of my mind for not telling me about this place,' said Angela half-laughing, half-annoyed. 'Minthami, if you, Sa-Lon and Roi climb up on those rocks over there, I'll try and set up my camera over here, and see what kind of picture we get.'

Afterwards Angela took off her boots and stockings and hoisting up her skirts, waded into the warm water.

'Tomorrow you must wear longyi like real Burmese girl,' Minthami told Angela. 'Then you can sit in water and be very happy.'

'I should like that very much,' said Angela, feeling she was in paradise. 'I don't think I'll go to Mandalay after all,' she laughed.

'Oh yes, An-Gel go to Mandalay. Mandalay very beautiful city. Minthami miss it very much when she live in Rangoon with Shwe Nat. Shwe Nat, he like jumping-cat with hot feet in Rangoon and always angry with Britishers for keeping him in right place at right time. He say Britishers not have imagination, they only go by Magna Carta — Minthami not know what that is at time and ask husband and he say it mean, Queen Victoria, I love you well, pray let me kiss your toe.'

'I haven't heard that one,' Angela said, amused by Minthami's imitation of her husband.

'No one hear that one,' Minthami replied. 'Shwe Nat, he say things not for other people to hear when he shout at Minthami for whole world to hear. He very funny man. ...' She went rushing off then to rescue her youngest son from drowning, the children's games becoming boisterous.

When she came back Angela said, 'It sounds as though Mr Vorne doesn't love the British very much.'

'Oh, he love them all right,' Minthami said, thrashing out her washing on the rocks, 'he just not like them very much. He say, they popping up in Burma like smallpox in India.'

Angela felt she ought to bring the subject of the Shwe Nat to a close.

That night at dinner Emmeline Lydell asked Angela if she had had an enjoyable day.

'Yes thank you, Aunt Emmy, very nice. You didn't tell me there were hot-springs in Loloi.' She had not meant to sound accusing, but her aunt's expression was one of injury.

'You didn't ask me dear ... and I never thought to mention it. I've always regarded it as being rather ... er ... native I suppose, a communal washing-place, breeding-grounds for germs and so on.'

'So is the ablution centre in the compound.' Angela reminded her.

'This soup is rather nice, Moke,' Miss Lydell said turning to him. 'Very nice indeed. What is it?'

'Shrimp, Miss Emmy.'

'That's nice ... Angela dear, what's the matter?'

Angela had pushed her soup-plate away: 'I think its disgusting ... oh no, no, not the soup, Moke,' she said hurriedly, catching sight of his hurt expression. 'I was meaning something else ...'

'Moke dear,' said Miss Lydell, 'I wonder if you'd go onto the verandah for a moment?' She knew he would still have one ear pressed to the flimsy wall, but something was obviously worrying her niece and she wanted to find out just what. 'What's disgusting, dear?'

'That Nathan Vorne is married to Minthami,' Angela blurted out against her will.

'Why dear? Because he's white and she isn't? Many European men out here take native wives and mistresses.'

'It's not that. Why, he must be approaching forty! And ... and married to a mere child! Well, a child to look at. She says Sa-Lon and Roi are her sons, I find that hard to believe because she only looks fifteen years old now. Sa-Lon she told me is six. Whose sons are they, Aunt Emmy?'

'Nathan and Minthami's dear. Who else?'

'Who else indeed! I thought ... oh, I don't know what I thought. I thought Sa-Lon and Roi were the children of the prince to whom Minthami had been given as a concubine — if that's the word. That they weren't hers, but she possibly looked after them for this prince of hers ... oh, I know I'm getting awfully muddled. But how can they be her children? She's not old enough.'

'Minthami's certainly of age, Angela dear. That's old enough to have children, surely? And girls in Burma ... anywhere in the East for that matter, mature much faster than those in the West.'

'But what you're really avoiding saying, Aunt Emmy, is she gave birth to Sa-Lon when she was only fifteen years old?'

'I assume so. I've no cause to dispute Sa-Lon's and Roi's ages.'

'And they're Nathan Vorne's sons?'

'To all intents and purposes.'

'That's what's so disgusting about it, aunt Emmy! A Christian whiteman should know better. To take a child-bride for no other reason than ... than ...' she remembered the hermit-phongyi's five sins. 'Lust, Aunt Emmy, is immoral. I doubt he would have bedded a fourteen year-old-girl in his native America. The law wouldn't have allowed it for a start.'

'I believe he has a very real affection for Minthami,' said Miss Lydell, mildly surprised by Angela's outburst. The girl obviously felt very strongly about Nathan Vorne's immorality and she wondered why she was so interested in his affairs.

'And living like a native too ... they sleep on the floor you know. How can a man who has obviously been bred

124

to better things live like a savage in the jungle?'

'I've never really given it much thought dear, Nathan and Minthami are hardly ever here. They're always flitting off somewhere or other, Rangoon, Mandalay, America — Loloi is only a convenient resting place since Minthami's people are here. How legal and binding their marriage is I wouldn't like to say. It's none of my business. But in Burma mutual agreement between the couple themselves and the girl's parents is all that's required. The Sawbwa obviously agreed to the arrangement and was pleased by it. He and Captain Vorne are great friends.'

'And Minthami being a rich and beautiful Shan princess obviously attracted the Captain. I still think that a man of his age, to all accounts a Christian gentleman, should not have seduced a fourteen year old ... child! Excuse me, Aunt Emmy, I've had a long and busy day and I think I'd like to go to bed.'

'Goodnight, Angela dear ... and I rather think that if anyone did the seducing, it was Minthami. But you mustn't let other peoples' bizarre relationships upset you.'

'I'm not upset,' said Angela's muffled voice from behind the bamboo screen, 'and I wouldn't know about human relationships — I've never had any.'

Emmy Lydell detected a note of self-pity in that voice as a petticoat came flying over the wardrobe-line. 'What about that nice boy in Mandalay you came out here to marry?'

'Matthew? Matthew and I aren't engaged anymore. Goodnight, Aunt Emmy.'

Miss Lydell wisely refrained from saying anything more on the subject. Thoughtfully, she turned down the oil-lamp, the insects inside its glass dome frantically squittering as they singed. She looked into the faces of her six sleeping protégés and smiled tiredly as she kissed each one on the forehead: Doh, Ray, Mee, Fah, Soh, Lah, much easier to remember than their complicated Burmese names.

CHAPTER TEN

ONE

The next few days in Loloi were set aside for the Harvest Festival. Three days of holiday were given by the Sawbwa, so there was no school. Minthami had brought a very beautiful longyi for Angela to wear, and Miss Lydell could hear both of them laughing and chatting like a couple of schoolgirls going to a party. Behind the bamboo screen Minthami was showing Angela how to keep the skirt in place, while Sa-Lon and Roi had joined the 'boarders' for a bed-time story. Dark saucer eyes were fixed intently on the school-mistress's face, every nuance of her expression not missed by her admirers.

'And then, Little Red Riding Hood said to the Big Bad Wolf, Ooooh, what big teeth you have grandmother ...'

'Ooooh!' said the children, thumbs dropping from sleepy mouths to share the delights of the English language.

'Make him a tiger instead of wolf, Daw Lydell,' Sa-Lon urged. He spoke excellent English, but with his father's accent.

'And the Big Bad Tiger answered, all the better to eat you, my dear ...' The tiny tots began to nod off one by one and presently Miss Lydell closed the book. 'That's all for tonight children. Roll down your sleeping-mats. Sa-Lon and Roi, you wait out on the verandah please, your mother won't be long.' Although it was late, Minthami was taking Sa-Lon and Roi to the night-time

126

revelries. Burmese children kept very late hours which Miss Lydell disapproved of. But Sa-Lon and Roi were not her children so she did not interfere in the way they were brought up. Doh, Ray, Mee, Fah, Soh and Lah were a different matter altogether and were her special responsibility.

Angela was having difficulties. The heavy black satin longyi embroidered with Chinese temples, birds, flowers and fruit, edged with an elaborate border of emerald silk and silver thread, was not doing as it was told. She felt reluctant to wear it in case she spoiled or tore it. But Minthami was so insistent, she had no choice.

'It strong best silk from Siam. Very good present from husband who bring it home from travels.'

'All the more reason why I shouldn't borrow it. I was taught at school, never a borrower or lender be.'

'Then I give it to you Amagyi-Angel,' Minthami said, holding fresh flowers in her mouth ready to put into Angela's hair. Angela was touched by the Shan girl's words. Amagyi, she had learned meant 'big-sister' in Burmese, and to be called anyone's big-sister was a term of endearment. 'This longyi not fit Minthami anyway,' she went on to say. 'Husband buy things for wife without knowing size. He think everyone high as he, and Minthami a giraffe-woman with long long neck to fit longyi. It mean cutting off pretty border, and that great shame, so you have longyi as present, Amagyi-Angel.'

'I couldn't ... no really I couldn't Minthami ... besides, I can't seem to keep it up — without it slipping ...'

'Come, Minthami show you how. First you bring it this way, to right, like this, so it fit very tightly,' she poked Angela's hip with a long finger. 'Then, all this here on right, you bring back other way. You must hold hand so, to make front pleat, then quickly to left again ...' And with a deft flick of the wrist that beat the eye, she twisted and tucked the pleated material into the cotton waistband. It appeared secure enough but Angela was a little dubious.

'Are you sure it won't fall off? Oughtn't I to put a pin

in it? I don't want my skirt to drop in front of the Sawbwa's eyes.'

Minthami laughed, 'No, it all right. Also plenty room to walk, see.'

Angela kicked a leg and pulled a face. 'I don't think it does for me what it does for you. Especially with this very English blouse. But never mind. I hear sounds of impatience from your two sons so we'd better be off. I have something for you in return for letting me borrow this longyi.' She took some photographs out of the Shan bag she had bought in the Loloi market, and sorting them gave one to Minthami. 'That one's yours, Minthami. You may have it.'

Minthami took the picture of herself seated on the rocks above the lotus-pool, her arms draped around the shoulders of her two grinning sons. She was so overwhelmed by the beauty of the picture, tears sprang to her dark eyes. 'Oh, see here is flower and here is Roi with wide teeth smiling, and on pool is lotus-blossom, and patterns of Minthami longyi ...' she clasped the picture to her breast. 'Amagyi-Angel, I thank you,' and one knee behind the other, the Shan princess curtsied to the commoner.

Angela turned away and took up the other photographs lying on her cot. 'These are mine, but I don't mind your borrowing them for the moment as I know you'd probably like Captain Vorne to look at them.'

'Yes, yes,' said Minthami eagerly, peering over Angela's arm to look at the hermit-phongyi on the steps of his pagoda and Miss Lydell's schoolchildren sitting in the compound having their lessons with her. 'Minthami very careful to bring back. But first she show husband, father and wives and children ... also new baby which Minthami soon to have ...' she added the last shyly, lambent eyes glowing with deep inner happiness.

'Oh, that's splendid news, Minthami ... I'm delighted for you.' Angela turned away so Minthami couldn't see her face. 'Now I think its about time we went, don't you?'

On his verandah, the Sawbwa sat in all his Chieftain glory. He wore his formal hat called a gaung-baung which he had worn in King Mindon Min's presence. Apart from that Eastern headpiece, the rest of him was clad in a Westernized style of suit made of white satin. Trousers and jacket were so ludicrously tight on his enormously fat body, he reminded Angela of a gigantic cream puff oozing from the edges. Squashed into a chair too small for him, he was grotesque, amusing, regal and ridiculous, and Angela did not know whether to burst out laughing or curtsy to him. She did the latter. Enormous rubies winked from his fingers as he waved his cheroot in greeting, his smiles broad and red like his rubies. They were given chairs among the Sawbwa's wives who were seated on mats. 'There are so many of them,' Miss Lydell whispered in Angela's ear as she drove her palm-leaf fan at the vicious mosquitoes. 'Chief wives, head-wives, half-head-wives, lesser wives and under-privileged wives, it's a job to remember all their names. But they're a wonderful help to me and keep the boarders' clothes washed, pressed and mended. I do wish he wouldn't eat that awful betel-nut, though. When he talks to me I'm reminded of tuberculosis.'

'Hardly,' said Angela with a smile, 'he's too gross. Look, he's waving his cheroot again ... do we wave back?'

Miss Lydell came out from behind her fan and glancing in the Sawbwa's direction, his male relatives gathered around him in equal splendour, fluttered her fan at Minthami's father. 'Doesn't the village look pretty dear? I do love those Chinese lanterns, and the smell of all that cooking has made me feel very hungry. Moke assured me there would be plenty for us to eat at the Pwe, and got out of cooking for us for the next three days. What a pity you can't take a picture of all this.' She waved her hands airily, embracing the Sawbwa's compound and the place circled off for the night's entertainment. Nathan Vorne, standing among the mango trees on the opposite side of the compound thought Miss Lydell was waving to him and brandished his pipe at her. 'Oh, there's Captain Vorne dear ... it is Captain Vorne, isn't it? I can't see too well in this dim lighting.'

'Yes, it's Captain Vorne, Aunt Emmy. Sa-Lon and Roi are with him. I wonder where Minthami's got to?' She glanced around, but couldn't see her in the crowd. 'Don't Burmese men and women ever sit together, even on a sociable occasion like this?' Angela asked.

'Oh, no dear. It simply isn't done. Women remain on one side and the men on the other. The only time men and women are alone with each other is if they're married or there are relatives present.'

'That seems rather odd when one considers the other kinds of liberties Burmese women seem to enjoy. I mean, they appear to be boss in their own right, in the home, in the market, with the children, everywhere, while the men remain inconspicuously in the background.'

'True. They also run businesses and are allowed into educational establishments, and take responsibilities women in the West are denied ... ah, here they come, the dancing troupe. Now hush dear, let's watch. There's Minthami!' The village band, comprising the kye waing, circle of gongs, the lin gwin, cymbals, pa tala or Burmese xylophone, saing waing and saung gauk, drums and harp, loudly and joyfully brought children into the torch-lit circle, Minthami leading the procession. Then followed a contemporary drama in song and dance called a Pyazat. Feathery headdresses of pampas grasses and bright green costumes sewn with seed pearls depicted the growing rice-plants. The children acted out the story of the seasons. Amid much music, laughter and amusement, each child rice-plant wriggled through brown gunny sacks in imitation of sprouting through the earth. Buckets of water were thrown over them by enthusiastic stage assistants; this was the monsoon season. The harvest-time brought out a golden image of Buddha noisily trundled around the arena on a cart pulled by two real water-buffalo who ran amok in the crowd until fetched back into the limelight by stalwart fathers whose sons were the buffalo drivers.

The Pyazat concluded on a note of thunderous applause, the Sawbwa and his family cheering, beaming, clapping, footstamping, loudest of all.

Next came the real Zat performance, a religious story symbolizing love, sorrow and rebirth. Minthami was the leading Zat dancer. She wore a silver-white costume that shimmered and shivered in the lantern-light, glass jewels sewn to her satin longyi turning her into an ice-maiden. Breathtakingly lovely, she indeed was that fairy princess, lithe and graceful, and Angela could not help sneaking a look at Nathan Vorne to observe his reaction to his dancing princess. His face was in shadow. Angela brought her attention back to Minthami, sweeping her partner and everyone else off their feet as her long, blue-black hair, left unbraided, swept the dusty stage.

'You know dear, Minthami actually means dancer,' Miss Lydell murmured behind her fan. 'I wonder if the old Sawbwa named her before or after she was taken to the Court of Ava?'

'Maybe he consulted an astrologer at her birth. How are her hands able to twist in these extraordinary movements and positions?' Angela whispered back.

'They break and dislocate finger-bones of any girl-child destined to be a Zat performer,' explained Miss Lydell.

Angela, shuddering, did not wish to know more on the subject, fully aware now of why Minthami's hands were so strangely flexible. Afterwards, bhodi flowers were scattered into the audience. When the last clashing echoes had died away, music and dancing were forgotten as the men, first in line, headed for the feast. The Sawbwa and his menfolk were served where they sat. Plantain-leaves of rice, curries, fish and fruit were brought to them on flat basket-trays by the women. Only when the men, hunkering on their heels, had finished eating did the women partake of what was left.

131

'I think,' said Angela in disgust while waiting for supper, 'it's quite the worst show of bad manners Buddha could have devised! I mean, men filling themselves to bursting before the women get the left-overs. It's unfair ...'

'I disagree,' said a deep voice from the shadows. Nathan Vorne came into the pool of lantern-light in which Miss Lydell and Angela were standing. Angela noticed he did not carry a plantain-leaf plate piled high with food, only his pipe in his hand. 'Why, Captain Vorne?' Angela asked, her voice tight.

'Why what, Miss Featherstone?' He feigned innocence.

'Why don't you consider it bad manners men eating before women?'

'Because I'm a man I guess.'

'And a Buddhist perhaps, Captain Vorne?' said Miss Lydell, matching his bantering tone. She could see that he had been teasing her niece, though Angela could not.

'I can't say in all honesty I'm a Buddhist, Miss Emmy. Leastways, Minthami'll tell you I'm not. She's always beating me with the broomstick for wearing my shoes indoors.' His tobacco smoke kept the mosquitoes and other insects at bay. It smelled quite nice after all the garlicky and fermented saltfish smells wafting around them.

'So you and the Sawbwa had no success with our friend the Loloi tiger, eh Captain Vorne?' Miss Lydell asked.

'None at all, Miss Emmy. However, after the harvest thanksgiving's over, we're organizing another shikar. Only a couple of nights ago some livestock was savaged over at Ku, which means he's back on the prowl.'

'Captain Vorne,' Angela said, trying to curb her excitement, 'I'd dearly like to take some photographs of a tiger-hunt. May I accompany your party? I can use a gun.'

Before he had a chance to reply, Miss Lydell said to her niece, with a look that conveyed she thought Angela had taken leave of her senses, 'I wouldn't conceive of you doing such a thing, Angela! Why, you might be killed before you got anywhere near enough to the tiger to take his picture. I've never heard of anything so irresponsible in my life. Besides, it will be an all-male party, and Burmese men don't like women getting in the way — especially English women. Is that not so, Captain Vorne?'

He scratched his head and contemplated his pipe, an unwilling victim in a women's argument. 'Well, Miss Emmy,' he said in his lazy drawl, 'it's a question of the tiger finding us if we don't put a mind to finding him first. Half the reason why we don't manage to finish him off is because the darn Buddhists run away rather than shoot the crittur. And if Miss Featherstone here can use a gun like she says, then there's no reason why she can't come along. She looks like a pretty sensible female to me.' His blue eyes swept her cunningly, and Angela wondered why she felt suddenly enfeebled by a look from him that held her unwillingly captive for those few seconds.

She swallowed. 'Thank you, Captain Vorne. I promise I shan't let you down by fainting away or doing anything stupid.'

'Angela, I firmly forbid such a thing!' Her aunt, helpless between the two of them, looked from one to the other. 'My dear girl, what would your father have thought of my irresponsibility in letting you go on such a trip?'

'He would have thrown me into the arms of the tiger to get a good picture for the Delhi Camera Club.'

'Captain Vorne, you don't know what you're letting yourself in for.'

'Oh yes I do, Miss Emmy,' he said, his piercing blue eyes still fastened upon her niece's green ones, 'and I'll beat the hell out of her if she lets me down.' He seemed to realize suddenly where he was and to whom he was talking. 'Don't worry, Miss Emmy,' he continued, turning to knock his pipe out on the trunk of a mango tree,

Miss Featherstone'll be perfectly safe with me ... now, any of you ladies know the whereabouts of Sa-Lon and Roi? Minthami made me promise not to let them out of my sight while she was doing her dancing bit — but you know what kids are like, Miss Emmy.'

'I certainly do, Captain Vorne,' she said, still angry with him for taking Angela's side, 'they bleat at all the wrong times and have a habit of being everywhere but in the place you're looking. The last I saw of Sa-Lon and Roi, they were climbing the roof of your father-in-law's house.'

Observing him saunter off in search of his sons, Angela remarked; 'Sometimes he looks to be in genuine pain with his feet — as though he's treading hot coals. I wonder what happened to him?'

'Captain Vorne, my dear child, is always going from one scrape to another. I daresay a tiger snapped at his heels when he got too close with his pipe. But you're a naughty girl, my dear, for going against my wishes concerning tiger-hunting.'

'Aunt Emmy darling,' said Angela linking her arm in her aunt's as they drifted towards the last of the food, 'don't be angry. For a souvenir I'll let you have a framed photograph of the tiger-hunt.'

'Make no mistake my dear, the Burmese refer to him as a devil. And I think the Shwe Nat is every bit as his name implies.'

THREE

As soon as the harvest-festival celebrations were over, Angela decided to return Minthami her lovely longyi for fear of becoming over-fond of it. Her aunt's boarders were going on a picnic with her, Moke driving the ox-cart with the children grinning in the back. 'I think we'll be going to the big lake at Ku, dear. So don't worry unduly if we're late home. Take care of yourself and Moke says there's jaggery if you get hungry before dinner this

134

evening. Oh, by-the-way, Angela, if you're going to Minthami's, would you mind dropping in a parcel of childrens' clothes to be mended at the Sawbwa's residence? Ask for the Maha-Devi, and she'll distribute the sewing among the lesser wives.'

Her voice was all but swallowed up in the squeal of ox-cart wheels, noise being very necessary in Burma to ward off all kinds of evil spirits. They deliberately left wheels unoiled, just for that purpose, and Angela's teeth were set on edge.

Angela dropped in the parcel of mending for the Sawbwa's wives, then she met Sa-Lon and Roi scuttling along the road like frightened rabbits from the direction of the basha hut. 'Hello,' she greeted them, 'where are you two going in such a mortal hurry?'

'Go to Pwe,' said Sa-Lon, kicking up the dust with his bare toes.

'But the Pwe's over,' Angela reminded him.

'Papa says go to Pwe.' Sa-Lon insisted.

'Here you are then.' Angela gave them some of Moke's jaggery.

'Thank-you-amagyi-Angel,' they chorused, not forgetting their 'English' manners as taught by Daw Lydell. Angela had to smile at their seriousness. They were pretty little boys, but she still couldn't relate them to Nathan Vorne who was as fair as they were dark.

Angela arrived outside the basha hut only to hear raised voices coming from within: it sounded more like an all-out fight than a heated argument. She turned, ready to creep away lest she be caught eavesdropping when Minthami came rushing through the kus-kus tatties at the door, down the verandah steps and almost bumped into Angela before she became aware of her in the compound. She caught hold of Angela's arm in a grip that pinched, whirling her round to face Nathan as he stepped out on the verandah.

'Here now ...' she screeched at him like a fish-wife. Angela couldn't believe this was the gentle Minthami. Her eyes were red and swollen with weeping and her

135

hair unbound and dishevelled. She looked like a wild woman, not the beautiful princess of the Zat performance. 'She is here ... Amagyi-Angel is here ... you tell her. She is brought by your evil spirit to hear this thing to sadden her ... go tell!'

'Minthami, what on earth's wrong?' Angela glanced from one to the other in bewilderment and embarrassment.

Minthami glowered at her husband; 'Tell her, *kala!*'

Nathan Vorne shrugged. 'Miss Featherstone, take no notice of her. She's in one of her silly moods again. She gets herself all worked up about nothing.'

'*Nothing? Nothing!* You call tearing up Minthami nice pictures of sons, nothing! I give you *nothing ...*' she ran up the steps and punched him.

He caught her flailing fists and shaking her, said, 'Stop it, you silly little Buddhist bitch!'

Minthami kicked him and Angela took a deep breath: 'Captain Vorne ... Minthami ... I know its none of my business, but if its anything to do with the photograph I gave you, I'm very sorry.'

'Not only sons' picture, all of them, see ... I show you Amagyi-Angel,' and wriggling herself out of her husband's arms Minthami rushed into the living-room. She was out again to shower Angela with a snowstorm of photographic paper. 'Not only he tear up picture of Sa-Lon and Roi with Minthami, he tear up Buddhist phongyi and Miss Lydell schoolchildren!' Minthami cried, weeping in an agony of frustration. She threw herself on the top step and pounded the boards with the palms of her hands in a truly theatrical gesture.

Angela looked from the stricken Shan princess to her seemingly indifferent husband observing his wife's histrionics with an absolute air of insouciance.

'Why, Captain Vorne?' Angela asked, her voice icy.

'Two of those photographs happened to be my property, Captain Vorne. I gave only one to Minthami to keep. The one of your sons taken at the waterfall.'

'Miss Featherstone, if they were your property or

Queen Victoria's, I'd still have got rid of them.'

'How dare you, Captain Vorne!' By now he really had put her into a towering temper. 'All your wife intended to do with those photographs, taken at great cost and developed myself with even more patience, since photographic materials are hard to come by in this country, was to show those pictures to you and her family before returning them to me. It was to be a surprise to you, as ....'

'That, they certainly were Miss Featherstone! I can't tell you how much of a surprise. But the fact remains, I'd be much obliged if you refrained from taking anymore pictures around here. It isn't that I don't appreciate your artistic talent, but I object to any invasion of my privacy — by anyone!'

'Your privacy!' She was beginning to sound like Minthami, he was driving her to such fury. Angela took another deep breath and modulated her voice, 'Goodness me, Captain Vorne, what has an old hermit-phongyi and a few native school-children got to do with your privacy?'

'Everything, Miss Featherstone, so perhaps ma'am you wouldn't interfere anymore in things between Minthami and me.' He jabbed the stem of his pipe at her in a manner that would have made her slap his face had she been standing near enough to him. 'Take it or leave it, Miss Featherstone, but that's how it is. I'm not giving you my reasons, I'm just telling you to put your camera away until you get to Mandalay. Now, if you'll excuse me please.'

Before he had a chance to disappear behind the rattans, Angela asked, 'Why Captain Vorne, do you object to my taking photographs in Loloi? Has the Sawbwa issued a decree I don't know about?'

He looked at her as if he would have liked to toss her out of his compound, but she was not ready to depart yet — she wanted a proper answer from him first.

'Miss Featherstone, I'll thank you to mind your own business and leave me to mind mine.'

'Very well, Captain Vorne. But I find your behaviour unjustified ... and ... totally offensive. I won't intrude on your precious privacy, anymore. If Minthami wishes to see me again, I'll be happy to receive her in my aunt's home. But I shan't come here again. Minthami, I've returned your longyi. Thank you for letting me borrow it.' Angela placed it on the bottom step.

'Ohhhh!' Minthami cried, and leapt up from the verandah to launch herself once more at Nathan. 'Now you offend Amagyi-Angel. You very bad man. Your wife hate you very much, Thakin!' Her fists like small hammers pummelled his chest. 'Minthami go away,' she sobbed, 'she run away far, and never come back. But first she take Sa-Lon and Roi ... you truly Shwe Nat of Mandalay like they say and Minthami have no wish to live anymore with kala and ludu who not real husband but American Captain!'

She turned and rushed down the steps in her tight longyi, fleeing past Angela to the Loloi-Ku road as if the Loloi tiger were after her. Angela did not know whether to go after her little Shan friend or not. She turned to the husband; 'Captain Vorne, I'm truly horrified by your conduct toward Minthami who has great affection for you and her sons. If I'm to blame for your quarrel, then I apologize. I had no idea some innocent photographs would be the cause of all this trouble. I'm upset because Minthami's upset and she ought not to be in her condition. Don't you think you'd better go after her and bring her back? Running like that she's sure to bring on a miscarriage.'

'I beg your pardon?' He took his pipe from his mouth to glare at her in astonishment.

'She ... she's ...' Angela felt a lump in her throat that wouldn't be shifted, and he was glaring at her so balefully she felt foolish. 'Don't you know, didn't she tell you about herself?' She spoke to the banyan tree, unable to look at him.

He waved his pipe at her again. 'What's Minthami been telling you Miss Featherstone?' he demanded.

Angela closed her eyes and swallowing hard in the hope she was not interfering again said; 'Minthami told me she was expecting a child.'

'Did she now!'

When she opened her eyes he was looking at her with a grin on his face that infuriated her.

Shaking his head he said; 'Poor Miss Featherstone! I have no wish to disbelieve my dear little wife, but believe me when I tell you she lies like a trooper. Having babies every other week is all in Minthami's mind, nowhere else. Ever since Roi was born she's wanted a daughter. Because she doesn't seem able to beget one, she goes to Lord Buddha to answer her prayers — rather like our Lady of Lourdes, if you get my meaning. Minthami can't have any more children, Miss Featherstone, but thinks she can through faith in Buddha.'

'I ... I'm sorry ... oh dear, I do seem to have put my foot in it today. I'll go now. I shan't come here again. I'll probably be setting off for Mandalay shortly. Goodbye, Captain Vorne.'

She felt an utter fool as she walked down the path knowing he was watching her, but not knowing what his thoughts were, only that he disturbed her.

CHAPTER ELEVEN

ONE

A ngela stood in the basha schoolhouse throwing things half-heartedly into an old tin trunk purloined from Miss Lydell. Her thoughts were confused: nothing belonged to her, not even the trunk — Blaize's clothes, Yoe's book, her father's camera, photographic materials supplied by Sir Edwin. All she, Angela, owned was what she stood up in, her boots. Even they were beginning to wear thin and had mildew spots on the leather. She sighed, melancholia weighing heavily on her soul this bright morning. She had made up her mind to go to Mandalay, having decided to tell Matthew the whole story. If he wanted to marry her despite everything then she supposed it would be to her everlasting good fortune. If not, she would return to England. Childrens' voices suddenly silenced, Angela listened. She heard her aunt talking to a man. Her heart did a tiny somersault and she told herself not to be stupid. Why would he come here? She moved to the window and cautiously peeped into the compound. A low and animated conversation seemed to be taking place between Nathan Vorne and her aunt, while her aunt fed his horse with jaggery. His appearance was so altered this morning, Angela hardly believed it was the same man. He wore a white shirt and cravat, jodhpurs and riding-boots. Under his arm he carried his sun-helmet. He looked, for a change, the epitome of a gentleman. Her back pressed flat against the wall so that she couldn't be seen if they looked up, she listened with one ear at the open window, but she could only make out the muted hum of their voices. Miss Lydell gave a little laugh, then nodding, brought the children out from under the house to say good-day to Captain Vorne. Angela watched him shake each child's hand, very seriously, Doh, Ray, Mee, Fah, Soh and Lah.

She was puzzled. He seemed to be on familiar terms with them. Despite Miss Lydell's vague attitude in the past to Nathan Vorne and his affairs, watching her now, Angela realized she was actually on very good terms with him. To her horror, she saw them coming towards the house, leaving the children and the horse in Moke's care.

'Angela ... Angela dear, could you leave your packing for a moment? Captain Vorne's here to see you.'

Biting her thumbnail, Angela looked round the room. Petticoats and other articles of a personal nature were strewn on chairs. The table was littered, and she was at sixes and sevens. She wondered how he always managed to induce this sense of panic in her.

'Can you spare a moment dear? I know you're busy,' Miss Lydell came inside the living-room and swept up two petticoats and a pair of pantalettes with lace frills from a chair which she offered to the Captain. Rolling Angela's clothes into a bundle Miss Lydell tossed them out of sight and took two crystal tumblers from a little cabinet — her only two — and a bottle Angela did not know her aunt had hidden away. She felt her answer ought to have been: Yes, Aunt Emmy, I've lots of spare moments, but none for him!

Instead, she murmured something polite and remained like a mute against the bamboo screen separating bedroom from living-room. Her Aunt Emmy obviously knew how the Captain liked his whisky, two burra-pegs and no water. Watching her fuss round him, Angela wondered how often he came to indulge his very un-Buddhist habit with her. Miss Lydell helped herself to fresh lime juice, and only then remembered to ask

141

Angela if she required a drink to refresh herself.

'No, thank you, Aunt Emmy,' Angela said haughtily.

'Won't you sit down, Miss Featherstone?' Nathan Vorne said, and waved his hand to a vacant chair. Angela resented his attitude, verging on rudeness.

'No, thank you, Captain Vorne.' She had a tiny feeling he was laughing at her behind his whisky glass. 'So, you're off to Mandalay?' he asked, looking at her strangely.

'Yes.'

'I'd no idea Mr Hawes was your uncle and Matthew Sinclair your fiancé,' he said. Placing an arm along the top of the chair next to him, he tilted his own seat back to regard her fully. 'Not till just now that is, when your Aunt Emmy told me.'

'Adrian Hawes is my father's step-brother, Matthew Sinclair is not my fiancé anymore. We ... I broke off the engagement two months ago.'

He cleared his throat as his eyes flickered to a point over her right shoulder and then back to her. 'I'm sorry ... anyway, Miss Featherstone, the reason I'm here is about those photographs I destroyed yesterday ...'

'Please don't explain, I think I understand.'

'No you don't! You don't understand a thing, Miss Cleverboots, so please sit down and listen to me.'

She flushed. 'Captain Vorne, I've no wish to quarrel with you again, but I resent your tone of voice and ...'

'Sit down please Angela,' Miss Lydell said quietly.

Angela looked at her aunt. Grey eyes were not twinkling but commanded her as only a school-mistress could. Angela swallowed hard and sat down.

'I want you to promise me you won't mention a word of what I'm about to tell you.' Nathan Vorne began.

She opened her mouth but he held up a hand: 'Shut-up and listen, Miss Featherstone ... I'm sorry Miss Emmy, but you've sure as hell got yourself a mighty big-mouth niece...'

'Captain Vorne! I'm not sitting here listening to your insults ...'

142

'Those photographs were destroyed for a reason — a damn good one. The most important one was the picture of Miss Emmy's six boarders seated in the compound with her — and I didn't want that to fall into the wrong hands especially in Mandalay! They are royal children, Miss Featherstone, placed here in the Sawbwa's protection for reasons you'll presently find out.'

Her jaw dropped, she gaped incredulously, unable to do anything other than utter a little gargle of apology. When she had collected her wits she said: 'Goodness me! No wonder Aunt Emmy's always been so cagey about those children, never letting them out of the compound or strangers near them. I thought they were the children of some Raja or Shan Chieftain elsewhere ... so whose children are they Captain Vorne?'

'Mindon Min's very own. They were removed from the Court of Ava, by me, in secret and with only the King of Burma's knowledge. It was done for their own safety. Incredible as this all might seem to you, Miss Featherstone, on the accession of every new King and Queen to the throne of Burma very great bloodshed and unrest has been incurred in the past. Mindon Min did not want his reign to end in a holocaust of tyranny and blood-letting, or his golden city destroyed in an internecine struggle. I'm well acquainted with my facts, Miss Featherstone ... I landed, penniless, in Mandalay ten years ago and established myself as a trader up and down the Irrawaddy with King Mindon Min's full backing. In the course of my work, and the nature of it, I often had to approach the King in matters of legality, monopolies, etcetera, which I won't confuse you with, but suffice it to say, through all that, I came to know the Burmese King well; he was a just and good man. I also got to know the Einshemin, the Crown Prince of Burma who was not told of his appointment as his father's successor until the very last minute. That is a Burmese custom, too, because Mindon Min's own brother was assassinated before he took the throne of Burma. Therefore, because all royal relatives closest to the throne of

143

Burma are "removed" to allow for no opposition, I would ask you to say nothing about the children in your aunt's care when you arrive in Mandalay.'

'You mean they'd be ... murdered?'

'I mean they'd be murdered. So you see why I had to tear up your photographs?'

'I do indeed ... does Moke know about the children?'

'No one, except your aunt, the Sawbwa and myself ... and now you, know their real identities.'

'What about Minthami?'

'Minthami least of all. She thinks as everyone else, that the children are the progeny of a wealthy nobleman somewhere down in the south. Nothing to do with the Court of Ava. Why should anyone think otherwise? Mindon Min, if he wanted to banish his relatives, sent them to India.'

'Then why didn't he? I mean, send them to India?' Angela asked, still flabbergasted by all this.

'He wanted them to remain in Burma so that when the Einshemin was crowned King, he could reinstate them as his own *loyal* relatives. Loloi's merely a temporary arrangement, because as soon as things are settled in Mandalay, the children will go back to the Court of Ava — once Queen Sinpyumashin and the Taingda, who is a wily individual whom she has promoted from Chief of the Palace Guard to her right hand man in the Hlutdaw Council — are banished. The Crown Prince fears that she will retain too much power and be a constant source of annoyance to him were she to remain at the Court ... however, I digress. To get back to the subject of Minthami, it's a long time since she herself left the Court of Ava, so she wouldn't know these youngest offspring of Mindon Min and his minor wives. I had to destroy the picture of Sa-Lon and Roi, as well as the one of the hermit-phongyi at the Loloi pagoda, because I didn't want her to suspect anything ...' he shifted his position, stretching out his long legs under the table and with an eyebrow quirked towards the whisky bottle, helped himself to more. 'Minthami would've wondered why I tore up that particular photograph and not the others when I told her I was damn angry with you for taking them all in the first place. Forgive me.'

She couldn't do anything else in the light of his smile, especially with such well-calculated charm behind it.

'I would ask you though, to destroy the negative-to-positive plates in your possession and any other photographs you might have taken of the royal children. Those of Minthami and the boys perhaps you'd keep in mind to take again at a later date. I'll reimburse you for the expense — and trouble you've gone to regarding those photographs ...'

'There's no need, Captain Vorne,' she said testily.

Nathan tossed back the rest of his drink. 'Now,' he said, standing up and taking his sun-helmet from the table, 'I must be off ... The Sawbwa and me are trying to organize a hunting party and its proving to be mighty difficult. I've never known such cowards as the Burmese ... but, let me just say this much, Miss Featherstone, I take you to be a completely trustworthy lady, but, if one word of this conversation gets out, I'll know who's responsible. I'll take you apart piecemeal with my bare hands, got that?'

He towered above the school-teacher, dominating everything around him. Miss Lydell, remaining seated at the table, watched her niece and Captain Vorne with a rapt expression on her lined face. Here were two very strong personalities, tugging a little in this direction and then that, charging the atmosphere around them with tiny sparks. Miss Lydell was not fooled for one moment. She had felt a tension between these two people on the night of the village Pwe.

Angela set her shoulders and said frostily: 'Captain Vorne, I'm not a complete and utter simpleton! I know the gravity of the situation, and the danger my aunt is in through harbouring Mindon Min's children. Believe me, nobody's going to know who I am or what I've been doing with myself prior to my arrival in Mandalay — except perhaps my uncle Adrian and Matthew Sinclair.

You can rest assured I shan't breathe a word of all this to them, — or anyone else. Loloi's secret is perfectly safe with me. Thank you for being honest with me regarding the photographs. I know you needn't have said anything at all about them, or furnished me with an excuse for your ... for your conduct yesterday. However, I'm gratified you've thought sufficiently of me to have placed me in a position of trust. Good day, Captain Vorne. I must press on with my packing,' and abruptly, she went behind the bedroom screen.

The following morning Angela received a message from Nathan Vorne, conveyed by Sa-Lon: 'Dear Miss Featherstone. I have no objection to your photographing an up-country tiger if you so wish. A young lad from the village of Ku, tending the animals not two miles from here, was savaged last evening, and lies in a coma. Therefore, we set off at first light tomorrow as the animal now has the taste of human blood and must be destroyed. I fully understand if you cannot join the shikar, since you're in the midst of preparations for Mandalay. If so, safe journey, and one day we will no doubt meet up again in Mindon Min's golden city. Yours sincerely, N. de Veres-Vorne.'

Angela put the note in between the pages of Prince Yoe's Theravada Texts, and pondered on what she should do.

TWO

The Sawbwa decided at the last minute not to accompany the shikaris, and left the hunting-party in his son-in-law's capable hands. Nathan intended to go on horseback part of the way — as far as the other side of Ku where, in the hilly jungles, the tiger obviously had its lair. Then they would switch to elephants. Outside his basha hut Nathan dismounted when he saw his two sons come running down the path to meet him. He picked them up, one under each arm, and jog-trotted them back to

Minthami who stood on the verandah. Angela sat patiently waiting for him while the rest of the hunting-party progressed slowly toward Ku, further up in the hills. The toywa people gathered along the roadside to see them off and wish them luck. She rubbed her eyes, already feeling gritty with dust.

Angela was suddenly aware of what all the women like Minthami — not discounting her aunt's thoughts — must be thinking of her. A lone woman, to go after a tiger in the company of men only, it did not seem correct. Oh poof! she said to herself, as she spurred her horse forward, its not as if I've anything to lose!

Angela and Nathan picked up the rest of the Shan escort from Ku and proceeded eastward, upcountry. They progressed slowly, resting during the hottest part of the day. When they made camp at night, Angela found it extremely cold. She was reminded of Nepal and Assam when, in the Quentin camp, they had had to wrap themselves in thick blankets and shiver in the Himalayan atmosphere.

On the second day they came into the foothills that progressed to the mountains of China. Wonderful valleys and jungles opened out from rock-gorges.

Milky-white waterfalls poured like champagne from bottles into rivers far below. Through Nathan's field-glasses she was able to see the dark jungle where their tiger lurked. They were three or four thousand feet above sea-level; to the east lay Tonking, to the north Yunnen, and to the very far north, discernible only as blue smudges, were the snow-capped mountains of Tibet, like bruises on the face of heaven.

That day, the tiger's tracks led them in a semi-circle, leading them north-east and then bringing them to face west again.

'The way our intelligent tiger-friend goes, is beginning to look like the Choonbatty Loop at Darjeeling,' said Angela while they made evening camp. She was hot, dusty and weary, and thankfully gave the horse over to a syce. Removing her sun-helmet, she shook out her thick hair. Sweat and dust clogged every pore, her eyes, mouth and nose were gritty, and she longed for the hot-springs of Loloi to make her clean again. She hung her skirt and jacket on a convenient thorn tree. Using Nathan's riding-crop she thrashed the dust from her clothes.

'My, I hadn't realized how hungry I was until the cook started cooking,' Angela said.

Nathan took his pipe from a leather pouch containing his tobacco. 'Panthé Kaukswé,' he murmured through his pipe, 'thank God we've a Chinese cook in camp and not a Burman.'

'Don't you like Burmese food?' asked Angela.

'Only when I can see what's in it. Chicken and noodles one can distinguish, but half the concoctions Minthami puts in front of me defy the imagination. I've never been to Darjeeling, tell me about it,' he settled himself more comfortably and added with his arms folded, smoking peaceably behind his pipe, 'They tell me it's another Simla and a favourite place with Britishers who always seek a little hill to turn into a green and pleasant land during the hot weather season. Rather like the Burmese I suspect, only instead of sticking a pagoda on it, they stick a Union Jack.'

'Is that wrong?' asked Angela, hitting out at her clothes so hard, Nathan winced.

'Not if one's an Imperialist.'

'What about owning black-slaves on sugar-plantations in places like Louisiana and the West Indies?'

'So, someone's been doing their homework ... nothing to do with me, Miss Featherstone. Slavery was abolished when the Yankees won, and any black man staying on — women and children included — became a friend of the family. After my father died, my younger brother Courtney inherited everything. My father cut me off without a penny you see — for trying to liberate one of his darkies, well, quarter-darkie anyway. When she turned out to be a kind of relation of mine, he didn't like it. If you ever meet Nanette Gideon in Mandalay, Miss Featherstone, she'll tell you the half and more. Now tell

148

me about Darjeeling.'

'They've started to build a railway system to link Darjeeling with the plains. It's a remarkable feat of engineering. Although there wasn't an actual railway in operation when I was there — a few months ago — preparations were going ahead to put the engine to work within a few weeks. It should be functioning now. It was all too much of a climb for the poor pack-animals, but worth it to see the Himalayas. I tried to take a picture with my camera, but a negative-to-positive plate of one dimension could never have done justice to that view, so I discarded the idea. But that was truly the roof of the world, and God's own country, Captain Vorne.'

'And I thought America was.'

'I'm sorry ...?'

'Oh nothing, just talking to myself. Where are your parents?'

'Both dead.'

'No brothers or sisters?'

'No.'

'What are you doing travelling the world alone?'

'I started out as a missionary. I worked with the Hindus — among the girl-children dedicated to the temple-gods. But my success story wasn't spectacular I'm afraid. I used to get very despondent when only one or two would be able to see sense, and against vast millions of them it seemed a hopeless task.'

'But even one sheep ... eh, Miss Featherstone?'

'Yes, I know. But I decided instead to come out to Burma.'

'And what do you make of it?'

'When I've been to Mandalay, I'll tell you ... now then, do you think our tiger is much further ahead?'

'I think he's right about here somewhere. As we came down the valley with thick jungle on either side, where I pointed out the ravine and water-hole to you? that looks like tiger-country to me. If we don't flush him out today, I think tomorrow we'll go down to the ravine. I didn't want to, its too enclosed and therefore dangerous if

149

there's a tiger there.'

'Couldn't it be a panther, or leopard?'

'Could be, but I've a feeling not ... my guess is, our tiger's also a family man, and if he's got a mate around the place, we've got to be extra wary. Where were you figuring on standing when you take your picture of him?'

'Why, in the howdah of course! Right beside you, so that while you shoot from one elephant, I'll be taking a picture from the other.'

He chuckled. 'Some hopes the lady has! Anyway, if you're intending to use that great gun of yours, then aim for the spot behind the ear. Any other place and it isn't instant death to the tiger — which is mighty dangerous to the men on the ground with their nets. Always aim deep into the brain, and that's right behind the ear.'

'Thank you for warning me. I'll do my best with my Fox-Talbot in one hand and an elephant gun in the other.'

'Just warning you, Miss Featherstone ... hell, can't we start calling each other by our first names? All this fancy British stuff, isn't me after a while.'

'I've no objection ...' she turned aside, unable to address him familiarly, just yet. She was glad the cook banged the gong to tell them supper was ready.

The following day they knew they were on the tiger's tracks for sure — and Nathan was right, there were four of them.

'Sometimes tigers get flushed out of their natural habitat for a number of reasons, drought, fire, food shortages, denuding of the forest or jungle, so he'll take up residence outside his natural territory. That's what our tiger and his family have done, because, as you were quite rightly told, Amagyi-Angela, tigers don't usually come around Loloi.'

He had been examining the paw-marks in the soft mud at the bottom of the ravine. He suddenly looked up and frowned, watching the sky for kites and vultures.

'Is something wrong?' Angela asked.

'No ... I guess not.' He shrugged. 'Just a funny feeling about those birds, that's all. We'll set the machans up around here. The two big tigers are the problem, getting them together — one without the other is curtains for somebody, because the mate will get so darned mad for the other's death. Anyhow, you settle yourself over there ...' he pointed out a place safe enough in which to set up her camera and tripod, 'and let's hope he and she do their bit by taking it nice and easy down to the waterhole with their cubs so's we can catch them.'

The smell of human beings would flush them out soon enough, and content that all they had to do was wait for the tigers to come to them, Nathan settled himself down to wait. He chose the watering-place, close enough to keep an eye on Angela. The rest of the hunting party were in their look-outs, chosen by Nathan who had given orders on how and where the machans were to be placed, who were to be the beaters and flushers, and who were to trap the tigers in a circle of nets when they were spotted. Then he put his bush-type hat over his face and to all intents and purposes went to sleep under a thorn tree. Six feet above his head, couched in the sturdy tree twisting out from the gully-sides to overhang Nathan's reclining figure, a man called Than Sein kept watch.

Angela wondered if Nathan could be wrong about the tigers. This lower point of the ravine where the jungle met in the shape of a V, was hotter than anything she had yet experienced. Steep sides caught and held the afternoon sun, baking it again in the belly of the rocks which flung it back a thousand times. Heat and humidity, insects and flies, lizards and spiders, scorpions, snakes and leeches, all Buddha's creatures. Angela, dropping asleep on those thoughts, jumped awake, her nerves tingling as her eyes flew open. Rivulets of perspiration trickled down her neck, between her shoulderblades, her breasts, into her eyes, from her hair and into her ears, until she felt as limp as a gutted fish. Her petticoat and skirt clung damply to her legs, her blouse to her back and armpits. She shook herself, the sound of cicadas and other tree insects like a fever in the head, the

151

rotting sour smell of the jungle not far away, making her fidgety in the prickly heat of suspense. Nathan had told her that the tigers would be sleeping off their lunch of black doe so wouldn't show themselves at the watering-hole until sundown. She picked up her 12-bore and marched purposefully to the thin sluggish trickle of brown water forcing itself between rocks and jungle.

Angela dipped and re-dipped her handkerchief in the water, then held it to the back of her neck. Her front buttons she unfastened, putting the cooling dampness into her cleavage, unaware that the tiny bejewelled good luck charm Minthami had given her, reflected its brilliance from around her neck straight into the watchful eyes of a tiger.

Nathan slapped at a lizard making a nuisance of itself. He missed, and it scuttled away in fright. Suddenly birds and tree-insects became silent, the fever-pitch of background jungle noise held on a pinpoint of hot drawn breath. Butterflies dropped out of sight, playing for dead like crisp autumn leaves . . .

Nathan tensed, and hissed through his hat: 'Than Sein! I see him . . . don't budge an inch, just cover me.' His fingers were on his rifle. The tension in him coiled like an unreleased spring. He had the tiger beautifully in his sights, the spot behind the ear infinitely vulnerable. In that instant too, Than Sein's gun went off, fired to avenge the mauling of his young son. The great beast, propelled by a shaft of pain in its side, with a snarl of fanged fury, leapt the narrow gorge towards the irritating light in its eyes, and the shikaris with their nets could do nothing.

Angela was only aware of a rainbow of orange and black arching the water-worn gully, her gun at her feet. Her scream swallowed up in the foetid breath of the killing animal, she raised her arms to protect herself and was engulfed in all things dead and black.

Nathan fired again, desperately this time, hitting the tiger behind the ear. Angela, knocked aside by a blow from its mighty paw as the animal plunged to its death, lay unconscious beside the tiger.

152

CHAPTER TWELVE

ONE

The camp cook solicitously brought to the flap of the tent some Pazoon Kyaw for Angela. Nathan shook his head and Wu-Han went off again with his prawn-in-vegetables. Nathan had had to give Angela a strong dose of laudanum to take away the pain and to help her get some sleep. Revelry in the camp had already begun. The shikaris were happy with their trophies; four tiger skins, and so much meat and offal Angela, had she been conscious of it all, would have been disgusted. Any excuse for a celebration and the hunters were soon enjoying themselves, making such a terrible din with their Lin Gwin cymbals, clappers, nhai pipes and gongs that Nathan had to tell them to tone down the noise.

Angela woke up once, and found him hunched cross-legged in the entrance to her tent, flicking through Prince Yoe's Theravada Texts. He became aware she was watching him and put the book aside. 'Interesting,' was his comment, 'I didn't know you understood Burmese.'

'I can't — but I shall someday.'

'Fair enough. But now, how're you feeling?'

'Very strange ... as if I'm floating.'

'You almost did — straight to heaven. If you weren't an invalid, I'd thrash you for going down to that watering-place the way you did — without saying a word to anyone but marching off into the teeth of tigers as if they were domestic pets!'

153

'I'm sorry ... you didn't tell me they were lurking so close. You said they'd show themselves at sundown.'

'Well, I was wrong. And you mustn't go around believing everything you're told. Didn't they teach you to think for yourself at school?'

'No. Maud and Ida Bloxham did the thinking for us ... is there any drinking water? I seem to have a wretched thirst.'

Her tongue felt over-sized, useless and she knew her words were slurred although her mind seemed lucid enough; she remembered the tiger very clearly.

'Here ...' he brought the chatty to her lips, helping her to drink from it by supporting her. 'Fine! Now I know you're alive and kicking I'll leave you to get some more sleep. I'm going to join the party. Goodnight Amagyi-Angela.'

'Goodnight Captain Vorne.'

In the first stirring of jungle dawn, the sky turning from indigo to mother-of-pearl, Angela was wide awake and refreshed. The birds were singing, taking over from the other kind of song and dance which went on through the night. She raised herself awkwardly on her bedroll and the sudden movement made her dizzy. She fell back, lightheaded, numb down one side. Her shoulder had been bandaged expertly, and a sling put on under her blouse not so expertly, for the blouse was on back-to-front. Then she realized that was probably the most sensible way for it to go since it couldn't be buttoned-up. She tried sitting up again, willing herself not to faint, as the call of nature was becoming most insistent. Finding her shawl, she wrapped it round her and stepped out into the pale rush of morning sunlight.

Angela was surprised to see Nathan up quite so early as the night's celebrations had only recently concluded. He seemed to be engaged in some industrious pursuit, picking seed pods off a tree. He wore no shirt, his trousers had been rolled up to the knee. Keeping her distance, she called to him cheerily; 'Good morning,

154

Captain Vorne, thank you for all you did for me yesterday.'

He turned to face her beneath the tamarind tree. His pipe in his mouth, he said, 'You're welcome. Without the luxury of a camp doctor, it was the least I could do. Minthami's ointment will stop any infection from the tiger's claw.' He turned back to picking the tamarind pods which he was dropping into a basket at his bare feet.

Curious about 'Minthami's ointment', and what he intended to do with the tamarind pods, she drew nearer, one arm hugging herself against the fresh morning air. She stopped in horror. 'Leeches,' she said faintly, 'Captain Vorne, your back's covered in leeches!'

He reached for his shirt hanging from a branch of the tamarind. 'They do look like leeches, I grant you. But they're not.' He tucked his shirt into his belt with a kind of briskness to his actions that denoted end of subject.

Angela said: 'What on earth have you done to your back if those aren't leeches?' Then she realized his back was covered with purple-red weals, not leeches and comprehension dawned. She was tongue-tied.

'You coming? I believe breakfast's in the making.' He picked up the basket of pods. 'Don't take it too much to heart, Angela. I don't.'

'How?' she asked, feeling stifled.

'Would you really like to know?'

'Yes, I'd really like to know.'

'Spotted Faces, ask them.'

'Who on earth are Spotted Faces?'

He gave a harsh, raw laugh. 'You well might ask! They're human beings, honey, like you and me, like the Queen of Burma and her ilk, like a lot of other people with the mark of corruption on them. But they were just doing their job, honey, just doing their job.'

'Keeping a man fettered while they flog him?'

'That and more ... but can we change the subject?'

'Oh, how I *hate* this savage savage country!' she said with passion. 'I hate its climate, its barbaric customs, its

155

food and its religion. I hate its pagan primitiveness ... I hate its people ... how you can choose to live your life here, is beyond me. I wish I'd never come out East, I wish I'd stayed in England ... I wish ...'

He put down the basket. 'Angela, you mustn't think like that ...' he moved a few steps towards her. 'Honey, yesterday's near-mauling has obviously worked you up. Listen, it's no more savage, pagan or barbaric than any other country. Just different, that's all. You must learn to know it first, then accept and finally to love. That's the only way you can begin to face up to a lot of things.'

'I'll never understand. What did you do that was so terrible they had to treat you like an animal? No, worse than an animal, for animals aren't chained and whipped like that.'

'I stole, Amagyi-Angela, I stole royal children from Mandalay. A kidnapper, in other words, a serious offence in any language. Now can we go and eat? I want to get back to Loloi.'

'Nathan ...'

He glanced up, his hand on the basket handle. 'Yes, Amagyi-Angela?' Deadly serious, he waited expectantly.

She smiled: 'Thank you for taking a picture of the dead tiger for me. I realized you had ... but ...'

'But not that I knew how to use the Fox-Talbot? It's all right? I didn't mess it all up — I hope ... what do you want Than Sein?' Nathan asked, as the man approached them sheepishly.

'Very sorry, Thakin Vorne, for causing accident yesterday.' He sidled a glance in Angela's direction.

'I'm still damn angry with you, you know that, don't you?' Nathan told him.

'Yes, O Thakin master. But please, to give tiger-claw to English-lady for pretty brooch like many Ingalaik wish to have. It good one, smooth claw, not to hurt lady.'

Nathan appeared mesmerized by it; then he jumped up. 'Come on, let's get out of here ... fast. Hey, you there, Wu-Han, never mind breakfast ... Than Sein, get Missy-Sahib in the howdah.' He went running off like a man taken leave of his senses.

'Nathan, Nathan!' Angela, frightened by his appearance, ran after him, wincing in pain and having to bite her lip to sustain the jarring to her injured shoulder. 'Nathan, can't you tell me what's wrong?' She followed him to his tent where he sat on the ground tugging on his boots: 'Nathan, what's wrong, please?'

'What a fool I am! Jesus, nothing was right with this shikar, nothing! I've been wasting my time here when I should've been at Loloi. It's all been contrived, every bit of it ... how the hell did they find out I wasn't in Rangoon, or America? Four months, four months and they still won't give up! And I thought I'd given them the slip.' He had pulled on his boots and was on his knees rolling up his bedroll. 'Or at least that they'd pardoned me my offences by turning a blind eye.'

'Nathan! Will you please tell me what you're talking about!' Angela cried. 'What's all this frightful lather about?'

'Tigers — two big and two small, no more wild than you or me. Than Sein's boy, all on his own, wouldn't have been given a few scratches by a man-eater, he'd have been eaten on the spot if the tiger'd been that hungry. The same fellow who launched himself at you, he wasn't aiming to kill to eat. He'd had too much of a bellyful shortly before he leapt out of the bushes. They'd already eaten half a black doe, the rest of it where those kites and vultures were wheeling overhead. So he wasn't hungry, otherwise he'd have eaten the rest — or his family would. No siree, there's no black does around here either, and tigers with clipped claws don't do their own killing. So someone put them there — and I'm beginning to get a god-awful feeling why. If you're ready, let's go.'

He was already halfway to his elephant.

Given the gift of prescience, Angela would never have believed under what dreadful karma she was being drawn to Mandalay.

Around Loloi's gentle green slopes, paddy-fields behind their retaining walls of irrigation were black. It was more than just the mere burning of stubble after the rice harvest; it was a cremation. Basha huts were gone, and the Sawbwa's chalet only a smoking ruin from which an occasional explosion of an igniting spar sent fountains of fire into the air. Pi-dogs had come slinking back to the corpses of humans unable to run fast enough before the raiders entered their village. Nathan, in the van of the hunting party, left behind their pitiful cries and curses, as he spurred his horse forward to reach Loloi first. Angela, finding the slow-moving elephants tiresome, had also switched to riding a horse despite the pain and inconvenience of her shoulder. Flame-trees around the school compound stood like mute sentinels of death, pitiful reminders of their name. Everything, everything had been put to the torch. She ran, past him, overtaking him in her mad flight towards the schoolhouse and, Nathan in his own urgency, was hardly able to stop her. Gasping, he flung himself on her:

'No ... for God's sake, no! Don't go up there ... let me.' Mercifully the schoolhouse had not been set on fire like the rest of the village.

Angela swayed, perspiration wet and cold on her, beads of it on her top lip, her hair damp.

Nathan stepped over Moke's body lying across the threshold of the living-room, his shiny old man's scalp hideously battered, white tuft of hair stiff with dried blood in incongruous mockery of old age and the love he bore for his orphan children and Miss Emmy.

'Don't come up,' Nathan shouted to her, dreading to find what lay behind those bamboo walls. There were few reminders of the struggle that had taken place inside. A chair knocked over, a broken lamp, a few scattered clothes; Nathan let out his breath like a rasp from his lungs, painful but relieved. What he had been expecting to see, had not occurred.

'Nathan, Nathan, come quickly ... oh quickly! It's Aunt Emmy.'

He fell down the verandah steps, jumping them in his haste. The schoolmistress had managed to crawl underneath the schoolhouse. Blood had dripped from Moke through the boards of the verandah to spot her face and body like some horrible disease. She was still alive when Nathan and Angela found her.

'Dearest girl ...' she whispered, her lips bloodless, like the hands Angela held, 'so glad, so glad you went on ... tiger hunt. Other ... otherwise ...'

'Hush, Aunt Emmy, please don't talk, just let Nathan and me move you to a more comfortable place?'

'No.' She screwed up her eyes tightly, the pain thrusting through her. And on a tremble of effort said: 'No Angela, I don't want to be moved.'

'Miss Emmy,' said Nathan, taking one of her hands Angela had been clasping, 'if you can, just nod or shake your head ... don't tire yourself talking, but we have to know: The children, were they killed?'

She shook her head.

'Were they taken away?'

She nodded.

'By soldiers?'

'No ... Wu-tribe ... headhunters ...'

'Did they do all this? Did they destroy Loloi?'

She nodded.

'Could you possibly be mistaken, Miss Emmy?'

'Possibly.' She opened her eyes. He felt a tiny pressure from her fingers. 'Nathan ... I'm sorry.'

'Oh God, Miss Emmy,' he said with a sob as he brought her hand to his lips, 'I'm the one who should be sorry. Just tell me one more thing, were Sa-Lon and Roi here today?'

She smiled, waxen, shook her head.

His body slumped with relief. Angela whispered to

him, 'Nathan, you go. Go and find Minthami and your sons.'

He shook his head.

Miss Lydell murmured, 'Pray god ... they went ... Loloi pagoda ...'

'Oh Aunt Emmy, God!' Angela cried. 'What God? What God can allow this ... this sort of thing to happen! Go on, tell me!' In her blind rage, her impotence and despair she wanted to lash out, hurt herself, hurt anyone, hurt her God — never there when she wanted him.

'Don't — don't betray your faith, dear girl. Or yourself.' Miss Lydell's own implicit faith gave her the strength to face her maker, and while Angela knew as much, she wavered in bitterness. 'What faith? I lack faith, Aunt Emmy. I lack understanding. I lack the simple acceptance of a child. I only want to accuse.'

She bowed her head over her Aunt's body, bleeding its lifeblood into the bare earth. What price love and duty now, thought Angela bitterly. Yes, she wanted to blame someone, her soul had already been wrung out sufficiently between a Christian God's two hands — and he himself only knew the reason. She lifted her face to the floorboards above her head, feeling the last drops of a scarcely cold life ebb down on hers in a second savage baptism. She groaned aloud.

Sometime later she was aware of Nathan's fingers pressing her good shoulder. 'Angela,' he whispered, 'your Aunt Emmy's dead, honey.'

She nodded. But he had to ease Angela's stiff fingers from her Aunt's.

Nathan dug two shallow graves in the compound and Angela helped as best she could. They wrapped the bodies in sheets. Then they placed them in the graves, side by side and replaced the soil. They piled stones on top so that the jackals and pi-dogs would not dig them up. Afterwards Nathan took staves from the white paling fence of the compound and fashioned two rough crosses which he placed on the graves. There were flowers in the compound, bhodi flowers growing in profusion. Angela fell on her knees, unable to weep. 'She hated bhodı flowers,' she told Nathan, 'and there are no roses left.'

But she gathered the flesh-coloured orchids and put them on the graves. It was all of such little consequence anyway, Angela thought grimly, her missionary zeal at last swallowed up in this latest massacre. Nathan flung the shovel across the compound. His gesture angry, helpless and futile, his oath savage and despairing, served to bring him to his senses. 'Come,' he said, grabbing Angela's right hand, 'let's get out of here.'

Silently, they set off along the Loloi-Ku road. Some of the villagers returning to their homes in the aftermath of the massacre joined those men who had been on the shikar and all were now mourning their dead, scenes of outrage and disbelief unforgettable. When they were in sight of the basha hut, Nathan broke free from Angela and went running ahead, limping badly. He came out onto the verandah, the terrible fear gone from his eyes. 'I think they're all right. Nothing's been touched. They must have got to the pagoda in time — they'd have been safe there.'

But Angela wasn't paying him any attention. 'Nathan, look,' she pointed down the road. 'It's the hermit-phongyi ... carrying something on his back, my God!'

Nathan sprang three steps into the compound, and before Angela could run forward to meet the old man of the Loloi pagoda, had wrapped his arms around her, dragging her back into the barred protection of the banyan tree. Screened from the hermit-phongyi, Angela was terribly aware Nathan was trembling like a reed in a high wind. His arms tightly around her waist, his forehead pressed against her hair, he whispered; 'Wait ... please just wait with me, Amagyi-Angela.'

The hermit-phongyi stopped in front of the ancient banyan. He put down his burden. They were aware the sack was blood-stained. Fighting against Nathan's restraining arms, her shoulder on fire, Angela stepped out of the protection of the banyan tree and fell on her knees, sobbing: 'I can't bear anymore.'

With deep and terrible sadness, the hermit-phongyi looked at the tall, fair-bearded man who wore a mask of death. He spoke in Burmese to Nathan. 'Not Buddhists,' he shook his shaven head at Nathan: 'Not Buddhists, master. Paid mercenaries, that have no belief except that which lakhs of gold provide.'

Nathan could not speak, he could not trust himself.

Stooping, the hermit-phongyi reached into his sack and withdrew something so terrifying, so obscene, so human in its frozen smile of death that Angela, stumbling to her feet, bent double in the shadow of the banyan and vomited. Nathan's throat worked, his mouth full of spittle. Reluctantly, he extended a hand that shook, and withdrew from the face he knew well, from the red gash that was the Sawbwa of Loloi's mouth, a rolled and blood-stained parabaik.

He did not unroll it; he had no reason. He knew now who was responsible for the massacre at Loloi. He had suspected the moment Than Sein had handed him a claw to turn into a brooch. His anguish burned so deep, it had congealed into an ineffable hatred, a desire for revenge that would eat him like acid unless he did something about it. 'What have they done to my wife, Minthami?' he asked the old man of the pagoda.

'A prisoner,' said the hermit-phongyi. 'They have taken her as a hostage.'

'Who has taken her?'

'Royal troops.'

'And my sons?'

'They too. Taken with other children from the English school.'

'Who was responsible for all the killing and burning at Loloi?'

'Bandits, mercenaries, master, not Royal Troops.'

'Head-hunters? Wild-Wu? Kachin warriors? Who, old man, tell me who is responsible for severing the head of the Sawbwa of Loloi. Who?' His lips curled back over his teeth, a white-faced snarling animal, the hunted, not the hunter anymore.

162

The hermit-phongyi began to weep. 'I do not understand, master. I do not understand all this bloodshed. I am Buddha's disciple of peace, and know not the warring factions in this land.'

'Who ... damn you!' Nathan had grabbed the old man by the front of his robe; 'Spotted Faces ... were they Spotted Faces?' he cried to the monk.

Angela sprang up and ran to him: 'Please don't ... don't frighten him, Nathan. There's been enough violence for one day. He doesn't know who the real killers were. It might have been mercenaries, it might not.'

'Has my family been harmed in any way?' he asked, his voice cracking in weary hopelessness, all the passion in him draining.

The hermit-phongyi shook his head.

'Tell them,' Nathan said brokenly, 'tell them, I'll sign the parabaik. But first I want my wife and children back. Safe and unharmed. Go tell the soldiers of the Queen, old man.'

The hermit-phongyi shook his head again. 'I cannot. They have all departed. Royal Troops have returned to Mandalay with the Shan princess of Loloi and her two sons. I am left here to tell the Shwe Nat of Mandalay for each day he lingers one son will be flogged. One stroke today, then two, then four, then eight. Each time the number will be doubled until the child is dead. Next, the second son, and finally the wife, if she lives through the deviations of the Spotted Faces.'

Nathan swayed, his fists clenching and unclenching. His eyes closed, he turned and placed his forehead against the tortured branch-roots of the banyan tree. 'Old man, do you know what you're saying?' He groaned. 'A man can take a hundred lashings a day, but a child — who knows.' He raised his head, his fist against his mouth as he looked at the sky. 'Go away, old man, go away.'

The hermit-phongyi looked at the stricken white man, tears flowing down his withered brown cheeks. 'I am sorry, master, so sorry. But I am instructed by the Chief of the Queen's soldiers, the Taingda Mingyi himself, to tell the American Captain all these things so that he will come to Mandalay, and answer for his many crimes.'

Nathan nodded, 'I understand. Now go. Go and give the Sawbwa of Loloi decent cremation rites for the faithful Buddhist he was.'

The hermit-phongyi picked up his grisly burden and in the gathering dust departed to his ruined pagoda.

Nathan saw Angela kneeling on the ground, rocking herself backwards and forwards as though possessed. Her good arm clutched the bad in its improvised sling. Setting aside any further thoughts of travelling to Mandalay that night, he helped her up and supporting her, led her towards his basha hut. She shook her head, drawing back from the steps:

'No, not in there. I don't want to go in there.'

Leaving her in the darkening compound he went inside. Almost at once he reappeared with two sleeping mats under his arm. They could do nothing more tonight except try and get some rest before heading for Lashio. Taking her icy hand, he led her through the bamboo grove to spend the night at the hot-springs.

CHAPTER THIRTEEN

ONE

It was impossible to sleep. The ground was too hard, her shoulder too painful, the jungle too close and the moonlight too bright. She sat with her back against a mossy boulder and watched the moon through the trees fret the pool with watershadows. Nathan sat beside her, occupied with his own thoughts.

In the end he spoke aloud, 'I never for one moment imagined she'd discover Mindon Min's treaty with the Sawbwa of Loloi.'

'Who?'

'Queen Sinpyumashin — she's running things with the Taingda, her instrument of murder and mayhem. The Crown Prince is in Rangoon, trying to muster forces against her. The Shan States are independent, and that's why Mindon Min thought his children would be safe enough up here — but it appears nothing's sacred anymore.'

'How can you be sure she's responsible for the massacre?'

'Honey, I know. I haven't been in Burma this long not to know what kind of jungle I'm in. Don't forget, these people are descendants of the Mongol hordes that vandalized Asia not so long ago, and their Oriental minds are devious. Of course, I realize their cruelty and barbarism is like everywhere else in the world, no better, no worse, done according to expediency, customs and beliefs. It's when it gets personal, it's hard to take.'

165

'I know,' she said. 'I know exactly what you mean. But how did they find out about the children, Nathan? It couldn't have been the photographs, surely? It happened all too swiftly and word would have had to reach Mandalay, then troops mustered. If Minthami had shown the photograph to a spy here in Loloi, it would have taken more than three days for the message to be passed on and soldiers to get here. We were only away from Loloi three and a half days looking for those wretched tigers.

'Five days,' he murmured, 'plenty of time to get here from Mandalay. Don't forget, the Pwe was over two days before we started off on the shikar, and Minthami must have shown those pictures to someone in the enemy camp on the first night of the Pwe — or even the next night. Time enough.'

'So what you're saying in other words, is that it's all my fault.'

'It's nobody's bloody fault! It's probably mine, if anyone's. If I'd stayed away another couple of months, or at least until the Einshemin was on his throne, they wouldn't have followed Minthami and me to Loloi — or associated us with the Sawbwa, and his dealings in the past with Mindon Min. Queen Sinpyumashin and her Hlutdaw know everything that's going on, even as far as Rangoon. In Rangoon though, we were safe and far enough away from Sagaing death prison. Under British rule, Sinpyumashin and her Hlutdaw couldn't touch us. Then Minthami decided she'd had enough of Rangoon and since I told her she couldn't go back to Mandalay, she wanted to come to Loloi. I never raised too many objections because I thought everything had died down regarding my escaping the death prison, and that a royal blind eye had been turned on the whole business, so that Minthami and me would be safe enough here. Obviously I was wrong! The Court of Ava still have it in for me. Whether it was anything to do with your photographs wouldn't have mattered one iota. They'd still have got to those children — somehow.'

'And now they've got your two sons and Minthami as well.'

'Yep ...' he stripped a twig of its leaves, his manner distant. A monkey screamed in a tree, answered by the harsh cough of a jackal.

'How did you escape from Sagaing death prison, Nathan?'

'With cunning. It cost me five Queen's rubies and four bottles of best Scotch whisky thrown out by a certain Minister of the Gospel.'

She managed to smile. 'You said those tigers were royal immigrants from Mandalay, then how come the Loloi tiger was roaming loose before you and Minthami arrived in Loloi? I've been here seven weeks, and Aunt Emmy told me about the tiger long before I knew you and Minthami had come back.'

He shrugged. 'I don't know. Maybe Sinpyumashin with her telescope consulted the stars; maybe I'm all wrong about those tigers and an Indian Raja couldn't afford to keep them anymore in his royal menagerie, so he dumped them between Ku and Loloi; maybe Queen Sinpyumashin knew my mind better than I did and planned all this in advance of my movements, knowing I'd play right into her hands; maybe she found out about the royal children the moment the *Belle Hélène* had whisked them out of her sight, and bided her time until this moment to take out her revenge on the Sawbwa of Loloi. I don't know anything anymore, honey. Maybe, we'll never really know the full story. It's happened. Now why don't you get some sleep as we've got a mighty long way to travel in the next few days.'

'A few days, Nathan! Surely we must get to Mandalay quicker than that if Sa-Lon is to be spared?'

'Even four strokes from a Spotted Face's flail will cause blood-poisoning to settle in. I don't aim me to let that happen to Sa-Lon. In the morning, as soon as we get to Lashio, I can get a telegraph down to your Uncle in Mandalay. Adrian Hawes will intervene on Sa-Lon's behalf, and I guess he'll play merry hell with the Burmese if they lay a finger on a white man's child.'

She must have dropped off sometime during that awful night because she was awakened by a shower of rain. For a little while she couldn't move because her shoulder had become so painfully stiff. She wondered exactly what had been done to it, and intended to ask Nathan at some appropriate time. Her shattered grasp on reality restored itself gradually. She sat up, looked around, wondering where he had got to, hoping he hadn't left her alone to forge ahead with his journey to Lashio sometime during the night. But then she saw him sitting on a rock nearby.

'Nathan, I must wash and change out of these filthy blood-stained clothes. Uncle Adrian will have a fit if I arrive in Mandalay looking like this.'

'You're a typical woman after all, Amagyi-Angela. But rest assured. While you were asleep, I went back to the hut and packed a few things — among them a longyi — the one you borrowed for the Pwe as I assume that's the only one of Minthami's to fit you. Also some ointment for your shoulder.'

'Minthami's ointment?'

'Yes, why?'

'What's it made of?'

'Oh, tiger's whiskers and tiger's ...'

'No, seriously, Nathan!'

'I am serious. Tiger balm works wonders at curing all sorts of things. From headaches to toe-aches. It burns like hell, but it takes care of any infection.'

TWO

Thirty miles to Lashio, but they managed it by mid-afternoon the following day. Their mode of transport varied from ox-cart to mule to walking. But Nathan got his vital message through to Adrian Hawes in Mandalay and afterwards appeared a little more relaxed. They found transport on a raft-village floating graciously

168

down to Mandalay, so they spent the rest of the afternoon with families of hospitable Burmese who fed and watered them. At sundown, the village-people moored in a safe anchorage along one of the Irrawaddy's tributaries. The following morning Nathan became impatient with the slowness of their journey and decided to leave the floating village with its washing-lines, cooking stoves, and goats aboard. He had been hoping to get a ride in a Flotilla Company vessel going to Mandalay which would bring them more swiftly to the city. As no Irrawaddy Flotilla Company boat passed them, they transferred to a large sampan that appeared to be making faster progress than all the other river craft. Again Nathan and Angela were given a meal and refreshment in the way of coconut milk drunk from the pierced shell. She could not get over the hospitality they received. 'How on earth can she manage to cook such a lovely meal in this narrow boat, with no facilities to speak of?' Angela asked Nathan while the Siamese woman provided them, as well as her family, with a delicious meal.

Nathan shrugged. Cross-legged in tattered trousers, with the point of his pen-knife struck into the coconut shell, he appeared unconcerned about the way the natives lived on the Irrawaddy. 'Generations of being born water-people, I guess.'

'You guess at everything, don't you Nathan?'

He looked up at her. 'What's biting you?'

'Mosquitoes.'

Their eyes held. He flashed her a sudden smile. She was glad to see him less oppressed with thoughts of Minthami and his sons. She realized it was unjust to harbour malice at a time like this, but she felt very jealous because it was Minthami, Minthami the whole time! Minthami, she couldn't help feeling, was probably safe and sound and cosily installed in the Mandalay Palace with her sons — whom no one would touch because they would be too afraid — while she and Nathan were suffering untold misery on the Irrawaddy in defiance of time and the elements to get to her without delay. Her absolute exclusion in his thoughts, regardless of her injured shoulder and the death of a beloved aunt, made her resentful — resentful and jealous of Minthami and yet she asked herself why, why should she care?

Then the Siamese family with whom they were travelling decided on a whim to change their minds about the direction they wished to go, and turned round and headed back for Bhamo.

'Hey, you can't do that,' Nathan said angrily, 'you promised to get us to Mandalay by this evening.'

'Very sorry. We not go to Mandalay anymore.'

There was nothing more to be done except to wade back to the river bank and wait for another passer-by to give them a ride. Nathan at the water's edge waylaid a sampan. 'Hey, stop! You there Chinaman, we want to go to Mandalay.'

Whiskery-bearded, toothless, the wrinkled old Chinaman drew his sampan to the white man's feet and grinning said; 'You wanee go Mandalay by this evening I takee. Ying Ch'ang go very fast in the moonlight for one Tical — but no Chinese chop-mark. Many merchantmen bite in silver which mean it no good.'

'Ying Ch'ang,' Nathan said, stepping aboard, 'when it's the year of the inflated Water-Rat I'll pay you, but right now you'll have to make do like the rest of us with a few pieces of jaggery.'

Ying Ch'ang's sampan sank in the moonlight. Under his thatched roof at the time, happily unconcerned, he smoked his opium-pipe. Nathan and Angela couldn't keep pace with bailing out what was coming in through the holes of his boat so they abandoned him to dreaming in the sedge.

Angela waded waist-deep in the water. Exhausted, she flung herself on the river bank, her left side on fire. She lay face down, quivering with exertion, desiring only that her sling and bandages be removed, the mosquitoes stop tormenting her, the world to go away. Mandalay might as well be on the far side of the moon. Yet, she could also see the funny side of things.

Nathan fell down beside her on the smooth grassy slope. He let the river lap his bare feet, despite the mosquitoes in droves at the water's edge. His attention on his burning soles and the present hell they were in, he said; 'We'll rest up awhile. No point in killing ourselves — it won't help Minthami and the boys. Just don't cry about it, that's all. Do you want some more ointment on that broken neck of yours?'

Her shoulders heaved. She had difficulty snuffing out her choking sounds, her face in the grass. 'For God's sake, it's not helping matters ...' he reached over to turn her onto her back and discovered she had been trying to stifle laughter not tears.

'Oh Nathan ... I'm sorry! I shouldn't be acting so stupidly at a time like this, but it was Ying Ch'ang in his moth-eaten beard and tub looking so comical! You wannee go Mandalay, I takee ... Ying Ch'ang go very fast in moonlight for one Tical. ...' she smothered her amusement behind her hand, aware suddenly of his mood. He was not smiling. Instead, he looked at her as if seeing her for the first time.

The exhaustion trembling her limbs, the effort and forbearance of the past few days taking its toll from her, she was aware suddenly the quiver in her limbs had taken on a different significance. She jerked her head away, her breath catching in her throat. His strong fingers cupping her chin drew her back relentlessly, examining her soul; 'The Maiden, the Missionary and the Missy-Sahib, an interesting combination. I wonder what it would be like to make love to all three.'

He let her go and fell back to lie with his hands behind his head. Biting his lip he stared at the full-bodied moon on the river.

She sensed his mood. In the grass his hand searched for hers. 'Is this the good or bad one?' he asked without turning to look at her.

'The good one ... I'm not sure anymore.'

He took it up and placed it against his lips: 'It tastes of the Irrawaddy,' he said, 'pungent and racy.'

171

It hurt to breathe. A deep physical well of want grinding in the pit of her stomach, a crass betrayal of herself by her own body longing for not only the touch of his lips on her hand but on every inch of her skin when she had thought she would remain for the rest of her life beyond what the physical could bring her. This was not what she had experienced before. Then it had been total revulsion in a forced violation, a rape, a sexual lusting that had torn her out by the roots. Now, suddenly, her whole world in a few simple words, in the linking of gently powerful, sinewy fingers with hers, seemed to have acquired a new perspective. She wasn't afraid of him as a man, just herself as a woman.

She realized he was waiting for some sort of confirmation from her, negating the spectre of Minthami between them. She also knew it had nothing to do with Minthami but only what they themselves had felt, had wanted, from the day she had walked into his basha hut for the first time. Why else had she wanted so badly to go on that tiger-hunt with him if not to share and participate in his life for just one brief moment?

'Tell me, Miss Angela Featherstone,' he said, his voice part of the velvet darkness holding them in its cloak of secrecy, 'why an honest young lady like you has jilted a fine upstanding man like Matthew Sinclair?'

'I don't love him.'

A slight breeze drifting trailing vines clinging to the branches of the tree under which they lay, fanned them lazily while keeping the mosquitoes to the water's edge. 'Seems a sensible answer,' he said at length. 'Why then did you say yes to him in the first place?'

'I don't honestly know. I met Matthew aboard the *SS Tahara* sailing to Bombay. It was the first time I'd been anywhere on my own. Oh, my Uncle Adrian was there of course, to look after me and to hand me over to my father in Delhi. A ship-board romance was what I'd read about in cheap novelettes so I suppose it all rather went to my head. I knew nothing about love, the feelings of the heart, all that sort of thing one has to find out for oneself. When Matthew proposed to me in Delhi, just before he received his posting to Mandalay as Uncle Adrian's Secretary, I accepted. I only knew him three months in Delhi before he left for Burma. Not long at all to get to know the man I'd committed myself to for the rest of my life.'

'So now you've discovered you don't love him, when did enlightenment dawn?'

She wasn't sure of his reasons for asking such a question; wasn't sure if he was laughing at her or not — teasing, Aunt Emmy would have said.

'Why don't you answer me?' he asked. His voice full-bodied, rich, was very close to her. He had rolled over onto one elbow, an arm across to trap her, the hand of which traced her ear with an exploring finger. In the warm breath of an unspoken longing on her cheek, his power and attraction became irresistible.

She had never been kissed in the San Mukh cave, only used. When his kiss came she was stunned by it, his mouth shocking her into a submission totally acceptable in its gently wilful confiscation of any resistance she might have had — she had none.

The tide of emptiness within her ebbed, bringing in its return a floodtide of response, an impatient desire for loneliness to be assuaged, shame to be negated, love to be answered.

He unfastened the knot of her sling with fingers that were very sure of themselves. He removed the longyi. Lying with him under the moonlit tree she gave herself up to a never-ending spiral of time and movement controlled by him.

Lips, mouths, hands, long pale limbs entangled by the darker hardness of him, drawing her closer, deeper, the gentleness of his strength mindful of her injury, her throat arched to his final demand.

In the morning they made love again, a subtle, sensuous, slow, voluptuous postscript to remind them of the night without its urgency.

CHAPTER FOURTEEN

ONE

Nanette Gideon felt very faint. She fluttered her handkerchief in front of her flushed face. The nausea persisted; she wished she hadn't come.

Something funny was definitely going on in the Palace. Nanette had sensed it for the past two nights. Giddy had refused to attend the Coronation Celebrations for the new King and Queen of Burma, so Nanette had come alone; she wished she hadn't come at all.

The Zat performance was called *The Silver Hill*. Sneaking a glance at King Thibaw and Queen Supalayat, Nanette saw that they appeared to be enjoying it very much. It was hard to read what Queen Sinpyumashin, the Queen Mother was thinking, seated beside the Taingda, both of them enigmatic and very difficult characters to assess. San Dun the singer—actor was very good but Nanette found the music too loud. His softly sung words in the finale, without the background music, were infinitely more pleasing in their plaintive pure beseechings, and brought tears to Nanette's eyes.

'Do come, my darling,
Though your pretty feet are tender,
Please do not tire so soon,
Do come along, my darling.'

Her handkerchief pressed to her mouth, Nanette

174

hurriedly left her seat beside the French Consul after San Dun's song. Outside the ornate vermilion doors of the King's Theatre she fluttered her handkerchief again, the heat, smells and noise inside overwhelming. Nanette went in search of a glass of water.

She hurried to the Queen's quarters, having been there often enough to gossip and take tea with the princesses and other ladies of the Royal household. In the past Queen Sinpyumashin had encouraged Nanette Gideon's visits for a very important reason; Nanette imparted much useful information in her näive and imprudent fashion and, in return for flattery and privilege not granted to others, the Queen of Burma was kept abreast of what the foreigners in her Kingdom were up to.

It was while she was wandering down a corridor in search of her glass of water Nanette heard the unmistakable sounds of a child crying. She stopped by the door, then put her ear to it. Two female guards were in position further down the corridor; these were not the nursery quarters so Nanette became suspicious.

She turned to the guards, frowning. 'Open this door at once!' she commanded in Burmese.

The women continued to stare straight ahead uncomprehendingly, slant eyes and flat faces like dead wood. Nanette rustled her taffeta ball-gown as she went to them. Stamping her feet, she pointed an accusing finger in the direction of the door in question. 'If you don't git and open that door for me I'm going right now to King Thibaw to tell him the facts. If there's a child locked up in there I want to know the reason it's crying. And if the reason is because it's dark in there then I'm going to be hopping mad, for kiddies jest don't like the dark. I know ... I wasn't put in cotton bales head-down for nuthin'!' Nanette, struck to her very heart by any child crying, upbraided the women guards, flew to the ornate red-lacquer doors elaborately painted with chinthes, dragons and crocodiles, and pressing down on gold handles, pushed hard. The doors opened inwards. 'Huh!'

175

she said over her shoulder, 'it's lucky for you two these weren't locked!'

Inside the room the lamps burned low, casting ominous shadows on the high ceiling. Two little boys crouched on the floor, their arms around each other. The younger child wailed monotonously, the elder trying to offer what little comfort he could. Nanette recognized Nathan's two children and crouched on the floor beside them. 'What've you two been up to?' she asked, taking Roi in her arms and wiping his face with the hem of her skirts. 'Hush there now, honey, it's all right. Sa-Lon, perhaps you can tell Ma Nan here, why you two are locked up like as though you're a couple of naughty boys. Where's your mama?'

'Dancing for the King and Queen,' said Sa-Lon, glad to share his burden with Ma Nan. 'If she doesn't dance for the King and Queen, the Taingda will send someone to beat us again.'

'Well, I do declare that's about the wickedest thing I've heard and I'm absolutely incensed by it!' said Nanette Gideon, her sickness forgotten. 'Dry your tears. Be good little boys and I'll be right back when I've found Minthami. I'm going to find out what's been going on in this Palace, if it's the last thing I do!' She went marching into the corridor. 'Now you two listen to me good and proper! I want that door left open so those two little mites can see what's going on. If not, when I get back with King Thibaw, who's a good Buddhist King and declares love for his people — which means little children — you two're going to look sicker than a couple of separated chopsticks!' Jerking her head at them conclusively, she departed. Nanette knew where Minthami would be found if she were taking part in the night's entertainment. In the dressing-rooms behind the Theatre she encountered Royal Guards who would not let her enter without requiring to know her business. 'I've been sent forthwith by the Queen of Burma to assist the Shan princess Minthami dress up in her costumes.' They promptly stepped aside.

176

Nanette Gideon found Minthami in a state of near collapse. Her eyes lit up when she saw Nanette. She was dressed as a marionette, her face gruesomely painted with yellow Thanaka, sandalwood-paste for beautification. Nanette Gideon knew that marionette performances were the most gruelling. 'Why honey,' she said, bending down to Minthami's feet, 'they're red raw and bleeding ... what are they making you do, honeychile?'

'Two days and nights,' Minthami whispered, resting her feet awhile on a stool. They had to be careful. She knew suspicious eyes were watching the Gospel Preacher's wife. 'Two days and nights Minthami dance till she can dance no more. I have no sleep and worry for children, also for Shwe Nat — who receive message of cruel Taingda that we taken hostage again and brought to Mandalay.' Minthami put her head in her hands. 'Water please Ma-Ma Nan.' Nanette fetched some from a covered earthenware Pegu jar standing in the corner of the room, and while she was about it, drank some herself. She pretended to be attending to Minthami's feet. 'Ma-Ma Nan,' said Minthami, moistening her dry lips even after the water and casting fearful eyes about her, 'Minthami must tell you things ... it very dangerous here and we must be careful. While we dance and sing, princes and princesses, they are being killed in other part of Palace. I know this thing, I hear every night crying, crying, crying, and Minthami can do nothing, nothing! It is for reasons of State. Everyone who is threat to Dragon Throne is "removed" like they say. It is that Queen Sinpyumashin wish only for King Thibaw and Queen Supalayat, her very own daughter, to rule Myanma. All other princes and princesses close to them die meanwhile. It is with help of evil Taingda this thing happen, for he is Controller of Palace Guard. Prime Minister, the Kinwun Mingyi, who is good man, can do nothing ... nothing! because Taingda Mingyi is Queen's favourite and all powerful now.'

All the time Nanette Gideon's eyes were growing wider and wider in horror and incredulity.

177

Minthami took another sip of water. 'Please Ma Ma Nan, Minthami only have short while before she must dance again in Zat performance. She very afraid to say too much in case Sa-Lon and Roi again are whipped by Spotted Faces and die ... but please believe what Minthami tell. She know what very brave God Ma Ma Nan have as Christian of Mr Gideon, and so Ma Ma Nan brave too. Please to go to bandstand near favourite summerhouse in Palace gardens. By outside walls of Palace, she must hide. Hide well, Ma Ma Nan, for otherwise you too will die. Wait there, see what happen tonight. Tell no one. When everything quiet again, go straightaway back to Gospel Mission and give grave news of happenings to husband. Then tell Gospel Preacher to go to British Resident who know what to do. Do not go yourself Ma Ma Nan, for fear people of Taingda watch and see where you go, what you do. You must go home like nothing happen, but tell husband. Minthami would tell own husband, but Shwe Nat not in Mandalay. She very afraid he die. If Ma Ma Nan wish, please to do this thing for Christian benefit.'

Minthami felt she had said enough. Exhausted, she did not know how she would get through her next performance. She reached for her dancing slippers and winced with pain as she tried to put them on her swollen feet.

'Lordie, Lordie!' Nanette exclaimed weakly, 'I'm sure as hell dumbfounded by what you jest told me, Minthami. But honeychile, I ain't so brave I can do what you ask of me.'

'Yes, yes,' said Minthami impatiently. She tossed her long straight hair out of her eyes. 'You must do this thing Ma Ma Nan, or more people die. Minthami must go now, for she is to dance and sing with San Dun. Please to take very great care, Ma Ma Nan.'

Minthami left the dressing-room with her troupe of dancers. When Nanette was certain that everyone was more interested in what was taking place in and around the lavish theatre, she slipped away and collected her cloak. Escorted by Palace Guards to the Queen's Gate, she turned, clasping her hand to her head; 'Now ain't I jest the biggest fool!' Then she explained in Burmese to her escort that she had forgotten her evening bag. The guards, nodding jovially, allowed her re-entry. Nanette ran back to the lovely teak and glass palace which glittered like a jewel in the bright moonlight. Familiar with the Queen's apartments, she knew how to get into the garden without arousing suspicion. A door, used only by the Queen of Burma, gave access into a private courtyard which led onto the exotic gardens. Since the Queen of Burma was at the Zat performance, Nanette knew the door would not have a Royal Guard on it. The whole place seemed deserted; everyone was at the Zat. A golden key was usually left in the lock for the Queen to come and go in private. Nanette used the door, turning the heavy key, which squeaked atrociously. Holding her breath, she darted behind a heavy curtain, teeth chattering in fright. No one came and she slipped through into the Queen's own garden, gliding like a cautious shadow down to the Bandstand Minthami had mentioned. Close by, bright-white, she made out the favourite Summerhouse of the Royals. Nanette hid in a thick clump of oleander bushes and waited.

She waited for almost two hours. Twice she fell asleep in the bushes. She was beginning to get cramp and awkwardly moved her position. Nanette could not help feeling Minthami had imagined the whole thing: She wouldn't be at all surprised if Minthami was hallucinating after all she had been through. Nanette had just decided to go home to bed when noises in the darkness drove her to be cautious.

The moon by now had set. In the grey darkness she strained her eyes to find out what was happening. Underneath the Bandstand a ghostly light flickered. Sounds of smothered laughter drifted across the garden to where she hid amongst the oleanders. Another tiny lamp was lit. She saw men drinking, tipping bottles to lusty throats as though they did not know what drinking

179

glasses were. Squatting, spitting, grunting shadows sprawled across the grass, like hyaenas crouching over putrid pickings, Nanette realized with a nasty jolt just who those men were.

She wondered what the Spotted Faces were doing in the Palace gardens, and who had provided a party for them with liberal splashings of alcohol.

Then she felt the earth move.

It shuddered under her like an earthquake.

Into the darkness, plodding in sacred white luminosity came the King's own elephants. Singoung, elephant-trainers, led them to the Summerhouse. They stopped. Nanette could not make out why or what the head elephant men were doing, for it was too far away and dark to see properly. But through the stillness of the tropical night the unmistakable sound of link against iron link could be heard. Chains were being manhandled, man to man . . .

She waited, watched, petrified by what was happening.

Presently the Singoung and the elephants moved off again, carefully, as though hampered by heavy logs the common working-elephants were accustomed to dragging. But these were no common working-elephants, they were the Kings own sacred beasts. They lumbered forward, so close to Nanette, she would have been trampled had they moved off their prescribed pathway. Nanette saw that each hind leg lifted cautiously, had chained to it, not teak logs but live human beings. Nanette Gideon thought she would die of mortal terror. Her blood turned to water, her saliva dried in her mouth. Yet, the fascination of the macabre kept her eyes wide open, unable to move or turn away in the root of her dread: Palace walls, white elephants, prisoners dressed in white; she could not help but see the reflection of that scene which would remain burned into her memory until the day she died.

The prisoners, at least thirty of them, men and women, were muffled, blindfolded and chained to each other, the front person attached to the rear foot of an elephant. Three rows of ten were made to line up before a freshly dug trench against the outside walls of the Palace. Jostled into position, they were released from the elephants, the Singoung taking away the chains. Then, to her eternal disbelief, the confused prisoners who had hardly uttered a muffled sound between them, were set upon by the Spotted Faces, inflamed by alcohol. Heavy wooden cudgels ruthlessly murdered the helpless prisoners, most of them blindfolded and not realizing from which direction the next vicious blow would strike. Those escaping the cudgels were strangled.

Nanette Gideon knew, knew most certainly, that even for the sake of her Christian conscience, she could not have uttered one word, cried out, screamed, moved an inch to prevent what was taking place under her very eyes. Paralysed with an emotional shock that destroyed her mental stability and powers of coherent speech, she knew what her fate would have been had she been discovered hiding in the Mandalay Palace gardens that night!

So it was that she witnessed the bludgeoning and strangling to death of princes and princesses of the Alaungpaya-Konbaung Dynasty, some only girls and boys, others courtly young men and women, others still older, but all of them relatives of King Thibaw and Queen Supalayat.

It was a tradition, Nanette knew that much; she also knew that Royal blood could not be spilled by the sword to seep into the ground of execution, that too was a tradition.

Crawling victims, dazed and blinded, others lying motionless on the ground like alabaster images destroyed by a sudden earthquake, all were tumbled into the obscene trench. Dead or alive, kicked and beaten into the mass grave, the earth was quickly shovelled over them by the Spotted Faces.

Afterwards, the white elephants trampled down the heaving earth, impacting it so that not a trace of the night's activities could be seen.

Singoung and Oozies led away the elephants, not suspecting that an hour later they too would be dead, beaten and strangled by the Spotted Faces who had already had their own tongues cut out.

Bent double with a terrible pain in her gut, Nanette Gideon felt she was about to die with what was left imprinted on her mind. She would never forget that sight, never! Too afraid to move lest the Spotted Faces creep back and find her, she did not leave the oleander clump till cock-crow. Then as the Palace guests departed after the night's festivities, Nanette joined them innocuously, and went home to the Mission on Kyauktawgyi Road.

TWO

Mr Hawes was immensely grateful to Mrs Gideon for having saved her vapours until the end. While Mr Gideon and the Indian maid tried to revive Nanette with smelling-salts and cold compresses, Mr Hawes availed himself of the opportunity to inhale his amyl-of-nitrate. Mrs Gideon's very pathetic yet graphic ramblings concerning events that had taken place in the Mandalay Palace had left him in a state of shock. He was filled with revulsion, distaste, anger and a helpless rage because all his good intentions were frustrated. The Queen-Empress's Government of India and the Foreign Office had made it quite clear they did not want to get 'involved' in Upper Burma's affairs. Britain had too many committments on her doorstep already. The Afghan war required a concentration of British soldiers up on the north-west frontier and unrest with the Mahdi in Egypt meant another Army was needed. Troubles at home, especially on the Irish front, occupied and taxed the Government's strength and resolution while the rest of the Empire was stretched to its utmost limits to maintain law and order. Present expenditure could not therefore be increased by 'putting a military presence in the native State of Upper Burma.'

Mr Hawes had had his answer.

He had no words to describe fully the feelings engendered in him through Nanette Gideon's description of Thibaw and Supalayat's relatives being murdered on three nights running, while they sat through Zat and Pyazat performances to the everlasting glorification of Buddha; why, it was preposterous!

'What are we to do now, sir?' Matthew Sinclair asked from the arm of one of Mrs Gideon's drawing-room chairs. Mr Hawes continued to pace the length of the floor. He did not answer his Assistant's question because he was trying to think the whole tragic matter through. Since the British Government had refused him their support in the matter, he had to fend for himself ...

Four days ago he had received a telegraph from Lashio informing him that Nathan Vorne and Miss Featherstone would be arriving in Mandalay with the minimum of delay. He had been asked to intercede in the affair of Captain Vorne's wife and children, further grave news pending. He wondered what the further grave news could possibly be, feeling that he had had enough grave news these past few days to last him the rest of his life. He never thought he'd live to see the descendants of Kublai Kahn's Mongol hordes who had ravaged, pillaged and browbeaten Asia into submission, practising their barbarity in the nineteenth century! There was only one recourse left to him he felt, and that was to put the fear of a Christian God into heathen savages. He felt so strongly about the tragedy inside the Mandalay Palace, he did something he had never done before in all his years of office; he made an emotional decision.

'Mr Sinclair,' he barked, wheeling upon Matthew with a purpose of will altogether awe-inspiring. 'We must leave for the Residency right away.' He turned to the Gospel Minister; 'Mr Gideon, please don't wait upon us any longer, but attend to your poor wife. Kindly give her our regards when she recovers from her indisposition, and thank her most sincerely for bringing to the British Government's attention the events that took place in the Mandalay Palace during the Coronation celebrations. She is a brave woman. Good day.'

Once more inside his own domain, before he removed his helmet and placed his baton on the desk, he gave orders for the Union Jack to be lowered from the staff. 'At once! Mr Sinclair,' he barked, his emotions getting the better of him.

Matthew jumped to it and passed on the command.

'Incredible, barbaric, monstrous ...' he was still muttering to himself when he flung open his office door. He was in a towering temper and beginning to get palpitations.

Two people — who had not his sympathy for one moment — had been given seats in his sacred precincts. It was unfortunate for them they'd chosen such an inopportune time to present themselves, for Mr Hawes glowered at them menacingly.

Mr Hawes' reception of his niece and Captain Vorne was distinctly chilly; 'Good afternoon Angela, Captain Vorne, you've arrived at last.' With calculated precision he did not shake hands, but put his marshall's baton down and then his sun helmet — in the absence of servants who appeared to be keeping their distance. Nathan Vorne he observed sitting like a man racked beyond endurance on the edge of his chair, his knuckles white as he clasped and unclasped his hands while gazing at his feet. The biggest sin any man could commit was to come into his presence with a four day's growth of beard, with or without an excuse, so he was not prepared to forgive Captain Vorne for his disgusting appearance. He tried not to look at his niece too hard. He was utterly dismayed by her appearance. She had allowed herself to go 'native', dressed in a longyi and a man's collarless shirt that was torn, dirty and crumpled, sandals on her bare feet and a ridiculous coolie hat dangling around her neck. Her hairstyle was another source of irritation, drawn tightly to the crown of her head, braided and left to dangle like a rusty pigtail down her back, while her complexion looked as though it had taken a thorough grilling from the Burmese sun, ye gods!

'Is something wrong, Uncle Adrian?' Angela asked, disappointed by his lack of enthusiasm at her arrival. 'It's lovely seeing you again, though I'd have wished it to have been under happier circumstances.'

It wasn't a choice remark to have made in the circumstances and Adrian Hawes' face showed it. Angela lapsed into silence. He reached for the brass jug on his desk, found it was empty, banged the gong on his desk and shouted for Matthew Sinclair.

'Let me,' said Angela, taking up the jug. 'I expect Matthew's busy ... I saw him in the yard just now ordering the flag down.'

'Sit down, Angela! The window's open. Mr Sinclair might be blind but he's not deaf ... ah, there you are Mr Sinclair, I want you here as well. Shut the door will you?'

'Yes sir ... hello Angela, Captain Vorne.' Matthew came inside and quickly shut the door. Angela avoided meeting his eyes. The look on Matthew Sinclair's face did not slip past Mr Hawes unmarked; the young man looked decidedly deflated by Angela's coolness. Mr Hawes cleared his throat, romance would keep — he was more interested in Captain de Veres-Vorne and his activities. He listened to what his 'grave news pending' was all about, his only appreciable comment coming when Nathan described Miss Lydell's death. From a distance of courteous letters at infrequent intervals, he had known and liked the Loloi school-teacher, a relative only through the marriage of Angela father's, his step-brother.

When Nathan handed the torn and bloodstained parabaik of such a sad history over to him, Mr Hawes took it with distaste. He did not even deign to unroll it. He knew that this time Nathan Vorne was not going to play games with the lives of his wife and sons, and would have signed it.

185

'Mr Sinclair,' he passed the parabaik to Matthew, 'get this over to the Palace right away. I want an answer by five o'clock this evening.'

'Yes sir.'

Matthew returned an hour-and-a-half later, at four o'clock. He found Mr Hawes, Angela and Nathan in exactly the same way as he had left them, very sober, still sitting there awkwardly. They were having tea though there was an obvious chill in the atmosphere.

Mr Hawes wiped his moustache before opening the official communication from the Mandalay Palace. It was from the Taingda himself, stating that their Majesties, King Thibaw and Queen Supalayat would receive the following named people in the King's Audience Chamber at nine o'clock precisely. The names were, Captain Nathanial de Veres-Vorne, Mr Adrian Hawes, Miss Angela Featherstone — to pay her respects to the new King and Queen of Burma — accompanied by Mrs Gideon of the American Gospel Mission, as chaperone. All such foreigners to conform to the usual forms of obeisance before the Burmese King and Queen.

Mr Hawes was insulted and perturbed by the Taingda's artful communication. His name had been placed second to that of Nathan Vorne and nowhere had he, the British Representative, been given his correct form of address by the Burmese Minister, which was a veiled insult to Her Majesty, Queen Victoria's Government of India. The Taingda was also fully cognizant with British regulations concerning British Consuls making a laughing stock of themselves by crouching in bare feet on a dirty floor in a ludicrous act of homage, and the fact that his step-niece's very recent arrival in Mandalay had already been observed, proved how far indeed the Hlutdaw's tentacles reached. Mr Hawes tossed the scribed parchment on to his blotter. 'Hrrumph!' he snorted, taking out a damp and mildew-spotted handkerchief to wipe his clammy brow. 'Mr Sinclair, I shall be obliged if you will return to the Palace with my reply to the

Taingda — have this set down in its official form when you've penned your notes. We shall state something to the effect that from this day, at noon, the Union Jack ceased to fly over Mandalay. It is therefore quite beyond the British Resident's capacity to concur with the Burmese Government, as all diplomatic relations have ceased between the British Government and the Burmese Hlutdaw. The Court of Ava will be made aware of my profound disgust at the new administration — which appears to be worse than the last — only for goodness sake don't write that down!' He took a deep breath. 'If the Taingda Mingyi and the Hlutdaw think I'm going to openly condone mass murder by bowing and scraping before Thibaw and Supalayat — who have no right to be on the Dragon Throne in the first place — then they've another thing coming! Young man,' he barked at Matthew who had let his attention wander with woebegone glances in the direction of his ex-financée, she reluctant to meet his ardent glances, 'Pay attention, will you. You will take my place this evening, Mr Sinclair, but not as the British Resident's Assistant, since we have no more truck with the Burmese. You will be there merely to bring Captain Vorne into the custody of the Hlutdaw — for it appears he's still our responsibility until nine o'clock tonight. And *don't* crouch down too low in front of the Ava crowd, Mr Sinclair,' said Mr Hawes in one final gesture of defiance against the Burmese, but especially against the Taingda Mingyi who had been made Minister of the Interior in King Thibaw's new Government.

'No sir.' Matthew said with a wry grin.

Adrian Hawes then turned his attention to his stepniece. His frown deepened; 'Angela, I don't like what you're wearing. I hope you have a change of clothing because you cannot go into the presence of the King and Queen of Burma dressed like one of them, in that native long ... longyi thing.'

Angela's sigh was one of sheer exasperation, 'Uncle Adrian, I'm sorry, but my trunk I left behind in Loloi.

187

Even then I doubt there would have been anything suitable in it to wear before the King and Queen of Burma.' Her manner clearly indicated that she thought him unreasonable. 'Nathan and I left Loloi in rather a hurry you see, and ever since we've been travelling on sampans, rafts and sinking ships.'

He positively bridled at her — so it was Nathan now! Mr Hawes wondered if Angela Featherstone had taken leave of her senses altogether. 'I fully appreciate your difficulty, my dear,' he said in a voice that had once disconcerted King Mindon Min, 'but find something decent to wear. That's all I'm asking.'

'I guess Nanette at the Gospel Mission will oblige Miss Featherstone with some clothes,' Nathan suddenly interrupted, as he could see both Mr Hawes and Angela were getting rather hot-tempered.

'What?' Mr Hawes, feeling a little dizzy turned to the American. 'Oh, yes, yes, good idea.'

The man had a brain as sharp as an Indian chettyar's, Adrain Hawes reflected as he took stock of both his step-niece and the American who had a most unsavoury reputation where women were concerned. He hoped sincerely she had not become 'mixed-up' with the man during their enforced sojourn on the Irrawaddy. He was acquainted with everything that went on in Mandalay, no less the gossip that was bound to circulate in a small community and Captain Vorne's preferences for 'native' women had not escaped his attention — nor the attention of others. First it had been that quadroon girl Nanette he had brought with him from the States of America, both of them apparently cruising the seas with half the US Navy after him to charge him with unlawful abduction of an under-aged female as well as smuggling. When Edom Gideon had followed up his Yankee victory over the South and had married the little quadroon thereby turning her into a good woman for her salvation and Nathan Vorne's deprivation, he had turned to a child-bride, another native, the Shan princess Minthami. The Lord alone knew how many more there had been in between! But to see a relative of his 'gone native' while in the fellow's company made him shudder in apprehension. Nothing apparently stopped the man from getting what he wanted — he hoped he did not want Angela. He had not forgotten Captain Vorne's ruthlessness, his cold-blooded nerve in gaining his objective come hell or high water; there had been an example of it one night not so long ago when he, Adrian Hawes, had not sustained a complete heart attack on that night, but had come near enough to one. He remembered how three Buddhist phongyis, complete with saffron robes and begging bowls, had arrived on the doorstep of the Residency on the eve of Thibaw's and Supalayat's wedding. To discover that two of the phongyis supporting the crippled one in their midst, were none other than the Crown Prince of Burma himself with his younger brother the Prince Nyaung Ok, had made him, for the very first time in his life, take to the brandy bottle.

Thereafter, it had come to light that the American Captain had been the instigator of the outrageous plan to get the two Princes back to Rangoon and out of harm's way — a very ingenious plan he had grudgingly admitted at the time. The American had himself just 'managed' to escape the Sagaing Death Prison from which no man had ever walked out alive. Then, under the protection of the British Flag, and darkness, the two Burmese Princes had been 'smuggled' back to Rangoon aboard an Irrawaddy Flotilla Company boat, Nathan Vorne keeping them company. He had received word in due course that the American Captain was lying low with the British in Rangoon while the two exiled Princes were trying to return to Mandalay at the head of an army to wrench back the Dragon Throne from Thibaw and Supalayat. The man was clever, and he was also a packet of trouble! Adrian Hawes wished to draw this meeting to a close. He took out his half-hunter from his waistcoat pocket. 'Well now, if you'll both excuse me,' he said to Angela and Nathan, 'I have further pressing matters to attend to. Captain Vorne, as you're under house-arrest until nine

189

o'clock tonight, I'd be obliged if you'd remain on these premises. I'll send a boy to fetch any belongings you might require from your house.'

Nathan nodded and stood up. He extended his hand; 'I want to thank you, sir, for what you've done on my behalf. I'm deeply indebted to you.'

'Captain Vorne,' said Mr Hawes rising to take the proffered handshake, 'Mr Sinclair will furnish me with a full report of what transpires this evening between you and the Burmese. I hope everything will go well, and your family will be restored to you. I have it in writing that they won't be harmed if you present yourself at the appointed time.'

'I understand. And thank you again. Where do you wish me to park myself in the meanwhile?'

'In the reading-room if you don't mind. One of the servants will show you the way. Ring for any refreshment you might require — I do believe we have spirits on the premises, if that is your preference.' He opened the door of his office, ushering them out into the gloomy corridor. In a room across from his, he said to Matthew Sinclair busy with under-secretaries drafting out the reply to the Taingda's Mingyi's dispatch; 'Mr Sinclair, I want that in the Hlutdaw's hands by five o'clock sharp!' When he looked round again, he saw his brazen step-neice kneeling on a priceless black-lacquered and inlaid mother-of-pearl table from the reign of the first Alaungpaya. Not only her appallingly bitten bare legs were exposed to everyone's view, but she was intent on examining one bare shoulder in the ebony and gilt mirror hanging on the wall. Hands behind his back, Nathan Vorne, with a glazed look in his eye, seemed equally engrossed in watching her. 'Captain Vorne, here's my Bearer to show you to the reading-room!'

Nathan turned absentmindedly at the irate voice of Mr Hawes issuing orders right left and centre. 'Oh yes ... thanks ...' He followed the Bearer out.

'Angela,' said Adrian Hawes crisply, 'first thing tomorrow morning, I want a word with you. I want to

190

know why you've broken off your engagement to that nice young fellow Matthew. I refuse to take it seriously, and so does he. I want you to reconsider the matter. I think you're a very foolish young lady.'

'Yes, Uncle Adrian,' she said, sounding surprisingly meek.

'I'm going to send word to Mrs Gideon to present herself here within the next hour to kit you out for this evening. Meanwhile, wait here until I can find a woman staff-member to show you to your quarters ... and how did you manage to damage your shoulder like that?'

'A tiger, Uncle Adrian.'

'Hrrumph!' He went inside and shut his office door on her, wondering to himself which tiger, and determined to marry her off to Matthew Sinclair without delay.

CHAPTER FIFTEEN

ONE

Angela found it hard to believe she was actually in Mandalay at last. For so long she had lived on a knife-edge, she was unable to relax at this, her journey's end. She was caught up, irrevocably in events surrounding Nathan Vorne, who was stopping anyone around him from relaxing at that particular moment as, taut as bowstrings, they all waited to be received by the King and Queen of Burma.

Twice they had been notified there would be a delay in presentation. Nine o'clock came and went, and then ten. They continued to wait in the ante-chamber to the Hall of Audience. Angela stole a covert glance at Nathan. Remarkably presentable in a cream linen suit favoured by Americans in the East, he sat next to Matthew, who, himself, was smartly turned out in pin-stripe of worsted material that Angela imagined must be extremely uncomfortable in Mandalay's heat. They all sat rigidly on ornate gilt and brocade chairs regimentally placed along one of the red-lacquered walls — except for Nathan who never sat straight anywhere. He slumped forward, his elbows on his knees, his chin resting on his clasped hands while he stared at the floor. The minutes and the hours ticked by. He became tighter-lipped, pinched and paler, eyes very blue, like fired steel. Seated between Matthew and Nanette, he glanced up once and caught her eye. Angela tried a reassuring smile, but he didn't respond to her effort of trying to bolster his spirits. She turned away, deflated while wishing she did not look so much like a stick of candy-rock from Brighton beach. The only frock of Nanette Gideon's to fit her, it was a hideous pink-striped affair with so many frills and furbelows she felt overdressed.

At half-past ten, a Palace Official came to inform them they would not be received after all in the King's Audience Chamber, but another room in his private quarters. Angela suppressed her disappointment at being deprived of an opportunity to see the great Dragon Throne in the opulent Hall of Audience she had heard about, and hoped she would have an opportunity to view it on another occasion less harrowing than this. Before being taken into the King and Queen's presence they were asked to remove their shoes and leave them in the ante-chamber.

The room in the King's Quarters into which they were ushered was so thickly carpeted even their breathing seemed muffled; it was like sinking into an exotic sea-sponge. Curtains of orange and silver chequered-brocade hung in a triple-arched alcove. They were held back in softly draped folds by tufted silver tassels a foot long over a carpeted dais scattered with plump silken cushions. Behind the dais was a mural painted in vibrant colours. Brash and gaudy, the scene was very appealing to Angela, for it could have been no other view other than the banks of the Irrawaddy drawn from experience.

The King of Burma accompanied by his Queen and her sister entered the receiving-room via a secret door in the mural. The royal trio took their time in settling themselves comfortably and decorously on the dais. Crouching, as they had been instructed while the royal people took their places, Angela, while humbled herself, saw what diminutive figures they were, yet enthroned with a power that was quite staggering in the way they were revered, adored, and obeyed by those attending upon them.

Once the royal trio were seated to their satisfaction — their entourage behind them in a semi-circle hiding the

Irrawaddy mural — the rest of them were allowed to be seated on the cushions. Angela sank back gratefully. Crouching barefoot in Nanette Gideon's hideous frock which was too tight in the bust, trussed up in overlaced corsets she had grown out of the habit of wearing, had made her hot, bothered and extremely red in the face.

On the King's left, slightly positioned in front of the other attendants, a very regal Burman stood, wearing a gaung-baung in his official capacity as Advisor. Angela assumed this must be the notorious Taingda who had been rapidly elevated to a position of power. The Queen and her sister lazily examined them through gilded opera-glasses until Angela felt like a goldfish in a bowl being gaped at by interested children. The King was staring quite openly and unblinkingly at her. He was a handsome young man in a fleshy way, his wide flat face aping a Western-style thin black moustache not at all of the Buddhist habit. But the face was also that of a schoolboy's, bland and harmless, most definitely unlike the autocratic and harsh ruler she had imagined. Neither did he look to be an habitual drunkard who was reputed to drink gin-and-tonics all day. In a white silk blouse and blue and gold flowered-silk pantaloons, his bare toes hung over the edge of the carpeted dais in rather an un-Kingly and pathetic fashion. Around his wide forehead he wore a white muslin band to secure his elaborate blue-black coils of hair wound into a topknot. The King sported so many jewels on his hands, fingers, ears and clothes, he sparkled as much as his bright red mouth smiling at her, his eyes altogether vanishing in slits of secrecy. Angela realized suddenly why King Thibaw was smiling so provocatively at her and, flustered, lowered her eyes quickly, hoping she had not offended his Majesty by being over-bold by scrutinizing him — or, on the other hand, for not smiling at him in return for his obvious interest in her.

Thibaw's Queen, seated beside her sister — who was supposed to be betrothed to Prince Nyaungyan Min, arranged by the Queen Mother and the Taingda in order

194

to consolidate their hold on the Dragon Throne — had their legs gracefully tucked under them out of sight. The Queen and Princess were like twin dolls. Queen Supalayat wore an exquisite stole wonderfully handsewn with millions of tiny seed-pearls which she had draped over her right shoulder, and a choker-necklace a handspan in width, a solid encrustation of rubies, diamonds and sapphires, quite literally worth a Queen's ransom. Those two items were the only things Angela remembered about Queen Supalayat, her jewellery and her elegance.

She spoke in English, hesitantly at first, but gaining in confidence as she got used to the unfamiliar language learned of necessity; 'It is with pleasure we welcome and greet you, Mrs Gideon, Miss Featherstone, Mr Sinclair and Captain de Veres-Vorne. It is with especial acknowledgment we receive you Miss Angela Featherstone, as a visitor to our country. How long do you intend to stay in Mandalay?'

Angela was so taken aback by that sudden dart of a question she looked at Matthew, wondering what she ought to say. He kept his eyes fixed to the Queen's toes and Angela realized he could not answer for her as the Queen had not addressed him. The Palace Official had made it clear to them that no one addressed the King or Queen, or asked them questions unless first invited to do so. 'I ... er ... I wish to stay long enough to be able to take photographs of your exquisite Palace and city, Madam. Those outside Burma know so little of this country, it would be nice to have an album of pictures to show the world.'

The Queen smiled, the merest little deepening of a quirk to the right of her pale pink mouth. 'Such an excellent idea! You must show us some of your work so that we may be able to judge for ourselves the quality of your photography. My husband and I are also interested in photography. If we find you are good enough for what we would wish, then we would allow you to take pictures of Mandalay with our licence.'

Angela was overwhelmed, having received far more than she would have hoped from the Queen of Burma. 'Thank you, Your Majesty,' she murmured, eyes downcast.

King Thibaw said; 'This is very interesting to note. Photography is a fascinating new art form. I believe many excellent compositions are emerging from the camera obscura to rival that of traditional art. I myself find the idea of identical reproductions quite fascinating, for there is great potential in the camera, great potential. Who knows, but one day we might be able to have coloured photographs, Miss Featherstone, and then I think traditional painting will go out of the window.'

'That would indeed be a great step forward sir. But I feel it would be a miracle to achieve such a thing as coloured photography — independent of the art of tinting the developed photograph, that is.'

'Perhaps you are right, Miss Featherstone. Madam, the Queen, and our gracious mother, Queen Sinpyumashin, also have a great interest in photography though the Queen Mother prefers the art of astronomy. I have a new camera that was made in England,' he confessed smilingly, screwing up his black eyes and full mouth, a schoolboy proud of a new toy.

'That is interesting, Sir,' Angela murmured, trying to avoid the almond-shaped eyes intense in their scrutiny of her. 'Unfortunately, I've lost my camera now. May I enquire Sir, what kind of camera you have?' She forgot she was not supposed to ask questions.

The King of Burma did not appear to mind in the least: 'I have a Fox-Talbot, Miss Featherstone.'

'I also had one in my possession, Sir. Though it was nothing grand, it did take passable photographs.'

'Then sometime, Miss Featherstone, you must give me your opinion on the one I have in my possession, for it does *not* take passable photographs at all.' The King went back to chewing his thumbnail, staring at her unblinkingly, leaving the jewels in two life-size marguerite brooches pinned to the grosgrain sash of Kingship

196

across his breast to do the blinking for him.

The royal couple passed on to the others. They were familiar with Nanette and asked her very little of herself, only touching briefly on whether or not Mr Gideon had managed to gain anymore converts to Christianity.

'I guess not, Madam, Sir. I guess Buddhists are mighty hard to get hold of these days.'

Mr Gideon had warned Nanette to remain discreet when asked about converts to Christianity. If they knew he was taking too many, they would be bound to shut him down, his presence in Mandalay only tolerated by the Sangha because of Mindon Min's past benevolence towards the Christian community.

The King and Queen nodded approvingly and directed their attention to Matthew Sinclair. They addressed themselves politically to him, King Thibaw expressing dismay in that the British flag had ceased to fly over the Residency. Matthew nodded glumly, fidgeted with his glasses, and mumbled something about it being a sad but necessary gesture from the British point of view.

'Why?' Asked King Thibaw, blankly.

'Because Sir,' said Matthew unhappily, 'the British Resident is a very confused man. He is confused as he had hoped for closer co-operation from the new King and Queen of Burma and their Hlutdaw — and indeed, was given to understand that this would be the case. However, he now sees co-operation as not forthcoming, that his friendly voice falls on deaf ears, and that trading agreements are being ignored. The British wish to preserve detente with the Burmese, to trade Manchester cloth for Burma teak — a fair deal by any standards, but in view of recent internal happenings in Upper Burma, this is not now possible from our direction.'

Angela felt like applauding him; she could see Queen Supalayat and King Thibaw were suddenly on edge and that clearly Manchester cloth for Burma teak was not their priority. Queen Supalayat transferred her attention immediately to Nathan, while the King reverted to

197

playing with the tassels of his cushion.

'Ah!' exclaimed the Queen, clapping small hands in capricious delight, opera-glasses transferred to her lap. 'At last we have the pleasure of meeting with you Captain de Veres-Vorne. You are becoming a legend in your own lifetime, Captain. We have heard many things about you from almost everyone in Mandalay — our gracious mother, Queen Sinpyumashin, one of them. She has expressed her desire that this interview be conducted on her behalf, hence our intervention in matters concerning the Independent Shan States of Loloi, the subject of which we shall presently come to. We would like to say however, how much we have enjoyed the dancing of your wife Minthami, the Shan princess of Loloi. She should be encouraged to pursue the profession for which she was trained by us here at the Court. Minthami is a talented and beautiful artiste. Alas, she informs us she much prefers her simple way of life without servants and the trappings of luxury to which she has a birthright. She tells us that she cooks, sweeps and cleans all by herself with no outside assistance. Quite remarkable! We have been trying to persuade her to come back to the Court of Ava, and to have her sons Sa-Lon and Roi — charming boys — to stay here and be the companions of other little boys of the Court; Royal Princes, Captain. But alas, our suggestion for their education and upbringing Minthami rejected. *Quelle domage!*' The Burmese Queen smiled sweetly. 'Forgive my reverting to French, Captain de Veres-Vorne, but I speak the language a little better than English, and sometimes find myself lapsing into it. But then, I believe you have a French background yourself?'

'Way back, Madam.'

'On your father's side I believe?'

'Yes, Madam. When the French settled Louisiana.'

'And your mother?'

'She's Anglo-Irish, Madam.'

'So I heard.' All at once her patronizing tone vanished and was replaced by a different one. Angela had half

198

been expecting it, realizing that Supalayat had dished out treacle for the fly to step into. Like the little flicks of a snake's tongue, she continued to goad him. 'Now, Captain de Veres-Vorne, in the matter of your treacherous behaviour concerning the Burmese Royal Family, our gracious Mother, Queen Sinpyumashin, has asked us to intervene as it is bringing her much grief. She has no wish to upset the fine balance of things between East and West.' She paused deliberately, waiting for him to become her fly.

Angela had sensed him simmering all night, just waiting to get to verbal grips with someone from the Court of Ava. Social graces, she had discovered, were not part of Nathan's composition and, true to form, he dispensed with etiquette forthwith: 'Madam, at no time did I ever seek to undermine the authority of the Burmese Government by my actions.'

'You deny the presence of royal children at the Shan village of Loloi?'

So here it was, out in the open at last. The massacre at Loloi, the tiger-hunt to get Nathan out of the way, holding Minthami and the boys to ransom, it was all part of the plot. Angela did not know why she was surprised. What Nanette Gideon had told her Uncle Adrian and Matthew — who subsequently had passed it all on to her in a whispered conversation during moments they had had together before setting out for this audience — made her aware that if someone was capable of instigating such a monstrous deed as the elimination of their own relatives, they were capable of anything.

'I do not deny the presence of royal children at the Shan village of Loloi, Madam,' he said, 'but I deny the circumstances in which they were supposed to have been taken there. I didn't steal, kidnap, abduct, rob, pilfer or do anything else illegal regarding those children. King Mindon Min asked me personally to convey them to a place of safety. It was he who suggested the village of Loloi in the Shan States. The Sawbwa of Loloi made a treaty many years ago to support King Mindon Min at a

199

time of Shan uprisings. His own children were taken as hostage by King Mindon Min, in order that the Sawbwa keep his word — which he did. He was ever a noble and staunch supporter of King Mindon Min, so, for that reason, the six royal children were given into his care.'

Queen Supalayat held up her hand lest he carry on: 'We are well aware of all that, Captain de Veres-Vorne. But the fact remains the children were "kidnapped" as you say in your country. Nowhere is there a document to be found from King Mindon Min sanctioning the removal of his children from this Court. Can you yourself produce any such document? It will provide the necessary evidence we require.'

His fair brows drew together: 'No Madam. I have no such document signed by Mindon Min. I have only a piece of paper authorizing the banishment of six of his children to India.'

'You possess the duplicate of that authorization Captain, we possess the original. Now, on what authority were those children removed from the Court of Ava and transported aboard the *Belle Hélène* to Loloi?'

'On Mindon Min's authority Madam. The document of banishment was a foil. King Mindon wished for the utmost secrecy so that his children's lives would not be in danger.'

'Why would they be in danger?'

The tension in the room was tremendous. Angela shut her eyes and Matthew Sinclair wiped his steamy glasses. Surely to goodness Angela thought faintly, he wasn't going to come out with it and tell the Queen of Burma she was a murderess.

But even he hesitated: 'Madam, whatever danger King Mindon Min thought his children might be in, was his prerogative. I did not ask, I merely acted. He asked me to put my boat at the disposal of his family and I did as I was asked. No document exists for that reason. It was purely a verbal matter between the King of Burma and myself — as a subject of his. I served him to the best of my ability.'

200

The Queen did not mask her scorn: 'Captain de Veres-Vorne, was it really thus? My, my! You were sent for by King Mindon Min in order that you might do him a personal favour? I'm deeply impressed. Forgive me Captain, but why should the King of Burma choose you, a foreigner to his Kingdom, a non-Buddhist, a well-known mercenary and bounty-hunter, to do him this especial favour?'

'Maybe Madam, because I had a steamboat, a wife who was the Shan princess of Loloi, and a father-in-law who had sworn to the King he would ever be his loyal and faithful henchman. Maybe too, he trusted me as a neutral in his country.'

She moistened her lips. King Thibaw seemed bored by the whole business.

'Then how,' insisted the Queen, 'do you explain the fact that several thousand rupees worth of rubies were found aboard your boat the *Belle Hélène* if they weren't payment for the kidnapping of royal children?'

'I've no idea Madam. Maybe someone put them aboard my boat deliberately so I'd look guilty. All I got was Mindon Min's blessing. Any lahks of gold went directly to the Sawbwa of Loloi for the upbringing and care of the children, and payment to the schoolteacher who looked after and taught them.'

The three people on the dais flicked sly glances in Angela's direction. She now knew why she too had been 'invited' here. Anyone, it appeared, even remotely involved with Loloi, was suspect: 'The only rubies I had in my possession,' Nathan told them, 'were five given me by my father-in-law, the Sawbwa of Loloi, for merchandise he'd asked me to bring back for him from Canton.'

'Which brings me to another matter of treachery,' said the Queen. 'The Sawbwa of Loloi interfered greatly with matters of State — our State, the Kingdom of Upper Burma. As Overlord of an independent enclave, he had no business to do so. Any diplomatic negotiations should have been done through the proper channels. He had no right to harbour in his village our children, princes and

201

princesses of the Court of Ava. That he should do so constitutes an act of treason!' Her voice had risen to a shrill note of accusation, and in that moment she sounded just like her mother who had interrogated Nathan some months earlier.

In the uncanny silence following that final word from her, Nathan said calmly: 'And that's presumably why you had him beheaded by mercenaries, Madam. He who was ever King Mindon Min's faithful henchman acting on a bond between them.'

Oh God, thought Angela. She heard Matthew's swift intake of breath coincide with Nanette Gideon's as well as her own. Don't Nathan, don't! Don't flirt so with death all the time! she silently entreated.

King Thibaw began to fidget. Queen Supalayat put her opera-glasses back to her eyes and surveyed Nathan for a long time. Then she leaned behind her sister to say something in Burmese to the Taingda Mingyi. He came beside her and performed his deep shikkos at her feet before handing her the parabaik Matthew Sinclair had returned to the Hlutdaw that afternoon. The Queen of Burma unrolled it and held it aloft for them to see: 'You have confessed in this document to all the charges brought against you, Captain de Veres-Vorne.' Her smile was feline, triumphant. The Queen's eyes were so cold and implacable, Angela suppressed a shudder. Supalayat was not to be trusted. No wonder the King left all the talking and intimidating to her, and if the stories concerning Queen Sinpyumashin were to be believed, then Supalayat was indeed her daughter! 'Is this your signature?' she demanded tapping the parabaik with a long finger-nail.

'Yes, Madam,' he replied, undaunted even now.

'You maintain your innocence in all this? That none of these charges brought against you are true and you acted according to good faith and your loyalty to my father King Mindon Min?'

'Yes Madam.'

'Do you usually put your signature to things you

202

disagree with, Captain?'

'Frequently Madam. In Burma.'

They stared at each other. Then she looked away. Over her shoulder she handed the dirty torn scroll to the Taingda. 'Destroy it,' she said in Burmese.

Angela was not the only one present who at first did not understand what she had said. The Taingda looked at his Queen, tried to smile, found he could not, tried again, failed dismally and ended up staring blankly with an idiotic look on his face: 'I — I beg your pardon, divine Majesty? I have truly misunderstood ...'

'I said destroy it,' she snapped.

'At once, O Queen, at once.' He performed a couple of deep shikkos at her feet before moving backwards in a crouching position to take up his stance once more behind the dais.

They were perplexed, hardly daring to look at one another. The full import of her words certainly hadn't dawned on Angela until the Queen started speaking English again: 'Captain de Veres-Vorne, you are hereby given a full pardon and are free to go. The British Resident in Mandalay, who has taken such a great and personal interest in your affairs, will be informed immediately of our decision to pardon your crimes. It is only with Royal clemency you are allowed to walk away from here a free man. But in this month of coronation celebrations we are willing to pardon the offences of our subjects, together with those foreigners who have incurred our very great displeasure ...' she paused significantly. 'However, we wish not to detain you again in Sagaing, nor deport you for your pardoned misdemeanors, but hope you will remain with us in the Kingdom of Burma and continue to ply your trade up and down the Irrawaddy as you did in the time of King Mindon Min.'

She waited to see the dramatic effect of her words upon the four people at her feet. All four were suffused in smiles. Even King Thibaw smiled at Queen Supalayat's sister. The Queen herself did not.

'Captain de Veres-Vorne,' said King Thibaw, at once looking much relieved that this affair of the Shwe Nat was over at last, 'sometime you must come and tell me all about King Geronimo, the great Apache Chief of your country. I believe he is very brave and rides a horse like the historical warrior Tamerlane.'

Queen Supalayat said: 'Captain, we believe many new stores are opening up in Rangoon, run by the British. We are given to understand specialized merchandise from all over the world can be found in these big stores. We would greatly appreciate something like that here in Mandalay. There is a suitable plot of ground for an Emporium to be built out by the Sinzwe bazaar. You would be granted a special licence to open such a store.'

'Thank you Madam. But first I must ask the price of the land. I might not have enough money to buy or build.'

Queen Supalayat shrugged. She fingered her beautiful seed-pearl stole in an abstract manner, not meeting his eyes.

'The price has been paid,' she murmured. She turned away, wishing to bring the audience to a close, but Nathan said in the eerie space of time that had followed her remark:

'Madam, what price has been paid, Loloi? The English school-teacher, Miss Lydell? The Sawbwa of Loloi's head? The Royal children's lives? What price, Madam? It was to be my life for my wife and sons ...' then he blanched. Nathan came off his cushions as the full impact of her words struck him. Angela, agitated by this war of nerves, began to tremble when she saw the Royal Guards who had remained inconspicuous until now, step towards Nathan.

Matthew too scrambled off his cushions: 'Keep sitting, I beg of you,' he hissed under his breath to Nathan. 'Just let me handle this ...' He bowed to the King and Queen. 'Madam ... Sir ... it was understood that Captain de Veres-Vorne would give himself up in return for the lives of his two sons and his wife Minthami.'

'That is correct, Mr Sinclair,' Queen Supalayat said.

Because she said nothing more, Matthew stated: 'Then I trust they have not been harmed in any way, Madam, and would be grateful if they could be released into my charge without further delay.'

'Princess Minthami and her two sons have never been kept as prisoners,' the Queen said, looking as though she enjoyed playing cat and mouse games when the stakes were high.

'I — I don't understand, Madam,' Matthew said, perspiration dripping from his face, his glasses opaque.

Queen Supalayat began to laugh, the high shrill sound of capriciously tinkling bells. She clapped her hands in delight. Her sister smiled, followed by the King, unsure of himself in front of the foreigners. Angela began to feel pity for him, eclipsed as he was in the shadow of his tiny domineering Queen.

'I demand to know, Madam, what has become of my wife and sons.' Nathan glared daggers at her, recalcitrant as ever.

'Relax, Captain de Veres-Vorne,' Queen Supalayat smiled. 'By the look in your eye I gather regicide is intended, although I'm certain even you would not be foolish enough to start the Third Burmese War.' She ignored him then and turned her attention to Nanette Gideon: 'Mrs Gideon,' she said, still laughing gently to herself, 'what do you think of the new fashion my lady guards are wearing? Do you not think the Chinese style of trousers for women much more practicable?'

'Oh, much more Madam, for women doing a man's job. I never reckoned on them being much like women even in their Burmese skirts.'

The Queen, still smiling at Nanette, smacked her hands sharply together. The summons brought the Taingda mincing forward again: 'Issue orders to fetch Captain de Veres-Vorne's two sons to him at once.' Queen Supalayat then dismissed her Advisor with a flick of a wrist.

'What about Minthami?' Nathan asked, not deigning

to address her as he should.

'That is not possible ... oh, please, please Captain! Are all you Westerners alike, so fidgety the whole time?' She waved him back to his cushion. 'It is not I who with-hold Princess Minthami from you, but the Portuguese doctor attending her.'

'God in heaven, what's been happening now?'

'What sadly happens to women from time to time, Captain. She is miscarrying her child and cannot be moved.'

'In that case, may I see her, Madam? Because I don't believe you.'

Again she burst out laughing: 'I find your manners barbarous, Captain, but infinitely amusing. No you may not see your wife who is confined in the Queen's Quarters. No man is ever permitted there except the King. I will allow Mrs Gideon and Miss Featherstone to visit Princess Minthami and vouch that all is well enough with her. They will be escorted there presently. Mean-while your sons will come to you and you may take them home. Now we shall bring this audience to a close. Thank you for attending upon us. We bid you good-night.'

The royal trio made their exit; it was almost midnight.

INTERLUDE

The Sayadaw, the wise and learned teacher of the Pagoda Monastery and Convent of Sasana, had never had such a conscientious pupil. He had never had an Englishwoman come to him so desirous of taking the path of humility, abstinence, knowledge and final liberation. He had accepted, of course he had accepted. Meanwhile he kept his own counsel while observing her at her devotions, keenly, as a loving father would his child. The Sasana was there to provide knowledge concerning the teachings of Buddha, for that was what Sasana meant.

The novice in the Sasana library put away the parabaik containing the poems of a Buddhist King. The text had been inscribed in sacred Pali script found in the Shwegugyi Temple in Southern Burma. She was making a study of Pali, as she was making a study of her whole life: existence was unhappiness, unhappiness was caused by selfish desires and craving, desire could be destroyed by following the eight-fold path that would lead to final liberation ...

She had done enough study for one morning, she was hungry. It was time to go in search of food, for, after the hour of eleven before noon, a holy person fasted.

The bright sun outside hurt Angela Featherstone's eyes. But work brought its own consolation, a reprieve from wayward thoughts. Before feeding herself, however, she had to feed the sacred turtles in their pool by the Sasana Pagoda. It had become a regular practice with her.

Amagyi-Angela, the Buddhist novice, crumbled bread into the deep green water softly shaded by the trees on Mandalay Hill. Sunlight lay trapped in her red-gold curls, clipped short like a boy's. When she took her vows, the rest of her head would be shaven, her robe would become pink instead of white, and she would walk barefoot for the rest of her days. Sometimes, the very thought of liberating herself from the world into which she had been born overwhelmed her so much, she had to flee to the Sayadaw to restore her faith and resolution. He always did.

The whispered passage of many feet passing and repassing on the worn flags paving the pagoda areas, were like a prayer, a reverent breeze that fanned her mind anew. So many pilgrims, devotees, one could not help but be affected by such homage. Absorbed by the utter contentment around her of the disciples of Gautama Siddhartha Buddha, she fed her turtles. Her black lacquer bowl rested on a low stone parapet that surrounded the turtle-pool. Its lid off, ready to receive the offerings of the devout, she knew she would never starve to death in Burma.

An un-Buddhist tread, the scraping of shoe-leather on holy ground, disturbed her serenity. From the corner of her eye she perceived a hand that was all too familiar as he put cherries in her bowl.

'So! An angel without wings has learned the Oriental art of making God an instrument of expediency. How are you Angela?'

'Contented, Nathan. Buddhists don't have gods, only disciples.'

'To give you your due, I'd thought you'd only stick this whole business for two weeks and then call it a day. You're tenacious if anything. Stubborn would probably be a better word.'

She turned cool green eyes filled with sunlight upon him. The look was meant to convey tolerance. 'I shall enjoy the cherries, Nathan. Thank you for your gift. I'm sure you'll earn some merit for your thoughtfulness.'

'Why are you doing this, Angela?'

'Doing what?'

'Making Matthew a laughing stock in this city?'

'That had not been my intention.'

'You're also killing your Uncle Adrian by degrees. He's appalled by your behaviour — so am I.'

'Nathan, if you've climbed a thousand steps to torment me, please go down again and leave me alone.'

'I'm dying to know, honey, why you're doing this to yourself. A bald head and flamingo-pink is not a bird that will suit you. Besides, I know for a fact you're one of life's participators, not shirkers. You'll never be happy, or satisfied, behind nunnery walls.'

'Nathan Vorne! I refuse to listen to any more of your insults.' She picked up her black bowl, slammed its lid on, and picked her way through a puddle left by a recent mango shower. Angela walked a few steps down to a white marble parapet near a little Buddha shrine, hoping he would go away.

Nathan followed: 'For God's sake, Angela, the joke's gone far enough. Every indulgence has its excuse, but my advice to you is, you get down those steps fast and marry Matthew Sinclair who's as nice a man as any you'll find this side of Suez.'

She looked across the city, her elbows leaning on the retaining parapet. From here she could see far away to the cobalt-blue outline of the Shan hills in the East, to the south and west across Palace battlements to the Bund and the river Irrawaddy throbbing in loops and tributaries through the dense jungles beyond. Mandalay was expanding, building progressing inside and outside its fortified walls. 'I see you haven't wasted much time in staking your claim to a right royal piece of land in the best part of the city, Nathan Vorne,' she said with a dint of amusement. 'They're busy with the foundations of your new store already. You'll be scaffolding yourself to greater things soon.'

'What else do you begrudge me, Amagyi-Angela?'

She whirled upon him, not liking the sound of that

one bit: 'How dare you Nathan!'

'Ah!' he said grinning widely and holding up a finger in front of her nose, 'the old spirit is still alive after all. What is it the Buddhists teach — *As the dewdrop slips into the shining sea?* Honey, you're a long way from losing your individuality I'm glad to say. Now why don't you cut out all this hokus-pokus and go back to being Angela Featherstone, one-hell-of-a-great-female? You're wasting yourself, believe me. You're not designed to be a nun, but someone's girl-friend, fiancée, wife, mistress, mother . . .'

'How's Minthami?' she asked shortly.

'Getting better. Daw Khin Htay's medicine worked wonders when nothing else could. When she's able to climb a few thousand steps, she'll come and see you.'

'Tell her I'll look forward to that . . . I have to go now Nathan.'

The Convent bell had started to ring, summoning her to a period of meditation. She had learned to distinguish the Sasana bell from all the others ringing at the same time. Angela picked up her begging-bowl but he stayed her hand, awhile longer.

'Angela honey, I didn't come up here to quarrel with you. I just want you to know you're making a lot of people very unhappy by what you've decided to do. You're wasting your life by becoming a Buddhist nun. Life isn't meant to be lived behind solid stone walls. We've got to get out there and face it head-on, and fight for it if necessary; that's what life's all about. But, enough preaching from me, I'll leave that to Edom Gideon. What I really had to say was a temporary farewell. I'm off to Indonesia for a little sea-run, and to pick up a few odds and ends — the Queen of Burma isn't the only one who wants her thirty pieces of silver.' His smile was a little off-centre, yet it was designed to go straight to her heart, which she knew would lead her astray if she let it. She had made up her mind Nathan Vorne would probably leave her in as many pieces as Garabanda.

She lifted her head; all around her thousands of little pagoda bells were blown by warm breezes of the Irrawaddy, a thousand-thousand souls all clamouring to be heard at once by Buddha. It was cooler up here on Mandalay Hill than down on the flat plain below; the soft breeze ruffled her hair and his: 'What can I say except, may you go with happiness in your sails and return safely,' Angela said to Nathan as she smiled into his blue eyes, and knew that he was a million miles away from the core of her existence, a law only to himself and nobody's man.

'Sayonara, Amagyi-Angela,' he said, that lovely Japanese farewell, his clouded gaze containing a mixture of doubt, hope, relief and something else she could not quite make out. 'Sayonara, honeychile.'

Along the covered walkway back to her Convent, she thought about him. Life was only ever a bowl of cherries to him, Nathan Vorne. And she prayed for him too, prayed the winds of Java would blow him safely back to Mandalay.

PART II

River of Gems 1884-1886

CHAPTER SIXTEEN

ONE

'*Anicca, Dukkha, Anatta*: Impermanence, suffering, egolessness: Life is change, life is desire, life is sorrow. When desire ceases then so does sorrow.' The nun meditated.

Hot winds were in the tamarinds. Ragged banana trees fanned themselves breathlessly. Jacaranda and mohur sacrificed mauve and gold blossoms, and the flame-of-the-forest stood stark naked. Coolies slept in dried pineapple trenches while leathery lizards scuttled in search of water, and the nun and her camera came intrusively into the Burmese way of life.

The King of Burma had given his old camera to the Amagyi-Angela because it 'did not take passable photographs.'

How well Angela remembered his remark. She could hardly believe five years, nearly six, had gone by since that memorable day — her first in Mandalay.

Her camera just would not stand up in the high wind! Angela decided she would have to pack up and return to her convent to wait for a less windy day to take her photographs of the Shwe Emporium.

Queen Supalayat, from whom Angela had received a Commission to take Court photographs, wanted pictures of the grand new store built by Captain de Veres-Vorne in her city. She had seen an article in the *Rangoon Gazette* concerning the first de Veres-Vorne Company of Rangoon, and did not wish to be outdone. She told Angela she desired to take Mandalay from its 'native backwater' status to bring it recognition from those in the South — perhaps even as far away as London, England. She therefore required a portfolio of Mandalay to be started, with Angela to do the photographs.

When reviewing one or two 'tentative shots' as Angela had called them, Queen Supalayat and the Taingda Mingyi had hummed and haaed over them, finally rejecting them as being not 'quite' what they wished to pass on to the outside world.

'We would wish for something a little more "original" so the Britishers can put it in their London pipes and smoke it,' the Queen told Angela — who did not know what to make of that remark. All she knew was that Queen Supalayat could be very very difficult to please. She delighted in making people run her errands, sending them here, there and everywhere on a whim, sometimes as far as Paris to obtain scent, jewellery or clothes, she had seen in some fashion magazine or catalogue; if they did not please her, she sent them right back to Paris!

Ramur, the Dravidian, and Shwe Emporium's doorman on a par with the best commissionaires of Bond Street and Fifth Avenue, grabbed her camera and stand, which the high winds tried to topple. Bowing, he handed them back to her with a big smile: 'It is Krakatoa again making big indigestion in sea like last year. That's why we get these tail-end belching noises and much wind in Mandalay. Amagyi-Angela, it is better you go home and leave pictures for another time.'

'I think that's a perfectly sensible idea, Ramur. Would you mind helping me gather my things together? Good morning, Mrs Wandersmeith, Miss Stuttgart, my isn't it breezy!'

They dropped two annas into her bowl: 'I thought nuns were supposed to be celebrate,' said Vanda Wandersmeith to Nancy as they pushed into the Emporium's glass double-doors to get out of the dust blown up on Mandalay's streets. She jerked her head toward Ramur preoccupied with the British nun and her belongings.

'Celibate, dear, celibate,' said Nancy glancing nervously over her shoulder. She knew how Vanda could hurt people's feelings by talking too loudly.

'That's fish, Nancy!'

'No Vanda, that's halibut.'

They bumped into a gentleman walking out of the Shwe Emporium, sola topi under his arm. Grinning broadly, he bowed charmingly and then kept the doors open for them to go through.

'Why if it ain't Captain de Veres-Vorne!' said Vanda while Nancy seemed flustered. 'I'm glad you're back in town Captain. I've been meaning to tell you your Notices don't work ...'

'Otis, Vanda, Otis!' Nancy smiled at Nathan Vorne. 'She means your elevators, Captain, the steam ones.'

'Oh, what seems to be the trouble?' he asked, eyebrows raised, 'I've just been in them myself, up one, down the other. They seemed to be working fine to me. But if in doubt, Ramur will show you ladies how ... excuse me, I've got a boat to catch.'

Outside the Shwe Emporium he saw a hastily departing nun, her pink robes hardly disguising her unmistakable figure. 'Amagyi-Angela,' he ran after her, 'hey ... what's the mighty hurry?'

'Good morning Nathan ... I didn't know you were back in Mandalay. How are you?'

'Fine Angela, fine. How're you? Here, let me carry some of that equipment. You look over-loaded ...'

'No, no, thank you,' she said breathlessly, 'I can manage perfectly well.'

'Then at least stand still and talk to me for five minutes. I'm damned if I'm running after you in this hurricane.'

Head down, robe wrapped like a shroud around her long legs, her hood whipped away from her shaven head, she felt the blood pounding in her ears. 'Go away, Nathan, and leave me alone,' she muttered fiercely. 'Five years is a very long time ... I think I've forgotten the art of talking to you.'

'And I guess I never thought you'd stick to your guns, Amagyi-Angela.'

'You never really knew me, Nathan.'

'Damn you Angela! Will you stand still ...' He grabbed her elbow, halting her furious flight along the streets of Mandalay back to her hill-top retreat. 'Why are you running away from me?'

'I'm not. I have to get back to the Convent. I've some Pali scripts to work on for the Sayadaw.'

'Damn your Pali scripts ... and the old man you bribed to keep you in the Sasana.'

'How dare you, Nathan Vorne!'

'Oh, come off it Angela, the whole of Mandalay knows you parted with your inheritance — your father's and your Uncle Adrian's to keep you in that ludicrous outfit. Why Angela, that's what I'd like to know?'

'You'll never know. Now please leave me alone Nathan. Go back to Rangoon or wherever else you've been these past five years.'

'America, Ireland, Java, Canton, I've sailed the seven seas, Amagyi-Angela, does that answer your question?'

'I'm really not interested, Nathan.'

'Yes, you are, you're bloody interested.'

'Oh God! You're more conceited than I ever imagined.'

'Shouldn't it be "Oh Buddha!" seeing how you've slipped into his shining sea?'

They stood on the pavement glaring at one another.

'The Maiden, the Missionary and the Missy-Sahib ... how wrong I was Angela,' he said. Sadly, she imagined. Of course she was being stupid. 'Don't ... don't please.' She pulled her hood on, bending to pick up her unwieldy camera thrown down in a rare fit of temper, when she thought she had learned by now to control her emotions.

'Still taking pictures I see,' he remarked wryly.

Oh God, she thought again, what a futile conversation after five years! But what does one say when there are too many things to say? Nothing, nothing ...

'For royalties or for charity?' he asked when she

remained silent.

'Both. The money I'm supposed to earn for the photography, goes to the Convent. I say supposed to, because Supalayat's now in charge of the treasury and she's a notorious non-payer when it comes to her own bills.'

'Then I guess I'd better start charging her account at the Shwe Emporium for the privilege of using my store to bolster her prestige in the eyes of the outside world,' he said, suddenly his face softening from its grim aspect of a few moments ago. 'I assume that's what you were doing? Trying to get the absolute correct angle for my double-doors with Ramur in the middle?'

'I was. Until Boanerges' two old trumpets came along.'

He grinned. 'Amagyi-Angela, I've missed you. Listen, I'm putting on a little show at my house tonight. Since it's Christmas and all that, please will you come? I'm asking you nicely as a favour to me. Most of the people invited you already know.' As soon as he'd said it, he realized that was one reason why she might not accept his invitation; she wouldn't want to get involved again with people she had known in the past.

'I'm sorry Nathan, I can't. The Sayadaw only allows me to go out on "royal errands". I have to be back inside the Convent by six o'clock.'

'What rot.'

She ignored that low remark: 'Besides, as a Buddhist I don't believe in Christmas anymore.'

'Rot again. Then it's a house-warming party. We'll celebrate the christening ... I beg your pardon, but one forgets how many 'Christian' words creep into the vocabulary ... the naming of my new house on the Bund; Whitewalls. How about it Amagyi-Angela?'

She took a deep breath. 'I'll think about it Nathan.'

'No thinking ...' he took her hand, and for a split second the fire and the desire was back. 'No thinking, Angela,' he said. 'I would like you to come.'

Angela looked up at him: more beautiful than ever;

more alarming, more arrogant, more treacherous, more everything. She pulled her hand away. 'I don't know Nathan. Now I really must go.' She retrieved her things, including the food bowl with two annas, courtesy of Edom Gideon's converts.

TWO

Angela did not know she could be so nervous.

They were all gathered at Nathan's house that evening, the Sinclairs, the Tennent-Brownes, recently come to Mandalay on behalf of the Boundaries Commission, a young man called Buchanan, the Sundevavas, Ma Ngwe, prosperous Minkdaw married to a lawyer in the Hlutdaw, U Po Thine. The Gideons were missing, but Angela realized Edom Gideon was probably at his Gospel Hall holding a special Christmas service for his congregation.

When Nathan met her inside the beautiful marble hall of his grand house overlooking the river Angela asked;

'Nathan, where's Minthami? I was expecting to see her.'

'Roi had pneumonia last month. She didn't want to move him all the way up here until he was fully recovered, so decided to stay down in Rangoon.'

'Oh, I'm sorry, I didn't know your son was ill.'

'How could you? Ah ... here's Leigh, come and meet him.'

This Nathan, as host in evening dress, was someone she had not met before! Having been taught at her Academy only to associate the word 'nice' with food, she described him to herself as looking very nice and then put him quickly out of her head by thinking instead of the Three Baskets of the Buddhist Scriptures.

Angela did, however, have the honour of being placed on his right hand, with Lady Bee on his left. Mercifully the Sinclairs had been placed at the other end of the long table with Sir Edwin.

For five years Angela had paid little or no attention to her appearance, but tonight she felt terribly conspicuous in 'flamingo-pink' as Nathan had once rudely remarked. Even Blaize Tennent-Browne's gushingly obvious comment was designed specifically to make her feel yet more embarrassed.

'Darling, you look divine in that costume. How clever of you to think of fancy dress. Mrs Sundevava, don't you think the Amagyi-Angela's lace headdress is a clever idea? So pretty — as a disguise.'

After that ascerbic comment she went on to monopolize the rest of the conversations taking place around her, interrupting and, Angela had no doubt, annoying Nathan's guests. Lady Bee, with the ruthless attention of a surgeon's scalpel dissected each person's past, present and future. She began with Leigh Buchanan.

'What do you do for a living, Mr Buchanan?' She asked the attractive young man seated on her left, who appeared to have eyes for no one save Milly Sinclair, Matthew's pretty sister.

'Er ... telegraphy, Lady Tennent-Browne.'

Blaize smiled dazzlingly, her pink gums and large teeth rather daunting, though not in any way unattractive, as she was a very presentable young woman, her dark hair and blue eyes and deep dimples made full use of where the opposite sex was concerned.

'Do call me Bee, Leigh. Everyone did in Manipur ... so different to Mandalay! What's this thing telegraphy? I know what it is, but how does it work exactly?'

'By sending messages of Morse Code along a wire, ma'am.'

'Heavens! It sounds like a washing line ... Captain de Veres-Vorne, so nice of you to invite Edwin and me to dine with you. I do adore Christmas Eve, don't you? Although it's never the same out East as it is in Tunbridge Wells. Such divine soup. Bird's-nest, isn't it? I know, because we were invited to a Chinese banquet last week and bird's-nest soup was on the menu — along with fifteen other courses. One does realize however it

221

isn't quite the same kind of bird's nest one finds in an English hedgerow. Would you mind awfully if we called you Nathan? Captain de Veres-Vorne is such a mouthful with the soup.'

'My pleasure,' he murmured, his face perfectly straight.

'You work for yourself out here, don't you, Nathan?'

'Yes, ma'am, I'm my own boss.'

'Ah!' She exclaimed, her blue eyes alight with enthusiasm. 'The spirit of free enterprise at last.'

She made him sound like one of his boats coming into dock, and Angela lowered her smile to the bird's nest soup which tasted remarkably well of asparagus. Matthew was looking at her with a very odd expression, not paying any attention to Edwin's statistics of traumatic glaucoma out East, a little out of date since he had retired from being an Army Opthalmic-Surgeon for a number of years now. Matthew's wife however, a thin whey-faced creature who had come out East via the Fishing-Fleet, seemed remarkably interested in infant mortality rates for India and Burma. Angela noticed her third child seemed about due.

'Matthew's ayah was the one responsible for his bad eyesight,' she informed Edwin earnestly. 'She allowed the flies to crawl over his face when he was a baby, thus causing an eye infection — his mother told me all about it. That's why we don't trust Indian ayahs. Milly has come from Coimbatore to help look after the children for that reason.'

Angela seemed to be catching Matthew's glances rather a lot across the dinner table, he too very conscious of the absurd direction their lives had taken.

'Yes,' said Matthew, clearing his throat awkwardly while Angela went on unconsciously crumbling the bread-roll on her side-plate. 'Milly's a marvellous help with the children.'

Blaize Tennent-Browne had gone back to the subject of Nathan's occupation. 'Yes, but what do you do exactly, apart from sailing up and down the Irrawaddy in that little boat of yours?'

'Nathan owns the Shwe Emporium, Rangoon and Mandalay, Bee,' Angela informed her as Ko Lee, Nathan's Chinese houseboy, stood beside her elbow with a dish of yams. 'Thank you Ko Lee.' She helped herself.

'Trade, how interesting,' said Lady Tennent-Browne sounding rather deflated by the whole concept of trade.

'Bee thought you were at least the American Ambassador to Mandalay, Nathan.' Angela concentrated on her food.

'Angela, how could you! Really darling, sometimes I wonder why you're making yourself look a fool in that nun's habit. What made you entertain a notion of putting a store like the Shwe Emporium right in the middle of the jungle, Nathan?'

'Well ma'am, God created the world in six days and on the seventh added Burma as a postscript. The way I see it, if he'd had a Shwe Emporium around, he could've bought his tools cheap, and cleared his own jungles instead of leaving it all to us.'

'It must be awfully difficult conveying everything from the coast?'

'I have me my steamers.' Nathan said.

'Steamers? How interesting. Forgive me Nathan, but I happened to hear a little rumour on the jungle grapevine ... you know how it is ... that you're related to Countess Keir?' Her knife and fork hovered expectantly.

'She's my mother.'

'Oh now, that *is* interesting! However, I thought your family were connected to cotton plantations and all that sort of thing one hardly dares talk about since emancipation.'

'I am. My mother remarried again after my father died. She went back to live in Southern Ireland and married into Anglo-Irish nobility from Tipperary — God help her. Back to her roots, Lady Bee, if that answers your question.' Nathan said very straight-faced.

Angela could see underneath he was tickled pink by Lady's Bee's blatant inquisitiveness. She could also see

223

that Nathan Vorne had gone up a notch — several notches — for being related to the British aristocracy after he'd gone down for being associated with that bourgeois word, trade.

'Do you sell thimbles, Nathan?' she asked, going off at a tangent.

'Not personally, but I believe the Shwe Emporium stocks such items.'

'Thank heaven for that. No one seems to have heard of a thimble out here. Leigh, where were you educated?'

'The Woolwich Military Academy, Lady Tennent-Browne.'

'Oh yes. That's interesting. Where are your parents posted in India?'

'They were in Calcutta, but have now retired to Dehra-Dun.'

'Ah yes, the Forest School place. Full of teak-wallahs. This is awfully good wine Nathan.' It looked as if it had gone to Lady Bee's head for all her remarkable talking. 'Where do you go to school, Miss Latchkeerandi?' she asked the Sundevava's teenage daughter who, together with Milly Sinclair, appeared to be tittering over something and not sharing the joke with anyone.

'Latch-mi-randi, Bee,' Angela said, hoping someone would silence the garrulous Blaize.

'Damn fine wine, Captain!' Sir Edwin boomed from the other end of the long rosewood table gracing Nathan's dining-room and covered with the best silver and crystal. 'The French appear to be getting everywhere in Upper Burma. But, they know how to lay down a classy cellar!' He held up his glass. 'Happy Christmas everyone! Mr Po Thine and I've had a most illuminating conversation. We're having the devil of a job to get the Hlutdaw to co-operate with the Calcutta Boundaries Commission. Mr Po Thine here — who sees things from both sides — assures me the Burmese are all hot air about attacking the Indian boundary posts over this disagreement on the new frontier with India. I'd like to believe him, but it doesn't get away from the fact such

224

threats from the Burmese is damn nigh anarchy!' Edwin concluded, as red as a turkey-cock on good French wine.

'I believe you were at the October meeting of the Rangoon Chamber of Commerce, Nathan?' Matthew asked. 'What were their directives?'

'There were three main resolutions,' Nathan told them. 'Upper Burma being grossly mismanaged by King Thibaw and his Hlutdaw, entails unwarranted misery and distress to the inhabitants of the country, therefore HM's Government should step in to restore law and order since Lower Burma and Upper Burma are inter-dependent. They proposed that Upper Burma should be annexed, or failing that, a Protectorate should be estab-lished with one of the exiled Princes reinstated on the throne — preferably one sympathetic to the British. The trouble is, The Nyaungyan Min in Calcutta where he was removed by the British for his own safety, is not the right person to step into Thibaw's shoes at this moment. His younger brother Prince Nyaung Ok, also in exile and living in Pondicherry, is finding it hard to escape the clutches of the French despite all the money being raised to get him to return to Mandalay at the head of troops.'

'The damn French,' Edwin said angrily, 'will be the ruination of Indo-China, which includes Upper Burma! You mark my words, the moment the British let go, they'll be establishing their own Empire out here. That's what they're aiming for, control of these countries.' He was getting carried away in the heat of the moment and Angela thought he ought to have stuck to the fruit juices U Po Thine and Mr Sundevava were drinking on account of religious principles. She herself was only sip-ping a little iced-water with her meal, her meticulous scruples concerning the hours of fasting, dispensed with for this particular occasion by special permission from the Sayadaw.

'What do you think about those proposals from the Chamber of Commerce?' Matthew asked Nathan.

'To be honest, I don't see what right your Govern-ment or any other Government has in the management of Upper Burma,' Nathan said. 'It would be different if their atrocities and mismanagement directly affected the British — but so far they've only rioted, looted and killed among themselves. The British can't simply step into someone else's country, dethrone their King because they don't like or don't agree with the way he's running things, and pinch it for themselves. That's how I feel about it. Bring the pudding and dessert, Ko Lee.'

'Yes Cap'ain.'

Had Nathan forgotten so easily Loloi, her Aunt Emmy, his own father-in-law the Sawbwa of Loloi, the princes and princesses of the Court of Ava, to all accounts done away with never to be seen or heard of again? And what about the things done to himself and to his Minthami and their children? Angela looked to him. He looked at her. The question mark in her deep green eyes asking, Why Nathan? He seemed to give an almost imperceptible shrug, as if to say, I don't really care anymore, I've got what I want.

'Would anyone care for some crème caramel? There's also almond soufflé, or fresh fruit? Bee ... what will you have?' he asked.

'Crème caramel if you please, darling. Almonds always bring me out in hives. That was a most delicious meal, Nathan. Congratulations to your cook. I haven't tasted quail done like that since ... since last week. Do you play polo, Nathan?'

'No ma'am,' he replied distantly as he directed Ko Lee.

'Such a shame! Edwin adored playing polo with the Raja of Manipur. Didn't you darling ...? I said, Edwin darling, did you not adore playing polo with the Raja of Manipur? Thank you Ko Lee that will do ... the caramel looks divine, not too overdone. Do you play polo, Leigh?' She sampled the crème caramel, placing a tiny portion on the tip of her tongue to test it first lest it bring her out in hives. Angela observed her with as much amusement as did Miss Latchmirandi and her mother.

'No, Lady Tennent-Browne,' Leigh replied, 'I don't

play polo either.'

'Lord!' she wailed across the tazza 'does no one play anything in Burma?'

'Only patience,' Nathan replied, holding her to ransom across the tazza. 'Too hot and steamy in the afternoons for anything else.'

'Dear me, I can see I'm going to have to change a few things around here.' Reluctantly she withdrew her gaze from his. 'Angela,' she said, sounding a little breathless, 'how is it you're allowed such liberty? I mean, darling, no other nun appears to go wandering around Mandalay with a King's camera and gilt-edged invitations in her pocket both to the Palace and to Whitewalls? It appears being a Buddhist nun in Burma can't be all bareheads, feet and sacrifice.'

Nathan cleared his throat, coming to Angela's rescue before she got herself tied up in explanations that had nothing to do with anyone, least of all Blaize Tennent-Browne. 'Ladies, if you'd care to adjourn to the drawing-room ... this way ...' He left the table, hosting them out. 'Tea and coffee will be served in there.' His hospitality, like his smile was gracious.

'Yes, of course darling, we know the way.'

Leaving the men to their brandy, port and cigars, Angela hoped she could soon take her leave, wondering why on earth she had given into temptation after five years; this was not at all an adventure a Buddhist nun undertook, with or without royal licence.

Graceful French satinwood furniture adorned Nathan's drawing-room, which was both comfortable and elegant. White walls, white marble floors, windows from floor to ceiling to trap the light were also designed to keep the burning heat beyond the cool shady verandah. Doric columns supported the high ceiling where lethargic pull-punkas circulated the air and provided the only real incongruity in an otherwise beautiful room.

'Do you ever see Minthami, now Amagyi-Angela?' Ma Ngwe asked, plumper than ever in her prosperous marriage to an eminent lawyer. Ma Ngwe lit a long thin cigarette — most Burmese women had a smoking habit, especially a Minkdaw like Ma Ngwe.

Angela smiled at her, 'Rarely these days, Ma Ngwe. Minthami is so seldom in Mandalay now.' She sat down on a couch covered in expensive white vellum.

'I'm very sorry your uncle, the British Resident, died from so much worry in those bad years we had,' Ma Ngwe said.

'It's sometime ago now ... but yes, I do miss him. He wasn't all crusty old bachelor. He could be surprisingly human sometimes. I'm sorry, too, your aunt Daw Khin Htay died.'

Ma Ngwe, her cheeks like two bright pink apples, said sweetly and sadly, 'Daw Khin Htay has not found her peace yet. Sometimes Ma Ngwe hears her spirit in Hope Tree where she would sit and talk to her child and her King.'

It sounded all rather far-fetched and superstitious to Blaize Tennent-Browne who changed the subject. 'Tell me, Angela darling, about that delicious man Nathan Vorne who seems to occupy a little place behind your veiled eyes — oh, don't scowl at me like that darling, a woman can't hide her feelings for the man she, shall we say, admires? What was I saying? Oh yes, is he really married to some sort of native princess?'

'She's a Shan princess, Bee.'

'*C'est la même chose,*' Lady Bee murmured. She put down her cup and saucer. Leaning back, she patted her dark hair and beneath languid eyes looked curiously at Angela — the oddest Buddhist nun she'd ever seen. 'How can a marriage like theirs be legal? I mean, presuming he's a Christian and she's a little Buddhist princess, very devout to all accounts, the Church wouldn't sanction their marriage unless she became a Christian, and apparently she's not, so legally they're not married.'

'I've no idea, Blaize. What Nathan Vorne and Minthami do is their business. It concerns no one else.'

'Darling, you may like to pull the wool over your own

eyes, but you can't pull it over mine. I've seen the shifty little glances you two give each other when one or other of you thinks no one is looking ... Oh look, you two girls,' she said to Milly Sinclair and Miss Latchmirandi, 'Why don't you go and play mah-jong or i-ching or something! This is an old woman's conversation not suitable for your tiny ears.' Reluctantly they moved away into a corner where they amused themselves by playing the piano.

Claire Sinclair, unfortunately, remained beside Mrs Sundevava and Ma Ngwe, all agog as to what Lady Tennent-Browne meant to say to the nun. 'I'm talking about the legitimacy of a Christian-Buddhist marriage. There isn't any. They can't have got married in a church, it wouldn't have been permitted if she hadn't renounced her Buddhist doctrines, and the Burmese don't commit themselves to marriage as we do — why, the women don't even take their husbands' names when they marry. Ask Ma Ngwe. He's only living with her, therefore their children are illegitimate — bastards in other words, without wishing to shock anyone.'

Clare Sinclair gasped and turned pink as she held her small thin hands over her enormous abdomen. Angela did not know why, but she took an instantaneous dislike to Matthew's 'miserable little wife' as she mentally viewed her: If he had required to marry anyone off the rebound, she felt he could have made a better job of it.

Mrs Sundevava adjusted her sari from the umpire's corner and watched with deep interest the game being played between the nun and the lady. She had encountered many Memsahibs like Blaize Tennent-Browne — though perhaps not quite so flamboyant — sallow-faced, spiteful, frustrated women with no interest whatsoever in the East. With all the time in the world at their disposal while husbands and servants pampered them, they had nothing better to do with their narrow lives than pose with the poisoned tongue and tear limb-from-limb those unfortunates who happened to be 'tainted-with-the-tarbrush' on the maidan of Empire. It was doubly

229

unfortunate tonight that their host, Captain de Veres-Vorne, had been made their target, or rather, his two olive-skinned sons. So Mrs Sundevava reflected and waited. Ma Ngwe began to look on a little unhappily and Clare Sinclair gloated as she viewed Matthew's ex-fiancée with envy and jealousy.

Angela put down her empty cup, keeping her composure remarkably well she thought, in view of Blaize's vicious remarks that were hardly the kind of conversation propriety demanded. On this occasion — done for sensationalism and her own spitefulness — Angela felt that the kindest thing she could do was to say goodnight to everyone present and thus put an end to Lady Bee's pleasure. Relinquishing her comfortable seat on Nathan's white couch, a commotion on the verandah at that moment, drew everyone's attention.

THREE

'It's all right everyone! Just go back inside, it's only for Matthew.' Nathan ushered them all back to his drawing-room and furnished them with more drinks and sweets. 'Sing Christmas carols, if you wish,' he said before shutting the double doors on his guests.

Out on the verandah Matthew, in a conspiratorial whisper to the Burman who had crept up the verandah steps like a dacoit, said: 'Ba Say, I'm very angry with you coming here to Captain Vorne's house like this. If anyone finds out what you're doing we'll all be for the chop.'

'Ba Say very sorry, Thakin Sinclair,' he whispered in the darkness, moving his white muslin scarf away from his mouth, 'but very grave things Ba Say have to tell British Assistant of Mandalay.'

'Very well, get on with it then,' Matthew said peevishly, taking off his glasses and wiping them. Nathan was standing close by, listening to what Ba Say had to tell them.

'They start many riots again in city. Much burning, many people dead in massacre. They try to burn down Gospel Mission, but Preacher-man he and many followers able to put out fire before it do much damage. Also, Pathan Sundevava, he have warehouse go up in flames.'

'Is that all?' Matthew said, replacing his glasses on his nose and repocketing the cloth he kept to wipe them.

Ba Say looked offended, not realizing that the man he was speaking to had not meant to sound facetious: 'Ba Say risk very bad danger with secret news from right inside den of lion's mouth to tell Thakin Sinclair there is secret treaty now with French for ruby mines and even Shan States.'

'Why didn't you say so in the first place? All right Ba Say. I'm coming back to Mandalay immediately. Buzz off now.'

Ba Say crept back into the darkness of the trees shadowing the house. 'I suppose we'd better tell old Pathan about his warehouse,' Matthew said to Nathan who had been standing like a shadow, smoking his pipe in the background. 'I'll have to get back, Nathan. I'm sorry.'

Nathan nodded: 'Duty calls us all. I'll fetch Sundevava.'

He was back presently with the Indian gentleman. 'Oh my goodness me!' exclaimed Pathan Sundevava. 'They have done for me good and proper now if my sugar goes up in flames. It is these wicked Bos, these leaders of vicious bands of thugs in the pay of the Taingda Mingyi and his corrupt ministers. For a long time now I have refused to give into their system of bribery and corruption, not put my hand in my pocket to give the Bos-Colonels this so-called 'protection' money they want from me to safeguard my premises. If they have now set fire to my warehouse, the next time it will be the house in which my wife and child live. It is very wicked. I must go. Please excuse me Captain Vorne. I must flee to the scene of the crime straightaway.'

'Nathan,' Matthew said, 'if these racketeers are setting

231

alight to property out at Go Wain, what about your own warehouses up-river?'

Nathan's lips, pulled tightly back from his teeth in more of a grimace than a smile, made no bones of the fact it would be more than the dacoits bargained for; 'My own racketeers will see to it those warehouses stay intact. I'll soon get to hear if there's any monkey-business with the de Veres-Vorne Company. But I will get over there as soon as the party's over — when I can decently get everyone out of Whitewalls without scaring the hell out of them.'

'I think the party's over — for tonight anyway,' said Matthew with a heavy sigh. 'Sometimes I wish Adrian Hawes was back in his old seat ... I'll go and tell Clare to prepare to go home. Thanks for a nice evening, Nathan.' He held out his hand.

Nathan's concentration was on the Mandalay sky. His left hand coming to rest on their handshake, he said to Matthew, 'Hang fire a moment — the glow up there tells me it isn't the Star of Bethlehem. I think the ladies would be far better off remaining here tonight than try to get back through the city.' Removing his pipe from his mouth, he placed it in an ashtray on a wicker verandah table. 'Fee Tam will be around to make them comfortable. That'll provide me with an excuse to accompany you back to Mandalay. I want to find out what's happening — they'd better not have set fire to the Shwe Emporium, otherwise Supalayat and her Hlutdaw can pay for the damage.'

'Edwin and Leigh won't want to stay behind,' Matthew said unhappily. 'I'm awfully sorry we've broken up your party like this, Nathan.'

'Not your fault,' Nathan said briskly. 'We can go and give poor old Edom Gideon a hand with the fire-fighting.'

Angela refused to remain at Whitewalls when she heard about the rioting. 'I must get back,' she insisted out of hearing of the other women present.

Nathan hissed at her in the glow of lamplight on his

verandah, 'You're surely not walking back barefoot through the streets of Mandalay tonight!' He stuck his face close to hers for emphasis.

'I surely am, Nathan. If there are injured people in the streets, then I can be of assistance — that's what nuns are for at times of distress. I'm often out with others from the Convent if we're needed at night for some reason.'

'Not this night, its too dangerous.'

'I've lived with danger for the past six years. I'm used to it,' she continued stubbornly.

His eyes narrowing, Nathan looked at her steadily. Then he said, tight-lipped, 'My word Amagyi-Angela, if I was that old Sayadaw of yours, I'd have tanned your hide and sent you back to England years ago. What a sting in the Kuthodaw you must be to him.' He glanced up then and saw Matthew's wife silhouetted in the verandah door-way, the light thrown all around her, appearing to him like the Virgin Mary.

'Matthew,' she said, sounding like a death knell as her eyes sought him out in the semi-darkness, her hand clutching her over-burdened stomach, 'I — I think ... the baby's coming.'

Nathan swore, his head sinking between his two arms levering on the wicker table while standing there arguing fiercely with Angela, 'Christ! That's all we need!' Angela, smiling at him, said: 'I shouldn't be at all surprised. It is after all Christmas Eve!'

CHAPTER SEVENTEEN

ONE

Angela felt her whole life was being spent in mopping up other peoples' perspiration. A cold compress in her hand, she bathed Clare's face.

The men had done a disappearing act the moment Clare had announced her condition, Nathan whisking off with Matthew, Leigh and Edwin to investigate the situation in Mandalay. The Sundevavas and Ma Ngwe and her husband had also departed. Angela could not forget, nor forgive Nathan his look of undisguised relish in gaining the upper hand at her expense while he announced softly in the lamplight, 'Well now, Amagyi-Angela, since it's Christmas Eve and it looks like we've a third coming on our hands, I suggest you make yourself useful here rather than on the streets of Mandalay. Fee Tam will get you all the hot water you need, clean sheets and anything else, like lots of black coffee, hot and strong, because its going to be a long, long night.'

Why me? she asked herself, pulling off the silk cord draping aside the heavy bedroom curtains, I don't even like the woman! Angela tied the cord to the foot of the guest bed and shoved it into Clare's hands.

'Here,' she said, 'grab hold of that when the pain gets unbearable. Scream as much as you like. All the men have gone, including your husband — and Blaize Tennent-Browne won't hear you, she's asleep.' Angela realized she was being very unfair to Matthew's wife, but she was still furious that Nathan Vorne had had his moment of triumph as he imposed his will on hers.

As it was Clare's third child, the labour progressed steadily and without complication. Clare behaved herself remarkably well, doing exactly as nature had shown her twice before, helped along by the Amagyi-Angela's rather intimidating manner. Angela issued her orders briskly and with a no-nonsense clause to not only Clare but also Fee Tam shuffling in and out on stunted feet. Half-an-hour before the baby was born, Milly Sinclair emerged sleepily to lend her assistance, for which consideration Angela was grateful — young Milly was a girl after her own heart.

Another daughter was born to Clare and Matthew at seven o'clock in the morning. She had come without any fuss. By the time Matthew arrived back with Nathan, at eleven o'clock, the hour of tiffin, the house and everything else had been restored to order with Clare sitting up in bed nursing her baby.

Angela sat on the front steps of Whitewalls, a steaming cup of coffee in her hands. Matthew went upstairs to visit his wife and child and to reassure Clare the other two children were being well looked after by faithful servants who had removed them to the safety of the British Residency, in view of the fact that Kyauktawgyi Road, where the Sinclairs lived, was not a safe place to be. He was still in evening dress from the night before, now somewhat bedraggled, as was Nathan, indolently leaning against a pillar, eyes bloodshot, his face and shirt grimy and with a wide grin showing chimney-sweep's impish white teeth. With a flourish he produced something from behind his back. 'Happy Christmas!' he said, handing her a bunch of tight-fisted Burmese roses, peach-pink and sweet-smelling.

'Why, thank you Nathan,' Angela said, pleased as well as touched by his gallant gesture. Her confusion made her say the wrong thing, 'But oughtn't these to go to the lady upstairs?'

Something alien flickered in his face and without another word he turned on his heel and went inside his house.

235

Angela buried her face in his roses, cursing herself for her clumsy handling of such a delicate situation. But she saw only an empty chair, an empty place at an elaborate Christmas dinner-table, and a beautiful marble house empty of the wife and hostess for whom it had all been intended ...

Matthew came outside. 'Hello Angela,' he said, seeing her bowed form huddled on the top step of the verandah in an attitude of abject weariness. He cleared his throat; 'Thanks so much for what you did for Clare last night.'

Angela raised her head, turning slightly to look at him standing behind her shoulder in an attitude of unforgiving rigidity that still dogged their meetings. His tired eyes flickered from her face to the roses, then back to her face. Angela said; 'No trouble at all Matthew. It's a lovely baby who made no fuss. What are you going to call her?'

He hesitated, fumbling with his glasses, taking them off before moving away to stand with his back against a supporting pillar. 'Clare and I haven't decided. I'd like to name her after you for having brought her into the world ... that's if you have no objection.'

Angela could not meet his eyes, but instead turned her face to the garden and the monkey-puzzle tree, blue-black against a golden sky. 'I'm flattered. But I don't think it would be a good idea. Clare might not like it.'

'Yes. You're probably right.' He put on his glasses again, his expression reverting to one of studious official-dom disguising the gentle sensitivity underneath. And because he always made her feel so damn guilty, she found herself always being short with him — or distant!

After a while Angela said; 'How are things in Mandalay?'

'Getting from bad to worse.' He pulled a wry face. 'Not content with burning Bhamo to the ground a few months ago, now they're trying to do the same to Mandalay.'

'But why Matthew, why? What *do* these people

236

want?' Angela looked up at him, her expression angry and bewildered.

'What we all want I suppose. The stability and fairness that comes with good government.'

'Well then, the right-thinking Burmese had better get Prince Nyaungyan Min back from India to give it to them, because Upper Burma won't get it with Thibaw and Supalayat who are only out for themselves. I've seen how those two sometimes behave, just like a couple of young children who become bad-tempered when they can't get any sweets. Its not Thibaw as much as Supalayat though. She and the Taingda Mingyi run this country according to their own laws.'

Matthew nodded. 'Don't I know it. They're both pro-French which doesn't make my task any easier. The French themselves are fanning the flames of unrest because the moment Upper Burma's at her weakest they'll walk straight in from Tonking and take over.'

'What are the British Government doing?' she asked him since he was in the forefront of diplomatic affairs going on between Mandalay and Rangoon.

Matthew concentrated on the toes of his scuffed and dusty shoes. 'Nothing. For the moment. They're not prepared to interfere unless it directly affects us.'

'Oh, come off it, Matthew! Five years ago it directly affected us. We both remember the wave of revulsion that swept Rangoon and London when the papers revealed what had taken place in Mandalay during three Coronation days proclaiming Thibaw and Supalayat as the new monarchs of Upper Burma. I'm not saying anyone should have stepped in to interfere or to take over the country for themselves as France — and ourselves — might have wished. All I'm saying is, with all the mass-murder taking place — condoned through silence — a firm stance should have been made to get Thibaw and Supalayat off the throne they'd usurped and hand it back to its rightful heirs. Either the Einshemin, or his brother Prince Nyaung Ok if Nyaungyan Min was too old or sick to rule. That's all I'm saying. But now,

237

five years hence, it's too late to do anything about what is happening here. Thibaw and Supalayat are too firmly ensconced on their Dragon Throne.'

Matthew gave her a shrewd glance. 'Five years is no time at all when other people are all the time after your power, glory and wealth. It's no time at all in the life of a country, but it's a very long time in government. Thibaw and Supalayat have tried to do away with everyone who poses a threat to them. Even exiled princes are hounded wherever they are until they conveniently vanish. Anyone remotely suspected of furthering a pretender's cause is eliminated, especially those involved in financing Nyaung Ok's claim to the throne. Things can't go on in that way. The reason why we're witnessing all this bloodshed and unrest now is because a great dissatisfaction is sweeping the country through government mismanagement and corruption. Leigh Buchanan tells me he hasn't been paid for four months by Thibaw. Soldiers, Royal Troops, they're left in the same predicament as are all those in Thibaw's employ. No wonder gangs of thugs roam loose, looting and burning. The Bos-Colonels have everything their way, so dissatisfied customers join them. And as long as a blind eye is turned as far as racketeering and profiteering is concerned, with half the money seeing its way into the pockets of corrupt Ministers, then Upper Burma will seethe with rebellion. Things are bound to come to a head sooner or later.'

'Well as long as it isn't our heads,' Angela said, suddenly very tired of everything.

Matthew took out his handkerchief and wiped his streaming brow. 'How nice it would be to see some snow today,' he remarked with a touch of nostalgia.

Angela regarded him sympathetically. 'Matthew, I should try and get some rest. Clare and the baby are fine, but you look dead on your feet. I'm sure Nathan will give you a couch somewhere so you can put your head down for an hour or two. Milly will take care of things if I can't keep my eyes open — like you.' She smiled one of her rare and beautiful smiles, her eyes yellow-green in the sunlight, her concern for him genuine.

He seemed to take a deep, deep breath, his lips inhaling tightly, while his shoulders hunched themselves into a knot of pain he was desperate to rid himself of. 'You know, I think the reason why I fell in love with you aboard the *SS Tahara* was your ability to make me feel so good even when I knew I was unworthy of you.'

Angela set down her coffee cup on the marble step and gathering up her pink robe, ran without stopping until she was out of sight of Whitewalls. Only then did she slow her pace to walk with some dignity back to the Sasana Pagoda to feed the sacred turtles.

TWO

Three months later Milly Sinclair pushed along a wicker baby-carriage on an expedition which led her effortlessly to the river, and Nathan Vorne's house out on the Bund. It was very early yet, not six o'clock, and Milly needed to get the day's exercise done and out of the way before the heat made any exercise out of the question.

She had her eyes on the lovely white house set on its green hillside above the river, all but invisible through a park of trees. Tall Sailor Palms imported from Singapore, feathery white bamboo, golden mohur, mauve jacaranda, flame-of-the-forest, the purple-green monkey tree, a perfect setting for a palatial house. An impressive porticoed facade, verandahs on either side at ground level. Another verandah sweeping around the first floor rooms with their long shaded windows. More arched windows on the second floor. It was all so symmetrically pleasing. Milly could almost see the graceful Southern Plantation house on whose lines Nathan Vorne must have built this one. After all the flimsy bamboo, mud and thatch, Whitewalls seemed a Palace, and not even the best residential homes cropping up fast in Mandalay's suburbs were a patch on Captain Nat's Whitewalls.

Milly became aware of two men on horseback. She

had been walking the river-road on her early morning jaunts from the baby Sarah's sixth week in early February, and had met neither Nathan Vorne nor Leigh Buchanan. This morning she ran into them both.

'Good morning, Miss Sinclair,' Nathan and Leigh greeted her cheerily, and not without some astonishment. They dismounted and doffed sun helmets. 'You're up early and far from home, Miss Milly,' Nathan said.

'Yes,' said Milly shyly, 'but it's good exercise and fresh air for the children. There's smallpox in the street so I thought it best to keep out of harm's way as much as possible.'

'Well, I guess that's a good enough excuse,' Nathan smiled down at her. Chestnut curls tumbled from under her sola topi, her grey eyes like a misty morning by the river.

Milly had not been aware that Nathan Vorne was back in Mandalay. Most of the time he appeared to be down in Rangoon with his wife and sons, who were being educated there — or so she had heard through the inevitable gossip-mongers.

Leigh Buchanan said, 'You know Miss Sinclair, you oughtn't to come out so far by yourself. It's dangerous in view of all the cut-throats roaming at large these days ... especially along this lonely river road.'

She smiled up at him in her mild and gentle fashion, her extreme youthfulness tempered by an air of practicality. 'I don't think, Mr Buchanan, we can live our lives in total fear all the time. Besides, no cut-throat would find much to rob from the likes of me, squalling children and ayah.'

In a peculiarly distant manner, Leigh reverted to stroking his horse's neck, thinking how totally wrong charming Milly Sinclair was.

Nathan said hospitably, 'Why don't we all go inside and have some chota-hazri instead of talking out in the road? You can't have breakfasted yet, Miss Milly, and it's a long time to tiffin. You and the children must be in need of a drink.'

'Thank you, Captain Vorne,' Milly said, 'but I'd better turn round and go home now. It wouldn't be fair to impose ourselves on you in such a casual fashion. Besides, they might start getting worried at home if we're away too long. But thank you all the same.' She turned away.

Leigh was disappointed. He had thought a great deal about Milly Sinclair during the past three months, and had welcomed this chance meeting to renew his acquaintance with her. Verity, God bless her, settled the matter for him.

'Verity is very hot and thirsty and wants to go to the bathroom. She doesn't like sitting in the bushes like Jubela.'

'Verity!' Milly scarlet-faced in confusion, scolded her brother's four-year-old daughter who was too precocious by far! Peter, the next oldest, sitting at the other end of the new baby's carriage, took his thumb from his mouth and lisped in agreement with his sister:

'Thirsty too. Want orange juice.' He stuck his thumb back into his mouth.

Nathan laughed, 'Come on then, bring them up to the house, Miss Milly, I think you're outnumbered!'

'Verity wants a ride ...'

'Hush Verity,' Milly whispered.

'No indeed, she shall ride a cock-horse to Banbury Cross ... get up here, whoops-a-daisy!' He mounted, keeping her in the saddle in front of him, where Verity giggled delightedly.

Leigh seized his opportunity and walked beside Milly to the house while Jubela brought up the rear with Peter and the baby. The horses were handed over to a syce who had come out as soon as he heard hooves scrunching on gravel. Nathan asked Ko Lee to attend to breakfast for everyone, and to bring fresh fruit-juices for the children. Afterwards he disappeared, whether through necessity or design, Milly did not know, only that she suddenly found herself alone with Leigh Buchanan.

She knew she had no right to be here. Feeling horribly

conspicuous, she stammered an excuse; 'I really feel I'm imposing on Captain Vorne. I oughtn't to be here uninvited ...' She faltered, stood up, sat down, not knowing what to do except pretend to be anxiously keeping an eye on Verity and Peter rolling on the grass while the baby slept contentedly in its carriage. Milly was only glad he continued to study the marble tiles at his feet.

She stood up again: 'I — I mustn't stay. Please would you convey my apologies to Captain Vorne, Mr Buchanan.'

'Leigh ... please call me Leigh, Milly.' He lifted his head to look at her then, and became suddenly aware of her distress. 'Please don't go, it's all right Milly, Nathan won't think you're imposing on him, he's not like that. And if you're worried about being alone with me, the ayah is six feet away and we have been introduced ... haven't we?' He smiled, gently persuasive, trying to put her at her ease. 'Come on, sit down and tell me why and how you come to be in Mandalay. We didn't get much of an opportunity to talk the last time we met, what with riots and babies being born. Please Milly?'

Reluctantly she sat down again. Four places had been set at the breakfast table. As she did not think the fourth place was likely to be Jubela's, Milly felt somewhat relieved that Minthami was at home to be her chaperon.

Ko Lee came onto the verandah, immaculate in white linen jacket with shining brass buttons, his black trousers well pressed. Always the 'Captain's right-hand man', Ko Lee was very conscious of it. Silver bowls of fruit, pawpaws, limes, mangoes, bananas, plantains, apricots, peaches and pineapple, the variety was infinite, all set down on a snowy cloth. Fruit juice came in crystal jugs with beaded muslin covers to keep off the flies, and from the kitchen quarters she could smell fresh-baked bread and ground coffee. Pretty chintz covers and cushions adorned the white wicker and wrought iron furniture, plants and shrubs in huge clay pots spilled colour and greenery onto the verandah.

Conscious of what Milly must have been thinking while her dreamy eyes took in her surroundings, Leigh

242

coaxed her out of her shyness. 'Do you like Burma, Milly?' he asked, while Nathan's servants and Ko Lee hovered around them.

'I don't know whether I do or not, Mr Buchanan. It's all rather ... I think primitive is the word. I don't know. I haven't been here very long, and I don't suppose I'm staying that long. It was only supposed to be a temporary arrangement. My real home's in Coimbatore where father is District Commissioner.' She kept her grey eyes firmly upon her clasped hands reposing in her lap.

Leigh Buchanan thought Milly Sinclair to be the sweetest girl he'd ever met. It was like finding snowdrops in Mandalay, sweet, cool, pure and infinitely pleasing. He wished to know more, much more about her.

'Tell me about Coimbatore,' he said.

'Oh, there's nothing much to tell. We're from a large family — eleven children. Our eldest brother is fifteen years older than Matthew. We came last. Matthew's nearest to me in age and even so, there's seven years difference. But we've always been rather close. Are you in the Army, Mr Buchanan? I only ask because I heard something about your being in Thibaw's Army when we were at Captain Vorne's dinner party.'

'No,' he smiled. 'I'm in nobody's Army in the true sense of the word. I'm a civilian. It's true to say I started out my career at a Military Academy, but then I got side-tracked into the Post and Telegraph Service. I'm by profession a Telegraph Engineer–Operator, but I also teach. I got a posting in Thibaw's Army as a civilian instructor, laying down the foundations for a full and comprehensive telegraph service throughout Upper Burma. I have to rely on the co-operation of the British in Rangoon and the Burmese up on the Northern frontiers to do my job at all. It's difficult at times, but also a satisfying challenge. At the moment the Irrawaddy is the main form of communication here, and that's a slow old process. What telegraph that does exist is not enough. So that's my job, to speed up communication in this country.'

243

'I see. I suppose a railway would help as well?'

'That's coming too.'

'It's all rather exciting. To live in a country and in an age where we can see all these advances taking place right under our nose.' Milly had unconsciously relaxed in his company. They were so engrossed in talking to one another they were hardly aware of 'the voice' coming along the verandah until Blaize Tennent-Browne intruded upon them.

'Well I never, a lovey-dovey little tête-à-tête, how sweet! Good morning Leigh, Milly. Darling what on earth are you doing here so early in the morning? Oh, don't answer that question if it embarrasses you two lovebirds ... but naughty, naughty Leigh — I know now who's been putting the love-light in your eyes.' She wagged an accusing finger at them, and thoroughly dismayed they both turned scarlet while Leigh silently cursed Lady Tennent-Browne's flat-footed approach calculated to scare Milly off faster than anything.

Oblivious to the embarrassment she had caused, she turned as Nathan re-emerged for breakfast. He held her chair while she seated herself decorously, first depositing an attaché-case she had brought with her under the table. She removed riding-gloves before placing a well-laundered white table-napkin in her lap. Milly, half-standing, half-sitting like Leigh, both of them not knowing what to do with her sudden descent upon them, had the oddest feeling Lady Tennent-Browne had breakfasted here on more than one occasion.

'Do sit down you two,' Blaize said, waving them back into their chairs.

Only when Verity fell down and cut her knee in one of her boisterous games on the gravel path, did Milly have an excuse to jump up from the table. Leigh quickly gulped down his hot coffee. 'I think I'd better see Miss Sinclair back to Mandalay,' he said in rather a rush. 'Not a safe place to walk alone with the children.'

'Good idea,' said Nathan, chewing a crust with deep concentration. Leigh turned aside, feeling rather hot around the collar and thanking Lady Bee for it. 'Take Danny Boy,' said Nathan helping himself to marmalade, 'Verity can ride home with her bad knee.'

'Oh, please don't go to so much bother for us,' Milly said. 'Ayah and I can manage perfectly well and you don't have to come at all Mr Buchanan. It's six miles there and back, and you must have other things you'd rather be doing.'

He couldn't tell her there was nothing he would rather do than walk her home. 'I insist,' said Leigh. 'Come on Verity, let's go and find Danny Boy.' He took the little girl's hand so there was an end to the argument.

'Thank you, Captain Vorne,' Milly called, waving to him from the path, 'the chota-hazri was delicious.'

'Pleasure,' Nathan called from the verandah. 'Give my regards to Matthew and Clare.' He turned back to Blaize who was eyeing the little scene with extreme amusement, her dimples deep and naughty. 'Lady Bee, if you breathe one word that might embarrass Leigh and Milly, you'll be hoist by your own petard.'

'That darling,' she said drumming long buffed fingernails on the back of his hand, 'is a petard I shan't be able to resist.'

He withdrew his hand to pour himself more coffee. Lounging back in his curved chair he looked her in the eye. 'Business first, pleasure later. What's in Edwin's briefcase this time?'

She brought it out from under the table. 'He wishes me to impress upon you the utmost secrecy surrounding these papers. Darling, in other words, this very confidential information must not fall into anybody's hands except the C.C.'s.'

'Seeing how I'm your half-wit messenger boy,' he said gruffly, 'when I lay me my neck on the chopping block, I make good and sure the knife's nowhere in sight. What kind of bomb have Matthew and Edwin put aboard my boat this time?'

'Arms darling. Being smuggled in via Tonking. Martini-rifles by the cartload.'

245

He threw back his head and began to laugh loudly.

Blaize affronted, drew herself up. 'And what may I ask is the cause of such hilarity? Contravening the Treaty of Yandabo is hardly a laughing matter, Captain Vorne!'

'I agree. From where I sit on the sidelines I can't see if you Britishers are being deliberately stupid as far as the Burmese mentality is concerned, or underneath your seeming naivety you're as devious as the Burmese. Smuggling of arms, men, drugs, secrets, anything you care to mention has been taking place ever since the British and the Burmese signed their first commercial treaty and the road to China was opened up to them. Putting your foot down now regarding arms coming in from across the northern frontiers, isn't going to stop the Burmese smilingly agreeing to British demands while carrying on in exactly the same way as before.' He helped himself to more coffee. Blaize's fingers walking up his shirtsleeve while he was drinking it made him aware of another direction this chota-hazri was taking.

'Darling, I love it when you get so angry! All that passion behind those blazing blue eyes, lips and tongue on the rampage. Mmmm, golden hair like a crusader's halo. All that wildness can surely be put to better use? Now that we've dispensed with business ...' Her hand slipped into the warm dark shadows his open-necked shirt afforded her touch. Her eyes narrowingly seductively against the crisp tickle in the palm of her hand, she pouted prettily. 'We have all the time in the world. Edwin isn't expecting me home till tiffin, so darling ...?'

Hand-cuffing her wrists in a grip that made her wince he jerked her closer to his chest, bringing her nose to nose with him. 'So darling,' he drawled in lazy Southern tones unpracticed though not forgotten, 'as much as I'd love to jump into my bed with you this very minute, I have me a boat to catch, orders to give, and darn me if I haven't forgotten to feed the turtles at the Sasana!'

Nathan walked off along the verandah, his shout, demanding Ko Lee, made her blood curdle.

CHAPTER EIGHTEEN

ONE

Nathan hoped to reach Rangoon in six days — hopefully five — allowing for the idiosyncrasies of a river jam-packed with all kinds of craft from sampans and sedge rafts carrying whole villages to the I.F.C.'s double decked steamers.

As much a water-gipsy as any Inle leg-rower, he never liked the journey south as much as going northward to Bhamo, his last trading stop on nine hundred miles of navigable river. Nowhere was there scenery like that, following the river through Burma's jungles to rocky gorges and soaring mountains, waterfalls plunging hundreds of feet into the valleys of the Salween and Irrawaddy. Up near Lashio and Loloi, in that Shan country of green hills, mountain air, misty lakes, he felt his best, satiated by the kind of life the Shans offered.

He looked to the wash of the *Belle Hélène II*, his brand new, fast steamboat; to Findebar, Ko Lee, Tonsin and the rest of his crew; to coolies, wading in and out of the water in wide pointed hats of straw; to elephants chained to the mighty teak, felled logs tumbling to the water, where they were lashed into rafts floated by the rivermen of the Bombay-Burma Teak Corporation to Rangoon. With the adventurer's bubbling enthusiasm and inquisitive eye, Nathan knew that the stimulus the East gave to his soul would never diminish.

Nathan presented his papers for inspection at Thayetmyo on the border between Upper and British Burma.

Twenty-four hours later he reached Rangoon and found an anchorage in that magnificent harbour of the South where impressive warships of Her Britannic Majesty, Queen Victoria, danced side by side with humbler vessels like the sampan, steamer, and fishing-boat. Rangoon defied Nathan, it always had. It hurt him, mocked him, taunted him and drove him back to the heart of the real Burma every time — Mandalay. Rangoon was not his city. Nor was it Minthami's. Ever since they had become Supalayat's targets, one moment all favours from her, the next reprisals, uncertainty had driven them to Rangoon. Like so many under Thibaw and Supalayat's yoke of oppression, Nathan had decided it was best to be prudent by dwelling in Rangoon for the time being. Dull — yes, exciting and challenging — no. Nathan knew which he preferred, but for the sake of Minthami and his sons accepted the freedom anonymity in Rangoon spelled.

Sunlight lanced flames from Mindon Min's wonderful golden-jewelled hti of the Shwe Dagon, dazzling his eyes and his heart. He crossed the Pazundaung Bridge to stroll round the lake, view the orange-gold Pagoda Mindon Min had endowed with a diamond orb, jewelled vane, cone and hti encrusted with more jewels, then to wend his way back into the heart of the city. He always took this route when coming off his boat, finding his shore-legs again after a week on the Irrawaddy, refreshing his memory, blowing away cobwebs, musing upon over-dressed British in suited boater and sola topi, upon the longyi and guang-baung, the parasol and golden umbrella, bare feet, clogs and Burmese sandals stepping off pavements to accommodate Northampton leather. A city of contrasts, a hybrid, a Noah's ark. He was the observer, the neutral, the sceptic, and he shuddered at the price of Colonialism.

Gharrys, rickshaws, tongas fought for customers and deafened him. So did the bells of the Shwe Dagon vying with the golden thin finger of the ancient Sule Pagoda close to Chinatown where he and Minthami rented premises. Street-vendors, kaka-shops, opium-dens, bustle, corruption, noise, heat, smells, he had come back to a part of town as far removed from the elegant British Port Authority Building, as Rangoon from Mandalay.

He was hot, tired, dusty and a little bit irritable by the time he arrived home. The Sino-Asian quarter fascinated as much as it appalled him. Nathan ducked his head under the clothes blowing on the wide walkway of verandah leading to his own apartment. God, he thought to himself, while shifting his kitbag from one shoulder to the other in search of his doorkey, why had he ever let Minthami sweet-talk him into living in this slum?

Between two sets of dingy washing strung across the verandah, he and another man collided. Dressed in a white satin jacket with jewelled buttons, a checked longyi denoted him to be a man of rank. The Burman, startled, muttered a hasty apology — more through instinct than deference, Nathan guessed — as he stooped to retrieve his fallen key. Too late he realized the Burman had fled into the lines of washing, descended the verandah steps, and disappeared into the crowd milling about underneath the over-hanging verandah balcony. Nathan swore, wondering about the man's business.

He let himself into his apartment, his mood not enhanced by that brush with the cocky Burman. He slammed the door harder than the man going out had done, his temper getting the better of him. Minthami came running into the entrance hall, a canary-yellow towel worn turban fashion round her long black hair, another yellow towel draping her like a short sarong from bosom to thigh. Her eyes lit up when she saw him 'Sa-Lon,' she said, calling him by the name of water-gipsy reserved only for moments of great affection, 'you back!' She flung creamy arms around his neck, nose nuzzling his in the Burmese way of kissing. Sometimes he enjoyed her behaving like a colt, other times, not. Right now he felt as if she'd punched him where it hurt most. He untangled her arms and flung his kitbag into a dark corner of the tiny vestibule from which four thin-bamboo doors led off into other rooms.

Observing the mood he was in, Minthami sighed help-lessly: 'So, you not want wife, she make supper for Thakin Vorne.' On the threshold of the kitchen she turned back with a pout. 'Why you not tell Minthami you come home? No wire, no letter, no nothing. Min-thami hear nothing for weeks, and always she think American Captain drown in river.' She clucked her tongue disapprovingly. 'Minthami, she very lonely with-out Shwe Nat but he never care. He always away some-where making more money and more money.'

'Who was that man?' he asked.

'What man?' Minthami put on her blank expression. 'Minthami not know any man ...'

In two blind strides of rage, he crossed the hall to grab her by her bare shoulders: 'Quit playing games with me Minthami! I've known you long enough to know when you're lying. I saw a man, a too-damn-smart Burman leave these premises. I want to know who he is.'

Her eyes flashed dangerously. Minthami did not like being handled like a woman he might have picked up off the streets. She pushed his hands away. 'Minthami not know where you are, what you do, what women you have, and you come home five minutes and accuse wife of being with other man. You crazy!'

'Who was that man?' he asked evenly.

It was a tone of voice Minthami had learned to recog-nize. When the Shwe Nat looked at her with eyes of fire and white pinched face, his voice deep from inside, she knew what to expect. But Minthami was not intimidated by him, not like some. She ignored the danger signals. 'Shwe Nat crazy,' she said, dismissing him to make tracks inside their tiny kitchen.

His hand shot out and grabbed her arm. 'Minthami, that man, that pompous Burman with a smirk on his flat face and a licence into *my* house. I want to know what he was doing if he wasn't licking the cream off *my* saucer — so you tell me and tell me darn quick what his dirty business was?'

250

'No Man!' she shrieked knocking his hand aside. 'Why you always talk dirty? Why you always think dirty? No one see, no one know, no one care, you crazy American Cap ...!'

Her head snapped back as he struck her.

Her yellow turban dislodged, brought her long hair cascading over her shoulders. Mute, they stared at one another. Nathan felt sickened by his action. For fifteen years they had lived together and never once had anything like this happened between them. Never once had he lifted a finger to her while she might bite, kick and scratch him. Never!

Minthami was aghast. For anyone to strike her was beyond recall. No man, no woman, no child ever laid a finger on another person's head, the highest place of honour. For the Shwe Nat to strike her face was the greatest form of dishonour imaginable. She knew, in those final moments, that the crisis in her relationship with Captain Vorne had come to a head.

Nathan took her arm and led her into the bedroom, Minthami so meek and mild, he felt a little tongue of fear lick his spine. He made her sit on the bed with him. 'What's his name?' he asked.

'U Hla Hla Han.'

'What is he?'

'He Princely blood ... Shan son of Sawbwa.'

'Where from?'

'Taunggyi.'

'He doesn't sound very Shan to me.'

'That not his real name.'

'What is it then?'

'That his stage-name.'

'What stage?'

'School of Dancing Burmese make for British.'

'What was he doing here?'

'He come to see Minthami.'

'Why?'

'Minthami lonely.'

'What else?'

251

'Nothing else. Only present.'

'What present?'

'Sacred relic of Buddha to place in shrine of house.'

He had been studying the floor at his feet, his head bowed over clenched hands, knuckles white. She, staring ahead to the square patch of blue sky beyond the window.

'Has he touched you?' Nathan asked.

She turned to him, her face scornful: 'What you mean touch?'

'I mean, you silly little Buddhist bitch, has he tumbled you in *my* bed to father you with some princely Burmese phongyi while I've been working, or ... or some butterfly spirit of daughter you're always carping about?' He thumped fists down on the bed. 'Because if he has, then I'm chucking you out right now into the Street of a Thousand Whores ... so go!' He pushed her roughly towards the door. 'Go, you ... you ...'

Minthami trembled. She shrank into herself, moving as far from him as she could. Clutching the towel to her body she said with great dignity: 'Minthami go, Captain Vorne. She not like to live with ludu and kala anymore. She not like shouting in uncivilized manner. She not like to hear evil and dirty things. Minthami, Shan princess of better culture than American Captain of no breeding except what money buy. She is no more wife of Shwe Nat of Mandalay. Her heart for him now dead, so she go with very great pleasure. This time Minthami does not come back like other times. Minthami think she know what drive American Captain to behave like crazy man and she not wish to bring him any more suffering. So he free again. Pyan-dor-may, goodbye!'

It was the most withering speech he had yet heard from her. The measure of her disdain came with the command: 'Please, to go out of bedroom while Minthami dress.'

Pale-faced, he brushed past her. 'Damn you, Minthami, I never want to see you again. You go, and by the time I get back I want you and your poisonous little

252

Buddha images out of *my* house!'

Nathan stumbled down the verandah steps, desperate to get away from the one person in the world he had respected beyond measure. He went to look for Finde-bar and Ko Lee on the water-front. With luck a liquor-bar, another Asian whore or even half-dozen of them, might take the bitter taste of fidelity out of his mouth.

TWO

The Amagyi-Angela knelt before the Queen of Burma, while the Queen amused herself on her carpeted dais. In a corner of the Queen's chamber, a Frenchwoman knelt at the piano, its legs foreshortened to accommodate lady-pianists who came before the Queen of Burma to entertain her with their music.

Supalayat sat barefoot, surrounded by little mounds of gold coins. Before her dais, Burmese women knelt to take away as much money as their two hands could carry, payment for past services. It was amusing to observe. Some of the women Angela recognized as having been the laundry-women Supalayat had had whipped only the day before in an adjoining chamber. Angela had been taking group photographs of some of the princesses far enough down the scale of lineage to present no threat to the Dragon Throne. Listening to those poor women crying and wailing while the stick was wielded on their backs for having returned badly laun-dered linen had sickened Angela so much, she had deliberately pushed her tripod into a porcelain vase, knocking it over and smashing it. Supalayat had dis-missed her immediately for being clumsy. Angela hadn't been able to get out of the Palace fast enough.

Today the Queen had summoned her again, her forgiveness spreading largesse all around. 'Amagyi-Angela,' she said, smiling sweetly as she looked up from the photographs she had been studying in the centre of her bounty, 'you have done well with these pictures. We might be persuaded to incorporate them in our album. We wonder, might it be possible for you to undertake a little journey on our behalf?'

'Where to, Madam?'

'We have heard of a big store that is well established in a place called Knightsbridge. We would greatly desire some albums to be brought to us together with one or two other little items.' She did not look up, but kept her face to the photographs strewn amongst the money.

Angela had no intention of going to Harrods in London. Her eyes lowered to the birds of paradise on Supalayat's carpet, Angela murmured: 'Madam, if I had the honour I'd be delighted. However, the pull of my homeland might be too great for me to resist, and I might find myself never returning to Mandalay with your albums.'

'In that case we shall send someone else.' The Queen dropped the photographs and smacked her hands sharply together. 'You there at the piano, we have had enough of your music today. You are dismissed. Amagyi-Angela, take away these photographs and put them in my portfolio of Mandalay. Now you may also go. We are tired. Send away everyone,' she told her ladies-in-waiting. 'What money is left put into the teak chests. Those who have been too slow in taking the money can go without. Now we wish to sleep, so draw the curtains.'

Leaving the Palace, Angela went across one of the wooden bridges that spanned the wide Palace Moat and took the South gate down towards Mandalay's markets, bazaars and shops. She had been asked by the Head Nun of the Convent to purchase some new black lacquer bowls at the Shwe Emporium.

Inside the Emporium, Angela, her arms filled with black lacquer bowls, side-stepped Mrs Wandersmeith and Nancy Stuttgart rushing in Edom Gideon's direction, and collided with a baby carriage. Her bowls crashed to the marble floor, startling everyone.

'Oh, I'm so sorry ... I do beg your pardon,' Matthew's apology was drowned by his screaming children.

Angela was so surprised to see Matthew wheeling the baby-carriage, she forgot to be angry with him for running over her bare feet. 'Matthew! What on earth ...?' Her question remained suspended. She did not want to embarrass him more than he already was. 'Haven't you any servants?' she asked, taking control of the situation.

'Er ... Milly's around here somewhere,' he looked around him, totally disorientated, his glasses steamed up. 'Clare's sick,' he took off his glasses and wiped them. 'Milly's supposed to be helping with the shopping but she seems to have disappeared with Verity.'

Angela refrained from telling him that his sister was in the arms of Mr Buchanan somewhere amongst rattan garden furniture and flourishing indoor palms. She only hoped Edom Gideon's two old trumpets hadn't seen them, otherwise, the whole of Mandalay would know within the next ten minutes. Angela's heart went out to Matthew. Hapless, helpless and harrassed she could have killed Clare for subjecting him to this indignity. 'Where's your houseboy? Haven't you got one? anyone at all who can do the marketing for you?'

'The boy's sick ... cook's scalded himself ... Excuse me Angela, I must get on ...'

'Matthew,' Angela said, stooping to retrieve her bowls, 'let me help. I'll take the children home. You get back to the Residency if that's where you're supposed to be.' While she was on her knees she stuck her head into the pram, 'you baby can stop that racket ...' She caught its tiny fist and shoved Sarah's thumb in her mouth to stop her crying. Peter, sitting at the other end of the carriage looked at her with round eyes, his thumb already back in his mouth as Angela glared at him, daring him to utter another sound. 'Matthew, what's wrong with Clare now?' Angela asked, sweeping her bowls into her Shan bag looped across her shoulder.

He seemed a little reluctant to speak. 'Er ... Clare's indisposed.'

'If it's something catching, then I'd better know.'

255

His lips flickered, a momentary ray of genuine amusement striking upon his thoughts. He said; 'No, you needn't worry, Clare's having another child.'

'My goodness, what a little rabbit she is.' Angela realized it wasn't a very tactful remark to have made and changed the subject quickly. 'I think I see Milly and Verity over there by the garden furniture. If you want to get to the office, I'll finish here with Milly and drop by the house to see Clare.'

'Thank you, Angela. I can't tell you how ... how grateful I am.' Looking much more relieved, Matthew left his ever-increasing family to her, and dashed off towards the exit.

Espying Edom Gideon bearing down on her, no doubt to tell her what God thought of her for having renounced her Christian religion, she whisked baby-carriage and contents to where she could see Milly Sinclair innocently fingering some lace, her cheeks, glowing pinkly and her eyes very bright.

Angela looked down at her foot and saw it was bleeding from a very nasty gash across her ankle. Thank you Matthew, she thought with a grim smile, I suppose it's only what I deserve after what I've done to you. 'Good morning, Milly,' she said as Milly looked up with a little smile of recognition, 'your brother's gone to do the job of work he's supposed to be doing for the I.C.S. I'm helping up at the house today if everyone's sick, so let's go.'

'Amagyi-Angela,' said Milly with a sudden surge of radiance transforming her whole being, 'Leigh has asked me to marry him. Nobody else knows as yet, only you.'

'Hmmm!' Angela grunted as she wheeled the tribe through the Shwe Emporium, 'I hope you said yes.'

CHAPTER NINETEEN

ONE

F ive hundred miles away from Mandalay, the owner of its most prodigious store woke with a start, his bed damp with perspiration. The nightmare remained with Nathan. He lay in the steamy darkness under his mosquito-net, going over in his mind recent events. He told himself he was behaving like an idiot, that no woman was worth the wits going wool-gathering. By the lake of ten thousand reflections echoing the prayers of ten thousand souls borne on the bells of the Shwe Dagon, he had drawn another blank. Everywhere these past three weeks, blank stares, blank faces, blank shaking of impatient heads — and when it came to the Oriental shielding his own, Nathan knew it was like trying to prise a tick from a dog's under-belly. Once he had thought he'd seen Minthami in the local fruit market. He had run after her, pushing and dodging, cursing in frustration to catch up with her against crowds pushing him the other way. The girl with the long hair as silky as a raven's wing, orchids in her hair, he wanted to find her again ... but when he caught up with the girl in the bazaar, she had presented the raddled face of an Eurasian prostitute. He had turned away, disheartened.

Nathan was unable to separate nightmare from reality. To help him, he reached for the bottle of rum he had taken to bed. What had the Amagyi-Angela told them at his dinner party? Life was Impermanence, Suffering and Egolessness? The Buddhists might not be

257

so bloody wrong! he reflected miserably.

What had brought home to him the finality of Minthami's departure was the removal of her little alabaster image of Buddha she kept in a shrine in the living-room. She had never taken her Buddha relics before. And so Nathan was afraid. Afraid that Minthami had taken him at his face value this time and had gone off permanently with her Buddhist boyfriend. It had taken him three weeks to come to his senses, to realize what it must have been like for her to be left alone for long periods, not knowing his whereabouts, what he was doing, who he associated with. Downright lonely was what he felt right now with only his pipe and rum to keep him company. Damn Minthami! He thought again, the gnawing ache of uncertainty weighing upon him. There were a million and one holes in which she could have disappeared, the city a blank-faced jungle of humanity greedy to swallow up a young and very beautiful woman, never to be seen or heard of again.

It was then Nathan remembered Edwin Tennent-Browne's attaché-case and the papers he was supposed to have handed over to Charles Bertram, the British Commissioner: 'Jesus Christ ...' He tumbled out of bed and stumbled into the hall.

In his kit-bag, thrown into the corner the day he'd got back, he found the attaché-case at the bottom where he had concealed it under his clothes. Taking it with him, he climbed back into bed, shoved the attaché-case under his pillow and slept with a headache for the rest of the night.

Nathan was kept waiting by the Britishers for over an hour. He had foolishly, if honestly, declared that no, he had not made an appointment to see the Chief Commissioner. He was told he would be 'slotted-in' when time permitted.

Curious, he observed sceptically the machine of grand government. The to-ing and fro-ing of all the busy little bees going about their alloted tasks in keeping the Union Jack flying from the Khyber to Cape Negrais: a hive of

Empire as solid in mien and as immovable as the Rock of Gibraltar — which also belonged to them. Grudgingly he admired them while cursing their queueing system.

'Captain de Veres-Vorne?'

'That's me.'

'The C.C. is ready to see you now, Captain. This way please.'

Nathan, attaché-case under one arm, followed the Chief Commissioner's Secretary along a maze of corridors. He was finally ushered into a very business-like room. A heavy tooled-leather desk seemed surprisingly uncluttered for the work the Chief Commissioner was supposed to have been engaged in. Polished pynkinado floorboards had their nakedness covered by bright Indian carpets. Cumbersome armchairs and tables looked bulbous, and in one corner a top-heavy aspidistra hung lethargically over the edge of its brass bowl. Behind the Chief Commissioner's desk, three long windows were heavily shrouded in lace and damask, the outside shutters half closed to filter the atmosphere inside the room into the consistency of a tropical fish-tank. Nathan felt stifled and automatically eased his tie from choking him to death. A picture of the British Queen stared coldly back at him, fanned by the pull-punkas.

Charles Bertram shook hands with Nathan. Waving him to a chair, he said abruptly, 'I was expecting you three weeks ago.' Eyebrows framed the question, so what happened?

Nathan cleared his throat, 'Yes sir ... er ...' his teeth gnawing his lower lip in a self-conscious little smile, he apologized. 'I'm sorry, but I got delayed.' Nathan quickly handed over Matthew Sinclair's and Sir Edwin's despatches.

The Chief Commissioner sifted through them swiftly, and then laid them to one side. 'I'm grateful, Captain de Veres-Vorne. It's not the sort of stuff we can send on the telegraph, and reliable couriers coming from Mandalay are hard to find. Looks like things are hotting up.'

'You might say that,' said Nathan. 'It's mighty unsettling for the merchants, us traders, as well as the people living there.'

The Chief Commissioner sat like an Archbishop, finger-tips playing gentle pat-a-cakes with each other while he deliberated. The situation in Upper Burma had become the most pressing issue on his desk these days. It appeared the Taingda Mingyi was intent upon remaining un-cooperative, Thibaw vacillating, and Supayalat a downright pain in the neck.

The British Government and the India Office were urging him to decide matters one way or another regarding the annexation of Upper Burma. He was reluctant to do so, hoping in the meanwhile the matter would resolve itself and that affairs in Upper Burma would sort themselves out without British intervention.

Under cover of Upper Burma's affairs Charles Bertram was also taking stock of his American 'courier'.

It did not escape Nathan's attention — he disliked being scrutinized so closely by people in high places. Automatically his hand went to his tie again, straightening it a little.

The Chief Commissioner leaned forward and punched a little brass desk-bell in the form of Buddha seated in the lotus position, summoning back his secretary from an adjoining room:

'Mr Gosney,' said the Chief Commissioner. 'Would you kindly fetch Major Radcliffe in here for a moment or two? Tell him I shan't detain him long.'

The door closed. Turning back to Nathan the Chief Commissioner said: 'You were in the Sagaing Fortress were you not, Captain de Veres-Vorne?'

Startled, Nathan's manner was as constrained as his answer. He had no wish to be reminded of Sagaing. 'Sure,' he said, 'I was there once. It was one time too many.'

'I understand,' said the Chief Commissioner and Nathan reflected irritably he wouldn't have understood given a million years under the Bo Tree. 'I'm given to understand you managed a remarkable escape from there,' the Chief Commissioner persisted.

'Yes,' said Nathan cautiously, feeling that he was being taken slyly along paths he had no wish to tread again.

The door opened and Mr Gosney ushered in a khaki-uniformed Major whose Sam Browne belt was aligned to a hair's breadth of perfection.

Known to the Regiment by the nickname of Raj, Major Jeffrey Arthur Radcliffe, British Military Intelligence, Dum-Dum, Calcutta, made Nathan feel decidedly nervous. More so when Charles Bertram turned to him with the adjunctive:

'Major, Captain de Veres-Vorne has brought us some valuable information from Mandalay concerning the smuggling of arms through the State of Tonking as well as some other very interesting information. He is also in the unique position of being the only European ever to have escaped the Burmese death prison at Sagaing — and lived to tell the tale. After a detention period of ten days or thereabouts in the hands of the renowned Spotted Faces, he managed to walk out of their front gates unmolested. Quite an amazing feat I think you'll agree.'

Nathan winced, the Chief Commissioner's unfortunate use of the word 'feat' conjuring painful pictures Charles Bertram knew nothing about. 'I think, in the circumstances, he's just the kind of man we're looking for,' concluded the Chief Commissioner.

'Just wait a minute, gentlemen,' said Nathan, backing away from the two official Britishers who seemed to know enough about him to make him very suspicious. It was one thing to do them an occasional favour by acting as unpaid courier, quite another matter when it began to get personal. 'This is your war, not mine,' he told them bluntly. 'I'm an American neutral who has promised the Burmese to keep his nose out of their affairs — the promise extracted in the Sagaing death prison. I don't aim me to return there, not ever. Sorry gentlemen.' He made for the door.

Unfortunately Major Radcliffe still stood up against the heavy teak panelling. Arms folded regimentally, he had almost a feline smirk under his well-manicured moustache. Even the Chief Commissioner seemed to purr as he laid a friendly hand on Nathan's shoulder. 'Relax, Captain de Veres-Vorne,' he said. 'We are not at war with the Burmese. Whatever gave you that idea? Major Radcliffe, however, is rather interested in the layout of the Sagaing Fortress, and the character of the Irrawaddy loop that takes in Ava and Sagaing. In view of your knowledge of the place, we would be awfully grateful if you'd oblige us with a little information ... now if you'll kindly excuse me gentlemen, I must press on. Thank you so much for your help, Captain de Veres-Vorne. Good day.'

It was all done so subtly, so smoothly and in such a 'gentlemanly' fashion, Nathan was still gasping at their sheer audacity when he found himself in another part of the building, staring blankly at a map of Burma on Jeffrey Radcliffe's wall. How the hell, he wondered stupidly, had he got himself mixed up in British field operations for the intended invasion of Upper Burma? He was always to rue that day.

'Captain de Veres-Vorne, any information, you can let us have on the layout of the Sagaing Fortress, will be of immense value to us as we have no intelligence on the place. I take it these walls ...' he tapped the spot with a long pointer 'would be impossible to breach either from the landward or the riverside?'

'That's right, Major. But if you had a machine that could drop cannonballs out of the sky, then I reckon you might just succeed in routing Thibaw's army holed up in there.' He then wished he hadn't made a joke of it.

Major Radcliffe scratched his moustache with the pointer, his face plainly betraying the fact he thought American frippery in this instance quite out of place. 'Quite,' he bit off the word, laid down the pointer and took out a cigarette-case. Opening it, he offered Nathan first choice.

'Thanks Major, but I only smoke me my pipe.'

'We're working on all sorts of things at Dum-Dum,' he informed Nathan as he inhaled deeply. He picked off a strand of tobacco from his tongue and concentrated on flicking ash off a knife-pleated khaki knee. 'Captain de Veres-Vorne, you do understand the necessity for utter discretion in what we say in here?' He looked up, perched as he was on the corner of his desk, his eyebrows raised.

More of a statement of fact than a question, Nathan felt irritated by the man's superior attitude. 'I understand that much, Major,' he said brusquely. 'Information I don't mind buying and selling, as I am not partial to the Burmese Royals. The rest of the Burmese are fine — happy, polite and in general a harmless bunch if you know how to handle them. They, like all human beings, prefer to be handled gently. But — and this is a mighty big but with me — I don't want to get mixed up in anything that might involve my family. We've tasted the Queen of Burma's whiplash once too often, so I don't need my neck on anyone's chopping board a second time round. Any information coming from me, I don't know anything about. I'm neutral, remember.'

Jeffrey Radcliffe gave a big smile. He gracefully sprung from the edge of his desk, wiggled his top lip, and pointed to the kite-like cartography of Burma, peppered with his own little flags, markers and pins. 'Do you happen to know the strength of Burmese arms and men, and the position of their batteries around the Sagaing Redoubt?'

'I can only give you what I vaguely remember,' said Nathan frowning at the map. 'It's more than six years ago, Major, and I don't reckon much of their positions sunk into my skull at the time, only their cudgels. I'd have to draw you a plan. The whole fort is a warren of passageways, watchtowers, ramparts, surrounding a central compound. It's an impregnable fortress for anyone trying to get in from the outside — in fact, it's easier to get out than it is to get in. Anything aiming to shoot upwards at it from the water below the Redoubt is a sitting duck for the Burmese manning the Sagaing walls with their big guns. And it's not only Sagaing, its Ava and Amarapura to think of as well, because the way the river turns and twists in this triangle is bad enough for boats concentrating on navigation without being shot at as well.'

'That's why it's imperative we know the precise strength of their army and navy,' said Major Radcliffe. 'If you'd work on drawings for me Captain, I'd be much obliged. Let me have them first thing tomorrow. In a month of Sunday mornings,' he said, pacing the floor of his office with his head bowed and hands behind his back, 'we've just *got* to be able to know everything there is to know about the Irrawaddy fortifications — everything. Otherwise we can't possibly hope to sneak a flotilla of the size we're contemplating past the Sagaing Redoubt. I would dearly like to have more information too on this gun-running business — how much of the stuff is getting through under the noses of the Chinese Black Flags. Gun-running through Tonking has increased, although the Burmese deny any such thing. But we've got to be sure of our facts. Facts, Captain!' He wheeled a hawk-like look on Nathan. 'Any ideas?'

Nathan said uncomfortably, 'Well, er, there is a chap — a Britisher, who might be able to get you facts, Major. He's in the Telegraph Service, presently in King Thibaw's employ. He's up Bhamo way. He has his ear pretty close to the ground — wire, I should say.'

'Oh good, good, get him on it ... but I want facts!'

Nathan had the oddest sensation Major Jeffrey Radcliffe wasn't really listening, that he already knew to whom he, Nathan, referred. It was possible. Every Britisher more or less knew everyone else's business out East — railway-carriages as much gossip-shops as their clubs and cantonments.

'Let me have your sketches at your earliest convenience, Captain, there's a good chap,' he repeated. 'Draw the river exactly as you know it. Any little detail, even

264

what you might consider to be the most inconsequential, might not prove to be so in the long run. We even want to know which leg the pi-dog cocks to piss against Sagaing's walls in case it suggests something. Have they got cannon on the Sagaing ramparts?'

Nathan rubbed his chin: 'There are cannon up there, but so old I reckon they were used in the first Burmese War. What make, I couldn't even begin to guess. Number and poundage I'd have to work on when I get my memory in order again. The way I see it though, if you're intending to breach these forts,' he tapped his finger in the triangle of red markers, 'Ava, Sagaing, Amarapura, you're going to have one hell of a job. This stretch of the Irrawaddy is a skipper's nightmare. The river channel between Ava and Sagaing has a long reef extending out from this loop ... to block the channel about here when the water's low. The water levels fluctuate immensely. In the monsoon season from June to September it's about twenty to thirty feet above its lowest level in December — and that monsoon level can remain high until about mid-October. Depth readings have to be taken all the time through the Ava loop which can slow a boat tremendously, down to two or three knots, otherwise there's the danger of scraping the bottom on one of the numerous sandbars concealed below the surface level of the river. Below the Sagaing Redoubt itself there are more shifting sand-banks, so, if the leading boat gets stuck the rest following can't go anywhere. If that happens and the whole of the navigable freeway gets gummed up, the Burmese will blast the hell out of your fleet from all the way along the embankments.'

'And that's precisely what we wish to avoid, Captain. Facts. All of them. I eat them for breakfast.' He gave a fleeting smile.

Nathan returned it. 'Well, I guess there's some consolation in all this Major — that's if you're still not at war with the Burmese. You might not have to fire a single shot. The Burmese are medieval monks most of the time, and when it comes down to brass tacks like shooting at something, they'll run a mile. They're Buddhists, not soldiers, even if they like to think they are. Once they see British warships coming up the Irrawaddy they'll go crashing off into the jungle to their nearest pagoda to ask for Buddha's help. You can sail in and stick the Union Jack on Sagaing ramparts with no trouble.'

Again his flippancy was not appreciated.

'Captain de Veres-Vorne, one thing we never do in the British or Indian Army is underestimate the enemy. In the past, tragic mistakes have been made by scorning the opposition as being vastly inferior, native, archaic, ignorant etc. Now then, that's about it for today. But do let me have your info as soon as possible. Get those plans drawn and let me have them ... let's say I'll be expecting you about this time tomorrow. Come right up without waiting downstairs. Ask for Corporal Duckett and he'll show you the way in — and now the way out.'

The hearty team-spirit was all there, so obviously bred on the playing-fields of England. Jeffrey Radcliffe opened a door that led to an inner office. Poking his head round the edge of it, he said to someone Nathan could not see, 'Corporal Duckett, return Captain de Veres-Vorne to Mr Gosney's office, pronto, there's a good chap.' He came back inside his own domain as Corporal Duckett appeared in the adjoining doorway.

'Goodbye, Captain, nice to have met you. Thanks for coming along to help.' He went back to studying his map, puffing his second cigarette while contemplating the intended invasion of Upper Burma.

Nathan could not restrain a tiny flicker of amusement while he followed the bandy little Corporal through a congerie of offices and corridors. Major Radcliffe had made him sound like an interdepartmental dossier — return Captain de Veres-Vorne to Mr Gosney's office, pronto! Thinking about it, Nathan decided that he probably was a file marked 'Confidential' as of the moment, knowing the British and their rapacious appetite for pieces of paper — which they were always making him produce at Thayetmyo.

Mr Gosney, before handing Nathan over to a lesser mortal to show him the way out to the street, presented him with two well-sealed buff envelopes. One was marked for Surgeon-General, Sir Edwin Tennent-Browne KCMG, KCVO, and M Sinclair Esq, Charge d'Affairs, ICS (Mandalay).

'The C.C. would be awfully grateful if you would put these despatches straightaway into the hands of the two gentlemen concerned. Hand them to no one else. Good day, Captain de Veres-Vorne.'

Lizard-like, he smiled sleekly and it was on the tip of Nathan's tongue to tell the well-oiled Mr Gosney that despite being an American he could still read English and why didn't he get someone else to do his dirty smuggling work!

He thought better of it. He chafed, but he also put the papers in Edwin's attaché-case. He was one big fool, and knew it.

TWO

Outside the High Commission Nathan wiped an arm across his perspiring brow and made haste to rid himself of the winged collar Fee Tam had put so much starch into that it cut his throat like a razor-blade. Bundling collar and tie into his pocket, he breathed more easily. From his waistcoat pocket he extracted his Max Minck and regarded the time. It was almost two o'clock. It had been an awful morning as far as he was concerned. He felt hungry and decided to do something about it. His chota-hazri had been revolting as well as rushed, with tepid tea and soggy bread slipping away on lashings of ghee. He could quite truthfully say that the hardest thing he found in Burma was getting used to the food. Nathan scratched his head, wondering where to go and what to do. He did not want to eat alone and had no wish to eat in the company of Findebar, Tonsin and Ko Lee. He very much desired to return to Mandalay.

In the end he decided to take his sons to lunch. Perhaps too, they could spend the rest of the day sailing a boat on the lake, a fishing-boat rather than the kind he was used to. He set off via Fytche Park to the English Boys' School, not far from the Royal Lakes.

Sa-Lon, Roi and he spent a pleasant enough half-hour and then Sa-Lon's sulks became too much to bear. 'What the hell's the matter with you Sa-Lon?' Nathan snapped. 'I thought you'd have been pleased to see your father.'

'I'd have been very happy if it had not been this after-noon father. Today we have our most important cricket match of all. I would have gained the most runs for my house as I've been practising very hard at my batting, and now I can't play because you took me out of school.'

'So, Sa-Lon de Veres-Vorne must show everyone he's not all brown and no brawn, eh? Last time it was brain, wasn't it Sa-Lon? A bad mood with me on account of your not gaining top-marks in some examination or other, hmmm? The excuses are wearing a little thin, so if you'd rather I kept my distance, say so now.'

Sa-Lon grated his teeth. Nathan heard. Approaching fourteen, Sa-Lon was getting too big for his boots in Nathan's opinion. He decided he required taking down a peg or two. Somehow, he had always sensed trouble brewing with Sa-Lon who was spoiled rotten by Min-thami. Thank God he'd rescued both the boys from becoming namby-pambys, and had put them into a decent school rather than some Phongyi-Kyuang Min-thami had had in mind for them. Nathan came to the conclusion that Roi was far the better character of the two. More stable, less volatile, more respectful. By the end of the afternoon, his patience sorely tried by his eldest son's mood, Nathan was exhausted.

'Have you seen your mother lately?' Nathan asked cautiously.

The three of them stood before the statue of the British Queen sitting in a bed of roses with orb and sceptre.

'Yesterday. Why?' Sa-Lon said, casting him an odd glance. 'Haven't you been home yet?' he added impudently.

Nathan wanted to box young Sa-Lon's ears, but resisted the impulse. 'As a matter of fact I haven't.' He cleared his throat. 'As a matter of fact I came straight from the docks to see you lads first before going home.'

'That's funny,' Sa-Lon said, not waiting for Nathan to finish, 'mama said you'd been home three weeks.'

Nathan cleared his throat again, sticking his chin far out at being caught lying. 'Er, did she now ...' he regarded Queen Victoria's Hanoverian nose, 'I don't suppose she, um, she said where she'd been ... I mean come from ...' Abashed, he glared at Sa-Lon. His patience snapped. 'Oh, for God's sake Sa-Lon, forget it will you!'

He walked away. Roi caught up with Nathan, pulling his jacket sleeve to gain his attention, 'Papa, is something wrong?' he asked, skipping along to keep pace with his father's long strides.

'Wrong?' Nathan looked into the troubled young face. 'No, of course not Roi. Why should anything be wrong?' He stopped, turned and waited for Sa-Lon. Nathan rumpled Roi's dark hair in an affectionate gesture, 'come on you two sporting fellows,' he said, forcing himself to be cheerful for Roi's sake, 'it's getting dark. I don't want to get the stick from your headmaster for keeping you out later than your pass.' His paternal indulgence stretched to its limits, he gave Sa-Lon a beaming smile. 'Don't scowl Sa-Lon,' Nathan said, 'if the wind changes you'll be stuck with that look.' He took out some money. 'Here you are you two, pocket-money, so don't say I don't think of you occasionally.'

It was rather more than both boys had expected.

'Papa,' said Roi outside the school-gates, 'the English boys say we're half-castes because our father is a white man and mama is black ... I said, mama isn't black, she's a creamy-gold colour which is nicer than white, and the fellows simply laughed. Sa-Lon had a fight and received a black eye and then the stick from Mr Whitehead for being aggressive. Old Crumbs, the head-prefect, ragged us again and said the reason why we're in trade is because half-castes can't do anything better.'

Nathan was appalled.

'Shut-up, sneak!' Sa-Lon dug Roi in the ribs before running off up the school drive.

Nathan did not know how to answer his young son. In the end he said, 'Roi, you shouldn't care what other fellows say. They're ribbing you because they're jealous while you're rich. I guess their parents shop in the Shwe Emporium, so you can tell them that being in trade also means being clever, since they have to pay while you get it all for nothing from your trader-father.'

Nathan had to leave it there. He couldn't begin to explain to Roi the implications of the word 'half-caste'. There were some things one simply didn't talk about.

Roi smiled a cheeky grin and Nathan felt a whole lot better. 'Well then, papa,' said Roi, 'I guess I'll have to tell them all that and put them in their place.'

'That's my son. Run off now and catch up with Sa-Lon.'

Nathan stood a long time at the school gates after his sons had disappeared from view. Angry and saddened, he wondered what good this very expensive English School was going to be to Sa-Lon and Roi if they were made miserable on account of the shade of their skin. It might, in the long-run, have been better for Sa-Lon and Roi if Minthami had had her way and sent them to a Monastery School.

CHAPTER TWENTY

ONE

Nathan pushed aside the drawings and other bits of information he had been concentrating on for Major Radcliffe from Dum-Dum. He reached for his pipe on the bamboo table beside his bed, and had to admit to himself how disgustingly full and dirty the ash-tray and everything else was.

The details of Sagaing prison were easier to recall than expected though he had never thought of the horrors of the fort since the night he had walked out of it. But ten days inside those walls must have been etched on his mind in blood, because he was able to summon every detail of the place including the position of the stand-pump in the compound. He had spent enough hours, God knew, confined in stocks, observing the comings and goings of everyone and everything around him.

He puffed his pipe. Lying with his hands behind his head, his eyes upon the fly-spotted ceiling of the bedroom; he had never really given this apartment he rented more than a passing glance before. He realised after three weeks of being cooped up in it, how very sordid it was. He had allowed Minthami to choose the place where they should live in Rangoon, and she had chosen Chinatown of all places. He presumed it had been on account of the Loloi Shans being closer to their Thai and Chinese neighbours than the Rangoon Brit-ishers. But, for all that, he thought she could have chosen somewhere better. Here, all he had discovered was humanity spitting, coughing, fighting, fornicating, eating, defaecating and swindling. God, he must have been mad to have contemplated even paying to live in this garbage-dump! Well, at least he could get rid of it now. Minthami wasn't coming back and he certainly had no intention of living here by himself. As for the boys, he'd send them to America in a few years time to complete their education.

He went back to his neat drawings. Cannons, shoals, shallows, bamboo stockades, gun emplacements, he was being a traitor to the Burmese who had feathered his nest and the only reason he was doing it was because he hoped the British would blast the hell out of the Burman who had pinched his woman! Nathan dismissed the thought of having been bought a second time round.

His drawings in the hands of Corporal Duckett, he begged forgiveness that he could not see Major Radcliffe as agreed because he had an urgent appointment, but hoped the information supplied would be of some use. Afterwards Nathan paid a courtesy call to his office to check that all his hirelings were behaving themselves as they should, bought a tin of toothpaste at the Shwe Emporium and while he was at it, some Wilkinson's Sarsaparilla.

'Essence of red Jamaica, the wonderful purifier of the human blood.' He smiled at the salesgirl. 'I'll buy it, I've got everything it says here, torpid liver, debility, eruptions — and the etcs they mention.'

'You're not paying, are you, Captain de Veres-Vorne?' asked the girl.

He smiled again, 'Why not? Can't get everything for nothing in this world.' He gave her small change. 'I shouldn't stay in business long if my kyats and pyats didn't do a bit of circulating.'

He spent the rest of the day drinking lassi-yoghurt on his crumpled bed, spilling ash and tobacco everywhere, and went to sleep early.

First thing in the morning, he was setting sail for Mandalay.

TWO

Wilkinson's Sarsaparilla had such a good effect on him, Nathan did not awake until tiffin-time and then only because his feet were being molested. The skin on them was fragile like his back. Sensitive after what the Spotted Faces had done to him, six years later his nerves still flinched. Reluctantly he opened his eyes.

The vision draped in mosquito-net made him groan.

'Minthami, where the hell have you been!' he said sinking back onto his pillows.

She went on massaging his tender feet in the way only she knew.

He spoke to the fly-spotted ceiling: 'I thought I told you to clear off. I didn't want to see you again.'

She still did not answer. It wasn't a dream, for her hands were sending real messages through him. His eyes wide open now, he said angrily. 'Damn it, Minthami, clear off!'

'Minthami go presently. She come only to find pair of shoes for Sa-Lon. He require them today and so Minthami come to look in house which Captain Vorne make into trashcan.'

'Oh God.'

'Why you say, Oh God?'

He cleared his throat. 'Because I felt like it.'

She looked divine. Dressed up in an elaborately woven ceremonial costume, he could only imagine it had been done for stunning effect.

'Why are you all dressed up like that?'

'Like what, Captain Vorne?' she asked innocently.

'Like that ... all those open fancy skirts and whatnot ...' He wagged a finger at her. 'Don't tell me you walked through the streets like that.'

'Why you worry? You throw Minthami into Street of

273

Thousand Wars where everyone fight all day, so why you care now?'

He struggled to sit up against the cheap brass bed-head he had had to live with for so long. 'Minthami, where have you been all this time? I demand to know.'

She giggled, and then gave a little twirl for his benefit. 'You like me Captain Vorne?' She began to imitate the disjointed movements of a marionette dancer. She did it so well, her body obedient in every movement the brain willed. Fascinated he watched, her ability to drive him to the heights and depths of passion unchanged. 'How much American Captain pay for Minthami today?'

'Minthami,' he said, clutching his head, 'please, please don't do this to me! Quit lying for a change. Tell me where you've been. I've been going out of my mind these last three weeks wondering what had happened to you.'

'You very funny man,' she said. 'You hit Minthami, beat her, slap face — which very bad thing to do as it make wife feel husband have no respect for her any-more, call her rude name, throw her out in street, then send Findebar, Ko Lee and Tonsin all over city looking for her because American Captain frightened of what become of her,' she finished on a high sing-song note of complaint and confusion.

She began soothing his feet again, leaning over the footrail to do it, the mosquito-net caught over her headdress like a bridal veil. He cleared his throat: 'I'd still like to know where you've been. Have you been living with the man who gave you Buddha's relics, Ha-Ha-Hands?'

Her hands snaked along the insides of his bare legs.

'God Minthami ... don't do that!'

'Yes, Minthami live with him.'

He took hold of her arms and pulled her over the footrail so that she was on top of him: 'Now I want the truth!'

'Minthami here all the time. Downstairs in house of Hla Hla Han who Minthami half-brother. He come from Moulmein with wife and second wife to live in Rangoon.

Minthami and half-brother live in Court of Ava as children hostages of Mindon Min. They give much help and comfort to each other when Queen Sinpyumashin who is now Queen Mother get angry with them. Now we see each other again. He work where Minthami work, in Culture school which makes much dancing and festivities for British people who not understand Burmese culture.'

'Why the hell didn't you say all this before?'

'You not give Minthami chance. You only believe what is inside evil kala mind.' She tapped his skull. 'Hla Hla Han bring casket of make-believe Buddha relic which we use in Zatpwè at Culture School. We make many performances and much busy while Shwe Nat in Mandalay. That is only way Minthami not lonely, now Sa-Lon and Roi in English boarding school. That is why you see him inside house on day you come home. He mean nothing. Minthami mean nothing. After he go, she get undressed to put on clothes for evening performance at Culture School.' Again the childish crescendo of indignation that he could have misjudged her so much.

'Oh God, Minthami ... I'm sorry ...'

She ran her long fingers through his bright hair that had always fascinated her. 'You always say sorry Big Sa-Lon, and sometimes it not enough ...'

'Then let's get these things off before I give you the hardest lay you've ever had,' he began removing her clothes impatiently, his need for her suddenly unbearable.

'It not enough,' she insisted, 'for sometime Minthami ...'

She was unable to finish what she had been going to say because he suddenly filled her mouth with kisses. Her hair, silky, black, loose, swamped him in essence of jasmine and roses. He took her so quickly, he was left gasping long after the relief her body afforded him. She was left gasping with indignation. 'Big Sa-Lon, if you like that, why you not buy woman?'

He smothered his laugh in the pillow: 'I want you, no one else. I've missed you.' He rolled on his back and

275

reached for his tobacco pouch. He became conscious of the funny look she was giving him. He paused, his hand on his pipe: 'What's that face supposed to mean?'

Close to him on the single cot, she stared up at him, a strange light in her eye: 'Minthami think Shwe Nat lie about not wanting other woman. It pity American Captain not Buddhist, then he have *ma ya nga*.'

'I don't want a second wife,' he lit his pipe.

'Minthami think Shwe Nat need second wife.'

'I don't care what the hell Minthami thinks, I know what I think.' He sucked his pipe.

'Lesser wife of Buddhist, she do things for husband first wife not always able to do.'

'What's that supposed to mean?' Frowning he looked down at her, her face on the pillow by his elbow.

She caressed his chest, his dark-blond mat of hair, to her, intriguing and unusual in this land of smooth-chested men. 'Sometimes Minthami think Shwe Nat and Amagyi-Angela ...'

'For God's sake, Minthami, stop that!' He got up from the bed to pull down the rattans at the window because the sun streaming through turned the tiny room into an oven. 'And another thing, we're getting out of here. Either we get a decent house out by the lakes somewhere, or live permanently in Mandalay.'

When he turned from the window she was kneeling on the bed, her shoulders moving rhythmically to the sensuous swing of her perfumed hair. Her dances were not always confined to the religious. Her body movements and poses could be as suggestive and as erotic as any nautch girl's, or Indian temple-dancer's in worship of the phallic symbols. Her desires and sexuality apparent in the way her thighs were slightly apart to reveal to him the place still moist with his own lustings of a moment ago, she held her arms out to him: 'Come,' her lambent eyes heavy, she drew him to her, 'this time it also for Minthami. She make Shwe Nat very happy again so he not want other woman.'

He had missed a day's sailing time. A longyi wrapped round his middle, his chest bare, he stood regarding her with a glass of warm East India pale ale in one hand and his cold pipe in the other.

Minthami lay on a day-couch in all her naked glory assiduously muttering prayers to Buddha. Slender dancer's legs tightly crossed in fierce protection of the seed in her womb, she moved her prayer-beads in time with her lips.

'Crazy woman,' he muttered while he gazed on her slim and almost breastless body, the cylindrical shape Burmese and Shan woman culturally desired.

Nathan went in search of ice. The zinc-lined tundice was empty. 'Minthami,' he yelled from the kitchen doorway, 'there's no damn ice left!'

Because there was no reply, he went to the couch. 'Minthami, did you hear me?'

'Shhh!' she hissed fiercely, her eyes still shut. 'You frighten butterfly-spirit of daughter Buddha make for Minthami.'

Leaning over her he whispered against her shuttered eyes, his hand resting on the triangle of her butterfly-spirit, 'Minthami honey, is it too much to ask you to see to it the chokra-boy fetches ice from the Shwe Emporium? You know how I *hate* warm ale.'

'Minthami not forget. She order plenty ice from ice-machine at Shwe Emporium before husband come home. But when Shwe Nat come home in bad temper without telling Minthami anything, he drunk, drunk, drunk every night! Minthami know. She watch him from downstairs apartment-house of Hla Hla Han but he never see her.' She opened her eyes. 'He very silly. Never think to look in same house, but only brothels and bazaars and silly places Minthami never go.' She closed her eyes again. 'Bad, very bad, and house so dirty! So ice go.'

'Ice go ... I see.' He nodded. 'Well, while you're

about it, would you mind saying a little prayer for me, something like getting Buddha to send round to the Shwe Emporium for more ice, please?'

'It too late. Shwe Emporium closed, Managers require to sleep if Shwe Nat still awake. Anyway, Buddha enlightened one, O Thakin Vorne, and so he not answer such prayers. He not drink Scotch whisky, Jamaica rum, Indian beer and American ice.'

'I guess,' said Nathan straightening his back, 'you're getting about as saucy as young Sa-Lon. So Minthami honey, you're coming back to Mandalay with me — first thing tomorrow morning. We live together at Whitewalls from now on, not in this Chinese laundry.'

'Anything, O divine Thakin. Minthami try not to miss many friends and relations who like to live in Chinatown because of good food and much happiness. She make Culture School in Mandalay if that is wish of Thakin Vorne.'

He grunted. Warm beer in one hand and a cold pipe in the other, he flung himself down on his freshly made bed. One thing could be said for having her back, at least the place was clean and tidy again, his washing done and his food cooked — even the scorpions in the wash-house along the verandah did not know what had hit them when fresh soap and paper arrived.

Crazy girl, he thought again, in his mind quite certain that despite all Minthami's cravings for another child — 'a butterfly-spirit of daughter' as she euphemistically put it — Daw Khin Htay's potent medicines to save her life six years ago, when she had miscarried their last child, had put paid to any further chances. Minthami, at twenty-eight, was still young and lovely, but to know her body had become only a piece of sterile equipment unable to conceive any more children, would destroy her. For someone who knew so much about the anatomy of her body and what it could do and feel, she was remarkably naïve of its biological functions. He wondered if she would still enjoy and participate in their sex-life as much, if she realized there could never be any child now, as the by-product of consummation. On his part, he'd rather have his tongue cut out by a Spotted Face than let her be aware of his suspicions.

'Minthami, why did you come back to me?' he asked from his bed.

'Minthami have no more money,' her musical voice answered from the living-room. 'She have very important position as Apyodaw at Water Festival and require new ceremonial costume of *achaeik htameins*.'

'What's wrong with what you were wearing this morning?'

'It belong Ma Ma May who is second wife of Hla Hla Han at Culture School. Why you smack so rudely Minthami's face that day?'

'Because I'm a crazy kala I guess.'

'Big Sa-Lon, Minthami very sorry, but she unable to go to Mandalay till after Burmese New Year waterfestivities of Thingyan. It very great shame for Minthami not to be in Rangoon for Zatpwé at Culture School when she work so hard at performance.'

A tight knot settled around his heart. 'Minthami,' he said levelly from the living-room doorway, the dark-blue sky in the open window framing her like a picture while she reposed languidly on her cane couch, 'I have no intention of eating my heart out over you for the next three weeks. I'm returning to Mandalay in the morning. I have two barges and the *Belle Hélène* loaded to the gunwales with stuff for the Shwe Emporium ordered from England, which they're waiting for. If you accompany me back to Mandalay, you'll make me very happy. If not, then you can have your *achaeik htameins* and enough money to pay off the chittys, the boys' school fees and anything else you want money for. But you won't see me again — not for a very long time. After Mandalay I'm going to Bhamo and the northern tributaries — I might even go to Yunnen.'

She seemed none too perturbed about another lengthy separation. She smiled, her eyes drowsy with loving. 'Minthami have much to keep busy and try not to miss husband. Next time he come home maybe she have gift for him. Maybe she will be big with Lord Buddha's child to give as offering to Shwe Nat.'

'Maybe. But aren't you getting your deities rather mixed up?' He asked, trying to maintain a level tone. 'It's Lord Buddha who should receive your offering. After all, I'm only flesh and blood, he's the one with the golden penis.' He eased himself away from the door jamb while she reached angrily for her robe.

Winding her hair into a thick rope she fastened the heavy coil with a broken comb. 'It very hot up here tonight. Minthami think she go downstairs to have breakfast with Ma Ma May and family.' She tightened the sash around her slender waist.

'Honeychile, it's eleven o'clock at night!' he reminded her.

'That is time Chinatown wake up. You like Minthami bring you back egg noodles?'

'I would like Minthami to wake me up at five o'clock if she's still having breakfast or saying her prayers. Now I should like to get some sleep — after I've cleaned my teeth with my new pink toothpaste.' He moved away to the bedroom.

'If Minthami awake she use bamboo-clappers to wake Shwe Nat who sleep like teak-log. But if she too sleeping, please not to wake because she have very busy day tomorrow as important Apyodaw at Zatpwé. Afterwards — after New Year Festival — she will come back to Mandalay and live in Shwe Nat's grand house.'

He closed the flimsy rattan door of the bedroom, the noise outside deafening, the smell of cooking, of rancid ghee, of the hot spicy Orient, high on the night air. Once again Rangoon had vanquished him.

'Man-da-lay.' Even the sound of it was more pleasing!

CHAPTER
TWENTY-ONE

ONE

F ive months later the monsoon season had set in with
a vengeance. Shafts of rain hammered the parched
ground, drummed on plantain leaves waving like angry
elephant's ears, pock-marked the Mandalay moat so that
the water-hyacinths closed ranks and cowered beneath
the onslaught.

Clare Sinclair had requested her day-bed be moved to
the verandah where she could watch the play of water on
water, the nearest she would ever get to England. She
looked forward to the Amagyi-Angela's visit in a curious
way. While being intimidated by her aloof bearing, Clare
found the English nun's Buddhist serenity infinitely
reassuring. When Clare had used the word 'different' in
relation to the Amagyi-Angela, 'magnetic' had been the
word Matthew had used. She did not know exactly what
he had meant, but in a way she felt that the woman with
the green eyes who had once been betrothed to
Matthew, did have a certain presence. But she still did
not like her.

Clare stared dully at the water. Kyauktawgyi Road
ran along the northern boundary of the Palace moat, the
back of the house looking out on it. To the west, three
quarters of a mile away, was the Residency. In exactly
the opposite direction, three-quarters of a mile to the
east, was Edom Gideon's Gospel Hall. Clare knew that

the Amagyi-Angela was bound to come from that direction, down the covered walkway of a thousand steps to the foot of the Kuthodaw, then past the Gospel Mission and the Kyauktawgyi Pagoda to this house they rented for an extortionate sum from relatives of the Taingda Mingyi. It was a dismal house, Clare hated it. Gloomy and damp, its thatched roof in urgent need of repairs, the timber rotting, she wished the whole house would fall in the moat. She wished for the umpteenth time she had never heard of the Fishing-Fleet. She sometimes wished she did not know who Matthew Sinclair was.

She turned her pinched face to her husband who sat in a peacock chair in the corner with Verity on his lap. He was reading to her from a child's alphabet book. Her hands went to cover her stomach. Each pregnancy seemed more uncomfortable and terrifying than the last. She had been devastated to learn one could still fall pregnant while nursing the previous child. Someone had told her it was impossible. Clare had discovered nothing was impossible where making babies was concerned. She hated it. And she hated Matthew most of all for subjecting her to such a procedure.

'Indeed! And I do recall that fine lady, Mrs Wandersmeith going as purple as a plum because of such a naughty thing,' Matthew was saying to Verity, the storybook closed. 'Naughty mama too. We shall have no more practical jokes after church, but shall behave instead with pious prévenance as befitting Reverend John's little flock.' He pretended severity, but his daughter was not fooled. She tittered behind her hand.

Matthew had to smile too, imagining Mrs Wandersmeith's face when Verity had gone up to her in the street with a collecting-box for the Anglicans. At that moment Bhuti, the Parsee servant, shuffled onto the verandah in barefeet to announce that the Amagyi-Angela had arrived.

'Excuse me please, Clare,' Matthew lifted Verity off his lap. 'Now that Angela's here I'll be getting along to the Residency as I've got a lot of catching up to do with work that's getting neglected.'

'I wouldn't have thought there was much work for you to do in view of the fact there's no official communication between Rangoon and Mandalay,' Clare said peevishly.

Matthew refrained from answering that remark. He was almost glad to see Angela.

'Hello Matthew,' she said cheerfully. She shook out her umbrella into the moat, regardless of the drenching she herself had received even with the umbrella. She still walked around in bare feet Matthew noticed.

'You should dry yourself thoroughly otherwise you'll catch a chill and make yourself very sick,' he said.

Angela laughed. 'Goodness me Matthew, if I took a chill every time I walked out in the monsoon, I'd have nothing to complain about in the hot season.' She settled herself beside the pile of sewing and mending Clare had put out for her — though why Clare couldn't do it lying there all day long like the Queen of Sheba, Angela did not know. There was nothing wrong with Clare's fingers as far as she could tell.

'Well,' said Matthew, his hands behind his back, seeming to be dancing with impatience to be off now that his lunch break of attending upon his wife was over. 'Please excuse me. Duty calls.'

He gave a half-hearted smile, but his eyes behind his glasses when alighting upon her, Angela noticed, contained the same hard glint of despair and anger, still unforgiven, still unforgotten. She sighed. It must seem like rubbing salt into the wound to come here every afternoon but, as he and Clare had insisted, she felt she could not deliberately turn down a cry for help.

An hour later the sun burst through the lowering clouds and formed a rainbow over the moat. It steamed in the heat and so did they. Then the mosquitoes came in droves, wretched little things pinging their way to destruction. Angela felt unable to remain another moment in Clare's sulky company when a familiar voice echoed through the house.

'Coooeee! Only me ...' Blaize Tennent-Browne sauntered onto the verandah. 'Not all asleep I hope. Hasn't it been a beastly week? Angela darling, I thought I might find you here doing your good deed for the day. How many lives have you stored up for yourself now? I would have thought making purgatory of this one would have put you off any others. Lord above, Edwin's getting such a grouch these days I had to leave his athlete's foot and bald patches to get a little fresh air. Darlings, when I marry again it will be to an adolescent Subaltern — I blame my father for panicking me into the arms of another old man. Seven daughters was his purgatory, poor old darling.' She flopped into the peacock chair, her elaborate organza hat full of silk flowers and ribbons tossed onto a side table. She wore an extremely charming white lace frock that must have cost Edwin the earth. Angela, threading her needle, took stock of Lady Bee kitted out for an English garden party in the summertime, instead of a Mandalay verandah in the rainy season.

'Darlings,' she gushed, 'do look at these shoes of mine.' She displayed trim ankles for their inspection. 'The mildew here is worse than in Manipur. The same thing has happened to my too, too expensive white kid gloves. Riddled with green spots, simply everything! Now I resemble a mouldy leopard when I go anywhere — too funny for words. Goodness, aren't the water-hyacinths a sight when they open after the rains? So blue-blue, they're almost the colour of that delicious man's eyes. Of course I know you know to whom I refer, Angela darling, so don't pretend you've never heard the name. Talking of him ...' she fiddled with her crimped fringe while gazing vacantly across the moat, 'did you know he's back in Mandalay? Oh, you didn't know? How silly of me, I imagined you'd be the first to hear that the King of the river is back in his marble palace while the King of Burma meditates in his wooden one. What fun! Anyway, *this time*, he has his little native princess in tow.' She gave Angela a dimpled smile.

Angela, head bent to her needlework said: 'Is that so? I had no idea Nathan and Minthami were back. My goodness me, I'll have to turn out my best hat for the occasion.'

Clare tittered.

'Touché darling,' Blaize gave a throaty chuckle. Swinging her crossed leg under elegant lace skirts she said to Clare: 'Darling, you're the size of a house already. What are you and Matthew producing this time, an elephant?'

Clare flushed. Biting her lip she looked about ready to dissolve into tears. Blaize continued; 'So don't be tiresome darling and keep the secret all to yourself — we get such precious little excitement in our lives in this wretched little city. When are Leigh and Milly getting married?'

Angela thought Clare was about to have an attack of the vapours and passed her the smelling salts on the table beside her.

'I'm sorry,' Lady Bee said. 'Have I said something I should not? It's just that I heard something in the European Club the other day ... you know how gossip gets around, especially among all those crude little teak-wallahs on leave from their elephants. I wouldn't have believed a word about Milly and Leigh being lovers, only that I happened to see Milly one morning breakfasting at Nathan Vorne's house ... Oh goodness! How could you ... really Angela, I'm soaked ...!'

'So sorry, do forgive me Bee ... I'm getting so clumsy ... it was Supayalat's vase the other day.' Angela frantically mopped up the spilled water on Clare's table with the bib she had been stitching, then turned to Blaize's assistance:

'Don't! Please don't ... you're making matters worse with that wet cloth.' Lady Bee stood up, shaking out the water in her lap.

'Oh dear, I do hope the lace doesn't shrink Bee ... such a pretty frock too. I should get home at once and lay the dress out flat to dry. On no account hang it up otherwise you'll ruin it.'

Blaize had recovered her composure. Matching the Amagyi-Angela's cat's-paw wit, she said, 'Don't worry darling, I can take a hint. The dress won't spoil like the pink-thing you're wearing. Remind me to lend you some patterns sometime. You might like to pass them on to your Head Nun to attract more custom up at the Sasana ... anyway darlings, I must fly. I've promised to cheer on Nathan, Leigh and Edwin playing polo against the natives. Would you believe, those clerk-wallahs from the Shwe Emporium and Nathan's godowns are actually good at it, in a native sort of way! Goodbye Clare dear, do try and drink up the nerve-tonic Edwin prescribed. It will make you less watery and more milky. Goodbye Angela, I'll tell Nathan I ran into you.'

She departed with her hat.

TWO

At the sunset hour when the land turned from gold to crimson, Nathan strode along Kyauktawgyi Road. At its eastern extremity he turned left, past Mindon Min's seven-hundred-and-twenty-nine pagodas inscribed with the Pali texts of the Kuthodaw.

Gigantic statues of crested lions guarded each of the two breathtaking staircases leading to the top of Mandalay Hill. Two covered walkways wound up the hill from the south with plenty of stopping areas to gain second wind. The view obtained was always worth the climb, an almost three-hundred-and-sixty degree vista over the plains and as far as the Shan hills. At this hour he hoped to find Angela feeding her turtles. He was looking forward to seeing her again.

The Chinthes with fierce open jaws seemed almost to snarl at him as he, the irreverent kala, walked their sacred steps without removing his shoes. Almost at the top of the hill, he met Buddha turned to bronze and gold with his hand outstretched over Mandalay and, close beside him, the statue of a woman holding in her hands her amputated breasts as an offering to Gautama. It was a statue he never much cared for. Nathan, perspiring with the effort the climb entailed, took off his sun-helmet and wiped his brow.

The man who had been following him from the time he had entered the city via one of the lesser west gates, darted back into a niche. Nathan adjusted his chin strap, seemingly preoccupied but not missing a thing. He put on his sun helmet though he did not require it at this hour, and continued into a little covered arcade. From one of the stalls selling joss-sticks, gold-leaf, flowers and Mandalay slippers, he selected an ivory and silver comb for Minthami. Then he passed along to a fruit stall, taking his time in pressing, discarding and choosing some mangosteens, his favourite fruit. Nathan glanced over his shoulder. The man still lurked in the shadows. Nathan walked on a few more yards, paused, made certain the man was not in sight before dodging into a recess containing a brilliantly adorned Buddha whose lower half sagged with the weight of gold-leaf pressed on him by his followers. The comb in his pocket, Nathan placed the mangosteens at Buddha's feet.

The man came abreast, furtively looking to right and left. He paused, seemed uncertain, his face well concealed in the scarf of his turban. Nathan grabbed him from behind.

With a savage wrench on the man's arms, he forced him backward into the recess so passers-by could not see them. 'If you don't tell me who you are and why you've been trailing me, I swear I'll slit your throat!' he hissed in the man's ear.

The muffled figure writhed, squirmed to get out of the strangulating arm around his neck, a knee in his back. 'Stop ... stop please Thakin Vorne ... it is I, only Ba Say ...'

Nathan pulled away the muslin scarf. 'Christ, Ba Say you frightened me half to death. What the devil do you think you're doing? I thought you were some Dacoit-Bo

287

about to put his *dah* in me.' He released the Burman. 'Why are you following me?'

'Thakin Vorne, Ba Say has heard very bad things in Council Meeting today. News of arrests ...'

'Look, before you go spilling any beans to me, I'm not British. The man you want is the British Charge d'Affairs, Mr Sinclair.'

'Ba Say know, Thakin Vorne, but it does not behove Ba Say to tell him of these things since it affects him. I come from Taingda Mingyi's Hlutdaw where special meeting is held on situation here in Mandalay. It is very bad. Many names are put on list. All those who are called "suspect foreigners". Thakin Sinclair, he is one of them.'

'Who else?'

'Many others. Ba Say remember few like Thakin Buchanan of Telegraph Service, Thakin doctor-fellow who is called Brown Tent ...'

'Tennent-Browne. Who else?'

'Many, many others ... Ba Say have good memory, he write down ...'

'No, for goodness sake don't write anything down, Ba Say, otherwise you'll be pinned to the Palace Watch-tower for spying.'

'Ba Say already whipped and bad things done to family by Taingda Mingyi and Dacoit-Bos he pay.'

'That's not the point. Was my name included on the Taingda Mingyi's list?'

'No Thakin Vorne, that is for sure.'

'Oh well, I suppose that's something. Very well Ba Say, make yourself scarce, and for God's sake next time don't creep up as if you're about to stick a knife in me. Besides, it looks damn suspicious. Don't worry, I'll warn the suspect foreigners to watch how they go. And many thanks.'

'It very great pleasure, Thakin Vorne. May you walk with happiness in your stride.' Ba Say, with extreme courteousness, backed away from Nathan, and then ran off into the arcade. The last thing Nathan felt in his stride as he went downhill to warn Matthew Sinclair of the danger he was in, was happiness.

Nathan found Matthew at the Residency, seated in Mr Hawes' old place of office. Matthew was drinking alone. Embarrassed because he had been caught behaving in a very un-Adrian Hawes manner, Matthew sheepishly greeted Nathan.

'Don't mind me,' Nathan said happily. 'I'll join you if I may.'

'Rather ...' Matthew waved Nathan to a seat before ringing the bell to ask the bearer to fetch another glass and more whisky. 'And I don't wish to be disturbed for the next hour or so,' he told the bearer who was not very good at taking orders. 'What can I do for you Nathan?' Matthew asked, polishing his glasses, when the door had closed.

'I've just been talking to Ba Say who was at this afternoon's meeting of the Supreme Council. Apparently, the Hlutdaw have drawn up a list of names under the heading of suspect foreigners. Your name is on it.'

'That's to be expected.' Matthew replaced his glasses, able to see Nathan more clearly. He reached for his drink of whisky, chota-pegs taken neat like Nathan.

'You know about it?' Nathan asked, disgruntled on account of having walked all the way down Mandalay Hill and a mile-and-a-half along Kyauktawgyi Road with second-hand information.

'I've known for sometime now that something like it was bound to happen. My name would be at the top of the Taingda Mingyi's list, that's obvious. However, this has all come about through France trying to establish her own commercial interests in Mandalay. Because of it, London and Paris are hardly on speaking terms. The new French Consul here has also been fanning the flames of discontent between Rangoon and Mandalay. Ever since the Franco-Burmese treaty was signed in January the French have done nothing but step on our toes. All that business of the two-and-a-half million pound loan for a railway link between Mandalay and Taunggyi, with the same amount being offered to set up a Currency Issuing Bank, the French have one because they're determined to get the better of us. The Taingda Mingyi and Supayalat as you know are pro-French in any case — though in my opinion the Taingda's a xenophobe if anything and wants Burma only for the Burmese. Anyway, it's all a nasty business, especially over that arms deal the French and Burmese made behind our backs. H.M.G. has written to the British Ambassador in Paris regarding the precautions necessary to prevent confusion in the affairs of "semi-civilized dependent states" — Lord Salisbury's words, not mine.' Matthew paused, sipped his whisky while Nathan remained silent.

'But the fact remains,' Matthew continued, 'the Hlutdaw have now gone one step further in wishing to keep us in our place — second to the French. You've presumably heard about this Bombay-Burma Trading Corporation business and how it's dragging on? They're insisting now on fining the Corporation for the alleged — I say alleged because the C.C. maintains it's utter fabrication after inspection of the B.B.T.C.'s books — alleged appropriation of revenues from the Ningyan forests they say should have gone to Thibaw and the foresters. The sum of £106,666 they're disputing, must be paid off in the next four months otherwise they're threatening to seize the Trading Company's timber supplies. U Po Thine, who is one of the lawyers involved in the case, informs me the Hlutdaw are rejecting an arbiter being brought in to settle the matter. We're just waiting to see what's going to happen. That's why I'm not too perturbed about the Taingda Mingyi's lists and threats. He won't touch a hair on the head of any of us until this B.B.T.C. business is resolved. Half the time it's mere posturing by the Burmese. They don't really want to upset us, but merely desire to poke us back into our place to prove whose country it is. We're ploughing too much money and industry into Upper Burma for them to do anything really foolish where we're concerned. It's taken me long enough to find out that much.' Matthew drained his glass and refilled it.

Nathan let out a low whistling-sigh through his teeth. Rocking backward in his chair, one leg crossed over the other, he rubbed his chin and declared, 'What a hell of a state of affairs.'

'It is at the moment,' Matthew agreed. 'It's just a question of calling their bluff. The only reason why trouble didn't come earlier was on account of the defeat the French sustained at Lang-son in March. The subsequent fall of Ferry's Government because the French people made a hue and cry over the cost of their participation in the war with Indo-China, was fortunate from our point of view in that Salisbury's Government declares a forward-thinking policy at this very moment when France has backed down.'

'So what are you going to do?' Nathan asked Matthew.

'Sit tight for the moment. I haven't been recalled yet. When that happens, I'll go home. Meanwhile, I sit here and sweat it out ... the whisky does help.' He gave a rueful smile and tapped the bottle.

'Happy days then,' said Nathan, raising his glass. 'I'm just glad I'm neutral in all this.'

'I'm just glad you're such a fast and reliable runner,' Matthew said, feeling very relaxed and contented in Nathan Vorne's company. He wasn't such a bad hat as people tried to make him out to be, Matthew reflected. 'I hear it was a good match this afternoon,' he remarked sociably.

'If one likes being energetic at five in the afternoon,' Nathan said, adding, 'The field was so damn wet after the rains it was water-polo if anything.'

'Who won?'

'We did of course.'

'Who's we?' Matthew grinned.

'Us neutrals.'

'Of course! Oh well,' Matthew glanced at his watch and pulled a face. 'I suppose I'd better steal off home, otherwise Clare will be fretting. Good to see you, Nathan. Many thanks for letting me know what Ba Say eavesdropped on this afternoon. I'm glad he's still on his toes. But why didn't he come to me in the first place, instead of this roundabout fashion through you?'

'You know the Burmese. At times they carry their politeness so darn far you feel like giving them a kick up their shikkoing backsides. I guess he didn't want to hurt your feelings and preferred me to soften the blow. There we are.'

They shook hands on the verandah before going their separate ways.

Matthew was very sorry he had decided to go home at all. Clare met him in the drawing-room and accosted him without waiting for him to hand his hat and umbrella to Bhuti. It was the first sign of life he had seen in her for months.

'Matthew, your sister is nothing but a little tramp!'

Matthew stepped back in alarm as Clare launched her blistering attack on Milly. He looked at Clare as if she had taken leave of her senses. 'That is one thing Milly is not! And I'll thank you to keep a civil tongue, Clare.' He hadn't felt as angry as this in his entire life. Hurt and upset yes, but never angry like this. But Clare had something to say and she was determined to say it.

'I've sent Milly to her room. She's to stay there. I've forbidden her to leave the house or to have anything to do with our children.'

'Why may I ask?'

'Not before I tell you I got Bhuti to take the riverboat to Ava with a telegraph message to your parents. I wish them to recall Milly to Coimbatore and told them why.'

'You did what?' Matthew was aghast.

'I was not going to let that sneaky Mr Buchanan handle the wire because he's the cause of all this. That's why the telegraph message was conveyed from Ava and not Mandalay.'

She seemed to be congratulating herself on her cleverness and Matthew felt the room swim. He wished he had not drunk so much whisky. He collected himself. Taking a deep breath he asked: 'Will you please tell me what Leigh Buchanan and Milly have done to you that you should behave in this vindictive fashion towards them?'

'I'll tell you Matthew. Your cheap little sister has been seeing him behind our back. Everytime he's on leave from the jungle, they're seen together until the tongues are wagging all over the place. I'm surprised you've heard nothing, as you seem to hear most things going on around you. She sneaks off to meet him in other peoples' houses. I won't have it, Matthew! I won't have your sister disgracing my house by her wanton behaviour. I won't have her seeing that Mr Buchanan again. I don't want her in this house with my children another day. And as for that Captain Vorne, why he's been encouraging those two all along in their illicit behaviour, allowing them to use Whitewalls to indulge their ...'

'Stop!'

She had never heard him shout like that.

'Stop. Not another word!' His hand raised for silence, he paced the floor, one hand behind his back, 'I don't want to hear another word from you regarding my sister. I am going now to talk to Milly to find out the truth of the matter.'

'The truth of the matter is she's a slut.'

'No Clare, she's in love. That's something you wouldn't understand.' Matthew turned on his heel and walked out of the drawing-room.

FOUR

In the moonlit distances the wide river gleamed like a landed mackerel curiously mottled in silver. The trees were tinsel shrouded against the deep velvet night sky and fireflies stabbed the shrubbery with little pencil-darts of brilliancy.

Nathan and Leigh sat on the verandah at Whitewalls drinking in the night's loveliness as well as their liquor. Minthami's incense sticks kept the mosquitoes away to a degree, and the smoke of Nathan's pipe helped. There was so much beauty in this country, so much opportunity, yet always marred by a feeling of uncertainty. Always walk cautiously in these dark unpredictable lands, was a theme that kept repeating itself inside Nathan's head.

Nathan had thought it only fair to warn Leigh that his name too had been placed on the Taingda Mingyi's list of suspect persons. Leigh's reaction, as Nathan half-expected, was much the same as Matthews, that the Burmese would not arrest anyone at the moment because they had no reason to do so. That would only further blacken their reputation with the outside world. 'The Burmese are not so stupid they would deliberately alienate themselves from the civilized countries on whom they most rely,' had been Leigh's opinion, 'but if either the Burmese, or the British, declare war,' Leigh had gone on to say, 'then I suppose we'd better watch out. But I'll go carefully, don't worry. And thanks for warning me.'

'Don't thank me, thank Ba Say for "sticking head right inside den of lion's mouth",' Nathan had quipped.

Nathan got up from his chair to go and stand by the verandah balustrade. He had been conscious of a slight vibration under his feet, his thin Burmese sandals disguising nothing. His hand on the balustrade felt the same vibration. He looked at the hanging lamps on the verandah but they seemed perfectly steady and everything pinned on the walls had not moved either.

'What's the matter?' Leigh asked. 'Earthquake?'

'I don't know ... I just felt a drumming in the ground ... horses! Christ almighty! Leigh, grab the guns ... there on the wall behind you, they're all loaded.'

'Dacoits?' Leigh asked springing into action.

'You bet your life.' Nathan took his rifle down. 'The Bos around here have been after my hide because I refuse to kow-tow to their system of easy-pickings ... I'm going to tell the servants to lock up and warn Minthami to stay out of sight,' he ran off, shouting along the verandah to his household staff.

Leigh felt dizzy. He parked himself behind a marble pillar, his mouth feeling like sand-paper, an awful feeling upon him that Nathan was right to be perturbed about the Taingda Mingyi's threats, for the man wasn't to be trusted. He eased the barrel of the rifle in-between the balusters of the verandah, wondering to himself where Nathan and his men had got to.

The pounding along the Bund increased, growing louder, drawing nearer. The first horse and rider came into view, not pausing but galloping at breakneck speed along the driveway. Leigh took careful aim. He waited a hairsbreadth of a second for the dacoit to reach a space between the trees, sighting him in the bright moonlight which helped to target him, and fired. The horse reared, throwing its rider to the ground.

Not a movement. Good. He had hit the first one, first time round, Leigh waited for the others.

Nathan at the other end of the verandah, his men hidden in the bushes flanking the house, heard the dacoit's terrified horse plunging off to the back somewhere. Waiting for the second wave of them, the rest of the gang in one bunch, was interminable.

Then Nathan saw Leigh creeping across the grass: 'Leigh,' he hissed 'don't be a bloody fool ... it's their kind of tactics to draw us out. The others will come.'

Leigh's hoarse cry through the darkness made Nathan freeze. Christ, he'd been warned! The dacoit had probably been shamming anyway. Nathan leapt over the verandah and, crouching, made use of the shadows to go to Leigh's assistance, dreading finding him with his throat slit by a slashing knife.

The two figures were locked together. Nathan could not make out what was happening. 'God, Oh God, Oh God ...' Leigh moaned in the darkness.

'Leigh, what the hell's going on?' A small feathered toque rolled to Nathan's feet. He became aware that the body in Leigh Buchanan's arms was a woman's. 'Milly ... it's Milly, Nathan. Milly, I've killed her. She's covered in blood, can't you see?'

'Christ Almighty, get her to the house ... no, don't you, I will. Just fetch Ko Lee to me ... no don't bother ...' He had already scooped Milly Sinclair into his arms and was running to the house. Nathan placed her gently on the white couch. 'Stay with her.' Leigh had followed. 'I'll get Minthami ... I'll send Ko Lee for a doctor.'

He could see Leigh had gone to pieces and was useless. Nathan himself, dry-mouthed, had an awful feeling in his gut.

Minthami, who had been back at Whitewalls for the past month, now came running down the stairs, tying her sash: 'What, what? What is happening?'

'Milly's been shot. Her head's covered in blood. Do something Minthami for Christ's sake. Leigh's like a madman in there ... Ko Lee go run, run I said! Fetch the bloody doctor.'

Minthami pushed Leigh away. On his knees with his head on Milly's breast, both arms clasped her lifeless body. 'Move, let me see her.' She glanced up at Nathan, 'Take him please and give him brandy before he too die.' Minthami gently touched the wound on Milly's forehead. She moved aside the chestnut curls so she could see exactly what damage had been done. 'Fetch smelling-salts and brandy ...'

'Dammit all Minthami, you can't give her brandy when she's not breathing.'

'She is breathing very nicely. Do as Minthami say please, Shwe Nat, and presently she will be all right, but for now she is concussed.'

'You mean she's not shot?'

'No, she not shot. Just graze on head where she fall on gravel. I think it horse who is shot, for he squeal very badly when I hear him just now. You go look after horse, I look after Milly.'

Leigh, white and trembling in the armchair in which Nathan had shoved him with a drink of brandy, simply could not still the tremor of his two hands clasped round the glass. What Minthami had just said began to register with him. 'She's not dead . . .?' Ashen-lipped he spoke like a voice from the tomb.

'She alive. She lucky. You men, always playing with guns to kill people, then think afterwards, it very silly. Fee Tam, please to bring cotton-wool, cloth and bandages,' she ordered the old Chinese woman who had come into the room. 'I think her eyes begin to open . . .' Minthami detected a movement from the corner of her eye and waved Leigh down again. 'No, please not to talk to her till she better.' She smiled at Milly who stared back at her in a daze, wondering who she was. 'It all right Milly. I am Minthami, wife of Captain Vorne. You in his house. You remember what has happened?' She presently asked the girl when she seemed less torpid.

Milly put her hand to her head: 'I think the horse threw me.'

'Good!' Minthami beamed. 'She very fine, not lose memory. Milly, you hurt anywhere else except in head?'

'I don't know . . . no, I don't think I do . . . yes, I do . . . I'm sorry. I shouldn't have come here like this.' Milly raised her head, wincing as she tried to move.

'Don't please . . . you lie still for little while longer,' Minthami said, easing Milly gently down again so her head rested on the arm of the padded couch. She bathed and dressed Milly's cuts and grazes and then made her sip a little brandy.

Half-an-hour later Ko Lee panted in with a lady-doctor and Minthami ushered Leigh out. The doctor pronounced that no bones had been broken, Miss Milly's head was not too badly damaged, but she would have a very bad headache and black eyes in the morning. She left after having prescribed a sedative. By the time Nathan came back into the drawing-room with Leigh, Milly Sinclair was sitting propped up with cushions, smiling, chatting and drinking Minthami's China tea.

Nathan exploded; 'Milly Sinclair! Thanks to you riding in here like a damn dacoit tonight, someone's good horse has just had a second shot put through its head to put it out of its misery.' He turned on Leigh,

'And as for you, what a bloody awful marksman you are! Clean through the eyes your cock-eyed bullet went. In one side, out the other, blind as a bat but not dead, the poor dumb beast, God!'

Milly shuddered, Leigh flinched and Minthami waved her hands at Nathan.

'And don't you tell me to shut-up, woman! I want a full explanation from Milly Sinclair as to what the devil she means riding out in the middle of the night as though dacoits were after her. You deserve the spanking of your life, young lady, and I'm going to tell Matthew to give it to you.'

'Nathan please ...'

'Shut-up Leigh, this is my house. Well, come on Milly, explain.'

Milly burst into tears.

'Nathan, I won't have this.' Leigh went to Milly's side. 'Can't you see she's upset?' He held her hand.

'So am I. So are we all. She might have got herself killed as well as her horse. And you would have done the killing Leigh Buchanan, so make no mistake!'

'I'm sorry, Nathan, I can't take that, I'm leaving, and Milly's coming with me ...'

'No, Milly not come!' Minthami said firmly. 'Doctor say she must not be moved. Please everyone to sit down and drink more whisky and brandy. Everyone very upset, but now it all over, and no bad harm done. Leigh, you must not take Milly back to Mandalay tonight, but you go tell Matthew she all right.'

'No, please don't,' Milly interrupted, 'I don't want to upset them anymore. They don't know I've left the house. They were all asleep when I crept out. I've run away, Leigh. Please don't be angry. But Clare has been so beastly, I couldn't stay there another minute listening to the awful things she's been saying about us. I told Matthew, and he understands. But Clare has sent a wire to my parents asking them to come and fetch me back to Coimbatore. It's such a disgraceful request, and Matthew himself was very upset about it. If I could just remain here tonight, perhaps Leigh could have a word with Matthew tomorrow regarding what has happened. I'm terribly sorry I've caused so much trouble, but really, I'd rather die than go back to live with Clare.'

'You nearly did, Milly Sinclair,' Nathan glowered at her but Minthami silenced him. She put an end to the confusion. Clapping her hand she ordered her servants about. Milly was put to bed in a guest room, while downstairs Minthami instructed the two men: 'Please, in morning which is very soon now, you two have chota-hazri and then ride to Mandalay so no one thinks bad that Leigh and Milly sleep under same roof when they not married.'

'Get on with it Minthami,' Nathan prompted impatiently.

'Captain Vorne to tell Mr Sinclair of poor Milly living with much unhappiness in house of sister-in-law, and please to treat Milly with little more respect and kindness because she good girl. Also to ask parents in Coimbatore to give blessing for Milly to marry Mr Buchanan so she have her own house to live in.'

'So easy,' Nathan growled from his chair. 'Supposing they say no?'

'Then they silly peoples,' said Minthami without further ado, climbing off the arm of the chair where she had been perching: 'Now Minthami go to bed. In morning we talk again. When sun shine, it make everything look different so we worry no more.' She left them alone.

Nathan and Leigh exchanged glances. Leigh, a wing of dark hair falling across his brow, his blue eyes troubled, said: 'I can't ask Milly to marry me when my throat's about to be cut. I want to marry her, of course I do, more than anything else in the world. But it wouldn't be fair on her right now. What would happen to her out here alone, if something happened to me?'

'What happens to us all out here,' said Nathan standing up. 'If we're strong we lick it, if not, then it licks us. Well, are you coming to Mandalay for breakfast, or not?'

CHAPTER
TWENTY-TWO

ONE

Nathan supervised the transference of his stocks of rice, coal and pulses to his storage houses at Bhamo and Rangoon. It was one extreme to the other since Mandalay, in the middle, was now the centre of dacoit aggression. The removal of his coal reserves caused him the greatest headache. One spark, and the wharf would go up like Dante's inferno. His boats were already overloaded in both directions and he wanted desperately to get his coal down to Rangoon where the British would pay him a very good price if they were inching their way toward a third Burmese war. Nathan wondered where he could lay his hands on some more flats, every single one of them having been expropriated by the Burmese Government during the past few weeks. His thoughts and activities were interrupted by Mr Sundevava who minced along the wooden jetty at the high-water landing point where everyone was busy.

Mr Sundevava removed his straw torai, mopped his swarthy brow with a mildew-spotted handkerchief and said to Nathan, 'Good morning, Captain de Veres-Vorne. It is very foggy this morning, is it not? All this dampness is not good for my health, and it does not look as if the mist is likely to clear before midday.'

'It usually is a little murky on the river about this time of year, Mr Sundevava,' Nathan said, thumbs in the two

300

top pockets of his shirt, fawn cavalry drill trousers tucked into black boots thick with river mud. Head uncovered, the river breeze that was gently dispersing the mist, ruffled his fair hair.

'Captain de Veres-Vorne, is it possible you have any space, any space at all for a consignment of raw cane on one of your barges going up to Bhamo?'

'How much raw cane, Mr Sundevava?'

'Oh not a lot, not a great deal at all, a few tons, that is all.'

''Fraid not, Mr Sundevava. The last of my barges went on its way to Rangoon yesterday.'

'Oh then I am done for! The sugar represents a great sum of money to me — very personally. In this instance, I was hoping too to get my wife and child away if there is to be a war between the British and the Burmese. It is terrible that this should come to Mandalay in our time. I don't know if you were there, Captain de Veres-Vorne, but I myself was at the meeting of the Chamber of Commerce in Rangoon when it was simply urged that Upper Burma should be annexed by the British. And now this ultimatum to the Burmese Government to send the Bombay-Burma Trading case to arbitration is really throwing the cat in with the pigeons. And what are the Hlutdaw going to do regarding this British insistence about regulating themselves as well as a new Resident to Mandalay with no bowing and scraping attached? I do not think the Hlutdaw will wear that, nor that the British Resident have a private steamer at his disposal — I think that is so he can make a quick getaway in future. Meanwhile, while the British are desirous of keeping open their trade routes between Bhamo and China, we all have to suffer, we neutrals.'

'That's about the gist of it, Mr Sundevava.'

'It is going to inconvenience we businessmen quite considerably, Captain de Veres-Vorne. I shall be rendered destitute if I am caught inbetween the devil and the deep blue sea.'

Nathan grinned. 'I shouldn't worry too much, Mr

301

Sundevava. It will all blow over and be done with across the chota-hazri table. King Thibaw won't put up too much of a resistance and will accept the British ultimatum. He doesn't really want to fight them. He's off already to his Palace at Shwebo where he'll bite his nails, drink his gin and mull over his Pali scripts. In the end he'll prefer meditation to gunfire, just you wait and see.'

'Do you really think so, Captain de Veres-Vorne? Because, if you think that is the case, then I am a happy man again.'

'Why sure. But look here, if you're really worried about your sugar — and your wife and child — there are three flats the Burmese haven't pinched as yet. They're hidden in a creek just up from Go Wain. I should go and see old Dimitri the Greek about hiring them. Mind you, they'll need some running repairs on them first.'

'Thanking you, oh so gratefully, Captain de Veres-Vorne,' gushed the Indian gentleman. 'I will go and talk to Dimitri as of this very moment.' He replaced his torai and sloped off. Observing the little man's slippery departure in his crumpled cream suit, Nathan's grin broadened. Poor old Dimitri's flats were in a little creek all right, lying at the bottom of it because they had been overloaded. Anyway, Nathan thought, good luck to old Pathan Sundevava if he could dredge them out by the morning. As for his sugar, like hell he was worried about it — he was mighty worried he wouldn't get his raw opium in exchange for raw cane — a nice little lucrative deal he had going with the Chinese Black Flags on the northern border!

TWO

Matthew was sorting out his office and putting his papers in order when Clare burst unceremoniously into the Residency. Breathless, she confronted him, lips thin, her face flushed. Her bonnet and shawl were awry and she looked most unattractive in this, the eighth month of her pregnancy: 'Matthew, what's this note you sent by one of your orderlies to get the house cleared? What do you mean pack my things?'

'That's right Clare. Pack your things. Pack the children's things and tell Milly to pack her things. You're all leaving on the *Belle Hélène* to Rangoon — first thing tomorrow morning.'

'Why?'

'Because, dear woman, I have been recalled. We have all been recalled. The Burmese Government has turned down all but two of the clauses in the British ultimatum. They have no wish ...' he picked up the communiqué that had arrived that morning, 'quote, to regulate external relationships in accordance with the advice of the Government of India,' therefore it is assumed by H.M.G. that the Burmese have chosen to fight us for possession of Upper Burma. All the Europeans are leaving on the steamers, and you don't want to miss your chance of leaving with them, do you?' His look was stern, his manner toward her cold and aloof. Clare knew it was all on account of Milly and Leigh Buchanan, Matthew having chosen his sister's side rather than his wife's. Matthew had brought Milly back to live with them in Kyauktawgyi Road, had made Clare apologize to both Milly and Leigh and had extracted a promise from Clare to treat Milly a little more civilly. The only comfort Clare had derived from the whole miserable affair, was that Milly and Matthew's parents had not given their permission for Leigh Buchanan to marry their daughter as they had never met him, and as Milly was under-age, she would either have to wait until she was twenty-one or Mr Buchanan would have to travel all the way to India to meet the Sinclair family before they gave their approval to a union with their daughter. To date, none of that had happened. Clare could gloat in private.

'I cannot go,' Clare said to Matthew. Her hands were laced across the bulge of her skirts. He tried not to look at her. She did nothing to please him.

'You will go,' Matthew said, 'because I wish the children to return home to Coimbatore.'

'I cannot travel in my condition,' Clare said stubbornly. 'You wouldn't want me to give birth in the middle of the Irrawaddy, would you?'

'No Clare, I would not. However, the child is not due for another four to five weeks, and you'll have plenty of time to reach Rangoon before that happens. Nathan has made the offer of his new house which he and Minthami have bought by the lake, so you'll be well taken care of there. Minthami is already at the house — which I believe they have named Zayat — so rest assured your confinement will take place in a very suitable place!' He fidgeted. 'Nathan thought it best she return there for her own safety ... Mandalay is not a safe place at the moment, Clare, and I don't have to tell you why, so be like Minthami and obey your husband.'

'Are you travelling with us?'

'No. I must stay here until the last person who wishes to leave Mandalay of their own free will has done so.'

'Supposing the Burmese arrest you in the meanwhile?'

'Then that is my misfortune. But I cannot leave this office until I know that everyone under British protection has been taken to safety.'

'That's noble! All right. I'll go to Rangoon, but I expect it's like any other native city, dirty. I wish you had made arrangements for me to go on some other boat, I don't like Captain de Veres-Vorne.'

'You don't like anyone, Clare.'

'Don't be nasty, Matthew.'

'I'm stating the truth. Why did you marry me Clare?' he asked, glancing across at her for a brief moment, his attention while talking to her held by the two telegrams on his desk.

'Because you asked me.'

'Did I? How very thoughtless of me.'

Her lower lip trembled, her fingers plucking the fringes of her shawl. 'If I'd known you didn't love me, I wouldn't have said yes. I would have married someone else. Someone less ... less miserable!' she flung at him before hurrying out of the Residency. She would have run home but for the weight pressing on her legs.

THREE

Angela, from her vantage point on Mandalay Hill could see lines of fire streaking along streets of wood and thatch.

No one had expected violence would erupt so quickly on the heels of the British ultimatum being rejected by the Burmese Supreme Council. Everyone had expected King Thibaw and his Government to go back to the British with further talks. Now there was a mad scramble for the boats. Away toward the Bund Angela could almost feel the urgent activity taking place as the European populace fought to secure passages on the last of the steamers going down to Rangoon. She hoped Matthew's little family would go safely with Nathan at first sailing light, and before the Burmese closed the river.

Refugees were flocking into the Sasana Convent, terrified of the mobs rioting in the streets. She went to help.

Edom Gideon, among those who had chosen to stay in Mandalay, despite the inflammable situation between the Burmese and the British, relied on his neutrality as an American subject to protect himself and his little flock.

The Dacoits, their Bos-leaders and those with a grudge against the British, did not respect Edom Gideon's neutrality — he was white, he spoke English, he behaved like a Britisher and to all intents and purposes he was one of them. They threw stones at his Mission, hurled insults and waved their lighted torches threateningly. His congregation, a handful in number, were on their knees in prayer when several windows were broken, showering them all with glass. A shard cut him above the right eye and blood ran down his face. Nancy Stuttgart screamed. The rest followed suit and a general panic ensued as everyone stampeded toward the heavy teak doors at the back of the Hall.

'Stop!' The minister bellowed from the rostrum. 'Bolt those doors from the inside! Let not another person move from this place of worship, for, where one or two are gathered together, there shall the Lord be found. Mrs Gideon, I'll thank you to set a good example and be the first to drop to your knees.'

Nanette, now in her middle-age, held her beloved child in her arms and sank to her knees. Two year-old Duke Gideon did not like that one bit and set up a squall, his face buried in the curve of his mother's neck.

Minister Gideon wiped the blood from himself with his handkerchief, his face animated from within with a power and glory not witnessed in such dimension before. The Light of the World shone all around him, and indeed, if he were to be ignominiously blinded in both eyes, his congregation knew that this was *the* moment of truth written on wondrous pages they had all been told about;

'Mrs Wandersmeith, Miss Stuttgart, Mrs Gideon, the rest of my beloved ones, we are here to witness an historical, nay a biblical moment! We are the privileged. We are here in a heathen land of golden bells and pomegranates wherein the sands of time have been merely the preparation to this one glorious moment of our lives — the moment of truth! The Lord shall Christianize the heathen, he shall cast down their pagan idols, their graven images, and their devil worship; Buddha shall not prevail. We shall not be found wanting when this land is set free from the curse of irreligion to the dawn of the new millenium. Let us pray. He who is our salvation, our tower of strength in these troubled times, Lord, Lord, we call upon thy name. The Lord is a man of war; The Lord is his name. Pharoah's chariots and his host hath he cast into the sea; his chosen captains also are drowned in the Red River ...'

'Red Sea, Mr Gideon, not river,' whispered Nanette tremulously, 'Exodus do say sea and not river.'

'Mrs Gideon, I'll thank you to keep that child of yours quiet and not interrupt me when we are in prayer through the Holy Gospel ... the people shall hear and be afraid, sorrow shall take hold on the inhabitants of Mandalay ...'

'Palestrina, Mr Gideon. The Lord will not hear our prayers if we do not tell the truth ...'

'Ahem, Palestrina ... the dukes of Edom shall be amazed. Mrs Gideon, gather up your child and remove him to the back of the Hall. I cannot make myself heard ... God help us ...!'

Nanette screamed. She clutched her boy to her breast, her body curled over his to protect him as the doors gave way and the mob poured into the tiny hall with their dahs, sticks and lighted torches.

The leader of the mob, only a youth, raised his slashing dah ready to strike down on the heads of Nanette and her child, but a chilling voice held his sword-arm paralysed in mid-air. '*Kin Byar!*' The Kachin youth looked to the man who had shouted at him:

Edom Gideon, his hand holding the Holy Bible aloft spoke to the ruffians in their language. '*You* will not strike down my people lest the Lord God of Hosts strike *you* down dead at the very spot on which you stand. Put down your swords and sticks and let my people go. We shall depart this place in peace ... come, follow me ...'

Stepping down off his platform, his right hand still holding the Bible high for all to see and follow, he led his little band from the Mission Hall while the trouble-makers fell back to allow passage of the Christians in their midst.

Edom Gideon crossed Kyauktawgyi Road and climbed the steps of the pagoda after which the street had been named.

'Why is he bringing us in here?' Nancy Stuttgart whispered to Vanda while she cast terrified glances at the colossal marble Buddha with his eighty disciples in

307

shrines all around. 'I thought pagodas were part of Babylon.'

'Exactly, Miss Stuttgart!' Edom Gideon said, over-hearing her whispered words. 'As the Lord spoke against Babylon to Jeremiah the prophet; "Babylon is taken, Bel is confounded, Merodach is broken in pieces; her idols are confounded, her images are broken in pieces. For out of the north there cometh up a nation against her which shall make her land desolate, and none shall dwell therein." We are here to set up our standard, to publish and declare, we shall do so in the midst of our enemies. Let us fall upon our knees, O my beloved, and give thanks to the Lord who has safely delivered us this day from evil.'

FOUR

Kyauktawgyi Road was a scene of confusion and fire.

Clare Sinclair lay on her bed, her children hiding under it. She could hear the frightening mob howling for them outside in the street. She had no wish to be stoned and abused. Clare chewed the end of her handkerchief and drove Milly insane.

'Why doesn't he come? Why? He should be here now, helping to protect us against those savages out there in the street. I want him here ... go and tell Bhuti to fetch him. Tell him to come.' Clare, tossing her head from side to side whined miserably.

'Of course he can't come, be reasonable,' Milly begged. 'Matthew has a duty to keep the Residency open for all those requiring his help.'

'We are his first priority. Why doesn't he send for us so that we too might shelter there?'

'Because, if you got up off that bed and looked out of the window, you'd see why. We wouldn't get beyond the front gate let alone three-quarters of a mile down the road. It's alive with hoodlums making trouble for every-one, even their own Burmese people. We're safer off inside the house than to venture out there. We must stay here. Captain Vorne will send someone if he does not come himself to escort us to his boat. We have to keep ourselves ready, Clare, and not panic.'

'It's easy for you to talk. You're not in my condition.'

'Please Clare, try and get a little sleep until it's time to leave.'

The old Parsee servant Bhuti tapped gently at the bedroom door, the only servant left in the house, all the others having fled, including Jubela the ayah. 'Memsahib ... Missy-Sahib, they have set alight to houses in street. House next door is smouldering and sparks fly on roof. It is not safe anymore to hide in bedroom right underneath roof. You must come downstairs to verandah where it is safer.'

Milly had been aware for sometimes of the smell of burning but had tried not to let her thoughts dwell too much on it. But if the house did catch alight, they would stand no chance with all the wood and thatch around them.

'Clare,' she whispered in the darkness, 'Please will you try and help yourself a little more? I'll look after the children if you can manage to get yourself downstairs onto the verandah. I'll ask Bhuti to help you.'

'No, I don't want to move ... I can't move, my legs won't hold me ...'

'You must try, you must, for the sake of the children.'

'You go, you take the children. I'll stay.'

'You can't Clare, the roof will fall on top of you and you'll burn to death.'

'Oh God, Oh my God ... why did I ever come to Mandalay?'

'I don't know why, But now you're here it's up to you to make the best of things. I must take the children downstairs — you wouldn't want them to die horribly, would you? So, do come on, for their sakes.'

Clare moved her bulk sluggishly as Milly went to the door. 'All right Bhuti, we're coming.' Verity and Peter were curled-up on the floor, fast asleep on their stomachs, the baby Sarah kicking and cooing in her cradle. Milly put Peter into Bhuti's waiting arms, shook Verity to wake her and put her hand in her mother's. 'Clare, you take Verity, I'll bring the baby.' She wrapped Sarah in her shawls and followed Clare downstairs through the smoke-filled house. The dampness of the building saved them for the moment as it only smouldered. Milly hoped it would not suddenly burst into flames like the others she could see along the length of Kyauktawgyi Road, for then it would not take long to devour itself and them. She was worried. She did not think that even on the verandah they would be safe. Milly was in a dilemma, not knowing what to do, wondering whether it would not be better to brave the street and to try and get to the Residency where they might be better off with Matthew — presuming he was still there and not in the Taingda Mingyi's hands. Milly did not want to risk it.

The flurry of people fleeing their houses by paddling across the seventy-five yards of water to safety, made up Milly's mind.

'Bhuti,' she said, 'Sahib has a little fishing-boat hasn't he?'

'Yes, Missy-Sahib, tied to posts of house at foot of wooden steps.'

'Yes, I know where it is. But is it still there? He hasn't used it for a long time and I just wondered.'

'I will go and look ... one moment Missy-Sahib.' He put Peter in the peacock chair, fast asleep still with his thumb in his mouth. Bhuti padded to the end of the verandah where steps led down to the moat. Matthew had had a gate put across to prevent the children falling down into the water, the verandah steps open to danger when they had first come to live in the house. Milly heard the bolt squeak as Bhuti opened the little bamboo gate. His voice called back, 'Boat is still here, Missy-Sahib.' He came up again.

The smoke and smell of burning now dense, the children began to cough and splutter as eyes and lungs filled with the pungent fumes of smouldering dahni-

310

palm. 'Bhuti,' Milly said, 'I'll want your help to get Memsahib in the boat as I shan't be able to manage her on my own. If you can get her seated in the boat first, then I can hand in the children.'

Bhuti looked dubious. 'Missy-Sahib, you brave girl. But I think it is not wise. Small boat will topple everyone into water if children move.'

'We haven't a great choice Bhuti. We either stay here and burn to death, or we face the mob outside and get stoned to death. I think we'll have more of a chance on the water.'

'Missy-Sahib, have you ever rowed rowing-boat before?'

'No, I haven't. But I know what to do. You simply have to get the oars to move in the direction you wish to go.'

'It's not so simple, Missy-Sahib. You will drown baba-log and yourselves.'

'No, Bhuti, I shall not. Now please help me ... we're being smothered as it is.' She turned to Clare on her daybed, her eyes closed, seemingly unconcerned about everything going on around her. 'Clare,' Milly shook her. 'Come on, we're leaving. We can't stay here, the house is burning around our heads.'

'Where are we going?'

'Into the rowing boat ... don't argue with me Clare, please!' Milly cried in desperation. 'Please, don't Clare ... now listen. I'm putting those children in the rowing boat and we're getting away from here. Stay if you like, I don't care. But those are my brother's children and I'm not letting them burn to death when there's a chance to get them away via the moat. Come on Bhuti, help me.' Milly marched purposefully toward the steps leading down to the water, the baby still in her arms. 'Bhuti, bring Peter, Verity, you hold onto my skirts and don't let go — your mother's not coming with us.'

'Yes, yes I am ... I don't want to be left alone.' She managed to move fast enough then, and Milly said grimly: 'Bhuti, wait ... take Memsahib down first, and then come back for Peter.'

311

She waited and watched while Bhuti with great patience and tact helped and guided Clare down the slippery wooden steps that were beginning to rot away. Milly prayed they would not snap under their combined weight. 'Memsahib, please to hold with both hands on rails, I will help, so do not be afraid.'

Gently he coaxed the terrified woman into the boat. Clare finally sat in the middle of the canoe type craft. It took only a matter of a few minutes to get the children in the boat, the mother ten times more difficult to cope with.

'Bhuti,' Milly whispered to the faithful old servant leaning over the rail to see them off, 'don't stay here. You will be safe enough as the Burmese are only against the Europeans. Try and go soon, because I think the house will burst into flames at any moment. Don't try to save anything inside the house, your life is more important.'

'Yes, Missy-Sahib ... I will go to Residency and tell Sahib you have taken the family to safety ...' he paused, 'where I tell him you take them?'

'The only way I can go is to the east. I'll try and get to the north-east end of the moat, and then we can go from there across the bridge that will bring us out at the foot of the Kuthodaw. I want to try and get to the Sasana Convent. They'll give us sanctuary. If anyone comes for us from Captain Vorne, tell them where we've gone. Goodnight Bhuti.'

'Goodnight Missy-Sahib ... Memsahib and baba-log.'

Milly, terrified they would all drown before they had gone two yards, was more terrified of fire. It gave her courage to come to terms with the oars. Far more difficult than she had imagined, the long nosed boat kept following its own nose in circles. Milly was stuck, unable to move. She gave a plaintive cry for help: 'Bhuti ... I don't think we've cast off! The boat is still tied to the post.'

She did not see Bhuti put his hand to his head in alarm. All she heard were his scrabbling hands in the darkness as he untied the boat from its moorings. Milly plied the oars again and this time the boat shot forward into the water. They wobbled dangerously. Clare gave a

312

gasp of fright, almost smothering her baby in her lap as she huddled over it. Only Peter and Verity appeared to be 'enjoying the unexpected boat-trip and began to bounce up and down on the seat. Milly, her back bent, plied the oars, her concentration on both the water and the children who would tip them all out. 'Be still ... don't move an inch ... Verity, look after Peter.' She began to get the hang of what she was supposed to do. Finding she was going toward the west instead of to the east where the tiny lights of Mandalay Hill beckoned her, she managed to turn the nose of the boat and get it to go where she wanted. The oars felt unwieldy, heavy as lead, and she thought her shoulders would snap with the effort of getting the boat through the water — and Matthew had told her rowing was easy!

Dipping into the murky water, she felt the blades tangle in weeds and hyacinths and almost wept with frustration and anger. Clare did not help one bit but sat like a mute; her only use at the moment was her lap for the baby. Three minutes later, the scene behind Milly became silhouetted in lurid detail and the house they had just left exploded in spiralling flames.

'Please, please let Bhuti have got out in time, please ...' Her eyes screwed tight, Milly rested on the oars for a moment while she caught her breath. The children began to whimper, only the baby happy with her mother. Then they started to fidget. 'Aunt Milly,' Verity whispered, giggling behind her hands and squirming with delight. 'My feet are wet.'

'So are mine, Verity.'

So are Peter's and Mama's ...'

Milly murmured, 'Row a yard, forward a yard, backwards forwards, pull, pull pull ... back, forward, pull ... smoothly, go smoothly!'

'Aunt Milly ... the water's right over my ankles.'

'Oh God, Verity! Don't say that.'

Milly looked down and was horrified to see the glint of water in the bottom of the boat. It had not been there when they had started off. 'Bail ... quick ... use your hands and shoes. Both of you, Peter and you, throw out the water. Wait, here, under the seat ... see if you can find something to soak it up. Something ... anything! Row a yard, throw a yard, mind the other boats doing the same thing. Oh Clare, won't you please help? I think there must have been a hole above its normal level in the water, and our combined weight has made it that much lower. We'll end up in the middle of the moat unless you do something to help me, your children, and yourself. See if you can find something to get rid of all this water ... we haven't far to go, I hope. ...'

Clare managed to stir herself sufficiently and found a rusty tin can Matthew had used to store his bait. Slowly but ominously water seeped inside, weighing them lower into the moat. Please God, please God, was all Milly was able to think of as she kept her prayers to the rhythm of her shoulders while her arms strained to snapping point.

It was a nightmare she never wanted to relive. How far, how far? Milly did not know how far three-quarters of a mile was on water, only that it was half the length of Kyauktawgyi Road which she kept on her left as she rowed toward the north-east bridge. A hundred years later she saw the dark hulks of barges at their moorings. At the landing stage, she slipped the unobtrusive rowing boat between some steps and a gigantic State Barge glittering with gold. Milly had to sit quietly for a few moments, her body quivering with exertion. She realized she was damp and clammy right through to her skin. Her hair stuck to her scalp and her forehead, while she had the most tormenting pain through her eyes. Any undue stress brought on her headaches — ever since she had been thrown from her horse in Nathan Vorne's driveway. Presently Milly felt a little better, conscious that if they all sat there for much longer they would be paddling in the canoe. 'Clare,' Milly said, 'take some deep breaths to steady your nerves, it does seem to help. Then you must help me to get the children up the steps to the landing stage. Give me the baby ... no, I think a better idea would be if I went first onto the steps and you guide the children across to me. I'll put the baby down on the ground when I help you out. Give me your hand, Verity, there's a good girl. You Peter, sit still till I come back down the steps for you. Verity, please watch the baby carefully, don't let her crawl off the edge while I help your mother.' Milly was exhausted.

The royal boatmen were either asleep or did not care about anything going on around them. Milly was glad that there was precious little happening at this north-east sector of palace walls, the mob violence seeming to be confined to the other end of Kyauktawgyi Road where the British Residency was situated. She hoped Matthew was all right and that the Burmese still respected the small patch of ground the British owned in Mandalay, and so would not actually enter its compound.

Standing on the wooden landing stage with Matthew's difficult family on dry land once again, Milly's knees trembled with relief. She hoped she could manage the Kuthodaw steps.

Verity took her mother's hand. Peter on the other side of Clare clutching her skirts, his thumb never away from his mouth. He was sleepy and irritable and Clare snapped at him because he wanted to be carried.

The sleeping baby over her shoulder, and quite a weight at ten-and-a-half months, Milly said to Peter; 'Mama can't carry you, Peter, so be good. If you're very good and don't cry, the Amagyi-Angela will give you some jaggery when we get to the top of the hill.'

Two Burmese women solved the problem for them. On their way to take refuge in one of the pagodas, as all the rest-areas and sanctuaries were full of Mandalay's inhabitants because of danger in the streets, they took it in turn to carry Peter up the thousand steps. Clare, able to climb only a few steps at a time, made the journey ten times more laborious. They rested frequently, every five minutes or so. It was midnight when they finally arrived outside the Sasana Convent, its gates wide open to receive refugees. The climb had taken them an hour-and-a-half.

CHAPTER
TWENTY-THREE

ONE

'Amagyi-Angela, Amagyi-Angela! Come quickly, there are English people asking for you and I can't understand a word they're saying — only your name.' The Head Nun found her feeding a little blind boy. 'Go,' said the Buddhist lady, taking the spoon out of Angela's hands, 'I will attend to these people. You see to them.'

'Milly, Clare ... goodness, what a state you're in!' Angela greeted them with dismay. 'What's been going on? I thought you were going to Rangoon with Captain Vorne?'

'We are,' said Milly, slumping on the ground in utter exhaustion. She sat there looking up at the Amagyi-Angela with her big soulful eyes. 'Only no one came for us. The house was burning down around our heads and we had to get away. We came via the moat.'

Angela, silently admiring plucky little Milly, said, 'sit there all of you ... let me have the baby, Clare. I'll fetch you something to eat and drink, then you must sleep.' She took the robust Sarah from her mother's arms. The other two children were already asleep on ground-mats placed in the covered rest-area full of people.

'I'll just have a drink of water,' Milly said, 'Clare and the children can stay here but I must get to Whitewalls.'

'Milly Sinclair, have you taken leave of your senses?' In astonishment Angela looked at her.

'I suppose I must have,' Milly said wanly, 'otherwise I don't think I could have managed. But I have to see Captain Vorne and get him to postpone his departure or he will leave without us.'

'Captain Vorne would do no such thing Milly. If you're supposed to be sailing to Rangoon with him, then he'll wait or come looking for you himself.'

'But he won't know where we are. The servant Bhuti was supposed to take a message to Matthew telling him that we were making for the Sasana. Matthew would have let Captain Vorne know of our whereabouts, but minutes after we got the boat away the house seemed to explode in a ball of fire. I don't know whether Bhuti got out alive or not. That's why I'm worried in case no one can find us and the last boat leaves without us. I know it's all confusion and terror in Mandalay, but the rioters seem to be gathered mostly in the west end near the Residency. If I take the West Staircase down the Hill and cross the open land, I can reach the river without going anywhere near the city. It won't take me very long.'

'You are not going alone, Milly. I shan't let you. It will mean going through the shanty end of town where all the meanest elements of Mandalay gather along the swamps.'

'You go there, Amagyi-Angela,' Milly countered, 'so it cannot be altogether bad.'

'It isn't altogether bad Milly, but there are some rough people who dwell down there. And I go in amongst them because of who I am. It will be different for you, a young English girl alone, walking the north part of the city without any protection. Sheer madness! I will not allow it.'

Shades of a speech her Aunt Lydell had once made regarding a certain tiger-hunt, came back. At that moment, she sounded just like her. Angela hesitated. 'Milly, if you really are insistent on this, I'll come with you. The children and Clare are safe enough here — they're already asleep. Besides, Captain Vorne will be able to tell us what's going on and find out more about

317

Matthew at the Residency. I know that will put your mind at rest — and mine.' She smiled: 'We're not going to get any sleep otherwise.'

Angela gave the baby Sarah into the care of a young Burmese nun, and in a little while returned with a robe for Milly. 'You must get out of those wet clothes, Milly. Put this on. It will make it easier for us to go through Mandalay without drawing attention.' She handed Milly the white robe of a novice.

The Head Nun raised her eyes in mild surprise when she heard of the Amagyi-Angela's plans, but kept her own counsel. She was fully aware that the English woman would do what she had to do, and was not going to interfere with her conscience.

Angela decided that Milly's idea of taking the West Staircase was probably far more sensible than going through the disrupted city and out of it again via one of the bridged-gates. All entrances and exits were, in any case, being guarded by Royal Troops. They would make faster progress out to the Bund by going through the sleeping village of straw and mud on the north-west side of the hill, behind Kyauktawgyi Road.

It was almost two o'clock in the morning. While the rest of the city rebelled in violence, the shanty-town outside Mandalay's walls appeared to be slumbering undisturbed. A pi-dog howled in the eerie stillness. It was too quiet. Angela, her hood concealing her head and face, felt uneasy as she and Milly picked their way through muddy puddles, dirt and litter. Here diseases prevailed in all forms. Matting huts leaned one against the other like houses of cards. Only a puff of wind was required to blow down that straw village beyond Mandalay's gilded gates.

Palace washerwomen poured out of the main North Gate, taking with them bundles of dirty linen. They would wash it in the morning down by the riverside. At ten o'clock each evening the washerwomen returned to the Palace to spend four hours inside sorting their loads, then left again at two in the morning. The guards in their

318

pyatthats manning the gates knew exactly the womens' routine and left the gates open at those hours to allow them free passage.

Angela and Milly, arms tucked into their sleeves, heads bowed in lowly demeanor, hastened through the village of the washerwomen when along one of the alleys to the north a band of dacoits rode into view. One after the other, four, five, six of them, heading for the main North Gate they knew would be open at this hour.

Aroused from sleep, the people of the village poked startled heads from doorways. An old Burmese woman, her white top-knot catching the moonlight, senile and blind in her extreme age, wandered into the alleyway. Dust and noise blown past her, she was caught in the whirlwind of riders while her shrill railings kept a tryst with the demons of darkness who haunted Mandalay. Leaning from his saddle, speed unchecked, one of the dacoits slashed viciously downward as if he would have her head, and the frail creature with upraised arms and unseeing eyes who blocked his path, had her arm sliced cleanly by his dah.

'Ohhh, Ohhh!' Milly Sinclair caught her breath, her face instinctively turning against Angela's shoulder while Angela silenced Milly by a swift hand across her mouth. They had drawn themselves into the shadows, backs fearfully pressed against thin rattan walls as the dacoits raced past them. Scattering the groups of chattering washerwomen with their heavy bundles, the dacoits rode toward the open city.

The Burmese woman's white top-knot unfastened, her hair straggled like a ghostly mist around her as she lay in a pool of blood with a bloodstained hand clawing the air, the other lying dismembered beside her. She breathed in shallow rapid gasps of pain. Shocked villagers gathered around. Milly, her eyes closed against such a pathetic sight whispered, 'Tonight is like a judgement. I can't believe this is happening. Amagyi-Angela, what are we going to do?'

'We must help her, Milly. We can't walk away from

here and leave her like that because there's a boat to catch. Captain Vorne will wait. See if you can find some clean-looking linen we can use to staunch her wound. I don't think the dacoits will be back as they've got inside Mandalay by now, so we'll be safe enough to show ourselves.'

The Burmese woman was in a lot of pain. Low moans rising to a crescendo of agony made them all grit their teeth in that tiny hut, while the bewildered old woman clutched herself in frenzy. Haemorrhaging badly from the open end of her amputated arm, her bindings rapidly became soaked in blood which Angela and Milly renewed as fast as they could. The bleeding just would not stop: Angela whispered in English while the woman's family wept and wailed by her side, 'We've got to find a doctor! I can't do anymore for her, she needs laudanum to knock her out. There's a lady-doctor in Kyauktawgyi Road who will come out to her. It means I'll have to leave you here alone with these people. I'll try not to be too long. Will you be all right, Milly?'

'I'll be all right, but will you, Amagyi-Angela? I don't think you ought to go.'

'I must Milly. We can't let her die so dreadfully. At least the laudanum will ease her out of this world without much more suffering.'

Milly nodded. 'Very well, I'll sit here and do my best for her.'

Daughters and grandchildren gathered around Milly whom they believed to be a nun like the Amagyi-Angela. The only communication was by smiles and actions. Milly felt wretched. She could not remember a time when she had felt more wretched. She wished she were with Leigh, she wondered what he was doing and where he was; he might even be in Mandalay for all she knew — so near and yet so far.

Angela, not far from the North gates, passed a small Buddha shrine made of Sagyin marble from local mines and, like Nathan's house built of the same marble, it shone in the moonlight. From the grove of mango and palm trees surrounding the shrine, a man stepped into her path.

Angela instinctively kept her head down, her arms tucked into her sleeves. She forced herself to remain calm, for the shadowy creature skulking so suspiciously in the grove was surely a dacoit. Usually, however, dacoits never bothered women, their main concern that of looting, and so Angela hoped he would leave her alone, especially as she was protected by her nun's habit.

But he was not going to leave her alone. His face and voice concealed by scarves, he approached her with muffled request:

'As a holy woman, it is permitted for you to nurse sick men. My man is bleeding from a bullet wound in the chest. Please come inside and attend upon him with the skill and wisdom of your calling.' A dah in his hand made his message perfectly clear, and Angela, not so brave she could afford to ignore the threat of beheadment, followed him into the shrine.

In one corner of the shrine, joss-sticks illuminated not only the gold-leafed Buddha, but a man lying on the impacted earth floor. He was coughing blood. Angela knelt beside him. Blood trickled in a steady stream from one corner of his mouth.

She turned back his blouse to discover the site of perforation, a small black hole that had staunched itself. 'He's bleeding internally into his lungs,' she tried to explain, 'there is nothing I can do to save his life. I'm on my way to Kyauktawgyi Road to get some laudanum for an old woman who is also badly injured, and I'll bring some back for this man too.'

'The medicine you speak of, will it save his life?' The Bo leaned over her, the flickering joss-sticks throwing his gigantic shadow across the arched roof of the shrine. 'Or will it be better that I should put him out of his misery now?'

Angela, on her knees, looked up at him, answering his question with sincerity, 'No, but it will stop his pain.'

The Bo seemed to be riveted, his deep black stare penetrating into her green eyes, and in that instant, recognition was born on both sides. Though his face was muffled she knew he was no Burman, for, in the harsh belly-laugh of disbelief bursting through his nainsook scarves, a shattering explosion inside her own head dispersed fragments of revulsion all through her body to tear her out all over again by her very roots.

He tried to pull the hood from her, but her hands clawed against his, his laugh, behaviour, vileness, resurrecting from the dead something she had kept deep-hidden in the Sasana Convent for six years — an act of murder and she the murderess atoning for a crime she had not in the first place committed.

Against her knee she felt the cold hard pressure of metal. Her skirts had hidden the pistol tucked into the injured man's cummerbund as she knelt by his side. Her brain cooler, sharper, clearer than it had ever been, she took and held the pistol steady with two hands while her head and hood were dragged backward by the man who was Garabanda. She shot him in the forehead. This time she made certain he would never stand up again to torment anyone. This time, she had nothing to pay.

Angela ran out of the shrine and all the way back to the injured woman's hut. Her chest heaving, laden with red-hot iron, she could not breathe and was hardly aware of what she was doing.

Milly, her head on her knees, was half-asleep when Angela burst in panting unevenly. 'I'm sorry you had a wasted journey,' Milly said, rising stiffly to her feet, 'she stopped breathing about ten minutes ago so I think she must be dead — her family seem to think so, but you see for yourself ...' Milly broke off, aware suddenly of Angela's haunted face, eyes and lips utterly colourless,

'Amagyi-Angela,' said Milly disquieted by Angela's appearance, 'you look as if you've seen a ghost, what's happened?'

'Nothing, nothing ... come on Milly, let's get out of here. Run, please run, we must get to Whitewalls.'

Ko Lee answered her urgent summons on the great brass bell outside the double front doors of Whitewalls. He was alarmed by the sight of the women on the Captain's doorstep. 'I go find Cap'ain, ladies, one moment please.'

Nathan was swift on Ko Lee's heels, still in his day clothes though it was the dawn hour. 'My God Angela!' he said striding across the hall, 'What's been happening to you? Why are you covered in blood? You, Milly Sinclair! My dear girl, I've spent half the night looking for you, and I've only just returned from Mandalay. What the hell's been going on?'

'Shades of Loloi, Nathan ... but take Milly inside please. She's dead on her feet ... she'll explain everything, I must go.'

Angela turned and ran down the verandah steps. Milly, past her last reserves of strength practically fainted in Nathan's arms. He scooped her up and placed her for the second time on the couch in his drawing-room. He told Fee Tam to look after her. Then, nimble-footed, he took the steps of the house and raced across his gardens in Angela's wake. He caught up with her halfway along the grey river-road, but in the opposite direction to Mandalay.

'For Christ's sake, Angela.' His breath caught in harsh gasps, he grabbed hold of her elbow and pulled her round with such force she slammed into him, taking the wind out of him and what little she had left in herself.

To Nathan, she sounded like a wounded animal with all the hounds of Hades after her. His arms came around her while she panted her jagged breath against his shoulder. He held her close and soothed her as he would a frightened colt.

The knotted rigidity of her body slowly melted out of

her as he held her tightly, tenderly. Then suddenly he bent his mouth to hers and silenced her rasping breath in a kind of loving that tilted her whole world to meet the yearning inside her. Hungrily she clung to him, feeding from him as he himself searched and dragged and prolonged their kisses into an eternity that harboured only themselves. Starved for so long of any feelings of affection, she could only drown in the deep dark well of velvet into which they had both slipped one Irrawaddy night when he had proved to her what a beautiful place the world could be, their bodies pledged to one another, and that without him, she was incomplete. Then his actions changed, his desire heightened to the searching greed of a lover, hands smoothing her robe against her supple length, feeling the need of her. Loosening the gown to the softly firm upthrust of her breasts, he pressed her to the cotton thinness of his shirt, to the frenetic graspings of flesh and more flesh, to the desire and the impermanence and the sorrow that must come with the parting.

With a cry that was halfway between desperation and pain, she wrenched herself out of his arms and, free of him, pulled her robe over her shoulder. She knew it would always be like this, the furtive guilt, the incompletion and the uncertainty that would always haunt them, thrusting them further and further apart because there was no other way for them to go.

While the grey-wash pearl of dawn lifted the ebon-green palms to the tinge of the new day, he stood looking helplessly at her. Defeated and shaken too, his elbow shielded his mouth as though he would wipe the scourge of her kisses away from him.

'What's the matter?' he asked, bewildered yet again.

Quivering like a spent arrow, she could only accuse. 'You deliberately mock me, Nathan.'

'How?'

'By ... by ...' She could not put her feelings into words.

He supplied them, angrily, 'By still desiring you even

though you have a shaven head? By daring to thrust beneath the holy robes of your estate? By taking advantage of a weak, weak moment in the life of Buddha's most respected, most untouchable, most upright nun? Come off it, Angela! Be a bloody hypocrite with others, don't try it on me. You've just proved to me how wasted you are in your Sasana on the Hill. What happened last night that you should throw yourself at me with such wonderful abandon after throwing only cold water in my face for almost seven years, huh?'

Her eyes narrowed to venomous slits of green glass. 'I took a pistol from a dying man and shot his Bo right right between the eyes. Bang! Dead centre of his forehead. He didn't bleed. He just looked at me in rather a surprised manner. Then he fell crashing on top of the man with the bleeding lungs. I did it in cold blood. Premeditated, and without any remorse. I did it with great enjoyment. A trigger-finger, singing to the melody of revenge! It was very sweet! And I'd do it all over again. That's what I did this night. So you see, you know me very, very well Captain Vorne, this Amagyi-Angela with blood on her hands and all down her nun's robes. Yes, I am a hypocrite, damn you!' She almost snarled at him, only that the snarl became a sob.

He sank to his heels under the Bo tree behind him. She stood out in the road, her weight seeming to press her down on one foot while she hovered on the verge of outer darkness in the look he gave her, unable to grasp the enormity of her extraordinary confession. Angela's fists clenched, she faced him:

'That's why I must return to the Sasana,' she told him. 'I must tell the venerable old Sayadaw of my crime.' She pulled her hood over her head and turned her back on him. 'To take a life, any life, even the life of a mosquito is a mortal sin, isn't it Nathan? That's why I have to seek the Sayadaw's forgiveness.'

His voice had a hollow ring to it when he asked; 'Why did you kill him?'

She shrugged. 'Why does any woman want to kill a man?'

325

'I don't know, I'm asking you.'

Over her shoulder she gave him a scornful glance: 'Because he was out to harm Milly and me. He was not Buddhist. The Buddhists respect women.'

'I still think the last person you ought to go to is the Sayadaw. You will put him in the position of having to take your confession to the Sangha. The Sangha would deem a man's life to be more important than a woman's and would hand your case over to lay authorities.'

'The Burmese can't try me, I'm British.'

'Bloody hell, Angela! It's a bit late to think of that now, isn't it? You're a Buddhist nun, though for what reasons you ever became one, defies my imagination.' He shook his head in despair. Picking up a tiny pebble, he threw it away angrily. 'What did you do with the gun?' he asked.

'I think I must have thrown it down again, I can't remember.' Angela closed her eyes to shut out scenes of the Jainta Pass — the dead Minister, his wife and Felicity Quentin. It was all the same now, whoever it was, the past having become so confused and intermingled with the present, herself, Felicity, Milly, Aunt Emmy, Moke, the Sawbwa of Loloi, revolving and revolving and revolving on a perpetual theme of violence.

'Hell!' Nathan took a deep breath. 'But you're not going to the Sayadaw, that's for sure. The Sangha will pass you over to the Taingda Mingyi and he's just itching for any old excuse to lock away as many Europeans as he can at the moment, and that means Britishers — which is what you still are despite what you think you are, Amagyi-Angela! Believe me honey, Sagaing prison isn't worth the trouble of saving your immortal Buddhist soul, spirit, egolessness or whatever else is supposed to happen to one after death. Those women of Sagaing are just as bad, if not sometimes worse, than their Spotted Face menfolk, and I'd hate you to sit in stocks all day long. The way I see it, nobody's going to miss a couple of dacoits better off dead than alive. If the gun you shot him with is still in the shrine close by the bodies, it's going to look more like a squabble between two bandits, or else they got their just deserts at the hands of the soldiers. No one saw you, did they?'

'I don't think so. In fact, I'm almost sure. There was too much happening in the shanty-village and at the North Gate for anyone to take much notice of a concealed shrine.'

'Then don't be an idiot all your life, Amagyi-Angela. Just forget the whole business and give up Buddhism for the love of God.' Again he picked up a pebble and tossed it away in contemplative moodiness as he hunkered on his haunches, and pink blossoms from the Bo tree drifted upon his head like rosy snowflakes. 'I guess I can forgive you everything — except for having all that glorious hair of yours chopped off. That to me is a worse crime than dacoit-killing,' he said, staring up at her.

It wasn't a smiling matter, but Angela gave a crooked little smile and said, 'Your unhelpful comments still leave me a prisoner of my own conscience.'

'Then that's between your conscience and yourself, honey. I've never suffered from one, but I guess it must be hell. Will you come with me to Rangoon, Amagyi-Angela?' he asked, contemplating her, his strong face expressionless, but his eyes striking the flint-sparks of something deep inside him. 'The *Belle* is waiting.'

'Why, Nathan?'

'So that you won't do anything else foolish while I'm gone from Mandalay. I don't want to see Sagaing again, but if you're insisting on being as naïve as Nelly O'Kelly by moonlight through opening your big mouth to tell the Sayadaw about last night, I must just have to get you out of there, and that won't make me happy.'

'Why Nathan?'

'Hell honey. I don't know! You're just a darn awkward woman I seem somehow to have got myself all tangled up with — just like Minthami! I told you years ago you ought to have married Matthew Sinclair, if only to get out of my hair, and Clare out of Matthew's.'

'Please don't, Nathan. That's not fair to anyone.'

327

'I'm sorry.' he stood up, his eyes watching the sky. 'It doesn't look like I'm going to be sailing at first light. Come on, let's get back to the house and get some organization into our lives. Otherwise the Burmese will close the river to any further traffic and we'll all be stuck up the gum tree ... well, at least your lot will be, I'm neutral. I'm also supposed to be picking up Blaize and the Sinclair ayah who ran off into the arms of the Tennent-Brownes last night. Did you know the rioters burned down Edom Gideon's Mission Hall?'

'No. That's awful. I hope none of them were hurt.'

'I think they all got away inside the Kyauktawgyi pagoda. What gave me the devil of a fright when I first arrived in Kyauktawgyi Road, was seeing the Sinclair house going up in a fireball. I imagined them all burning with it, but there was only the old man inside, their Parsee servant. You know, you Britishers really are messing up the lives of everybody who is not British and only want to live a quiet life in Mandalay.'

He looked at her quizzically as they walked side by side through his gardens and back to his house. Angela could not bring herself to say anything for the moment. She had been fond of the old Parsee servant Bhuti, as faithful to the end as most Indian servants. Green parakeets and fantails sat in the trees, bul-buls sang their hearts out in the golden rush of morning sunlight. Mimosa and jasmine scented the sweet air while the Irrawaddy emerged through the jungle of night like a silver snake shedding its skin to the newborn day.

'Will I ever see Mandalay again?' she said aloud. But it was asked of herself more than of Nathan, their tired eyes registering each other in the participation of a common ground, that of living their lives in the vibrant throb of the golden Orient that would always haunt them. Why was it that palm trees against a blue sky engendered in one's soul such feelings of languid contentment even when that contentment was about to be rudely shattered by the anxious uncertainty of what the future held? Those were Angela's thoughts as she and

Nathan ascended the marble steps of Whitewalls. She sighed. 'A very beautiful house in a very beautiful land of very unpredictable citizens,' she remarked ruefully.

'Rest assured honey, if the British ever win their cold war, hot war or chilly war against the Burmese, they'll make Mandalay so darn predictable, Queen Victoria will be able to sit on Mandalay Hill with her hand out- stretched over the land Buddha gave to Mindon Min, and not even Edom Gideon will be able to shift her ass.'

'Nathan,' Angela said with a little laugh, hoping they hadn't disturbed Milly who deserved all the sleep she could get, 'apart from being predictably outrageous, will you also be so kind as to find out what's become of Matthew when you fetch his wife and children from the Sasana?'

'Sure honey ... Ko Lee, bring us some coffee. Hot and black and then get your tail over to the *Belle Hélène*. We're leaving not later than tiffin-time.' He turned back to Angela, the gallant gentleman once more as he held her chair while she sat down at his verandah table. 'Matthew was doing a grand job by not panicking when I last saw him at roundabout three o'clock this morning. Don't worry, if the British are all like him, they'll be arriving from Thayetmyo with the dâk-mail.'

CHAPTER
TWENTY-FOUR

ONE

The last of the steamers had left Mandalay for Rangoon.

Matthew Sinclair, unable to see his wife and family off on Nathan's boat, had passed on his messages and good wishes to them when Nathan had appeared to tell him they were safely aboard the *Belle Hélène* and due to sail within the hour. That had been twenty-four hours ago.

Now, Matthew, Edwin Tennent-Browne, a Scotsman named Dave MacAbee and a French engineer, Robert René, were the only Europeans left in the Residency. They had barricaded themselves inside, wondering how long they would be confined under house-arrest before the British Flotilla heading for Thayetmyo eventually appeared in Mandalay.

Virtually under seige, it was, for the moment, no great hardship. Food and water was smuggled in to them every day and their slops smuggled out. All in all, with the Residency's stocks of spirits and cigarettes to bolster their flagging spirits during the heat of the day, the first twenty-four hours passed without undue stress.

The following morning, after thirty-six hours of seige, Ba Say brought news that the Taingda Mingyi had ordered two Italians to mine the river at Minhla so that the Flotilla would be blown up before it ever got as far as Ava.

Horrified, Matthew could only stare owlishly at Sir Edwin. 'That means the steamers too — they won't have reached Minhla as yet, and they'll be blown to bits with women and children aboard. We've go to do something, Edwin. We can't just sit here keeping this sort of news to ourselves. They've got to be warned.'

'And how do you propose to do that in view of the telegraph being censored?' Dave MacAbee asked gloomily, adding, 'You know the Burmese won't let us use it anymore.'

Edwin said to MacAbee, 'You're a friend of that Buchanan chap aren't you? Both of you in the same outfit?'

Dave nodded.

'Where's Buchanan now?' Edwin asked.

'The last I heard, he was supposed to have disappeared into the jungle somewhere. The Burmese have no more use for us. Leigh being suspect alien number one because of the kind of work he was engaged in in Thibaw's army, had to make himself scarce mighty quickly. I was already on leave here in Mandalay, so I honestly can't tell you more than that.'

'Have you any idea where he might go?' Matthew asked, polishing his glasses thoughtfully. He breathed mist over the lenses, his concentration on that small and monotonous chore allowing him time to put his thoughts in order.

Dave MacAbee, his feet up on a table, took his time in considering his glass of whisky. Irksome inactivity for so long had made him sluggish. 'Leigh often stays at a toywa near Senyat when he hasn't enough leave to spend in Mandalay. I think he's on pretty close terms with the Thugyi of Senyat who supplies him with all kinds of information. If he needs to hide anywhere, he'd go to the Thugyi.'

There was a heavy guarded silence.

In the end Matthew said to Edwin. 'Are you thinking what I'm thinking?'

'I do believe I am, old chap,' Edwin said, lethargically

331

swatting flies with a long-handled swingle. 'And anything is better than dying of rustification in this place. I've just been observing the movements of all our pani-wallahs and sweeper-boys looking after us despite the Taingda Mingyi's threat to have our guts, and I think we can get away to the jungle to join Buchanan as I have a little ruse up my sleeve.' He got up from his chair and went to the window. Sticking his head out, he saw an orderly curled up on a sleeping-mat snoring his head off. Edwin reached further over the sill and prodded the Burman awake with the swingle. 'Come inside, fellow,' he said.

The man sleepily obeyed.

Edwin instructed him; 'Look here, we want to get a message to Ba Say who is clerk-wallah at the Hlutdaw. But you must do it on the sly. We want Ba Say here tonight, understand?'

The orderly nodded, 'Thakin master, I will fetch him secretly this very night.'

'Good, that's settled that,' said Edwin, making himself comfortable again on the leather chesterfield of Adrian Hawes' days.

'What had you in mind, Edwin?' Matthew asked.

'Dear chap, these Burmese are in and out of here as if it were a pagoda rest-house. Nobody seems to give a fig we're in the Taingda Mingyi's black books and can't step outside even to piss. It won't be too difficult to do a bunk if we disguised ourselves as one of them.'

'You mean just walk out of here in fancy dress?' Dave MacAbee asked, grinning broadly and liking Sir Edwin's idea very much. Even the handsome Frenchman stopped drinking long enough to pay attention.

'I mean just that, old fellow. We'll join forces with Buchanan. He's bound to come up with an idea as to how we can tap the Burmese lines. After all, that's what his job is all about. But Matthew's right, we must let the British at Thayetmyo know of these latest developments concerning Burmese mines — which no one even knew they had.' Edwin scowled at Robert René. 'I don't know

332

what you're doing here with us René, but it's your bunch who are probably responsible for the Burmese laying their hands on ballistic weapons.'

Robert René, quite blasé about the whole affair, shrugged in typical Gallic fashion and went on drinking his whisky.

Mandalay's recent Chargé d'Affairs stopped polishing, put on his glasses and announced, 'I think your idea is simply splendid, Edwin. Let's just hope we don't have too much trouble locating Leigh.'

'Amen to that,' said Sir Edwin.

TWO

The *Belle Hélène* steamed toward Pagan. On either side of the Irrawaddy, across thirty square miles of the plains, hundreds and hundreds of ruined pagodas and temples lay abandoned in the fields. They had been destroyed along with the religious fervour that had built the Kingdoms of Pagan when Kublai Khan and his Tartar hordes had ransacked Burma. Nathan never ceased to be amazed at the sheer zeal which must have gone into the building of Pagan and, in an extraordinary way, still lingered in its ruined stones nine centuries later. Blaize Tennent-Browne entered his wheelhouse and put an end to his private and peaceful reverie spent watching the world go by him.

'Darling,' she said, sidling in and shutting the door, 'May I have a word with you?'

'Nope. Sorry Bee, no offence, but I make it a rule of mine, no ladies in my wheelhouse.'

'Then I'm exempt. Nathan darling, is it really true our Angela has at last seen the error of her ways and has abandoned Buddha for a far greater cause, that of providing light relief on this voyage?'

'Something like it,' he said, his teeth clamped to his pipe.

'I must say, it's about time. Darling, that robe of hers, well, it was too too much! One simply couldn't get within ten paces of her without smelling the whole of Burma on it. I asked Tonsin to drop it in the Irrawaddy — oh, not Angela darling, the robe. She's now wearing a decent frock of mine and apart from her head, seems almost human. She has had the sense to keep it covered I'm glad to say. For one horrified moment, I thought Angela had managed to convert our Milly to Buddhism, but thank the Lord it was only a disguise. What luck I decided to pack a large suitcase. Everyone on this trip appears to have been dipping into my wardrobe — darling, I shall simply have to run up some more chittys with you, or rather, with the Shwe Emporium for some new clothes.'

'Is that so?' Nathan remarked absently, his eyebrows forming arches of impatience. 'Now, if you'll excuse me honey, I've work to do.'

'Not at all, you go right ahead and blow off as much steam as you like darling, because you're not going to like what Angela's just sent me up here to tell you.'

'Out with it, woman!'

'Well, let's just try and put it as delicately as possible shall we? The reason for Clare's extraordinary perkiness this morning has been attributed to her becoming a mother for the fourth time ... ah! No violence please, darling.' She stepped back a pace.

'Goddammit Bee!' Nathan snatched his pipe from his mouth and yelled full blast, almost sending her through the door: 'What did you say? I won't believe it. No woman, no woman, can give birth twice in one year! Can they, can they, can they? Tell me they can't. Go on, tell me they can't! I can't stand it ... that ... that woman cannot, she simply cannot, be giving birth on *my* boat, with *me* around, with a *war* around, with the *Irrawaddy* around — she simply cannot *do* this to me. I am *not* a maternity-home!'

'Oh dear, I knew you'd be angry.'

'I'm not angry. I'm merely finding this all too much to

believe. I'm merely being used. I'm merely becoming a pawn in a lot of women's hands. I won't have it! I am my own master!'

'Don't shout darling ... you'll frighten Clare. Angela thinks it must have been the Kuthodaw steps or Clare got her calculations all wrong.' Blaize, forced backward to the wheelhouse door, cowered.

'Where is she? Where is she? Ko Lee ... *Ko Lee*, get your tail in here and take the wheel ... just lead me to her. I'm going to tip her and her calculations straight into the Irrawaddy.'

Ko Lee took the wheel from him while he stormed along the deck, and Blaize, fluttering beside him, said, 'Calm down, darling. I know you're all hot air and don't mean a word of it ... after all, it was last December, and this is November and it only takes nine months ... Nathan! You simply cannot go in there. Clare is in labour.' Her back to the cabin door behind which Clare and Angela struggled for the second time, she tried to protect the women. 'Angela is having a very hard time of it, she wouldn't want a man around ...'

'I'm the Captain of this boat, and who the hell is giving birth, Angela or Clare?'

'Darling, don't get shirty with me. It's a breech birth — or so I've been told by one who seems to know everything — the baby's stuck and won't come out and that's why Angela's perspiring in your cargo hold. Clare is being difficult as usual.' She gave a quick grimace of clarification, 'You know what I mean.'

'Mind out of the way, Bee. I do know something about breech births — Roi was one. And Angela can probably do with some constructive help.'

'My, my!' said Blaize in fiendish admiration. 'Not only does he sail a good ship, but he's also an accomplished accoucheur who knows how to handle breech babies. Aye-Aye, Cap'ain!' Saluting him, she smartly stepped aside to allow him in. 'But remember, it's the mother and not the midwife, Cap'ain, who needs her hand held.'

335

'Cut it out, Bee,' Nathan growled as he opened the cabin door, and wished he had not.

THREE

Milly Sinclair paced the floor of the hot little cabin, perspiration beading her smooth brow as she crooned to Sarah who had been screaming with stomach pains. Next door, she could hear the awful sounds of Clare's confinement. Milly did not know who was having the worse time of it, the mother or her assistants.

'Nini baba, nini. Muckan roti, cheeni. Hamara baba sogya, muckan, roti hogya,' she crooned to the child in an age-old lullaby of the East, sung by ayahs to their charges from time immemorial. Milly remembered it from her nursery days in Coimbatore, 'Sleep baby, sleep.'

'It no good singing,' Jubela announced mournfully from her corner. She sat on the floor, Peter and Verity both asleep in her ample lap, their heads on her shoulders while she rocked them soothingly to the swish of water cleaved by the *Belle*. 'It no good singing,' she repeated, 'baba require mother's milk. If not requiring of mother's milk, then goat's milk. But baba need milk. If English Memsahibs pay attention to Jubela, they will know to sit mother on hot brick to make baby come right way up. So much screaming and shouting on this boat, old man Findebar, he run into embankment like the whole world gone mad.'

'Shut up, Jubela,' Milly said wearily. 'Just tell me where we can find a hot brick in the middle of the Irrawaddy?'

'Plenty bricks round Pagan. We can send men to bring back ruined pagoda brick. I tell Memsahib Bee, she tell men to bring goat on boat and we have milk for baba, but she tell Jubela to shut-up too because we have no room on boat for goat. English Memsahibs, they always worry about things that do not matter, but things that do matter, they do not worry about. Jubela happy to

336

sleep with goat if it mean milk for baba-log.'

'Then you sleep with it, Jubela. I'm putting Sarah in her basket. It's Lady Tennent-Browne's turn to nurse her. I'm tired and want some fresh air.'

Jubela looked up in alarm, her brown eyes reminding Milly Sinclair of two prunes in custard. 'Missy-Sahib,' she whined, trying to get her hands together in supplication round the children. 'Please, I beg of you, do not send that woman in here. I will nurse all three babas, goat and mother, but promise me, not that one with the English dimples and a tongue like a cobra.'

Milly smiled to herself as she went in search of Lady Tennent-Browne.

Blaize sat languorously in a deckchair reading a book under the boat's striped awning when Milly disturbed her. 'All right darling,' Blaize snapped, putting the bookmark in her page, 'What with that wretched woman who still hasn't given birth and her screaming child, I haven't had a wink of sleep all night! Good-morning, Mr Findebar,' she smiled as he came up on deck. 'Run along, Milly dear, I'll be along presently. I'm sure Jubela doesn't need me this very moment.'

Leaning over the rail, Findebar hoicked his rusty lungs into the Irrawaddy. 'Mornin' ma'am,' he greeted Blaize by doffing his navy-blue cutter's cap, scratched his white thatch and replaced his head-gear. 'Be in Rangoon soon at this rate, ma'am.'

'I sincerely hope so, Mr Findebar. Two days on this boat, and I'm sick to my stomach already. I don't know what I shall be like after six. Let's hope we don't bump into the Flotilla in the dark, because then I think I will have experienced everything there is to experience on this trip. It really is *not* the kind of voyage I had expected.'

'Oh ma'am, I'm sorry to hear that. What had your ladyship expected, if I may be so bold as to ask such a question?'

'I had at least expected this voyage to be conducted with more "bienseance", and that the food would be a

337

little more — well, recherché. I had not expected prawn chop suey on the menu, Mr Findebar.'

'You're right ma'am. If you're feeling sick to the stomach then it's all to do with Ko Lee's prawn chop suey because it makes me feel sick to my stomach. When you've travelled on this boat as many times as I have ma'am, and got served with prawn chop suey that many times, it's like having your guts — pardon the expression ma'am — wrapped around the smoke-stack in a north-westerly. Besides, the fish that Chinaman dredges up is always suspicious. What he used in last night's dinner surely came from that dirty ole sedge village floating by us yesterday forenoon. And I hear tell they have the typhoid at Myede. Stale as last year's ale those prawns, and Ko Lee knew it.'

'It's up to you to complain to the Captain, Mr Finde-bar. After all, I believe you are his ... I think the expression one uses is, first-mate? Therefore it's up to you to inform your Commanding Officer of his cookboy's methods of shopping. Obviously he is not to be trusted and must pocket the difference between good house-keeping and bad. In India it was called 'dastur', a word closely akin to dastardly! Ko Lee's dishonesty in purchasing sub-standard food for his own pocket and our ill-health, is something Captain Vorne should be made fully aware of.'

'No ma'am,' said Findebar shaking his grizzly head, 'I couldn't risk sticking my neck out where Ko Lee's concerned. Bin with us years has the lad, and the Cap'ain's mighty fond of him in his own way ... oh no, ma'am, not in that way I assure you! The Cap'ains most respectable and so is his Chinese boy.'

'Well, Mr Findebar, whichever way it is, our stomachs are the sufferers. I see him now, taking over from Tonsin in the wheelhouse: Obviously, his graceful aristocratic hands could not stand the baby on it's head and he's given up again. Excuse me, Mr Findebar. I'll have a word with Captain Vorne myself, regarding his Chinese boy's prawns.'

338

Gracefully she gathered up her skirts and taking h. .
book marched with the light of devilment in her eyes to
what Findebar considered to be the holy-of-holies,

'You'd think,' said Findebar to himself as he spat
through a big grin into the Irrawaddy, 'our ladyship was
a paying-guest!'

FOUR

At Senyat toywa Leigh was rudely awakened from his
sleep. 'Thakin ... Thakin, wake up please,' whispered
the headman of the village in which Leigh was hiding.
The Thugyi breathed curry and garlic odours all over his
guest which brought Leigh to his senses more quickly.

'What's up?' Leigh asked in alarm.

'Four Ingalaik come from Mandalay. Ba Say fellow,
he run away from Hlutdaw and guide Ingalaik through
jungles with very much trouble. They ask for Buchanan
man. You wish them to find you?'

The old Thugyi was no fool. Leigh sat up cautiously.
'What men? Did they give their names?'

The Thugyi wrinkled his brow. His white topknot
shook while the candle in his hand guttered in the
downward draught from the gaping hole in the thatched
roof above Leigh's head. The Thugyi tried to recall what
the Burmese guide had told him: 'One man very sick
with fever ... Sin-care, his name ...'

'Sinclair?' Leigh was disturbed. Fully clothed when he
had lain down on his bed-roll to sleep, he only had to
put on his jungle boots. Leigh followed the Thugyi to
another run-down hut where he encountered Milly's
brother in the grip of malaria, Sir Edwin Tennent-
Browne in a towering temper, and Dave MacAbee and
Robert René, the French engineer, all looking sadly the
worse for wear in their Burmese clothes.

'Damn glad we managed to find you at least, old
chap,' said Edwin, adding with a vicious look in Ba Say's
direction. 'Ba Say knows the jungle about as well as he

knows Buddha's backside. Got any quinine in your pack? We've run out.'

'Somewhere in my hut — I'll fetch it.'

'Before you disappear, is it safe to hole up here for awhile, just until Matthew's over the worst of this?'

'Not really,' said Leigh. 'General Gyi San Wun, who is the big noise around here, is due at the Senyat garrison at any moment. I've discovered the Burmese have got a secret arsenal of weapons stored up here.'

Edwin let out a long low whistle of astonishment.

'So I'm not staying.' Leigh continued. 'He's not going to think it's an English picnic going on under his nose if someone lets slip Englishmen are hiding in the jungle. The Thugyi knows of a better place to hide, and I was intending to leave first thing in the morning.'

Edwin asked Leigh, 'Listen old chap, the reason why we got out of Mandalay was not only because we'll be of more use to the British by staying out of the Taingda Mingyi's hands and fighting as free agents from the jungle, but because we've got to get some info down to Thayetmyo before the Flotilla reaches Minhla. Is there any chance of using their telegraph around here?'

Leigh frowned. 'Senyat is where I've been operating from. A new Company of Thibaw's troops will be taking over the garrison in a few days time under Gyi San Wun who is the Taingda Mingyi's noble cousin or something. He's not a man to tangle with I believe, so any messages will have to be tapped through before he gets here.'

'Can you do it for us?'

'Do I get any choice?'

'No.'

'Then I suppose I'll have to. You'll have to let me work something out because my face is very familiar around here and they're going to wonder why I want to use the telegraph when I've had my marching orders.' Leigh turned to the Thugyi and said in Burmese, 'The damp floor of this hut is not a good place for the sick Ingalaik to lie. Is there anywhere else he could spend the night?'

The Thugyi's elaborate Burmese topknot shook in agitation. 'Thakin-masters stay in big house of stilts belonging to wives. I will wake them all up to attend upon Englishman. Please, you wish all of you, to hide from General Gyi San Wun?' The Thugyi could not contain his anxiety, and though he had not understood what the Englishmen had been saying amongst themselves, he had a fairly shrewd idea of what was going on.

Leigh nodded, and the Thugyi replied quickly. 'Then here it is no good to hide. Too near Senyat garrison. It is better you all go straightaway to place in jungle where it plenty safe. You trust me please, and we will make preparations to go immediately. We carry sick man on palanquin.'

Leigh nodded. 'Very well, if you're sure you know what you're doing in the dark'

'In two hours it will be light,' said the Thugyi. 'Then it becomes unsafe, for many soldiers pass this way through jungle. Trust me Thakin, and we will go safely before the sun rises.'

Leigh knew how worried the Thugyi was for the safety of his family, and toywa-people to whom he was a father. Despite his hospitality and willingness to help them, it was understandable he wanted to see the back of them in case the new Burmese Commander, Gyi San Wun, discovered that four fugitive Englishmen were hiding in Senyat toywa. He put himself and the others in the venerable old Thugyi's hands.

FIVE

That evening, just as jungle shadows tentatively fingered the edge of the overgrown compound surrounding a decrepit dâk-bungalow to which the Thugyi had taken them in the dawn-light, Leigh listened to the noise a tauk-té lizard was making in the corner of the rotting verandah; 'Tib-tib-tib, ibbett-ibbett-ibbet,' the lizard insistently demanded attention along with the rest of the jungle's clamour. Monkeys and parrots screeched. Below them in the compound Ba Say had turned his hand to being camp-cook. He squatted over a fire on which he had set up a cooking-pot. The appetizing aroma of chicken curry made Leigh feel extremely hungry. Robert René moodily whittled away at a piece of bamboo with his pen-knife while Matthew, with the help of the quin-ine, was sleeping without shaking. Leigh was disturbed by all that Edwin and the others had told him. He knew he would have to try and use the Burmese telegraph that same night, otherwise it would be too late. He had also to pass on his own information, that of Senyat's secret arsenal the British knew nothing about. It was going to be risky, he knew that much; but he also knew it was imperative the Flotilla Commander had prior knowledge of what he was about to run into once the fleet sailed from Thayetmyo.

Leigh got up off the damp floor-boards where he and the others lounged on the verandah waiting for Ba Say to hurry up and produce his culinary masterpiece supplied by Senyat's toywa people in the shape of two strangled cockerels. He wanted to stretch his legs which had become stiff with inactivity.

'Where are you off to?' Edwin growled, glancing up. 'We don't want you to go advertising the fact we're holed up in this place to Gyi San Wun, or his men who might be lying in wait for us.'

'Don't worry. I'm not going further than the fringes of the compound. I've got cramp, that's all.'

'I will accompany you,' said Robert René, throwing aside the stick he had been whittling.

Once out of earshot of the others, René turned to Leigh and said; 'Well, *mon ami*, what is it you wish to say to me that you have no desire the others should hear — according to your little billet-doux sweetly passed across to me, eh?' He made eyes at Leigh.

Lianas, thick as a man's ankle, roped them as they both meandered along the scarcely visible pathway trod-den by the feet of the Thugyi of Senyat and his handful of trusted men who had guided them to this secret hiding place.

Leigh asked carefully, 'You were working with those two Italian chaps in the Taingda Mingyi's pay, weren't you?'

'You mean Corini and Mageler?'

'I believe those were their names.'

'What of it, mon ami?'

'The Taingda Mingyi is pro-French. So what is your excuse for fleeing Mandalay?'

Robert René, momentarily nonplussed by the Britisher's veiled accusations, did not know what to say. Leigh pressed his advantage — he trusted the Frenchman about as far as he could throw him. 'I would have thought,' said Leigh, 'you would have been delighted to stay in Mandalay to observe the British being kicked out of Upper Burma. You and your countrymen could have taken over without fear of any commercial competition.'

The Frenchman came to a standstill on the gloomy jungle path. He resented the Britisher's tone and his face showed it:

'You are accusing *me*?' Both hands curled into his breast he looked injured. 'You think I too am in the Taingda Mingyi's pocket just because I'm a Frenchman?'

'Aren't you?' Leigh asked.

Robert René threw back his crisp dark head and laughed loudly. Humming-birds hovering over bushes took fright and disappeared deeper into the jungle. A mynah bird somewhere imitated René's laughter. 'That is rich, *mon ami*,' he said.

Leigh remained composed. He shredded a leaf with concentration while he waited for the Frenchman to clear himself.

'Oh, no, no, no,' said René at length. 'I am the last man to be deemed a hireling of that Burmese Minister — or monster if you prefer. I do my job of building bridges over rivers, engineering their railway system and sinking wells for Mandalay's water supply, so never fear my friend, the Taingda Mingyi is no personal friend of mine.

The only money I take from the Burmese is for the work I do for them. If you think I'm all for kicking the British out of Upper Burma, you are wrong. I have nothing against them. I do not care who runs Burma as long as I get my salary paid to me each month, kyats or rupees, I don't care which, as long as it's in gold sovereigns at the end of the day.' He grinned widely, showing white even teeth against his tan.

'Plus a very handsome sum for reinforcing the Burmese fortifications along the Irrawaddy, eh René?'

The Frenchman shrugged with open palms; 'So,' his lower lip jutted out indifferently, 'it is my job.'

'Is it also your job to know exactly how much has been smuggled into Sagaing, Minhla and Gue Gyoun Kamyo, all with French assistance?'

René said nothing.

'Come on, René,' Leigh said, coldly relentless, 'I know what's going on between you and the Taingda Mingyi's Government. Half the French, Italians and Portugese are paid handsomely for doing what is not in their contracts of employment. The illicit smuggling of arms across the Indo-French border is contravening the Anglo-Burmese treaty — but we won't go into that. I'm more concerned with the clever engineering you do in other ways, Monsieur René; like the fortification of Burmese strategic defences along the Irrawaddy, mining rivers and bridges — that kind of stuff the Burmese wouldn't have a clue about. All of which earns you lakhs of gold sovereigns no doubt. So come on, René, tell me, why are you here now with us? To spy on us perhaps?'

'What would that achieve, Mr Buchanan?' the Frenchman asked with a smile. 'But you're a man after my own heart. As an intelligent man, you must realize the offence is only committed where there is proof of the crime. I've done nothing the Burmese haven't asked me to do.'

'Fair enough. But I've plenty of proof where you're concerned, René. Like illegal gun-running under the noses of the Chinese Black Flags, like opium deals, like helping Corini and Mageler mine the Irrawaddy, like being here now to drop us into Gyi San Wun's bag.'

'You are a most suspicious man, Mr Buchanan. But tell me, who will be in the fire if the British lose their little war with the Burmese, me or you?'

'We won't lose, René. When, as opposed to if, the British arrive in Mandalay, General Prendergast will doubtless open the season by asking a lot of questions concerning the underhand activities of the French prior to his arrival. Questions like who supplied foreign arms and ammunition to the Burmese against all sorts of agreements and treaties? Why were our men and steamers blown to bits at Minhla and Sagaing? Who helped the Burmese to this end? Where will your kind of engineering be then, Monsieur René?'

Again the Frenchman's infectious laugh brought the jungle noises to a standstill. 'Very clever, Mr Leigh Buchanan! But you did not have to resort to that kind of subterfuge for your answers — I'd have readily given you all the information you wish to worm out of me. To show you my loyalties are very divided, I will tell you without playing games with you that a force of eight to ten thousand soldiers of the Burmese Army is at Sagaing. The same number is being despatched to Minhla where a supply of weapons has just found its way from Senyat. The arms are arriving from Tonking. They are brought here to the garrison in the jungle — you know about it, I am sure. The British, I hear tell, are all set to take Gue Gyoun Kamyo, the biggest fortification on the Irrawaddy. But they should concentrate on Minhla. The Italians you see, namely Corini and Mageler, have placed mines in the water below the Minhla Redoubt. The mines will be detonated from the shore as soon as the Flotilla is sighted. So, *mon ami*, it is not I who should be under suspicion, but the Italians. Your honest eyes betray you my friend. I know very well your pincer tactics to trap me have only been a fumbling in the dark. Fortunately, I have been able to assist you because, shortly before Corini and Mageler disappeared, I was

345

looking for the plans of the Irrawaddy fortifications, as I'd been asked to survey and structurally attend to their defences. It was then I discovered the elaborate plans the Italians and Burmese had worked out concerning future underwater mining of the river.' René paused, looking at Leigh with his head on one side. He tapped his pocket. 'The plans are here — copied by me. You will have your proof.'

'How much, René?' Leigh raised his eyes to where the sun was beginning to depart the scorched earth, its fevered renderings of the day purpling the dark-green glade to the approaching night.

Robert René grinned again; 'I would still wish for my salary to be paid me in gold sovereigns when the British arrive. I have my own interests to protect after all. Let's say, I will give you Corini and Mageler's plans of the mining of the river and any other vital information you require, if you will forget my, er, little featherings of my own nest?'

'It's not up to me,' Leigh replied.

'You are a greedy man Mr Buchanan.'

'No René. I'm only protecting my own nest. I'll get those plans off you one way or another — it's four to one against, in this instance ...' Robert René found himself looking at Leigh Buchanan's pistol. 'I'd like those plans, René,' Leigh said, calmly surveying the Frenchman.

'Put the gun away, Leigh,' he said, unfastening his shirt pocket to take out his slips of paper. 'I am not a violent man, nor I think are you. I promised you these. I hope I'm not stupid enough to believe the British will lose their battle with the Burmese, so let us behave like gentlemen and not resort to guns. I know when I'm beaten.'

The plans of the Irrawaddy defences in his hands, Leigh put away the pistol — carried with him whenever he was in the jungle, if only to shoot snakes.

Having exercised their limbs while coming to terms with each other the two men turned back to their jungle hut. They heard Burmese voices. Cautiously hidden

346

behind trees until their visitors' business had been established, Leigh was relieved to see it was only the Thugyi and his four henchmen bringing water, kerosene and food to them. Leigh knew they had nothing to fear from the peace-loving Karens of Senyat, a mild and hospitable race, for, like most toywa people of Burma they did not care who sat on the Dragon Throne in Mandalay as long as they were left in peace and happiness.

'René,' Leigh said, 'I want you to do me another favour.'

'What's that, my friend?' asked René with raised brows.

'I want to send a wire down to Thayetmyo, but I've got to have help. I'll have to relay my message from Kadaw, not Senyat.'

'But why?' asked René, puzzled. 'Kadaw is four miles from here. It might as well be on the other side of the moon in this jungle. What prevents you from using the telegraph hut on Senyat Hill where you have always operated from? The Burmese know and trust you at Senyat, and since General Gyi San Wun has not arrived as yet, a few subordinates of yours now operating the field telegraph, are unlikely to ask questions of the man who taught them their trade — even if he is British,' René concluded with a smirk.

'I don't wish to use Senyat for reasons of my own. Will you help or not?'

The Frenchman scratched his head thoughtfully, his dark eyes on the Englishman. 'How?' he asked.

'A fault will have developed on the line between Senyat and Kadaw. It happens all the time; stirrups, wheels, porcelain insulators stolen by the Burmese to sell to the Chinese, or else monkeys chewing through the wires. We're going to do the repairs.'

'Are we?' said René, not at all enamoured of the idea.

They entered the compound and only then did René give his actual assent:

'All right, *mon ami*, I'll help you. But every favour has its price — as you and I already know.'

'Come on then, René, let's have it,' Leigh said.

'The little daughter of the village who follows her grandfather the Thugyi, and who cannot take her eyes off your handsome body while she nurses a papoose at the nipple, if you must cold-shoulder her, then send her to me. Tell her another handsome man, a Frenchman who invented love, so knows far more than an Englishman about it, waits for her behind the Banyan tree.'

Leigh gave a short laugh, 'René, you'll get me pinned on the end of the Thugyi's spear!'

'But you British are always so capable of defending yourselves,' René replied with a hearty slap on Leigh's back.

They came into the compound where Ba Say, seeing them coming, began to dish up his chicken curry. Leigh was so hungry he could have eaten an ox. He hoped Ba Say's cockerels were edible. 'René,' he said, 'tonight you need your strength for other things.' They spoke in low voices out of the hearing of the others eating on the verandah.

The Frenchman sighed dramatically, '*C'est la vie!* There is no romance left in the heart of a Britisher. All they think of is war. We French, we make love first, then think about war.'

'That's why you always lose against us, René' Leigh replied. 'We do it the other way round.'

'The other way round my friend, is always dangerous.' Robert René put out his hand to receive his offerings of chicken curry dished up on a plantain leaf from Ba Say; 'I might be the loser, but I won't be a dead loser. You, *mon ami,* will be dead if Gyi San Wun catches you at your monkey tricks.'

'Us, René us!'

CHAPTER
TWENTY-FIVE

ONE

'For if we believe that Jesus died and rose again, even so them also which sleep in Jesus will God bring with him. For this we say unto you by the word of the Lord, that we which are alive and remain unto the coming of the Lord shall not prevent them which are asleep. For the Lord himself shall descend from heaven with a shout, with the voice of the archangel, and with the trump of God, and the dead in Christ shall rise first. Then we which are alive and remain shall be caught up together with them in the clouds, to meet the Lord in the air: and so shall we ever be with the Lord ... Amen.'

Nathan closed the Bible and handed it to Findebar.

Not a ripple marked the sheet-metal surface of the river save where the *Belle Hélène* cleaved the milkwash of her progress. The fitful sun occluded in its own baptismal burial. It was still, very still, so still and silent even the breath of God seemed held in abeyance on river mists shrouding in death the little knot gathered at the rail of Nathan's boat.

Angela tossed wreaths of yellow tuber-roses and white jasmine picked by Milly, Blaize and herself from an embankment garden, onto the river to mark the spot where two corpses had been dropped side by side. Milly was devastated, as were they all. She wiped away the tears. 'She was always such a good baby,' she said.

'Always so fat, happy and bouncing with health. I can't believe it.' She began to weep again overwrought and emotionally drained. Sympathetically Angela put her arm round Milly's shoulders. 'Milly dear, I think we should all try and get some rest. Perhaps Ko Lee, you'll bring us a little tea in our cabin?' She raised an enquiring eyebrow and Ko Lee gave a nod, his own face tragic in the light of recent events. 'I bring, Amagyi-Angela.' He said, disappearing to the galley.

'It was the goat,' Blaize insisted. 'Its milk was infected. But nobody would listen to me when that stinking creature was brought aboard this boat. Sarah died because of milk-poisoning. It wasn't so traumatic where the other baby was concerned because it never knew it was alive, what with being strangled by its own birth-cord and the rest ... my God! Am I glad I never produced.'

'Bee, why don't you pipe down for a change?' Nathan said wearily. He could truthfully say this had been one of the worst sailings of his life. Four days, and they were still no nearer to the border. What with the Burmese, and Lady Bee on his back, he was almost looking forward to seeing Rangoon again.

'Darling,' Blaize said heedlessly, as snappish and as irritable as everyone else, 'does it make you feel powerful to be prince, priest and privateer?' Her blue eyes under impeccable dark arches were maliciously vindictive. Nathan knew she was itching for a row. 'Not content with exerting your prestigious influence on the pregnant mother's inelegant abdomen to turn her baby on the Amagyi-Angela's words of wisdom, you now turn to baptising and burying all in one effortless sweep. I never cease to be amazed by your sheer versatility, Cap'ain. What a pity you're such a gowk when it comes to women. You're emotionally terrified of them, Nathan darling, despite all appearances to the contrary. Go on, admit it!'

Both sets of blue eyes clashed dangerously.

'If you're feeling sea-sick Bee, why don't you go and

lie down for a little while,' Nathan said, refusing to lose his temper with Blaize who had been getting on everyone's nerves and his in particular.

'What do you see in her for heaven's sake?'

'Who? What the hell are you talking about?'

'The Amagyi-Angela. It's as plain as a pike-staff for all to see, but really darling, surely you could do better than wanting to bed a bald, freckled-nosed woman whose figure is the ideal shape to take the depth-readings in this river?'

He looked at her steadily, 'I could do a lot worse, Honey-Bee. I could take me to bed a woman who'd kill a man's ardour stone dead by talking him through it.'

Ignoring her efforts to detain him further by fair means or foul, he sought refuge in his wheelhouse, knowing that Lady Bee, in a frustrated little temper, was stamping her foot behind his back.

Ko Lee, standing at the wheel, said, 'Cap'ain grinning very big. You think something funny, eh Cap'ain?'

Nathan took out his pipe and tamped tobacco into the bowl. Thoughtfully he drew on it, 'Yes, very funny Ko Lee. Just take my advice and remember to marry a woman who is fat, fifty and faithful. That way you can both grow old together instead of before your time.'

'See here, Cap'ain,' said Ko Lee, fishing something out of his pocket and handing it to Nathan, 'It very nice, yes?'

'Jeese, Ko Lee! Where the devil did you pick this up?' Nathan weighed the brooch in his hand, 'This must be a King's ransom at least.'

'It sure one big ransom,' Ko Lee agreed, nodding vigorously while he steered the boat.

Nathan held the margarite up to the light. It almost blinded him in its diamond brilliance. 'Come on Ko Lee. If you stole it, I'll have you keel-hauled.'

'No steal, Cap'ain. It sitting velly happily in bottom of river where washerwomen take clothes of Palace to wash everyday.'

Nathan, his pipe not in his mouth, whistled through

his teeth; 'So that's where the crafty little viper's hiding the Crown jewels!' His grin broadened. 'Ko Lee,' he said, putting his hand on his boy's shoulder, 'If the British do happen to win their silly war against the Burmese, you and me are going diving for treasure-trove, m'lad.'

'Solly Cap'ain. No divee, no swimee.'

'No payee, either,' said Nathan.

TWO

Sixty miles from the frontier, Nathan studied his charts in the wheelhouse while Findebar took the wheel, leaving Tonsin to stoke the boiler. A shout from Finde-bar as they passed in the shadow of Gue Gyoun Kamyo on one side and Minhla on the other within a two mile stretch of the river, drew Nathan from his charts.

'Steady Findebar, steady!' he yelled, wrenching on the fog-horn.

'It was him, Cap'ain, not me! Coming out of the fog like that, he needs his brains tested,' Findebar yelled back. 'Watch it yourself an' all, Cap'ain,' Findebar warned when Nathan took over. Both hands gripping the wheel, teeth clenched hard on the stem of his pipe, Nathan brought the *Belle* hard to port and dangerously close to the shallows on the Gue Gyoun side of the river which they had been trying to avoid. Although there was plenty of room to pass, the Commander of the Burmese steamer coming toward them towing four flats in convoy, seemed determined to cut across their bows. Nathan and Findebar observed that each flat-bottom barge had been purposely embedded with teak piles as sharp as needle-points.

'What the hell's he doing?'

'He's trying to sink us, Cap'ain, that's what!' Findebar broke out in a sweat. 'Christ Almighty, he's doing it again! Watch it Cap ... we're scraping bottom ... out, out!' Findebar on two dancing feet waved his fists at the

Burmese steamer. 'Lord God, there's another two of 'em coming up behind us through the fog,' said Findebar, his head stuck through the glass windows of the wheelhouse.

'Get below and put some steam into this thing,' Nathan said grimly, his wits trained to starboard and portside simultaneously while the Burmese steamers tried to sandwich him in the middle and another cut his bows. 'Right, so they want to play musical boats in the fog, we'll show them, but we've got to get past their batteries on the hill as well — if they don't knock the hell out of us first.' Nathan again dragged the wheel to port, beginning to sweat like Findebar.

'Looks like they intend to do that without the aid of their batteries, Cap'ain ... that critter's sneaking up again on our stern ... wait till I get us the pressure going, Cap'ain, and we'll leave him in the shallows instead!' Findebar, almost purple in the face with indignation at such rough treatment in a dangerous stretch of river, blasted the fog-horn.

'Then for Christ's sake do it, Findebar, instead of mouthing off ... the *Belle* can out-run anything on this river — but just remember we're neutral!' Nathan said over his shoulder as Findebar crashed open the wheelhouse door and almost fell down the steps.

'Cap'ain,' he yelled back happily. 'I'm going to hoist the stars and stripes so blooming high, them blind Burmese bastards is going to mistake morning for night.'

Burmese guns opened fire, peppering the water with grapeshot as the armed steamers tried to prevent the *Belle*'s progress. Weaving in and out of the other boats, Nathan was determined to get the better of them. Blaize, terribly shaken at the sudden gunfire, fell inside the wheelhouse. 'Nathan ... what on earth is going on ...?'

'Get down ... on the floor!'

From the floor she said: 'Are they shooting at us?'

'Right first time ... scarper ... on your knees woman! They'll blow your head off ... and tell the others to stay below. That's an order.'

'Oh yes, oh my goodness, yes indeed ...' On all fours

Lady Bee went quickly back to her cabin.

Through a loud-hailer Nathan heard the Burmese Commander of the river-launch drawing alongside them, telling them to pull the *Belle Hélène* into the Gue Gyoun Kamyo shore.

Over my dead body, thought Nathan, and was thankful when Ko Lee materialized beside him.

'Wantee help of Chinese navy, Cap'ain?'

'Grab this . . .' Nathan thrust the wheel into his hands and taking up his own loud-hailer answered the Commander of the *Shwebo*: 'Ahoy! Stop your firing at once. There are women and children aboard this boat.'

'Then kindly reduce speed and let us come alongside, Captain Vorne,' the Burmese Commander replied.

'Over my dead body, Ko Lee,' Nathan said, withdrawing his head. He had the awful feeling that that would probably be the case if he did not comply with the orders of the Commander of the *Shwebo*. He brought his loud-hailer up again: 'We are a neutral vessel, Commander, and you have no authority to detain us.'

'I have every authority, Captain Vorne. I wish to examine your papers. We are fully aware you have British women and children aboard your boat. That is not a neutral act, Captain, so kindly pull into the Gue Gyoun Kamyo shore, otherwise we shall open fire again.'

'Heathen savages,' Nathan retracted his head and pushed his cap to the back of it in frustration. Then he stuck his angry head out again and called: 'Commander Bodaw, the *Rangoon Gazette* and the *Times* newspapers would dearly love to get hold of this story. They'd enjoy relaying throughout the world how Burmese sailors opened fire on helpless women and children. If you proceed to attack an unarmed vessel carrying the neutral flag of the United States of America, then you'll never hear the end of it.'

'Captain Vorne, I am warning you!' came back the eerie hollow-tube voice, 'the river ahead of you is mined. You will be the cause of the deaths of your passengers, not the Burmese navy who are only seeking to warn you of the danger. We have no wish to harm you or your passengers. And now that you have been sufficiently warned, please pull your steamer into the Gue Gyoun Kamyo shore, otherwise you will run the risk of being blown to bits by our mines. We are advising you of this for the safety of yourself and your passengers.'

'Hell, Ko Lee, what do we do now!'

'We obey, Cap'ain,' said the Chinese youth with a resigned shrug of the shoulders, but at that moment Findebar, with an oily rag in his hand, burst into the wheelhouse; 'Don't listen to 'em Cap'ain! They're lying in their red teeth. Don't do it sir. They wouldn't know how to mine a river and that's a blooming fact. We'll beat 'em all the way to Thayetmyo, take my word for it Cap'ain. But if you do as they want it'll be the sodding worse for all of us.'

'Leave Cap'ain to make own worthy decisions,' said Ko Lee imperiously.

'Cap'ain Nat.' Findebar implored, ignoring Ko Lee, if you surrender to them Burmese bastards, they'll do you down like the day you were taken off the *Belle* at Sagaing. You'll rue the day. They're lying little toads and they only want our boat to rig up against the British. If you surrender, I quit!'

'Stow it, Findebar, nobody's surrendering. I just don't think they're lying in this instance, and I don't fancy the *Belle*, with us on it, blown sky-high out of the water.'

'Aw Cap'ain, they're bluffing! They're heathens. What do they know about ballistics and things that are all new to 'em? Mark my words, sir, if you get tough with them, they'll back down. They always do.'

Nathan reached a decision; 'Findebar, forget about putting knots into this thing. Ko Lee, swing her round to Gue Gyoun.'

'I never thought I'd live to see the day when Cap'ain Nat Vorne surrendered to some Burmese loudmouths — unconditionally!' Findebar in disgust flung his oily rag to

355

the floor before making himself scarce.

Nathan brought the *Belle Hélène* to a graceful if ignominious berth alongside the wooden landing stage just below the impressive red fortress known as Gue Gyoun Kamyo. He and his crew were armed with pistols when the *Shwebo* and her sister launch the *Mingun* anchored alongside.

'You have chosen a wise course of action, Captain Vorne,' the Burmese Commander said after he had descended with all pomp and ceremony from the deck of the *Shwebo* to the quayside. 'You will not suffer for it.'

'I shouldn't damn well think so!' said Nathan. 'Listen to this, Commander Bodaw, we don't budge one inch from this boat which is American neutral ground. Neither do your sailors put a foot aboard until I'm assured of a safe passage to Thayetmyo. I want two bullock carts, signed passes for safe conduct, and enough food and drink to furnish our conveyance by land to the frontier since your navy has rendered the Irrawaddy impassable.'

The Burmese Commander smiled placatingly. He waved an airy hand at Findebar, Ko Lee and Tonsin, all pointing their guns at him: 'Captain Vorne, you are in no position to bargain with me. What can four pistols do against the crew of the *Shwebo*, *Mingun* and *Pagan* with their machine guns? No, no, no, Captain, you might be a courageous man, but you're also a very foolish one if you seek to shoot down the whole of the forces opposing you at this moment.'

'I don't think that at all, Commander Bodaw. But we can and will take the officers who command the *Mingun* and *Pagan*, as well as your good self, if any of you step aboard the *Belle Hélène* without an invitation.'

'And what then of your women and children?' asked Commander Bodaw, his patronizing tone changing to one of long-sufferance. 'I do not vouch that they will have safe conduct, should anything befall officers of the Burmese Navy — who are only trying to reason with you. Your best bet and most sensible one, Captain

Vorne, would be to come along with me without any-more fuss. You, your crew and the British women and children, will be quartered quite comfortably in the Myowun's residence at Minhla where you will be treated as guests of the Burmese Governor. After the British forces have been vanquished forever from Burma, you will be free to go your own way once more. Until that time, please place yourself in honourable hands.'

'Ko Lee,' said Nathan without taking his eyes off Commander Bodaw, 'go below and stay below with the Memsahibs and children. The moment you hear shots from up here and know the Commanders of the Bur-mese steamers to be dead, you shoot the women and children and then yourself. They will not be allowed to fall into Burmese hands alive. Do you understand?'

'Aye, aye, Cap'ain. Ko Lee understand perfectly. He go now to carry out wishes of Cap'ain for velly last time.'

'And that leaves three shots for three Burmese Commanders,' said Nathan eyeing all three of them. 'I'll do it too, Commander Bodaw, so never fear I dally with you.'

Commander Bodaw had not thought that for one moment. He hesitated. They, everyone of them standing around those boats, knew the scandal of such a thing would be too dishonourable to bear. Captain de Veres-Vorne's reputation up and down the Irrawaddy had not diminished in nearly two decades, but rather, had increased in notoriety. The legend of the Shwe Nat of Mandalay was formidable. A man capable of defying the Queens of Burma as well as garotting a Spotted Face within the very shadow of the death prison, was capable of anything. Commander Bodaw's decision was a respectful one. He wavered; 'Captain Vorne, there is no need for all this play-acting.'

'Oh, I do assure you, Commander Bodaw, nothing is further from my mind.'

By the look on Captain Vorne's face, Commander Bodaw did not think so either. 'Very well, your terms are agreed. Two bullock-carts, free passes, food and water, and you may proceed on your way to Thayetmyo.'

'In writing, Commander Bodaw,' Nathan insisted. 'You will state that we will not be molested in any way on our next few miles to the frontier, that the *Belle Hélène* will not be touched at her moorings or requisitioned as a gun-boat by the Burmese, and that we will have our bullock-carts and our food and water.'

'I cannot guarantee the safety of your boat, Captain Vorne. There is no knowing what might happen to it in the approaching naval battle against the British. But I suggest you remove yourself and your party without any further delay. Otherwise, should the British Flotilla be sighted within the next few hours, I cannot guarantee you a safe conduct to anywhere. It will be arranged for the bullock-carts and provisions to be brought to you here — though I still think it would be more prudent of you to accept the offer of Burmese hospitality in the Governor's Palace across the river than to risk infantry guns and dacoit assaults on the way to Thayetmyo.'

'We'll take our chances,' said Nathan, two feet planted firmly and squarely on his own territory. 'I should also like a pallet of straw to be provided for one of the carts as I have a very sick lady aboard. I think she too would prefer to die on the road to Thayetmyo than in a bamboo stockade in the Governor's compound.'

'You do the Burmese an injustice, Captain Vorne,' said Commander Bodaw in an injured tone. 'The Burmese do not fight women and children, and indeed, it is not they who have started this war but rather have been forced into it by the British. We are defending our own country, Captain Vorne. Is that a crime?'

'Without getting involved in any politics, Commander Bodaw, I don't like being caught in the middle. If you'd kindly furnish me with what I've requested, I'd be much obliged.' said Nathan.

The Burmese Commander bowed low, and without distressing himself any more over the fate of Captain Vorne and his passengers, hurried back to the safety of his own steamer.

An hour later, Commander Bodaw's aide presented himself smartly to Nathan aboard the *Belle Hélène*. He had with him all the appropriate passes and papers to accommodate their journey to the frontier. Two bullock-carts, one with a palliasse and two mules laden with provisions waited on the embankment. The fate of the *Belle* had been ignored, but as Nathan had no wish to abuse his luck, he accepted what had been granted him. Ko Lee, Findebar and Tonsin, still sported their weapons, and after seeing Commander Bodaw's aide off the *Belle*, handed the women and children down into the waiting carts.

'I hope the British Flotilla blows them to smithereens,' Lady Tennent-Browne remarked as she stood twirling her silk parasol over one shoulder while glowering at the Burmese boats and sailors watching their departure. 'This is simply too bad darlings! As though we haven't suffered enough on this voyage by our odious circum-stances. How they expect us to travel through their savage jungles in ox-carts I can't imagine. What safety are we guaranteed, Nathan? You know as well as I how useless their bits of paper are when it comes to winning. Why can't we continue aboard the *Belle*?'

'Because they've laid mines in the water to blow the Flotilla up, that's why.'

'How do you know that?'

'I've just been told.'

'They might be lying.'

'They might be. But I'm not risking finding out.'

'Nathan, I refuse to travel in that first cart with that abominable Burman who keeps turning round behind his scarves to ogle me. I shall sit in this second cart with you, Angela and the children.'

'Up front Bee, with Findebar and Milly. Then you can lend Milly a hand with Mrs Sinclair.'

'Nathan, I refuse to be dictated to as though I were a child!'

Not stopping to argue, he lifted her bodily and dumped her on the tailboard of the first cart, accidentally hooking her petticoats on a large splinter. He left Findebar to sort her out while he assisted Ko Lee and Tonsin carefully carrying Clare on a makeshift stretcher. Angela and the ayah were busy organizing the two children into the second cart.

'Mr Findebar, it's no good pulling at the material, you'll tear it! This is a Paris gown and most expensive. Milly, move along the seat, there's not going to be room for all of us with that wretched mattress on the floor ... if that bullock-cart wallah turns around to leer at me once more, I'll ... I'll I don't know what I shall do. Haven't you managed to unhook me as yet, Mr Findebar? I'm waiting.'

'No ma'am ... I can't ...' His tongue between his teeth in concentration, his fingers were clumsy on the fine material. 'Pardon me, your ladyship, but if you'll only stop bobbing about a bit, I might see what I'm doing.'

'I am not bobbing, Mr Findebar! Now who are all those men coming down the hill?' She directed her parasol towards the red fort.

A detachment of Burmese troops in their eye-catching uniforms were seen descending the hill path from Gue Gyoun Kamyo. Their Commanding Officer rode in front, seated on a mule.

'Hut-hut-hut!' He tapped the animal along with a stick. Coming up to Nathan's small party, he bowed from the saddle, a fat little man with his short legs splayed out over his fat little mule. He said in a high-pitched cadence without an appreciable pause; 'Commanding Officer of Gue Gyoun Kamyo much regret mix-up but request to see Captain de Veres-Vorne and prisoners immediately. Orders of noble General, Commander-in-Chief and son-in-law of most illustrious Taingda Mingyi, as well as Keeper of Royal Barges and mighty warrior of divine Majesty, King Thibaw of Burma!'

'Dammit! What prisoners?' Nathan asked furiously. 'There are no prisoners here and you can get back to your noble Commander and tell him I said so. We have just been issued with free-transit passes to the frontier, signed by Commander Bodaw himself.'

'Please, Captain Vorne', insisted the comical little Burman on his mule, 'do not argue with Burmese soldiers of illustrious Burmese Army. Commander Bodaw is Naval Commander of Irrawaddy who has no authority on land which is jurisdiction of Noble Hlethin Atwinwun who commands fortress of Gue Gyoun Kamyo.'

Equally incensed by the delaying tactics of the Burmese, who, in Findebar's opinion, ought not to have been trusted, he turned around from the tailboard of the cart, one hand still concealed in Lady Tennent-Browne's lace hems as he tried unsuccessfully to extricate her. The Burmese infantry officer, misconstruing Findebar's motives, raised his gun and fired at him.

Findebar reeled, blood spattering Blaize. Nathan with a hoarse cry leapt on the Infantry Officer and himself was dragged down by Burmese soldiers. In the riot and confusion the children and ayah screamed, Jubela covering them all with her sari. Milly fell to her knees to help Findebar who lay spreadeagled half in and half out of the cart. Stunned, Angela could only stand petrified like Ko Lee and Tonsin, who almost dropped Clare Sinclair to the ground.

'Oh God ...' Angela, her hand to her mouth, moved to help Milly with Findebar, but Burmese soldiers stepped in front of her with their guns held threateningly.

Findebar's body slipped to the ground and Milly, on her knees beside him, took up his navy-cutter's cap from the mud and clutched it tightly to her.

In silence, Nathan's pathetic little party were herded together and forced at gunpoint uphill to Gue Gyoun Kamyo, escorted by a very subdued Infantry Officer.

Clare Sinclair, sick and weak on her stretcher, was pushed unceremoniously beside Findebar's body. The tailboard was slammed shut and the ox-cart — driven by a Burmese soldier, because the two terrified Burmans from whom the carts had been requisitioned had already fled downhill back to their toywa — trundled in the wake of the Hlethin Atwinwun's prisoners.

The noble Burmese General ordered his prisoners — so fortuitously come by — to be incarcerated in cells facing the river. From that position, they would most certainly be in line of British gunboat fire. He also ordered the dead sailor to be thrown into the Irrawaddy, after which the Hlethin Atwinwun sat down and personally penned a missive to Commander Bodaw congratulating him in having placed such valuable hostages in his hands, though that had not been Commander Bodaw's intention at all.

CHAPTER TWENTY-SIX

ONE

At dawn on the 13th November, a rather strange greetings telegram was intercepted by the British. The message was in Burmese and tapped out in Morse Code from Kadaw, approximately fifteen miles from Mandalay. The young Telegraph Operator who had received it, shook his head, shrugged his shoulders and handed the English translation to his Duty Officer.

'Happy Birthday to you, Happy Birthday to you, Happy Birthday dear Harry, Happy Birthday to you.'

The Duty Officer promptly put the message forward to the de-coding room. Later in the day that signal, along with several others, was put in the hands of General Harry North Dalrymple Prendergast, V.C. who had arrived at Thayetmyo that afternoon aboard the *Thambyadine*. In the signals handed to him for his attention, he deemed the one from Kadaw to be of as much importance as that sent from the British Foreign Office, Whitehall. The Foreign office communiqué he proceeded to act upon immediately. It urged an immediate advance upon Mandalay since King Thibaw had rejected Britain's final ultimatum, all answers from the Burmese Government proving unsatisfactory.

The bad news from Kadaw he transferred into the hands of one of his Staff Officers aboard the *Thambyadine*. Major Jeffrey Radcliffe, baton under his arm, twitched his moustache like a rabbit, read and digested the important information he had received, and proceeded to act accordingly.

The British Flotilla set sail.

On that November day, so awe inspiring was the sight and might of British arms and invincibility as it steamed up the Irrawaddy for a distance of five miles, Burmese villagers left their homes to run to the river banks where they were better able to wave, shout and cheer the British on to Mandalay.

The Flotilla had been fitted out with great forethought. Sailing vessels, large and small, had been requisitioned in Rangoon. Behind the steamers came the large barges, or flats. These had been converted to accommodate the artillery while the smaller steam launches hired from the Irrawaddy Flotilla Company had also been fitted with guns. Troops were accommodated in steamboats of the Company or in private vessels refitted with arms-racks, accoutrement-hooks, latrines and water-supply tanks. Hospital ships too were extremely well equipped, a number of instant field hospitals easily and quickly able to be assembled close to the battlefields. Nothing in any way had been left to chance, for the Army had learned a tragic lesson at great cost thirty years before on the battlefields of the Crimea.

This time, the British were taking no chances in the capture of Mandalay. The main force of troops consisted of 10,000 soldiers divided into three Infantry Brigades, six Companies of Sappers and Miners, three Batteries Royal Artillery and three Mountain batteries from India.

Hitherto, Jeffrey Radcliffe had only seen the river Irrawaddy on the walls of his Rangoon headquarters, a flat uninteresting brown and green contoured coil of immense strategic value. Having pinned flags, markers and drawing-pins into, all over and around the one dimensional picture that was his bird's eye view of Burma, he saw it all now in the reality of its savage splendour, and could not help but be affected by it.

General Prendergast V.C. was not boasting when,

sixty miles from the frontier and within sight of the invincible red walls of Gue Gyoun Kamyo which dominated the river for two miles, in answer to Jeffrey Radcliffe's remark, 'We'll never breach those walls in a month of Sunday mornings, sir,' the General had made the pragmatic reply, 'But sir, I intend to do it in *one* morning.'

'Any luck and the Burmese will be too busy picking themselves out of the water at Minhla, blown to bits with their own mines,' Major Radcliffe chuckled in delight while he swept Minhla ramparts in his field glasses and saw the Burmese flag flying defiantly above their heads.

'Good work there, Major, in sorting out that damn queer message that arrived from Kadaw, damn queer stuff! We wouldn't have known a thing about it if we'd sailed straight into their mines. Nasty business too about Senyat bristling with armaments to defend Mandalay, while Minhla bristles with Royal Troops — since we'd been given to understand it was water-logged and therefore abandoned. Good work on your chap's part, whoever he was. He'll get a mention in despatches.' Harry Prendergast lowered his glasses once more and went below to start organizing his Officers in their simultaneous attacks upon Minhla and Gue Gyoun Kamyo.

Brigadier-General Foord's Brigade of Royal Welsh Fusiliers and the Madras Army had already disembarked eight miles downstream at a place called Patango. The Madras Army had long experience and knowledge of scaling difficult stockades with rope and bamboo ladders, practised on the assault-courses at Dum-Dum, Calcutta. The Liverpool Regiment and the Madras Army were to attack from the East while the British gunboats, the *Irrawaddy* and *Kathleen*, were to keep the Burmese soldiers inside the fort occupied from the front. Meanwhile, The Bengal Brigade under Brigadier-General Norman were to land at a place called Maloon on the right bank of the river. Their objective was to disarm Minhla, and, while they were about it, make certain they captured the Burmese Governor and his high officials. Thick jungle thicket, narrow twisting cart-tracks, made the attack upon Minhla harder than expected. A Burmese villager informed Colonel Baker of the Queen's Own Bengal Infantry that Royal Troops had arrived the day before and were entrenched around the town. Added to Colonel Baker's difficulties, his small Company of men comprising the Bengal 11th Infantry and the 12th Madras Infantry, were not reinforced by Brigadier-General Norman's Royal Welsh Fusiliers because they did not arrive at the landing point in time to take part in the capture of Minhla.

Finding themselves ambushed, Colonel Baker's men came under heavy fire from the Burmese who had made a determined stand at the Burmese Governor's palace. Big guns pounded away at the British. Eventually, after heavy bombardment, a small group of officers and men from the Madras and Bengal Infantry led an attack over Burmese entrenchments of carts and bamboo until they gained the stockade. The Governor's palace was set alight, the troops reformed, wheeled to the right and advanced eastward to the town of Minhla itself. Casualties had been heavy on both sides. The confusion was not helped by the slow progress of the hospital ships, nowhere near Minhla where they were most needed. Wounded and dying lay out in the hot Burmese sun until medical attention duly arrived.

Early on Tuesday, 17th November, and only four days after setting out from Thayetmyo, Brigadier General Foord and his men left Patango village via a very good cart-road that led northwards. Through eight miles of dense jungle, hacking their way rather than marching, they reached the east wall of Gue Gyoun Kamyo.

Burmese guns were still directed at the *Irrawaddy* and *Kathleen* whose long-range Nordenfeldt and Gardner machine-guns bombarded Gue Gyoun Kamyo with nine-pound and twenty-pound shells. The Burmese, their undivided attention concentrated upon the river, had not envisaged a rear-guard action. The assault force of the Madras Army led the way followed by the Liverpool Regiment, scaling parapets, breaching the mighty red walls and eventually storming the East gate. The routed Burmese fled to the river where they were shot by Sepoys.

It was subsequently discovered that the main Gue Gyoun Kamyo force under the noble Hlethin Atwinwun had evacuated Gue Gyoun as soon as the *Irrawaddy* and *Kathleen* had tried to breech its west wall.

By one o'clock on that Tuesday, Gue Gyoun Kamyo fell to the British. General Prendergast aboard the *Dowoon* observed the white flag of surrender hoisted on the white pagoda East of the great red fortress. The gunboats *Irrawaddy* and *Kathleen* were ordered to stop shelling Gue Gyoun Kamyo and to turn their attention to Minhla where the fighting between Burmese and British troops was savage and bloody. The Burmese were putting up great resistance and were fighting valiantly to the last man.

'There sir,' General Prendergast said, his pale eyes strangely luminescent as he turned to Major Radcliffe, 'I have done it. Gue Gyoun Kamyo is ours. It's only a matter of time before Minhla is also in our hands.'

Major Radcliffe, in addition to his appointment as Staff Officer in the Department of Military Intelligence, had been appointed Liaison Officer to the Burmese since he spoke the language fluently. He was ordered by General Prendergast to go at once to Gue Gyoun Kamyo and to bring back a report on the extent of British and enemy casualties, the number of weapons and prisoners taken and the general conditions prevailing inside the fortress.

Transferred from the *Dowoon* by tender, he was more than astonished to find British women and children insensibly incarcerated in the bowels of Gue Gyoun Kamyo. After that incident he learned not to be astounded by anything he might run up against in Burma beyond Thayetmyo.

'Good God!' he exclaimed when the door of their cell

had been pushed open by a couple of young Welshmen who had confiscated the keys from Burmese guards, 'What on earth are you lot doing here?'

'You may very well ask such a thing, Major!' Lady Tennent-Browne said as she stormed out of the cell where they had been subjected to all sorts of monstrosities in the shape of rats, spiders and scorpions that had plagued them, 'We thought you'd never get here!' Undiscouraged by a filthy blood-spattered frock Paris would have wept over, a dirty face, broken fingernails, unkempt hair and a body that had been kept unwashed for several days, she did not mince matters; 'You certainly took your time about it.'

'Ma'am,' Jeffrey Radcliffe apologized hastily, 'we came as soon as we could. I think you'd all better come along with me and put your complaints to General Prendergast himself.'

'Like this?' Countered Lady Tennent-Browne in dismay, feeling that meeting a General in her present *déshabillé* appearance was not quite the thing to do. She regarded the dapper Major in alarm. 'Certainly not, Major!'

'Yes ma'am, exactly like that ... excuse me.'

A shout from one of his men drew his attention away from the ignominiously treated Memsahibs whose spirit it appeared, despite all, remained unquenched. Further along the dark wet passageway green with condensation he encountered yet more prisoners who were not Burmese; two servant-boys and one American Captain he had once met in Rangoon.

'Good God!' Jeffrey Radcliffe repeated a second time, 'Captain de Veres-Vorne, what are you doing here?'

Nathan, despite his misery over Findebar's death and everything else that had transpired from that moment to this, grinned in pleasure, the first time he had felt remotely like smiling over anything:

'Major Radcliffe,' he said. 'It's sure good to see you and your boys. Now, you get us out of this hell-hole as

fast as you can and take me straight to your Commanding Officer. I want to fill him in with what's been going
on around here, and then maybe he'll shift his ass a little
quicker to Mandalay!'

TWO

In the hot blue stillness of an oppressive room in the
private residence of Senyat's Commanding Officer,
Leigh Buchanan felt cold.

Perspiration had dried on him many times over. He
felt icy cold, so cold it was difficult to stop his teeth from
chattering. The pain in his hands had diminished to a
numb-throbbing ache. He could hardly remember the
agonized fire of the morning when one by one his fingernails had been removed with sharpened bamboo splin-
ters and tweezers.

General Gyi San Wun, his patience fast dwindling
with the Englishman who would not talk, asked again,
'What was your purpose in riding to Kadaw in the
middle of the night?'

Dulled behind a red mist, his occluded brain had
mercifully imposed an impediment upon his speech.
Leigh could not think, his articulation was bad, Gyi San
Wun could not understand him even if he did crack
under interrogation. 'I ... I ...'

'Remind me again,' said the cultured Burmese voice
as the man took snuff from the back of his soft white
hand. The eyes were Chinese, dead eyes; they shrank
Leigh's soul.

He tried to think what it was he had told Gyi San
Wun earlier in the day; something like, I went out to
inspect the telegraph wires and to make sure everything
was operating correctly at Senyat and Kadaw ...

'Senyat and Kadaw,' he remembered murmuring.

'Why?'

Leigh remembered the night. Distantly he remembered the night, he couldn't remember anymore, he

couldn't remember what it was he was supposed to have said.

They took him away and brought him back an hour later.

'Why did you ride to Kadaw in the middle of the night?' asked General Gyi San Wun.

'The storms ... typhoon earlier. Lines were down. Happens all the time, I was responsible ...'

'You *were* responsible. But why did you go all the way to Kadaw to send your message to the British?'

'No message to British ... checking lines, that's all.'

'What else?'

'Nothing else. At Kadaw I said my farewells to Ko Ba Wan ...' Leigh took a deep breath and tried to sit up, 'Ko Ban ... no Ko Ba, yes Ko Ba Wan. He had been at my Senyat classes ... but posted to Kadaw. I had to wish him goodbye ... good fellow. Good friend. Wife had a baby, a son. I went to wish them happy birthday, congratulate him on birth of son ...'

'So you rode four miles in bad weather, along treacherous and water-logged jungle tracks, in the middle of the night, only to give Ko Ba Wan such a simple message? Why did you not use the telegraph from Senyat?'

'It was not operating,' Leigh said wearily.

'For reasons that you and the Frenchman had previously been tampering with the Senyat line?'

'No.'

'*You lie Englishman!*' Gyi San Wun thundered, slamming both his fists on the table so close to Leigh's blackened finger-stubs he cried out before he could help himself. Leigh bit hard on his crusted lip, trying to sustain the jarring agony through his whole body. He forced himself to look up and to behold those terrifying eyes of Gyi San Wun.

In the look the Englishman gave him, General Gyi San Wun realized that to lose his composure would only undermine his authority and lower his esteem in the eyes of the Britisher. They, like the Manchurians when seeking to intimidate, remained collected and invincible for maximum effect. He wished to emulate them in the transmission of fear. Therefore, he lowered his tone and reached for more snuff from the gold and vermilion lacquered box the Queen of Burma had given him. 'It was specifically to relay messages to the British Commander at Thayetmyo you rode four miles in bad weather, was it not? Why did you not wish to use the telegraph station at Senyat? Was it because you feared my imminent and untimely arrival, eh Englishman?'

'Why ... would I wish ... to do all that when, when ...' Oh God, Leigh felt his tongue would blather all sorts of things if he were not more in control of his wits. Again he tried to breathe deeply, but all he seemed capable of taking into his lungs was the sickly odour permeating throughout the ghastly room.

'I am asking the questions, Englishman,' said Gyi San Wun mildly over the snuff, 'You have just told me the lines between Kadaw and Senyat were faulty so you could not send your messages from Senyat Hill.'

'Yes ... that's why Monsieur René attended to them for me. As an engineer, he know ... he knows more about it than others ...'

'But Monsieur René is a civil engineer, not a telegraph operator, so what would he know about it?' continued the smooth voice in Leigh's ear.

'Water,' Leigh whispered.

'No. Why did you not enlist the help of one of the soldier-engineers at Senyat?' Gyi San Wun persisted.

'None available. General Maung Laik took all his skilled men with him to Myingyan.' Leigh shifted his position awkwardly, the lightheaded feeling on him coming and going in a way that made him feel sea-sick, nauseated, so that he thought he would throw up in front of Gyi San Wun if he had to smell his smell for much longer. Dully Leigh registered the word opium. The man smoked opium from the hookah beside him. The knowledge of Gyi San Wun's addiction made Leigh cringe from the sadism linked to that addiction.

Leigh tried to conjure Milly's dear sweet face before him, but he could not. He could not remember a thing about her except her eyes. Great grey misty eyes containing her soul so that when he had looked into them he had wanted to drown in them. Yes, to drown deep down in Milly Sinclair's lovely eyes; he loved her, he loved her so much, he would fight his way out of Gyi San Wun's clutches so that he might see her again — Milly, dear Milly, he silently cried over and over again. Tired, he put his head down on Gyi San Wun's table; so tired, because he had not slept for days and days, he thought his mind would split ...

'We know you rode to Kadaw on the Thugyi's mule,' droned the voice, 'and the Thugyi will also be punished.'

General Gyi San Wun filled the entire universe. Mighty, towering, un-Burman, his tall spare frame and cruel hawklike Taingda Mingyi features presented a mask of death. Adorned in silken robes of scarlet and gold, his black satin and gold-braided gaung-baung sat regally on his head. He had been about to retire to bed when he had learned of the exciting capture of two foreigners interfering with the telegraph lines between Senyat and Kadaw. They had tried to escape, to remain hidden in the jungle, but a pi-dog had sniffed out their hiding place and had led his soldiers to the foreigners. Now, he was greatly enjoying himself with the young Englishman who had so much more meat on him than the insipid Frenchman who gave way to a woman's tears and puked before anyone had really got their teeth in him. General Gyi San Wun's eyes were no more than slanted slits of malice in his dissolute noble features as they dwelt unemotionally on the Englishman's dark, downbent head and bloody fingers. He was brave and foolish. General Gyi San Wun admired and despised the foreigner. 'What information did you relay to the British via a secret coding?' His voice was a cat's purr caress while gently tapping the back of Leigh's crusted hand with a long steel nail-file he used for paring his finger-nails.

'I relayed no information.'

'Why did you ride to Kadaw?'

'To wish Ba Wan Happy Birthday ... new baby. Congratulations in order ...'

'He was a great friend of yours, this Ko Ba Wan?'

'He was a friend, yes ...'

The file flashed viciously.

'*No* ...!' Leigh's whole body jerked, his injured hand remained pinned to the table. He was too far gone to do anything except utter a little moan and pass out as his head fell forward.

Gyi San Wun nodded, and the two soldiers standing behind the prisoner's chair removed him to his bamboo cage.

Senyat's noble Commander reached for his opium-pipe.

The Telegraph Operators at Senyat and at Kadaw had been questioned concerning the 'birthday message', but their information had proved unproductive. None of them had any knowledge of how or from where the message had been tapped out on their lines. Ko Ba Wan had sworn that the Englishman had only been whistling the familiar British tune when he had appeared in his telegraph hut to say goodbye, and to congratulate him on the birth of his new son. He had never been left alone for one moment — well, one moment perhaps and that was when Ko Ba Wan had gone outside of his tiny relay station at Kadaw to relieve himself on the outside wall. But the lines had been out of order at the time, and therefore the Englishman had not been lying. No messages had been received or transmitted via the Morse Code because of the fault. Gyi San Wun pondered the confusing incident. But he felt certain that somehow the Englishman *had* interfered with the Burmese telegraph system and relayed a message in code to the Britishers at Thayetmyo concerning Burmese military movements. For a long time his noble cousin, the Taingda Mingyi had entertained suspicions regarding the activities of this Englishman Buchanan. Staying so often in the marble house of the wealthy American Captain known as the Shwe Nat of Mandalay — that in itself was incriminating evidence, for the Shwe Nat himself was not to be trusted. Then there was the business of the Sinclair family, the British Chargé d'Affairs — another man whose mild appearance belied a shrewd intelligence. The Englishman Buchanan was known to be entertaining notions of marrying himself into that well-known family who had such great influence in Anglo-India. In Mandalay itself, this tight little knot of foreigners had stood together to undermine Burmese morale and to establish themselves as a kind of hierarchy in opposition to the Dragon Throne. But they would not succeed!

Ah, but that milksop General, Maung Laik, had refused to acknowledge the Englishman Buchanan's duplicity, viewing him only as an 'honourable' English gentleman who would not bite the hand that fed him. Now see the damage done for trusting foreigners! He had passed on secret and vital information through the very Burmese he had taught and who trusted him. Definitely, he had tampered with coded messages, disrupted the censored military telegraph system of the Burmese, bitten the hands that had fed him. Gyi San Wun wondered if General Maung Laik would still consider the Britisher to be honourable and trustworthy — he was not as easily foiled as his predecessor, and that was why he had replaced the Maung Laik on the Taingda Mingyi's orders.

General Gyi San Wun smiled to himself and went on paring his long nails while dreamily smoking his opium-pipe. And another matter, he told himself, the Frenchman's version of the confused Senyat-Kadaw incident had differed considerably from the stories of Ko Ba Wan and Ko Toe Myint, one the operator at Kadaw, the latter operating from Senyat Hill. He preferred to believe the Frenchman's story for there was real truth in fearful truth and Monsieur René was afraid enough to sell his own soul to the devil ...

He asked his crippled servant to instruct the soldiers

to bring the Englishman back.

When Leigh was once more placed in a chair in front of him, Gyi San Wun began again; 'You lied to me, Englishman, when you said Ko Ba Wan and Ko Toe Myint were friends of yours. Your people do not have the Burmese as their friends. You only wish to rule them as you do the Indians. We shall therefore call Ko Ba Wan and Ko Toe Myint colleagues of yours. Or better still, children of yours as you were their teacher. Yes, good little Burmese children. So, it was easy to bribe your children to send your uncensored messages via the Burmese field telegraph. How did you bribe them?'

Leigh observed thin blue cords of smoke from the Sino-Burman's cheroot tangle with the vapour from his oil-lamp. Next to the oil-lamp was a heavy brass-gong the General struck to draw the attention of his crippled servant who shuffled in and out on stunted feet ridden with a disease of the bone. Hoisted by the roots of his hair to face the Sino-Burman because he had not answered, he felt the Burmese soldier's heavy breath on the nape of his neck. Leigh said: 'Water ... thow yea ... drinking water ...'

'No,' said Gyi San Wun.

The brilliance of the lamp hurt his eyes. Hot so hot in here, and yet he felt so cold inside. Leigh wanted to be sick. 'Water ...' he pleaded. 'Sleep,' he pleaded, but he could not make himself heard against the nausea over-taking him.

General Gyi San Wun said, 'What are these?'

Because his head had once more fallen onto the table, the Burmese soldier behind him pulled his head up again by his hair. Leigh tried to focus his unwilling eyes. A codebook had been pushed into the circle of light from the lamp. A page had been torn out of it, singed at the edges. Leigh remembered he had tried to burn it in the shadow of a Bo tree he and René had been sheltering under when four Burmese soldiers had leapt out of its branches, the pi-dog yapping at his and René's heels. 'My codebook,' Leigh murmured drowsily.

General Gyi San Wun smiled cruelly. At last he felt he was getting somewhere with this obstinate Englishman.

'A codebook of your own secret signals, yes, Englishman?'

'Yes,' said Leigh uncaring.

'What kind of secrets are contained in these closely scribed pages of Burmese and English?'

'All sorts of secrets.'

'Transcribe them.'

'Too many ...'

'Then some of them. This one here ...' Gyi San Wun tapped a pointed fingernail on the place.

Leigh squinted, his eyes watering, his mind confused. He took a deep breath and tried hard, hoping afterwards they would give him some water and let him sleep; 'The dots and dashes of the Morse Code are transmitted ... by varying the time the transmitter key is depressed.' He had to stop and lick his dry lips. His tongue felt too large to fit his mouth. Gyi San Wun nodded to his servant who shuffled forward with a glass of water in his hand. Like a madman, Leigh's lips hovered and trembled on the rim, but they would not let him take more than a sip.

'Mmm ... many operators find it difficult to learn the time signals acc ... accurately.' He experienced a loud ringing in his ears, on and on and on, like deafening pagoda bells.

'And this one ...' General Gyi San Wun turned another page in the *Handbook for Telegraph Operators*.

'One has to ... has to take account of accents and the inter ... international range of languages,' Leigh muttered with pain and desperation running through him. 'Thus, in Burmese ... the jux ... juxtaposition of those letters most used, h-l-a, n-g, g-y-i, can be grouped together. When transposing English groupings, ing, ch, sh ... same principal applies ... I can't read anymore ... can't see ...'

'Enough! What then is the purpose of such a codebook?' demanded Gyi San Wun who had gleaned nothing at all from that rigmarole of words concerning the Morse Telegraph, whose functions and mechanics baffled him.

'It's merely for my-my own use when teaching operators English techniques in use of Morse. You see ... English and Burmese, vastly different languages; very difficult because groupings are nothing alike. Letters and sounds are pronounced quite differently. Nor are there same combinations of letters of alphabet ...' His voice had faded away until it was scarcely audible to Gyi San Wun. 'Dots and dashes ... most used letters, groupings, being also quickest to transmit,' he rambled disjointedly.

'Give me an example,' insisted Gyi San Wun.

'I cannot ... not if ... not if you do not speak English.'

'I speak English, Englishman!' shouted Gyi San Wun. Then, with a calculating smile that did not reach his hooded eyes he said in English; 'Happy birthday to you! You see, Englishman, so now I would wish to know what that means translated into Burmese Morse Code!'

'In Burmese,' said Leigh desperately, with the room going round and round him and his tongue choking him half to death, 'it means, the phongyis are all gathered around a beautiful birthday cake and are dying to blow out the candles but the King hasn't arrived yet.'

'What does that mean?' asked Gyi San Wun quietly.

Leigh murmured, 'It means, the phongyis are all gath ...' The nailfile silenced him.

Presently Gyi San Wun asked; 'Your father, it is true he works for British Military Intelligence, Dum-Dum?'

'He did,' Leigh said. 'But he's retired now.'

'And you, you are the same?'

'Yes, you might say I've been retired by the Burmese.'

'I did not mean your employment with the Burmese. I meant in connection with British Military Intelligence. I think Englishman, you deliberately choose to misunderstand me. I also know your grasp of the Burmese language is not so minimal you misunderstand a simple question when you teach others the intricacies of it. So don't be deliberately stupid, Englishman, for your toes

377

still retain the feeling your hands did a little while ago. Not only will you be unable to send Morse messages, but you will also be unable to walk to your places of intrigue. So tell me quickly, in what capacity have you operated for the British within our Burmese network? Are you a British spy working for their Military Intelligence Department?'

'I've worked for the Burmese Government and their Royal Family irrespective of any military organization, British or Burmese.'

'What was your purpose in working for the Burmese?'

'To widen their knowledge of the Electric-Magnetic Telegraph now in operation throughout most civilized countries of the world, and to improve Burma's communication network in this area,' Leigh replied stoically.

'Why?' demanded Gyi San Wun.

'For money.'

General Gyi San Wun fingered his smooth long chin. This Englishman Buchanan was too intelligent by far, and too erudite to be tricked into giving something away through his failure to grasp the Burmese language. He knew it as well as he did his own language. 'You consider you were well paid by the Burmese and that was the only reason why you worked for them?'

'Yes,' said Leigh. 'That and because I like Burma ... did like Burma ...' He coughed and a fleck of blood clung to his lip. Leigh began to feel curiously detached as he looked up at the pale Sino-Burman seated opposite him like a devil simmering in a smokescreen of iniquity. The fumes of the opium-pipe were making him feel nice, very detached, non-caring, free of pain and even happy. Milly's face drifted in front of Leigh, woven in the coils of lazily drifting blue smoke swirling all around his head. Leigh reached up and touched Milly's face and she smiled back at him, her misty grey eyes soft with love ...

'Why did you try to burn your codebook if it contained such helpful information for the purposes of teaching your classes?' Gyi San Wun asked Leigh.

Leigh, intent on catching hold of Milly through the

tendrils of mist coming between them, did not hear Gyi San Wun.

The Burmese Commander waited for the disorientated man to stop moving his arms. When he could not, he asked for him to be taken away. Tomorrow would be time enough to get to the real core of the Englishman. Right now he felt very tired, his senses satiated. General Gyi San Wun closed his dead eyes and let his mind dwell on many things.

The world was full of traitors. There were three more Englishmen hiding somewhere in the thick jungle surrounding Senyat and Kadaw. The man Sinclair was of special importance to the Taingda Mingyi as he harboured much information concerning the Burmese. But he, Gyi San Wun, would track him down. He would track them all down sooner or later; what he had in mind for the Frenchman tomorrow would lead him straight to the hornets' nest. And then, the quiet Englishman Buchanan, observing his friends' plight, hearing their cries, would himself reveal all, yes all — what 'Happy Birthday to you' truly meant!

He opened his Sino-Burmese eyes and lit his hookah. Relaxing to the bubbling sounds of the water in the vase, he sucked contentedly on the tube. He dwelt too, on the possibility of another gold medal from King Thibaw. He presently called for his ancient Chinese servant by banging the heavy brass gong supported by the facing trunks of two huge ivory elephants. They were the sacred white elephants of jewelled Myanma. The foreigners would not steal away the Kingdom of gold they had desired desperately from the moment they had first trodden upon the golden shore — he would make certain of it by putting traitors among traitors.

Gyi San Wun's smile was truly enigmatic when he murmured through his contented bubbling, 'Bring me the volume of *The Life of the Manchurian Inquisitor.*'

'At once, Honourable and Noble Master,' and bowing his way out backwards, the Chinese servant hastened to obey the wishes of Senyat's new Commanding Officer.

CHAPTER
TWENTY-SEVEN

ONE

In the Myowun's abandoned palace across the river, Angela, Milly and Blaize awaited news from Nathan who had accompanied the Flotilla to Mandalay. He had promised to send them back word the moment he heard anything concerning Matthew, Leigh and Edwin.

Major Radcliffe had been instrumental in finding the women lodgings at Minhla and allowing Nathan to 'tag' along with the Flotilla on account of his invaluable knowledge of the Irrawaddy. One of the tasks allotted to Jeffrey Radcliffe and his men was to make the river below Minhla safe so that the rest of the fleet might pass without fear of Burmese mines. The American Captain, Jeffrey Radcliffe was sure, would be able to give them information as to where and how to mark out the mighty rivers with buoys in avoidance of shallows amongst other hazards to be faced.

Blaize fanned herself vigorously with a palm-leaf. Seated on the verandah of an upstairs room not gutted by the fire that had destroyed so much of the palace as well as the town of Minhla with all its wooden houses, she exclaimed in delight: 'Isn't this nice! What a pity so much of the palace went up in smoke. But it does serve them right for having cannon on the roof aimed at our poor boys who were being slashed to pieces by those awful Burmese dahs. Did you see that handsome peacock Angela darling; strutting pompously through the gardens with his harem of peahens following him? I do think that was how Buddha and his disciples got their idea of this male supremacy business which allows them to have so many wives it's postively immoral. They must have stalked like that in the Garden of Eden.'

'Buddha or the peacocks, Bee?'

'Oh, too, too funny Angela darling. Milly dear, I do wish you'd stop moping because your lover hasn't penned you a letter for at least a week. I daresay he's busy hacking his way through the jungle to you this very moment. We all go through it out here darling, so accept it. We're grass-widows half the time and totally exploited the rest. Men are so incredibly thoughtless. Angela, have you taken a peek yet into those upstairs rooms along the fretted balcony untouched by the fire? My dear, absolutely crammed full of *the* most delightful silks and satins imaginable. Such finery to make your mouth water, and far superior to Parisian quality — we could make dresses galore. It's about time you cheerfully said goodbye to that horrid black thing you borrowed from me. I only bought it because I was in mourning at the time.' She turned on the Myowun's carved throne, brought upstairs from his gutted Audience Chamber, to say to Clare, who languished on a day-couch just inside the verandah doorway, 'Clare, you look positively wretched in that drab colour. Yellow on a woman with a sallow complexion always makes her look like a mango with swamp-fever. Only my opinion of course, so don't weep darling. We all know you're anaemic and touchy after being through purgatory. My word, after listening to you for three days, I'm so thankful I never produced.'

'Blaize, Blaize ...' Angela cleared her throat warningly and frowned at Lady Bee who insisted on being deliberately tactless. 'I think Bee, we shouldn't touch those materials. It might be considered theft.'

'Nonsense darling! Let's just say the spoils of war.'

If she had not been Lady Blaize Tennent-Browne, she would have been the Queen of Sheba. 'Where I wonder,' said Angela trying to change the subject altogether, 'has Jubela got to with the children? This place still isn't safe for them to go wandering off at large.'

'Calm down, darling. Anyone would think they were your children the way you worry about them. Clare doesn't seem too bothered, so why are you? Milly, if you don't smile soon, I shall become most awfully vexed.'

'Leave her alone Blaize,' Angela said, softly insistent.

'Very well. But we all have a little cross to bear. If it's any consolation to anyone, I'm still grieving very deeply over the death of Mr Findebar. It was such a blow. He was such a nice man and I know Nathan was simply devastated because they had been together for a long time. But really, if we dwelt constantly on thoughts of death in this country we'd take up permanent residence in a cemetery. The Burmese are a very violent nation ...'

'No more violent than the British,' Angela interrupted. 'It wasn't exactly a pleasant sight to see all those poor Burmese soldiers running out of the fort to get to the river, being gunned down by our soldiers. Or knowing that the Sepoys were blowing Burmese brains out once they did manage to reach the Irrawaddy. They should have been taken as prisoners, not murdered.'

'Whose side are you on darling?' Blaize asked with raised brows. 'And one doesn't call it "murder" in a war.'

'Then what does one call it?'

'Dear me, darling. Let's not get involved in a philosophical argument on the ethics of war. That's too, too much in this heat. But at least we had a grandstand view of everything didn't we? My, wasn't Nathan angry when from his cell window he saw the *Belle* being blown up by *our* gunboats. What a hoot! I could hear him shouting all down that gruesome corridor. And what he wasn't considering doing afterwards to poor Commander Clutterbuck of the *Irrawaddy* when he discovered *he* was the man responsible for the sad demise of his precious *Belle*! Well, I simply had to take myself away and laugh into my handkerchief. I do hope Edwin remembers to change

382

his socks as I'm not with him to remind him. He's prone to athlete's foot you know — excessively overactive sweat-glands, the Army doctor at Manipur told us. But after all, Edwin is a remarkable man for his age — he'll be sixty-five this year you know, darlings. Which reminds me, very soon I shall be approaching my own hill — still, we shan't talk about such a depressing subject, I'm not there yet. But I'm so glad I never produced. Simply ruinous for one's hour-glass figure — that oughtn't to worry you in the future, Angela darling, as any difference in your weight is bound to be an improvement. Did they not teach you to eat up all your nasty green vegetables in that Academy of yours? I do hope Nathan arrives safely in Mandalay without getting himself blown to pieces just like his poor *Belle*. Yes, Ko Lee? What is it you want, creeping up on us like that? Can't you see we're busy?' She frowned at him from the cushioned comfort of the Myowun's throne.

'I not notice, Lady-Memsahib Bee. Ko Lee knock velly velly loudly but ladies too chatty-chatty to hear ...'

'Get on with it boy — and don't pretend you can't speak intelligible English! Has Captain Vorne sent us a wire?'

'Too soon. He not allive in Mandalay yet with Blitish soldiers who do not fly like bird. It is illustrious Blitish Army doctorchap comes knockee-knockee on ladies door. He want to speak most urgently and wait outside please.'

'Show him in then, Ko Lee, don't keep him hovering on the doorstep. I expect he's here to enquire after our health,' Angela said, getting up, but Blaize met the Medical Officer first.

'Good morning, Captain Brierley!' Lady Tennent-Browne greeted him with deep dimples and a languid hand. 'Do forgive our shabby appearance but I'm afraid my luggage blew up with the *Belle Hélène*. We're all making very good progress after our ordeal, Captain, if you're here to follow-up our thorough medical check-up by your Superior Officer. Mrs Sinclair appears to be the only one in need of a tonic.'

Captain Brierley felt Mrs Sinclair's pulse, nodded his head and said; 'Yes, I might be able to find a tonic, somewhere ... however, that's not the only reason I'm here, ladies. May I ...?' He took the arm of the Myowun's chair while Blaize hovered behind Clare's day-couch because from there the Captain was in direct line of her vision. Milly and Angela looked at him attentively.

'A grave situation has occurred at Minhla,' he began, his lean face creasing apologetically. 'Because of the erratic weather conditions we've been experiencing of late, cholera has broken out among our troops. Reported cases have been isolated aboard one of our hospital ships in the middle of the Irrawaddy — where it will remain to receive further cases. We have also managed to requisition a number of monastery and pagoda rest-houses in the area in order to accommodate our sick men. We're doing everything we can to contain this outbreak otherwise the effect on our troops will be devastating. You'll appreciate the difficulties we've run up against, the climate, food and conditions which our boys are not used to. However, cholera in Burma — as you're all possibly aware of — is of such a nature as to afflict one half of the room whilst leaving the other half contagion free; its manner is always endemic and unpredictable.' He gave a little smile and cleared his throat. 'Which brings me to the reason why I'm here ... oh, besides that of seeing everything is well with you ladies.' The smiles flashed on and off in quick little spasms of embarrassment. It had been a long time since he had had to deal with female ailments. 'I know it was your intention to proceed to Rangoon as soon as the river was re-opened to public transportation, but I must ask you to defer your departure until the cholera epidemic has abated. Otherwise there is a risk that you take the cholera with you down to Thayetmyo and perhaps risk the lives of our soldiers.'

'And what about your soldiers risking our lives,

Captain Brierley?' Blaize asked, her eyes flashing. 'Did your men not wear their cholera belts? You know how imperative it is everyone adheres strictly to the rules of the East if poisonous odours are not to be passed on to others? If your men were given a diet of oysters, then that accounts for the cholera as oysters are known to transmit that poisonous disease. Besides, we have children with us. We cannot stay at Minhla another moment but must proceed to Rangoon in order that the children might not pick up anything from your sick men.'

'Ma'am, I'm afraid that this area has already been made an out-of-bounds zone which means that no one who is not already within this boundary may come in, and those inside it may not leave. But you are all pretty well isolated enough here at Governor's palace.'

'I'm sure that we would be delighted to co-operate with you and Surgeon-General Monelly by obeying your orders to remain here until given permission to leave,' Angela reassured him.

'Thank you, Miss Featherstone.' He smiled in gratitude. 'I'm sorry that this has occurred to inconvenience you ladies, but you must understand our reasons for the restrictions. Widespread cholera would wipe out the entire Expeditionary Force overnight. Having come so far, we would then end up losing this war against the Burmese. In this heat, with the intolerable conditions our men have to endure, there would not be many left to take Mandalay after all our concerted efforts to get an organized Army into Upper Burma.'

He felt he had made his point. He drummed up courage to face his next task. The young Medical Officer diverted his gaze to the smoke-blue distances of jungle-clad hills and tall palm trees beyond the Burmese Governor's palace. He brought his attention back to the ladies on the verandah and running his finger inside the collar of his high-buttoned khaki tunic, addressed himself to Angela in particular, as he felt she was the most sensible one to handle the situation. 'The Deputy M.O. wishes this residence to be turned over to the use of er ... as a temporary hospital for some of our less sick men. Sunstroke, snakebite, heat-rashes, food-poisoning, that sort of thing. We wish to keep our minor ailments away from our more severe casualties, those men wounded on the battlefields. Naturally, the contagious diseases would not be brought here either.'

Again he felt very uncomfortable with Lady Tennent-Browne's dagger-looks directed at him, and once more ran his finger inside his restricting uniform collar.

'Does this mean we're to be ousted from our quarters without consideration to the welfare of Mrs Sinclair and her children? I refuse, Captain, here and now. I simply refuse to be re-housed in some filthy godown, rest-house or native compound. You may return to the Deputy M.O. with my answer. No.' said Blaize.

'No, indeed, Lady Tennent-Browne,' he said almost biting his tongue as he tried to reassure her. 'We intend to use only the ground-floor room undamaged by the fire. You ladies may remain in these upper rooms where we will see to it that your privacy is respected at all times.'

'I'm glad to hear it. I for one will not budge from here. How many of your "minor afflictions" are we to have imposed upon us for the duration?'

'About ... I would say, about half-a-dozen or so, ma'am.'

'That's simply wonderful Captain Brierley. Cholera on our doorstep and minor afflictions inside the door. What else have you in store for us besides a war, cholera and imprisonment?'

'Captain Brierley,' said Milly Sinclair who had listened to everything with great attention. 'I don't mind in the least offering my help for what little it's worth while we're cooped up here doing nothing. If you'd like bandages rolled or anything minor like that I could be of some use. I'll gladly lend my help. I know you and your medical orderlies must be very hard pushed at this particular time, what with cholera to add to your worries. I know nothing about nursing serious wounds, so I would not be much good for that, but I could manage the little tasks.'

Blaize and Angela had both turned to her with open-mouthed astonishment, and in the temporary silence put up by the vanquished ladies of more mature years Captain Brierley rushed in with a beaming smile; 'That's very handsome of you, I must say Miss Sinclair, and I'm overwhelmed by your offer. Any kind of help would be greatly appreciated by myself and the M.O. who have better things to do than put calamine on sun-burned noses or attend to scorpion-stings. There would be nothing sent here you couldn't cope with. Just a few silly lads of ours who can't stomach the food, or have laid their hands on spirits before sundown, the sort of thing a few days rest and quiet will soon remedy. Most kind of you to offer your services, Miss Sinclair, I know the Deputy M.O. will himself be awfully grateful. Now then, I'll come along first thing tomorrow morning with some of my bandsmen and we can get some organization into this place. I shall also give strict instructions that these upper floors are to remain out-of-bounds to all Army personnel, and any man caught snooping into your privacy or inconveniencing you ladies in any way, will be court-martialled. Good day Lady Tennent-Browne, Miss Featherstone, Mrs and Miss Sinclair. Thank you so much, Miss Sinclair,' he said again whilst warmly shaking her hand, 'so kind of you.' And before anyone could change Miss Sinclair's mind, Captain Brierley hastily departed.

'Well!' Blaize exploded after he had made himself scarce, 'Millicent Sinclair! Do you realize what you've done? Really, my dear girl, you are getting far too big for your boots in making *my* decisions ...'

'Milly dear,' said Angela before Blaize Tennent-Browne got carried away further, 'if you wish to lend a hand nursing our injured soldiers, then I shall assist you. I think seven years in the Sasana Convent has taught me one skill at least, and that is the care of sick people.'

'You do realize don't you, Angela, what you and

Milly will be called? Oh, you don't know! Well, I'll tell you since I have great experience with our little Army up and down India and know all about Regimental gossip. You will be called camp-followers by the common little soldier-boy bred in the gutters of our cities — if the Officers don't call you such names themselves. Really darlings, I wonder what on earth has possessed you to do such a thing! It might have been different if you'd decided to nurse Officers who are a little more graceful in their manners and breeding, but all those uncouth little tommies with their coarse ways, really darlings, you must be raving mad, the both of you.'

'Have you quite finished, Blaize?' Angela asked coldly. 'Now I wish to say a few words. The only reason, Bee, you are called a lady is because of dear Edwin,' Angela got up from her chair on the verandah and left Blaize's presence.

Milly, in tears, ran after her.

TWO

With incredible speed and efficiency, Captain Brierley set up his little hospital ward under the Deputy Medical Officer's orders. Angela and Milly soon settled into a routine nursing their 'minor afflictions', which became a standing joke between them. Both of them had been glad of the diversion, hands and thoughts kept busy while the Burmese and British fought it out on the 'Maidan of Empire'. Milly especially was grateful for the diversion, Leigh's unnatural silence causing her a great feeling of disquietude. She was fully aware he could not possibly have known about their enforced sojourn at Minhla, for Nathan would not yet have arrived in Mandalay with the Flotilla to put Leigh, Matthew or Edwin in the picture. Uncertainty prevailed. Milly told herself not to be foolish, Leigh was safe enough wherever he was. She only wished she knew where. She just hoped they had all managed to get some place far enough away from the

Taingda Mingyi's clutches, that was all.

Yet her feeling of foreboding continued, and the only way to defy it was to keep busy, busy, busy.

Out in the middle of the Irrawaddy a hospital ship lay at anchor with the cholera cases aboard. Most of them succumbed to the disease within forty-eight hours. Those who by some miracle survived that most feared scourge of the East recuperated in nearby monastery zayats or resthouses. Serious casualties and cases requiring more complicated surgery or medical attention than the field hospitals or hospital ships could provide, were shipped downriver to Thayetmyo where two Base Hospitals had been set up to receive Army personnel, one for the British , the other for the Indians.

Such cases as heat stroke, snake-bite, food-poisoning and scorpion stings, were nursed at Governor's palace by a handful of medical orderlies with Angela's and Milly's assistance as Captain Brierley's original half-dozen cases turned out to be two dozen. In the end too, Lady Tennent-Browne stopped turning up her nose at those to whom she had referred as 'common little tommies'. Having decided their company was far more preferable to that of Clare Sinclair's, she left Clare to Jubella.

CHAPTER
TWENTY-EIGHT

ONE

While the British Flotilla steamed slowly toward Mandalay, rapidly the rate of disease and death increased. If Gue Gyoun Kamyo and Minhla had been British victories to crow over, then after Myingyan morale fell very low. Not only did the raw British soldier have to contend with the threat of sickness, he was unused to the exhausting climate that produced unknown fevers like cholera, dysentery, typhus, smallpox, quite apart from the minor discomforts of prickly-heat rash and sunstroke; his monotonous staple diet consisted of rice and saltfish; mosquitoes plagued him to death, he was far from home and soon he began to wonder if the capture of Mandalay was truly worth the effort. The feeling in the 'zenana' ward at Governor's Palace was one of general depression after the battle of Myingyan because it was suddenly realized that more, many more, lives were being lost off the battlefields of the Irrawaddy than actually on them.

Then one morning Orderly Larcher came into the ward with a beaming smile and a hale and hearty manner he had not had for over a week. 'Lady T-B,' he said, marching up to her medicine trolley, 'guess what our boys are saying now?'

Her attention divided between castor-oil on the one hand and kaolin on the other, her tongue between her teeth as she concentrated on spooning out the correct amounts for each patient, she presently asked; 'What are they saying now, Larcher?'

'That Hlethin fellow ma'am, had it all wrong. What he telegraphed to the King of Burma was all lies ma'am. Kicked the bottom out of his barges we did — and not the other way round as it was put about to lower our morale. Orf he went with a flea in his ear from Myingyan Hill, complete with golden umbrella and earrings, quiet as a lamb to give Queen Souplate back her golden mugs. She'd asked for them back, you know ma'am, when she found out the real truth of the matter. And now the King's been asking for his golden medals too because he's in a right huff with the Hlethin for walking out of Gue Gyoun and telling lies about Myingyan.'

'Well I never,' said Blaize Tennent-Browne, 'I'm sure Mr Larcher, Queen Supayalat will be most put out by it all while she remelts her golden mugs. But you don't want to believe everything you hear. There's always two sides to every story you know, and we're just as capable of propaganda as the rest. Now then, I'm finished here, so if anyone comes looking for me in the next twenty minutes I'll be on the verandah sorting the linen which that wretched ayah was supposed to put away last night. I now have to make beds with mildewed sheets. You can finish this medicine round, Mr Larcher, because I can bear the smell of it no longer. Oh, and by the way, Miss Milly has gone off to try and find some sugar and lemons because of that silly business of the Deputy M.O's of giving the men lemon juice and sugar to counteract scurvy — as though we're not going to enough expense and bother already by shipping boatloads of cabbages, sprouts, live goats and pigs from India to Rangoon so that our men might be better fed!' She swept regally from the room, and Bines said to Larcher with a big grin, 'Cor blighme, ain't she just priceless!'

'Now-now, m'lad,' said Orderly Larcher, 'none of the lip. Won't have a word of disrespect I won't concerning them fine females who don't mind putting up with your face.'

'Sorry, Mr Larcher. That one in the black dress wot keeps her head all done up, is she bald like they say?'

'I couldn't begin to say, Bines. And it ain't none of your business either. For all that, she ain't a bad-looker to my way of thinking — and she keeps her mouth shut when it doesn't need to be opened. Not like some I can mention — and that means you.' He wagged an admonishing finger. 'Even if the M.O. do say it's blood-poisoning, I know a lead-swinger when I see one, Bine's m'boy!'

TWO

Milly had gone across the compound to the kitchen quarters where Ko Lee and Tonsin were acting as chief cook and bottle-washer. She found Ko Lee in an act of near-murder, beating Tonsin with a broomstick and shouting at him in a manner terrifying to the timid.

'Sillee fellow, sillee fellow, you have sense not even in place where you sit upon ... what you do, huh? What you do? You tell me quick or I beat you again. You tellee Ko Lee why you sleep at very important time, or he make short work of you like you do his curree, huh? Now I see why Cap'ain and Findebar always kick your pants, huh?'

'Ko Lee,' said Milly in astonishment, 'what on earth's going on here?'

'Huh, Missy Milly, this sillee half-black half-white fellow burn Ko Lee curry for tommies. Now what will happen huh? Ko Lee, he get kicked in pants by Blitish soldier who get blame for being Chink-cretin like Cap'ain call him when he do things wrong. Now, this time, it not Ko Lee fault. Now I start all over again and much time gone and no chicken left, huh!' He put aside the broom he had been wielding and stood with arms folded, glowering menacingly at Tonsin cringing in the corner.

'Ko Lee,' Milly said, 'we've run out of lemons and

sugar for the men, so please can I have some more for the ward?'

'No lemons, no sugar, no nothing left, sorree Missy Milly. We run out of everything in cookhouse because this sillee fellow here ...' He raised a foot and hoisted a kick into Tonsin's buttocks. 'He forget to collect supplies of important meat and vegetables and everything which come on tender all the way from Rangoon. No lemons, no sugar, no chicken, no nothing for Blitish soldier. What they eat this evening, huh?' He lifted his foot again but Tonsin dodged it.

'Ko Lee, leave him alone,' Milly said, rescuing the lad from Ko Lee's venom. She gently chided Tonsin; 'Really Tonsin, you must be more responsible and meet the tender when it's due in at Minhla, otherwise everything gets put out. Why did you forget to collect the stores this morning?'

'No good asking him, Missy Milly, his tongue too big for sillee mouth and all he do is make chin wet with drooling like baby. He not to be trusted with anything, that is why Cap'ain and Findebar kick his pants. Now we very late for tiffin, and Blitish fellow kick me in tail. I go, I start again, excuse please but I make chop suey for dinner tonight.'

Milly looked dubious. She did not think their patients would appreciate chop suey at all — certainly not Ko Lee's. 'I've a better idea,' she told the cookboy, 'I'll go myself to the Quartermaster's store at the Garrison and bring back the things we require. I'll try and get some more chickens and then you can make another curry. You and Tonsin had better start preparing the vegetables and other ingredients in the meanwhile. I shan't be long.'

It was Ko Lee's turn to look doubtful. 'Missy Milly,' he said frowning, 'you not able to go alone to carry all things back by yourself. Everything too heavy for little lady like you.'

Touched by his concern, Milly reassured him, 'I'll take the little wooden cart one of the men made to trundle Mrs Sinclair's children in, and half-a-mile is no distance for me to walk — why, I used to walk three times as far before sun-up in Mandalay. Please get started Ko Lee, otherwise we'll be in trouble from our starving patients.'

She took the little handcart on wheels and set off to the Quartermaster's store at Minhla Garrison. Milly was confident she was not breaking any rules about straying out of bounds, for she was going nowhere near any zayat resthouse or other accommodation housing Captain Brierley's recuperating cholera patients. The track she took was the swampy half-mile pathway to Minhla Garrison, whose flag she could see fluttering above the trees. Usually, the supplies for Governor's Hospital were unloaded from the river-side onto the wooden landing stage below the Myowun's palace, the swampy road making passage difficult for a lot of supplies to be brought from the Garrison via that route. But for an emergency, she would not have come this way — Milly countenanced this occasion as an emergency.

She could smell the awful gases given off from the mangrove swamps which lay beyond the immediate trees bordering the road to Minhla. She kept the Union Jack as her landmark so that she would not become disorientated and lose her way.

Bombadiers Fields and Martin had taken a wrong turning somewhere and had got themselves hopelessly lost. Detached from the main body of their Company out after Burmese snipers, they had panicked and ended up in the mangrove swamps from where they had seen the Union Jack fluttering. Whooping with delight they galloped in the direction of Minhla Garrison and burst onto the same pathway at the same time that Milly, humming cheerfully to herself, trundled the handcart.

Fields dropped his half-smoked Wild Woodbine onto the muddy path and crushing it under his boot in front of Milly's little cart said with a pleasantly surprised smile, 'Hello there, what have we here? Looks like a little blue-bell, don't she Boosy? Now what's a pretty little flower like you doing walking all by yourself, eh luv?' He came a bit too close for Milly's liking.

'Please excuse me,' she said, 'I'm on my way to Minhla Garrison to get some stores for the Hospital.'

'Oh, so you're one of them fancy nurses the fellows are on about up at Gov's Orspital. Nice.'

Milly made to pass him but he took her arm; 'Not so fast then darling.' He fingered her crisp white headdress Blaize had made to match her dress from material found in the Myowun's boxes ... 'Real sight for sore eyes, isn't she Boosy? What's your name then, luv?'

'I'm not telling you,' she grew alarmed, more so when he noticed the bracelet on her wrist and said smoothly, 'Nice gold bangle you got there. Where'd you get it?'

'That's no business of yours. Besides ... it really doesn't belong to me. I'm keeping it to give to the Sasana Convent when I get back to Mandalay.'

'Why're you wearing it then?'

'An old Burmese woman gave it to me.'

'A likely story. Ain't she cute, Boosy?' He chucked Milly under the chin while his companion stood moodily at the side of the road, waiting for him. 'Come on then, if we're all going the same way to Minhla, let's go. You and me can take a little stroll together, eh luv?'

'I — I'd rather go alone — if you don't mind ...'

'Oh, but I do. Cummon darling, be a sport,' he put an arm round her shoulder.

Cautiously, Milly said, 'You may have the bracelet, I don't want it ...' she began tugging it off.

'Not so fast luv, not so fast,' Bombadier Fields laughed. 'Nobody's interested in the bangle. It's what it's decorating I'm more interested in.' Again he began touching her in a familiar way.

'Aw knock it off chum,' said Bombadier Martin, growing impatient by the side of the road, 'let her get on if she wants to. Cummon, me feet are fair killin' me after all that running through the jungle after wogs.' He started to march off down the track but a stone thrown by Fields hit him in the middle of his back-pack. He stopped and said angrily, 'Knock it off I said!'

'Just a minute Boosy, just a minute. Don't be in such a flippin' hurry. Ain't you got no feelings no more?'

'Look mate,' Boosy said angrily, 'you know what toffee-nosed Brierley said about court-martials if we go interfering with them women up at Gov's, so cut it out and leave her alone.'

By now Milly was in tears. Desperately she said to Fields. 'You take the bangle if you want.'

'Not the bangle luv, just a kiss. Just a little kiss and no harm done, eh?' He brought his face close to hers and she smelled strong tobacco on his hot breath.

'Let me go ... please! If you don't I'll scream ...'

'Go on then, scream.' Grinning, he clapped his hand over her mouth, his other arm capturing her waist while he dragged her off the path and under a tree. He breathed in her ear, 'Now then, like I said, just one little kiss and some harmless fun, and no one gets hurt.'

Above his hand her terrified eyes implored his friend, and Bombadier Martin, angry, tired and miserable from blistered feet in boots issued to him in the wrong size, lunged at Fields, pushing him in the back of the shoulder so that Fields' forehead slammed against the tree trunk, stunning him. 'Knock it off I said,' Martin shouted at him, 'You bloody stupid or something? Cummon, let's get back, I'm tired ...'

'Sod off!' A fist shot out and connected with Martin's chin. Rifles and back-packs forgotten, the two of them fought it out while Milly fled.

Her skirts tripping her up, she ran the remaining distance to Minhla Garrison. Only outside the main gate did she compose herself. Trying to contain her speech and her uneven breathing she asked to speak to Medical Officer, Captain Brierley, determined to bring to his attention the man who had assaulted her so that he wouldn't try anything like it again. She told the guard on the gate she was from Governor's Hospital with an urgent message for Captain Brierley and she was escorted immediately to his office. The Orderly Officer told her that Captain Brierley was not in at the moment,

396

having gone down to the riverside to see off the tender taking patients to the hospital ship for transference to Thayetmyo.

'He won't be long, Miss,' he tried to reassure her, seeing the young lady had got herself into quite an agitated state, 'if you'd care to wait inside here, I'll fetch you a cup of tea, Miss.'

'Thank you.' Breathless, Milly sat down in Captain Brierley's office and the Orderly Officer shut the door on her. Milly looked around the drab stone walls, the window set high so she would have to stand on tip-toe to see out of it, but guessed the view was of the river. She hoped Captain Brierley would not keep her waiting too long lest her courage fail her and she could not mention anything of the incident on the path to Minhla. In five minutes the Orderly Officer had brought her the promised tea and she took it gratefully, while he tactfully left her in peace to drink the hot sweet brew. Milly, restless and agitated by the unnerving incident on the Minhla road, began to wander round the gloomy office, the desk littered with files and medical chittys, while the hastily made shelves hanging more off the wall than on, were bowed down by medical books and journals.

Idly, the cup and saucer in her hand, Milly walked round the desk, her attention inquisitively drawn to personal photographs belonging to Captain Brierley, their silver frames in prominent display, lovingly polished. There were two pictures, an elderly couple, the woman seated and the man standing rigidly behind her chair, the other of a small shaggy-coated black dog. She put out her hand to take up the photograph of the pretty dog and her arm brushed across a medical-record in a blue file. The name on the outside seemed to come up off the desk and hit her a blow between the eyes. The tea spilled in her shaking hand and hastily she set down the cup and saucer on a corner of the cluttered desk.

Milly opened the file that had been lying on top of all the others and began to read the Medical Record: 'Agent: Leigh John Buchanan, Age 28, Special Intelligence Department, Dum-Dum, Calcutta, India. The date written had been the 20th November 1885, a week ago ...

Milly read of Leigh's capture by General Gyi San Wun, a Sino-Burman given to drug-addiction and sadism. She read of Leigh's torture and abuse in Gyi San Wun's hands and of his extraordinary escape staged by Matthew Sinclair, Edwin Tennent-Browne and a Burman, Ba Say.

Milly read of Leigh's physical condition when brought out of the Senyat jungles, and how the toywa people had helped to get him into British hands after the battle of Myingyan to put on one of their hospital ships to take him to Thayetmyo ... and Milly Sinclair, unable to read anymore because a fist had been plunged into her chest to rip out her heart, rose from Captain Brierley's desk with no recollection of what happened to her after that.

'You all right, Miss?' the guard asked, anxiously peering at the young nurse walking glassy-eyed out of Minhla Garrison. He received no reply. Milly couldn't remember which sinous path she was supposed to take back to Governor's Palace.

She heard footsteps running behind her, the soft pad-pad of bare feet. Milly, over her shoulder, saw a man with a stick. Automatically she too began to run, the grunting noises behind her the only thing to mark her conscience. She ran because she was compelled to, completely disorientated, unable to see in which direction she was going. With all the trees closing in on her, she only knew she had to keep running to get out of the thick black mud that already had choked the life out of her in Captain Brierley's office.

THREE

Flimsy white draperies caught up in pinnacled reminders of little white pagodas made Angela smile as she wheeled the food trolley between the two neat rows of mosquito-netted beds. The avenue of hospital beds reminded her of the Kuthodaw at the foot of Mandalay Hill. She wondered if she would ever have the courage to face her old Sayadaw again. She missed the Sasana. Often she had browsed among the white marble canopied shrines of Buddha and felt an immeasurable peace steal over her so that she was able to look right inside herself, to take hold of the central core of her life and to guide her destiny in a way she had not thought possible. Meditation into her own experiences and attitudes had made her come to terms with herself. She paused now at the foot of one of the soldier-shrines with her trolley. Blaize and Ko Lee assisted her in dishing out the evening meal. Lance-Corporal Bines she observed was not on his bed where he ought to have been. They saw him creeping back sheepishly into the ward.

'Bines!' Lady Tennent-Browne said angrily. 'Where do you think you've been?'

'Only out to the latrine, ma'am,' he replied, shamefaced.

'You know very well Bines, Captain Brierley's orders were complete bedrest on account of your blood-poisoning.' She prodded him back to his bed. 'You should have asked Mr Larcher or one of the other Orderlys to fetch you a commode. You don't wish to get a bad heart, do you?'

Bines, red-faced in the midst of the other men's laughter, said sulkily, 'Wot's me bleeding heart got to do with me spots?'

'Everything Bines,' Blaize furnished him with a ready answer. 'Your bleeding heart is doing exactly that, pumping around a lot of poisoned blood all round your body from your spotty face to your odious little toes, so if you ever wish to see Mandalay, you'd better start doing as you're told for a change.'

'How do you know all that Lady T-B?' he asked, respectfully.

'Because Bines, my husband used to be an Army-wallah just like our Deputy M.O., and so I know all about little boys who get sick through disobedience.'

Angela paused by the foot of his bed, 'Soup, Lance-Corporal Bines?'

He looked up again. 'No thanks Miss Angel. What else is there?'

She lifted the lid of the heavy government-property dechi and sniffed. 'What is it, Ko Lee?' she asked, glancing at him suspiciously, not liking the look of what she saw in the dechi.

He displayed all his teeth in a very wide smile. 'Stew Missy-Sahib Angela. Just like English boys have back home,' he said, proud of his achievement and eager to please.

Angela was less impressed. 'What did you put into it?' she asked dubiously.

'Everything, Missy-Sahib Angel.'

'It certainly smells like it,' Blaize agreed, taking some stew to another patient not quite as fussy as Bines.

'Well Lance-Corporal, do you wish for some stew?' Angela asked, the ladle poised above what she hoped was not skinned cat in Ko Lee's version of stew.

'By the look on your face, Miss Angel, I don't think I will,' he grinned back at her.

'But you must eat something,' Angela insisted.

'My goodness me!' Lady Bee snapped, taking the dechi-lid out of Angela's hands and slamming it back onto the container. 'You are a difficult man to please, Bines. Ko Lee, what else can this soldier-boy have to eat?'

'Nothing else, Lady T-B. Missy Milly not back with chickens and lemon as yet.'

'Miss Milly?' Angela turned her attention to Ko Lee. 'What are you talking about Ko Lee? Isn't Miss Milly upstairs with Mrs Sinclair and the children? I thought she was resting.'

'Not sure, Missy Angel,' he shrugged. 'She go to Minhla Garrison this afternoon for chicken and lemon and sugar for soldiers because Tonsin, sillee fellow, forget to collect supplies when tender arrive and sail away again because they think we want nothing. So we have nothing, and Miss Milly set off for Quartermaster's stores to fetch things in babycart.' He put his hands together, 'Please to forgive Ko Lee, Chinese boy who forget such things earlier, but he velly busy without Tonsin who he send to look after Miss Milly on road to Minhla. But he not back yet either, so solly.'

'Stop fooling around for a change and talk properly,' Lady Tennent-Browne snapped again.

Angela said frostily, 'Ko Lee, what time did Miss Milly set off for the Garrison?'

'Perhaps after tiffin-time which very late today.' Ko Lee said hurriedly, 'Maybe it was two o'clock today as everything so late.'

'Good heavens, Ko Lee,' Angela said, glancing at the clock, 'that was five hours ago! Why didn't you mention all this before.'

'Very sorree, ladies, I forget with everything so late and nothing to cook.'

'And so you should be! You deserve to be horse-whipped ...'

'Bee please! Let's not get carried away. Ko Lee, which way did she go?'

'Swamp-path, Missy Angel.'

'You are irresponsible!' Blaize fumed.

Angela, aware that no one was paying the stew any attention and all ears were flapping, especially Lance-Corporal Bines', said to Ko Lee; 'You dish out the rest of the meal. Come with me, Blaize.' She began to discard her pinafore. Outside in the corridor she said, 'You look in the other rooms, I'm going to go across to Clare.'

Angela hurried across the compound to their rooms in the Myowun's part of the palace. Clare had not seen Milly all afternoon and nor had Jubella. Angela ran back to the ante-chamber of the zenena, her shawl and over-boots in her hand. Blaize glanced up from pouring out two cups of coffee. 'Where do you think you're going at this time of night?' she asked.

'To Minhla Garrison, where else?' Angela said, flinging the shawl round her shoulders before tugging on her boots.

'Be sensible darling, you can't go alone. Why, if anything unspeakable has happened to Milly, you don't want to run the same risk, do you?'

'Risks don't bother me anymore,' Angela said tightly.

'Darling, you're being an awful bore, you know. You're not a Buddhist nun now but a frail woman, as are we all. If you must go to Minhla Garrison, then take Orderly Larcher with you. He's a good reliable man with daughters of his own. But let's not get carried away, Milly might only be gossiping with that nice Captain Brierley who's looking for a wife — haven't you noticed the way his eyes follow her around everywhere? No? Well then, I have. She's probably having a nice cosy little tête-à-tête about the patients, at his office in the Garrison.'

'For five hours Bee?'

'I do admit that's rather a long tête-à-tête.' She shrugged, 'Well then darling, he might have invited her to have dinner with him.'

'Don't talk rubbish Bee.'

'Whoops, sorry. I know we're all here to do a job of work and not fraternise, but if it stops you tearing your hair out ... so sorry darling, my mistake again, then I'll tell Larcher to fetch his hurricane lamp to guide you to Minhla. He's no doubt having his break at the moment which means char and dog-ends in the zenana bathroom.' She removed herself and her cup of coffee to the threshold of the ante-chamber and in strident voice appealed down the corridor, 'Larcher, Mr Larcher! If you please, do come out of there, we have an emergency on our hands and require your hurricane lantern.' She came back inside the room. 'There, that should shift him from the throne-room. Do stop foaming at the mouth, Angela darling. You look as though Milly has already been ill-used like that Felicity child you brought to us in Manipur ... ah, there you are Mr Larcher! I hope you didn't choke too deeply on your butt-end but we require

402

two lanterns and your services. You are to accompany Miss Featherstone to Minhla Garrison to fetch Miss Milly home. She went to the Quartermaster's store to collect some rations and hasn't yet returned.'

'Right you are Lady T-B. Be with you in half-a-tick Miss Angel,' Larcher said, his fatherly face and mutton-chop whiskers suddenly a warm comforting sight. He went off in search of storm lanterns, a very queer feeling in his stomach that wasn't anything to do with Ko Lee's stew.

Halfway to the Garrison they discovered the children's cart overturned by the side of the road. It was empty.

'Looks like she didn't get to the Garrison, after all ma'am,' said Orderly Larcher. 'It would've been full of stuff if she'd been on her way back from Minhla.' His brows drew together. 'Miss Angel, ma'am, I reckons she was frightened off into the swamp by the looks of all these prints in the mud churned about round about here. If you like, Miss, I'll go on alone and try to find out what's been going on.'

'I'll come with you, Mr Larcher. If Miss Milly ran into the swamps, then you might need my help. Don't worry about me, I'm not afraid of the dark or of mangrove swamps. I'm very used to Burma now, Mr Larcher.'

'That's a blessing Miss. It doesn't do to have a weak stomach in these parts of the world ... mind how you go Miss Angel, it's as slippery as muddy treacle so only treads where I tread.'

'Mr Larcher,' Angela could hardly voice her fears, 'could she possibly drown in the swamps — if she did happen to come this way?'

'We shan't think about such possibilities ma'am. If something did frighten the lass bad enough to send her flying off the path, it's likely she would become lost in here somewhere. If we can't find her soon, we'd be better off in the long run fetching out a proper search party ...'

'Oh no! No, no, Mr Larcher,' Angela said quickly. 'It

403

would be better if we could find her ourselves. The less people who know about this, the better.'

'I understand Miss. But don't fret yourself. We'll find her, I'm sure.' Larcher had that awful sinking feeling again, even while he tried to sound convincing for the sake of the stoic young woman with him, that whether they did or did not find Miss Sinclair's body in the mangrove swamps, either way it was going to be an all round bad business. He kept to himself the discovery of a mangled cigarette on the Minhla path, those few shreds of tobacco in a grubby piece of white paper smelling like the familiar Army-issue brand for the Officers, most of the tommies rolling their own.

Half-an-hour later they came across Milly's white headdress picked out by moonlight shining through the trees, all but a corner trampled into the thick black mud which oozed and sucked alarmingly at their feet. Not far away, at the edge of the swamp where the smell was appalling, they found Milly against the twisted roots of a tree. She was covered from her feet to her hair in the thick green-black slime of the quagmire, her large grey eyes wide open staring vacantly at the silver face of the moon through the mangrove trees.

Orderly Larcher carried her across his broad shoulder while Angela led the way, holding high both lanterns to light their footsteps back to Governor's Palace.

CHAPTER
TWENTY-NINE

ONE

Major Radcliffe lowered his field glasses, thick fog rising like the hot breath of river-gods to obscure his vision of Sagaing. Innumerable white pagodas and temples studded the forested hills around Ava and Sagaing, visible to his eyes only when the wraith-like tendrils momentarily parted by an unseen hand allowed him a glimpse of what lay beyond the immediate river. Adverse weather conditions had hampered the progress of the fleet for days now.

Thirteen miles from Ava the Flotilla was forced to drop anchor and to remain there for some little time, visibility now so bad, they were fearful of running aground or into each other. Brigadier-General White had already been issued with orders to lead an attack on Ava should General Prendergast's last minute talks with the King and his Hlutdaw fail. The British ultimatum stipulated, the King's personal surrender, with no repercussions on the British populace remaining in Mandalay, and any further disputes he might have to be conducted in the proper manner pending orders from the British Viceroy. The King's Great Burden-Bearer returned to inform General Prendergast that the King of Burma required more time to think about an armistice. The Royal Wungyi was informed that sufficient time had been granted already, that there would be no armistice, only a dignified surrender to be negotiated.

Once again the harrassed Wungyi departed in his State Barge, the King's Peacock Banner limp beside a white flag of truce with no breath of air to stir the silk or the British from their intention to capture Mandalay.

A dejected figure, the Wungyi sat slumped beneath his golden umbrella of State wondering how he was supposed to bring back an answer to the British General by four o'clock the following morning before the threatened British bombardment of Sagaing and Ava took place. The Wungyi was afraid. He wept silently to himself when he thought about Ava, that former glittering capital of the Alaungpaya Kings of Burma whose mighty palaces had been lined with gold, encrusted with precious gems, steeped in so much fabulous wealth even the British had come in fear and awe to King Bagidaw of Ava, and had bowed, scraped and shuffled before him while begging trading favours from him. And now, those very same descendants of the kala were threatening to destroy Burmese history. The little Wungyi put his head in his hands and despaired. His fear encompassed his King and his country, his fear encompassed himself, because whichever way the coin fell he was going to be the loser. Bad news to his King would most likely mean the loss of his head and bad news to the British would indubitably have the same result.

By ten o'clock the following morning the Great Burden Bearer had failed to materialize out of the mists. No reply from the King of Burma had met the British ultimatum so General Prendergast ordered that the Flotilla advance on Ava, but for the time being only as a threatening gesture, while the Burmese continued to procrastinate. As the fleet approached Ava, it was discovered that the Burmese had done exactly as they had at Minhla, blocking the river by sinking some flats embedded with sharp teak spikes so that nothing could pass. In addition, the narrow Ava-Sagaing passage was dammed-up by a sunken steamer and other small rivercraft. It had been hoped by the Burmese that such delaying tactics would allow more time for the Taingda Mingyi to consolidate Mandalay's defences against the British while the Prime Minister, the Kinwun Mingyi, searched desperately for a more rational and civilized way to save Upper Burma. The Kinwun Mingyi however, feared that matters had been left too late. He begged King Thibaw to negotiate fresh terms with the British General.

Meanwhile, Major Jeffrey Radcliffe, jovial enough in the circumstances, said to Nathan Vorne, 'Right ho Captain, here's where we begin mopping-up operations as we did at Minhla Redoubt — just as well those Burmese mines didn't stretch right across the river to blow us all up, but only the tail-end of the *Kathleen*. Thank God too we managed to catch those Italian chaps detonating the mines from the shore — they got their ears well twisted for it! Any ideas on how and where we can squeeze through this graveyard of amorphous monsters?' he asked Nathan, looking at the glass surface of the river with its scuttled Burmese vessels sticking out of it like so much dead wood from a sunken forest.

'Major, see that long-armed sandbank stretching out from Ava to the Sagaing inlet? There, where the river sweeps round?'

'Captain Vorne, all I can make out at this precise moment is the Loch Ness monster and her babies scuttled in the mists of Drumnadrochit,' was the Major's reply.

Nathan smiled, 'Then I guess you're looking in the right place Major. Now, if that sandbank hasn't shifted like the Continental drift during the past seven years, I reckon I know where I once trod deep water — very deep water!'

Major Radcliffe lowered his field-glasses and said, with an unfeigned smirk of trimmed moustache, 'My word, Captain, don't tell me you lost *another* boat of yours in the Irrawaddy?'

'That, Major, is a darned sore point with me,' said Nathan, not wishing to be reminded of the loss of

Findebar and the *Belle Hélène II.* 'I reckon you fellows owe me several lakhs of gold sovereigns for having smashed up my boat. Mighty bad shots, I reckon, hitting a neutral vessel at anchor with the Stars and Stripes showing as big as a bedsheet.'

'Well Captain, all I can say is, let's wait and see how much Thibaw has stashed away in compensation for all the expenses incurred in this war. Now then Corporal Duckett, where are those charts the Captain worked out for us?' He stretched an arm behind his back and Corporal Duckett placed them in the Major's hand. Jeffrey Radcliffe kept his attention on the river ahead, he and Nathan Vorne reconnoitring a safe passage for the Flotilla in one of the smaller steam launches of the I.F.C.

TWO

General Prendergast's patience was fast running out. He felt that he had given the Burmese enough time to come to terms with the British and, exasperated by their wishy-washy approach to serious business in not honouring the time agreed upon to negotiate a peaceful surrender, gave orders that Sagaing and Ava be disarmed immediately. Brigadier-General White and his men were instructed to take Sagaing.

Nathan's drawings and descriptions of the Sagaing Fort, given to Major Radcliffe in Rangoon, provided invaluable details and ground intelligence so that the task of disarming it was greatly simplified. Sagaing's vulnerable spots were breached without difficulty.

At that eleventh hour, too, King Thibaw's State Barge loomed through the mists which at one o'clock were still as thick as early that morning. The Minister of the Interior, the Taingda Mingyi, on much prodding and pushing by King Thibaw and the Kinwun, had sent word via the Wungyi for the Royal Troops inside Ava and Sagaing to lay down their arms immediately and surrender to the British.

Brigadier-General White would have been forgiven a feeling of deflation in the anti-climax of his 'taking' of Sagaing which General Prendergast was relieved to know had been accomplished without unnecessary bloodshed. The fat Burmese Commander of Sagaing, happy in the middle of his dinner, sent word to Brigadier-General White requesting the British General's permission to let him finish his dinner before leaving Sagaing; Brigadier-General White refused.

Soldiers in khaki landed at Mandalay on the following afternoon, the 29th November, just eighteen days after their advance from Rangoon.

King Thibaw, in his favourite Summerhouse in the Palace gardens where, seven years before, Nanette Gideon had been an unwitting witness to the bizarre and despotic massacre of his royal relatives, signed the surrender documents handing Upper Burma to the British. Afterwards, the King turned to the giant negro in the group of officials witnessing the signing formalities of dethronement, and asked if he were the executioner. The King was reassured by the British that no, he was not the executioner, but they did urge him to leave Mandalay forthwith. King Thibaw refused to oblige; he wished to stay put in his capital city and, despite the entreaties of his own family and Hlutdaw Ministers, he had made up his mind that Mandalay was where he would remain.

Exasperated beyond measure by the obstinate King, Brigadier-General White ordered a guard to be put on him. The 67th Hampshire Regiment, without removing their boots, marched into the Mandalay Palace to take control of the Burmese King's sacred person.

Many hours later, much later than the British had intended King Thibaw to leave Mandalay, he informed them he would leave, but would not be insulted by the offer of a hospital-doolie on which to travel — if his gilded coach could not be found, he would walk.

With great dignity he set off for the riverside, his route lined by British soldiers as a large crowd had gathered to bow before the King and bless him, and the British feared there would be trouble or the King might escape. The long walk however became too much for King Thibaw whose handsome appearance seven years before had impressed many ladies at his Court, but now had dissipated to obesity and weakness. In the end he was put into a bullock-cart, Queen Sinpyumashin the Queen Mother, and Queen Supalayat, with the Prime Minister, the Kinwun Mingyi beside them, also travelling by bullock-cart to the Irrawaddy river where the *Thoreah, The Golden Sun*, waited to receive the dethroned King and his family. A Naval Brigade, and the Liverpool Regiment provided the King's escort, his last glimpse of his golden country seen from the decks of the boat taking him to Rangoon and thence to Ratnagiri on the Kolkan coast of India to spend the rest of his life in a sad exile.

THREE

Several days after the fall of Mandalay, Nathan encountered Major Jeffrey Radcliffe again, this time on the steps of the Shwe Kyaung, the Golden Monastery. The Shwe Kyaung had been the gilded and lacquered Royal Apartment in which King Mindon Min had died. When Thibaw gained the throne of Burma, he presented his father's royal bedroom as a Monastery for the Buddhist Monks. It had been removed in its entirety to the foot of Mandalay Hill.

Behind him, Major Radcliffe had a small detachment of Royal Welsh Fusiliers who were hot and bothered as the conscientious Major assigned the mammoth task of correlating the work, contents and protection of Mandalay's glorious cultural treasure. 'Hello there,' he greeted Nathan after they had almost bowled each other over. 'Ever been inside?' Jeffrey Radcliffe asked, his thumb toward the Shwe Kyaung meant to convey the conquering hero's spoils of war, but only succeeded in irritating

Nathan. 'That was part of it I believe, very pukka!' the Major continued. 'It's going to take a month of Sunday mornings to sort out everything. I thought Buddhist Kings were supposed to be ascetics like the monks of the Sangha.'

Nathan, concentrating on the odd little job of adjusting the strap of his sun-helmet hoped he was not emulating the conqueror's boastfulness when he said, 'I've been in there, thanks, Major. Only that was in the days when it was a Royal bedroom inside the Palace and not outside.'

'So you actually met the old boy, Mindon Min?'

'Several times Major.' He put on his helmet and smiled tautly. 'In those days too, I didn't mind doing a bit of bowing and scraping before a mighty decent King — who'd turn in his mosaic tomb if he saw your lot here today.'

Jeffrey Radcliffe wriggled his moustache uncomfortably before he changed the subject, 'Some bedroom what! Must have been a guilty conscience made him turn it into a Monastery — forty eight sons and goodness knows how many daughters. Those were the legitimate ones too by all accounts, so how many were there on the wrong side of the blanket, I ask myself. Makes one wonder from where he got his energy, as Buddhism seems to me an exhausting religion. However, as I said, it's going to take a month of Sunday mornings sorting out every single article of value in Mandalay, but Prender wants the impossible and I suppose he'll have it.' He lowered his tone and glancing over his shoulder to make sure none of his soldier-boys could overhear what they were saying, sidled closer to Nathan who stepped back a pace. 'You should just see what they're shipping off to England. Thibaw's best Crown jewels for Her Majesty — including his Crowns for ceremonial occasions, Supalayat's jewels — a necklace that would make you gasp for what it's worth, solid gold Buddha for the Princess of Wales and ivory tusks for H.R.H. The Prince of Wales ... spoils of war, what!' He winked at Nathan.

Nathan himself wondered at Major Radcliffe's sudden indiscretion. An Army Intelligence Officer was hardly going to divulge State secrets without an ulterior motive. All he could assume was, the crafty Major was taking out an indemnity for the future by testing American trustworthiness. Right now, the British were going to find it even harder to find friends, Nathan guessed, and would require all the help they could get from neutrals like himself. He put out his own golden apple; 'If you ever want to know where the rest of the loot went, Major,' Nathan said, 'they don't call the Irrawaddy the river of gems for nothing.' He returned the Major's look of astonishment with a reciprocal wink.

Major Radcliffe's finger and thumb removed an eyelash from the corner of his eye. Squinting into the sun he remarked, 'Watching Thibaw waddling out of his Palace with such a pathetic dignity about him was rather an odd experience. I couldn't help feeling then he wasn't as much a gin-soaked alcoholic as a confused and mismanaged young man. Going off meekly with his two Queens beside him, they looked just like naughty children caught at the sweet jar.'

'Don't you believe it, Major, those two sweet-looking ladies with him — Thibaw wasn't so bad mind you — had snake-juice in their veins and were about as nice as their Alaungpaya ancestors. Ask the workmen who repair Mandalay's walls from time to time and they'll tell you what kind of skeletons the Konbaungs keep in their cupboards. I just hope your General can make a better go of things than Thibaw did. This isn't an easy country to govern Major, as no doubt your lot will find out sooner or later — sooner would be better for all our sakes. The last three days have been as bad as the days that went before the King's dethronement. Nobody, I'm afraid, is going to behave in a very civilized way until your General Prendergast makes up his mind to take a firmer stance in regard to all this nightly rioting and looting that goes on here. It's no good him marching off up to Bhamo because he's worried about what China's doing, because the Black Flags couldn't care less about who is inside Burma as long as they don't cross the Yunnen boundary. But if Mandalay remains in a state of turmoil, then dissatisfaction is going to spread far and wide with contenders for the Dragon Throne only making matters worse while they pay the Bos to perpetuate a state of unrest. It doesn't help things either, Major, when the very man who was the real culprit behind all the corruption and murdering going on here, now works hand in glove with the British as their most trusted Burmese Minister!'

The American's remarks made Major Radcliffe feel even more uncomfortable because he knew how right he was. The glory of a bloodless victory would be swallowed up very quickly if murders continued to happen in broad daylight, arson and looting rife, and the populace oppressed by the cut-throats who appeared to dominate the country. Prender would of course have to put his foot down and show his teeth if there was ever to be law and order in the wake of Thibaw's departure. It was one thing to get here, another to keep it. Kyauktawgyi Road jammed full of Monastery schools and pagados containing valuable cultural treasures, had been the scene of last night's burnings, the destruction of Pali scripts just part of the mindless activity that went on in crimes of violence against the community. Major Radcliffe, because he was aware of all that, had no wish to be reminded of it by an American. His manner lost its warmth and became one of chilly aloofness; 'Do excuse me now Captain de Veres-Vorne. I'll be jogging along with these lads of mine as we've a mountain of work on our hands which will keep us all busy for a month of Sunday mornings. I daresay we'll bump into each other again since we're here to stay.'

'If you want some help with cataloguing all your finds, Major, I know just the lady who can give you invaluable assistance regarding the Pali treasure-trove held in Mandalay's religious places. She and her camera have been at work for seven years recording Mandalay's history, and there's nothing about the Kyauktawgyi, the

Sandamuni and the Kuthodaw she can't tell you. Angela Featherstone, Major, one of the ladies you rescued from Gue Gyoun Kamyo.'

'The ex-Buddhist nun you mean? That's interesting. Thank you, Captain.' He touched his baton to his boat-shaped military cap and departed with his helpers.

Nathan climbed the Kuthodaw stairway, fully aware that Ba Say was creeping up on him from behind. He stopped in the balustraded rest-area where they had first met on the night of rioting three weeks ago and when Ba Say was close enough, Nathan said without turning round; 'It's all right, Ba Say. There's no need to creep up on me anymore. The Taingda Mingyi's being a little more civilized by working for the British not the Burmese Government anymore.'

He turned around and grinned at the thickly concealed Burman whose legs appeared to be shaking. Ba Say had lost weight too. 'What've you to tell me this time?' Nathan asked, intuitively smelling trouble.

'Ba Say not used to being free agent, Thakin. He still is much confused over many unfortunate things that happen in Senyat jungles with Englishmen who escape from Taingda Mingyi before British arrive. I am asked by Thakin doctorman who is named Tent-Brown to contact tall riverboat Captain and bring him to Senyat toywa which is not too terrible distance from Mandalay. Thakin doctorman has much weakness from jungle-fever and fears to die, but he wish to tell first American Captain of many things. Please to follow Ba Say, and he will guide you to place of hiding where there has been much trouble.'

Later in the day, Nathan and Ba Say left Mandalay together for the jungles of Senyat.

FOUR

Angela sat in the ante-chamber of the zenana ward, her elbows on the desk, her chin cupped in her hands while she stared meditatively at the de-bunked Myowun's pretty porcelain clock on a lacquered table in front of her. For three days now Milly had lain comotosed and Angela was exhausted trying to think up new excuses to give to Captain Brierley concerning Milly's indisposition and non-appearance in their little ward. She had asked Larcher to remain discreet and he had. Milly could tell them nothing about what had happened to herself on the road to Minhla Garrison and Clare was being very nasty about the whole business. She had insisted they call a woman doctor to find out if Milly were still a virgin.

Angela, appalled at such a suggestion had fought it out with Clare, 'You cannot, you simply cannot subject Milly to that kind of humiliating procedure Clare!'

'I can and I will. I am responsible for her welfare. She is under-age. If she was assaulted by a man — or even men — on her way to get the stores, then we've got to know the truth of the matter. Since she seems to have lost her mind and can't speak, that's the only way to be certain. Anyway, it might not have been soldiers but Burmese guerillas, who are said to be hiding all over the place.'

'The Burmese do not rape women, Clare. They are mostly Buddhists and respect women.'

'That's what you say, you're prejudiced.'

'I'm telling the truth. I walked around Mandalay for seven years, night and day, and no Burman ever molested me ... that kind of social violence comes from the ruffians tagging along with them. However, we are assuming that Milly was attacked, that might not be the case at all. She probably wandered off the path of her own accord — you know how she's always gathering bunches of wildflowers to brighten the ward — so she might have seen an orchid or something she wished to pick, and got lost by straying too far.' Angela wished to get off the subject, but Clare was being especially vindictive over the whole affair.

'And there's that half-caste who's half-mad with it, Captain Vorne's stupid stoker.'

415

'His name is Tonsin, Clare, and he's not mad. He has a stutter that's all.'

'It might have been him. He's been missing for three days.'

Angela with no defence on that score had come downstairs to sit in the office and go over in her mind again the reason for Milly's behaviour. From the night they had washed the mangrove mud off her and put her to bed, she had remained like a rag doll whose life came only from the hands that supported it. The clock ticked the hour away and still she sat meditatively, knowing that she would have to go sooner or later into the ward to dish out supper as Blaize was busy upstairs sewing another new frock from the Myowun's materials.

Scuffling at the door brought her attention back to the things on hand, and an insistent rapping on the wood made her answer, 'Yes, come in.' Skirmishing and muffled oaths continued, so she got up from the desk to investigate.

Orderly Larcher and two soldiers forcibly restrained a mud-caked brawny youth trying to fight them off while they held him by the scruff of his neck, forcing his arms up behind his back and his head down so he could do nothing except dribble on the floor.

'Tonsin!' Angela exclaimed, shocked to the core.

'We've found him ma'am,' said Larcher, beckoning the soldiers inside the room and quickly shutting the door. 'Begging your pardon ma'am, I took the liberty of organizing a little search party these past two nights since we found out about Miss Milly.'

'Larcher ... when?' Angela, wide-eyed, could only stare at him.

'Sorry, ma'am, while you ladies were asleep was the only time the men could creep out and ...'

'From their beds?'

'Yes, Miss.'

'Larcher, do you know what will happen to us all if Captain Brierley finds out what's been going on in this out-of-bounds area?'

416

'That's nothing to what'll happen ma'am if the Commanding Officer finds out there's been a rape and one of our men is responsible,' Larcher replied. 'Anyway, Miss, now we've found him ... with this in his pocket.' He placed Milly's gold bangle on the desk. 'It's proof enough who did the dirty deed and we'll see to it he never attacks another woman again.'

'You'll do nothing of the sort, Larcher!' Angela said, her manner and authority making them all aware that nobody was about to get away with lynching. 'Release him at once,' she told the two soldiers who manhandled Tonsin between them. They looked to Orderly Larcher as the father-figure. His bushy brows drew together, but with a curt nod he reassured them.

They let Tonsin go and he fell on his knees, drooling and clutching Angela's hem. She flicked the material from his clawing hands and went to stand behind the desk. 'Where did you find him?' she asked icily.

'In the swamps, Miss.'

'Did these two soldiers find him?' She waved her finger at them.

'Yes, Miss.'

'What are their names?'

'Bombadiers Fields and Martin, ma'am.'

'How did they find him?'

'They were out on manoeuvres, ma'am, searching for Burmans. They found this fellow under one of the trees not far from where we found Miss Milly.'

'Are these two men to be trusted?' She glowered at the two soldiers. 'Why, and how did they know to bring him to us if they were looking for snipers? Why didn't they take him straight to the Garrison?'

'Well ma'am,' said Larcher looking sheepish. 'I took the liberty upon myself to make some discreet enquiries of my own. It transpired that these two lads were on the same road as Miss Milly on the afternoon of the attack. They'd just come out of the swamps and were returning to Minhla when they saw Miss Milly on her way to the Garrison. When I started asking my snooping questions like, they realized what I was driving at and came to me of their own accord about the sighting of Miss Milly that afternoon and, to be exact ma'am, the sighting of a Burman in the area wielding a lathi — a big stick ma'am.'

'I'm fully aware of what a lathi is Mr Larcher.'

'Yes ma'am. It turned out to be this Eurasian fellow, Miss, a stick and the gold bangle in his possession,' Larcher concluded almost triumphantly. 'All of us here at Gov's Orspital, Miss, are real cut up about this Miss Milly affair — some of the lads couldn't help overhearing what was going on over the supper-trolley the other evening, and they wanted to be sure the culprit would be caught before it got even more nasty for everyone concerned. What do you want us to do with him, Miss Angel?'

'You'll leave him here with me, Larcher.'

'But ma'am, if ...'

'No ifs and buts, if you please, Mr Larcher. I shall handle this, not you. I've known Tonsin for a very long time, and I'd like to hear his version of the story before I decide either to take it to Captain Brierley or to a higher level.'

'But ma'am, he can't speak a word of English.'

'But I speak Burmese, Larcher. Now, if you please, take these men away and leave me to talk to Tonsin alone.'

'But ma'am, with all due respect ...'

'With all due respect, Larcher, if you continue to argue me down, I'll see to it that if Tonsin is not the man responsible for Miss Milly's condition, you and the rest of Minhla Garrison will come before your Commanding Officer.'

'Yes, ma'am.' Cowed, he ushered Fields and Martin from the presence of a lady he considered in the light of an avenging angel. It took fully an hour for Tonsin to furnish Angela with his version of what had happened on the road to Minhla. In his hesitant stutterings she gathered that he had been sent by Ko Lee to see no harm befell Milly, but Ko Lee had warned Tonsin not to let

418

Milly know that he was following her in case she sent him back to help with the cooking. Tonsin had dodged from tree to tree in Milly's wake. He had seen two soldiers come out of the mangrove swamps. They stood talking to Milly on the path until one of them took hold of her and dragged her off the path under the trees. Tonsin told Angela he was going to use his stick on the man, but the other man came back and started a fight so that Milly then ran off in the direction of Minhla Garrison. Tonsin waited for half-an-hour, he said, for her to come out again and when she eventually appeared she looked sick. She did not take the turning back to the hospital half-a-mile away, but another one through the swamps. Tonsin had followed her to warn her of the danger she was heading into. He had tried to call out to her but his tongue wouldn't let him, and the only noises he seemed to be able to make frightened her so that she ran faster. He told Angela how Milly had gone into the mangrove swamp and fallen in the thick mud that dragged her down. She had screamed, and he had taken her arms and tried to help her out. He had been pulling on both her arms when her bracelet had been dragged off and, for safe-keeping, he had put it in his pocket while he tried to rescue her. He managed to pull her out and laid her against a tree where she could breathe properly, but forgot to give her back her gold bangle.

'But why didn't you come back and tell us what had happened Tonsin?' Angela asked. 'Surely you realized how guilty you would look through running away and leaving us to find her?'

He did not answer but kept his head down and cried against his mud encrusted knees.

'Were you very frightened?' Angela asked more gently. He nodded. 'The two soldiers who caught you, were they the ones Miss Milly was talking to on the road to Minhla?' Tonsin nodded. Angela asked next, 'Were you frightened of them?'

Tonsin shook his black curly head.

'Of me then?'

No, Tonsin was not afraid of her. 'Of Lady Bee?' Asked Angela in desperation. Again he shook his head. 'What then?' asked Angela. In the end she gathered Tonsin was very afraid Milly was already dead, and he would be blamed for neglecting to look after her properly by allowing her to lose herself in the swamps. 'Oh Tonsin!' Angela, shaking her head, placed a hand on Tonsin's heaving shoulder. 'Dear me,' she sighed, 'what a mess we seem to have got into. Don't cry any-more Tonsin. I know how much you respect Miss Milly, and how fear can make us do strange things.' He clutched her skirts again, his gratitude pathetic. 'All right, I won't let the soldiers take you away. Leave this to me.' Angela went to the door and opened it. 'Orderly Larcher, come in here.' He had been in the ward and came out to her summons, Larcher informed her that Fields and Martin had returned to Minhla Garrison before they were missed. When the door had once more closed on them she told Larcher of Tonsin's version of the story, at the end of which she said in a tone of voice he had learned best not to argue with, 'And as I'd prefer to keep an open mind on the subject, Larcher, I'd be grateful if you would do the same. I am not going to say anything for the moment to Captain Brierley, or the Garrison Commander. I'd like you to warn Fields and Martin, and the men involved in your midnight search party — of which I know for sure Bines was a member — that if they breathe one word of this to anyone, or lay a finger on Tonsin, I'll take it upon myself to see life becomes very uncomfortable for every one of you from Minhla to Mandalay. I know General Prendergast personally, and I know too what a stickler for protocol he is, so be warned Mr Larcher, because I hold you personally responsible in all this.'

'Yes ma'am. I'm sorry ma'am, but it was a question of doing my duty to everyone concerned.'

'I know you acted from the best motives, and I'm not saying anything against that. I just don't trust those two men you brought in here, and I'd rather not believe their story just for the moment. Miss Milly will get better given time, and then she can tell us herself what happened to her on the road to Minhla. We might all be jumping to the wrong conclusions in this instance — even if they do seem to be the obvious ones at the moment. Now leave Tonsin with me. He's given me his word he won't run off again, and I trust him. Let's not rush into things and in a few days time I'm sure Miss Milly herself will throw some light on this. For the moment she is in too great a state of shock to do anything. Thank you, Mr Larcher, for your co-operation. You may go now.' She held the door open for him. 'And no more midnight sorties, please Larcher.'

'No, Miss Angel,' his fatherly face dissolved into grins of relief as he twisted his cap in his hands; 'Thank Gawd Miss Angel, you're not going to kick up a song and dance about this. I was most afeared of our reputations as all of the lads here are a decent bunch.'

'I'm sure they are, Mr Larcher, and no one is blaming anyone at this stage. Goodnight.'

'Goodnight Miss.'

Angela took herself straightaway to Clare whom Jubella was impatiently settling for the night. 'Out, Jubella,' Angela said holding the bedroom door open. 'I'll call you back in a moment or two.' She turned to Clare. 'You're right Clare. The only way we can be certain that Milly hasn't been sexually assaulted within the last few days is for a doctor to give her an internal examination. A lot of suspicions will be cleared out of the way and we might find out why Milly has reacted like this.'

Clare's smile was feline and gloating.

God damn you, thought Angela furiously, knowing Clare was dying to hit back in some way at Matthew for the humiliation she had suffered earlier in the year over his sister.

'I'll arrange for a lady-doctor to see Milly tomorrow,' Angela muttered before slamming the door on Matthew's wife.

421

CHAPTER THIRTY

ONE

Angela managed to locate a Burmese lady-doctor in the area, and she was smuggled into Governor's Palace under a cloak and dagger secrecy. Angela knew it would be more than her life was worth to be caught disobeying the Deputy M.O.'s orders. Angela ensured the Burmese lady gave Milly a strong sedative so that she would be unaware of what was happening to her, the poor girl being in a bad enough state of shock as it was without adding insult to injury.

The doctor was very thorough, even to lifting Milly's shuttered eyelids to peer at length into her pupils, then pulling out Milly's tongue with her fingers, staring at it thoughtfully and finally putting away her instruments to say with a beaming smile; 'Nothing wrong with little lady.' The Burmese doctor, a congenital deformity twisting her back, was unable to stand straight as she looked up at Angela. 'She will be better in a few days time. It is sudden shock to brain which does not wish to face up to many things of moment. If she fall in swamp, then that is great shock, but not altogether to do with what is happening inside her head and body.'

'What is happening?' Clare asked flatly.

'She is taking refuge in a flight from her life. It is something she wishes not to face and her brain makes her sleep for this effect. But nothing to worry about,' she reassured them again, handing over a little phial of medicine to Angela. 'Give her this. It will restore her to

422

healthy life once again. She will be ready then to be strong mother in six months time.'

Clare groaned and Blaize reached for the smelling-salts which she thrust into Clare's flaccid hand. Clare said weakly; 'I knew it ... Milly was always wandering off and not behaving herself. And for her disobedience we all have to suffer. I warned Matthew his sister was nothing but a little slut, and this only serves her right.'

Angela wanted to laugh in Clare's face, she found her so puerile and affected. Instead she snapped; 'If you don't shut-up Clare, I'll tip cold water on you.'

Clare struggled into a more upright position on the day-couch on which she lay: 'As for you, I never did know what Matthew saw in you. You're a vicious-tongued creature who has always encouraged Milly to go against me. All I can say is, if Milly's going to have a rapist's child in a few months time, then Nathan Vorne is responsible for harbouring vermin aboard his boat by the company he keeps ...'

Angela's hand took Clare off guard, the smack of her fingers leaving four red weals on Clare's white cheek. She fell back swooning against the cushions while the Burmese doctor twittered; 'Ladies, ladies, please do not fight over the poor child who cannot help all this!' She took up her bag and scurried toward the door, Blaize about to open it for her when Clare, loathe to let anything die gracefully, opened her eyes and said: 'Doctor, I wish to know the truth ... has my sister-in-law been physically abused?'

The Burmese doctor looked bewildered. She turned to Angela: 'Please, I do not understand? What does she mean, abused?'

'Go on Clare, tell her,' Angela said grimly, her arms folded while she and Blaize both glared at Clare.

Clare, her fists bunched, hammered on the sides of the couch; 'Doctor, I wish to know if my sister-in-law has been physically assaulted within the last few days ... you say she is not a virgin, but is to have a child. I wish to be sure of my facts so that my husband, her brother and guardian, might be informed in order to take the necessary steps to bring to justice the man responsible for her downfall.'

'No assault, no bruising, no damage except to what happen inside brain. She is not virgin it is true, but neither has she been with man in recent days. Three months ago, yes, for soon, in six months she is to be made a mother and by then she will be plenty better. I can say no more, for I do not know what has happened to make brain sick except for falling into mangrove swamp, yes ladies?'

'Yes, thank you Doctor, I think we understand perfectly.' Angela saw her off the premises after paying her fee and raced back to Milly's side where she guessed what would be happening. Blaize, bearing the brunt of Clare's tirade, raised despairing eyes to the ceiling as she quickly drew Angela inside the room.

'Leigh!' Clare breathed through clenched teeth, her narrow eyes habitually remaining closed when she wished to emphasize the point her fists were making, 'I knew it, I knew it! He was not a man to be trusted. He seduced Milly and made us a laughing stock — Matthew especially, who trusted him even as far as taking Milly's side against mine. It serves him right. His sister has truly paid back his trust with that awful lecherer called Leigh Buchanan.'

Angela took a deep breath and willed herself to say calmly, 'Milly's baby will be absolutely legitimate if that's what you're wishing to gloat over.'

Her eyes flew open. Angela was aware that even Blaize hadn't uttered many words in the prevailing tension. 'What do you mean?' Clare said, sounding quite rational despite her readiness to resort to hysteria at the least provocation.

'Milly and Leigh are married.'

Clare blanched. Blaize's jaw dropped. Astounded, they both gaped foolishly at Angela.

'Married ... when?' Clare asked.

'Three and a half months ago.'

'She can't ... she hasn't got anyone's permission. She's under age and her parents haven't given their consent. The marriage can be annulled. Matthew wouldn't allow it ... Nor his parents ...'

'I hardly think Milly's parents will object to Leigh Buchanan when she's carrying his child,' Angela said quietly. She crossed the room to stand by the window where the lowered jalousies kept the sun off Milly's sleeping face. Remarkably peaceful under the effects of the soporific drug she had been given by the doctor, sunlight and shadow played across her features, striping too, the wooden floor like a tiger-rug. 'Milly and Leigh,' Angela went on to say, 'are quite legally married. Milly has her marriage-lines and her wedding ring to prove it — they are kept in her reticule. Edom Gideon performed the ceremony aboard the *Belle Hélène II*. Nathan, his crew and I, were the witnesses — ask Ko Lee if you don't believe me. But more importantly, Matthew was also there representing his parents. They had telegraphed their consent for the wedding to take place. As Milly's guardian, he gave her away — to Leigh Buchanan.'

The silence was protracted on that last little flourish of Angela's; it had given her the greatest pleasure to vanquish Clare once and for all.

In the end Clare said with the first ounce of spunk they had yet glimpsed in her. 'Why wasn't I aware of all this? Why didn't Matthew tell me, I who am his wife and next-of-kin?'

'Because Clare, you were only ever concerned with yourself — never with Matthew or Milly. Or your children come to that, since you handed over their welfare to Milly and then blamed her when things went wrong. You didn't want Milly to be happy with the man she loved because you were jealous. You were jealous of love. I'm sorry your marriage to Matthew never worked out the way you wanted, but don't blame me for his lack of love where you're concerned, or take it out on Milly and Leigh.'

'I don't know whether to believe you or not,' said

425

Clare, Angela's finger-marks still stinging, dull pink in the pastiness of her face. 'When and how could they have got married? And when would they have been together? Milly was always with me and the children — Matthew saw to that.'

'Remember that mad dash of hers in the middle of the night? You were going to keep her locked up so that she could not see Leigh when he was home on leave, but Milly ran away and ended up at Whitewalls with Nathan and Minthami? Remember that she stayed with them for a week until Matthew got you to apologize to her and promise to treat her with more kindness? It was during that week Leigh and Milly got married. Nathan lent them the *Belle* for a few days to have their honeymoon. After that, they saw each other at Whitewalls whenever they could — all legal and above board, Clare, and nothing sordid at all in their love for each other, no matter how much dirt you wish to throw at Milly. So there's nothing you can do to put the clock back. They are in love, they are married, and they are expecting their first child in six months time, *fin!*'

In the stillness a crusty green lizard plopped from ceiling to floor.

Blaize applauded loudly. Having hung on to Angela's every word to the total annihilation of Clare, her clapping hands rang with her laughter: 'Oh my God, too too funny for words, darling! I think this has been the best afternoon of my life and I wouldn't have missed it for the world. Only the Shwe Nat of Mandalay can seduce a Buddhist nun far enough in the cause of love to make her overturn the laws of God, and man. I congratulate you and Nathan on Milly and Leigh's behalf, what champions they have in you two! And, of the next two people in this world who thoroughly deserve each other, you and Nathan, darling, are superbly matched in villainy. What a pity, Amagyi-Angela, his little native princess stands between you and total happiness.' She went off into another shrill peal of laughter not shared by Angela or Clare. In the end, wiping her eyes with a corner of a lace-edged handkerchief, she enquired: 'Well darlings, as it appears our Milly has only been attacked by the man she loves, what happens now?'

'Now Blaize,' Angela said, 'you can please yourself what you do between looking after Milly and Clare — to whom I have nothing more to say regarding the disgraceful and suspicious way she's treated Milly. I'm going across to put poor Mr Larcher's mind at rest, and to get him to explain to our "common little tommies" as you once put it, with hearts by the way, of pure gold, that Milly is all right and the only harm done was that she lost her sense of direction and ended up in the swamp. So, if it wasn't for poor frightened, half-witted Tonsin pulling her out, she would be dead!'

TWO

A few days later, Captain Brierley's Orderly Officer appeared on the threshold of the ante-chamber to the zenana ward. He had come via the supply-tender from Minhla Garrison, the boat awaiting his return at the wooden landing stage below the hospital. Angela was frantically busy scribbling names and figures into columns of recent admissions and discharges to hand to Captain Brierley.

'Begging your pardon ma'am, I can come back for all the chittys later in the day,' said the Orderly Officer, 'but right now ma'am, with Captain Brierley's compliments, he hopes he's not putting you to any trouble, but he would like you to come to Minhla Garrison straight-away. I'm to be your escort back in the tender ma'am.'

Angela glanced up, dismayed; 'Oh dear, there's nothing wrong is there?'

The Orderly Officer stared straight ahead, to a point somewhere above her, and his stern pale face with an over-long jaw reminded Angela very much of uncooked wet tripe nobody wanted. 'Sorry ma'am, it's not my place to say,' he murmured.

'No, of course not, I'm sorry. Just give me two minutes to have a word with Orderly Larcher before I leave, and two more minutes to fetch my shawl and boots.' She gave him a bright smile, hoping to cheer him up a little. 'It's always so muddy down by the river.'

'Yes ma'am.'

She wondered why all military men had a habit of referring to a woman as 'ma'am' as she followed him through river-mud and mosquitoes. The journey to Minhla Garrison took ten minutes by tender. Angela, stepping onto the landing-stage just below the Redoubt, observed that all the wreckage left after the battle for Minhla, flung into the water by the retreating Burmese soldiers when their mines had failed to do the job required, had now been cleared away and the river was once again open to transport. She wondered what on earth Captain Brierley wished to say that could not be said on one of his routine ward-rounds. The amusing thought flashed into her head that perhaps Blaize was right and he was looking for someone to whom he could 'pop the question'. She hoped sincerely not, as she had no wish to hurt his feelings by turning down a proposal of marriage.

The Orderly Officer took her through a maze of corridors in the red brick fort, up several flights of stairs and eventually to a tiny office at the top of the building not far below its ramparts. She was ushered in, but it was not only Captain Brierley who rose to his feet to greet her.

'Nathan! What on earth?' Bewildered, she turned to Captain Brierley and then back to Nathan, 'I thought you were in Mandalay,' she said, sounding almost accusing.

Captain Brierley cleared his throat, flashed her an apologetic smile and murmured; 'Please excuse me, Miss Featherstone. I've some new patients docking-off, and I have to get over to the Zayat receiving them. I know Captain de Veres-Vorne wishes to talk to you alone, so I'll be disappearing to do what I have to.' He shook

hands and scurried away, a sheaf of files under his arm
and the corners of his white medical coat flapping in the
urgency of his departure.

'Come and sit down, Angela,' Nathan said, after the
Orderly had shut the door on them with the promise of
tea shortly.

'Nathan, what's wrong?' Angela asked, the look on
his taut unsmiling face the prelude to some bad news.

'Angela honey, I wanted to talk to you first because I
know you're going to be able to cope with what I have to
say better than all the others ...'

'What Nathan, what!' she urged as she sat down,
tense as wire, and wary of this unexpected visit from
him.

'Just give me time, honey,' he said desperately. 'I've
never sailed the Irrawaddy so fast in all my life — two
days ago I was still in Mandalay ... besides, I've got to
find me the right way of saying all this to you.' He paced
the room like a caged lion, his index finger rubbing the
side of his nose in a gesture of hopelessness. 'Angela', he
came and stood beside her, 'honey, I'm sorry, but Leigh
and Matthew are dead.'

'Oh God ...' Her head fell forward to her lap as she
bent double with an awful pain inside her heart.

He waited for her to pull herself together. Presently
she took her hands from her ravaged face to seek out
blindly his own set lines and pallidness lit only by those
blue eyes flashing brilliantly while he too tried to come
to terms with fate.

'How?' she whispered.

He licked his dry lips and resumed his pacing. 'Two
days after we left Mandalay on the *Belle*, Matthew,
Edwin and a couple of other men who had barricaded
themselves inside the Residency managed to escape from
the Taingda Mingyi's clutches by dressing up as Burmans
to disappear into the jungle. A Burman, Ba Say,
employed as a clerk in the Hlutdaw used to give away
State secrets to Matthew, who passed his information on
to Leigh Buchanan, who, in turn, kept the British

informed via the Burmese telegraph network ... Leigh, you see, worked for British Intelligence ... however, to get on, Ba Say led Matthew, Edwin and the others to Leigh who had been hiding in the jungle to avoid internment at Sagaing prison because the Taingda Mingyi had put out a warrant for his arrest. The toywa people at Senyat hid Leigh as best they could, Ba Say managed to get Matthew, Edwin and the rest to him. They asked him to try and get a message down to Thayetmyo warning the British of the mining of Minhla. Leigh himself had some vital information concerning Senyat's secret arsenal for the defence of Mandalay and the future harrassing of the British if Mandalay fell to them, so he managed to interfere with the lines, and with the help of a French engineer called René, was able to relay some sort of coded "birthday" message to Major Jeffrey Radcliffe at Thayetmyo. Unfortunately Leigh was captured with René.'

Nathan paused and took a deep breath. 'To cut a long story short, Edwin, Matthew, a Scotsman named MacAbee and Ba Say, made a bid to get Leigh and René out of the clutches of some sort of madman named Gyi San Wun who had taken over the command of Senyat Garrison. You see, he'd resorted to torturing the truth out of his poor bloody prisoners ...'

Angela gave a sharp exclamation of horror and Nathan, looking hard at her said, 'If you want me to stop say so now. It gets worse.'

She raised a hand. 'No ... no, just tell me all there is to know. Don't spare me the details if it has to be said.'

'Gyi San Wun was an opium addict and a dyed-in-the-wool sadist with it. After having removed Leigh's fingernails and twisted the hell out of his limbs in the old Burmese method of torture they used at Sagaing — bamboo poles levered through a fellow's manacles to dislocate the joints — if they didn't snap first — he set about emasculating the Frenchman and ...'

'Oh my God, Nathan, please stop!' Angela put her hands over her ears. 'Please don't tell me anymore ...

just get on with the rest of what I'm supposed to know, though God knows why you're telling me all this ...'

Grimly he cut her short: 'Honey, you've *got* to take it! Every ghastly damn word I want you to hear, just so's you know who started all this in the first place and who had to finish it by picking up the pieces of men I respected, but more than that, who were *my* friends too! So here goes, because you'll be the one to tell Milly, Clare and Blaize, not me, no siree, not this time. So can I get on now?' he concluded harshly.

She nodded.

'Matthew, Edwin, Ba Say and the Scotsman, with the help of the toywa people, got inside Senyat Garrison and blew it sky-high, their task made considerably easier by several hundred gallons of kerosene oil stored inside the stockade. René, in his bamboo cage close by the arsenal when it blew, couldn't be saved. But they did manage to rescue Leigh who was inside Gyi San Wun's private house at the other end of the compound where Wun was having some more fun with him when Matthew and Edwin arrived on the scene. That's about it. Gyi San Wun, a Chinese servant and two soldiers guarding Leigh were shot, and in trying to get out of Senyat gates with Leigh aboard a bullock cart, Matthew, driving the cart, was shot in the head by a Burmese soldier.'

She nodded, her eyes screwed tight, her shaven head decorously concealed beneath its nursing-sister head-dress to give her a more pleasing appearance. Nathan admired her self-possession in that moment, when he allowed his thoughts to dwell on her.

'Edwin managed to take over the cart and with MacAbee's and Ba Say's help got out into the Ava-Senyat road where the toywa people were waiting for them. They guided them back into the jungle to hide, though Leigh was taken by river to try and find a hospital ship that would convey him to Thayetmyo. Matthew was buried in the jungle. Edwin, MacAbee and Ba Say got away, but then went down with jungle fever. Edwin's better now and is back in Mandalay, and the

431

Scots chap too, I believe. But Edwin's terribly cut up over the whole affair and seems to have turned into an invalid overnight ... however, that's neither here nor there. I came to give you this ... Edwin asked me to hand it over to Clare, but I somehow gathered for myself it wasn't meant for Clare at all, but you. There's a note inside.'

In the handkerchief he had thrust into her lap several small articles had been kept together. Matthew's half-hunter, his glasses with lenses smashed and frames bent, some keys, and the pearl and opal engagement ring he had given her in Delhi, which subsequently she had returned to him. A little scrap of paper with rusty blood-stains had a few scribbled words done by a shaky hand; 'I've always loved you ... I see your face, your eyes, your hair even when I'm with another ... I love you now and I will love you till I die.'

A sob held deep down in her throat, Angela transferred the ring to her finger, the other items she tied together again in the handkerchief and stood up. Her legs shaking, she turned toward the door 'Clare need not know ... she's still his wife and these belong to her. I'll only keep Matthew's ring.' She looked up and caught his eye on her, a nerve in his jaw pulling at a corner of his lower lip, he appeared to be fighting down some conflict within himself.

'You haven't asked me about Leigh,' he said brittle as glass as he took stock of her. 'How and when he died.'

She shook her head, her tearful eyes searching out the high-grilled window above his head. 'Leigh's dead — that's enough for the moment. The rest will keep till later. I don't know how Milly found out, but I'm sure she knows it too. She is ... I'll tell you some other time Nathan, but right now I want to get back. ...'

'Leigh died just two hours before the hospital ship he was on pulled in to Minhla to take on board some more men going down to the Base Hospital at Thayetmyo. Captain Brierley told me that. Leigh's medical record had been forwarded to him among others. He had to check up on the passenger-list of soldiers going down to Thayetmyo and to separate the dead from the dying and anything else it fell to him to do. You might also mention to Milly, when she can take it, his body is being sent by the military back to Calcutta ...'

Angela seemed to crumble before his eyes. She put out a hand to steady herself against the door while the other shielded her face. Fighting to hold inside the tears that Milly would know for the rest of her days, she forced her teeth into her lower lip, her green eyes beseeching. 'Tell me why it had to be Milly? Tell me!' She wrenched open the door, her tears flowing freely, but in two strides he had pushed the door closed to take her by the shoulders, shaking her to stop her rising hysteria.

'Angela, pull yourself together,' he hissed, 'you've got to, for Milly's sake if not your own.'

'Her favourite brother *and* her husband! Milly's going to have Leigh's child, Nathan, and he knew nothing about it.'

Nathan took a deep breath. Filling his lungs, he looked up at the ceiling which was only the yawning arch of all man's aspirations, stretching up and up and up, and just as one began to touch the centre of that arch with the tips of one's fingers, it gave way and crashed down on all one's hopes and dreams. Poor little Milly Sinclair. And the only consolation he had at that moment was in knowing that the girl weeping her own heart out against his shoulder was human afterall.

He wanted to say a lot of things to her in that moment; but in his heart knew too, this was neither the time nor the place. One hand pressing her head against him, the other in the small of her back, he let her fight her own devils while he could do nothing more than help cushion the total desolation the greedy winds of war brought with them.

When she was a little calmer he said, 'Let's have that tea now honey, before it gets any colder?'

'Nathan, I must go back to the Convent. I must, It's

433

the only place in which I feel safe. I must get back to Mandalay as soon as possible and tell the Sayadaw what I did to Gar ... to the man in the Buddha shrine. The Sayadaw will be able to advise and guide me. Milly will never return to Mandalay now. She and Clare will go to India with the children ... and with all of them gone, another anchorage that was given me in a moment when I required it, has again been taken away from me. I feel I need the abiding security of the Sasana.' She looked up at him, her tear-stained face, he thought, strangely beautiful when she could defy life's tears in that tender smile of acceptance. 'Don't look at me like that, Nathan,' she whispered, 'it weakens all my resolutions.'

'How else should I look at you honey?' he asked in a hopeless gesture of defeat, his thumbs caressing away the tears and the freckles adorning the bridge of eyes and nose, disarmingly appealing simply because she was utterly without vanity. 'How else should I look at you when thoughts of you fill every hour of my day, yet still you keep me at arm's length?'

FOUR

'Amagyi-Angela,' said the venerable Sayadaw at the Sasana Monastery, his bald head bowed, cataracts on the glazed windows of his mind, 'You have told me the story of the murder of the man called Garabanda and with-held nothing. I know how much courage that must have taken. Through one such act your whole life has been altered, taking with it the lives of others. Yet, it is for us to experience these crossroads great and small, for there is sorrow in all life's journeys, each one, no matter how momentous or how insignificant, affecting us forever. But to take another person's life is the ultimate sin. Though Garabanda be a murderer himself, though he maim, kill, abduct, assault and violate, gives no one the right to take away his life. And, in that same regard, I have no right to take away yours. You will suffer and grieve for what you have done, for I know too, that to be the captive of your own conscience is a far greater torment than any punishment I can inflict upon you. You will be punished enough without my intervention and without that of the Sangha — they will not hear of this thing from me. With the power invested in me as one of Lord Buddha's disciples, I will take responsibility for your confession and in the mercy given, merit is also received. But you must work out your own salvation by turning your back on the temptations that came your way. Go child, away from here. The Sasana is unable to receive you back until you are cleansed from the sin of blood through that atonement which is only attained on that worldly path of perpetual struggle to be born again without sin. You will reach again that point of yesterday wherein you were the innocent victim and not the guilty wrong-doer. Then return to me. Leave me now as my spirit is sad in that I have failed you.'

'If I can no more remain in the Sasana Convent as one of Buddha's holy nuns, might I not assist you as a lay-person in the work I was doing in the Sasana library? In that way I will be able to achieve merit again in the eyes of Lord Buddha as there are many ways to find that path which leads us back to the "oneness of the all."'

He bowed his shaven head. His thin gnarled hands lay in repose in the lotus cup of his lap while his unseeing eyes marked the spot of her kneeling supplication.

The venerable Sayadaw raised his hands in a blessing: 'Very well, my child, your heart is good and that is all that matters. Since my eyes can no more do the work for me, I will be glad of the eyes Lord Buddha has sent back to me in this his hidden purpose. I will look forward to hearing again the readings of the Amagyi-Angela who attends to the care of the Pali parabaiks with such devotion. Though I may call you Amagyi-Angela no more, I have missed the English lady who has been my eyes. We will still talk together upon the many interesting things of your precious culture in the school of your Christian God. So come child, sit.'

435

The venerable Sayadaw smiled benignly, his toothless gums stained by the habitual chewing of betelnut, and he made a request: 'Repeat to me of your knowledge so that I am reassured you have not forgotten the things you have learned on that eight-fold path of endeavour which is of the Lord Buddha's teachings.'

'Sila, the precept, Samadhi, equanimity of mind and Panna, wisdom and insight, and the eight actions of my evolutionary process are, right speech, right action, right thought, right-exertion, right attentiveness, right concentration, right aspiration, right understanding.'

'That is good my child. But remember, there are many states of spiritual development before the ultimate goal is reached.'

FIVE

Beyond the library windows of the Sasana Convent, the Shan Hills were misty blue. Peace had settled back in Mandalay, even if it were only an uneasy one between the Burman and the Britisher. The Convent doves warbled contentedly. Angela smiled to herself. In her hand she held a letter from Milly Sinclair who had returned to her family in Coimbatore, Southern India. While Milly refrained from dwelling on the past, and never mentioned Leigh once, Angela sensed in Milly's letter that she had, at least, come to terms with her life. Her baby son was six months old now and thriving, Milly's consolation and her future when it had seemed the poor girl had no future left after Leigh's death. Milly also wrote to say that Clare had left Matthew's two children, Verity and Peter, with the family at Coimbatore and had returned to England. They had since heard that Clare had remarried, her new husband having his own cooper-business in North London. 'So, Angela dear,' Milly wrote, 'you mentioned in your letter about our girl of the Fishing-Fleet going home with the label "returned sour" instead of "returned empty" as Clare's sort are usually described. But now, at least, she's got her pint and by the sound of things her cup runneth over! Naughty of me, I know. However, I'm glad she's got over my brother's death so quickly, and has settled down again to a way of life she understands . . .'

Poor Matthew, Angela could not help reflecting then, and all because of her, his short life had also been an unhappy one with sour Clare! But, she also reminded herself as she looked out on the Shan Hills, life is desire, life is sorrow and life is impermanence; it has to be, for there is no other way to find the sunlit ridges of the journey.

TO SLAY A
CRESTED LION

1888

CHAPTER
THIRTY-ONE

ONE

Nathan had been away four months to Macau and back to Mandalay. He wished he had stayed away another four months when he saw the mountain of correspondence awaiting his attention and the noise that greeted him after stepping off at Mandalay's low-water landing point to take the road home to Whitewalls. The banshee wails in his front garden made him wince as he walked up the drive and continued to make him wince while he took a bath.

He came out of the bathroom towelling his hair dry, another towel round his midriff, and almost trod on a green lizard as it scuttled away from his bare feet. Delicate bracts of bougainvillaea trembled as he leaned over the verandah balustrade to shout down to Minthami: 'Get rid of those god-awful Sadhus Minthami, and quit making that racket, I can't hear myself think.'

'Minthami cannot get rid of music-makers O divine Thakin, who always come home in very bad mood after being on long voyage. We make very grand entertainment at Culture School in Mandalay for anniversary of British, when Upper Burma annexed to British Queen and Country,' she shouted back above the noise of one old man blowing his nhai-pipe and the other banging his wahlet-khoke, bamboo clappers while Minthami's troupe of young dancers wove in and out of the bushes with shrieks of laughter. Nathan, with a sigh of resignation, turned back to the bedroom and sat down on top of his letters. Eyeing them all with distaste, he wished fervently for the time when Sa-Lon could take over this side of the business, his empire of commerce having grown by leaps and bounds since the British claimed victorious management of Upper Burma. His unwillingness to tackle the more mundane aspects of that commercialism had also increased by leaps and bounds, as he considered paper-work to be a sheer waste of his time.

'Personal, Personal, Private,' he muttered to himself, throwing letters aside at random, 'For the Attention of Captain de Veres-Vorne, Personal, Private and Confidential ...' He felt no more the master of his own destiny. He hated begging letters, bills and complaints. To feel the water beneath his boat, bows cleaving a specific passage, to stand beneath the mizzen mast on a full-rigged ship ploughing the ocean, the wind in his hair, the sun on his back, the salt tang of the sea on his face, to be able to breathe freely and deeply of God's open spaces as in the days of Findebar and the first *Belle Hélène*; that was what life was all about. Not this bondage to desk and chair which was beginning to destroy his imagination, his soul, so that in the end he would die just another pen-pushing petty bureaucrat suffering from galloping consumption of the written word.

Teak for Scandinavia, silk for Arab ladies, rice for three-quarters of the world, tea and gold and japanned boxes for the luxury markets of England and America ... how had all this happened? He needed more than a couple of secretaries, he required a whole empire of them with Sa-Lon in overall management.

Nathan tore open a flimsy envelope because it had been hand-delivered and seemed more interesting than all the other correspondence. 'Dear Nathan,' it read, 'This is just a brief note to let you and Minthami know that I'm shortly to be married ...'

Stunned, he leapt off his bed and hung over the verandah to wave the letter at Minthami; 'Minthami, do you know anything about this?' he yelled.

'Know what, O divine Thakin?' She looked up at him with a face full of smiles.

'This ... this horrible little note from Angela informing us of her intention to marry ... to marry ...' he scanned the page for the name but all she had written was that he was a military man, and that omission infuriated Nathan even more because it was as if she were ashamed of what she was doing. 'Minthami, if you don't get that tribe of yours to stop making their infernal racket, I'm coming down there to throw each and everyone in the Irrawaddy!'

She clapped her hands sharply and silenced them, dismissing the children to the shadows of the trees where they tittered amongst themselves.

'Do you know who she's supposed to be marrying?' Nathan demanded.

'Minthami know Amagyi-Angela marry someone she meet at Minhla, that is all. Maybe he doctor-fellow from hospital where she work. Amagyi-Angela does not come often now to see Minthami because she keep very busy with library-work for Sasana and also teaching British and Burmese schoolchildren about Mandalay.'

'I guess I'm a monkey's uncle when it comes to a woman's mind,' Nathan muttered furiously.

'If you always wish to stick nose where it is not wanted, you must expect pain when it is bitten off,' Minthami told him.

'And what the devil's that supposed to mean?'

'It mean, O divine Thakin, it very great shame you do not marry Amagyi-Angela as second wife, for then Minthami too very happy because she left in peace half the time by Shwe Nat who always interrupt Minthami when he come home!'

She clapped her hands again and with even wider happier smiles, gaily recommenced her dancing rehearsals. It appeared that next to Buddha, dancing was the most important thing in her life. 'Minthami,' he said, 'I'm going into the city, so don't bother to get me anything to eat, will you!'

Since her banishment from the Sasana Convent, Angela lodged with Ma Ngwe, her husband U Po Thine and their children, in the old home of Daw Khin Htay's bordering the White Monastery on Mandalay Hill. When Nathan called upon Ma Ngwe she informed him Angela was not at home.

'Do you know where I can find her?' he asked.

Ma Ngwe, blossoming nicely to the plumpness of her late aunt, smiled and nodded, 'She has gone to feed sacred turtles in Sasana pool.'

'Thanks Ma Ngwe,' he dumped a bale of French silk in her arms, 'From Macau,' he winked before taking the Kuthodaw steps two at a time.

Angela was seated on the low stone wall surrounding the turtle pool. Sunlight glinted off her autumn-tinted curls escaping the edges of the smart little toque she wore in jade-green to match her two-piece outfit piped in navy-blue. She turned to him and took the rest of his breath away while his heart pounded to the beat of Mandalay steps.

'There you are ... what the devil's this?' Rudely he flung her letter back at her.

Her fingertips drifting idly in the water, her head on one side, she smiled into his eyes and her smart little hat-feather seemed to wave defiance at him. 'Hello Nathan. When did you arrive back?'

'Exactly two hours and five minutes ago.'

'My-my, you must have flown up here.'

'Cut it out Angela, and tell me why you're doing this?'

'Doing what, Nathan?' As infuriating as Minthami a short while earlier, he felt like shaking her brains up a little.

'Dammit all Angela, getting married!'

'Don't you want me to be happy, Nathan?'

'Of course I want you to be happy,' he shouted, 'but I don't want you to get married to some ... to some ...

444

some Army fellow to be happy. I thought you had dedicated your life to Buddha, not Mammon.'

'Well, I've changed my mind. I've decided, you see Nathan, I don't want to be left on the shelf after all, a spinster everyone talks about behind their hands. Anyway, I'm tired of living at Ma Ngwe's ...'

'Minthami and I offered you Whitewalls, but you turned your nose up at that offer!' he reminded her.

She laughed. 'Dear Nathan, what as? Your ma-ya-nga at Whitewalls? No thank you. When Jeffrey asked me to marry him, I ...'

'Jeffrey? I thought it was that Minhla doctor, Captain Brierley?'

Again she gave a little laugh, 'Oh no, not he ... Major Radcliffe, Nathan, though he's recently been promoted to Lieutenant-Colonel'

'God Almighty, Angela! I don't care if he's Viceroy, you can't marry him.'

'Pray tell me why Nathan?' she asked, her eyes narrowed in feline smiles while she continued to aggravate him by her placidly unruffled airs and graces put on specially to keep him in his place.

'Because you can't that's why ... besides, you don't know him.'

'I've known him for almost two years over Pali scripts and Government tea. He's a very intelligent man and we have a lot in common.'

'That's wonderful. But he's still not your kind of man.'

'What's that supposed to mean?' She glared at him. Ruby lips, cream complexion prettily flushed in anger, her figure filled out as he had never seen before; now perfectly accentuated in her green dress, her brilliant emerald eyes cut him in two. And because he had never seen her looking so beautiful or quite so desirable, he was suddenly jealous — inexplicably jealous — of Jeffrey Radcliffe. 'You're wasting yourself on him,' he said bluntly, 'he's not your type.'

'Too late, Nathan. Jeffrey and I were married at the

Garrison Church about ... oh, let me see,' she looked at her father's gold watch hanging from a chain around her neck, 'about two hours and five minutes ago,' she said flippantly.

Stricken by that announcement — he had firmly believed he could get her to change her mind — he sank on the stone wall beside her, too devastated to say anything. Inside him he cursed and cursed her foolhardiness.

'Jeffrey was as lonely as I. After the death of his wife ... I know she's been dead a long time now, but he said he still misses her companionship, a woman to come home to ...' She twisted her gloves, unsure of what she wanted to say. 'He has a young daughter at home in England. As he's unable to look after her without a wife, she's ... she's cared for by other people. Of course he minds about it terribly. So you see, he's had a very lonely life too. We can be of comfort and help to one another in many ways.' Her voice faded away in rather a dismal manner.

'Do you love him?' Nathan sounded hollow-voiced.

'I'm ... fond of him ... we're good friends ...' Still she twisted her gloves in a frustratingly fidgety mood that irritated him.

'I asked if you love him.'

'I don't know.'

'Then you don't. Being good friends isn't going to count for much when you don't like him in your bed.'

'That's all you think of, isn't it Nathan?'

'What else is there to think of in the dead of night?'

'Oh you!' She flicked turtle-pool water at him. 'You're supposed to be happy for me, not make me feel miserable on my wedding day.'

'Well you've made me darn miserable. Where is he now, this great lover of yours?'

'He's just attending to things, paying off the Padre and such-like. I said I'd come up here in the meantime.'

'Edwin and Blaize there?'

'Yes.'

446

'Why didn't you invite Minthami and me to your wedding?' Nathan was rewarded by the uncomfortable glance she shot him before she got up and in order to avoid his look turned her back on him; 'Oh, I thought you wouldn't be back in Mandalay in time for the wedding and I didn't think Minthami would want to come alone.'

'What a bloody hypocrite you are Angela. You didn't invite us because you didn't want us to show you up in front of your grand military hierarchy whose scruples didn't prevent them from buttering up the murdering Taingda Mingyi in Thibaw's wake!'

'That's unfair Nathan!'

'Is it? You tell me what's fair then?'

'You're making me feel very very miserable on my wedding day.'

'And you're going to stay that way honey, for a long time to come. I just don't understand you Angela! My God, Brierley might have been a better chap for you to marry, not Jeffrey Radcliffe who's more interested in what his soldier-boys do with their spare time.' He pulled his head back but her hand found its mark and the sharp echo of her slap caused one or two passersby to regard them with amusement.

'Temper,' he said, the light in his eyes mocking her. He put up his hand and touched the smarting flesh while he held her captive by the look he gave her. 'Now, why, I wonder, did you do that. The Maiden, Missionary and now the Memsahib ... like I said, character will always come out. You're too hot-blooded to be a nun or Jeffrey Radcliffe's wife, and someday honey you're going to come to terms with yourself instead of messing up your life over and over again by running away from what you really ought to face.'

'And what is that, Nathan?' she asked, almost hissing at him as she bent closer.

'That's for you to find out, not for me to tell you. Now then, seeing as how you've gone from one extreme to the other, where are you and your fine husband intending to spend your honeymoon?'

'If that's another personal question in order to insult me, go away.'

'Honey, I'm only asking out of genuine interest, not because I wish to insult you. As Minthami and I didn't have an opportunity to offer you a choice of wedding-presents I'm putting one forward now. How would you two lovebirds like to borrow the new *Belle Hélène* to take you on a cruise? A real honeymoon, honeychile, nine-carat sailing yacht with crew attached. She's in Rangoon at the moment having her last dash of spit and polish but she's yours the moment you say the word. I dare say Jeffrey's got leave enough stored-up to take you away for the time of your life, what ho!' He waved a hearty almost derisive hand in the air, taking Jeffrey off in a rather facile way.

'You'd better ask Jeffrey,' she muttered, looking everywhere else rather than at him. 'We had talked about going down to Rangoon for a few days as I've never seen the Shwe Dagon.'

'Then here's your chance.' He shrugged lightly, his manner still breezy. 'My present to you just to prove I'm not the hard-hearted devil you think I am. Minthami and I wish you every good fortune in your future life as Mrs Radcliffe, Amagyi-Angela, so may you walk with happiness in your stride.' He took her hand and placed it against his lips; 'It smells of turtle soup,' he commented before standing up. 'And now I'm going home to get me some sleep. I might bump into your husband on the way down the steps so I'll try to put a brave face on things as I hand over the keys to my heart's delight while asking him to pay off his mountain of chittys after the honeymoon ... Shwe Emporium jade suits you much better than nunnery pink, Amagyi-Angela. Sayonara, honey.'

His sun-helmet under his arm, he made haste to get out of the covered walkway. The last thing he wanted to do was congratulate Jeffrey Radcliffe on his marriage to the Amagyi-Angela.

THREE

From the sunken mountain chain of the Andaman islands, through the Strait of Palk between Ceylon and Southern India, Angela and Jeffrey cruised to the Laccadive Islands. They spent a few days exploring coral-reefs and lagoons stretching all the way down through the Arabian Sea and Indian Ocean in a chain of atolls reaching to the Maldives. On Kavarrati they went sightseeing. They wined and dined, shopped and laughed, and generally did all those things honeymooners were expected to do, except that each night Angela retired to her own bed and Jeffrey his.

The mutual arrangement agreed upon before the wedding, discussed with no sentiment or reservation, suited Angela admirably. Her respect for her husband was enhanced rather than diminished for, in his gentlemanly fashion she realized he was giving her time to sort out her feelings. 'Dearest,' he said one bright morning while they stood at the boat's rail observing ebony-skinned Arab boys diving for the exquisite coral off the shores of Kavarrati, 'I'm rather fed up of all this sailing round and round in circles. We've seen all there is to see, let's go home.'

The word 'home' encapsulating Mandalay, sounding so tender, made Angela smile. 'As you wish Jeffrey,' she replied, breaking off pieces of bread to throw over the stern of the *Belle* while enjoying the sight of flying fish, their enormous pectoral fins making them appear like irridescent birds leaping through the water. She brushed her hands together to rid them of crumbs and turning to him, added, 'I'm sure I too have had more than enough sea water. I don't mind curtailing our honeymoon. Perhaps we could spend a few extra days in Rangoon before returning to Mandalay?'

'Whatever makes you happy, Angy.' Leaning over the taffrail, smoking a cigarette, he turned his head sideways to return her smiles. 'What I love about you,' he said, 'is how adaptable you are. All the women I've ever met in the cantonments throughout India were fat whining bores who never made an effort to do anything except whine.'

He turned back to the coral-divers, flicking ash into the water while waving at the participants of the swimming-gala put on especially for their benefit. 'Wow! did you see that one, Angy?' He pointed to the Arab dhow. 'That fellow went from the top of the mast, clean as an arrow. Bravo, well done!' His applause was loud. A few curly black heads bobbed up alongside the *Belle*. Narrowing his eyes against the haze from his cigarette smoke, Jeffrey shook his head at their blandishments.

'You require, pukka-Sahib, coral necklace for preety m'lady?'

'Well why not!' He threw some money into the water for which they all dived greedily. One of the boys tossed up the coral necklace. 'I bet it's not coral at all,' Jeffrey muttered through his cigarette, his eyes creasing in amusement as he flung the souvenir at Angela, 'but just like French pearls we found in the Mandalay Palace after Thibaw and Supayalat were kicked out. Crumbled to dust! Such swindlers, the French!'

'I think coral-diving from that height is awfully dangerous for them, Jeffrey. Tell them I don't want to see them do it anymore. They can burst their lungs in the sea if they go down too far, and it's not right to encourage them to risk their lives for money — even if they are poor.'

'Don't you believe it. They do it for money yes, but not because they're poor. I think they do it to show off, and to enjoy the element of danger — what's life if there's no excitement in it? Neither is prostitution the oldest game in the world ... for nothing! There you are, rupees for your exhibitionism, boy.' Grinning at them, he dropped one by one his coins into the open mouths of the young divers.

Jeffrey moved away from the taffrail, suddenly bored by their antics. Angela and he spent the rest of the morning browsing in the Kavarrati Arab market, bargained vociferously for their purchases and afterwards lunched on the *Belle Hélène III*. Jeffrey had hired the services of a French chef in Rangoon, who had come aboard with his galley-slaves to provide them with their meals during the cruise. Jeffrey had told Angela he did not trust half the places in which food was served and desired to know who was feeding him so that he would be sure who to blame if ever he went down with food-poisoning.

'Do be careful,' Angela murmured drowsily when Jeffrey announced his intention to take out a rowing-boat to an inlet where there were some ancient and interesting caves. 'The currents are particularly treacherous around these reefs, Jeffrey.' She had declined his invitation to accompany him as she had a headache induced by too much sun, sand and sea.

'Yes, ma'am,' he said in a hypogean voice, touching his Malacca walking-cane to his straw-boater to make her smile. She preferred him in mufti, though his soldierly bearing could not be disguised. 'Pukka-Sahib tell black-boy to row him dashed carefully through water m'lady!'

'Is Janum going with you?' she asked. Janum was his personal servant who had accompanied them to attend to their domestic comforts.

'No, I'm leaving Jan here to look after you. Just in case you decide to flirt with the crew in my absence.'

'No fear of that,' she yawned. 'This morning has made me too tired to raise an eyelid let alone a smile.'

Angela dozed off and slept heavily for the rest of the afternoon. Waking at half-past five, she felt peculiarly lethargic and dull-headed despite her good sleep. The cabin was very close and stuffy, which had made her perspire heavily during her siesta while, against the fly-screens at the portholes, the monotonous drone of insects sounded like a zoo in her head. She thought she might take a bath to revive herself.

Nathan had spared no expense on this, his latest boat, so it was wonderful to have the luxury of water straight from taps in the bathroom en-suite to the two cabins, Jeffrey's door and hers both entering it from opposite sides.

Angela soaked herself leisurely.

Half-an-hour later she felt considerably better, the sun going down helped to draw more air through the boat. She stepped out of the bath wearing a towel like a sarong and went back into her cabin, loath to put on restricting clothes which would bring her out in another sweat. Angela knelt on the bed beside the porthole to watch the sky's mutations — carmine, orange, crimson and gold as it died in its own suttee while sea-breezes leapt into play, ruffling the water and coolly fanning her burning skin. The *Belle Hélène* had been anchored out in the bay rather than in the harbour with its noise, smell and bustle. Angela thought how beautiful it all was with the sea-birds swooping and diving for fish in the shot-silk merging of the Arabian Sea and Indian Ocean, on whose rose-gold coruscations dhows, caiques, feluccas and numerous other small craft crowded the off-shore islands with lateen sails cinnabar in the light of the setting sun. No wonder, Angela mused, Nathan was such a water-gipsy. Thinking about him then only made the empty ache inside her worse, for, everywhere she turned on the *Belle Hélène III* she was reminded of him. She told herself not to think about him because yearning for recognition from him would be about as frustrating as yearning for Buddha to provide her with a female Nirvana.

She heard Jeffrey's cheerful whistle from the small boat bringing him back to the *Belle* and then his neat tread on deck. Angela made haste to sort out what she would be wearing for dinner that night, her trousseau hastily furnished by the Shwe Emporium, Mandalay.

Jeffrey walked straight into the cabin without knocking. He usually did knock, so, taken back, the towel to her nakedness, she looked at him with reproach in her eyes; 'Jeffrey, you didn't knock!'

'I'm sorry dearest ... do forgive me. Angy, I've

452

brought you something.' Flushed and excited by the offering he had to give her, he took little notice of her scantily clad person. Fumbling in his pocket, he drew out a pretty red coral necklace.

'Jeffrey,' Angela said in exasperation, 'that's the fifth red coral necklace you've bought me in a week. They're all the same, so please don't waste your money on any more. A green one, or yellow one or even sky-blue pink, but not red as it simply does nothing for my kind of colouring!'

'What's the matter Angy? You're not whining are you?'

'I'm sorry ... I have a very bad headache that's all.'

'Just let me put this on for you, dearest ...' and he stepped behind her to fasten the clasp. She lowered her head, smelling tobacco, alcohol and the Arab market on him. Perturbed by his strange behaviour she lifted her head and felt a strand of hair pulling in the clasp of the necklace. Angela winced, a pain shooting through her neck and down her shoulder:

'What's the matter?' he asked in alarm, 'You're not ill are you?'

'No, I'm not ill, just hot and bothered, that's all. Please leave me to get dressed now, otherwise I will be ill from the draught.'

'Oh, how thoughtless of me, yes of course.' He stepped smartly towards his own cabin, but turning on the threshold remarked, 'Angy dearest, I know I'm a lucky fellow in having such a pretty wife. I want you to know too how much I respect you for being so natural. None of those awful boned-things — corsets I believe they're called — which other women seem to wear to contain their fat, but firm, long, straight limbs just as God intended. And don't let those nice curls of yours ever reach the stage of becoming so out of hand they require pinning and prinking with combs and things to dig into a chap's chin, will you dearest? Dashed glad we're going back to Mandalay a week earlier than arranged as the work will be piling up to keep me busy for a month of Sunday mornings. Can't stand these Kaffirs either, a real menace some of them.' He went out and shut the door.

Angela, shaking her head, did not know what to make of it all, so with a wry smile hastened to get dressed. She wanted to look her best for Jeffrey and decided upon a pretty blue-and-white striped chameuse dress, also from the Shwe Emporium, Mandalay. But even while she was dressing, thoughts of dinner made her stomach queasy, the French chef's expert cuisine failing to whet her appetite ... she stumbled and fell.

Angela hit her head and lost consciousness. She remembered nothing more for a very long time.

CHAPTER
THIRTY-TWO

ONE

Intense light from another world forcibly struck her eyes. Quickly she shut them against the rude awakening but found nothing could shut out the pain and confusion as, even with her eyes closed, the disembodied images hammered blood-red fists against her shuttered eyelids. Weird voices tormented her, distorted screechings of merciless requirements were shouted inside her ears to make her cry; 'Stop, stop, leave me alone ...' But they came again, ghoulishly slipping through nets of infernal darkness, prodding and poking her, chopping off her new grown hair, poisoning her by forcing their vile potions down her throat. She screamed, 'Go away! Let me die in peace.'

'I think she will be all right now.' The gong rang in her head.

'Who? Who will be all right now?' Angela answered herself and did not know it. She turned her head to the clamour, lifted it to the burnished gold beyond the windows of darkness and wept while she craved for the tender blueness of an English sky.

'In the winter we had to scrape the ice from our beds, would you believe that? And the water was so frozen in our dormitory bowls we would have to bang it with the heels of our shoes before we could wash in the mornings ... I could do with some of that iced-water now ...'

'Come drink,' said a softer voice, hands raising her to

the rim of the glass. The shadows beside the bed took substance.

'Thank you, Minthami ... Minthami?' Exhausted, Angela sank back onto the pillow. Her mind was too confused to ask the questions trembling on the edges of her consciousness, and besides, she lacked the energy for such effort. Angela closed her eyes again. She wondered what Minthami was doing at the 'Misses Bloxhams Academy for the daughters of gentlefolk in Bath'. Maud and Ida Bloxham were very snobbish — although a foreign princess might 'just' be acceptable, were she rich and pale enough. 'Minthami, what are you doing here?' Angela murmured while trying to piece the jigsaw together.

'Minthami live here, Amagyi-Angela.'

'Oh, but that's not my name anymore, Minthami. I'm Angela Featherstone ... no I'm not ... I can't remember who I'm supposed to be now. Could I have another sip of water?'

'It not water, Amagyi-Angela, but cooling drink made from tamarind-pods which is very healing for stomach.'

'Oh, so that's why Nathan was picking them off the trees when we were on shikar! I always meant to ask him what he was doing but never did — because of Loloi and what happened there ...' She drank the refreshing juice that tasted better than the water she had drunk on Kavarrati. 'Where am I Minthami?' Angela asked, suddenly feeling very tired.

'At Whitewalls, where else Amagyi-Angela?'

Where else indeed! After a while she asked, 'What's been happening to me? Why am I here?'

'You very sick Amagyi-Angela. But now you much better. Doctor Suseela, she just leave and say you much better. Minthami tell everything tomorrow when you little bit stronger. Now you must sleep like clever Indian lady-doctor say. I go now to Culture School near Mahamuni Pagoda and later on Minthami come back to see her Amagyi, all right? Good Chinese nurse stay to look after you with Fee Tam. Minthami very glad you much better Amagyi-Angela.'

She faded again, her iridescent longyi reminding Angela of the flying-fish in the Indian Ocean. She slept peacefully.

True to her word, Minthami returned the following afternoon to sit with her. 'Only little bit talking each day till you strong again, say Indian doctor, so Minthami obey rules.' She gave one of her attractive little gurgles of laughter which brought Angela a thousand times nearer to living.

'What's been wrong with me, Minthami?' Angela asked as she tried to sit up and found she could not. Minthami promptly placed another pillow under her neck, plumping it comfortably as she fussed. 'You have typhoid-fever Amagyi-Angela,' she said, reseating herself beside Angela's bed.

'Then how long have I been lying here like this?'

Minthami held up a hand.

'Five days?'

Minthami shook her head.

'Five weeks? No, that's impossible!' Angela groaned. 'Where on earth have I been in that time?'

'Yes, Amagyi-Angela,' Minthami nodded sagely, her face cupped in her hands while her elbows rested on the bed,' it long time to be sick, but you very sick and keep coming and going away from us many times. Shwe Nat, he have to sit by bed to take turns wiping perspiring fevers from Amagyi's head which burn her very much and make bad ulceration in stomach like Indian doctor tell us.'

'Nat ... oh Minthami,' Angela groaned again, feeling very feeble and stupid, 'You don't mean to say Nathan was here?'

'Where else he go, Amagyi-Angela? This his house too.' She smiled and patted Angela's hand. 'You shout very loud for him to come, so he have to come. Shwe Nat make very good nurse when he think Amagyi-Angela going to die of typhoid-fever. He very angry with husband who not warn of danger of drinking dirty water

457

from islands in Ocean. Like water in Burma, it have to be made clean by heating on fire, then you drink. But when doctor Suseela tell him Amagyi-Angela soon better and not die like expected, he give thanks to Christian God and not care anymore. He go back to minding own business which Minthami grateful for because, when he inside house, he make much confusion and shouting to servants and everyone else — which not good for patient lying upstairs. Minthami, she too give thanks to Lord Buddha who answer her prayers, because Amagyi-Angela who's not like other English persons in Mandalay, she understand Burmese culture, and is friend of Minthami own heart.'

'Oh dear Minthami,' said Angela, feeling unusually weepy about everything, 'you're very sweet ... where's Jeffrey?' She asked as a sudden thought struck her concerning the man she had married but who somehow had slipped her memory so that she almost smiled at her lack of conscience concerning her husband.

'When you at Jaffna, he telegraph Shwe Nat with much bad worry over wife for he does not know what to do. So Shwe Nat tell him to come back in boat to Mandalay so you get well again at Whitewalls. Then British Army wish him to go straightaway up to Myitkyina because after death last year of Prince Nyaungyan Min who is supposed to be new Einshemin but he die, there is much trouble in Northern States. They say he die while in Calcutta in British hands and they not know whether it because of real sickness or poison and so now there is new pretender for throne which is Prince Nyaung Ok who is younger brother. Prince Nyaung Ok, he raise Peacock banner once again and many Burmese people rally to help fight against British. Many other pretender princes too, because they all fight for Dragon Throne. So Jeffrey and British soldiers, they go to keep peace on borders. He say he sorry he cannot stay with sick wife but it more important he keep Burma safe for her.'

Angela had to smile at Jeffrey's logic, so typical of

him. 'I understand,' she murmured, in her heart relieved, yet feeling ashamed of those feelings concerning the man she had accepted into her life.

'I go now, Amagyi-Angela,' Minthami said. 'Doctor Suseela, she get very angry with Minthami for keeping patient talking too long. I go to Mahamuni Pagoda to earn merit with Buddha with gold-leaf and many prayers. Ko Lee, he bring little boiled fish and plain rice for weak stomach like doctor Suseela say. No fruit to eat please Amagyi-Angela,' Minthami warned.

'You and Nathan have been so kind to me, Minthami,' Angela said, 'and I don't know how I can ever repay that kindness for, without you two, I think I would have died.'

'No need to repay, Amagyi-Angela. That is what friends for, to help without reward.'

'Where's Nathan so I can thank him too?'

'He go away again. This time back to Java. He send wire from Rangoon Office to say he fed up with writing letters all day long, so he think he go back to sailing ship in sea. He have plenty to export he say, so he leave poor Mr Secretary Jehan in Rangoon and poor Secretary Maung Ing in Mandalay to look after business. All Minthami know, many bills and letters come requiring signature of Shwe Nat, and he never here. He wait for day when Sa-Lon finish education and take over business, but Minthami know in heart Sa-Lon not wish to be trader like father. Ah, it is all very stupid business, this making of de Veres-Vorne Company bigger and bigger with more money and more money and everyone working hard and very unhappy doing it. Minthami not understand. She have no time to worry about husband and sons who not worry about her. Husband, he always go here, there and everywhere, boys do not wish Burmese mother to come to English school, so Minthami come to Mandalay to be happy in Mahamuni where she put her gold-leaf and joss-sticks.'

Angela felt a pang on Minthami's behalf because she knew how she had devoted herself to Sa-Lon and Roi —

sometimes more than to Nathan.

'Soon, Amagyi-Angela,' said Minthami, scraping back the chair as she rose to her feet to squeeze Angela's hand in farewell, 'Shwe Nat he come home. Then we have no time to talk like this, for he is always like how you British say, Tom-cat with hot feet, yes?'

'Yes,' said Angela, smiling at such an accurate description of the Shwe Nat of Mandalay.

In the following days Angela's strength gradually returned. After a fortnight she was allowed to sit out in a chair beside her bed, then on the verandah. When she first tried to stand on her feet after such long weeks of being an invalid she could do no more than cling to the doctor and Minthami as they helped to get her mobile again. She realized that she had gone back to her former stick-like proportions and sighed with frustration at her own bodily shortcomings — how true she told herself fiercely, that the spirit was willing while the flesh was weak. But she drove herself to pick up the pieces of her life and to start living again, determined that though she might take two steps forward every time and get pushed back three, she would get there in the end.

'Softly, softly catchee monkey,' said doctor Suseela one morning when she came for her routine house-call and found Angela exercising with the aid of a walking-stick along the verandah.

'Now I know what it feels like to be as ancient as Methusela,' said Angela, disgusted with her slow progress and the indignity of the walking-stick — without which she was certain to totter and fall.

However, by the time Nathan returned home she could walk slowly to the end of his drive and back to the verandah. She knew the master of the house had arrived late one afternoon when she was resting on the top of her bed reading a book. Everyone appeared suddenly to have gone mad as they rushed hither and thither while accomplishing very little. The sounds of fervent activity reached her through the open bedroom windows and, from where she lay, if she craned her neck, she could see

Tonsin and Ko Lee labouring up the path bowed down with everything they carried on their backs. With a little chuckle to herself, she wondered if the Shwe Nat ever passed through Mandalay unremarked.

TWO

Minthami, negotiating her way between a Borneo head-hunter's grotesque mask, a stuffed baby crocodile, a jade figurine of Amazonian proportions, dried squids and enough China tea to supply their English visitors for years to come, took herself to Nathan's office on the ground floor. As Nathan insisted only Mr Secretary Maung Ing was allowed to go in there during his absence, the room was left shuttered and untidy. Snagging her longyi on some wooden crates stacked with boxes and trunks and bales of Indian cotton outside his door, Minthami was not happy in contemplating how anyone as beautiful as the Shwe Nat could also be so barbaric.

'Amagyi-Angela wish to speak with you,' she said in a very off-hand manner, frowning at him because he had been shouting for his secretary, his pipe, his wife, his dinner, a clean shirt, socks and his Chinese houseboy to bring him whisky laced with ice. He had found his pipe, she noticed. He sat at his cluttered desk tamping down tobacco in the bowl, his face very bronzed, his eyes very blue, his hair very bleached and his mood irritable. Minthami herself was angry because he had not sent her a wire informing her of his arrival and so she had missed her afternoon with Buddha in the Mahamuni Pagoda.

'Tell Angela she'll have to wait, I'm busy right now,' he said, setting a flame to his tobacco.

'She ask Minthami very especially to ask Shwe Nat to see her when he arrive home.'

His eyes, narrowed while he drew on his pipe, flickered up at her. She had perched herself on the arm of a chair, her barefeet resting on the cushioned seat. 'What

461

does she want?' Nathan asked, looking at Minthami's toes curled pinkly and prettily into the chair. Minthami shrugged. Her chin cupped in her hands she said, 'To die in peace O Thakin Captain. You make so much noise in household and disturb everybody, we all cry. I go now to Mahamuni. It very late but I not miss merit from Buddha because American Captain not tell wife he come home today. Ko Lee bring food as Minthami not needed by Shwe Nat.'

'Minthami honey, I'm sorry. Come here and give ole man river a rub on the nose.' He stretched out an arm but she ignored him and, just then, a sweep of the fans across the ceiling drove everything off his desk so he had to lunge for his papers. 'Who the hell told the punka-wallahs to do that!'

Minthami giggled. 'It like Hindu ghat in here, so hot and smelly, Minthami tell punka-boys to put air inside room.'

'Well you can go and tell punka-boys to take air out of room,' he said, retrieving his papers off the floor. 'And while you're about it tell Angela I'll see her tomorrow. Today I'm too busy.'

'That is what she wish to see you about. But never mind. It not important if you not think it important. Amagyi-Angela, she is still weak inside body, and mind also not yet strong. She say many silly things which later on she change her mind again when she feeling more sensible.'

'Like what?'

'Oh, Amagyi-Angela wish to behave like men because her hair short like boy and just when it grow nicely Suseela say it must be made shorter for reasons of typhoid illness. She wish to take place of Mr Secretary Maung Ing here in Mandalay and repay kindness of Shwe Nat and Minthami.'

'Honey,' he said wearily, 'I don't know what the hell you're talking about. Has Angela had a relapse, is that what you're trying to tell me?'

'Oh, she have many relapse. Minthami feel very sorry

for her. She maybe have another one now you home. She is much confused.'

'Aren't we all ... Minthami, shut the door will you. Either come in or go out but the draught is playing havoc in here — and get those fans stopped. Have I got a pair of clean socks and a shirt anywhere?'

'Since when Minthami look after washing? Fee Tam have socks, not Minthami. I go now. I come back later on when it time to sleep. Maybe, if you too busy and too tired, Minthami stay in own room as usual when husband away. Then she not wake up in morning with eyes on floor to go to Culture School because she too tired when Shwe Nat come home after long time away.'

'If you mean what I think you mean,' he said with a wide grin as he viewed her in the doorway, 'I'm not that darn busy.'

She gave a heavy sigh, 'That is what Minthami afraid of. I go now to say prayers to Buddha. Pyan-dor-may.'

'Say a little one for me ...' But she had already gone out and shut the door.

An hour later a timid little knock disturbed his peaceful whisky drinking, his feet up on the desk. 'Come!' he said, frowning at the person about to enter. When he saw Angela, he removed his feet off the desk and got up to help her to the chair on which Minthami had had her feet. 'Angela, how are you honey?' he asked solicitously, taking her stick from her and placing it on his desk. He sat down again and picked up his drink.

'Getting better, Nathan.'

'What can I do for you? Minthami said you wanted to speak to me.'

'I know you're probably wishing to settle in first before you get waylaid by me, but I had to come and see you before I lost my courage to ask you what I'm about to ask you. But first of all I want to thank you and Minthami for all you've done for me. Secondly I wish to repay you.'

He shrugged off her suggestion. 'You don't have to do that.' He repeated what Minthami had said earlier,

'What are friends for honey, if they can't lend a helping hand now and then?'

'Thank you Nathan, but it doesn't make me feel any better for having scrounged off you for the past two months. I know Jeffrey hasn't sent you anything for my keep ... and I know too, he never settles his bills with you. I don't suppose he's sent anything from Myitkyina?' she asked lamely while eyeing the correspondence piled up on his desk.

'Haven't opened this lot as yet ... but he doesn't have to insult me you know. I don't expect payment from my guests.' He gave her a smile. 'I'm not a hotel proprietor.'

She knew Jeffrey had remitted Nathan nothing, not even for her doctor's bills. Neither had he penned her one line from Myitkyina. She kept her embarrassment to herself and said; 'Nathan, I know how much medicines and doctors cost, and it's sweet of you to consider me as a guest under your roof, but I'd rather remain independent if you don't mind. It's not fair that you have to feed, clothe and look after me in sickness or in health, so I've come to you with a proposition. I'd like to be given the opportunity to manage your business affairs here in Mandalay. I know that as far as your paperwork is concerned — ledger-books, accounts, invoices, all the chittys involved in the every day running of a business the size of yours — it's in organized chaos at the moment. If you don't mind a woman in charge, I'd like to take over the running of the de Veres-Vorne Company, Mandalay. I'll put your business affairs straight and in the long run save you a lot of time, money, custom, quality and temper. I'm sure a great deal of corruption and underhand fleecing must go on without your being aware of it — or perhaps you are aware of it but can't be in two places at once. That's what I'm driving at. I'll be your other half in Mandalay, and I don't require a salary until I've proved I'm worth one. In that way I'll be able to repay all your kindness and sympathy. When your profits soar and can rival that of Rangoon's Shwe Emporium, then we can come to some terms.'

Knowing him as she did, and having steeled herself to fight it out with him, she still wasn't prepared for his reaction: A blast of laughter almost blew his letters off his desk a third time. '*What!*' he shouted, tickled to death by what she had just said. 'Oh God, Angela, that's priceless! No, honestly honey, you're out of your mind ... Minthami was right ...' He hooted with mirth, 'Go back to bed, Amagyi-Angela and I'll fetch doctor Suseela.'

Angela, biting down her chagrin, used the tone of voice she had practised many times on the men at Minhla — it seemed to have worked then and she was determined to put Nathan in his place too; 'I assure you Nathan, I'm deadly serious. You might find it a laughing matter, I don't! I've come in all humility to ask you to give me a chance to repay you and Minthami for what you've done for me, and to help sort out your business affairs, so I don't find a slap in the face at all amusing. I want to become the first woman-manager of the de Veres-Vorne company, Far East, Pacific and Orient, South-East Asia, whatever you call it and wherever you trade. It needs someone at the helm right here in Mandalay!'

'You want ... you ... oh honey, that's rich! That's pure uncut diamond!' He slapped his thigh just to prove how rich she was and then guffawed with renewed verve so that Angela felt like tossing his whisky in his eye. 'Oh Amagyi-Angela, just let me get this straight ... you want to be my *woman*-manager? Cripes honey, I've only got one woman who requires managing, and I doubt even you could do that ...'

'Take that masculine smirk off your face Nathan Vorne, and just stop fooling around for one moment. I'm not asking to be made a partner in your Company — not yet anyway. I'm asking for a chance to prove myself and an opportunity to repay you. At the risk of repeating myself Nathan, I want a managerial position in the de Veres-Vorne holdings because I know I can do the job! And don't look at me so patronizingly, it's not very flattering.'

'You never cease to amaze me Amagyi-Angela! When I thought I'd learned everything there was to know about women, you come up with something like this, Jeeze!' He shook his head. 'And I'm not looking at you in any other way than in sheer blatant admiration. To go for the jackpot by wanting a managerial post before you've learned to count the gunny-sacks in the godowns, I like that. That smacks of ambition and can't be at all bad. I appreciate your sentiments honey, but even if I were willing to say yes to such an intriguing proposition, what would your husband say?'

'Jeffrey and I have an understanding. Neither one interferes in the other's life. That was our bargain, our kind of marriage-contract ... for reasons I'm not prepared to divulge to you, but it suits Jeffrey and me admirably. I lead my life, he leads his, and when the twain do meet, it's by mutual consent.'

'Amagyi-Angela, I salute you.' He shook his head and tossed back his drink. 'Listen honey, I'm delighted you want to help me out, but I'm not going to be delighted at the end of the day when a column of important figures hasn't been added up straight, or some little lady's forgotten which barge is arriving with what on board so it goes away again unloaded because the Bills of Lading have been filled out all wrong. Tilbury, Hong-Kong, Bombay, Calcutta, Cape, New York, Timbuktu, that's only half of where we stretch to, until I don't know myself whether I'm on my head or my heels — and I've been doing this job for the last twenty years. But you, my dear girl, want to jump right in the deep end and sort it all out for me overnight, that's rich!'

'Not overnight, Nathan.'

'Without one wit of experience in any kind of business whatsoever except in the translation of Pali and earning your living through begging.'

'That was un-called for Nathan.'

'Yes, it was, I'm sorry. Anyway, I've underestimated you Memsahib Radcliffe.' He helped himself from the bottle of Scotch whisky on his desk.

'Nathan, I promise on my word of honour I shaⁿ t let you down. I would study and learn everything there is to know about the kind of business you're running. I'm numerically sound — and to keep books is something I could learn if someone shows me how. I know how to read and speak the Burmese language. All that must be helpful in some way, and I'm very good at writing letters in a legible hand as everyone I knew when I was at the Academy lived on the other side of the world so I had to spend my time doing nothing but write letters. What I don't know I can easily pick up. You require someone to run the de Veres-Vorne Company in Mandalay more efficiently than it's being run at present, so ...'

'How do you know that?' he interrupted with a frown.

'Minthami told me.'

'Minthami only knows one thing about my business and that's if we're making enough gold-leaf to stick on Buddha's belly.'

'I just think I could fit the bill better than anyone you've yet employed in the way of secretary or manager or whatever,' Angela persisted.

'How do you know that?' he repeated with another frown.

'Minthami told me all your office and godown managers are useless as well as corrupt.'

'Is this some kind of joint-stock takeover by you and Minthami to put me out of business? Listen, Amagyi-Angela, when I want a second wife, I'll ask you personally, not through Minthami ...'

'Don't flatter yourself, Nathan,' she smiled wanly after her verbal tussle with him. 'Please just let me try for a little while at least. If, after the first six months I haven't been able to grasp a thing and your profits have slipped, then sack me.'

'I haven't employed you yet.'

'Please Nathan,' she held up her hand, 'let me finish first before you start deriding me. Let me prove myself, that's all I'm asking. I'm tired of doing nothing and want to use my abilities and talents to some advantage. I'm not uneducated and could be of tremendous help to you.'

'I know that. But I can think of better ways to use your talents,' he said flippantly, eyeing her over the rim of his glass while he rocked back in his chair.

'My God Nathan, you're so stupid sometimes, it's a wonder you ever made a success of the de Veres-Vorne Company in the first place,' she said scathingly. 'Women to you are only objets d'arts!'

He stopped rocking, and snapping back to his desk smiled and said, 'Which just shows one doesn't have to be clever to be wise. So my dear, while you're as thin as a bamboo pipe and need a stick to walk with, how do you propose to be my woman-manager? Right now Amagyi-Angela ...'

'Will you stop calling me that! I left the Convent years ago.'

'Right now, Mrs Radcliffe, you're not fit to tackle a boiled egg. Forget it honey. Some other time. Now if you'll excuse me ...'

'No Nathan, I will not! I want an answer from you before I leave this room. Yes or no?'

'No.'

'Please Nathan, please just give me one tiny chance. I promise you you'll never regret it.'

He rubbed his chin and regarded her penetratingly. A good sign, she thought, but kept those thoughts to herself. 'Well, I don't know,' he murmured which was the second sign of weakness as far as she was concerned. 'I don't think Jeffrey's going to like the idea of his wife earning her own living.'

'He'll be delighted I've found something to do while he's away chasing dacoits and making short work of the Burmese. I've as much brains as you and Jeffrey, and I'll prove it to you if only you'll let me prove myself.' Angela realized that that was probably not quite the right thing to say just then, but changed her tactics and disarming him with eyes and lips and feminine wiles, added, 'Please say yes, Nathan. You won't regret it, I promise.'

468

'Well I don't know. I'll think about it, and certainly I wouldn't consider anything until the doctor's pronounced you one hundred percent fit.'

She breathed out, the gamble having paid off; 'Aye-Aye Captain,' she beamed.

'No promises mind. No verdict until I see how you can get rid of a rice mountain without losing me my commission, or trace unpaid chittys of several months standing, and account for every single gunny-sack and de Veres-Vorne kerosene drum that's gone missing.'

'Aye-aye, Captain. Now if you'll kindly pass me over my stick I'll be putting it away in the elephant-stand on the verandah.'

'I'm not a very nice person to talk to when I lose my temper and I hate failure,' he warned, handing her the stick.

'Don't I know all that Captain Vorne! On that foundation we both know where we stand, so you and I should make a formidable duo where big business is concerned.'

'You're pretty formidable on your own, honey.'

'I don't know whether to receive that as a compliment or not. Whatever you meant, thank you, Nathan, for having confidence in me. My gratitude and appreciation will be shown by proving to you you've just employed the best woman-manager you've ever had.'

'I don't doubt that for one minute,' he said, holding the door open for her, 'But not until doctor Suseela gives the go ahead do I employ one single curl on that head of yours. And now Mrs Radcliffe, as you're putting away your stick into its elephant-leg, would you care to take my arm and let me escort you in to dinner as my wife won't be joining us this evening?' He extended his elbow in a gallant gesture.

'Delighted, Captain,' she murmured.

Angela, with reservations, linked her arm in his and he helped her to the dining room where dinner had been set for three.

CHAPTER
THIRTY-THREE

ONE

A bright crocheted rug wrapped round her knees,
Angela sat on the verandah outside the bedroom in
which she had helped deliver Clare and Matthew's child
Sarah, who had died aboard the *Belle Hélène II*. Somewhere in the house Tonsin's pet monkey chattered
volubly, while Nathan's garden steamed in the monsoon
rain. A white dove settled on the balustrade warbling
deeply and Angela crumbled a tea-cake which the bird
did not hesitate to take from her hand. It did not move
its position but with dainty rocking movements dipped
its beak to the crumbs while keeping one lazy eye winking at her. In her lap Angela had two letters, one from
Milly Sinclair in Coimbatore where she was bringing up
Leigh's two-year old son, and the other from Blaize and
Edwin who had returned to England because of Edwin's
health. Angela missed them all, and hoped Bee's
remarks about Edwin hating the miserable grey clouds of
Cheltenham Spa, and how he longed for the sun, might
induce them to return to Mandalay so that Edwin's
retirement could be spent with the sun warming his old
bones. As for Milly, Angela was happy to know that
Leigh's parents and her own vast family had helped to
cushion the blow of Leigh's death and had rallied around
her to bring up Leigh Junior.

Nathan appeared on the balcony and the dove flew
away to its dovecote in the garden. He tossed a buff
envelope in her lap.

470

'What's this?' she asked, suspiciously.

Nathan leaned against the verandah, his arms folded, one leg crossed over the other nonchalantly. 'Open it and see,' he said in an off-hand manner.

With a puzzled frown Angela read the Title Deeds to a property a short walk away from Whitewalls. 'What's this Nathan?' She looked up at him in bewilderment.

'A little bungalow I had in mind to make over to you and Jeffrey. I bought the land dirt cheap when nobody else wanted it, but now it appears the whole of Mandalay wants to come out here to live on the Bund. The Burmese family who had been occupying the place are leaving to go down to Moulmein, so I thought Jeffrey and you might like it.'

'But we're entitled to Army quarters.'

He shrugged. 'Please yourself if you'd rather live in a rat-hole at the Garrison. But the bungalow is still yours. You can rent it out if you like, if you don't wish to live there.'

'But why are you doing this Nathan?' Angela asked.

Again he shrugged carelessly, a typical Nathan gesture when he wished to disguise the softer side to his nature. 'A wedding present,' he stated.

'But you've been more than generous with wedding presents where Jeffrey and I are concerned. We can't take this property Nathan. Why, it's worth a lot of money.'

'It is. Now. So don't look a gift house in the mouth honey, only its front door waiting to welcome you.' He grinned. 'It's an opportunity to possess your own home, Angela, right beside Vanda and Nancy from Edom Gideon's church! As I said, the whole of Mandalay is itching to live out here now, so take the house while the going's good. In a few years time there won't be any land left to build on, so I'm darn glad I made me a few shrewd investments a while back.'

'And how am I supposed to explain to Jeffrey this generous gift from you?'

'You can always tell him it's a down-payment on the

471

best woman-manager I'm going to have one day.' He cleared his throat. 'Let's rephrase, "have to employ." Otherwise I might get my face slapped for unintentional use of the wrong word.' He stretched his arms above his head and looked down on her with a lazy half-smile. 'If Jeffrey were killed — perish the thought — while fighting the Burmese, the Army would kick you out of married quarters and you'd be left homeless again. Here's your insurance policy against that happening.'

'Thank you, Nathan, you're too generous. But Jeffrey and I couldn't take it for nothing. We would give you rent for it, or pay off a mortgage.'

'Listen, Amagyi-Angela, it's a gift. I don't want you to start paying me off anything. Why are you always so goddam snooty the whole time? Why can't you accept something at its face value without turning your nose up at it?'

'I'm not turning my nose up at it Nathan.'

'Yes you are!'

'I just don't like feeling I'm your kept-woman, that's all!'

'Oh ha-ha-ha, that's most amusing! You're about the least kept-woman any man could lumber himself with — you're too damn prickly to get nearer to than a hundred yards before you go screaming into your corner crying *rape* every time a red-blooded male comes near you ... hell, no wonder you married Jeffrey Radcliffe! You're perfectly safe with him, Amagyi-Angela, he's the Buddhist monk to your Buddhist nunnery, you're both about as warped as each other.'

'Get out of here, Nathan!'

'I'm going.' He strode to the verandah doors. 'No, I'm not, this is *my* goddamn house.' He came back to tower above her, '*You're* the one who's going. Either out to Sequoia, the deeds of which lie in your lap, or else to some rat-hole in the cantonment, but I can't stand having you under my roof when all I get from you are accusations and recriminations. You've never quite forgiven me have you, Angela, for what happened between us after Loloi when you were seduced — quite willingly might I add — in the aftermath of some moth-eaten boat sinking! You are trying to emotionally black-mail me over and over again for that immoral act, aren't you, you poor blameless, misused woman! But I'm not being taken in any more by feelings of guilt over what happened to you, or to Matthew Sinclair, through some cock-eyed notion you had at the time that I'd corrupted you, therefore you weren't pure enough to marry Matthew Sinclair in case he found out he wasn't marrying the virgin he was supposed to, huh?' He thrust his face close to hers. 'The face is right here Angela, slap it if you must, but don't give me your righteous indignation any-more.' He moved aside and turned his back on her. The sun lanced the garden in bright shafts of light piercing the rain clouds. 'If I wasn't so afraid your bones would rattle in your skin, I'd shake you to get some sense into you,' Nathan muttered.

When she still hadn't uttered a word in her defence, but observed him frigidly like a wax lily thrust in a vase of water, he turned around to say; 'I'm giving you *Sequoia* because I like to house members of my staff in better conditions than the British Army. But if you're not ready to be my woman-manager in a month from today, I'm sacking you on the grounds of ill-health.' He turned on his heel and left her to her own devices, the deeds to the bungalow still in her lap along with the two letters from Milly and Blaize.

TWO

Five weeks later Angela began to question the folly of her ways. What on earth, she asked herself miserably, had induced her to try to get the better of Nathan Vorne! Every night of that first week working for him, she had ended up in tears, hating him for his relentless, superior, masculine attitude that saw her only as some-thing decorative, to be picked up, handled, admired and

473

put back in its place with no more thought given than to a jade figurine discovered on his wanderings! While cursing him silently, she also admired his enormous appetite for non-stop work that had taken the de Veres-Vorne Company from one leaky boat to a flotilla sailing the seven seas. Even so, while rendered weak and exhausted after only seven days, she still vowed he would not get the better of her and that she could match him any day!

Angela realized Nathan was trying to prove to her — not very subtly — that she was incapable of the task she had set herself, and that she simply was not cut out to take over the management of something on the scale of the de Veres-Vorne Company. His undisguised cynicism regarding a woman's capabilities outside the bedroom gave her the incentive to carry on rather than go to him with a white flag of surrender. Exhausted, she fell into bed each night, promising herself, come hell or high-water, she would do what she had set out to do — come to terms with profit-margins on tonnage per flat and steamer loaded with such-and-such a commodity going to such-and-such a place, transposing it all into pounds, shillings and pence, dollars and cents, rupees and annas, kyats and pyats . . .

And, in the morning, she would wake with the thought of hundreds of miles of trading routes at such-and-such an exchange rate so, if the Irrawaddy Flotilla Company hired out flats at fifteen rupees per ton per month, and steamers including coal at forty-five rupees per month, could the de Veres-Vorne Company under-cut their prices so that at the end of the day the de Veres-Vorne Company got the orders and not the Irrawaddy Flotilla Company or the Bombay–Burma Teak Corporation?

Of course it could!

The Bombay–Burma Trading Corporation and the Irrawaddy Flotilla Company had had the monopoly for far too long, and only competition from someone like the de Veres-Vorne Company could ensure a more healthy economy in Upper Burma. After all, to be competitive spelled a more efficient and profitable business which in turn provided greater stability, quality, custom and prosperity to the country, didn't it?

Of course it did!

Angela, chewing the end of her pencil regarded Nathan in the office godown; 'Nathan, your flats have *got* to operate on twelve rupees per ton and your steamers forty-one.'

'Why?'

'Because we've got to beat the I.F.C. at their own game and we can't do that without undercutting their prices.'

'How, when coal for the steamers costs the same for us as for them?'

'Then we've got to go one better — I'll go to Kalaw myself and get a Contract from the Burmese supplying us with our coal to give us a better deal — lower than the I.F.C.'s, much lower.'

'Honey, if you can win us that kind of concession I'll eat my hat — and up your salary while I'm doing it.'

'I'm not receiving one at the moment,' she reminded him.

'No, that's true.'

'I'll do it, Nathan, I'll do it!'

She did. He did not eat his hat, neither did he put her on the payroll, but as far as Angela was concerned, his grudging admiration was enough for the time being.

THREE

Angela, who had been busy in her front garden planting flowers, put down her spade, took off her gardening-gloves and went inside to study the ledger-books she had brought home that day from the Shwe Emporium.

The following morning she set off early to the godowns along the river. When she got inside the tiny office with its corrugated iron roof which magnified the heat so it became like an oven as the day wore on — that was why she preferred to come early to do her work — the familiar smell of Nathan's tobacco greeted her.

'Hello,' she said, removing her hat and sticking the pin back into it before placing it on top of the rusty filing cabinet. 'You've beaten me to it this morning. Did your trip to Bhamo go well?'

He occupied the seat of honour and did not budge from it. Billows of pipe-smoke filled the room and she began to cough.

'Honey,' he said, contemplating her through the haze, 'you're looking a little peaky to me. Why don't you take the day off and go on home now that I'm back.'

'What's that supposed to mean?' She stood beside the filing-cabinet with her elbow on it, the back of her hand against her mouth to stop herself from coughing.

'It means, Angela honey, I think it's all getting too much for you ... look at you. You're as pale as Aunty Mabel on an African safari and coughing like a consumptive.'

'That's because you're not helping matters by adding to the unhealthy atmosphere in this cast-iron henhouse of yours. Why don't you get some punkas installed, Nathan? You can't expect your workforce to give their best in evil conditions like these ...' She swept an expansive arm around his premises.

'They've done fine up till now with no complaints. Anyway, punkas in this office haven't been necessary, nobody's ever used it much until you arrived.'

'That's been very obvious to me from the state of things in the place!' She pulled open a rusty drawer that protested furiously as it hung limply on the drawer below. Two pieces of paper lay in the bottom of it. 'If that's your filing system Nathan, no wonder everything's in such a mess. Before I work in here, I want new equipment, punkas, and a pen to write with!' She glared at him. 'I'd also appreciate it if you'd put another chair in here ... and ... and smoke your pipe elsewhere.'

He got up leisurely and offered her the office chair.

Placing himself on the corner of the wooden desk whose legs had been eaten mercilessly by white ants so that it wobbled precariously, he said through his pipe; 'You asked me if I had a good trip to Bhamo, the answer is no. The answer is no because I had to pacify a very old and very good customer of mine on the brink of taking his custom away from me to give it to the B.B.T.C. Reasons being that he'd been sent a boatful of yinma instead of padauk, and he can't work with yinma, which in turn sent *his* business hay-wire while he waited for a new delivery of padauk — from the B.B.T.C. Do you get the point I'm trying to make Amagyi-Angela?'

'Perfectly, Captain Vorne,' she replied, her arms folded while she declined to take the seat he had unwillingly vacated. Her green eyes narrowed; 'Why don't you come out with it straight Nathan? All this business about looking peaky, and go home and rest! Just stop patronizing me in that 'poor-little-woman' voice you use on Minthami. It doesn't do anything for me except make me very angry.' She turned round, opened another drawer from his so-called filing cabinet and thrust an invoice under his nose: 'U Tha Tay, Bhamo — a delivery of yinma ... whose signature is that, Nathan?'

He appeared to be short-sighted while he scrutinized the handwriting: 'Did *I* send him yinma?' Incredulously he met her eyes.

'You did.'

'Instead of padauk?'

'Yes, Nathan. It hasn't taken me twenty years to mistake yinma for padauk.'

'What a fool I am.'

'I suppose you told U Tha Tay your *woman*-manager was responsible, the new little female you'd employed and wished you hadn't, eh Nathan?'

He hadn't the grace to look sheepish and Angela could have shut his grinning head in his rusty filing-cabinet.

'Well now, I guess I did kind of shift the blame a little

... honey, you're doing a grand job here. At least now I can read and make sense of the numbers I see written down in front of my eyes. The way those Burmans write their numbers looks like they've deliberately gone mad with a doodling-pen to confuse me. Now then, while we're face-to-face upon the subject, I want you to get through Mr Pathan Sundevava's thick skull that if he doesn't stop undercutting my prices for groundnut oil, he's going to find himself squeezed right out of the market so that not even an Indian chettyar will bail him out when he finds he's got more peanuts on his hands than even a monkey wants. Because I'll get them from the U.S. of A. for the real price of monkeynuts!'

'Do you wish me to tell him all that in those precise words, or shall I rephrase them slightly so that he doesn't call your bluff?'

'Honey, you tell him *exactly* that.' He took his pipe from his mouth. 'How do you know I'm bluffing?'

'Nathan Vorne, at the Women's Academy I went to, a Saturday evening was the only time we were allowed to play games. Usually, the game we played was called hunt-the-kipper. Two trails were laid, one true one false. The right answers to all the clues led to a large marshmallow that improved the taste of watered-down hot chocolate no end. The wrong answers led to a smelly herring filched from the senior Miss Bloxham's cat. It was a spiteful if pretty thing. I collected quite a little store of herringbones and it stopped scratching me everytime I went near it. So, to coin a phrase from you, one doesn't have to be clever to be wise.'

'Put down hot chocolate and marshmallows on the Buyer's list at the Shwe Emporium ... hey!' He jumped off the edge of the rickety desk to tap on the glass partition separating office from godown. Angela looked in the direction he was waving his pipe while shouting at the godown manager through the glass; 'Maung Sang Aye ... he can't load rice like that ...' Nathan turned back to Angela. 'The fellow's got yaws all over his legs and shouldn't go clambering over the rice. Make sure he goes off work until his sores are healed.'

'Does he get paid while he's away?'

'Don't be an ass.'

'I'm not the ass, you are. How is he going to support his family if you put him out of work?'

'That's his problem, not mine ...'

'Nathan, you are corrupt! You are corrupt, and that's how you've made so much money! You are exploiting your workforce in conditions not fit to house ... to house cats!'

'Remarks like that from any other person would have earned them the sack.'

'You can't sack me. You're not even paying me.'

'You're fired!' He jabbed his pipe at her.

'Good!' She jabbed her finger at him. 'Now that you've done what you've been dying to do for the past few weeks I'm going to tell you how much of a fool you are to yourself. Yesterday, a whole consignment of crockery from Stoke-on-Trent was smashed to smithereens and resembled nothing but the mosaic decorations on Mindon Min's tomb when it was unpacked. Now then, it wasn't the fault of the coolies here, because I observed the way they were unloading those crates arriving at Go Wain. The coolies were very careful — and they don't get extra rupees for being careful. However, I've since written to the potteries to make quite certain they understand the fundamentals of long-distance packaging and storing. I've informed them that if we continue to receive inadequately packaged goods we shall take our custom to China. I've despatched a similar message to the masters of the merchant ships conveying our cargo and have asked for their co-operation in the matter of loading and securing in order to withstand choppy seas and storm damage, and unloading at Rangoon. So, wherever the negligence is occurring, it ought to stop. You must be losing a great deal of profit on that score alone. There is just one other matter to which your attention ought to be drawn before I take my hat and go, and that is, the Scandinavian Government have given us another substantial order for teak, and would require delivery to reach Göteburg by midsummer. Can we meet that sort of deadline — or do they go to the B.B.T.C.?'

'Sure! Why can't we meet their deadline and everything else? Tell them the de Veres-Vorne Company can do anything now they've got themselves a reinstated woman-manager. Well, I'm off honey.' He took up his sun-helmet from the desk. 'I've got a rubber-man from Kuala Lumpur to see, so, if you require my urgent assistance within the next few hours, I'm at Whitewalls. Otherwise get Muckerjee or Maung Sang Aye to sort out your problems — that's if you have any.'

'No, I don't think I will have any problems — especially when it comes to yinma and padauk.' She sat down at the desk.

He smiled: 'I'm delighted you're in Maung Sang Aye's place, Amagyi-Angela. You're so much better looking than he is.'

She ignored the bait. 'Does this mean I'm here to stay, Nathan?'

'Seems like it honey.'

'For a monthly salary?'

'That depends. I'm still convinced you're here to bankrupt the de Veres-Vorne Company. I don't trust you Mrs Radcliffe. Anyone who prefers dead herrings to marshmallows has to be distrusted.' He opened the door. 'I'll reconsider in a couple of months.'

'Nathan ...'

'Angela?' He turned back on the threshold to regard her with a glint in his eye.

'Nathan, even kipper-bones can be the means to an end and serve a better purpose than marshmallows. My purpose, seated here at this desk, is not to prove anything to you or to anyone else, only to me. I want to do this job to the best of my ability, the fourth of the eight-fold path, right effort or exertion, something I have to prove to myself because ... because I have to I suppose. I don't expect you to understand.'

'No, I don't understand you, Amagyi-Angela. I

understand Minthami all right, she's Shan and Buddhist. But you, you've twisted me in mental knots till I'm not sure what to expect from you anymore.'

She smiled secretively; 'Don't let me confuse you Nathan. We all of us have to do what's right for us. Please can I have a fan in here and a new desk now that I'm staying?'

'Angela honey, if you've made up your mind to go after the goddam moon because it's on the eight-fold path, who am I to argue with Buddha? Just fill out some chittys and hand them to Sang Aye and maybe one day you and Minthami can tell me what Lord Buddha's got that I haven't.'

He went out, and through the glass partition she observed him having words with the man with yaws. His name was Maung Da Wara and after Nathan had gone he came nervously to the half-glazed door of the office but would not step beyond the threshold because his religion and culture forbade him to remain in the presence of a woman not of his family.

'Yes, what is it Maung Da Wara?' Angela asked, feeling that the words trembling on his lips must be of grave importance to him.

He addressed her in the masculine gender which always took her aback, even when realizing that it was done out of polite consideration for the kind of work she was doing, a man's work in the eyes of the simple workers. 'Sir, I have come from Thakin Vorne to ask for my sick money while I am getting better at home.'

'Sick money?' Angela asked, mystified. 'Oh sick money!' She sprang up from the chair to take the petty-cash box from the filing cabinet. 'How much did Thakin Vorne offer you Maung Da Wara?'

'A quarter of my healthy earnings, sir.'

'Then that will be twelve annas, won't it?'

'That is right, sir.'

Angela gave him twelve annas. 'It's not much, is it?' She enquired, feeling rather sorry for Maung Da Wara with his yaws and meagre pay.

'No sir.'

'How many do you have to support in your family?'

'Eight people, sir.'

'Are any of them able to share the financial burden with you?'

'Yes sir. We all earn money to contribute to the family. I will now be able to offer my services to Mr Pathan Sundevava while I am getting better.' He took his twelve annas and departed.

Angela, sinking back into her chair, felt very deflated as well as foolish. She hoped to goodness Thakin Vorne would never get to hear of her charitable efforts to supplement Maung Da Wara's and Mr Pathan Sundevava's pockets at the expense of his!

CHAPTER
THIRTY-FOUR

ONE

Angela was delighted to hear from Blaize and Edwin that they had decided to return to Mandalay early in the New Year, their last Christmas to be spent in Cheltenham — where Edwin was bored rigid — before returning to the golden shore.

'Darling,' Blaize wrote in her gushing manner, 'I can't wait to say goodbye to this one-horse town — and I'd imagined Tunbridge Wells to be the most dreary place on earth! Simply can't wait to get back to see you in your new role as godown-superintendent. What a woman doesn't do in the name of love! Darling, whatever will you think of next. P.S. Is there a law that prevents a Buddhist woman having two husbands?'

While ignoring the majority of Blaize's remarks, Angela was glad to know Blaize and Edwin were returning to Mandalay. *Sequoia*, the house Nathan had given she and Jeffrey as a wedding present, went unremarked by Jeffrey who passed through life as though the whole world owed him a living. He arrived home on leave a week before Blaize and Edwin were due to return to Mandalay. He brought with him an exquisite pigeon-blood ruby necklace for her to wear at the Annexation Ball on the 17th February. Angela was aghast at the amount of money he must have spent on such a pretty bauble she had no need of, when the unpaid chittys were piling up at the Shwe Emporium and elsewhere because he had sent her no house-keeping money. She had never forgotten the one caustic little note he had written her from Myitkyina when she had asked him for some money: 'Dearest, so glad you're being well taken care of at Whitewalls. I'm short of the ready at the moment in view of the fact there are no banks in the jungle to cash my drafts. If you're that desperate for money, ask Nathan for a few annas, I'm sure he'll oblige until I get home.'

The fact that Jeffrey considered her to be worth only a few annas rankled most. Angela took the ruby necklace with a smile and kept her anger in check when dressing up for the one glamorous occasion on Mandalay's social calendar. Her dress she had made herself, rather than buy one from the Shwe Emporium. A white satin and silver trimmed creation, she designed it for maximum effect, pleased that her slender waist could still be drawn in to eighteen inches while her corsets pushed up her bustline to present a decent bosom above her décolletage. Against her creamy shoulders, Jeffrey's ruby necklace was displayed to perfection. While her hair was still not long enough to put up into an elaborate coiffure, she did the next best thing and held her curls back with fresh flowers and ribbons prettily laced through. Amazing, too, what uniform did for a man — glorifying him while covering the defects underneath.

On the night of the third Annexation Ball held in Mindon Min's former Hall of Audience (the Mandalay Palace now renamed Fort Dufferin and British Army Headquarters) Jeffrey, resplendent in scarlet Mess dress and cavalry moustache brushed to perfection, epitomised all that Empire stood for. He introduced Angela first to the Garrison's new Commanding Officer, Colonel, Sir Boland Dawlish and his wife, Lady Dorothy.

'What an exquisite necklace, my dear,' said Lady Dorothy in a rather vague and endearing way as she peered shortsightedly at Angela's bosom while her glass of champagne was in danger of following her line of vision. 'If it's Burmese though, you want to take it to a reliable jeweller Jeffrey,' she told him emphatically. 'You must make quite certain you weren't palmed off with spinels — though they can be quite valuable, especially the deep-red variety. Boland brought me a lovely ruby bracelet from a Mogok merchant, but alas, they were discovered to be glass stones and not even of the spinel type, so one can't quite trust anyone East of Suez in my opinion. But the jade and silver-work is rather clever, and genuine. Jeffrey tells us you do a little job of work my dear ...' She beamed myopically at Angela, her manner one of expectancy as she waited politely for Angela to enlighten her.

'Yes, I work for the de Veres-Vorne Company in the capacity of ...'

Jeffrey interrupted her swiftly, 'Yes quite! Well, we mustn't monopolize the good Colonel and his lady-wife all evening must we, Angy? Do please excuse us ...'

Lady Dorothy halted his hasty departure with a tap of her fan on his arm; 'Don't take Angela away from us just when we're having such a delightful conversation Jeffrey.' Turning back to Angela she said; 'One simply must set a good example to these poor souls out here and I do admire spunk and enterprise in a woman. If you require my support and assistance in your welfare work, or help raising funds for a worthwhile and charitable cause, don't hesitate to ask me, will you, my dear?'

Sir Boland bent a little from the waist to regard her from behind his monocle and mutton-chop whiskers, his hands clasped firmly behind his back. His smile was warm and fatherly, reminding her a little of Larcher at Minhla. 'Charitable works, good show!'

Angela had been about to answer him but Jeffrey did it for her, 'Oh yes quite! No question about it being charitable. Hasn't received a penny for her good works, eh Angy dearest? Need an English script in these native offices, what! Dashed frustrating to cope with illiterate beggars all day long. I can't imagine how the American chap does it, what!' He laughed effusively.

'Would you care for this dance Lady Dorothy?' He

swept a finger along the luxurious moustache he had grown in place of his little brush and Angela wondered why on earth Jeffrey was so nervous this evening, his speech and behaviour quite erratic.

'No thank you Jeffrey, the next one perhaps.' Lady Dorothy smiled at him as she spilled a little more champagne down her own bosom this time. 'I'm just so interested in your wife and all her good works. I've heard a little about her work, and how the Burmese hold her in such esteem here in Mandalay — you know how gossip circulates in small areas. Tell me Angela, this voluntary work of yours, what exactly does it entail?'

'I'm manager of the de ...'

'Manager of the interests of the community as a whole, eh what Angy?' Jeffrey said, frowning at her with pursed lips.

'A hobby?' Sir Boland Dawlish said, rocking towards her. 'All voluntary, good show.'

'Rather,' said Jeffrey, answering so much on her behalf Angela was beginning to think that Sir Boland and Lady Dorothy would think she was a deaf mute.

'I work for the de Veres-Vorne Company in the capacity of woman-manageress in their godowns and Emporium,' said Angela with a dazzling smile at all three of them.

Jeffrey turned as red as her ruby necklace and dared her to say one more word while the awkward little silence between Sir Boland and Lady Dorothy was amusingly charged with electrical currents unable to find a suitable path to take.

Lady Dorothy, in her rather horsy, untidy fashion, was the first to recover and with tremendous aplomb drew Angela to one side after remarking over her shoulder to Jeffrey, 'Of course you must dance with your charming wife, Jeffrey, but first of all I wish to have a little word in her ear.'

He, with acute embarrassment, stood rigidly to attention while Sir Boland attempted small conversation; 'How are things in the north?' To which Jeffrey, with a tepid twitch beneath his flamboyant moustache murmured something polite while Angela sensed all he wished to do was get his hands round her neck.

'What I really wished to say to you, my dear,' said Lady Dorothy, spilling a little more of the contents of her newly filled glass onto another lady's skirts while she confided in Angela, 'is that the best pair of English brogues I found out East was from the Shwe Emporium right here in Mandalay. I'm dying to get hold of another pair, but alas they didn't have another pair in my size. My dear, if you could attend to that little matter for me?' Her smile was gracious. 'There is another problem I have, that of underwear,' and she went into lengthy details of her requirements, after which she deposited Angela back beside her husband. 'Boland,' said Lady Dorothy, 'Angela, I now know, is Captain de Veres-Vorne's right hand person, his Secretary in other words, so clever of her! Captain de Veres-Vorne is quite the most charming man — I met him once in the Shwe Emporium when I required to make myself familiar with the store, and he was so obliging with his credit facilities. I did send him an invitation to this do, he being one of Mandalay's leading figures, but he didn't deign to reply to me — does he not like the British?' She turned to Jeffrey for clarification upon the subject. Her mild myopic eyes searched his face. 'Ma'am,' he said stiffly, 'Captain de Veres-Vorne was of tremendous help to us at Minhla and again at Sagaing simply because he knows the Irrawaddy River better than anyone else. As to his personal likes and dislikes, I couldn't say — he seems to favour anybody who might in the long run do him an even greater favour, and that's why I suspect he offered his services to us during the battle for Mandalay — Upper Burma now being an even more profitable place for him to earn his living, and far less barbaric.'

'The reason why Captain de Veres-Vorne does not attend these functions, Lady Dorothy, Sir Boland,' Angela smiled at them, 'Is because he considers them to be too snob.'

487

'Do excuse us! Angela must not monopolize your company the whole evening,' said Jeffrey, taking her arm. 'If I may, this happens to be one of our favourite tunes?'

'Of course, of course,' said Sir Boland Dawlish waving him away, 'one must dance sometimes. Come along my dear,' he said taking Lady Dorothy's arm, 'I think I can manage this one even with my creaking bones.' Firmly, he guided his wife away to the dance floor after she had hastily set down her empty glass on a Bearer's tray and knocked over two more in her fumbling clumsiness.

Angela smiled brightly in her husband's face; 'Jeffrey, you're holding me far too tightly and I can't breathe ... that's better!' She let out a sigh of relief. 'Now why are you looking at me so angrily? I was only speaking the truth.'

'What truth Angy?' he asked, twirling her round expertly to the music, a most accomplished dancer. 'Too much truth, dearest, can be very painful, and you wouldn't wish my career to be affected by opening your big mouth far too wide?' He looked with mildly scornful hazel eyes at her, and she noticed how nicotine stained his moustache was, his fingers too, for he smoked heavily.

'You know Nathan does not attend these functions because he considers them to be far too snobbish — and because of Minthami being excluded. There's always "them and us". Just look around you tonight. There are no Burmese people here, only Europeans who have key positions in the city or in the B.B.T.C. and I.F.C., but no real Burmans to whom Mandalay really belongs.' She emphasized the point she was trying to get through to Jeffrey.

'Well, you can't blame us for that surely?' he said derisively. 'Not when they're slaughtering us up and down the country so that ten thousand more soldiers are having to be drafted in to keep the peace.'

'The slaughtering is not one-sided, Jeffrey. We both

488

know how many the British themselves are shooting without fair trials, head-men of villages, rebel princes, even the monks who are fighting to get rid of an Army of occupation. You can't blame them when they thought the only reason Britain interfered in the affairs of Upper Burma was to place on the Dragon Throne another Burmese prince like Nyaung Ok, someone more sympathetic than Thibaw and Supalayat. To find out now that that was not Britain's intention at all, but that she sailed in to Mandalay to keep the country for herself by attaching it to India as an Indian province, when Buddhism was stamped out in that country centuries ago — no wonder the Burmese are rebelling against us!'

'I sometimes wonder on whose side you are, Angy. You're not turning native by any chance?' Jeffrey said laconically. 'I wonder too, whatever possessed you to become a Buddhist nun — you're not one of them still, are you?'

'Yes, Jeffrey I am, if you must know the truth. I might not be a nun anymore and wear a pink robe, but I still like to keep an open mind as far as Buddhism is concerned. I find it a very consoling and happy philosophy, especially the meditation.'

He smiled, eyelids heavy — until he raised them and his grin widened as he gazed over her shoulders. 'But sometimes, Angy dearest, truth can be confounded. Lady Dorothy's wish has been granted, for I spy with my little eye the backbone of Mandalay's trading section just being admitted into the Hall with his lady-wife in her longyi. In a month of Sunday mornings I never thought he'd have the nerve ...' Angela stumbled in her steps and his arm came round her too tightly for comfort. 'Steady Angy, steady!' He hissed. 'You're looking awfully pale all of a sudden dearest. I wonder, can it be due to the boss making such an untimely entrance, or for some other reason?'

His grip on her was suddenly crushing and Angela felt faint in the heat. 'Stand up straight my dear, you're letting the side down — and we can't allow that to happen in The Lancers, can we?'

'Jeffrey ... I can't breathe if you hold me so close.'

He smiled down at her in a way that made her feel that the ruby necklace and his other ostentatious gifts had all been in vain. 'You're looking very lovely tonight, my dear. More lovely than I can ever remember ... such sweet bright curls in that angelic fashion under its halo of pretty flowers, what a charming picture you make! What a pity your lover has appeared on the scene to ruin my evening. What's that you say? Not your lover? Well now Angy, Mandalay thinks otherwise. No, of course you don't listen to gossip. You ought to sometimes, it might make you a little more prudent as far as your behaviour is concerned. Now, I ask myself, what is Mandalay's golden boy dreaming of by bringing his little native wife into our midst this evening?'

'Jeffrey, don't be despicable! I wish to sit out the next dance if you please. I think I'd prefer to talk to Blaize and Edwin ...'

'Oh no you're not. You're going to smile dazzlingly at your golden lover-boy and his Shan princess ... come along, Angy, let me take you to them.' He held her arm remorselessly, his fingers bruising her elbow while he guided her across the room to Nathan and Minthami who were in deep conversation with Lady Dorothy and Sir Boland, both of them appearing animated and profoundly interested in what the exotic Shan princess was telling them about the Court of Ava and the palace of former days.

'We can't intrude,' said Angela.

'Why not, Angy? You've made such a glorious impression on Lady Dorothy as Mandalay's premier sales-lady.'

'Jeffrey, don't spoil things, please,' Angela pleaded, and was, for once, glad when Blaize poked her nose in.

She had detached herself from her close circle of friends to waylay them, forcing Jeffrey to mutter in an aside; 'Here she comes, blazing her trail as usual,' which brought a flicker of amusement to Angela despite her unsettled frame of mind.

'Angela darling, what a divine frock, so daring — for you. Shwe Emporium isn't it? Raj! My, but you look dashing tonight. Love the moustaches darling, simply too, too awe-inspiring. Angela, Reggie Rowanbottom and his fiancée are here, and I have their wedding-present list you asked for. Do come and say hello to everyone you two, and don't keep to your superior selves — we saw you currying favour with Sir B and Lady D, as Nathan's doing right now. What a hoot, darlings, bringing her here tonight. Too, too avant-gard for words.' She drew them towards her bosom pals, and Angela felt more stifled than ever, hating every minute of functions like this.

'Dashed Indians are infinitely better chaps,' someone was claiming, 'damn good soldiers too. Not like this lot from the jungles. I tell you sir, Upper Burma as a Province of the Raj simply won't work. This "pacification programme" is utter bunk.'

'No, not rupees, my dear sir, pounds sterling! Eighty thousand pounds was what Thibaw took by way of the fermented tea-leaf monopoly — let alone all the other monopolies. Corrupt, egad!'

Edwin, recovered in health, was in full fling with a fat cigar. He had put on weight again after his ordeal in the jungle, his holiday in Cheltenham had given him a new lease of life, and while he ignored the Adjutant beside him expounding on Thibaw's monopolies, was ruminating on his own bravado: 'Senyat, by George! Blew it sky-high! Damn near took off my eyebrows thanks to de Veres-Vorne and his kerosene drums ... must ask him what the devil he puts in his drums besides kerosene.

'The trouble is, the people in Rangoon have no idea that Mandalay is not like Rangoon. What a hue and cry there was when we kept on the old fellow, the Taingda Mingyi, to help get some organization into the place after Thibaw had left it in such a shambles. In the end the outraged voices had their own way and the poor old chap had to be sent packing off to Calcutta to keep

491

everybody quiet. I rather liked him myself, a shrewd, intelligent Burman who wasn't nearly as black as he was made out to be.'

Angela felt dizzy, the buzz of conversation, the music, laughter and chink of champagne glasses swamping her, so that she felt as though her head were being held underwater. She had kept to fruit juices during the evening, the last time she had touched any alcoholic drink was in the cave of the San Mukh when toddy-palm liquor had proved to be so effective. A magnificently uniformed Bearer with red and gold puggaree and cummerbund over his white jacket and trousers passed by, holding a tray of sparkling champagne-cup, and Angela, not stopping to think about it, lifted a glass and downed the champagne like medicine, with her eyes shut. The effect was pleasant. Opening her eyes, she realized that Jeffrey had noticed even if the others had not, engrossed as they were in their dull conversations.

'Angy,' he whispered in her ear, 'would you like another?'

'No thank you.' She turned to the person clasping her elbow.

'Mrs Radcliffe, if the little pink book dangling from your wrist has not been filled in for the next dance, may I have the pleasure? That is, with your husband's permission.' Blonde eyebrows quizzed Jeffrey.

'Well I ... thank you Nathan, but Jeffrey and I ... we ...' desperately she looked from Nathan to her husband, but Jeffrey with a smile and a flourish of the hand said;

'My pleasure. I hope she doesn't tread on your toes as much as she did on mine.' He drifted away to a group of fellow Officers.

'Darlings,' said Blaize, catching sight of them weaving toward the dance floor, 'What have you two naughty things done with Minthami? Oh, there she is, among the big noises. Nathan darling, you look simply divine if not sanguine in your penguin suit, lucky Amagyi-Angela! But don't forget to come back to ask me to dance, as I simply adore men in evening dress — and a handsome one like you just sends me all of a flutter ... coming, Major Braithwaite. Yes, I know this next waltz is ours.' She pulled a face and departed to her Major's arms.

'She never changes does she?' Nathan remarked, taking Angela in his arms. 'One of these days Lady Bee's going to burst into flames. I don't think I've ever had the pleasure of dancing with an English princess before, and honey, you sure look like one tonight,' he remarked chivalrously.

She inclined her head to his gracious compliment, 'Thank you Nathan, you really are a Southern gentleman at heart. However, this English princess could never hold a candle to a Shan one.' She added in all sincerity, 'And I'm not as real as Minthami, in fact, I'll probably vanish at midnight underneath my veil of English cold-cream.'

He chuckled. 'So that's the secret behind the freckles. Who's the Britisher behind all that insignia, regalia and what not?' he asked her, nodding his head in Sir Boland's direction.

'Goodness me, Nathan, didn't you know you were talking to Mandalay's new Garrison Commander?'

'Well I guessed he was pretty high up on the ladder of Britishers they send out here, what with everyone bowing and scraping in front of him. Puts me in mind of Mindon Min with shoes on — same difference, the hierarchy never change.'

She smiled. 'Didn't Lady Dorothy ask you what she asked me?'

'What did she ask you?' He looked down at her with one of his charmingly indulgent smiles designed to make her a little more dizzy. Through her champagne-touched breathlessness, she responded to his latent sexuality, doubly aware of it, while calling herself a fool for wanting to be enticed by him as, coolly, he pretended to a business partnership with her and nothing more.

'She would like the Shwe Emporium to stock brushed cotton underwear from Manchester. Her circulation's bad — even in Mandalay.' Angela said, deadly serious about Lady Dorothy's preferences.

'Honey, if she's the British Commander's wife like she says she is, she can have her drawers lined in ermine if that's what she wants.'

'No, I don't think she's that decadent. Nathan, why did you come here tonight when you've never before deigned to show your face at our 'British' functions which you're always making fun of!' She gave a little hiccough on the crest of champagne-bubbles she had swallowed too fast.

'Do I detect a typically "British" dig at me Amagyi-Angela? Well, if you must know honey, I came by royal command. Since your new Commanding lady included *Mrs* de Veres-Vorne on her gilt-edged invitation, I had to obey the voice of authority, didn't I? After all, I'm only an American in your country, ma'am, so I've got to mind my p's and q's now. I just thought I'd come along on this occasion to see what you Britishers get up to in your spare time when you're not chucking polo-balls, hockey-balls and cricket-balls all over the Maidan of Empire.'

'And now you know?'

'Yep, and now I know. Besides, I never miss me an opportunity to do a little business whenever I can. But I reckon I'll have to watch my step otherwise I can see that if I don't, some little lady with an eye to the main chance is going to come along and bite the hand that feeds her.'

'I'd never bite your hand Nathan, I require it to sign too many chittys. Where did you learn to dance? I thought you were always too busy to bother with the social graces you find so boring.'

'They are boring — that's why I ran away from home.' His blue eyes crinkled with mischief. 'Before I was seventeen years old ma'am, my lady-mother at Baton Rouge kept the slaves highly amused by trying to teach Courtney and me the social graces. She kept a dancing-master especially — among a lot of other kinds of masters who made my flesh creep. But I must say, it was never this enjoyable experience.' His arm tightened imperceptibly. At that moment too, the waltz finished

494

and with a disappointed shrug he led her back to Jeffrey standing among his brother Officers.

'But then, if we let them,' Reggie Rowanbottom's effeminate tones carried to them, 'the natives will get everywhere, and we can't allow that sort of thing to happen. Dash it all, I mean, look over there ... the gel in the blue longyi. Someone's native piece they've brought here tonight and dashed bad form in my opinion.'

Angela froze. Nathan's expression did not change, only the light in his eyes. He turned around to find out who had made such a remark. Blaize's little group of friends remained suspended, glasses and conversation poised in the balance.

Nathan laid a heavy hand on Reggie Rowanbottom's epaulette. 'Apologize,' he said between his teeth.

Adjutant Rowanbottom turned a plump red face to Nathan and pushing down his fat red lower lip in an attitude of disdain shrugged off Nathan's hand; 'Apologize? What for, sir?'

'Apologize,' Nathan repeated, cold and hard as vitrified enamel.

Adjutant Rowanbottom openly sneered in Nathan's face: 'To whom and for what must I tender my apologies, sir?' With a lordly air he looked down his snub nose at Nathan, thrusting out his jaw pugnaciously; 'I don't believe we've been introduced. Who and what are you sir?'

'I, sir, am Nathanial de Veres-Vorne, citizen of the United States of America and trader of goods in Mandalay. The *piece* in the blue longyi to whom you refer happens to be my wife, *Sir!*' He bellowed in Reggie Rowanbottom's face, their chins almost touching.

'I — I — I ...' Adjutant Rowanbottom's complexion changed from the colour of his tunic to puce. He turned to his friends; 'Is this upstart trades-wallah allowed to come in here and cause a scene like this? Bearer ...' He clicked fingers in the Indian's direction, 'Get this man out of here.' He turned back to Nathan. 'I'm not in the habit of apologizing on behalf of the native populace.'

Nathan's fist connected with Adjutant Rowanbottom's chin. The blow knocked him out and his eyes glazed as he crumpled into the arms of Captain Stiggins standing behind him. A woman screamed, the Bearer dropped the tray of brimming glasses and pandemonium ensued as two men leapt on Nathan to restrain him from punching a man who was already down.

'*Get those men out of here!*' Colonel, Sir Boland Dawlish commanded in stentorian tones.

Military police sprang on Nathan, dragging him away from the soldiers.

Angela, mortified, looked for Minthami in the crowd of disgusted spectators and found her abandoned, on the fringes of British and Anglo India's high society, her trembling hands pressed to her mouth as, wide-eyed and utterly stricken, she helplessly observed her husband being tossed ignominiously out of the Hall. Angela went to her side and, taking her hand, dragged her away.

Nathan, flung headlong out of Fort Dufferin, finished his fight with Reggie Rowanbottom's comrades on the West Bridge and thereafter found himself tossed into the moat to cool off.

Minthami wept uncontrollably, her delicate frame shuddering in misery. She had looked so beautiful, so proud and happy when she had entered the Hall beside Nathan. Angela felt she would never forgive him for this. She asked Jeffrey to summon them a tonga to take Minthami home and while he was searching for one, Blaize, who had rushed outside with portly Major Braithwaite, said breathlessly; 'I knew this was bound to happen. The moment I saw him bring her into the ballroom, I knew he was itching for a fight with someone. Darling, sometimes he really is a very stupid man.'

'I agree,' Jeffrey remarked, having found the tonga into which he assisted Minthami. 'He ought not to have subjected her to such a calculated insult. In a month of Sunday mornings I'll never understand the American mentality.'

Angela rounded on them both and said fiercely: 'Why

496

must you always talk about *her* in the third person? Why must you always pretend *she* doesn't exist! Look at Minthami, go on, take a good look at her. She's a human being too, flesh and blood, and not the outsider. We are the outsiders! This is her country and her city! Now just leave us alone, please. Go back to the Ball.'

'Angela,' Blaize said, not helping one bit. 'For goodness sake darling don't upset yourself so much. It will all blow over by tomorrow, just you wait and see. Everyone will forget all about this little gurrh-burrh by tiffin tomorrow, and I guarantee Reggie'll be around at Whitewalls to shake hands with Nathan — though it was his fault for having provoked him in the first place.' She fell back a pace as the tonga-driver got the horse moving and Angela heard her say; 'Come along Major Braithwaite, let's find my husband and ask him to try and salvage all our reputations with Sir Boland after this tacky end to what was a perfectly delightful evening.'

And the tackiness of the evening Angela could only lay at Nathan's door.

CHAPTER
THIRTY-FIVE

ONE

'Amagyi-Angela,' said Minthami, 'please tell tonga-driver to go to Mahamuni Pagoda instead of to house.' She said nothing more until the tonga-driver had taken his leisurely plodding time through the wide streets of Mandalay to the Mahamuni which was quite a distance from Fort Dufferin. Then, when they had drawn up in front of the Pagoda steps she patted Angela's hand. 'You good woman, Amagyi-Angela.' she said 'Sometimes it is they who do not understand us. But Minthami, she never understand Shwe Nat, never. Maybe Amagyi-Angela can do better job than Minthami who has not got Western mind like husband. I go now. Minthami will be all right and very happy with Lord Buddha who understand many troubles. Pyan-dor-may.'

She slipped down from the tonga and removing her pretty bejewelled sandals tossed them into the gutter before running barefoot up the moonlit steps of the Mahamuni where Angela knew she would find solace among her own people.

Angela, her hands clasped in the lap of her white satin gown sighed helplessly. Lady Dorothy Dawlish, mild and harmless, would no doubt be upset too, knowing she had been the cause of the fiasco by having unwittingly issued Captain Nathanial de Veres-Vorne his gilt-edged invitation as one of Mandalay's leading European figures, with no conception that Mrs de Veres-Vorne was a Burmese lady.

Angela asked the tonga-driver to take her to White-walls.

She found Nathan in his drawing-room dripping moat-water on his marble floor. Knuckle-grazed, blood-streaked and filthy, his evening-suit and silk shirt were in tatters, his bow-tie, undone, hung loosely round his neck. A wonderful plum-dark weal under his left eye proclaimed the start of a very ugly and painful face for the morrow.

Hearing the tap of her heels on his marble tiles he whirled to confront her, a glass of whisky in his hand.

'Ha! The pure white Buddhist nun has arrived in the guise of avenging angel. What can I do for you Amagyi-Angel? Tell me what I've been longing to hear all these years, how I can once more pleasure you by offering you the services of the *Nat*-stud of the year,' he sneered, swaying a little.

'You're drunk Nathan.'

'Just because your husband's a behind-the-curtain alcoholic, don't come in here preaching the gospel to me.'

'Leave Jeffrey out of this.'

'Go to hell, Angela. Go to hell with the rest of your snooty-nosed breed.' He flung himself onto his white couch, regardless of his wet clothes.

'You're a moral coward, Nathan. Just because the British rescinded your teak-export licence granted you by Mindon Min, you didn't have to use your wife to hit back at them.'

'What the hell are you talking about?'

'I know you by now, Nathan. And Blaize's right. You are a very stupid man sometimes. How could you have done it? How could you possibly have subjected Minthami to such a humiliating and ugly experience?'

His eyes blazing, he almost flung his glass at her. 'God damn you, Angela! Don't you talk about Minthami. None of you, not even you, are fit to mention her name — she at least is a lady. Go to hell, get out of here, go on! I don't want to see you again or your precious husband in all his fine regalia, badges and medals and whatnot like that fine Sir Colonel something or other and the rest — including the Tennent-Brownes, Rowanbum and his battalion of namby-pamby wet-chinned individuals who now run this country.'

'Don't be childish!'

'Christ, Angela!' He stood up, slopping whisky over what had once been a white shirt-cuff; 'You're as bad as the rest of them. You stood meekly by like that ninny husband of yours and said nothing in defence of Minthami or her country. Your lot took over as though it were your God-given right! I wasn't going to let some bumptious half-wit like that Rowanbottom get away with insulting *my* wife. You and your sort make me sick. Now get out of here and go home to your weak-chinned husband who can't cock it up in his wife's bed, only with his catamites!'

'How *dare* you Nathan!' She took great exception to his remarks even though she remained ignorant of the word catamite.

'Oh, come off it Angela. Don't be such a bloody hypocrite. Face up to reality sometimes will you. I know what kind of marriage you've got yourself, but that's probably the way you like it.'

She stepped forward and dashed his glass out of his hand. It went flying across the room to splinter on the tiles while he, as enraged as she, took her by the shoulders and tossed her back onto his wet couch while he stood above her and dared her to move.

'You listen to me Nathan Vorne,' she stormed, reviling him bitterly. 'Were I a man I'd do to you what you did to Reggie Rowanbottom. I can't begin to describe to you how despicable you are. You used Minthami — you used her for your own vile purposes like you use everyone. You came to Fort Dufferin tonight for one reason only, and that was to ape the grand master of Mandalay with your Shan princess waved like a banner in front of the British. But it didn't work, did it Nathan? You thought you'd go one better than they, didn't you? But when you found out you were nothing, nothing, in this city despite your grandiose claims to being Mandalay's magnificent millionaire and premier personage who can please himself, your nose was put out of joint. Your money and glamour proved not to be the calling-card you had intended them to be, eh Nathan? And the only one to suffer humiliatingly in front of everyone was your Shan princess whom nobody gives a damn about! I despise you.'

'By God, you're a patronizing little bitch.' He glared, pushing her down again because she had moved. 'Don't you talk to me about using people, Mrs Radcliffe. You've used Minthami and me. You used Matthew, and you're now using Jeffrey to get at me,' he told her, emphasizing every word with harsh precision. 'Sit down, damn you!' He flung her back. 'You're going to hear me out, Madam, before you leave this house. Now just you listen to me, my cold white Memsahib, I might look wet behind the ears to you, but I know the difference between what's a virgin and what isn't ... Ah!' His two hands thrust her shoulders roughly against the back of the couch. 'Don't say one bloody word about it because I don't want to know who did what to you as I'm simply not interested. Just get this into your head, Amagyi-Angela, the willingness of your capitulation into my arms on the banks of the Irrawaddy often made me wonder why, until I discovered you used me to take away some miserable experience whose shameful memories you wanted me to destroy for you. How fortunate for you that you actually enjoyed the experience a second time round, but next time it'll be on *my* terms not yours. So don't talk about my using Minthami — I know who I'd prefer in my bed any day, because you're dead Angela, as dead as a bloody herring and you're afraid of being resurrected.'

This time as her hand came up, he grabbed her wrist; 'You're getting mighty fond of doing that aren't you honeychile?' he said, taking both her wrists to haul her up beside him. His smile grim and determined, he held one arm behind her back for safe-keeping, the other he forced down between them, his leg pressing hard against her skirts so that her hand would be perfectly aware of him as a man. 'What's it to be this time, spiritual rape?' His mouth against her ear tormented; 'Go on if you must, kick, bite, scream, shout, oh yes, Amagyi-Angela, what a gold-plated little hypocrite you are. The Buddhist Convent was only the extension of that puristic Women's Academy of yours, wasn't it? So, whatever those places taught you about God's will, Allah's will or Buddha's will, they sure did one hell of a great job in twisting up your character, didn't they?' His mouth took hers without gentleness.

His fingers playing upon the soft roundness of her breasts thrusting above the low neckline of her gown, found the cold hardness of the ruby necklace. Raising his head to look at her in genuine appraisal, he slipped aside the low-cut shoulders of her evening gown, his smile one of supreme confidence in his assessment of her. 'I think "striking" suits you much better than any other word, Amagyi-Angela — yes, a striking woman. The kind of intangible beauty best left unadorned — or at the very least diamonds at your throat, not spinels ... though preferably lips. Don't fight me, I want you as much as you need me, honeychile ...'

Prisoners both on a sudden bright flame of desire, his lips against the pulse of her throat he murmured, 'Lust, Angela, pure unadulterated lust is what makes us both fight so frustratingly.'

She knew she would be lost in another few moments, the tunnel of retreat closed to her forever, the betrayal of everything she had striven for despite the odds, the measure of contentment she had at least gleaned by refusing to compromise on any score, fled on the folly of vain desires and promises. 'If you don't take your hands off me, Captain Vorne,' Angela said, chilling them both in the intensity of her scorn for him, 'I swear the moment I walk out of here I'll inform my husband of your behaviour, and then, it won't be the moat into which you'll be thrown, but a cell with bars for assaulting a woman of the Colonel-Sahib.'

Had she struck him with her bare hands a dozen times

and more she knew she could not have inflicted any greater pain on his battered flesh and ego. He stepped away from her in a daze, looking at her as if not quite believing she were the same woman and on the swift intake of pained breath silenced by the pressure of his thumb against his top teeth — a habit that came to him easily, said: 'My God ... Angela!'

With one finally withering glance that killed the flame forever in his deep blue eyes as he tried to make sense of her cruel rejection, he could only remain dumbfounded as she swept regally from his house.

TWO

The following morning at nine o'clock Jeffrey stormed into Angela's bedroom at Sequoia. 'Where the devil did you get to last night?' he demanded in a rare fit of unbridled temper. The fact that he had been riding did not make Angela feel any the happier, knowing who his companions were likely to have been. His arms full of equipment, he banged shut the bedroom door with the heel of his boot.

'Where do you think I was, Jeffrey,' she said, without looking up from her teacup and newspaper. 'At the Ball.'

'Playing Cinderella to Prince Charming, I suppose?' He flung everything, including her evening paraphernalia onto the unmade bed. 'I've just come from Whitewalls where I gave my horse into the care of Nathan Vorne's syce, since he offered me the use of his stables, and what do I find — relayed by a servant boy? That my wife has left her cloak, gloves and evening-bag on the master's couch! You deserve to be horse-whipped, Madam.' He brandished that article threateningly, the one item he had retained in his hand.

'And you'd just love to do it, wouldn't you Jeffrey,' she retorted, goading him, regarding him then as contemptuously as she had subjugated Nathan. 'I haven't been married to you for the past year without being aware of your moonlight shikars with Captain Groby. You weren't here last night, so don't you start accusing me of anything.' She turned her back on him and poured herself another cup of tea, her hand unsteady. Her breakfast tray placed on a bamboo table underneath the window, Angela cast weary eyes upon her bright front garden, noticing how the roses required to be dead-headed; later, she thought, later.

'You listen to me, my dear woman,' Jeffrey came behind her menacingly, his hands heavy on her shoulders. She shrank from his touch and her elbow knocked over the milk jug, the stream of liquid pouring into her lap, soaking her nightgown. 'I was a damn fool, to be taken in by your sweet innocent airs,' he said. 'You're no better than all those fat pasty-faced Mems with their vile tongues and gross bodies making trouble for everyone. You're just as filthy and tainted as they. You're not the moral, upright, good Buddhist nun I thought you were, are you Angy? Did you enjoy being on the receiving end of the Captain's prowess last night, eh Angy?' His smile was malicious.

Too much to bear, Angela flung the contents of her teacup into his face. 'Don't come here threatening me with your jungle-tactics, because it's you who have made a mockery of our marriage, not I. Neither did I know what ... what kind of pervert I had married,' she said bitterly.

He dashed the hot tea from his eyes with his sleeve before he took her chin in ruthlessly strong fingers. Even this early he had been at the bottle and Angela could smell the whisky on his breath. His bright spurs, polished for hours by Janum's painstaking hand to always keep his lord and master looking like a fashion plate, his high boots, jodpurs and once immaculate white shirt now tea-stained, everything to lend him such a lordly masculine appearance on the strength of his lush cavalry moustache, made her want to laugh in the realization of how little it all meant beneath the veneer.

Viciously he turned her head to face him. 'You are an

exciting woman when you're aroused Angy, my sweet. But I want you to be aware of two things. I married you for two very basic reasons; propriety and promotion. You came into my life at a very opportune moment. I required the respectability and stability of your dear little hand in mine at the altar, the dutiful presence of a wife beside me in my step up the ladder of ambition, a woman having her uses on occasions. But presence is all I require Angy, not body.' His hands slipped down to cup her breasts, fingers and thumbs cruelly teasing her nipples while he smirked. 'These simply do nothing whatever for me. However, what I do is no concern of yours — we agreed upon that — as we agreed that I would be marrying a good pure wholesome creature fresh from a nunnery. So, if I catch you at Whitewalls ever again, you see this hand of mine,' he turned it over in front of her face, 'full of callouses, square and blunted for its trained purpose? And this edge of it,' he placed his palm sideways against her neck in a cutting movement, 'has been used to kill a man quickly, quietly and cleanly. No fuss, no noise, no mess, just a gentle little exhalation of life because he wouldn't do as he was told. So don't flaunt that body of yours in front of other men and certainly not before the landlord, my dear, because just think what this hand could do to that pretty flower-stalk neck of yours.'

'You're mad, Jeffrey,' she pushed his hand aside.

He moved away and took out his cigarette case. Taking one, a little smile hovering, he lit up and inhaling deeply, blew smoke to the ceiling and sniffed. 'Oh dear, such a shame, fell down the stairs and broke her dear sweet neck ... it's been known to happen. Remember Mistress Amy Robsart and the Queen's lover? Why, even good Queen Bess accepted the broken neck story.'

'You really are mad,' Angela said, her nerves frayed after the row she had had with Nathan, destroying them both with an irrevocable wounding mightier than the sword. But to be accused by Jeffrey of some crime she had not committed was all the more laughable, all the more ironic. 'Go away. Go back to Captain Groby and your midnight drinking parties, but leave me alone.'

He picked a flake of tobacco from his tongue, using his thumb and forefinger in a neat gesture calculated to irritate her even more. 'What were you doing at his house last night, eh Angy?' He waited, arms across his soiled shirt while he smoked.

Too weary to argue with him anymore, her conscience perfectly clear despite what he and the rest of the world thought about her and Nathan Vorne, she turned back to the *Rangoon Gazette* and replied, 'If you settled your bills with him, I wouldn't have to do it — and I wish that were the truth of the matter!'

She was caught unawares, his reaction totally unexpected. He tossed his half-smoked cigarette out of the window and pouncing, lifted her bodily from her chair to fling her face first onto the bed. He held her down, his moustache tickling her cheek.

'So that is it? Wishful thinking? Mental adultery?'

'Let me go, Jeffrey. Release me at once.'

'I too have been doing some thinking Angy, and I've reached the conclusion I'm wasting you. All these lovely sweet curls — as pretty as a choirboy's.' He fingered her hair, snuggling his face into them, cooing the kind of blandishments in her ear she would rather not have listened to. 'Long straight legs, unfleshy hips. I think Angy, as I've got myself such a fire-cat wife, I'd better put her to some use even if she's not quite as pure as the driven snow. It's about time you and I had a child to stop the sordid little things people love repeating — although, if we paid any heed at all to the evil Mems and their gossiping tongues, there wouldn't be a brave fellow left to defend the Empire, would there?'

She hissed through her teeth while he kept her pinned flat, 'Go away! Get back to your ... to your catamites!' She tusselled with him while he tore her clothing, begging 'Don't Jeffrey, don't'. She sobbed as he reached for the riding-whip he had thrown on the bed.

She tried to escape him, but he only laughed in her

face as panting, she dodged him round the bed: 'If you use that on me,' she screamed, not caring if Janum, or Vanda next door could hear, 'I'll take you to your Commanding Officer and then let's see where your promotion will be.' She made for the door but not quickly enough.

'Oh no, that won't do at all,' he laughed as he locked the bedroom door and pocketed the key. He came towards her, crop in his left hand, the glint in his eye making her shudder. He looked so crazy and uncontrolled in a way she had never seen him before, his gentle and graceful manners replaced by this bizarre behaviour she was at a loss to understand.

'Don't ... you, not with that ... don't you strike me with that ... don't you lay a finger on me,' she gasped, cringing from him as he came stealthily for her, smiling cruelly, reminding her of a cobra ready to strike her down dead, or worse.

'Oh no,' he repeated, highly amused by her sudden fright, 'I'm not going to touch you, I'm not going to leave a single mark on you, I'm an Intelligence Officer remember?'

THREE

Hate and loathing encompassed her yet again. She did not revile him as much as she reviled herself for having taken the wrong path. Yes, she told herself in revulsion, she had indeed cut off her nose to spite her face.

In the lamplight, when the moths and other night insects flickered inside glass domes and Jeffrey had woken from the drunken stupor he had gradually worked himself into during the course of the day, she went to his bedside and standing over him said, 'Jeffrey, I want to tell you something.'

He blinked heavy eyes and raised his head to look at her, his chin unshaven, all his attractiveness dissipated in debauchery and drink. Resembling nothing like the man she had married a year ago, he put up a lethargic arm to

507

shield his eyes against the glare from the living-room in which she had been writing some letters.

'What, dear sweet Angy?' he asked, patting the bed. 'Come and sit beside me and tell me all about it as you were such a good obedient girl whom I have forgiven.'

'I'd prefer to stand,' she answered, her manner and voice filled with the frost of disgust. 'Jeffrey, I just want you to know that nothing you do shocks me. I'm immune to anything you can do to me. I know what some men can be like, and how far the human being can sink while the human soul shrinks and is lost beyond recall in its depravity. Some years ago, on my way from Delhi to Burma, the missionaries with whom I was travelling were ambushed and killed by a wandering band of thugs. The men were killed to be precise, while the girl with me, and myself, we were both raped by the Bo leader. I had a child, a daughter born at the Sasana Convent. When she was old enough, I sent her to England in the care of two Irish nuns who had been visiting the Sasana at the time, and they placed her with an elderly couple. She is ten years old this year. The nuns have written to me concerning Thania's unhappiness — her substitute parents are not only illiterate, but also unkind to her, and all they have is the money I remit to them each month. I haven't much money left to keep her in a better place as it has dwindled through the years. I'm not asking, but informing you of my intention; I want Thania to come to Mandalay to live with us and to be brought up as your adopted daughter — yours and mine. There are thousands of homeless children in England and we're offering our home out here to one of them — a common enough occurrence, so no one in Mandalay need ever suspect anything out of the ordinary by such an arrangement. I believe she's an intelligent child, so she will be told only the things we want her to know. When she's old enough I'll tell her the true circumstances of her birth. At the moment she doesn't know I exist because the nuns handle all the finances and everything else for me. When she comes here she will address us as her mother and father, and I want you to participate in that paternal role.' Angela took a deep breath and maintaining her unswerving stance said in conclusion: 'I'm writing now to the nuns to inform them of my decision to have Thania here with me. Now I know you have a daughter in England, Jeffrey, and I'm fully aware too of what kind of skeleton you're keeping in your cupboard. I happened to come across one day some papers of yours and while meaning never to pry, my attention was drawn to a letter while I was tidying your desk. It was asking for fees to be remitted to them, medical fees. Your daughter is sick with a mental disease you want no one to know about, and the fact that she's cared for in a mental institution in England rather detracts from the glamourous image you've built around yourself.' She paused. 'However, I fully understand you don't want any kind of gossip circulating around the Garrison, or Mandalay in general, regarding the imbecile child you fathered and were left stranded with on her mother's death. But if you raise any objections to having Thania here, or try to humiliate me anymore, I'll leave you, and the scandal I shall raise from here to Dum-Dum, will never get you the Colonecy you so badly desire. That's all I wish to say upon the subject.' Angela turned her back on him and banged the bedroom door on the way out.

FOUR

Five months later, when the monsoon season was in full spate, Angela took one of the I.F.C. ferries down to Rangoon to meet Thania's ship. The girl had travelled in the care of the ship's nurse, and Angela, reclaiming her daughter after nine years, experienced a stab of remorse plus an infinite sense of relief. Thania was so nondescript there was nothing in that frightened little stick of humanity to identify her with anyone. Her hair, severely parted in the middle, hung in two ropes of plaited straw either side of her pale little face while the colour of her eyes were lost to view in her constant squinting.

'Thania,' said Angela whilst shopping in the Shwe Emporium, Rangoon, for some decent clothes for the child, 'is there something wrong with your eyesight?'

'The light is very bright and hurts my eyes,' she replied, adding helpfully, 'I'm only used to the dark.'

Startled, Angela looked down at the little scrap; 'What do you mean, child?'

'My mother and father never let me have a candle madam. When it got dark I sat on the window-seat to read. I like reading. But when it got too dark to see anymore I had to put my book away — but I did try to stay by the light as long as possible.'

'Well, we must take you to see an occulist while we're in Rangoon and get your eyes tested. Would you like a doll instead of that horrid piece of dirty rag you're clutching?'

'No thank you madam,' said Thania, and for the first time, widened her eyes in alarm as she clutched her scrap of pink blanket closer in the only piece of loving she wanted. Not wishing to press the issue lest she upset the girl, Angela changed the subject; 'Thania, were you happy with the people you called mother and father?'

'Sometimes I was, sometimes I wasn't. They were very old and needed someone like me to look after them, I called them my mother and father because I had to.'

'What else did the nuns tell you?'

'They told me my real mother had given me away when I was a baby because she couldn't look after me, so that's why I had to live with my other father and mother till my real mother came back for me. But she would only do that if I was really good, then she wouldn't beat me or give me away again.'

Angela drew up short in one of the Shwe Emporium's aisles and stooping, took the little girl by the shoulders, 'Thania, look at me. No don't squint, look at me properly.' She did so, obedient if anything. 'I'm your mother,' Angela told her, hoping desperately she was doing the right thing.

'I know,' the child said simply.

'You know?' Taken aback by her perspicacity Angela asked, 'How do you know?'

Thania nodded like a little sage; 'Sometimes I can feel things when people tell me lies. I know when it's true or not. I know you're my mother but you don't want other people to know you're my mother and that's why you gave me away. But I knew you would come back for me when it was all right. Was it because my father died?' She peered into Angela's face, her own funny little face heartbreakingly endearing while she screwed up her eyes to see more clearly. Angela swallowed hard, feeling utterly demoralized in the presence of this little thing, her own flesh and blood; 'Yes Thania. But Jeffrey's going to be your new father now so you must address him as papa. For the moment you are our adopted daughter, because it will be far simpler to leave things as they are, now that everyone in Mandalay has heard Jeffrey and I are adopting a homeless child from England, since we have no children of our own. But only Jeffrey, you and I, know you're my real daughter, Thania, and we must keep it like that for the time being, do you understand?'

'Yes.'

'You're not unhappy that we brought you to this foreign country to live with us, are you?'

'Oh no,' she gave a little smile. 'I didn't like it where I was, specially when it was cold and dark in the winter and I'd have to get up early to light the fires and do the housework before I went to school. It's nice and hot here so I don't think I will get beaten so much if the fires aren't lit before I go to school.'

Again the knife twisting in Angela's heart sent her scurrying from emotional deadlock by thinking of something else to change the subject. 'Come along then, if you don't want that rag doll, let's go and find someone to test your eyesight.'

The Indian occulist examined Thania's eyes thoroughly and smilingly said; 'Nothing to worry about

Memsahib. Only a little weakness in one eye that will get better in time. She does not need spectacles. To exercise the eyes will be of far more value to the muscles. And of course to eat plenty of carrots.'

'I would prefer her to be fitted with glasses in order to prevent any more eyestrain when she reads,' Angela insisted.

He shrugged. 'That can be arranged, Memsahib. Come back in four hours time and I will have the spectacles ready for the little girl. But eat plenty carrots too,' he adjured, patting Thania's shoulder before they left the dispensary.

On the boat back to Mandalay Angela said to Thania, 'You must still go to school everyday, Thania, just like other boys and girls. When the new year starts in October I've arranged for you to attend a little English school at a nice town called Maymyo. It's not far from Mandalay, only about forty miles or so, and I'll come once a month to visit you at the school. Naturally you'll spend your holidays at Sequoia with Jeffrey and me — that's when he's home on leave of course. I can't have you at home all day because I have a little job of work to do, and I think you're far too old for an ayah — that's an Indian nanny. But I think you'll like Maymyo because it's rather like England though sunnier and warmer, although they do have frost in the winter and have to light fires, but you won't have to do any of that.' She looked down at the old head on young shoulders and asked, 'Do you think you'll be happy with that arrangement?'

Thania, peering over the boat rail with her new glasses because she wanted to see the flying fish in the river, put her pink blanket to her nose with one hand while the other she shyly slipped into Angela's hand; 'I promise to be very happy and very good madam.'

With a lump in her throat Angela said more sharply than she had intended, 'You may call me mama, Thania.'

WHERE THE CHINTHE ROARS

1896

CHAPTER
THIRTY-SIX

ONE

Nathan did not like the look of the water seeping through the retaining walls of his loading and unloading bays, saturating the floors of his godowns. Ten years before, when Mandalay had flooded badly with some loss of life, the Bund had been reinforced by British soldiers after the surrounding countryside had been awash for days. Flooding of the Irrawaddy had always been Mandalay's biggest problem as it had been built on such flat land. King Mindon Min, for that reason, had had the Bund constructed as a precautionary measure against the frequent flooding of the river that served his city. Nathan's warehouses along the upper stretch of the river past Go Wain had been severely damaged during that time ten years before, but they had been reinforced and the damage repaired. Since then, with the driving heat on corrugated iron roofs all day long, the stone walls of the godowns were beginning to show marked cracks and fissures, the rainy season also leaving a further legacy of damage as each year went by.

Ten years was a long time and both Nathan and Angela were dubious about any more 'patching' work to keep the godowns standing. After much discussion and costing they agreed larger and more modern warehouses were required. Nathan immediately set about calling in an English surveyor and Italian engineer, both men renowned for their ability in river-engineering.

Nathan asked for his old godowns to be temporarily

515

reinforced and repaired while the new building work was being carried out alongside so that he did not have to transfer his rice, grams and other perishable commodities elsewhere.

The experts' opinion was that his loading and unloading bays would have to be drained so that the retaining walls of the river could be repaired first.

'That's wonderful,' Nathan replied sarcastically, 'and how do we do that considering there's no lock-system on the Irrawaddy?'

'Hydraulic pumps and a rock-fill dam to hold back this quiet stretch of water, Captain Vorne, nothing at all elaborate. It will take hardly any time at all, so your boats won't be put to any great inconvenience,' the Italian engineer informed him.

Meanwhile the English surveyor had taken a good look round the old godowns and reached the conclusion that the stone walls could be strengthened with what he called deformed bars of twisted chamfered-square cross sections.

'That doesn't mean a thing to me,' Nathan told the Englishman. 'You do what you have to do. Get your recommendations into the hands of an architect for the new buildings and just do what you think is necessary in the meanwhile so that I don't have to mop up a gigantic rice pudding because the water's getting into my stocks. But just don't forget that at the height of the monsoon season, this river comes roaring full spate past these walls like a steam train across the prairies.'

'I've been working with this river, Captain de Veres-Vorne,' the Englishman said tersely, 'for the past ten years now, and I think I know what to expect from it.'

'Let's hope so,' was Nathan's comment, 'because I've been working with this river for nigh on thirty years and I still don't know what to expect from it.'

'Don't worry, Captain de Veres-Vorne, it will all be completed before the monsoon season next year. We'll make a start about November, December, when the river's at its lowest, and you'll have your new godowns by next May.'

'I just hope so — but I want the existing godowns repaired with the minimum of fuss and nonsense, so get your elephants down here as soon as possible — tomorrow if need be. Shift your twisted bars, blocks, pulleys and pumps and whatever else is necessary, but get moving because time costs me money.'

The two men disappeared with their tape-measures, pencils and notebooks, and Nathan turned to Angela who had come from her office to join him on the catwalk between the loading and unloading bays. 'I told you so, Nathan. I've been paddling in water for a week.' She smiled smugly as he had not wished to listen to her in the first place about the river undermining his godown foundations.

Observing the coolies still behaving like Holland's little boy by trying to plug the cracks in the retaining walls of the river with Portland cement, he smiled and said, 'So much fuss about nothing. Look at them Mrs Radcliffe. They're doing a grand job botching.' He turned on his heel and walked into her office. Nathan took out his pipe and tamped tobacco into the bowl. 'Honey, now you're sure you can cope with everything while I'm gone?' he asked with concern when she had reseated herself at her desk to go through a pile of invoices, an overhead fan driven by steam making her comfortable office a nice place in which to linger. He hesitated in lighting his pipe, sniffing something in the air with appreciation. 'What's the smell?' he asked inquisitively. 'It's certainly not eau-de-cologne.'

'Tsarevna. Jeffrey bought it for me.'

'What a wanton man! Getting back to my question, will you be all right while I'm in America?'

'Why shouldn't I be? Haven't I managed well enough in your past absences?'

'Indeed you have ma'am, indeed you have,' he said with one of his lazy smiles that hadn't changed with the passing of the years. 'I'll be away a long time this time, honey. Try and be a good girl while I'm gone and I might raise your salary when I come home. And mind they make me a good job of my godowns. I give you full permission to do what you think fit, but hold you responsible for any botch-up. I'll see you tomorrow honey, before I set sail for Rangoon.' He took up his sun-helmet, wasting time while he re-adjusted the chin strap and then, because she did not look up again or say anything else, he went out and closed the office door in rather an abrupt manner. Only then did she raise her eyes to his hasty departure, watching him with his sola-topi under his arm so that the shining glory of his head was revealed by the lighter strands of age as grey displaced the golden. His body too was heavier, maturer than the lithe young man of Loloi days springing up to rescue her from the claws of a man-eating tiger and, with a rueful little twist of her lips as destiny still defied her, she went back to what she was doing. She tried, as the Buddhists had taught her, to put the spiritual in place of the physical by the medium of meditation; she meditated upon the long curly rows of Burmese numerals on the piece of paper in front of her, but too many desires filled the spaces in between.

TWO

Jeffrey had arrived home three days earlier than she had expected. Angela was altogether dismayed to see him lounging on the verandah in his planter's chair, beside him on the wooden floor the ubiquitous bottle of whisky and an accumulation of cigarette butts. Every time he came on leave, he seemed a little more jaundiced and a lot more reprehensible. The jungles of Burma did not appear to suit him and Angela wondered why on earth he had volunteered to stay on to do the hard task of helping man the northern territories and keeping the peace among the warring hilltribes, when he could have had a comfortable posting elsewhere. Not that she minded, for the very thought of being uprooted from

Mandalay which she had made her home, filled her with alarm.

'Hello Jeffrey,' she said, trying to sound cheerful as she ascended the verandah steps without looking at his perspiration-soaked khaki uniform and unshaven chin, 'I wasn't expecting you home today.'

'That's perfectly obvious,' he said, reaching for the whisky bottle by its neck and pouring himself half a tumblerful. 'I couldn't find a damn thing to eat in the house.' He tossed back the whisky. 'Quite the working little Mem I see. Still enjoying your native work, eh Angy?'

'Yes, thank you.' She took off her wide-brimmed straw hat and jabbed the long hat-pin through it before putting the hat down on the verandah table. 'We've been very busy lately, the godowns are in need of urgent repairs. We've had to call in an engineer, surveyor and architect to put the place in order. In the coming months I'm going to be kept even busier as Nathan's off to America, after which he's going to visit his sick mother in Ireland.'

'You haven't asked me about myself yet, Angy? Remember, I've been away three months.'

'How are you, Jeffrey?' she asked, her back to the wooden verandah post while her gaze wandered to her garden where hibiscus, poinsettias, canna lilies and marigolds made a riot of colour. She had even planted a papaya tree for good luck. Angela thought about Uncle Adrian Hawes then, and his love of gardens, so much so that he had employed a mâli to turn the Residency compound into something more than a barren landscape. While she could not rise to the extra expense of a mâli and did most of the gardening herself, she did have a boy who came in occasionally to weed and to water the garden for her. 'I must get Nathan's mâli's son to water the garden again,' she said, more to herself than to Jeffrey. 'We've had such a hot spell lately, everything has dried up even after the rains.'

'The rebel armies in the wake of Nyaung Ok have

been slashed to ribbons at last,' Jeffrey informed her with a grim smile. 'All along the Chindwin and as far back as Mawlaik. We're going to kick them all the way to Imphal — or even to the Jainta Pass.' He watched her expression with amusement.

'Well done, Jeffrey. Your excellent intelligence work is doing a grand job in paving the way for annihilation and mayhem all through Upper Burma for years to come. The Burmese, you know, will never give up. Not until they've reclaimed Burma for themselves, no matter how many soldiers Britain sends out from England.'

'You talk like a bally native.'

'Maybe that's what I've become.'

'No doubt influenced by that native enterprise called the de Veres-Vorne Company,' Jeffrey sneered. 'Its boss in particular, eh Angy?'

'Why are you always picking on Nathan when he's been more than generous to us?' Angela said, turning her head to look at him.

'To you, madam, not to me. Generous I agree, and obviously as payment for services rendered.' He got off the long-sleever, and went inside the bungalow where their five year-old son, just roused from sleep by the ayah, was happily playing on the living-room floor with a clockwork train given to him by Nathan. The metal tracks running from room to room annoyed Jeffrey who had stumbled more than once over Theo's toys. The next minute Angela heard a howl from Theo who had had his ears boxed by Jeffrey, and before she could race to his rescue, Jeffrey stuck his unshaven chin through the bead curtain in the doorway.

'Keep that child under control or by God I promise you he'll be sent home to England and confined in an institution for the rest of his life. I don't want to see or to hear him while I'm on leave. If he insists on playing under my feet, then he must expect to get trodden on and his toys smashed because I'm not a ballet-dancer about to go picking my way through my own house. Goddam it madam, can't a chap come home to a quiet leave without all hell breaking loose everytime ... and what's more, you're more interested, I notice, in keeping your skirts up for the fine landlord in his godowns than in keeping food and drink in my larder. I won't have anymore of your slap-happy housekeeping otherwise we'll be tasting the whip-lash once more, won't we Angy my sweet?'

'Jeffrey ...' her throat worked convulsively while tears smarted behind her eyes, 'Jeffrey, must you drink so much?'

'Yes Madam, I must! When I come home to a filthy house, ants in the food cupboard and not a confounded servant in sight, what do you expect me to do but to take to the bottle in disgust, eh? In a month of Sunday mornings, my dear, I don't know what I saw in you in the first place. Get your brat out of my sight while I get some sleep.'

'He's as much your brat as mine, Jeffrey.'

'And how do I know that for certain? You're a bag of lies, Angy. I don't know what to believe, especially when I realize what kind of whelp Thania is. For all I know Theo is of the same breed, the product of a loose woman.'

Provoked by that final insult she flung herself on him. Jeffrey, with one swift push, sent her sprawling to join Theo on the floor where he was drumming his small fists in temper and tears. 'I've told you before, Jeffrey,' Angela said while she gathered her son into her arms, 'not to impose your vile behaviour on us. I won't have it anymore.'

'*You* won't have it, *you* won't have it! Who are you Madam to tell me what I won't have? I give you one more warning Angy. I want a clean and decent home to come back to. I want servants in attendance at all times and I want your brats elsewhere. Now get him out of this house and take him to your grand master at Whitewalls where no doubt he rightfully belongs.'

'Damn you Jeffrey, damn you, damn you! How I wish to God that were true ... yes, I say it! I say it a million times because I know now what I lost, for you! *You* get out of this house, it's not yours but mine — *mine*! Nathan gave it me and it's not I who should go, but you. *My* house Jeffrey, the Title is in *my* name, so you get out because *I'm* evicting you, not Nathan. Come Theo, hush darling, it's going to be all right, everything's going to be all right, mama's here now.' She cradled him in her arms before taking him up to go in search of the ayah who was probably hiding somewhere in fear of her life since Jeffrey's arrival.

She found Regina cowering in the bathroom and said to her, 'Take Theo to Whitewalls and stay with him until I get back. Don't bring him back here until I fetch him.'

'Yes Memsahib.'

Angela, while Jeffrey slept off the effects of his bout of drinking, took his horse from Nathan's stables and rode away without stopping to find out if Nathan were home.

Regina found the old Chinese woman who was almost blind and crippled, and in the kitchen quarters of Whitewalls gave Theo some food and drink. Afterwards, Fee Tam, shuffling in her dotage went to the Captain's study with the child by the hand and told him that the mistress of Sequoia had left Theo there to be looked after. Fee Tam crinkled up her Chinese eyes even more, to say through toothless gums, 'She maybe go as always to Talaing Temple which is not velly safe place because of evil spilits.'

'All right Fee Tam,' Nathan said tersely, 'just look after him till I get back with his mother.' He saddled his horse himself, and taking his rifle set off in pursuit, knowing exactly where to go. Halfway to Ava, along the river-road, he came into a gloomy forest where there was an abandoned Thaton Temple the Burmese avoided like the plague because they believed evil spirits dwelt there.

Angela sat on one of the crumbling steps wearing her office-suit, one he always admired because she looked her efficient best in that smart navy-blue zouave jacket and skirt trimmed with white, her bright hair back to its former glory usually pinned up under her hat, though she was not wearing her hat now. Nathan, from behind a tree stood a long time observing her, the Queen of the Rangoon Chamber of Commerce who had proved to sceptical businessmen and the rough-tough merchant-traders of the world that she was not only good-looking but could match them any day in shrewd intelligence and business acumen. Still wary of getting too close to her, thereby involving himself in another emotional tangle, these days he preferred to do as she did, keep their relationship purely at a business level — only that now, in silent observation, he did not turn away but went to her side. 'Angela honey,' he took her hands from her face with gentle firmness, 'I hate to see you so unhappy.'

Dry-eyed she observed him: 'How did you know where to find me?'

'I always know where to find you, even if you don't think I do. I know you come here to get away from Jeffrey. Sometimes I follow you just to make sure you're all right and the jungle hasn't eaten you. Honey, I'm going away tomorrow and I have to talk to you. Come with me to America. We'll take Theo with us.'

She shook her head emphatically. 'Please don't tempt me Nathan. Jeffrey would never let me take Theo away, despite all his cruel railings against us. Anyway, I've hurt Minthami enough by stepping so readily into the place she ought to be occupying — beside you whenever you're in Mandalay.'

A flickering smile, he said, 'I hardly think Minthami's cut out to be woman-manager of the de Veres-Vorne Company. Anyway, she's much happier doing what she's always wanted to do, and that's follow your good example along the eight-fold path to Buddha after her butterfly-spirit of daughter and everything else eluded her.' His fingers became pollen-stained shredding the petals of a yellow flower growing through the broken mossy steps of the temple. 'You haven't hurt Minthami, Angela, so get that silly notion out of your head. If

523

anyone has, it's me ... tell me what's happened this time to make you so upset.'

She shook her head. 'I don't want to talk about it. It doesn't help.'

After a while he asked: 'Shall I have it out with him and biff him on the jaw like I once did to Reggie Rowan-bottom?'

She smiled. 'No Nathan. That wouldn't do at all. He'd only tell you to mind your own business.'

The silence between them became oppressive. So many things to say but both unwilling to make the first move for fear of being rebuffed, pride and kindnesses struggling with the intangible power of both their personalities vying for supremacy. Neither would give in first and so, in the end, Nathan said, 'Right, let's go. I don't fancy the jungle *nats* or the militia Jeffrey might send out after me. And there's going to be no moon tonight.'

He took up the gun laid to rest on the step below his feet and turning, lent her a hand to descend the crumbling steps. The merest pressure of her fingers made him pause for an instant to look down into her face. It was soft, beautiful and very sorrowful:

'Nathan,' she said, 'thank you for always being so constant where I've been concerned.'

In that statement there was almost a yearning, a reaching out of tentative fingers to tear his soul apart.

'What are friends for, Amagyi-Angela?'

THREE

Jeffrey brought home the little fox-terrier ostensibly for Theo — for having smashed his clockwork train, he said. Angela did not know what to make of the peace offering rendered at the expense of a small defenceless animal, nor the genuineness of his bid to make amends for his behaviour, to stop drinking and to treat her less like the dirt under his feet. She had experienced these moods of contrition before — it was so typical of Jeffrey's character. He wavered between beastliness and kindness, love and hate, turpitude and scruples, the extremities of his moods so unpredictable she was at a total loss.

In one week, however, she saw a marked change in him. He cut down on his drinking, his cursing and the vile accusations which had no substance to them, and resembled once again the rational human being she first knew. His step became lively, his appearance as neat and tidy as on that first day she had seen him standing in the cell door at Gue Gyoun Kamyo, his speech unslurred.

Angela buried her own antagonism and put herself out to meet him halfway in order to salvage anything that could be salvaged from the unhealthy and love-lost marriage in which she floundered.

Marbles the fox-terrier came to stay and Theo adored him. One morning Angela saw Jeffrey taking Marbles and Theo for a walk along the river road, the dog leaping and yapping in excitement at Jeffrey's heels while Theo strutted along proudly beside his father. Through the open-paling fence Angela could see Jeffrey with his walking-cane, pointing out different things to Theo as they strolled leisurely in the pleasant warmth — six o'clock in the morning being the loveliest part of the day.

'Long may peace prevail,' she muttered to herself, going inside from the verandah to take up her hat and bag before she set off for the godowns. That tiny framed cameo of Jeffrey and their small son she treasured in her mind always.

CHAPTER
THIRTY-SEVEN

ONE

Sa-Lon de Veres-Vorne, conspicuously handsome in a white tropical suit, sullenly presented his own fugue in time among the shadows of his father's drawing-room. He could not take his eyes off the girl seated at the grand piano, her fingers and her concentration rapt upon Liszt while her mother sat on the couch with her needlework.

Seventeen-year-old Thania Radcliffe, home for the Christmas holidays from her girls' school in Maymyo, came almost every day to Whitewalls to practise her music while her mother chaperoned. Sa-Lon knew that his father had given them the run of his house while he was away in America, and that both mother and daughter used the invitation to full advantage in order to keep their distance from the drunken sot at Sequoia who, in Sa-Lon's opinion, ought never to have arrived on the British armada that had captured Mandalay ten years ago.

Unable to bear his frustrations any longer, Sa-Lon turned on his heel with a glass of half-finished orange juice in his hand and, unsmiling, left the drawing-room for the verandah. Thania, her soul in her music, lovingly fingered the dying notes. Expecting applause from the corner of the room she found none and, swivelling on the stool discovered that Sa-Lon had vanished. Not a girl given to great displays of emotion, Thania crashed both hands on the piano keys to sound a jarring discord, startling Angela who looked up from her embroidery. 'What was that for?' she asked, adding a little uneasily, 'Thania, you must wear your glasses when you're reading music. You'll strain your eyes again.'

'I don't need them, mama.'

'Yes you do dear. Now put them on. Where are you going?' Angela watched her daughter heading for the verandah. 'Oh dear,' she said in dismay. Perturbed by Thania's behaviour she untidily crammed her needlework into a Shan bag and hastened after her daughter. 'Thania,' she raised her voice, 'stop, wait for me, it's time to go home.'

'I know, that's where I'm going,' Thania called from the verandah. Angela followed and saw Sa-Lon leaning nonchalantly over the parapet, his arms supported on the coping while he toyed with his glass of orange juice. Thania was making off across the lawns back to Sequoia and he was observing her angry departure with a crooked little smile Angela did not altogether care for.

'Thank you for letting us use the piano, Sa-Lon,' Angela said, coming up behind him and catching him off-guard.

'Don't mention it, Mrs Radcliffe.' He turned to regard her with that half-mocking, half-playful smile around his fine mouth. In that moment too, Angela was aware that Sa-Lon's hostility towards her was no more concealed aggression — as in the past when Nathan had been around — but was now out in the open. 'I'm sure my father will be pleased to know someone's keeping an eye on his house during his absence,' he said languidly.

She smiled. 'When are you going back to Rangoon, Sa-Lon?' Her question, cold and aloof was meant to intimidate Sa-Lon whose supercilious behaviour towards Thania had vexed Angela.

'Soon Mrs Radcliffe.'

'Are you intending to go back to America?'

'No. I wish to set up my lawyer-practice in Rangoon.'

'I see.'

'So father has at last made you a partner in his busi-

527

ness!' Sa-Lon remarked, raising his glass of orange in a toast to her, the light in his eyes still hovering between amusement and scorn. 'He ought really to consider making it a Joint Stock or Limited Company in order to minimize the risks involved. I've been telling him that for years, but he won't listen to me. A loose assortment of private enterprises started up by father, the imaginative entrepreneur, is not a Company at all since he's solely responsible for all debts incurred should de Veres-Vorne ever collapse — God forbid. And now you, as his partner, will also be liable for those debts.'

'I don't think your father is about to become bankrupt if that's what you're concerned about Sa-Lon,' Angela said, unable to avoid putting him in his place.

He smiled Nathan's lazy smile. As dark as Nathan was fair, yet more attractive even than his father, Sa-Lon's tall handsome richness had earned him a reputation of being quite a philanderer already, with no mean record of broken hearts for his twenty-four years. 'No,' said Sa-Lon, 'I'm not worried about my father ending up bankrupt or not — his business is nothing to do with me. What I'm saying is, he ought to sell off shares in his so-called Company to make himself even richer. You and he would of course remain the major stock-holders, but with a limited personal liability in case anything unforseen occurs to wipe out his assets overnight. You might like to mention it again to my father because he's more likely to listen to you than to me. The last time I broached the subject he, as usual, got on his high-horse and, to use his own words, decided he did not want a bunch of thick-skinned, pen-pushing shareholders teaching him his business and talking down to him at share holders' meetings, and that 'de Veres-Vorne' was what mattered most, not what was tagged on the end of it.'

'Your father, Sa-Lon, will do what *he* wants to in the end,' Angela said. 'You and I both know that.'

Afterwards, back at Sequoia while Thania was getting

ready for bed she said to Angela, 'Mama, isn't he the handsomest man ever?' She peered through her glasses at Angela, her normally quiet reserve bubbling over with enthusiasm for Sa-Lon de Veres-Vorne shocking Angela into a sharp retort: 'Thania, stop talking like that at once! Sa-Lon might be the most handsome man in the world, but you're not to think of him in those terms ever again, do you hear me? I will not countenance it, so get him right out of your head this moment. Besides, you're far too young to be thinking about handsome men. If you disobey me I shall tell Jeffrey — and you know how he's just waiting for an excuse to send you back to England.'

It was the worst form of punishment she could think of for Thania, and hated herself for having to resort to such an unkind threat especially as Jeffrey probably could not care less one way or another as long as she footed the bills. Thania, normally so mild and caring, took Angela completely off-balance by her next remark:

'Oh, I understand perfectly mama. It's because he's not altogether white, isn't it?'

Angela, shocked to the core by Thania's tone, whirled round in amazement while Thania struggled to pull down the mosquito net over her bed. 'Thania, how dare you! The reason why I object to Sa-Lon de Veres-Vorne is nothing to do with the colour of his skin but what's under it. He's not a boy, he's a man of the world and has come back from America after having imbibed a great deal of American brashness, love of material things, love of himself, his own self-importance, and most of all love for women — any kind of woman at all.' She had to say it for Thania's own good. 'He might appear charming, handsome and dashing to you, Thania, but Sa-Lon's not to be trusted. He's also suave, sophisticated, smooth and very dangerous and will break your heart, make no mistake! But, I'm not going to let him. I forbid you to mention his name again and you will not go to White-walls to practise your music while he's there. Otherwise I will tell Jeffrey.'

529

Thania lay down under her mosquito net. 'Mama, don't get angry please. I won't do anything you don't wish me to. I don't want to hurt you and papa. So many things puzzle me though. Aunt Bee, before she married Brigadier-General Greenaway after Uncle Edwin's death and went back to Rawalpindi with him, told me Sa-Lon's mother was a Shan princess who had become a Buddhist nun. Is that true?'

'Yes, it's true.'

'Why did she do that?'

'For many reasons you would not understand. Neither can I explain them to you.'

'Was it to do with Sa-Lon's father loving an English-woman?'

Angela felt dizzy and put out a hand to steady herself against the bedroom door. 'Thania, is that what Aunt Bee told you?'

'No, I heard it for myself. No names were mentioned. But someone at school happens to come from Mandalay too, and she was saying something one day about her father knowing Captain de Veres-Vorne quite well because they did business together, and how the Captain had had an '*affaire de coeur*' with an Englishwoman, so his Burmese wife left him to go into a Convent and made him a laughing stock in Mandalay because of it. That was all. She didn't mention who the woman was.'

Angela did not wish to listen to any more. 'Thania,' she said, 'don't use the word affair, it's not a nice word for a young girl to use. Now I don't wish to hear another word from you so go to sleep.'

Angela went out and closed the door. Feeling drained and weak-kneed, she leaned against the wood, her brow clammy. Thania would be finishing at the Maymyo school next year when she would be eighteen; it was time for her to meet a nice young man to marry. But where on earth did one find a nice young man in Mandalay? There were not many Matthew Sinclairs around, most of the men being soldiers. There were of course the Officers at the Garrison, plenty of presentable young men doing their duty in Northern Burma. She would just have to attend more functions for Thania's sake, parties, gymkanas, picnics, polo-matches, the sort of thing she had not thought about for years because of her association with the de Veres-Vorne Company. But now she felt the time had come for her to consider her daughter and not herself. Naturally, she would be unable to make the introductions herself, or alone, and would have to enlist Jeffrey's co-operation in the matter so that Thania could be well-presented in order to meet the right young man for her.

TWO

The chilling shriek of an owl was answered by the harsh sounds of a nightjar protesting its antiphonal partner. Moonlight turned the night into day and the jungle into a theatrical setting. The horses whinnied and Thania giggled nervously as they drew rein before a grotesque ruined pagoda. Her fear had given a sharper edge to it on account of her disobedience of her mother's wishes. She tried not to let Sa-Lon see how afraid she was. 'How clever of you to find it,' Thania whispered into the jungle night that fascinated and repelled her in its terrifying mystique. She was glad Sa-Lon had brought his gun with him. Above her head, open-mouthed chinthe and hinthe towered in all their grotesque pagan imagery, their blind eyes seeming to be conscious of her every move while she herself returned their open-mouthed astonishment by staring up at them.

Sa-Lon dismounted and came beside her to help her from the saddle. Unable to take her eyes off the monsters guarding the entrance to the Talaing Temple, she allowed herself to be lifted down in Sa-Lon's upstretched arms. Threaded through his hands, Thania's startled glances came to rest on Sa-Lon's face as, in that moment, his hands carelessly brushed across her breasts and she recognized in his look a masculine regard for her

531

body. Lightly she touched the ground, unaware of having been put down. 'Sa-Lon,' she whispered, suddenly perturbed by much more than the night, 'how did you find out about this place? It's gruesome and I don't think I like it very much.'

He laughed lightly and took her hand, leading her to the pedestal steps of the ruined temple of the Thaton Mons. He sat down beside her, 'Don't be afraid Thania, the only *Nats* to hurt one are of the human variety. I found it one day,' he told Thania, 'when I was out riding by myself. It's so remote and eerie no one ever comes here, so you needn't be afraid we'll be discovered. Even the dacoits avoid it.'

'Sa-Lon,' said Thania breathlessly, 'I mustn't be too long. I promised my mother I wouldn't talk to you again.'

'You promised? Gee, you didn't tell her?' asked Sa-Lon in dismay.

'No, of course not. She doesn't know about tonight. I think she really would send me to England if she found out. But I don't like going behind her back and we won't do this again.'

'I wanted to talk to you, Thania,' he said, touching her cheek, his finger on the corner of her mouth making her shudder — though not in an unpleasant way. 'About us.'

Thania turned her head away, his ardent gaze upon her provoking utterly confusing sensations. Sa-Lon said gently, 'Don't be afraid of me. I wouldn't do anything to hurt you, you know that don't you?'

She nodded, her total innocence and charm making her so malleable in his hands. Sa-Lon's handsome smile was tender; 'You see, I had to talk to you about certain things. I know your adopted parents dislike me.'

'Oh no Sa-Lon, that's not true!' Round sea-green eyes had the moonlight in them reflected by the ugly spectacles she wore, and her pale heart-shaped face with plaited braids wound round her head in a severely unprepossessing style only emphasized the appearance of a tragic little moonflower sitting beside him. Sa-Lon took away Thania's glasses and placed them in her lap.

'You don't need those,' he murmured, 'and neither should you wear your hair like that.' Smoothly his hands took out her pins and unfastened her hair until it framed her in red-gold waves of incredible loveliness. 'Thania,' said Sa-Lon, a heavy weight on his chest as he looked at her, 'why does your mother force you to hide away behind those glasses and ugly braids?'

'What do you mean?' Thania looked at him, mystified, the ugly duckling become the swan so that Sa-Lon found it hard to control his emotions and only desired to sweep her into his arms. Instead, he smiled and chucked her under her chin. 'Honey,' he said, 'you're rather cute, and I think your mother — your adopted mother I should say — is jealous of the little beauty she keeps hidden at Sequoia. You're so much like her, it's uncanny.' He deliberately kept his teasing lighthearted but, Thania, biting her lip looked away. Then Sa-Lon de Veres-Vorne knew what he had always known, that this was the Amagyi-Angela's child, her real child and not some adopted nobody. 'On the subject of your adopted parents, Thania, whether you like it or not, they consider me a half-caste. My father is a white man married to a native woman who might be a Shan princess but nevertheless she's still black in their eyes. But that doesn't bother me one iota. I am what I am and proud of it. However, let's just put your parents aside for one moment because I couldn't care less what they think, only what you think.' He changed the subject on purpose because he did not wish to embarrass Thania, or himself.

'I don't care what colour you are Sa-Lon. I couldn't care less if you were skyblue-pink. I think you're a nice person, I really do.'

'If I asked you, would you ever consider marrying me, Thania?'

Thania was so paralysed with what Sa-Lon had just said she couldn't begin to formulate an answer. 'Oh Sa-Lon, if you asked me, I suppose I'd have to consider it, but it's really not up to me. I would have to ask my parents permission. I'm not twenty-one yet.'

'Honey,' a finger curling in one of her ringlets, his sultry eyes devouring her, 'I'd wait. I'd wait till Kingdom come if I knew you loved me and would one day marry me. Thania, I'm to be a lawyer, maybe soon a barrister and then one day a Judge of the Supreme Court. You know, sweetie, that's what we need out here, people who are educated on both sides of the fence and within the two spheres of black and white. Someone like me who can argue the fact that half black is not black enough for the black, and half white is not nearly white enough for either side. So here I am, fallen between two stools — the Socratic zebra in other words.'

Sa-Lon was fully aware he was talking to himself, Thania being too young, too unworldly and too ignorant in all her unblemished fair beauty to begin to understand what he was driving at. But he felt he had to talk, to get it out of his system, to tell the stars if necessary, who would better comprehend him than all the Thanias, the Amagyi-Angelas and even the Shwe Nats of Mandalay. He bit his fingernails, riled against being a bondman in his own country and smouldered against the injustices perpetrated against him every day of his life. Thania looked at Sa-Lon, at his handsome face and athletic young body, his velvet dark eyes and lowered lashes upon his cheek, while he got yellow pollen on his fingers shredding a moonflower on the crumbling steps where only spirits of the past dwelt — and she wanted to cry with the terrifying sweetness of it all. Held in that one moment of muted time, filled only with girlish dreams of love and romance, she never dreamt in that moment that there was nothing new under the sun; it was all hers — hers to have and to hold with Sa-Lon beside her, this forbidden assignation just the dawning of another creation in the thundering star-studded universe, the never-ending reaching out of hands touching hands, hearts touching hearts, fleeting desires seeking responses as she, Thania, the first wondering Eve held out the golden apple to the first Adam in their own garden of Eden ...

Tempted by Thania's adoration of him, Sa-Lon succumbed.

He took her in his arms and kissed her and Thania became Sa-Lon's captive audience.

Whenever they could, before she returned to Maymyo and he to Rangoon, he brought her to the Talaing Temple in the moonlight in order to become again Marcus Tullius Cicero speaking to the stars while Thania listened enthralled and thought him to be the most wonderful man on earth.

'It's just like the time they tried to woo the Chinese Emperor, Thania, at the expense of the Burmese people. Always at the expense of the Burmese people. They wanted the new Thathanabaing to be chosen by the Chinese Emperor and not the Sangha as had been the case since time immemorial. The British wanted more trading agreements with the Chinese, and also to keep them quiet about Lhasa — so near to Calcutta, three hundred miles if one discounts the Himalayas — as well as seeking their approval for annexing Upper Burma, never mind the Burmese people themselves. The Thathanabaing, however, has always been chosen by a Burmese King — but there isn't one anymore. So you see how the British have turned our laws upside down? They didn't take into consideration one big important fact — that the Chinese Emperor is seldom Buddhist and if he is, it's of the Mahayana School of Buddhism and not Theravada. The whole matter was dropped in the end, the British trying to save face because of their stupid ignorance. Now, what I'm driving at is this, if we had more good lawyers, educated enough to understand the Dhammathats as well as British Law, we'd be able to stand up for ourselves in our own Courts and tell the British where to get off when it comes to interfering with our social customs and sacred laws.'

Most of what Sa-Lon said to her went far above her head, his bellicose speeches and self-answering arguments, his dogmatic rhetoric and propaganda, but what

535

touched her most of all was when he alighted upon the subject of his mother. Then, the hard bitter young man kept as a second-class citizen by the mighty Raj who had captured his land and his people, softened in love. Then Thania realized how much he idolized his Buddhist mother, and how much Sa-Lon despised and hated his father for driving her into a nunnery.

In the early hours of the morning Sa-Lon and she would creep home. Safely deposited back on Sequoia's squeaky verandah floorboards to let herself over her bedroom window-sill, Thania kept her fingers crossed that her mother would not wake and discover her to have been in Sa-Lon's company when she had expressly forbidden it. Thania knew, without doubt, were that to happen all her lovely moonlight meetings with Sa-Lon de Veres-Vorne, whom she now felt she loved more than life itself, would come to a very swift end. If that happened Thania thought she would die.

CHAPTER THIRTY-EIGHT

ONE

Work on Nathan's new godowns was well underway by the end of February. Angela worked with the violent disruption all around her. It was imperative the new warehouses were completed by the start of the monsoon season, for the makeshift dam holding back the river whilst the loading the unloading bays and the river walls were strengthened would have to be removed as the rains greatly swelled the Irrawaddy, and building work would have to be halted. Normal business then could be resumed, Angela hoped. The constant hammering and banging one afternoon made her decide to take herself off to the Shwe Emporium where it was quieter and she could check their books in peace. She spent the afternoon there and arrived home at Sequoia rather later than she had intended. Jeffrey had been away six weeks and Thania too had returned to Maymyo so, expecting to see only Theo and the ayah on the verandah, Angela was rather surprised to see a strange young man wandering around her front garden in admiration of the flowers.

In the uniform of the 2nd Battalion Hampshires, he looked up when he heard the garden gate click, and came forward to greet her with outstretched hand: 'Good afternoon, Mrs Radcliffe, I'm Paul Monthavers. I've come from Fort Dufferin on the express wishes of Colonel Dawlish.'

'Has something happened to Jeffrey?' she asked, her

instant reaction to Captain Monthaver's presence one of alarm.

'No ... well, not fatally that is ... may we?' He waved a hand to the verandah and Angela re-collected herself and said, 'Yes, of course, do forgive me. I'll ask the ayah to bring us some tea.' She led the way up the steps and waved him to one of the verandah chairs, removing her hat before taking a seat opposite him.

'Mrs Radcliffe, your husband is in the Garrison Hospital at the moment and Colonel Dawlish wished me to convey his sympathies regarding your husband's indisposition — the letter will explain.'

His eyes flickered to the buff envelope in her lap. 'Mrs Radcliffe, I'm here also to say I have Marbles at my bungalow. Unfortunately Captain Pastheld who billets with me is allergic to animal fur and I'm afraid I can't hang on to Marbles until Lieutenant-Colonel Radcliffe is better and can take him on manouevres once more. It's a shame really because Marbles has become the Regiment's mascot. Shall I bring him back to you tomorrow morning?'

'Yes, by all means,' Angela murmured, reluctant to open Colonel Dawlish's letter in front of Captain Monthavers. 'Has Jeffrey been injured in some way?'

'A bout of jungle fever I believe. We brought him back with us from Myitkyina and Marbles was handed into my care by the returning column of the Burma Frontier Force. Lieutenant-Colonel Radcliffe is well enough — I assure you in that respect. I saw him myself yesterday as I'm one of the Staff Officers at Fort Dufferin, and he's making good progress. I did not want to leave Colonel Dawlish's letter in the hands of a servant so I hung on for you. What a nice garden you have, Mrs Radcliffe.'

'Yes, it is a nice garden. I don't know where the ayah's got to, but if you'll excuse me for a few moments I'll go and make us a cup of tea myself.'

'No, please don't go to all that bother on my behalf, really Mrs Radcliffe. I've got to get back to Fort Dufferin in any case.' He stood up with a smile and gave her his hand again. 'If I don't go soon you won't have a hedge left. My horse eats anything. Please don't bother to come to the gate as you must be tired. If there's anything any of us can do, Mrs Radcliffe, while your husband's recovering, I'm to tell you not to hesitate to get in touch with the Regiment. Colonel Dawlish's express orders. In any case I'll be along in the morning with Marbles.'

'Thank you so much for having looked after Marbles for us, Captain Monthavers,' Angela said warmly, rather liking his reassuring and down-to-earth manner.

'My pleasure.' He put on his helmet and took his leave.

After he had gone Angela read Colonel Dawlish's letter, several pages of a cramped hand she found hard to decipher. When she had read through it all, she sat back in her chair for several minutes so that she could assimilate the full facts behind his desire to communicate with her at a personal level.

In his closing sentence he had expressed a wish that she should come to Fort Dufferin to see him at her earliest convenience.

TWO

Angela did not go to the godowns the following day and, having forgotten all about Paul Monthavers bringing Marbles back that morning, summoned a tonga to take her into the city. It left her at the main gates to Fort Dufferin. Inside, it was hard to reconcile this horrible overcrowded cantonment with its huddle of wooden buildings with the fabulous palace in which King Thibaw and Queen Supalayat had ruled in such despotic splendour a decade earlier. Ten years; it seemed like a lifetime ago she had knelt at King Thibaw's feet and he had danced his handsome dark eyes at her. Kings and Queens, Princes and Princesses, all of them dead and gone or banished to a paltry exile on foreign shores far less golden. Angela wondered to herself if the relentless march of an Empire straining to grab more and yet more territory would have halted at these golden shores had Thibaw and Supalayat behaved less despotically. She sighed on the thought of how the mighty are fallen and on her own husband's fall from grace, and faced the Garrison Commander bravely.

'Are you feeling faint ma'am?' he asked, standing up behind his desk to rock a little towards her in a quizzical manner she found rather disconcerting. But his bewhiskered face showed only concern for her.

'Thank you, Colonel Dawlish, I'm well enough, though perhaps a tumbler of water?' she asked, for once her manner not composed but nervously twisting her handkerchief in her lap.

'Indeed, indeed my dear.' He rang his bell for the Bearer to bring fresh water.

'Mrs Radcliffe, ma'am', he said in due course, 'your husband has a very grave problem.'

'Yes, I know, Colonel Dawlish. I'm well aware of his drinking problems.'

'No ma'am, that's not what I wish to talk about,' he said. He gave an awkward little cough. 'There are two separate matters to be drawn to your attention. One concerns the events leading to your husband's breakdown, and the other is a Medical Report I have here from the Senior M.O. How would you like me to begin? With what happened at Chaukhai, or his health record first?' He was being very solicitous and Angela greatly appreciated his desire to save her any further embarrassment on the subject of Jeffrey's breakdown.

'Please tell me everything from the very beginning, Colonel Dawlish, and don't try to spare my feelings. I would rather know everything there is to know, and afterwards you can give me the M.O.'s report on the state of my husband's health.'

He nodded, and without further ado launched into the events that had led to Jeffrey's downfall at Chaukhai. As always, they had been short of men in the field, the 30,000 troops deployed for the Burma administration nowhere near enough as malaria, cholera, dysentery, jungle-fever and a host of other diseases took their toll on the troops. Ten miles from the northern border Jeffrey had been detailed to liaise with the Jinghpaws of the State of Kachin at a place called Chaukhai situated in lonely mountainous terrain bordering on China.

Two groups of Jinghpaws were engaged in a feudal battle, a blood-feud between brothers from neighbouring villages. The Jinghpaws were noted for their warring nature and even among their own tribes were always in a state of contention. Jinghpaw custom decreed that the youngest son inherited the right to become the leader or 'duwa' of his people, and not the eldest son as was customary elsewhere. The younger brother, when he assumed leadership, was then known as the 'thigh-eating duwa' because in ritualistic ceremony the tribal chief was always given the thigh-bone of an animal during the feast of celebration. The thigh-eating duwa's village then became known as the 'gumsa' or aristocratic-commoner village.

Colonel Dawlish explained all this to her as he related Jeffrey's bizzare story, and Angela would have found it all to incredible had she not lived through the massacre at Loloi and seen for herself the warring tribes-people of the northern territories.

When the younger duwa had established himself, the older brothers of the tribe would then take themselves away to start their own tribal or lesser villages called *gumlaos*. In Chaukhai, the elder brother of the thigh-eating duwa contested rights of overlordship because he and his brother had been born at the same time. But even the old women of the gumsa could not swear without falling out with one another as to the exact time of each brother's birth, identical twins claiming hereditary possession of the gumsa. The tribal war had started on that score, therefore, Jeffrey and his small band of men had been sent in to sort out the dispute and to establish the exact day, time and date of the Jinghpaw twin births. Unfortunately, the lesser Kachin tribes, in awe of the Jinghpaws through generations of territorial disputes, joined the war, and tribes like the Asti, the

541

Lashi and Maru became embroiled in the original Jingh-paw's hereditary dispute. The situation became inflam-matory. With the difficult country into which he had been sent on the one hand, and the suspicion with which the British were viewed on the other, Jeffrey had had to tread carefully. His written report bore out his caution.

As an arbiter, he had to liaise with all sides and get everyone to a 'parleying table' to sort out the various problems that had arisen. In his full report, Jeffrey had stated he had made contact with the leader of the gumlao or the secondary village first, and had come to an agreeable conclusion with him. The younger brother, the duwa, was being far more difficult to reason with, as he had declined to parley with the British and had no wish to arrive at peaceful negotiations with either his brother or the British. A few nights later Jeffrey's Company had been attacked in their camp and six men had been killed with several others wounded. They had no idea who had led the attack on them, only that it had been the extremely fierce warriors of the Kachins. Both factions of the Jinghpaws blamed the Asti, the Asti blamed the Maru, the Maru blamed the Jinghpaw gumsas and the gumsas blamed the Lashi — it became an intolerable situation until, in suppressing and questioning the rebellious tribes, Jeffrey learned through a Maru villager that the British Officers' little mascot captured during the attack on their camp, had been seen five miles away at the gumlao village of the secondary Jinghpaws. When the British soldiers marched into the village, they were informed by the elder brother that Marbles would be found at the gumsa of his 'parlous thigh-eating brother.'

Jeffrey had stated he knew full well Kachins were animists who indulged in the sacrifice of animals to propitiate their ancestral spirits or *Nats*. It was the primary function of every Kachin duwa to perform these rites and Marbles, the British soldiers' mascot, had been taken to appease the ancestral gods of the Jingh-paws whose misfortunes had been sent by the British.

542

'And so ma'am,' said Colonel Dawlish in summing up, 'Lieutenant-Colonel Radcliffe unfortunately did not see things in quite the same light as the Jinghpaws, the Asti, the Lashi or the Maru. All he saw was his little dog with paws and muzzle bound, ready to be put on a spit like a pig to propitiate some heathen spirits, and so he ordered his Company to fire and sack the gumsa. Therefore, it is felt, that his judgement being sadly awry and in question, it would be in his own interests were he to resign his command, Her Majesty having no further use for his services.'

Angela reached for her glass of water. Colonel Dawlish cleared his throat.

Angela composed her thoughts and tried to digest everything that had been conveyed to her. Jeffrey, whom she knew had worked up from the ranks to get where he was, his one ambition to get to the rank of Colonel before he left Burma, was finished, cashiered, kaput, Her Majesty having no further use for his services!

'I'm deeply sorry ma'am,' Colonel Dawlish said, 'I really can't express my feelings because I know what a damn fine soldier your husband was and how good, too, in his specialized field of Intelligence work. It would help you to know *why* he behaved in such a way — if you'd care to hear the M.O.'s report now?'

She nodded.

'I'll read it out exactly as it was written rather than try and explain in my own words as I'm not familiar with medical jargon.' He tweaked his monocle back into his eye and picking up a report from his desk read aloud:

'It is subsequently discovered that the here named Officer, Lieutenant-Colonel Jeffrey Arthur Radcliffe, Queen's Own Bengal Infantry, subsequently detailed to serve in Liaison Intelligence, Burma Frontier Force, is suffering from a condition thought to be of a hereditary nature. Whether or not the illness predisposes the said Officer's military actions at Chaukhai is, in my opinion debatable. However, with a personal interest in this case, I have taken it upon myself to conduct a little private research into his problem. I now put forward my discoveries together with material placed at my disposal by a certain eminent Swiss Professor at the *Clinique de Génètique* in Basle (to whom I referred this case).

'We are both of the opinion that the signs and symptoms displayed by Jeffrey Radcliffe come under the umbrella-term 'Mental Disorders'. Professor Ermental has termed this specific case as an 'Organic Psychoses' arising from certain bio-chemical disorders of the body. As yet, not a great deal is known about bio-chemical disorders which effect the function, consequently, of the brain. One thing emerges from studies into Jeffrey Radcliffe's case history is that the disease is exacerbated by bodily abuse, exhaustion, stress, malnutrition, alcohol and drugs. Jeffrey Radcliffe's case-history is an example of that psychotic state wherein two extremes of behaviour are manifest, excessive violence on the one hand with irrational fears on the other. When in the former psychotic state, an almost psychopathic violence might be associated with murdering tendencies. In the latter, a withdrawal from responsibilities — especially in association with the subconscious mind declaring something to be of an unpleasant nature. Toxic poisons are released into the bloodstream to upset the bio-chemistry of the body. In Jeffrey Radcliffe's case, a toxic-confusion was engendered through excessive and liberal imbibition of alcohol over a long period of time, thus producing the state of delirium tremens and amnesia.

'Therefore, in my summary, such is the diagnosis I am bound to make relative to the incidents that took place at Chaukhai in the State of Kachin; organic psychoses of an hereditary nature with an associated loss of intellect, personality deterioration and physical dilapidation, the chronic manifestations of which inevitably lead to dementia and early death. Signed, D.K. Willbride, Medical Officer, Fort Dufferin, February 1896.'

Colonel Dawlish left a decent interval of time for her to come to terms with all that had been thrown at her in such a distressing fashion.

544

'Alcoholism, therefore, was not your husband's whole problem, though it certainly did not help matters. The Medical Officer and I believe it was indulged in to escape from the knowledge of a disease for which there is no cure — the M.O. stumbled across some facts concerning your husband ma'am, and I don't know if Jeffrey ever told you, but he has a daughter in a mental institution in England.'

Angela nodded dumbly.

'Dashed bad business all this, dashed bad. No one likes to go through life thinking they might die a lunatic before they reach middle age. However, while we understand the circumstances of his irrational behaviour at Chaukhai, his illness no doubt made worse by the climate, conditions and everything else we have to put up with out here, we can't, ma'am, have room for mental degeneration and loss of intellect as far as an Officer in Her Majesty's Burma Frontier Force is concerned — no matter how insidious the nature of the disorder. You'll appreciate therefore why his application for extended leave in England was turned down and his resignation called for. Much the better way I feel to handle this tragedy, and the Commander General will ask no more questions concerning Chaukhai. Much better now, than later on when something else nasty might happen and the matter brought to light by a court martial, eh ma'am?'

Angela took a deep breath. 'Yes ... yes, I now understand everything perfectly — I think.' She moistened her dry lips. 'Thank you so much for your time and kindness in explaining all this to me. I know what a good record Jeffrey has behind him and I'm only sorry about what happened at Chaukhai. Did the M.O. mention how long this mental deterioration can take to run its course?' Angela asked, half afraid to raise such a question.

'I gathered by everything ma'am, that it's an insidious thing and there are periods of remission from it — especially if one lays off the drink and stuff. It would be a good idea if Jeffrey could be rehabilitated somewhere — perhaps the Cotswolds. The spa waters of Cheltenham, they say, work wonders for all kinds of diseases. I'm only sorry I have to tell you all this.' He endeavoured to think of something else to say to change the gloom surrounding Lieutenant-Colonel Radcliffe's fall from grace while he realized it would be a futile gesture. 'It comes to my knowledge ma'am, that you and a few other kind ladies did some extraordinary good work for us at Minhla in superintending a small unit when our chaps were rather hard-pushed.' He looked under his grey brows at her and his monocle almost slipped out. He tightened it back into his eye, and met her little smile of gratitude.

'Yes,' she said, 'but most of the time we only pretended to be nurses. None of us being professionally trained, we were only helpers who tried to do their best.'

'Good show, good show, that's what counts most, team spirit and a genuine regard for the article.' He closed the file on Jeffrey Arthur Radcliffe, Queen's Own Bengal and Burma Frontier Force — known as Raj to his friends — and to Angela it was like the placing of a lid on a coffin, the nails just hammered in very brutally upon her beleaguered senses and Jeffrey's career at the grand old age of thirty-nine.

Angela stood up. The Garrison Commander walked her to the door in his peculiar jerking fashion, hands behind his back and an air of deep concentration about him. 'If I can help in any way in getting Jeffrey rehabilitated in England, please don't hesitate to seek my help,' Colonel, Sir Boland Dawlish told her.

She knew it had been said through a sense of courtesy and nothing more. 'No indeed, thank you so much Colonel Dawlish for all your help.' Angela put out her hand and he held her lace-mittoned clasp for a second longer than expected.

'My dear,' said Sir Boland, 'don't take this to heart too much. Rum lot the Jinghpaws and their tribes. We've just got to be one jump ahead of them the whole time — this period of pacification is taking rather longer than everyone had envisaged when we first got here.' His eyes twinkled, then he asked, 'How's that scrap Marbles?

One gathers he's become rather famous overnight through all this.'

Angela forced a smile. 'Oh, none the worse for his escapade according to Captain Monthavers — which reminds me, he promised to bring Marbles back to us this morning and I completely forgot. Goodbye and thank you once again, Sir Boland. My regards to Lady Dorothy.'

In no mood to visit Jeffrey at the Garrison Hospital, she took a tonga home. Her mind had been made up on one score, there was no possible question of returning to England just yet. She could not conceivably walk out of her trusted position as superintendent of Nathan's business affairs in his long absence, and certainly never while reconstruction work was being carried out on his godowns.

As on the previous day, Angela found Paul Monthavers in her front garden. This time he had Marbles with him. Theo and the dog were having a marvellous time, Marbles' tartan leash — from the Shwe Emporium — trailing behind while Theo with screams and whoops of delight chased after it, nearly decapitating her flowers. Angela had never forgiven Jeffrey for having given the dog to Theo as his pet, then taken Marbles with him when he returned to duty. It had been a cruel thing to do and Theo had been weepy and miserable for days after. Angela smiled now at their games. 'Well at least he doesn't appear to have suffered from any ill effects for being so nearly the sacrifice to propitiate the Jinghpaw *Nats*,' she said to Paul Monthavers.

'No indeed,' he said, wearing mufti this morning and looking very presentable.

'I was so rude yesterday, Captain Monthavers,' Angela said. 'Please, won't you come inside and at least have a cup of coffee with me? I'm parched, so I'm certainly going to have one — oh, but that's if I'm not upsetting your plans. I've kept you waiting so long, you might have other arrangements?' she hesitated, looking at him enquiringly.

'No, I've no plans at the moment. I'm not on duty till a bit later on and would be delighted to have a cup of coffee.'

'Then let's go inside, shall we?' Angela turned and led the way. The ayah sat on the verandah keeping an eye on Theo, and because Nancy and Vanda hovered in their garden next door, eagle-eyes trained on her business, Angela preferred to go inside the house with Captain Monthavers and thus give Vanda something else to talk about while she at least maintained her privacy.

'Tea or coffee?' she called to him while he wandered round the living room taking an interest in her photographs.

'Oh coffee, please. Strong and black if I may. These are awfully good pictures, superb photography,' he said, taking the tray from her when she re-entered the room.

'Yes, I'm rather proud of them.'

'Did you take them?' he asked attentively, his eyebrows raised in surprise as he took his coffee cup from her.

'Oh yes. At last, I have a decent camera, a Kodak that uses a celluloid roll of film. So much easier than the old-fashioned method.'

'Theo tells me he has a sister. Is that her picture?' He asked, nodding at the silver-framed photograph Angela kept on her bureau.

'Yes, that's Thania. She was younger there of course. At the moment she's in her last year at a Girls' School in Maymyo, which is just as well as we'll soon be returning to England. Captain Monthavers ...'

'Please call me Paul, Mrs Radcliffe, I'm not on duty now,' he said with a warm friendly smile.

'Thank you, Paul. I went to see Colonel Dawlish this morning and he has left me in no doubt whatsoever about what took place at Chaukhai. Were you with Jeffrey's detachment of soldiers ordered to sack that unfortunate Jinghpaw village?'

'No, Mrs Radcliffe. I was on my way back from Myitkyina with my Regiment as we were due to take over a tour of duty at the Mandalay Garrison. Marbles was given into my care at Myitkyina.'

'I see.' She was so glad he had not been there.

Paul Monthavers stayed for a second cup of coffee. 'It's very pleasant out here by the river,' he remarked. 'It gets rather boring I'm afraid when one's off duty in Mandalay. Nothing very much to do if one isn't a Buddhist. Would you mind awfully if I sometimes came this way to take Marbles for a walk?'

'No indeed, I should be delighted,' said Angela. 'I certainly can't exercise him as I have no time. Yes, please do, anytime.'

He took his leave soon after and Angela reconfirmed her earlier regard for him. She thought him a very pleasant young man, no pretences whatsoever, no show, no loudness and not filled with his own importance, but just a nice ordinary young man who might be worth encouraging to the house for Thania's sake.

Angela did not go to the godowns as the day was too far advanced, and she didn't on the following day either as she went to visit Jeffrey at the Garrison Hospital and by the time she arrived back at Sequoia she had a splitting headache and only wanted to lie down. Jeffrey had been sullen and uncommunicative under his mosquito net. He occupied a small private ward off the main Officer's ward, and did nothing but smoke one cigarette after another while she sat beside his bed, his eyes fixed to the ceiling and never upon her. In the end, with a sigh of resignation and defeat, she got up and left him to his miseries. She did however have a long and illuminating discussion with the military nursing-sister in her little office. Jeffrey, pending his resignation, would remain in the hospital, and though she did not say so in as many words, Angela gathered Jeffrey was under military surveillance until his complete discharge — and the one consolation derived from it all was he would be unable to lay his hands on any more whisky.

Two days later a state of utter chaos greeted her when she returned to work. Maung Sang Aye, the godown manager, informed her that the Italian engineer had walked out after he and the English surveyor had lost their temper with each other.

'But he can't do that!' Angela said appalled. 'We've got to get the godowns finished by the time the monsoons arrive.'

Maung Sang Aye shrugged and left it to her as she was now back in the seat of office. Angela went straight to the house of the Italian engineer in Mandalay and waited there until he returned. 'It is impossible. I cannot come back while the pompous Englishman is teaching me my business,' the Italian said carelessly.

'But Signor, please! Mr Blackwood is attending to the godowns, I can't tell him to leave and go. Not that I would do so in the absence of Captain Vorne.'

'Then it is impossible. I cannot come back to work with him, Signora! I, Signor Luci, categorically refuse to return to the godowns if Mr Blackwood is to remain in overall charge of the building work. I have much else work to do in Mandalay and I cannot waste my time on people who do not know anything and refuse to listen to me.'

'But what's the problem?' Angela asked in desperation.

'He is the problem Signora! That man, the Englishman, he is my problem, nothing else!' He threw up his hands in a typically temperamental gesture and tapped his forehead. 'He is mad. I cannot work with mad people. Either he goes or I go.'

And since he could not be budged from his resolve, the Italian engineer went and Mr Blackwood stayed because Angela felt he was the more stable-minded of the two men. It took her three weeks to sort out the dispute and get the coolies to co-operate. The new engineer she found, in one mad rush to get the work restarted, was a German who promised to come out and look at the repairs so far done.

It took him another week to appear on the scene and by now it was getting toward the end of March.

He shook his head in dismay. 'Ja, ja, the water level is creeping up,' he remarked. 'Drainage in the bays must be complete if the Portland cement is to dry out thoroughly and the walls remain sound for years to come. We must put in a centrifugal pump to get out the water. Also, I have looked at the dam. We have problems at the toe.' He licked his forefinger and turned over the page of his notebook. 'The stability of the dam is impaired. The Italian, he has been much of a dopfkopf and got his sums wrong. This is a gravity dam, ja? So we have rock-fill construction, that is all right because it is built on moving places — the shift in the base of the river. Solid earth and heavy stones, that too is good. But we must bring again the elephants to reinforce the structure as here and there it is a little leaky, that is why we get water seepage into bays and godowns. We must prevent silt-pressure; it must not build up too much at the heel of the dam — then we only get much earthquake force behind it and kaput, we have no dam.'

'Oh please, please,' said Angela, her head swimming, 'you do what has to be done, Herr Truffen, but we must have all the work completed by the first week in June. Goodness, it's been long enough!'

'Nein, I do not think that will be so. There is much work left to do. But do not worry. I have a very good hydraulic systems and with my centrifugal pump we keep the water in the river where it is needed and not in places it is not needed, ja?'

'So you will take over the work?' Angela asked, still a little doubtful.

'Oh ja, ja. I will do the work. Very good it will be, but I must first correct the mistakes that have already been made, and that will take a little time.'

'Please,' she said, 'not too much time, Herr Truffen. Captain Vorne will not be a happy man if he comes home in October to find he is still without his new godowns.'

CHAPTER
THIRTY NINE

ONE

Angela congratulated herself on having found Herr Truffen, big, bluff and busy as he made order out of chaos. Work progressed well and by the middle of May Nathan's loading and unloading bays were nearing completion. Another two weeks Herr Truffen told her, allowing for a drying out period for the cement, and the water could be allowed back into them. Angela was thankful, because already the water level of the river was beginning to rise as the glaciers of the north began their summer melting to drain into the Irrawaddy and its tributaries. But she had every faith in Herr Truffen's ingenious centrifugal pump and hydraulics which kept the water diverted into another part of the river.

Because no flats could be loaded and unloaded from Nathan's godowns, further along the river Mr Pathan Sundevava and Dimitri the Greek allowed her to use their wharves for checking the flats that drew up with consignments of rice and pulses earmarked for the Northern Shan States. The flats arrived from Pagan where Nathan had another godown, and it was Angela's duty to make certain that what had been ordered there was heading, in the correct amount of gunny-sacks, for the right destination. In addition to the perishable commodities, oil-drums and coal also had to be accounted for, so, having to use other peoples' premises considerably confused the issue. Dimitri and Sundevava, in her opinion, had to be watched when several of

Nathan's barges came in together to Mandalay loaded with stocks, just in case they whisked away what was not theirs. One afternoon she arrived back in the godown office after checking consignments of sugar and coffee at Sundevava's godowns — one barge on its way to Singu, the other to be off-loaded at Mingon — and wearily sat down at her desk to go over some more chittys Maung Sang Aye had placed on her desk during her absence. An hour later he tapped again at her door:

'Thakin-Ma,' he said, his narrow hooded eyes disappearing altogether when he smiled, though Maung Sang Aye seldom smiled in her presence as he had great respect for her. 'Thakin-Ma, venerable nun wishes to speak with you.' The happy smiles Angela assumed were upon that score, for now they could all earn a little merit by feeding the nun.

'Venerable nun,' she murmured distantly, getting up to take some biscuits out of her bag, part of her midday tiffin she had not eaten. Then she noticed the water at her feet. 'Maung Sang Aye,' she said in alarm, 'I never noticed the water creeping in here like this an hour ago. It's quite a lot.'

His smiles increased, designed to reassure her. 'Thakin-Ma, it is nothing to worry about. Very clever pump, it breaks down this morning, but Herr Truffen, he makes it good again with many working-engineers. It is all in very good hand now and clever device is once again pumping out water very very fast. Next week, after walls have had one more week to dry in hot sun, we will have bays full of water again so everything is back too normal.'

'I hope so,' Angela said dubiously, not at all happy about paddling in an inch of water. 'Well, Herr Truffen obviously knows what he's doing even if we don't — but it still looks to me as though the water isn't dispersing but, if anything, coming in again.'

'New godowns Thakin-Ma, they are in very good shape,' Maung Sang Aye said happily. 'I have been along to see them and they are soon to be ready for occupation. Then we can take away all steel and iron bars and girders making supports in here and much confusion all round.'

'An understatement Maung Sang Aye, an understatement,' Angela murmured, taking her homemade biscuits to give to the waiting nun who turned out to be Minthami. Wearing her hood, she kept her distance from the workmen and coolies swarming the catwalks and godown premises.

'Minthami!' Angela said in surprise, delighted to see her little Shan friend after so long.

'Mayela shin?' Minthami said with a lovely smile.

'Yes thank you Minthami, I'm very well,' Angela replied in Burmese because Minthami had reverted to the use of her own language and not the interesting lilting English that had always made Angela smile. Minthami went on to tell her she had been given temporary permission to break her vows of silence. Because she belonged to a very strict religious order in Mandalay and not one as accommodating as the Sasana, Angela knew that what Minthami had to say must be of some importance.

'Minthami is very happy to see English friend and so she wishes to share happiness with Amagyi-Angela, but please, let us not talk here but away from noise which Shwe Nat always have in whatever he do.'

Angela returned Minthami's smiles; 'All right, just let me get my bag and boots and we can walk back to Sequoia. I haven't much left to do in the office and Maung Sang Aye is quite capable of looking after everything. Besides, I'm not happy paddling in an inch of river-water which may give me another attack of typhoid-fever,' she told Minthami with a rueful grin. Angela came back presently to join her, this time with her Shan bag and other bits and pieces she was taking home.

'Come,' said Minthami, making an offer to help carry some of her things, 'give to Minthami.'

'No, I can manage. I know how awkward it is to try

554

and hold anything else when one is trying to clutch that great big begging bowl at the same time.'

'Poor Amagyi-Angela,' Minthami said as they crossed the low-water bridge and walked along the foot of the embankment away from clattering and banging workmen, 'I think you have a very busy time with Shwe Nat away in America, yes?'

'Goodness me, yes! I'll never forgive him for abandoning me at a time like this — I think he did it purposely. It's possibly just as well though, because he would have lost his temper with everyone so often by now we would never have got the godowns finished — in a month of Sunday mornings!'

Minthami appreciated the humour. Laughingly she said, 'At least it is a happy thing Amagyi-Angela can joke at bad time.'

'Sometimes Minthami, I'd cry gallons if I didn't smile. Jeffrey you know, is in the Garrison Hospital. He's done something very stupid which has cost him his job. We might be returning to England, I don't know. I'm in such a muddle with everything ... but enough of my troubles. You're limping badly so let's sit here for a little while in the sun,' Angela suggested, adding heartily, 'I've got a picnic lunch for us, Minthami. Let's share it, and while we do so we can tell each other our troubles — well, my troubles and your happiness as your eyes are positively shining with joy, so let's hear your good news.' Angela sat down on the grassy bank beside Minthami, and fumbled around in her Shan bag for the fruit and packed meal she had set out with early that morning but had not had time to eat yet. It was such a beautiful day, golden and rare in the interlude between rain and shine, a treat, too, for her as she so seldom found time to relax these days with the rush and bustle of her working-life.

Minthami sat with her bare feet in the river-water, her pink robes pulled back over her shins while she and Angela munched through their picnic, Minthami having forgotten her fasting hours as well as her vows of silence. Angela was amused by the efficacy of Buddhism — she herself had succumbed so many, many times! Angela still found the Burmese easy-going approach to life remarkable, and exasperating — especially where the slow progress of the building work on the godowns was concerned, Burmese philosophy being that tomorrow was another sunny day! She listened to Minthami's bubbling enthusiasm based on that happiness and expediency inbred in Buddha's people, and found her company stimulating.

'Minthami will be very happy to see Roi again when he comes home from American University with Shwe Nat after they visit sick mother in Ireland. You know Amagyi-Angela, sometimes it seems very funny thing that Minthami never know of other side of family to which sons and husband belong. It strange world sometimes, yes?'

'Very strange,' Angela agreed.

'But Buddha always give much joy to Minthami. She is happy to know husband and sons happy also in things they must do for living lives themselves. Only one thing Minthami very sad about and that is because she have no butterfly-spirit of daughter to help and comfort in old age. That is why she go to Convent where there are many daughters and sisters to grow old and have happiness of talking times, for husband and sons, they do not talk like we like to talk and share of many things. They are too busy making money and more money. But Minthami is very happy to know she will one day soon have butterfly-spirit of grand-daughter to bless and look after in old-age.' She leaned over and patted Angela's hand. 'But Minthami always happy to have butterfly-spirit of sister in Amagyi-Angela who is great comfort. Sa-Lon, he comes to mother with much good news, for he tells Minthami he is soon to marry.'

'Oh Minthami, I'm delighted. That *is* good news. It's about time Sa-Lon settled down with a good girl who will make him happy. I know what a worry he's been to you and Nathan.'

'He is to set up lawyer-practice in Rangoon and new

English wife will help him, that is what he comes to tell Minthami.'

'An English girl from Rangoon! I'm delighted for all your sakes.' Angela was relieved to hear such welcome news, for an English wife was what Sa-Lon had always wanted.

'Then Minthami will be content. She will have Roi again, and butterfly-spirit of grand-daughter, and if Shwe Nat, he still make much noise in old age, Minthami not worry. She will nurse little baby again and remember happy days at Loloi when Sa-Lon and Roi cry all night to make Shwe Nat go to sleep in bamboo clump,' Minthami stated with one of her delightfully childish giggles.

Angela raised her head to the roar upriver and for a split second the world seemed to stand still. With a cry she leapt to her feet, 'Quick ... run ... run! The dam's burst ...'

A tributary of the Irrawaddy, held back too long from its normal course joined forces once more with the main river swollen with the volume of melting snows pouring down from the north. Furiously battered, the rock-fill dam began to disintegrate. A great tidal wave formed as the two parts of the river merged and water swirled and eddied back into the godown pools. Unable to contain the sudden deluge, un-set cement walls caved in, re-flooding the godowns.

'The Bund, the Bund ...' Angela cried, dragging Minthami with her. 'Hurry Minthami ... oh hurry, we must hurry ...'

'No, no, you go ... you go Amagyi-Angela,' Minthami wept. 'Minthami cannot climb, ankle is twisted ...'

'Yes, Minthami, yes! Oh yes ... we must,' Angela too began to sob, 'you can do it, you can! Please try, I'll help you.'

But Minthami's begging-bowl, still clutched to her stomach, fell from her frenzied grasp and rolled down the slope into the water pouring past in grey torrents building up and up, devouring the lower reaches of the

Bund. Angela tumbled down after Minthami whose one objective seemed to be to grab her bowl bobbing on the surface of the broiling Irrawaddy. It receded further and further from her grasp. 'Leave it, please leave it,' Angela cried desperately while Minthami took no notice but waded heedless into danger. 'Once the rest of the dam gives way we'll be caught between the Bund and the river ... and I can't swim ...'

With a superhuman effort Angela lunged at Minthami and managed to clutch a handful of pink robe, and while Minthami in a frenzy fought against her in total panic, Angela half-carried half-dragged her back to the slope of the Bund. And then the dam completely gave way under the pressure of the unleashed waters of the Irrawaddy, soon demolishing everything standing in its turbulent way. Workmen and coolies scrambled to safety in every conceivable direction, into trees, onto scaffolding, astride fallen spars. Retaining walls, loading and unloading bays, embankment walls, everything was destroyed by torrents of water viciously and relentlessly seeking free passage to undermine already weakened structural foundations. Steel and iron bars supporting the old godowns were swept away, so too the scaffolding on the new buildings. Stone masonry began to give way, the old godowns falling first to carry with them the new. Tumbled like toy bricks, debris gathered in the river, scaffolding bars like pieces of straw were hurled against uprooted trees, weakened embankments all along the river edges began to collapse under the pressure of the Irrawaddy which finally poured over the flat lands on either side of its course.

'Amagyi-Angela, I can run no more ... go please, you must try to save yourself ...'

'No, no, the Bund, we must try to reach the top of the Bund, it's our only chance ...' Angry cold waters made their skirts twice as heavy, dragging them down. Minthami's feet, cut and bleeding on river shingle could not support her as time and time again her foothold was taken from under her. The lower reaches of the great

558

earthen embankment began to disappear altogether and soon Minthami and Angela were back in water up to their waists. Angela began to claw frantically at the slippery slope of the Bund but was unable to maintain her grip as, with one hand, she held on to Minthami. She lacked the strength to drag her up with her, for every time she reached for those fragile boneless hands seeking hers, they slipped through her muddy clasp. Minthami fell back, sliding down the slippery slope and Angela, clawing for her, felt herself sliding. Reality began to slip away too as the bubbling cold Irrawaddy, mud-grey and black, reached as far as her neck. She could only see Minthami's pink robe and shaven head being pulled further and further from the shore, the river greedy for them both. With a super-human effort Angela threw herself towards Minthami and miraculously found one beautiful white hand seeking hers. Through the greyness she caught hold of it, gasping with the water that was in her eyes, her nose, her ears, mouth. Angela, unable to cry out loud, could only think in those desperate few seconds, Minthami, Minthami, why did you have to cut your hair, why did you have it all shaven off so that I can't even grab hold of that much to save you? She could hold on to her no longer ...

Anikka, Dukkha, Anatta, Life is Desire, Impermanence and Sorrow, and in her head Angela could hear the Shwe Nat of Mandalay damning and cursing in tears of blood when his Minthami too had given herself finally to Buddha.

The thundering water closed over everything. Angela gave herself up to it. Two white hands above the surface of the river held in the cupped-shape of a folded lotus-flower was the last she saw of Minthami, piteously crying, 'Help Amagyi — Angela, help, Minthami not swim either.'

TWO

'She's dead father, dead!' said Sa-Lon.

Nathan nodded.

From the jar the ashes were scattered, given back to the Irrawaddy that had always claimed her.

Nathan shuddered, Roi wept and Sa-Lon sought retribution.

THREE

The tonga stopped outside the paling fence. Moving away from the bedroom window overlooking the front garden, Angela began stiffly to put on her gloves. She pressed down hard between each finger in precise little movements calculated to draw the mind to the mundane rather than let it dwell on things that tore her apart. Angela noticed how the delicate crochet work of her lacy gloves had frayed and parted in places:

Yes, she thought, to become bogged down in trivia was best, it freed the passage of the day as the seconds, minutes, hours ticked away to the conclusion of a lifetime. The Buddhists had taught her to live only one day at a time — she ought to pay more attention to that simple advice, she told herself, by trying to do it more often. She blamed herself of course, for being so devoid of perception at the time. She regarded with cold hatred the face of her sleeping husband — in name only, God knew. The once distinguished Officer with his upright bearing, neat tread, precise manner and rows of ribbons and medals, he who had discharged his duties so carefully and conscientiously with only one ambition in mind, laid to waste. He had even married her on account of his career, for reasons of propriety and promotion he had said. And how are the mighty fallen when God or Buddha kicks over the pedestal, she could not help reflecting savagely: 'Why have I to give up everything I've built for myself in this country, just because of you?'

she asked him while his bloated face reminded her of an over-ripe aubergine traced by the red lines of his degeneracy. Mouth wide open in drunken stertorous breathing, one arm trailing the floor, he repelled her to such an extent she could not look upon him another moment. 'Janum,' she called sharply and Jeffrey's boy appeared in the doorway. 'I'm going now, Jan. Be sure and not let Sahib get hold of the whisky bottle when he wakes — if he ever does!' With a last sour look at the disgusting spectacle of her so-called husband, Angela walked past Janum on the threshold.

'Afsos!' Janum muttered. 'Memsahib, please do not worry about Colonel-Sahib, for Janum will take good care of everything.'

'I know that, Jan,' she said, placing a hand on the young man's shoulder. 'He's lucky you stay with him. No one else would.'

'He is like my own father or brother to me, Memsahib.'

'Poor you.' Angela went outside. She drew up on the verandah in pleasant surprise. Thania and Theo played on the lawn with Marbles. Thania, home for the summer holidays and not due back in Maymyo until the end of the monsoon season in October, chatted to Paul Monthavers who had strolled down from his bungalow and stood with a rapt expression on his face listening to her.

Angela held her breath, the diversion she had prayed for suddenly presenting itself in those few crystal seconds. Thania did not wear her glasses but held them in her lap while she sat on the lawn looking up into the face of the young man looking down at her. Her hair too, Angela noticed, was not worn in its usual severe braids wound round her head in matronly fashion, but had been pinned softly into curls and ringlets fastened with a blue ribbon. In her pale blue sleeveless frock she suddenly saw the reason for Paul Monthavers rapt attention upon her daughter. Why, thought Angela, she really is quite lovely, and in that moment forgot to chastise her for not wearing her glasses.

She pulled herself together and taking a deep breath went down the verandah steps. 'Good morning Paul. Not on duty today? My, my, Staff Officers up at Fort Dufferin seem to have a remarkable amount of time off these days.'

He smiled; 'I assure you Mrs Radcliffe, it's the first decent day off I've had for ten days.'

'How time does fly,' she remarked. 'Heavens, just listen to those turtle-doves! They breed like rabbits around here. Thania, don't take Marbles to Whitewalls today. You know how he yaps at the horses and frightens them.'

'I came to take him for a walk actually, Mrs Radcliffe, but didn't know your daughter was home to do the job for me,' Paul said.

'Thania, this is Captain Monthavers from Fort Dufferin. He sometimes comes to exercise Marbles for us. I'm sure he won't mind if you and Theo accompany him as he has taken all the trouble to come to visit us from Mandalay.'

Paul Monthavers appeared not to mind the suggestion in the least, nor Theo who often accompanied him on his walks, but Thania turned her head away and spoke to the trees, 'It's so hot mama. I think I'll stay here in the shade.'

'As you wish. Goodbye Paul. Thank you for coming to see us. Marbles is delighted and can't wait for Theo to put his lead on.'

She went out of the garden gate to the patiently waiting tonga. She liked him; she really liked him. He was, at last, a military man who did not call her 'ma'am' which she couldn't abide! A decent wholesome young man who had Matthew Sinclair's qualities. Then, reflecting upon Matthew Sinclair, Angela felt she had indeed lost out. They should have married on the firm foundation of mutual respect and understanding and, if passion had not abounded in their hand clasps, it might have materialized over the years to bring them both a measure of happiness. But she had thrown everything, her whole life away, because of one lovely, lovely moment on the banks of the Irrawaddy. As with other things, she put Matthew Sinclair out of mind. Angela, biting her lip while the tonga carried her to Mandalay, thought that if Jeffrey, in the separateness of their existence together, had never furnished her with one single thing of grace apart from Theo, then the bringing of Paul Monthavers into their lives might just save the day not only for Thania but also for herself.

FOUR

Nathan was already waiting for her outside the gates of Fort Dufferin. 'Honey,' he said, helping her down from the tonga, 'I hate to put you through this.'

She could not bear to look into his haggard face; a month after Minthami's drowning he was still a broken man. He took her elbow and led her into the Provost Marshall's Court where a Government Advocate was presiding over the Court of Enquiry regarding the deaths of several people in the bursting of Captain de Veres-Vorne's river-dam.

Angela closed her eyes. All she could see were the swirling waters of the Irrawaddy, Minthami's pink robe and her strange dancer's hands in her tomb of water being swept out of reach while the tidal wave that had borne down on them had taken one woman and tossed the other on the higher reaches of the Bund where eager waiting hands had dragged her to safety. Would to God it had been you Minthami and not me ... not me when the look on Nathan's face denies everything but you ... Over and over again she had tormented herself about what had happened, cried in the night with no hope of any comfort from anywhere — not even from Nathan, destroyed and parted forever from her on the ashes of Minthami's laughter so that she could not bear to think of the years she had lost in believing she held a place in his heart.

Sa-Lon, Angela noticed, was in the Courtroom. Their eyes met and held, and then Sa-Lon smiled through lambent eyes reminding her so much of Minthami. But the smile was not his mother's. It was cold, hard and calculating and Angela turned away from Sa-Lon's veiled accusations to look at Nathan with bent head engrossed upon what U Po Thine was advising him to do and say in a last minute rapid discussion before the Court finally got under way. Realistically, Angela had come to terms with the fact that if the verdict of criminal negligence went against Nathan, then the de Veres-Vorne Company of Mandalay would never survive the recriminations that would inevitably follow. Angela wondered if she were responsible for what had happened by calling in the German with his centrifugal pump and other modern equipment she knew nothing about, though in her heart she could not help feeling the Italian, Signor Luci, was basically at fault.

'Please tell us Signor Luci, in the simplest possible terms so that we might all understand, the basic construction of your dam.' The Government Advocate began his enquiry.

'A dam of earth, sand and gravel, it had a core of clay reinforced with concrete blocks, it is known as a rock-fill dam, your honour.'

Signor Luci went on to talk about hydrostatic forces, sedimentation and silt deposits, and steady discharge curves all of which left Angela far behind so that she found her mind wandering away from such factual data. She looked across at Nathan who sat back against his chair with his arms folded, absorbed utterly in what Signor Luci was saying. Would I, she wondered irrationally, have changed a moment of my life so that I would not have to stand up presently to account for my part in things that happened during his absence to tear us both apart, and of which he lays the blame at my door, if silently? Would I have changed a moment of it so that I would not now be here knowing, knowing, in this one final moment before Jeffrey drags me back to England with him, that every last moment was worth the fight? Answer me Nathan, answer me.

He looked up, drawn immutably to her. He beheld her steady green eyes and for a moment she was back again under the thick fleshy-leaved mango trees hung with festive Chinese lanterns in the Sawbwa's compound, her Aunt Emmy beside her, Nathan's pipe-smoke and the scent of bhodi flowers mingling on the soft night air with a look like this between them that had lasted forever and forever without another person in their field of vision. Searched, compelled, wounded by him, Nathan's strong blue magnetism accusing her of all sorts of things, Angela encountered Sa-Lon's dark eyes watching them greedily. God, Nathan, must your son also destroy me? she asked silently, savagely, gritting her teeth against father and son.

Angela felt unable to sit through another moment listening to centrifugal forces and linear impulses. She got up to go outside for a breath of fresh air because she felt faint — and because she could not bear Nathan's cold-shouldering another moment.

An hour later Nathan found her huddled on a bench outside the Courtroom. 'It's over for today. Back in the morning for the final verdict,' he said while Sa-Lon remained at his right hand, the only person he now seemed to want beside him.

She glanced up at him. 'Nathan, I'm sorry. If it was because of Herr Truffen ...'

He flicked a derisive hand in the air. 'Don't be an ass, Angela, it wasn't anything to do with Herr Truffen but merely a culmination of unforseen events. I'll see you in the morning as all the witnesses have said their piece, so we'll be required to attend the final summing-up. The G.A.'s now got all the relevant material at his finger-tips and should have enough time between now and tomorrow to mull over with his experts on whether I'm guilty or not of criminal negligence because I didn't get my godowns attended to before.'

'Don't,' she said, shuddering. 'You make it sound like

565

a death sentence.' She wished she hadn't used the word.

'Isn't it?' he asked coldly. 'If I'm found responsible, then I'm finished in Mandalay. Years and years of back-breaking slog for nothing!' he flung at her bitterly.

'*We're* finished in Mandalay, Nathan,' she replied, stung by his uncompromising attitude.

He looked hard at her: 'Come on Sa-Lon,' he said turning on his heel, 'let's get out of this hell-hole.'

FIVE

The Government Advocate took an hour and a half to sum up his findings, and that period of time was the longest Angela felt she had ever had to sit through; it even seemed longer than the time she, Nathan, Matthew and Nanette Gideon had sat in Thibaw's antechamber waiting for the Queen of Burma to pronounce sentence.

If the de Veres-Vorne Company folded in Mandalay on account of fifteen people drowning she doubted she could ever live with herself again. Nathan did not meet her eyes once, he had not spoken to her once, but kept to himself, to Sa-Lon and U Po Thine the whole morning. What about me? she cried silently. God damn you Nathan, what about me? Haven't I put in just as much over the last ten years to drag the de Veres-Vorne Company out of its native status to stand on a par with the Bombay—Burma Corporation? Don't blame me for what happened to Minthami, I did what I could. Depleted, she could only listen uncomprehendingly to the drone of the G.A.'s voice admonishing everyone from Signor Luci to Herr Truffen for criminal negligence.

Criminal negligence; death by hanging; death by garotting. Angela wanted to put her hands over her ears so that she did not have to listen to any more recriminations — because a verdict of criminal negligence upon the de Veres-Vorne Company, Mandalay would not only be Nathan's death sentence, but also hers.

'And therefore, in conclusion I'm bound to go by the findings of this Court wherein it is unanimously agreed that the de Veres-Vorne Company of Mandalay is found not guilty of criminal negligence.'

Nathan, tapping his pen up and down on the blotter in front of him, a deep and undivided concentration upon those precise little movements masking his equally undivided attention on the Government Advocate's concluding evidence, suddenly threw down the pen, picked up his sola-topi and without a backward glance left the Courtroom.

CHAPTER
FORTY

ONE

Outside Whitewalls Angela stepped down from the tonga and paid off the driver. Slowly she walked up the red-gravel drive, the coolness beneath the shading trees lining the grassy verges of Nathan's lovely gardens infinitely pleasant, soothing to the spirit. Turtle-doves warbled, out of sight but never out of mind. She paused for an instant to look at the graceful house of Sagyin marble from the mines of Burma. How intrinsically rich this land was she thought in those snatched moments of tranquil reflection — they seemed to come less and less frequently in these days of feverish activity which agitated her mind and spirit. Rich yes, in material wealth, beauty and culture — but the exploitation had already begun. Somehow too, she could not help feeling the spirit was gone, depleted through the intervention of an Imperial power so that it had all become as solid and as dull as Calcutta, Rangoon or London itself. Mandalay's uniqueness, that magic and magnetism bestowed on it by its native rulers, despite the despotism by which they ruled, had gone, leaving behind a heart lacking in the lustre of Mindon Min's and Thibaw's days. Nathan had been so right — Queen Victoria could dwell in peace and stability forever and forever on the top of Mandalay Hill.

'Ko Lee,' Angela said in the cool spaciousness of Whitewalls' entrance hall, having heard music drifting across the gardens, 'Is my daughter here?' She had come primarily in search of Nathan not Thania, but found her attention diverted to the splendour of Thania's music into which she seemed to be putting her heart and soul.

'Yes, Memsahib,' Ko Lee said with an eager smile, 'she is busy making happy tunes which make servants dance with happy feet in kitchen quarters.'

Utterly dismayed by Thania's uncharacteristic disobedience, having been expressly forbidden from coming to Whitewalls if Sa-Lon de Veres-Vorne was in residence, Angela sat down heavily on the nearest thing to her, a small round table of heavy Sagyin marble, upon which stood a jade figurine much admired by Nathan. Angela asked Ko Lee to fetch her a drink of water. When he brought it she asked, 'Ko Lee, is your master at home?'

'No Memsahib Radcliffe, he is at river making ready to sail soon to Andaman Islands.'

'Thank you.' She put the empty tumbler back on the tray he held for her. Angela thought about Milly and Leigh though she did not know why. She wondered if, had they met on the gentler meadows of England rather than on the maidan of Empire, would Milly have been a widow at the tender age of eighteen? Perhaps; perhaps not. What then of herself? Would her love too have been doomed from the very outset were it to have been found on any other shore save this strong passionate one, where everyday influences made living adventures spill over into what should have been the quiet currents of a happy contentment at this time of her life? Yet, was she not one of those adventure-seekers too, as much as Milly and Leigh, Blaize and Edwin, Nathan, all of them in pursuit of golden dreams? And would she not rather be here now than in some quiet English village happily darning socks on a wooden mushroom while she forgot how to dream anymore? She did not know, anymore.

'Something wrong Memsahib Radcliffe?' Ko Lee asked in consternation as he peered at her.

Angela smiled. 'Ko Lee,' she told him, 'you're getting as grey as your master.' He grinned and endeavoured to disguise his ageing looks by skipping off across the hall with a livelier spring to his step. Angela opened the drawing-room door, anxious to take Thania home with her. She froze on the threshold, her knees almost letting her down as she witnessed Thania and Sa-Lon locked in an embrace, the intimacy of which made her realize this could not have been the first time. '*Thania!*'

'Mama.' With a little whimper of fright Thania sprang from Sa-Lon and, biting her lip, blinked at Angela in red-faced shame, realized she was not wearing her spectacles, dragged them off the music-sheets on top of the piano and put them on. She blinked stupidly at her mother while Sa-Lon took out a gold cigarette case, tapped a white cylinder of tobacco on it, sauntered to the arm of a chair and sat down on it, everything in his manner and actions calculated to enrage Angela even more. Trembling as though she were in the raging grip of fever she said through her teeth, 'Thania, go home this instant.' But Thania made the mistake of turning to look at Sa-Lon and Angela, misinterpreting that look as one requiring confirmation as to what she should or should not do from Sa-Lon de Veres-Vorne, made Angela take two steps forward to strike her daughter for disobedience and impudence. She prevented herself just in time; 'Go home Thania, at once!' she said in such a manner as to drive the fear of God into Thania's soul.

The girl fled. Angela turned to Sa-Lon, 'How dare you Sa-Lon! How *dare* you treat Thania as though she were ... as though she were one of your common women!'

He blew his smoke to the ceiling, the smirk on his lean handsome face rendering Angela speechless with fury. White-lipped she confronted him, waiting for an explanation and an apology for his behaviour. 'Thania,' he drawled in his cultivated English-cum-Harvard accent with no hint of apology in his manner, 'would be the last person I'd treat as one of my "common-women". You see, Mrs Radcliffe, as soon as Thania's twenty-one, she has consented to be my wife. I'm prepared to wait that long.'

'Oh God.' So this was the English girl Minthami had meant! Angela choked silently while Sa-Lon got up off the chair and sauntered around his father's drawing-room, one hand in his pocket, the other holding his cigarette in a nonchalant attitude. 'So Colonel-Memsahib ... no please ...' he held up a deprecating hand, 'please don't say a word until you've heard me out. I know why you would not approve of your daughter ... I beg your pardon,' he dipped his head facetiously, 'your *adopted* daughter from marrying me. You and your husband call my breed — half-castes, I think is the term commonly used, or there is another endearing expression for half-breeds such as myself — an Eurasian, neither one thing nor the other, but only a mongrel, a hybrid, a potpourri. Though I wonder what I ought to be called in view of my American father ... an Amasian? Shanam? Or even Amor — short for American-Oriental. I think your greatest fear would be that if Thania were to become my wife, your pure white grandchildren would be brown, eh Memsahib Radcliffe? The kind they call in Anglo–India, tainted-with-the-tarbrush? That's what Roi and I are, Amagyi-Angela, tainted blood. Or is it that you have something else against me apart from the colour of my skin?'

'Sa-Lon,' Angela said, contriving to keep sane, 'once, not so very many years ago, you used the name Amagyi-Angela to me as an expression of love and respect. Don't use it on me now.'

'Why? Because it makes you feel guilty? Guilty that while my mother went into her Convent because she was a loving and true devotee of her religion, you used the Buddhists for your own designs, your own subtle schemes based on fraud and not faith?'

'What on earth do you mean?'

'I mean, Memsahib Radcliffe, while you hide your lovely innocent, trusting, daughter away behind her ugly glasses, hairstyles and drab clothes in that remote English school up in the hills, the whole of Mandalay still sniggers behind your back and your own incredible

571

näivety. Yes! Oh Yes! Look at her — no, you've already done that, haven't you? That's why you can't bear to have Thania loose when you're around. She reminds you too much of yourself, doesn't she?'

Angela swayed. Putting her hand out she found the piano stool. She sat down, white as a sheet. Sa-Lon, his face equally white, smoked his cigarette. 'I want to marry Thania,' Sa-Lon said. He turned to look fully at her. 'I, Amagyi-Angela, Sa-Lon de Veres-Vorne, an Eurasian with a highly improbable name, want to marry your daughter and she wants to marry me.'

Angela contrived to hold herself steady. 'Sa-Lon, where is your father?'

He shrugged indifferently. 'Where he always is I guess. After this morning he's a free man again and his own master. What a wonderful defence you put up for the de Veres-Vorne Company Mrs Radcliffe.' Sa-Lon's dark lashes lowered to his factitious compliments. 'I daresay he's at my mother's memorial stone buried deep in his garden along with six others. Underneath the Mohurs, Mrs Radcliffe, among my half-caste brothers and sisters, the scarce-formed bones of Buddha's children. By Minthami's monuments to love, he'll no doubt be shedding his crocodile tears and begging her forgiveness for having neglected her welfare of late by taking himself off to America instead of being in Mandalay to attend to her physical wellbeing. It's his self-imposed whipping block, damn him, for having been away from Mandalay when his bloody dam burst and drowned her.'

His voice broke and he turned aside. Sa-Lon dragged deeply on his cigarette, and when he turned back to her he looked her up and down with one of his supercilious smiles so that she could have smacked his beautiful face for insolence, 'If he's not at his memory-stones, Amagyi-Angela, you might find him at the Sasana offering cherries to other nuns, or at the Shwe Kyaung, the Mahamuni or the Kyauktawgyi. Anywhere where her ghost walks marble terraces so that he can catch a glimpse of her pink robe and shaven head going about in all humility because she was once a white man's whore.'

The next moment a blow she had been itching to strike sent him rocking. 'Sa-Lon, you will apologize to me for those words. You will apologize to me over the sacred ashes of your mother or, by God, I'll thrash you with my own hands — something your father should have done to you a long time ago. Don't you ever, don't you *ever* let your father hear you talk like that about Minthami because you'll rue the day, I warn you! Minthami loved you. She loved you and Roi more than life itself, so don't you ever insult her again in front of me. Sa-Lon de Veres-Vorne, were you the last man left on earth, I'd see to it Thania never married you, I swear it.'

He dragged heavily on his cigarette before viciously stubbing it out in an ashtray. Not looking at her he said brokenly, 'How can you, how can you even mention my mother's name when it was you who ultimately destroyed her? How, Amagyi-Angela?' He raised his head then, his golden cheek smarting with the red flash of her hand. 'You, pretending to be so moral and upright the whole time, wearing a Buddhist nun's robes, shaving off your brilliant hair in pious offering to Buddha, why Amagyi-Angela why, that's what I'd like to know?' He swivelled on his heel, away from her and, raising his eyes to the ceiling, lifted his hands in a theatrical gesture to remind her again of whose son he was though Minthami was never vicious like this. 'A couple of traitors, you and my father both. My mother was always too damn näive to be offended by what was going on between you two. Don't think, Colonel-Memsahib that because Sa-Lon de Veres-Vorne has two coats of paint on him, one that you can see and one that you can't, he has no eyes to notice what's going on under his nose, no brain with which to think and no feelings inside here ...' He thumped his breast savagely. 'Here, in a heart half black half white beating to the tempo of a million insults every day, the greatest one of them all is what my father did to my mother because of *you*!'

'Don't be absurd!'

'Oh, it's absurd now is it? Absurd because an Eurasian fellow, the random seed of a white man's lustings, voices his opinion in the face of a grand white Colonel-Memsahib who doesn't ever wish to hear the truth!'

'*Stop it! Stop it!*' she screamed, 'Oh Sa-Lon stop it.'

'No Colonel-Memsahib, I will not stop. Not now I've begun to say what I've been meaning to say to you for a long long time. You have been just like a pretty gadfly seeking to bite the hand of the unwary; just like the pretty blue grapebloom of the jungle that stings with poison in its beauty, you poisoned my father. Don't think I haven't noticed the way he looks at you — yes, even today, yesterday, the day before while my mother's ashes are scattered and his stupid tears mean nothing! As though she were of no consequence, her black feelings not worthy of consideration even now she's dead. Do you want to hear the real reason why she went into that convent and shaved off her hair, do you, *do you*?'

'No Sa-Lon, no! No. Don't, don't say anymore ... I'm going ... please don't say another word. It isn't true. Your mother wanted to dedicate her life to Buddha. You know how much your father pleaded with her to reconsider her decision, how he tried so hard to dissuade her from doing such a thing. And you're right, I became a nun not out of love for Buddha, or anything else. I loved nothing and nobody at the time, I did it as a matter of expediency. You know the truth of it, Sa-Lon.' She put out her hands as though she would ward off any more vile accusations he might make. 'Now, I want to speak to your father. Thania will never be yours, Sa-Lon, never.'

He came close, thrusting his face to hers, 'I want to marry Thania,' he hissed, 'and you won't prevent me.'

'Yes I will, Sa-Lon.'

His eyes narrowed, he glared hard at her, the look on his face vindictive. 'One day, Amagyi-Angela, this country will be mine again, and you won't have a right anymore to dictate to me what I should or should not do. One day, you and your meddling countrymen, the type you have the misfortune to be married to — pompous, unimaginative, medal-mad and drunk — will be kicked out of Mandalay never to return. While you massacre our monks, our princes, our village-headmen in your so-called "pacification programme" there won't be any peace here. While you and my grand rich father build their marble houses and teak bungalows to fashion and rule the world, there won't be any peace here. One day, Amagyi-Angela, the chinthe will open its jaws and roar so loudly, you'll be deafened as it tells you to get the hell out of Mandalay and everywhere else the tentacles of your Empire stretch, get out and go back to your cold grey dismal shores where your cold grey dismal people belong! But, when Thania is twenty-one, I will marry her, unless you wish to furnish me here and now with some legitimate reason why I cannot do so?'

Angela had difficulty in speaking and, swallowing, she said, 'Sa-Lon, that will never happen, not now, not even when Thania is twenty-one, thirty-one or forty-one. I wouldn't allow it. The chip on your shoulder would destroy you both. Now please move aside so that I might speak to your father.'

Sa-Lon straightened his back, moved away and said with a smile; 'He'll be on his boat if you wish to join him now that there's nothing preventing you and he from enjoying each other's company freely — except the fine Colonel-Sahib at Sequoia who doesn't know what time of day it is.'

'That's true, Sa-Lon. But the fine Colonel-Sahib still retains the power to deprive you of the signature you so badly require in order to marry my daughter.' And upon that parting shot she ran out of Whitewalls down to the river to find Nathan. 'Nathan, oh Nathan,' she cried, stumbling in anguish across the deck.

He came out of his cabin in alarm. 'Angela ... what the devil ...'

'Please, oh please ... I must speak to you. I know you've been deliberately avoiding me Nathan, but I've got to tell you something. Can we go inside? Shut the door.' Wildly distraught, she flung herself on him.

575

'Nathan, it's Thania.'

'What about Thania? Is she ill?'

Angela shook her head, swallowing hard to push down the lump in her throat that threatened to choke the life out of her.

'Here ... have some brandy, you look ghastly. 'He went to the decanter and while his back was turned Angela said:

'Nathan, Sa-Lon wants to marry Thania.'

He turned with two glasses of brandy in his hand and a smile on his face. 'Well now, that's wonderful news.'

'Shut up and listen to me. They can't marry, I won't allow it, they can't, Nathan, and that's all there is to it.' Oh God, she cried inwardly — what a terrible tangled web we do weave on that first deception! Her trembling fingers found the bulbous glass and while she drank to steady her nerves Nathan stood in front of her nursing the amber liquid in his glass. He regarded her steadily.

'I get it,' he said quietly. 'It's to do with his colour, isn't it? You and Jeffrey ...'

'*Damn you, damn you,* a million times! Thania is your daughter, *your daughter*!' she shrieked.

In the terrible silence that followed, he turned away to look out of the window at the river because he could not bear to look at her.

Sobbing she blurted it all out while he was like a man turned to stone. 'That's why Sa-Lon and Thania can't marry, don't you see now? Colour doesn't enter into it, only blood, only incest!' She turned away and began to bite her nails. 'The whole of righteous Mandalay knows whose child she is, but I wanted her back with me and so I didn't care because she was your child, *our* child Nathan. I even named her after you. I told Jeffrey she was Garabanda's child ... but even he guessed the truth, like Sa-Lon, like all of them ... Thania knows I'm her mother, but not who her father is.'

'I think,' he said, a grey voice rising from the tomb, 'you'd better start at the beginning and explain everything — including the truth about this man Garabanda.'

576

He still did not look at her but kept his elbow supported on the wide ledge above the window seat, his thumb against his top teeth as he stared numbly out of the window. 'From the very beginning, Angela, so that I know just how much you've deceived me and what it's cost us both.'

She told him about how she had met Matthew Sinclair aboard the *S.S. Tahara*, how they became engaged in Delhi and of her decision after her father's death to join Matthew in Mandalay rather than wait for him to get another posting in India. She told him about her journey through Northern India with the Quentins and how the little band of missionaries were ambushed in the Jainta Pass and what happened thereafter to Felicity Quentin and herself. She told him about meeting Blaize and Edwin in Manipur and what they did for her, and how afterwards, they had provided her with an escort to get to Loloi where she had arranged to visit her Aunt Lydell first before coming down to Mandalay. 'The rest of the story you almost know, Nathan, except that the man I killed in the mango shrine outside Mandalay was not unknown to me. At the time I thought it was some gross coincidence, but then I knew it was something that was meant to happen, that he, with others like him, run wild through northern Burma making trouble and so it was natural he would wish to grab what he could from Upper Burma's richest city — the Prince he had been serving was also from the Court of Ava, so Garabanda's presence here was not that out of the ordinary — just the time and place and my meeting again with him. I'd do it all over again too. He wasn't a Burmese dacoit, because I know they don't rape women but are only after loot and the excitement of killing other men who stand in their path. Garabanda was an out-and-out thug with only a small part of Burmese blood in him, the rest some sort of Arab–Indian mixture. I'm telling you all this because the girl who suffered the same fate as myself, Felicity Quentin, found she was going to have Gara-banda's child. Blaize saved the day for her. Without

577

going into any of the sordid details, that kind of realization gave me nightmares and I went into a kind of physical shock so that when month after month went by and nothing happened to me as it was supposed to each month, I thought I was going to have his child.' She composed herself by getting up to help herself to another glass, but this time she poured out a drink of water. Turning, she saw that he kept his face hidden from her. 'But I didn't, I had yours instead. Being incredibly näive at the time — having been taught none of the facts of life at school, only the spiritual, godly aspect of things, I couldn't bear to look at Thania as a baby in the Sasana Convent Refuge Centre because, in the circumstances, I wasn't sure in my own mind whose child she was. So I sent her away to England in the care of nuns where she was looked after by foster parents. The money my father and uncle Adrian Hawes left me was spent on donations to the Sasana who were my shield and anchor at that awful time. The rest gradually disappeared over the years to support Thania, to pay her foster parents and also the nuns in England who kept an eye on Thania's affairs for me. When I was able to sort things out in my own mind, and found there had been no need for my irrational fears and that Thania could be only one man's child, yours, I wanted her back here in Mandalay with me. But I had to have a husband for that to happen, so I married Jeffrey — purely a marriage of convenience because he didn't need me physically nor I him. But it still took me nearly ten years to find the courage to bring Thania back, right under your nose. When I saw her for the first time as a grown-up little girl aboard the ship that brought her out here I knew immediately who she was — because she's you in so many many ways. But you still didn't notice, did you Nathan? Others might have, including your own son — though God forbid even Sa-Lon would not be so callous as to trample on Thania's feelings ...

He found his voice at last. 'God damn you Angela, don't talk about anyone trampling over Thania's feelings! You have done the grandest job any mother could have done in screwing up one little girl's life besides so many more — yours, mine and Sa-Lon's for a start before we look any further.' He turned around then to face her fully, his eyes blue and passionate in an anger that burned so deeply, she was afraid. 'And what about Matthew's?'

'I wouldn't expect you to understand, Nathan.'

'No, goddamn it, I don't!'

'How could I have married Matthew when I was expecting your child?'

'You could have come and told me for a start. You could have given me the benefit of the doubt, you could have *trusted* me, Amagyi-Angela!' He got up and went to his brandy. Tossing it back, he said: 'Why, Angela, why? God, woman, *why* didn't you come to *me*?'

'I couldn't ... not when I had the daughter that Minthami wanted ... not when there was nothing left for me but the last vestiges of dignity.'

'*Dignity, dignity*!' he accused passionately. 'Confound your damn dignity, your pride and ... and your stiff-necked British upper lip. You are a fraud Angela. You are ... oh God, I can't begin to tell you all the things you are. You lied, you cheated, you stole ... yes goddammit, you stole Thania from me, eighteen years of her life for the sake of your dignity? I could strike you down dead this minute for what you've done.'

'Please don't shout.'

'I'll shout. I'll let the whole of Mandalay know what a hypocrite you are — if they don't already know it. You and your obscene little husband, pretending to have adopted some little waif and stray from the streets of London when all the time she was *my* child!'

'Nathan, before you go on accusing us, why did you not take a closer look at her for yourself? Yes, Nathan, why didn't you? I'll tell you why. You were always too wrapped up in your own money-making schemes, your own selfish desires while I at least tried to preserve Thania's dignity and pride, her name and reputation so that she wouldn't have upon her the stigma of bastard.'

'Do you think I give a fig what anyone calls her?'

'No Nathan, and that's the crux of the matter because you couldn't give a fig about your own children or who calls them names, cruel names like bastard, illegitimate, half-castes and everything else thrown at them just so long as you're happy doing what you want to. You don't think it matters to them, but take a look at Sa-Lon, really look at him. You are part of his destruction, Nathan, and he suffers a million deaths every day because of what he is and who he is. No, of course it doesn't matter to you, but Minthami felt it and Minthami suffered on behalf of her sons once the British got here ... it didn't matter before they arrived, did it? So don't start pointing the finger at Jeffrey and me because Jeffrey at least provided Thania with a name and a status.'

'And that's about all that's ever mattered to you isn't it?' he said bitterly. 'Pride, dignity, status, propriety, a good name, legitimacy, a place on the Board of Governors, a pillar of society, a woman of virtue. God Angela, go away before I get really angry.'

'I'm not going until we've sorted out what I've come here to sort out. I want you to tell Sa-Lon the reasons why he can't marry Thania.'

'I'm to do your dirty work now, huh?'

'Yes, Nathan, as I had to once on your behalf.' She put up her hands to defend herself because she thought he was about to give her a shaking for a remark she knew would cut him more deeply than anything else she could say. But instead he turned aside. 'Does Thania know who her real father is?'

'No.'

'But you're going to tell her?'

'Of course — now.'

He turned around to face her again, his glass in his hand. 'I congratulate you Angela. That poor girl who has only just managed to sort herself out after years of being shunted around from pillar to post, first with the Buddhists, then with strangers in England for God knows what mercenary purposes, then to be brought here as the adopted child of Anglo—India's upper crust, next to be told her adopting mother is her real mother after all and that her father, her real father, lives next door to her adopted father — but to cap it all, that the first man she falls in love with turns out to be her half-brother. Jesus! It's no wonder she's a corkscrew not knowing which way to turn!' In complete despondency he tossed down his brandy and said; 'You know exactly how to crucify someone don't you?' All the scorn and derision in the world was embodied in the manner in which he regarded her at that moment. But while she felt partially responsible, she could not accept the full extent of his abuse as she had done only what she had considered to be right at the time. 'Why the devil didn't you do the most sensible and logical thing and tell me about Thania eighteen years ago, not now when it's far too late?'

'Would you have married me then, Nathan?' she asked quietly.

His eyes faltered to the rim of his glass as he swirled the liquid round and round. 'No,' he said, raising his head then to look at her levelly, 'but I'd have made good provision for you and for her, just as I always did for Minthami and the boys.'

'I never doubted it.'

'So you thought of other ways and means of hitting back at me for having destroyed and humiliated you a second time around, is that it?'

'No, that's nothing to do with it. I did what I felt ought to be done in the best interests of my child and myself.'

'Yes,' he said very bitterly, 'in the best interests all round. You've always somehow managed to confuse the word love for sin because in your tiny inhibited little mind love has never been given any house-room. Just because you, Angela Featherstone, were emotionally starved during your childhood, shut away in some sterile Womens' Academy, you did not have to impose the same deprivations on Thania. Sa-Lon and Roi at least grew up with love and happiness surrounding them, so it's up to them now what they choose to make of their lives. But you, you've never been able to accept that because Minthami was a part of my life, you too could be included. You've never been able to understand that hearts and minds and souls aren't rigid little ballot boxes with votes thrust through the slots, and once filled, the majority is not declared the winner! I loved Minthami long before you came into my life, and when you did you added a new dimension to it. Nothing was subtracted, only added — Minthami knew that and accepted it. But you couldn't, because your upbringing made you too narrow to accept anything that might in some way be called unconventional.'

'So you wanted the best of both worlds, Minthami and me? Is that what you're saying?'

'Yes dammit.'

'At least you're honest — an honest Buddhist at heart, Nathan Vorne.' Angela had to smile despite her feelings. 'And you really are a man! You're a man, I'm a woman, and the rules are preordained — Christian, Buddhist or Gospelite — while the world will go on revolving as long as men like you make the rules to suit themselves, eh Nathan? I'm going now. I'll do my best to try and explain to our daughter how and why I mismanaged both our lives and I suggest you do the same for Sa-Lon. Jeffrey and I will be returning to England shortly and Thania and Theo will be coming with us. That's all I wish to say upon the matter — except that, after the de Veres-Vorne Company was vindicated this morning and freed of the slur of criminal negligence which caused all those deaths, I didn't deliberately set out to destroy Minthami for you.' She paused, waiting for him to meet her half-way, say something rather than accuse her all the time by his tragic silences. Angela swallowed, her defeat complete at his hands. 'I hope Roi will continue to keep up the de Veres-Vorne's good name here in Mandalay and that Sa-Lon will one day forgive me for everything of which I stand accused.' She turned her back on him and left his boat.

It was enough. She knew she had left him as desolate as she was herself. How and where, she wondered, had she strayed off the old hermit-phongyi's eight-fold path? She came to the conclusion it was the last one, 'right understanding,' as she hurried along the river road back to Sequoia. I did not understand in my jealousy, she told herself. I was always so jealous of Minthami, her happiness, her beauty, her popularity, her freedom and laughter and gaiety of spirit, her acceptance of the great issues of life without question, her humility — and of course her husband. Second wife, why that is laughable now, for I have never been anything to him, only his woman-manager — or perhaps I'm again lacking in right understanding. Maybe Nathan is right, love is not a compartmented word, maybe one can love twice and his love for Minthami has nothing to do with me, for he can love us both, equally and differently ... Buddhist reasoning again. Oh, I don't know. Right understanding though, that must be the utter receptiveness of mind and spirit. So, time to start again on that perpetual cycle of rebirth, time to pay attention, to take heed of yesterday's mistakes in order never to repeat them again on the next revolution of one's life, the next step forward to the next involvement with those whom we inevitably come to destroy, no matter how unwittingly and with the best one-time intentions, out of that first desire and that first deception ...

In a vague disorientated way, her thoughts cut off in midstream, Angela registered the presence of the doctor's carriage outside Vanda Wandersmith's bungalow and hoped neither she nor Nancy were ill.

On her own doorstep she encountered Sa-Lon with his arms around Thania. She was weeping bitterly against his shoulder. For one panic-ridden moment Angela's heart stood still, certain that Sa-Lon and Thania had followed her to Nathan's boat and had heard every acrimonious word shouted between them.

'Sa-Lon,' she said icily, regaining what little self-control she had left, feeling she had had as much as she could endure for one day, 'I thought I told you to leave Thania alone. Go to your father's boat, he wants to speak to you. Thania, come inside.'

'Mrs Radcliffe, I ...' Sa-Lon, his cheeks flushing and then paling as he fought down his conflicting emotions, gently disengaged Thania's arms from their desperate embrace. Angela could not believe her ears when he said to Thania, 'I'll handle this, go to Whitewalls, Thania, and let me talk to your mother alone.'

She nodded, and without looking at her mother, ran down the garden path, through the white gate and along the road towards Whitewalls.

'Sa-Lon,' Angela said, bridling at their behaviour, 'what's the meaning of this?'

'Please Mrs Radcliffe,' he said, a certain desperation about him so that she did not know what to make of him, 'I haven't come here to quarrel with you because this is neither the time nor the place. We've said what we have to say to each other, except this last — I want you to understand that I, in seeking ways and means to hit back at you — for reasons you already know — am the loser. Revenge doesn't taste as sweet as I'd anticipated. I apologize for having used Thania against you. I've guessed for a long time now whose daughter she is; I realize she's as much my father's daughter as yours ... oh, please don't worry, I haven't shocked her any more by telling her of such a thing, that's not my place but yours and father's. I just want you to be aware of how ashamed I am of myself, while realizing too that saying sorry isn't enough. However, once Thania's been told the truth regarding whose child she is, she'll understand ... she won't see me again as I'm off to Rangoon tomorrow. The only reason I'm here now is because Thania sent for me. The doctor is with your husband ... no, don't go inside!' Sharply he took hold of her elbow to stop her precipitous flight indoors. His Adam's apple bobbed with the difficulty of striking another blow against her, one which gave him no pleasure whatsoever and left him with as bitter a taste as trying to manipulate a sweet and innocent child like Thania against her own mother. 'The Colonel-Sahib had a fight with Janum. He got hold of the revolver Janum was keeping from him and shot himself through the head ...'

Angela clutched the empty air. She found her support on Sa-Lon. I must keep control, I must, I must, she told herself frantically as she pressed her face to the welcome shoulder of the one person she had come to despise. The rest of her world spun round and round, her wheel of fortune turning and turning and turning forever backwards, never forwards; the old Sayadaw in his Monastery, Buddha in his Pagoda, Jesus Christ on his Cross — all reaffirmed for her the one Karma over which she had no control. Whatever form sorrow took, it was hewn by other people, fashioned by them and nailed by them for the purposes of eluding her own faith and destiny. 'Jeffrey!' she cried, her fists against Sa-Lon, pounding him against this the final humbling of her spirit, 'Jeffrey ... why ... why? I must go to him ... help him.'

'No, you mustn't go to Jeffrey now,' Sa-Lon said, firmly gentle as he kept her away from the house. 'There's nothing more you can do to help him, you've done your best. Please go back to my father's boat and tell him what has happened ... he'll know how to advise you. Meanwhile, I'll stay here and do what I can to help.'

She nodded, dumbly, like a child.

Angela found Nathan where she had left him, his hands covering his face as he sat hunched in utter desolation on the windowseat in his cabin. She dropped to her knees in front of him. Her lips against his hands, foreheads together, their tears mingled.

'Nathan,' she whispered, 'I've come back and I don't want to go away from you again. Forgive me for being so blind.'

Presently she would tell him about Jeffrey, not yet, not yet. For now she wished only to savour this one precious moment with him, alone and unfettered, untarnished by words of sorrow or regret, gilded only by actions of love so often taken for granted in this the Karma she had made for herself.

Without moving he said; 'I was so afraid I'd lost you too Amagyi-Angela, my spirit, my driving-force, my life's counterpart. Without you I'm nothing; without you I began to ask myself that one helluva question no man likes to ask himself at this late stage in his life, what was it all for?' Then he raised his head to look at her fully, his face and voice no more muffled but clear in the crystal-blue mirrors of his heart. 'You've just answered my questions, Amagyi-Angela.'

Above his head she could see the soft blue-gold sky of approaching evening; she could hear the breeze trifle with pagoda bells in flirtatious music, watch it dally with the fronds of the ebon-green palms and ruffle the waters of the Irrawaddy that had joined them in love and commitment, and knew in that shining moment she would not have changed one step of the way, not one single step.

EPILOGUE — 1945

T he sun had set on Mandalay Hill.
Earth and sky were baptized by fire, consumed by fire, and in its deliverance Mandalay died in the flames.

As the last of the Mitchell bombers streaked away like black birds of prey into a copper-bronze sunset, the sky in the East settled to lemon and violet, shades of a lesser violence. A curious peace came to the land where once a city had been built to honour Buddha.

Eighty-eight years had passed since the birth of the golden city, a man's span in history, no more than the haunting scent of a bhodi flower. And a way of life had gone forever.

In the chaos and confusion, dust and debris, fire and fury, in the tragic aftermath of war, a remarkable coincidence occurred that had its beginnings half a century earlier.

On the 9th March, 1945, General Slim's 14th Army in Burma reached the outskirts of Mandalay. They found the Japanese dug in on Mandalay Hill, and occupying Fort Dufferin, the former palace enclosure of the Burmese Kings. Repeated infantry assaults across seventy-five yards of hyacinth-choked moat by the Royal Berkshire Regiment had been repelled time after time. On the hill of seven hundred temples, along the covered walkways and Kuthodaw staircases, a battle between Japanese and British soldiers was fought to the end.

Ten days later a heavy air attack was launched by the British. Mitchell bombers loaded with 2,000 lb bombs strafed Mandalay in an unprecedented air bombardment that lasted two days. The city was razed to the ground, nothing was left standing except Mandalay's red brick walls, Mindon Min's legacy to the Burmese nation. When the air attack stopped, six Burmans, railway officials in hiding from the Japanese, crawled through underground pipes and tunnels beneath Fort Dufferin to emerge on the other side of the walls bearing a white flag of surrender. The railwaymen informed the British Military Commander that the last of the Japanese troops had withdrawn two days earlier.

King Mindon Min's unique palace of carved teak, tiered roofs like the curving hands of a *Pyazat* dancer offering prayers to Buddha, was gone forever. Vermilion lacquer, burnished gold, lattice glass and mosaic decorations, all destroyed in the horrors of twentieth century warfare.

A young British Officer of the Royal Berkshire Regiment who had fought so hard for the liberation of Mandalay from the Japanese looked aghast at the scene of destruction. Close to him, near a crumbling parapet, a mighty chinthe sat beside its twin, guardians of the breathtaking staircase that wound up Mandalay Hill from the top of which could be seen the misty-blue Shan Hills. All at once, as if giving a mighty roar of disapproval at what had been done to its sacred city, the chinthe's jaw dropped open and shattered masonry fell at the Officer's feet. When the dust had settled he saw something bright sparkling in the bleak ruins of the stone image.

He stooped to retrieve the tiny jewel winking defiance at the broken land. It was a charm of a Burmese *Nat* spirit studded with precious gems. But something else caught his eye, a piece of paper fluttering on the ground, deliberately buried inside the chinthe's mouth along with the necklace. Scratched in sepia letters on the scrap of parchment a verse had been written in English. The signatures intrigued him more. *Amagyi-Angela and the Shwe Nat of Mandalay wish you, O lucky stranger,*

Happy New Year, 20th Century, 1900.

Astonished, he put both the necklace and the piece of paper in his pocket, his excitement unbounded.

Searching, searching, frantically searching through smoke and dust, through battered stonework and rubble, in flattened bamboo and thatch, in the matting of homeless refugees, with the cries and the screams, the bark of scavenging dogs, the whimper of the starving, the injured and the frightened beside him, he asked, pried, and searched. Everywhere he went he was met with the same numbness, the same glazed opposition to his questioning. Bruised and broken, the populace of Mandalay who had remained behind under the Japanese were shattered and stunned, and no one would furnish him with an answer. Always he was met by the same careless shrug of the shoulders, the terrible accusation:

'Dead. So many of them dead and gone. If not taken by the Japanese, then killed by British bombs, sorry.'

He despaired.

And then, so soon before his Regiment was due to move off, he ran to earth a surly Burman outside a rundown ka-ka shop that had miraculously escaped the bombing. Seated beneath a sacred Banyan tree, he sipped a greasy cup of tea.

Yes, he had heard of the legendary Mrs Radcliffe who had once been the richest woman in Mandalay. No, she had not been taken away by the Japanese to one of their concentration camps.

The young Officer's hopes soared.

The Burman, the son of a Burmese woman called Ma Ngwe and her lawyer husband U Po Thine, both of them contemporaries of Mrs Radcliffe, remembered being taken once to a grand white house out on the Bund and there, crouched beneath a grand white piano he had listened to an English girl playing beautiful music. He, young as he had been at the time, remembered it well. And then he dashed the young man's hopes.

'Mad,' he said, 'mad, mad,' repeating the word for impact as to the depth of the woman's madness. He stirred his greasy tea. His eyes dull and listless, he went on to qualify his statement, 'And that's why the Japanese didn't want her, like so many of her sort. They had no wish for a mad woman to disrupt one of their camps and give them more trouble than she was worth.'

'Is she alive now? Where can I find her? Will she still be at her house on Bund Road?' The questions tumbled one after another in his eagerness to find Mrs Radcliffe, mad or otherwise.

The Burman shrugged indifferently. 'House is gone. Everything has gone. Only white walls stand here and there like red walls of city which is all that's left. Nothing, nothing except bare walls everywhere.'

'And the mad woman?' the young officer asked, prompting the Burman into revealing more — and he certainly knew more despite his reticence.

Again the lazy shrug of shoulders disillusioned with the world; 'She is somewhere, everywhere ... in Mandalay, somewhere ... If she hasn't been killed by her own bombers. You will find her more easily if you ask for the Amagyi-Angela and not Mrs Radcliffe.'

'Amagyi-Angela,' the young man repeated, the verse and charm in his pocket like a good omen. 'Yes, I realize the legendary Amagyi-Angela is also Mrs Radcliffe — my grandmother told me.' He smiled. 'Thank you so much,' and with joy the Englishman thrust out his hand to the Burman.

But the forlorn Burman was looking instead into his empty cup, the British having caused him too many problems with the thoughtless placing of their bombs.

In anticipation, and with a spring in his step, the young man set off from the inner city to the river. He took the Bund Road as instructed, his footsteps taking him in first one direction and then the other while he looked and searched once again, but this time with greater hope in his breast.

Then he saw what he had at first supposed was a ruined pagoda, but no, closer inspection revealed the ruins of a spacious family dwelling. And there, exactly as the Burman had said, stood the bare bones of what must once have been the grandest house in Mandalay.

Congratulating himself on his abilities as a sleuth, he pressed the jewelled charm in his pocket as he strode along an overgrown, weed-thick drive over pink-gravel stones that had all but disappeared in neglect. Only the trees remained, tall sailor palms, mohur and jacaranda. He wandered through the neglected garden and was disappointed by the bleak desolation that revealed no woman, mad or otherwise. And then his footsteps brought him into a little patch of ground well-hidden by the trees. In its cool shadiness he came across an old nun with bald head, her pink robes crumpled and dusty. On her knees, she was viciously prodding the reluctant earth with a broken trowel at the same time thrusting seeds from a packet into whatever scratch she was able to make in the unyielding ground. Several white marble stones leaned crazily against a rusty wrought-iron fence that hemmed the family cemetery.

'Mrs Radcliffe?' he asked warily, almost whispering her name, fearful lest she answer in the negative or that she indeed was so mad he would be unable to glean any sense at all from her.

The old old woman stretched a long and pitifully wrinkled neck to he who towered above her in khaki uniform. 'Always uniform!' he thought she had muttered, but was uncertain.

Like a tortoise taking a peek at the world and finding it not to its liking, she retracted once more to the safety of her shell and went back to poking the stubborn ground.

'Mrs Radcliffe, please may I talk to you?'

'You're doing all of that, aren't you, young man?' the voice barked from the earth and the depth of it in that frail old body set him almost leaping for joy when he had been on the verge of despair. 'And now that you've found me Leigh Buchanan what do you want of me?' she asked, still digging painfully with her broken gardening tool.

He took off his flat peak cap and mopped his brow with a khaki handkerchief, his grin wide and friendly; 'Whew, I thought I'd never catch up with you before we moved out.' He extended a warm firm hand in greeting. 'But I'm not Leigh Buchanan, Mrs Radcliffe, I'm his grandson John Buchanan. Johnney, Mrs Radcliffe ...'

'Don't call me Mrs Radcliffe, Captain Johnney,' she said with energy, 'I haven't been called that for years.' She took her dusty hand out of his warm clasp. 'My name is Amagyi-Angela.' She rocked back on her heels to regard him with a terrifying curiosity. 'Talk about the venerable old Sayadaw's perpetual cycle of rebirth, you're the spitting image of your grandfather, Captain Johnney. He was a good man, a brave man — though bravery, citations and medals won't bring him out of the grave and back into Milly's arms, eh Captain Johnney? But those whom the gods love die young,' she lamented, rather fiercely he imagined. 'After my nine lives are gone, Johnney Buchanan, no one will ever hear of me again.'

Abruptly she set down her trowel, wiped her hands on the hems of her skirts and with a supreme effort of will, hoisted herself from her knees. 'Come Johnney Buchanan, a graveyard is no place for a young man to converse. Only we who are soon to be of the spirit world ourselves have that privilege. We'll talk on the verandah steps as I haven't a house anymore; the Japanese put paid to it in the early days of the war.'

Standing up on bare brown feet, he was surprised at her height. Having seen her stooped double among the memorial tablets in her little garden-cemetery, she had seemed so pathetically small and frail. But now that she stood erect, he saw her as rather a forceful creature, extraordinary looking with her bald head and aged face, and more than a trifle intimidating. She stooped again to retrieve her begging-bowl and spitoon. 'I knew you were a Buchanan the moment I saw you. How proud your grandfather ... ah, but I promised myself I would not dwell in the past. You must tell me Captain Johnney, what brings you to Mandalay apart from this wretched war. Come, we'll sit here on the verandah and pretend it is as it used to be. Such a beautiful verandah once ... where I believed your grandfather almost shot your grandmother ... but you must be brief, Captain Johnney, because at eighty-six I'm no chicken and tire easily.'

He came to the conclusion at once that she was not at all mad though her odd appearance might have led the onlooker to suppose she was. He was quite certain she could engender a wily madness if she wished — if it served her own interests better! Sparse white whiskers stuck from the dome of her sun-baked head covered in freckles, her skin, ravaged by the hot Burmese sun, fitted her skeleton bones uneasily and hung in the wrinkles and folds of a shrivelled brown prune. Sunken gums and ill-fitting false teeth presented an awesome image of the very aged, infirm and senile — perhaps too, that contrived madness which had intimidated the Japanese Commander to reject her from the rest of those led away to camps of death.

'What brings you to me, Johnney Buchanan?' she asked. 'Why was it so imperative you find me, a broken old woman who should have gone gracefully years ago?'

Again he smiled at her forthrightness. 'Yes, my Regiment did bring me here, but my real reason lies behind a curiosity that has been burning me for years. I want to find out more about my grandfather Leigh, grandmother Milly and the rest of them in Mandalay when it was ruled by King Thibaw. My fondest memories are of my grandmother Milly, and sitting at her knee while she regaled me with stories from childrens' books — but never about her own life.'

'I don't suppose she had any wish to talk about it — one never does about the sad things, Johnney Buchanan. Milly's life was all of that after your grandfather was tortured to death by a madman. Just one senseless madman, and that's what frightens me most, Johnney, the power madmen seem to acquire. Pain can be surmounted, humiliating cruelties inflicted on one's person can be overcome, but war waged by madmen is an incurable wasting disease that feeds off the weak and innocent long after the last gun has stopped firing — for it's always the innocent who must suffer the most in that first mistake that will inevitably lead to the last mistake, total destruction. Just look at what they've done to Mandalay, the waste and the emptiness of it all, to what purpose? Except for a stepping backwards in time instead of progressing forwards in harmony of the world, all because madmen have the power to destroy and destroy and destroy in their mindless acts of violence. But tell me about yourself now Johnney, for it must be a far nicer subject to talk about. Tell me what happened to your grandmother after we stopped writing — though I don't suppose you'll know. It was with great irregularity we corresponded — the fault lying entirely with me as I never was a good letter writer.'

'Grandmother Milly died just a few years ago. I remember her as a remarkable old woman. She never remarried, but lived her life to the end with my parents in Berkshire — where we all got back to after Coimbatore, the grass roots of the family at Caversham, where I had a pretty ordinary life — rather boring in a way. I have two sisters — both of them doing their bit for England as one's in signals and the other in the W.R.A.F. My father, Leigh Junior, fought on the Somme and got gassed later on in that war, after which he was always an invalid. So you see, I come from a military family so I suppose that's how I'm here now in Mandalay — rather an odd coincidence one might say. Grandmother Milly you see mentioned once the names of the Amagyi-Angela and the Shwe Nat of Mandalay, surprisingly the one and only time she did say anything about her early life in Burma, and that happened to be on her deathbed. The names stuck with me. When I knew I was on the road to Mandalay, I was determined to find out more. I'm afraid my parents never talked to me about anything really important, so I never found out much about grandmother Milly's life.

594

In repose, her face took on a kind of majestic beauty that transcended the ravages of old age and in her faded green eyes he became suddenly aware of what kind of beauty she must once have been. 'No ordinary coincidence brings you here, Captain Johnney,' she said. 'The liberation of Mandalay is just one of those extraordinary events in our lives when certain factors are brought together for a purpose — Karma, the Eastern races call it, an extraordinary force that guides and directs our lives on the doctrine that the sum of a person's actions decides his destiny in the life to come — you are part of your grandfather's Karma, Johnney Buchanan, and I believe that's why you're here with me now? Do you see? No of course you don't,' she smiled and patted his hand. 'I am an old fool who cooks up a lot of nonsense in her head, and always has done.'

'No indeed,' he said, 'tell me about your Karma … and the man they called the Shwe Nat.'

Low laughter deep in her throat made her less formidable. 'Oh, Johnney, Johnney, if I told you, I'd fill a volume not just a few minutes space.'

'Were you his wife?' he asked, fingering the charm in his pocket, the pieces of the jigsaw falling into place at last.

'Oh no,' she said after a moment's hesitation. 'He was always married to his peerless Shan princess — though there weren't any pieces of paper or wedding rings to prove anything — only a deep and abiding commitment which is as it should be. I suppose I was his ma-ya-nga as the Burmese say. Second wife, Johnney, and if that sounds shocking, it isn't. Not really. Minthami and I got on very well together and we never quarrelled … but after she drowned, then I had him all to myself. Twelve glorious years together, from Mandalay across the oceans, lovely, lovely times …'

She relapsed into a reverie in a land he was not permitted to enter. He could tell by her vacant absorption in something he could not see that moments like these must come more often now, her retreat into the past in order to escape brutal reality. 'Ah Johnney, John-ney, you will never know. You will never know the legend of our lifetime. He was part of that legend, Min-thami too. I can't be, not yet, but only when I'm dead — and sometimes I think I'm immortal as I go on and on and on digging beneath the Mohurs. Java, Sumatra, Macau, Bombay, sailing days, Johnney Buchanan, and always Whitewalls to come home to at the end of a voyage. He and I were alike, very alike, reflections of each other, made for each other though that sounds idyl-lic — it didn't preclude us from fighting wonderfully well as well as loving ... he drowned, Johnney, just like his peerless princess. A typhoon swept him away at a time when I wasn't with him. Lost in the China Seas one terri-ble terrible time ... but, it was the only way he could have died, as befitting a legend, for he was always the water-gipsy, the golden devil of Mandalay, part of the waters of the Irrawaddy that flowed through his veins ...' she turned to him, her face weird and wonderful as memories flooded back in colour and strength. 'But we had, all of us, an incredible good run for our money, Captain Johnney ... before they came and took it all away from us. Before they bombed and destroyed and captured the wealth of our golden city. Nothing remains anymore, no more golden days — for it's only when we look back at our lives do we recognize the gilding on it Johnney. Happiness you see, is seldom appreciated at the time, only in retrospect.' She became pensive and querulous then, 'No more de Veres-Vorne, its mighty commercial empire that was the backbone of Mandalay and the rest of the East. We had new godowns in the end ... after all that silly business with the Provost Marshall's Court — as though it were our fault the dam burst! They executed Roi in the end you know. The Kempai Tai got hold of him one day and beheaded him in front of us — right outside the godowns in full view of everyone — Ko Lee too, but they shot him through the head instead and he was an old old man — as we are all old in this savage place, because only the old are left. I fell on my knees to plead for Roi's life — he was an old man of seventy would you believe? I raised my arms to heaven, prayed to God and Buddha at the same time, gave the Japanese soldiers such a look because they were about to strike my head off too, they didn't dare after that. They locked me up for a little while without food and water, hoping to kill me off I dare say, but they didn't know how strong I was because not even typhoid killed me off.' She frowned, 'Sa-Lon of course, he was always anti-British. He married a Burmese woman in the end and not my beloved Thania. He had his own lawyers' practice in Rangoon and I never saw him again although I heard a great deal. He joined a political party to gain Burma her independence and was one of the leading figures instrumental in separating the country from India and the dominance of the Raj. He died just before the Japanese walked into Rangoon. So you see, Johnney, they've all gone and I'm the only one left.' She began to pluck her robe, the silence heavy in the drowsy heat. She slapped the mosquitoes from her. 'Do you feel it Johnney? The white marble silences of Whitewalls speaking to us?'

He felt the white marble silences weighing him down.

'Do you know the story of the fabulous Egyptian bird, Johnney Buchanan? The only bird who lives a certain number of years, at the close of which it makes its nest of spices, sings a melodious dirge, flaps its wings to set alight the woodpile and then burns itself to ashes? Mandalay is that bird. Whether or not it will ever rise again from its funeral pyre like the phoenix, I don't know. It doesn't seem very likely now, does it? A few days ago, Johnney Buchanan, I was very angry when I saw what our people had done to Mandalay. They were all gone you see, the Kempai Tai, all the Japanese soldiers, all retreated — did no one tell you that? Now, if Jeffrey had been alive to do your Intelligence work, he would have got his facts right first — poor, poor tormented Jeffrey. His cross to bear was a mental illness although, when I first met him he didn't have bats in the belfry — I don't suppose I'd have married Raj if he had

— that's what the Regiment nicknamed him — for Rad-cliffe, Jeffrey, Arthur ... a rather strange man, a haunted man was Raj. But he was every inch the British soldier, the pukka Sahib, and he would have told you there were no Japanese left on Mandalay Hill the day the bombers came. And now there is no Mandalay left. No palace, no city, no nothing, just smoking ruins. Sad, so sad and so very, very tragic. Nothing left to show of the golden city. Away the phoenix, away the beautiful legend, away Minthami and myself — born with the first spires of Mandalay ...'

She began to ramble then, making no sense to him while she fiercely clutched her begging-bowl in her lap and rocked herself with a faraway expression in her faded eyes.

'Are you very bitter, Amagyi-Angela?' He hardly dared frame the question, yet felt compelled.

She gave a little laugh. 'Bitter! Good heavens, what have I to be bitter about? No, no, Johnney Buchanan, bitterness is for only those with shallow vision. Worm-wood and gall only reverts on oneself in the end — I found that out to my bitter cost once, when I almost lost everything on pride and bitterness ... and lies. Bitterness poisons the mind, the body, that's what I've learned about bitterness. I'm an old woman now, too old to bear any grudges — though a few days ago I did feel my heart had finally broken when I saw what had happened to Mandalay. But there's no more time left for me to harbour grudges, I wish to be recycled you see Johnney,' she gave a deep throaty chuckle, 'and I don't want to come back in my next life as a fruit-bat or wormwood, do I? Oh no. But I wouldn't mind living this one all over again. Not many people you see have lived a legend in their own lifetime. I had that privilege. I've seen a bril-liant Empire dawn and fade. People, wonderful people, come and go in the traversing of their paths with mine through love and hate, peace and war, despair and hope, falsehood and truth, and now from suspicion to trust in you, Johnney Buchanan, the last of the breed, and pray God a more understanding one.' Her frail shoulders slumped forward. He thought she was about to give in to tears and steeled himself for the sorrows of an old woman with too many memories. But no, she meant only to lean a little toward him, peer into his smooth youthful face, touch his dark hair for a fleeting second and try to recognize in him something to remind her of someone; 'Yes,' she said, 'you've got your grandmother's eyes. Eyes you see, Johnney Buchanan, are the windows of the soul. Now and then the soul needs a window-cleaner but not too often I'm glad to say. How is Thania?'

'Thania?' Now he really did feel he was lost.

'Yes, Thania,' she insisted. 'My daughter. The Shwe Nat's daughter. You're from England, aren't you?'

'Yes.'

'Well, Thania visits England quite a lot. She didn't fare too badly in the end because when the Shwe Nat's mother died, some lady-Jane in her own right, she left him her estates in Ireland and he in turn left them to Thania ... he always did manage to land on his feet in the end, the cunning old devil! But he had imagination, guts and the sort of nerve that made him the friend of kings and princes — and of course princesses. He could also charm his way into the heart of a Spotted Face. What a man! Ah, now I'm becoming maudlin and boring. Thania married Captain Paul Monthavers from the 2nd Hampshires — you probably know him. He's a Brigadier-General now — retired of course. We're all old and retired ... such a nice boy and always most respectful toward me. They're often in London with the family — you must know them!'

He smiled, full of apologies. 'I'm awfully sorry, but I shall rectify the matter as soon as I get home.'

'You do that Leigh Buchanan ... you always were a tactful young man I remember, and even on your wedding day aboard the *Belle Hélène* did not ask the Shwe Nat if he had remembered the ring ... Theo ... darling Theo ... you remember darling Theo? He was killed at

599

the First Battle of Ypres in 1914 ... war, always war to take away our loved ones and our lives, so unnecessary ... war, war ... always killing, fighting ... quickly, quickly, I have to go Leigh. I hear the temple bells telling me it's time to hide. The Kempai Tai, they will come here again. Always searching, searching, Japanese soldiers everywhere searching the houses for Chindits. I must hide, and so must you, otherwise they'll put you in a camp, Leigh, and torture you ... quickly, come, otherwise they'll take us both like they took poor Minister Duke at the Gospel Mission. I must get back to my Convent, do come ...' She put out her hand to steady herself but dropped her begging bowl. Weeping and scrambling after it as it rolled down the steps and across the dirt compound in front of the house, he reached it before her. It was empty and he put his ration of chocolate in it, replaced the lid and handed it back to her.

'It's all right, Amagyi-Angela, it's all right. The Japanese aren't coming back anymore, that's why I'm here.'

She turned her terrified eyes upon him and he was forced to repeat his words of reassurance while she stood trembling like a water-reed with her two arms cowering over her bowl as though the Japanese would steal her chocolate. 'They're not coming back, you're safe. Mandalay is at peace now.' Gently he took her arm.

'Peace, Leigh? Peace. Such a beautiful word.' She relaxed slowly, her body quivering downward like a spent arrow whose independent power was stilled as it settled in peace. She stood on the hard riven earth and raising her head said: 'I hear the golden silences of Whitewalls ... do you know, these last few years have been the only time in my life I rejoiced that the Shwe Nat perished in his prime, for otherwise they would have done to him what they did to his faithful old servant. He would never, never have let them do this to his beloved Whitewalls which he gave to me ...' Exhausted she faltered, and whispered, 'Silence Leigh ... the firing has stopped, the bombs aren't falling anymore. No more awful war-noises but only the sound of turtle-doves and pagoda bells — as it was, as it used to be when we would walk out together in the soft shadows of evening, or beneath the moonlight that speckled the river like a big fat mackerel. The phoenix will rise again, it will.'

Johnney Buchanan raised his head and listened to the wild happy music of pagoda bells proclaiming peace on the very spot where, half a century earlier the legend was aided and abetted by the Shwe Nat of Mandalay and the Amagyi-Angela who had brought Milly Sinclair and Leigh Buchanan together on the wings of a romantic legend. He marked with fresh eyes how very golden were the Mohurs, how blue the jacaranda, how startling white the turtle doves and the marble terraces of a graceful old house called Whitewalls. He marked how the glazed depletion had gone from the old nun's eyes, presenting to him an inner beauty and defiant spirit that he now saw for himself was part of the legend upon which a golden city and golden dreams had been built.

His shadow thrown across her by the falling sun was substantial, familiar and very, very welcome. In the hushed wonderment of humanity holding its breath at a moment of rebirth, highlighted for the first time in that glorious evening peace which always came to White-walls, as purple shadows possessed those quiescent gardens of a bygone era, she asked him: 'Have you been to the top of Mandalay Hill, Leigh?'

Johnney smiled: 'Yes, I've been to the top of Manda-lay Hill Amagyi-Angela. As a matter of fact, I've just come down from there ... with this ...' He put in her hand the bejewelled *Nat* charm and observed her splen-did reaction, 'after many days fighting and many days searching.'

'Well I never,' she cooed, just like one of her white doves of peace, 'it's Thagya Min, King of the Major Nats. He comes each Burmese New Year, you know Leigh, at the time of the Water Festival to shower us all with blessings. I offered it one year to appease the gods ... I forget which year. The Shwe Nat laughed at my

601

superstitions — but in the end he always went along with my desires. How clever of you to find it,' she remarked, looking up at him fondly, pensively, so that he felt the time had come for him to take his leave of the Amagyi-Angela and her home, Whitewalls, all and more than he had expected.

'Thank you for answering my many questions, Amagyi-Angela. I hope none of them have been too tedious or impertinent, or that I've over-tired you by my unexpected visit.'

'No indeed, never. It's always nice to see one's own people, and old friends most of all. If you do go to the top of Mandalay Hill, Leigh, you must remember to feed the turtles.'

'Johnney,' he reminded her gently, a twinkle in his eyes.

'Forgive me, Johnney, names slip away easily from me these days. Such a nice young man like you mustn't forget to feed the turtles in the Sasana pool as the Japanese did — that's bad luck and probably why they lost. Peacocks are also supposed to bring bad luck, and that's why poor old Thibaw lost the Peacock Banner, I suppose. Come, Leigh, it's late. I only came today because the Shwe Nat asked me to put fresh flowers by her memorial stone ... she drifted away one day on the Irrawaddy, just like scattered petals of a bhodi flower, Minthami, the dancing princess ...' she put her hand in his, seeking his support in balancing on the step as she set down her begging bowl, to stand and look unimpeded one last time at her house of memories.

Golden light captured and held them both on the marble steps of Whitewalls, their shadows thrown long upon the compound.

She whispered in Johnney Buchanan's ear: 'I have many photographs and momentoes buried in the garden along with Nathan's silver. The Japanese would have taken everything had they been able to find anything. That's why they kept creeping up on me whenever I came here. But they could never trap me, I was too artful for them. I was always very busy planting flowers in the cemetery, but they never thought of looking among the headstones to find out what I was really doing. I have a medal too, hidden away somewhere — for nursing services rendered at Minhla would you believe! But my calotypes are better than my father's — though I never did win the annual prize of the Delhi Camera Club because I forgot to send them the picture of the Shwe Nat standing over a tiger that Thagya Min had caught by timed-exposure,' she chuckled, 'but that's another story.' Chatting away to him, she patted his hand in a very grandmotherly gesture. 'You're a good boy Johnney Buchanan. I know you've come to set free the bond. Though Mr Kipling could never have forseen in what manner his words would come true when he wrote his famous poem at the turn of the century, but only we in Mandalay appreciate. I'm glad British soldier, you've come back to Mandalay.'

'So am I Amagyi-Angela, so am I.'

'Then come, Captain Johnney,' she said, picking up her black lacquer begging-bowl, 'let's not look backwards anymore, but let's leave this place with only happiness in our stride.'

A strong young man's hand closed over the gnarled thin one of a remarkable old lady while turtle doves and pagoda bells proclaimed that peace had come back to Mandalay, and Johnney Buchanan's other hand touched the faded parchment in his pocket bearing, long dead, a Buddhist King's poem put in the mouth of a chinthe by the Amagyi-Angela and the Shwe Nat of Mandalay;

Tamed I would tame the wilful:
Comforted, comfort the timid:
Wakened, wake the sleeping,
Cool, cool the burning:
Freed, set free the bound:
Tranquil and led by the good doctrines
I would hatred calm.

GLOSSARY

Achaeik Htameins	Open woven skirts of intricate patterns worn on ceremonial occasions.
Amagyi	A mark of respect. Literally means 'big sister'.
Apyodaw	Dancer whose responsibility it is to placate all appropriate deities at start of Pwe.
Atwinwun	Palace advisor.
Baba-log	Children (hindi).
Basha hut	Small house on stilts with woven bamboo walls and thatched roof.
Bo	Leader, boss.
Bo tree	Sacred Banyan tree under which the Buddha gained enlightenment.
Chatty	Utensils for eating, drinking, cooking.
Chettyars	Indian money-lenders.
Chindits	The 'behind enemy lines' allied forces who harried the Japanese in WWII.
Chinthe	Mythical crested 'lion' guarding pagodas.
Dah	Burmese sword or knife.
Daw	Respectful form of address for woman, aunt.

Duwa	Kachin chieftain
Dechi	Saucepan, cooking vessel (hindi).
Eingyi	Woman's blouse.
Ghee	Melted butter for culinary purposes.
Godown	Warehouse, storage shed.
Gurrh-Burrh	Noise, fuss, tumult (hindi).
Hinthe	Mythical bird.
Hlutdaw	Royal advisory council, council hall.
Hti	Umbrella, upper portion of pagoda.
Jaggery	Sweet made of palm-sugar.
Kala	Foreigner.
Kutho	Merit.
Kuthodaw	Buddhist shrine, work of royal merit.
Ko	Brother.
Kyaung	Monastery.
Lakh	Indian word meaning 100,000. Used in Burma particularly referring to money.
Longyi	Man or woman's skirt-like garment, sarong.
Ludu	The common people.
Ma	Usual form of address for girl or woman.
Maha-davi	Chief wife.
Manuthiha	Half lion, half man mythical beast.
Maung	Usual form of address for man or boy.

Min	Prince or lord (retained by Kings after accession).
Mingyi	Great prince, title of most senior ministers.
Minkdaw	Wife of government official.
Mintha	Leading actor or dancer.
Minthami	Leading actress or dancer.
Myanma	Burma.
Myowun	Royal governor.
Nat	A spirit or devil.
Ngapi	Paste of fish or shrimp, fermented and pickled in brine. A Burmese delicacy.
Nhai	Read instrument like oboe.
Oozie	Elephant rider.
Parabaik	An old manuscript on soft bamboo paper.
Phongyi	Monk.
Pwe	Variety show, entertainment, festival.
Sangha	Buddhist monastic system.
Sawbwa	Shan chieftan, hereditary ruler of Shan state.
Saya	Wise man, teacher, doctor.
Sayadaw	Learned or senior monk, head of monastery.
Shikar/shikari	Hunt/hunter (hindi).
Sadhu	Indian holyman.

Shikko	To bow down low, kneeling, touching forehead to ground.
Shinbyu	Ordination, initiation ceremony of Burmese boy as novice.
Singoung	Head elephant man, above Oozie.
Stupa	Lower portion of pagoda.
Shwe	Gold/golden.
Shaitan	Wicked person.
Syce	Groom.
Thakin	Master, lord.
Thugyi	Headman of village.
Tonga	Two wheeled horse drawn vehicle.
Toywa	Jungle, or isolated village.
Tripitaka	The 'three baskets' of sacred Buddhist scriptures.
U	Form of address for a man, showing respect. Literally means uncle.
Viss	Traditional Burmese weight, 1.6 kg.
Wun	Government official, burden-bearer.
Wundauk	Hlutdaw assistant.
Wungyi	Royal minister of state, great burden-bearer.
Zat	Play or drama. Pyazat is similar, but with contemporary rather than religious theme.
Zayat	Monastery resthouse.

All Futura Books are available at your bookshop or
newsagent, or can be ordered from the following address:
Futura Books, Cash Sales Department,
P.O. Box 11, Falmouth, Cornwall TR10 9EN.

Please send cheque or postal order (no currency), and
allow 60p for postage and packing for the first book
plus 25p for the second book and 15p for each additional
book ordered up to a maximum charge of £1.90 in U.K.

B.F.P.O. customers please allow 60p for
the first book, 25p for the second book plus 15p per
copy for the next 7 books, thereafter 9p per book

Overseas customers, including Eire, please allow £1.25
for postage and packing for the first book, 75p for the
second book and 28p for each subsequent title ordered.